the Hollywood Trilogy

the Hollywood Trilogy

A COUPLE OF COMEDIANS

THE TRUE LIFE STORY OF JODY MCKEEGAN

TURNAROUND

THREE NOVELS BY

DON CARPENTER

COUNTERPOINT
BERKELEY

Library of Congress Cataloging-in-Publication Data

Carpenter, Don.
[Novels. Selections]
Hollywood trilogy : a Couple of comedians, The true [life] story of Jody McKeegan, and Turnaround / Don Carpenter.
pages cm
I. Carpenter, Don. Couple of comedians. II. Carpenter, Don. True life story of Jody McKeegan. III. Carpenter, Don. Turnaround. IV. Title. V. Title: Couple of comedians. VI. Title: True life story of Jody McKeegan. VII. Title: Turnaround.
PS3553.A76A6 2014
813'.54—dc23   2014022171

ISBN 978-1-61902-342-0

Cover design by Faceout Studio
Interior design by Sabrina Plomitallo-González, Neuwirth & Associates

COUNTERPOINT
2560 Ninth Street, Suite 318
Berkeley, CA 94710
www.counterpointpress.com

Printed in the United States of America
Distributed by Publishers Group West

10 9 8 7 6 5 4 3 2 1

A COUPLE OF COMEDIANS

I LIVE on a mountain. My ranch sits a couple of ridges below the top, just north of Jack London State Park. A couple of hundred acres of scrub manzanita, madrone and oak, with red and white opalized rock seldom more than a couple of inches from the surface, the whole thing tilted up against the mountain, most of it useless for anything but looking at.

The house is old redwood with lots of windows and a big porch around three sides, all looking out over the valley and the rim of low mountains to the east. Within spitting distance of the south porch is an old swimming pool that has been let go and is full of plants, mosquito larvae and frogs. A newer swimming pool is up the hill and away from the house. You can tread water in the new pool and look out over the Valley of the Moon.

The place used to belong to a screenwriter with a bad case of macho, who bought it from his wife's relatives, although he didn't know this at the time. I used to visit them up there when I was living in San Francisco. The screenwriter is a lanky ugly friendly guy who had grown up in foster homes all over the state. He kept a Thompson submachine gun by his bed, because the ranch is pretty isolated, but the only time he actually used it, at least to tell me about, was one night when there had been a lot of drinking and drug-taking and babbling about crazed bands of longhaired freaks in the hills, and my screenwriter friend was lying in bed later, a couple of hours before dawn, little blue bubbles popping in front of his eyes, with his wife next to him and their five or six children sleeping all over the premises and a couple of drugged up and boozed out Hollywood types on the sleeping porch with God knows what nocturnal habits, and he heard unusual sounds out in the trees. After listening to the noises long enough to work himself into a froth, the screenwriter got up and took his Thompson out onto the back patio. He heard the noises again, coming from the general direction of the trail up through the trees toward the swimming pool, and without thinking to check on his guests or the whereabouts of anybody else, he let loose a burst into the night, blowing his wife's cat into cat-heaven with an accuracy of fire that had to be seen to be believed. He always told the story on himself not I think to show how spooky it can get up here in the nights, or to demonstrate the need for caution when you have a loaded automatic weapon beside the bed, but for that accuracy of fire. "Just like pointing a finger," he told me.

Marriage problems caused him to sell the place back to his wife's family, and they leased it out to a woman psychiatrist who got herself mixed up with a real band of deurbanized crazies, and they pissed in the frog pond, drove nails into every wooden surface they could find, left dead animals and broken glass in the swimming pool and set fire to most of the rest of the place. Fortunately it was raining at the time and the house was saved. I picked it up from the screenwriter's former uncle-in-law at greatly reduced prices.

It's nice up here, even in the winter when it rains a lot. There isn't any television, and radio reception is no good except for a station that plays only country-western or religious programs. Things are pretty quiet. The garage is full of old magazines and books with titles like *Colonel Effingham's Raid, Beach Red* and *The Complete Works of Will James,* so there is plenty of stuff to read even without trips down to the general store in the valley where they have two racks of paperbacks and three of comic books.

After one full weather cycle things were getting back to normal. The neat rows of vegetables in the truck garden down in front of the house that had been the pride and passion of the screenwriter's wife were all gone to seed, what was left of them, and the raccoons came around every night in family groups to see what was happening and raid the garbage cans, and there is plenty of other wildlife, deer, bobcats, snakes, black widow spiders under the house and scorpions in the shower, tarantulas the size of your hand, shadowy bands of dog coyotes who never quite come out into the open; mayflies, dragonflies, horseflies, fruit flies and house flies, and of course way back in the hills the very real moonshiners making their own brands of wine and beer just to keep the recipes active until the next wave of prohibition, or so they tell me.

But generally it's quiet, very quiet, and when there's haze on the valley or rainclouds hanging low over everything, you'd think you were the only human on earth. Which sometimes is just the way I like it.

When spring comes to Sonoma Mountain it comes with ten billion insects, followed by everything you can think of that eats insects. The birds fly in and the frogs pop up out of the mud by the thousand, lizards, bluebelly stripers, snakes, come slithering and sliding down out of the rocks, in the warm nights you can smell the sweet slightly acid smell of romantic skunks, and the deer make so much noise snapping through the underbrush that you wonder why every tree in sight isn't peppered with bullet holes.

Just below the house is an old abandoned apple orchard with a couple of cherry and pear trees on the uphill edge, and these all come into bloom at the same time, the apple trees white and the others a pink soft enough to make you cry, and pretty soon the air is full of their smell and the night is full of peeping frogs and the messengers start clogging the road up the mountain with their telegrams, and I have to go back to Hollywood, to work.

Every year now I think about quitting, breaking up the act, just staying on the mountain and finishing the works of Will James, or maybe even getting that vegetable garden into shape—few rows of corn, nothing like fresh corn, some peas, mmmm, string beans, a couple rows of beets and carrots, pick 'em when they're babies and smother in butter, yum yum, and maybe a few of the artichoke bushes could be brought back to life (there were a dozen fine old artichoke bushes on the property, but the screenwriter with the bad case of macho imported a Mexican couple one year to take care of the place, and the man had sweated out in the hot summer sun chopping them down, and got most of them before the screenwriter could find the Spanish to make him stop) and I would plow and fence the orchard, and then would start thinking about the deer and the rabbits and the gophers, the bugs and birds that ate everything not under lock and key, and the messengers would start piling up in the mudslides, and so it would be either run for Hollywood or get into bio-chemical warfare with the entire animal kingdom, including William Morris.

By that time of year, mid-spring, my own relatives would be filling the guest-rooms and the kitchen, Buicks and Toyotas and white Chevy pickups sprawled in the gravel below the house, and they would *tsk-tsk* about me having to leave just as the good weather and all was coming, and so the morning would finally arrive. Six a.m. Six a.m. is the only time to leave this place.

The birds are just starting up and Grandpa is in the kitchen making oatmeal pancakes. It is bitter cold everywhere but in the kitchen. I try to get out of the house with just a cup of coffee, but Grandpa won't say goodbye if I don't cram a stack of his oatmeal pancakes into my face and grin and nod my head while he tells me how *damned good* they are, so, still chewing on the *damned good* but somewhat *dry* and *tasteless* pancakes, I come out of the house just as the sun is cracking the ridge across the valley, climb into the little Alfa that hasn't been down the mountain twenty times in the last three months and head for the Golden Anus of the California Dream.

JIM LARSON and I have a comedy act we put together in the 1960s. We used to play small clubs and do television, but for the last few years we make a picture every summer and do a month at the Golconda in Las Vegas. The movies never cost more than four or five million, most of that above the line, and if you can believe what you read in *Variety*, they usually return handy profits for all, so somebody out there must be having a good time. I can't bear to sit through them and Jim has a heart attack every time he passes a theater with Jim Larson and David Ogilvie on the marquee. We draw full houses most of the time at the Anaconda (as Jim likes to call it), so naturally what with all this popularity and money the little niggling problems of life manage to escape us, such as whether to order a hamburger or a cheeseburger and what kind of car to drive, where to sleep and what to do about holes in the socks, although both of us spent a certain amount of our lives wondering about just these very problems because in the wonderful language of the movie business, we couldn't get arrested.

After a couple of months in Hollywood getting up at six a.m. and hanging around the sound stages of the Burbank Studios, where there are four or five guys coming at you with problems for every minute you aren't actually out under the hot lights, playing the Anaconda is actually fun, because for one thing we are in front of a live audience and it is easier to make the jokes work, and when you're offstage you can tell people you are "exhausted"— although a couple hours on stage is far less exhausting than making movies.

Making movies is boring, and working Vegas is terrifying—that's the main difference. After nine or ten hours of boredom all I want to do is go home and watch television, but after a couple of hours of terror, the world seems like a wonderful place.

I'm talking about me, of course. Jim is entirely different, being neither bored nor terrified, to hear him tell it, and for that matter I believe him, because all day on the lot while we're making movies and rehearsing our act, Jim is busy, running in and out with people, making deals to make deals, entertaining ladies in his trailer, laughing and joking with everybody in that easy way of his. And in Vegas, while I'm going through flopsweat before every performance, Jim doesn't even show up until we're fifteen minutes late, then he comes in through the backstage door, talking with a mob of people that he somehow manages to keep from following him, winks at me and takes me by the arm and we go out under the pinkies while the band is still playing the number before our introduction and the poor guy backstage at the mike who's supposed to introduce us over the PA system doesn't get to do it because we're already out there and Jim has started to fool with the musicians and the audience begins that roaring sizzling sound that is like nothing else, and I'm not afraid anymore.

ONE TIME making the run to Hollywood I found myself in Los Banos at four in the morning, hungry, tired, bearded from a nice winter's solitude, dirty and unkempt. I went into the big all-night truck-stop restaurant, I forget the name of the place, Hinky Dink's or the Big Balloon or something. Rows of trucks were parked out in back on a big asphalt lot with gas pumps, oil racks and all that stuff, and inside, a few truckers were over in their private section of the place where they wouldn't be disturbed by the ordinary citizens, or *assholes*, as we are called. A couple of CHP guys were in with the truckers, but nobody in the asshole section except me. I sat at the counter and looked through the big plastic-coated menu with color photographs of the various leaders, the BIG DELUXE QUARTER POUNDER, etc., which sounded fine with me, along with some fresh coffee, and I only hoped that the french fries were going to taste better than they looked.

There were two waitresses, cute and young, a blonde and a redhead, both wearing bright red satin hotpants and white satin blouses, black mesh pantyhose and red heels; but of course they were in the trucker's den, one sitting with the cops and the other with some truckers. I could see in through the order area one of the cooks with his long homely face and white greasecap, and he looked up and winked at me: "Girl be along in a minute," he yelled, and I waved don't matter, no rush, and sat enjoying the quiet, the not driving, the different feel of the stool under my ass. I looked at the menu until the blonde came back of the counter, one of the pearly buttons of her blouse undone and showing a nice little slice of Playtex, her nametag saying DEBBIE, how unusual, I thought, ordered my burger, coffee and apple pie, why be a deviate at this hour?

"Yessir," she said nicely. I could see that she was tired of this night, her eyes a little glazed, her mouth pulled down at the corners. But polite to me, bringing my coffee right away and seeing to it that I had cream in my creamer, the order slapped up on the dolly, to be whirled and taken down by the frycook with another droll expression for me: "BIG DEE!" she yells at him going away, "BIG DEE!" he yells back at her and I hear the sizzle as my hunk of meat hits the griddle.

There was a murmur of conversation from the truckers' section, but that was all, no music. I took that first hot sip of coffee and swiveled on my stool to look for the jukebox. There it was, right between MEN and WOMEN.

A young couple came in through the door before I got up, early twenties, with a little baby in blue Dr. Dentons. They looked tired and worn from the road, and the baby was red-faced and irritated, making little noises of disgust. The couple settled themselves in a booth right behind me, and I turned to watch them, with their baby-bag, blanket, rattle toy, purse, coats, etc., murmuring to each other, "Can you get me the . . . ?" "Where's the lid?" "Hold him upright," and Debbie was right there helping them get all fixed up, Dad slipping out to go to the toilet while Mom gets the baby settled down and looks over the menu at the same time. Debbie lowered herself into the booth and took the baby, talking to Mom in a low voice, and then Mom went to the toilet, too. Debbie played with the kid and cooed and tried to get him to stop fussing, but nothing worked.

I turned away, realizing I had been sticking my nose too far into their lives, and bent over my coffee. I heard the couple coming back from the toilets and the waitress's laugh, and saw her come around the counter and slap their order up, although this time there was no yelling, so that must have been a little joke between the frycook and Debbie. I got up and went over to the jukebox. The truckers could see me better now, and I noticed a couple of them giving me the eye, seeing the beard and the shabby jeans, probably wondering what kind of hippie crap I was going to punch up.

Jim was all over the jukebox like a rash and just for the hell of it I played one of his older songs, "Let It Happen." The vamp started while I was still walking back to my stool, and I happened to be looking at the couple as the first strong notes of the bass began.

Their eyes lit up. They looked at each other as if they couldn't believe what they were hearing, and as Jim's voice hit loud and strong, full of all that romantic bullshit, the husband reached out for his wife's hands. God, I had accidentally played their song, and the fatigue was gone from their faces. They didn't get up and dance or anything, but it was worth a million dollars to see the way they looked at each other.

Debbie put my Big Dee down in front of me with a smile, and the frycook loudly sang along with Jim for a few bars, and even I was tapping my foot as I watched the redhead's hotpants cross the room and wag into the toilet.

Recognition, when it came, didn't spoil things. Debbie leaned over the counter and said to me in a low voice, "Aren't you David Ogilvie?"

"Yes, Ma'm," I said.

"You must love his music, too. That's wonderful," she said, and went to take food to the couple. They were having a merry old time, now that some coffee was inside them and the baby asleep, and after a while Mom got up and went to the jukebox and played a couple more of Jim's tunes. She smiled at me on her way back, shyly, and didn't say anything. The smile thanked me for rescuing them from the hell of four a.m. on the road.

Debbie thanked me, too, in her own wonderful way, out in the parking lot, and I guess now you know why I chose a career in show business.

THE FIRST time I saw Jim Larson he was on the bandstand in the Berkeley High School gymnasium playing for a noontime dance, only nobody was dancing much, because the band had gone, mostly, for a break and left a small combo—rhythm, a couple of saxophone players, and Jim with his silver-chased B-flat cornet. They were blowing their heads off. This was a while ago, and while swing was what the big dance band played, this little combo with no name was inspired by Max Roach, Dizzy Gillespie, Charlie Parker and those. I don't know whether it was the music or the performance that made the hair on the back of my neck stand up, but instead of continuing with what had brought me into the gym, which was the search for a girl named Chloe Melendrez, I joined the big bunch of kids gathered below the band and kept listening.

My musical tastes haven't changed much since then, my idea of a major trumpet player is Harry James, but even I could tell that these kids were just really very damned good. And they were so cool. One would take a solo and the others, instead of listening to him, would gather around the piano and talk to each other, tell jokes, paying no attention at all to the kid blowing his brains out, and then casually without any signal that I could see or hear, the whole combo would take up with the soloist and they would rant along like that for a while and then, say, Jim would take the solo and the others would leave him alone with the music (except the drums and bass, of course) and Jim would wander all over the stage in front of the empty folding wooden chairs and all the music racks from the full band, wandering with his head down and his trumpet held so that the bell was almost pointed at the floor.

He was dressed like the others, Levi's rolled to a thin line above his shoes, striped orange-and-yellow socks (I had on a pair myself), *huaraches* that had been dyed from their natural pale yellowish brown to a dark cordovan with an inch and a half of extra sole and heel added by the shoemaker (I had on a pair myself), white dress shirt, only instead of the leather flight jacket like mine or the baseball warmup jacket that nearly every Berkeley High School student wore if he didn't want to be accused of being a faggot, Jim and the other musicians were wearing either knee-length topcoats or sports jackets. Jim's was baby blue, two-button roll but hanging open, and his hair was done in the standard pompadour-into-duck's-ass that separated the *pachucos* from the goats (these are not racial terms, but social), and of course he and all the others in the combo were wearing the darkest sunglasses they could find.

I stayed for the rest of the lunch period and then rushed out of the building and across the street for a cigarette before class. While I was standing there wondering where Chloe Melendrez would be later in the afternoon (underneath a football player, as it turned out), Jim came out the side door to the gymnasium building and lit a cigarette and crossed over to where I was. We stood about five feet apart, sucking on our cigarettes while the hotrods rumbled and crackled up and down the street, radios blaring,

Open the do', Richard . . .
Open the do' and let me in . . .

or other popular hits of the day. I thought it would be nice if I complimented him on his playing, so I said:

"You're the trumpet player?"

"Huh?" He was so cool . . .

"That was great in there . . . the music . . ."

"Hey, well, yeah . . ." Or something like that. Jim was definitely in his cool period. After he dropped and stomped his cigarette he looked over at me and his mouth curled into a small grin: "Thanks, man . . ."

He scuffed across the street and reentered the gym.

"Hey, well, Oh gee gosh wowie," I murmured to myself, and the bell rang, so I ran across the slope and into the Academic Building for class.

The next time I saw Jim was at a dance at the Tennis Club up by the Claremont Hotel. The dance was given by a couple of the high school fraternities, who sold bids to anybody who would buy them. I might as well describe the bids because I don't think anybody uses them anymore, at least I haven't seen any since I left Berkeley High; they are little dance cards on colored silken strings that you buy to get into the dance and then give to your girlfriend, several pages, a flocked front cover (they were all different in design) and spaces inside to put the names of the people you danced with, except that it wasn't considered polite then to cut in or dance with somebody's date. Girls would collect them and put them up around their mirrors like Christmas cards. You had to buy the girl a corsage, too, so the darkened ballroom full of dressed-up kids would smell like a gardenia factory.

I had a date, Gloria Somerlade, who did not smell like gardenias because I had spent four dollars on an orchid for her, not because I had the four dollars to spare, but I thought it would show her a little class and make things easier toward the end of the evening. As a matter of fact, the orchid made her dance at a distance from me, to keep from crushing the flower. Jim was playing the dance, but like all the other musicians, working directly from the charts. He was not even the solo trumpet, that was a guy who sat next to Jim and who must have admired Harry James even more than I did, because he played just like him, at least so it sounded to me. I waved to Jim as I danced past once, but he didn't see me, even though he wasn't wearing his dark glasses.

WE KEPT running into each other on the #7 streetcar after school, except on the days he had practice, and after he had hit me up for a Camel several times, we got to talking and joking around. The streetcar was always crowded with kids standing in the back, and that's where we rode, sometimes getting on through the back door without paying, a dime was a dime, ⅕ of a drunk if you could get served. Another kid we knew named Bunky could work all the contraptions in the back of the car, which was just like the front, so that when the car got to the end of the line the driver just came back and set up and away we go. But with the thing packed and rolling along Grove Street, Bunky would take control and get us heading in the wrong direction. The driver would get up and fight his way through us kids with blood in his eye, while Bunky sneaked around outside and planted the track bombs he had stolen off the car in the first place, so that when the poor harassed driver finally got things calmed down, right away BLAM! BLAM! BLAM!

Jim and I thought this was pretty funny stuff.

Then we would spend weekend afternoons at his place, a tiny apartment in Cordenices Village, the housing project on San Pablo Avenue in West Berkeley, the worst part of town. He shared the apartment with his mother, but I never saw her. She was across the street at Knapp's Bar when she wasn't working, so we had the place to ourselves. Mostly we stayed in his room, drinking beer, smoking Camels, listening to Jim's record collection, my first exposure to the crazy people of rebop. Jim would lie across the bed looking hypnotized, listening to Charlie Parker or Howard McGhee, or he would pick up his trumpet, always there, and play along for a few bars, change the record and sing or play along with the new one. Some afternoons he would just practice, sitting on a turned-around kitchen chair, his sheet music on its rack (stolen from Burbank School) while I would either listen, talk to him or go through his collection of *Beauty Parade*, *Titter*, *Sunshine & Health*, etc., the best collection of magazines I had run into yet, although I had a better collection of funnybooks, which Jim ate up by the yardful.

Once while I was there somebody beat on the front wall of the building and yelled at Jim to shut up the goddamn trumpet noise and Jim leaped off the bed and smashed his hand against the wall and screamed like a maniac that if the bastard didn't like the goddamn music he could blow it out his ass, all at top volume, Jim sounding berserk but grinning, his eyes wild, and the guy outside went away.

And sometimes we would go around the project looking for the cheap girls who supposedly abounded in such places, but very seldom did we score, and once I got into a grappling contest with a girl bigger than me and was knocked over Jim's bed and cut my eye and damned near bled to death before Jim could stop laughing, and of course the girl got away.

One bad time I came over and Jim was practicing. He nodded and winked at me and I sat on the bed and lit up, but I could see he was having trouble. He would play a few notes, they sounded all right to me, and then play them again, interrupt himself, "Shit!" and then try again, playing the notes fast and high, getting more and more frustrated until finally he took the horn from his lips and stared at it with a look of dismay. "god*damn* it!" he said.

"What's the matter?" I said.

"It's this fucking *horn*!"

But it wasn't the horn. The horn was beautiful, kept polished and the valves lovingly oiled, everything in its place in the bright green velvet case, the spare mouthpiece, the little silver attachable music rack, the silvered mute and all. What was dismaying Jim was that he could *hear* the notes so well, could imagine what they should sound like, but could not play them.

But generally, a few bottles of beer, a few Camel cigarettes, sweet girlies in their underpants, and he could play like an angel. I got a real kick out of it, and never had so much fun in high school as over at Jim's.

WE HUNG around together for the rest of the school year and the summer, but then my family moved to the Pacific Northwest and naturally, I went with them, although the thought of leaving California for the backwoods made me sick. Late in the summer, not long before I left, Jim called me up one afternoon and said there was going to be a jam session in a barn up in the hills between Berkeley and Oakland, a real blowout with nobody trying to dance, just the music, and lots of musicians from all over the East Bay, and did I want to go, because nonplaying guests were going to be counted at the door. I was entering my own cool period at the time, so I probably said something like, "Hey, man, sounds like a groove, sounds real hep!" We were already making fun of people who said hep for hip.

To this day, Jim thinks of that night as the greatest evening of his life. It wasn't mine. I could think of ten thousand evenings where I had more fun, but I have to grant Jim his point, because he was up with the musicians and I was out with the drunks and fistfighters and bottlethrowers, the vomiters and screamers, the girlstealers and facekickers.

There were huge kid gangs in the East Bay at that time, and for all I know, still are—The Watchtrack Gang from Oakland, Jinio Reles and His Chinese Army (containing no Chinese), the beginnings of the Hell's Angels, and a lot of tough hombres who didn't belong to any particular gang, like Al deAlba or Billy Martin, but would stomp your ass if you looked at them funny. Once on an F train headed for downtown Berkeley, I didn't keep my eyes to myself properly when three zootsuited Pachooks made their way down the aisle, and I was forced, in front of my friends, girls, old people, etc., to eat crow—the head Pachook stopped in front of me and said, "I don't like your face."

It was a comment that invited response, and I suppose a bigger boy or one with braver friends might have said, "Yeah, well, *fuck you*, greaseball," and let it go at that. But the situation being what it was, I merely said, "Neither do I!" and, I think, saved the face in question from getting stomped on, because the three young zootsuiters laughed and left us alone.

My first job as a comedian.

I arrived at the jam session in the trunk of a friend's car, lying down in darkness for the entire ride up into the hills, but with consolation—Dotty McCarty was right next to me, my first date with her, and her reputation was that she would screw anybody who was halfway nice to her, so as the car rumbled and popped up and down and around the hills looking for the barn, Dotty and I got to know each other in the trunk, a few fond kisses, a certain amount of touching here and there, so that when we arrived and Forni, who was driving the car, opened the trunk and Dotty and I came out into the spotlights outside the barn, I was pretty jacked up, and ready for anything.

That night I was wearing a wine-colored cardigan sports jacket, that is, with no collar, a white shirt with a Mr. B collar, snappy necktie and a pair of charcoal chalkstriped pants that came up to my breastbone and were thirty-six inches at the knee and sixteen at the cuffs.

In the group milling around the entrance to the barn my clothes were a bit formal, but not unusual. There were other zootsuits, plenty, greasy Levi sets (Levi's, Levi jackets and field boots), plenty of topcoats and hats and sunglasses (including mine), lots of motorcycles, lots of chopped and channeled cars, some chopped and red-primered pickup trucks, evidence of cases of beer and pints of whiskey, a couple of shoving matches over by the door, and the sound of that music flooding out of the barn and making everyone who wasn't already inside with the insiders a little pissed off at the delays, the need for invitations (not on paper, just in the memory of the braincases at the door) so that the ozone was exploding with tension. My personal tension mounted pretty fast as I saw that Dotty was one of the few girls in sight, and that she was waving to quite a number of guys who were a lot older, tougher and drunker than I was.

So of course the trick was to get inside before anything happened. I pushed Dotty in front of me and used her as a battering ram to push through to the door, getting a lot of "Hey-what-the-fuck-oh-scuse-me's" from guys as they saw it was Dotty pushing them out of the way, but naturally Jim had forgotten to leave my name at the door, or the brilliant guys taking names had forgotten mine, but we got inside anyway because a couple of guys were trying to get in aboard their motorcycles, and this distracted the door-guards long enough for Dotty and me.

Inside was a different party.

It was a barn that had been turned into a theater, a stage at one end and lights on the performers. I had never seen so many guys carrying musical instruments as there were at the stage end of the room. The audience was lit up by a string of red and blue lights around the room, but it was pretty dark anyway, people packed into the place all bouncing to the music, smoking cigarettes and passing pints of whiskey around. Dotty and I got as comfortable as possible against the wall pretty near the stage, and I pulled out my own pint, which Dotty and I finished before long, since we had been nipping at it in the trunk of the car.

Even then the thought of going up onstage scared the shit out of me, but Jim was up there in front of the mob, loving it, bright-eyed, holding his beautiful silver-chased B-flat cornet with its glowing brass bell, onstage all the time I was there, through fistfights, guys yelling and vomiting, musicians coming and going. Later, when Jim's group was finished with their part of it, he saw me from the stage, shading his eyes, and waved for me to come on up, and then laughed because he knew I'd be scared, and started to leave the stage himself, but the leader of the new guys, a tall skinny black kid with a glowing saxophone, said into the mike, "Hey, Doctor Jim, may we detain you?" and to a hell of a lot of applause—every bit of it deserved—Jim came back onstage, waved his trumpet over his head as a kind of thank-you and they all took off into a version of "How High the Moon"—five or six black guys and Jim—that lasted at least twenty minutes and had everybody in the place screaming like banshees.

That's the way it was, and I can understand how Jim thinks of it as the best night of his life, although at some point during the early morning hours Dotty McCarty slipped off (or was kidnapped, what did I care?) and I saw her no more, not that I gave a damn about her, but Forni was pretty sarcastic all the way back to my neighborhood, and for that matter it wasn't pleasant to have on all those fine duds and end up alone. But hell.

I DROVE from Sonoma Mountain to Hollywood on a Monday, eating my way south as usual, pancakes with raspberry syrup, fried eggs O.M. with fried potatoes and bacon, rye toast with apple butter, always an eightpack of Coca-Cola on the floor of the car for me to uncork, draw off about half and put the bottle between my legs, five or six handrolled joints in my shirt pocket, a little bottle of cocaine underneath the rug next to the eightpack just in case I got sleepy; B.L.T. on toasted white bread with tall glasses of milk and french fries, lots of french fries, sometimes stopping at a McDonald's for a couple of big orders of french fries because McDonald's makes the best, but not ordering anything else because nothing else measures up to the fries; vanilla milkshakes, orders of fried clams, and when I stop at the gas stations to fill the tank I have to spend a little time getting the grease off the steering wheel, a little coke on my lip and away we go, up through the long hot run of the San Fernando Valley with the floor of the car awash in Coke bottles clinking against the unused seatbelts, hot, sick, stoned and tired, sticky and smelly, glad to make the turnoff at LAUREL CYN and whip up over the hill to Hollywood, the hotel, a quick checkin and up to my apartment and the icecold shower I had been dreaming about for the last couple of hours, with the window open in the bathroom so I could look down Sunset Boulevard toward downtown L.A. in the reddish twilight as I soaped the trip off my body.

But it was all a waste of time. I was sitting in the living room with a big white hotel towel around my middle, watching "I Love Lucy" on the color television set when the phone rang. It was Karl, our producer, and as usual he was in a state of panic, although he never liked anybody to know he was in a state of panic. We talked about this and that for a while, and then he said, "Jim's not here."

"He'll show up," I said.

"This is not the same," Karl said, making reference to the fact that Jim is never on time anywhere. But he wasn't exactly late. I always show up a few days early to get some of the garbage out of the way before we really start shooting the picture, like reading the script, going for fittings, etc., but Jim would just show up finally one day, take a look at his pages and step into the lights. This drove nearly everybody crazy, especially Karl. Right now he was telling me in his soft, well-mannered Ivy League voice that this time was different, Jim wasn't any of the places he usually was, he was really missing, and Karl wondered if I had heard from him or knew where he might be.

I had made it clear a long time ago that I would not be responsible for Jim, and he would not be responsible to me, and so I said no and told Karl not to worry. Then he wanted to take me to dinner at Ray Stark's house, and I begged off because I was tired, and then he offered to introduce me to a girl, an actress friend of his who happened to be staying at the hotel, and I begged off that, too, although I wouldn't have minded, but I tried not to take favors from Karl, and again I told him I was very tired and would see him on the lot tomorrow, and finally got off the phone. "I Love Lucy" was just getting rolling when the phone rang again, this time Karl's gopher, telling me that my appointment with Karl would be at ten-fifteen at his office, if that suited my convenience, and I said it did, and hung up the phone, walked down to the lobby to the Coke machine and got a couple of Cokes, passed a little time with the desk clerk, when he said, "You got a call, why don't you take it over in the booth," and I said, "Maybe I'm not here," and he said, "I think you want this one," so I went to the little phone booth across the lobby and picked up the phone:

"Hello," said Jim.

"Hello," I said back to him. I waited. There was a little crackling on the line. Long Distance.

"Where are you?" I finally asked him.

"I'm up at your place," he said. "On the mountain."

"That's funny," I said. "I'm down here in Hollywood."

"I know."

I waited. More crackling. Finally I said, "How's everybody up there?"

"Just fine," he said. "All but me."

I made noises like a violin but he broke in:

"Hey can you come up? I want to talk." After a little pause, he said, "I really feel bad, man."

"It's okay," I said.

"Oh, shit, I'll come down there. I'm acting like a goddamn baby."

"No, it's okay, let me come up there . . ."

So it was all a waste of time, me driving down alone. Every year it's something.

WHEN I flew back to the ranch all my relatives except Grandpa had pulled out. Whether from some kind of Okie delicacy or just because they all wanted to go to Laguna Seca and watch the automobile races, I don't know, but when the taxi pulled up at last in front of the ranchhouse there were unfinished projects everywhere in sight, piles of sheetrock, bags of cement and an old broken-down cement mixer from some previous tenant, a couple of the cars opened and spread about in mid-operation, several cans of paint and brushes left to soak. My relatives could rush into the middle of a project faster than anybody I ever saw, but then the pace would get leisurely, consultations would begin, and after a while everybody would be up on the porch in the shade of the house, sitting on the cushioned redwood outdoor furniture or on kitchen chairs dragged outside and brought back in at supper time, smoking and talking about their various projects. Grandpa alone failed to join these afternoon board of directors meetings. He spent most of his time out in the heat, cultivating the ground to get it ready for a second crop, having missed the first crop because I was up here alone at planting time and didn't plant anything. Grandpa went ahead and planted, after he had conditioned the soil, and then of course the rest of the summer would be spent in warfare. But usually I only heard about these things over the telephone, when Cousin Harold or somebody else would answer the phone (most of my relatives, including Grandpa, didn't like telephones), and so coming back like this, only two days gone and yet so much changed, was a little bit of a shock.

I paid off the cab driver and watched him bobble and slide his cab down the rock road until he was out of sight among the trees, and then turned and walked up onto the porch. There were all the chairs out from storage under the porch, the cushions already puffed and shaped to the behinds of the sitters. I looked around. Everything seemed dead, except for the chairs and the open French doors to the living room. Down in the orchard I could see Grandpa doing something at one of the trees, and I waved and yelled, but I don't think he heard me because he just kept on doing whatever he was doing.

I went in through the doors and into the kitchen, hoping to find something to eat. Jim was there, wearing an apron and huaraches and a pair of jeans, washing some dishes.

"I don't think I ever saw you doing dishes before," I said.

"Hello, Ogle," he said. "Everybody went to Laguna Seca for the races. They'll be back in a day or two."

"I don't miss them," I said.

"Neither do I," Jim said.

I poured myself a cup of coffee, Grandpa's coffee, took a sip and sat back. "What was for breakfast?" I asked.

"Oatmeal pancakes," Jim said. He kept doing the dishes. "All gone, though. Sorry."

"Another time," I said.

"I could call Grandpa in," Jim said. "He'd probably be glad to fix you a stack."

"I doubt if you could get him to do it," I said. "Does he know you're back?"

"I yelled at him."

Jim kept doing the dishes. He looked all right. I went out on the porch and sat in the sun, and after a while Jim came out with a cup of coffee and sat on the rail, looking down into the frog pond.

"This is nice up here," he said. "What do you do all winter?"

"Jerk off and read," I said. Knowing Jim, I knew he would get around to it after a while, or not. There was no prying at him, that's what most of the people who deal with him learn right away, don't push Jim.

"I don't blame you for liking this place," he said. "But don't you get lonely all alone in the winter? What do you do for pussy?"

"I go to town, just like everybody else," I said.

Jim took out a little gram bottle of coke, shook some out onto a fingertip and snorted it. He passed the bottle to me, and I snorted some, too.

"I haven't been to sleep in a few days," Jim said.

"Why not drink a fifth of whiskey? Put you right out."

"I tried booze, but all that happened was I got boozy and coky instead of just coky. Had some pretty bizarre fantasies. Let's walk down and see what Grandpa's doing."

"You better put on a shirt," I said.

We walked down to the orchard. Grandpa, wearing overalls and an old striped polo shirt of mine and a straw hat he'd had for at least ten years, was inspecting the trees. We said hello and kissed and he told me that my trees were going to rack and ruin, and that it was hopeless. I said I didn't care, and he told me I was a damned idiot for wasting fruit trees. I said he could have them and he grunted, which I took for a laugh, and, treating us like boys, shooed us away: "Go on, now, I'm *working!*" and me and Jim got out of the orchard.

"Have you ever seen the spring?" I asked Jim. He hadn't, so I took him across the drive to the edge of the woods where there was a big apple tree with a rock spring almost between its roots. A long time ago somebody had sunk a half barrel down around the spring, with a barrel cover, so that after lifting off the rocks put there, and taking up the cover, you had about two feet of icy cold spring water, even in the hottest summertime. We cupped our hands and drank, and then sat back in the shade of the tree. Everything was bright green where the spring leaked out and went back underground. The birds had pretty well stopped singing for the day, and the insects had taken over; they would go at it until about noon, and then everything would shut up, and all that might happen would be a hawk or vulture cruising overhead on the thermals. You can't tell me they're hunting, at that time of day. Nothing's moving at noon for them to hunt. I think they're just fucking around up there, staying out of the heat. I told this to Jim and he laughed and we had some more coke.

"I'm going crazy," Jim said after a while. "And it's no fun at all."

WE STAYED out by the spring for quite a while. Jim didn't mention about being crazy again, and I didn't push him. He wanted to talk about a Japanese girl. Jim and I had been in Tokyo at the same time, me at Tokyo International Airport (Haneda) and him with the Air Force band, stationed at FEAF headquarters downtown. Jim had a couple of rolled joints in his shirt pocket, and we smoked half of one of them. "Don't smoke too much," he warned me. "This is Hawaiian dope, the best in the world."

I said I would be careful.

Jim was in a mood to babble and fortunately I was in a mood to lay back and watch the birds circle, eating a couple of tight sweet-and-sour little green apples, and drawing up a double handful of icy water from time to time. Jim laid back too, and to look at him you'd think he didn't have a trouble in the world. He talked about the Japanese girl, calling her Shiroko, The White Hooker of Shinbashi, as if it was her title. She wasn't white but always wore a white *kimono* and seemed to always be drifting out of the fog just when Jim would be walking through that part of town. He knew all about her before he ever went home with her; she was famous, not just because of the white *kimono* and her incredible beauty, but because she was deaf and dumb, and could only make grunting noises. These sounds put a lot of guys off, but not everybody, and so once when Jim was really drunk he jumped out of the back of his taxi and went up to her, standing on one of the little stone bridges this part of town was full of.

"It was hard to make the deal," Jim said. " 'You speak how much?' was a little gross, with her grunting at you and holding up her fingers for you to count how much, 'Two hundred? No? *Two thousand? Yada! Nondemonai!*'"

We sat around for a while and listened to the wind in the trees.

"Am I boring you with all this bullshit?" he asked me.

"No, man, I heard about her," I said, and managed to keep myself from saying that I had gone home with her once, myself, and hadn't known all these years that Jim had. She was an incredible beauty, yes, true, and she *did* making squawking noises instead of talk, wore a white *kimono*, etc&etc., but the most important thing about her was her eyes. She had deep black eyes that looked at you from a hundred thousand miles away, and all the dirtiness, the embarrassment, the crude wrongness of the deal seemed to fill your mouth, even though she was polite and considerate and took you by the hand into her little hotel up one of the alleys off A Avenue, and you wished you hadn't stopped her, or after finding out she was deaf and dumb, you would smile and be a good guy and just give her some money and go away, but no, you couldn't pass up that incredible beauty, you couldn't let yourself not fuck her, and so you did, with her kissing you and grunting and groaning and giving you everything she had, but afterward you would look into those eyes and wish you hadn't. At least that's the effect she had on me. I didn't tell Jim any of this.

"I saw her in L.A., man," he said to me.

"Must be a lot older," I said, but the hair on the back of my neck stood up.

"No, not like that, I just saw her, walking down Hollywood Boulevard, wearing her same old white *kimono*. Back in Tokyo after I took her home that one time I went AWOL, man, lived with her for six fuckin' weeks. Then I went back and pulled an Article Fifteen and the band took off for the Embassy Run and I never saw her again, never went to Shinbashi again, man, that six weeks was really something."

First there was one big bird, then two, then three, all circling, their wings like dark outstretched fingertips, riding the thermals, drifting among the warm odors, waiting for that sharp, bitter smell of carrion that would mean dinnertime. We watched them for a while.

"How about seeing her on Hollywood Boulevard?" Jim asked me.

"Just one of those crazy optical hallucinations, I guess," I said back to him. "Happens all the time. Like these goddamn birds, do you really think there are any birds overhead?"

"Not if you say not, huh, Pal?" Jim laughed.

"Pretty scary, huh?"

"You goddamn fucking believe it," Jim said.

"That's the way we use to talk in the service," I said. "You don't know, *do* you!

"Huh?"

"Huh, *hell*, pay attention!"

"Scared the shit out of me, not that I believed it was her, you know, but just to be reminded scared me. I wonder how long she's been dead . . ."

"Does she have to be dead?" I asked, but my own sinking heart knew she was dead, long dead, Tokyo hooker dead.

"She's dead," Jim said with certainty. "Dead as a fucking doornail. Or why would she be haunting me on Hollywood Boulevard?"

"I certainly don't know," I said.

"That's not what's driving me nuts, though," Jim said. "It's everything else. If my life consisted entirely of seeing Shiroko on Hollywood Boulevard in the middle of a busy hot afternoon, I'd be the happiest man on earth, but no, there's more, there's lots more, Jesus, you must be bored by all this talk, I'm not a whiner, God knows, but I've got plenty to whine about."

Jim got carefully up, dusting the grass and dirt from his jeans, and sang one of his bestselling records, only with a really funny whine in it. I laughed after the first few bars, but he sang the whole song anyway, and then sat down again.

"That would sell shit," he said.

I agreed.

WE SAT quietly by the spring. It was one of those times you wish could go on forever, a little hunk of perfect peace. At the edge of the woods, away from the house and the orchard, one of the half dozen or so cats who lived around there was sitting on an old grey fencepost with just the tip of his tail moving slightly. The old cat seemed to be in a good humor, his eyes half closed, when I heard a whirring, clicking sound and saw a hummingbird hovering a few inches from the cat's face. Hummingbirds are tough little guys and with that vicious needle beak and that incredible speed, there isn't much for them to be afraid of. The little emerald bird whirred and clicked at the cat. The cat opened his eyes wide, looked at the tiny bite-sized creature, and turned away. A deliberate snub.

The hummingbird whirred off, clicking with satisfaction. I laughed.

"What's funny?" Jim asked.

Since he had just sung me a song, I felt it would be all right if I ogled him. I looked into his eyes, my mouth slightly open, my expression that of a man who is about to say something, something right on the tip of his tongue, if he could only just begin to get the words out, and held that expression, expectant, like troops at drill when the drill sergeant has yelled "FORWARD . . ." and everyone is set for "MARCH!" but the sergeant doesn't say it, and the troops lean forward, still expecting the sergeant to catch the rhythm and say "MARCH!" but he doesn't, and so the troops begin to fall down or relax or stiffen up, and then, when the timing is perfect to screw everybody up, *"MARCH!"*

Only of course Jim was used to it, hell, it was the basis of our act, me slow and him fast, me with not quite enough marbles rolling around in my attic;

him always with something to say, a song to sing, a little dance, but never making fun of me, never the songs or jokes at my expense, always my helpful sweet enthusiastic friend who would love me to be untonguetied, but him the straight man and me the one who, at the last possible minute, comes out with the word or the sentence or the grunt that makes the house come down.

But for now I just ogled him, my jaw getting gradually lower and lower until he had to crack.

We had been at it together for a long time but we still broke each other up, and I don't know about anybody else, whether painters or writers or actors or pratfall comics secretly love and admire their own stuff, but we sure did, and not all that secretly. People enjoyed that about our act, and told us so in their letters, and the best bit we ever did on the Tonight Show, the bit that got the most mail for us, was when Jim had been late as usual and Carson didn't think he was going to show up at all, even though Jim had been there all day rehearsing. Now he was gone, the staff was going crazy, Carson was doing his backstage burn, and finally the clock swung around and we were taping without him.

Carson called me out onstage first, because we were set to leave early, and Jim still wasn't there. I came out feeling fireants all over my body, and after the applause, sat down and listened to him improvise an excuse for Jim.

I didn't know what the hell I was going to do. We had material, but Jim did all the setting up, and my payoffs without his setups were less than nothing.

Finally Carson turned to me.

"Ogilvie without Larson," he said. "This is probably a show business first. What shall we talk about?"

Thanks, Johnny. Since I had no material I could use, I just ogled him, thinking he would take Jim's part, but instead he ogled me back, and Carson is a master ogler.

We ogled each other back and forth, with Carson giving the audience little side-ogles to bring them into it, and we were doing pretty well, getting a satisfactory volume of response from the house, when Jim stood up in the trumpet section of the band, holding somebody's instrument, and said, "What's the matter with you boys?" To the audience, once the lights and camera had pinned him, he said, "They both been eating peanut butter, look at 'em . . ." and the cameras came back to us, and we did our mouths-full-of-peanut-butter impression, and then back to Jim, who said to me, "Well, what is it? Bubble gum? What are you boys chewing on that makes your faces so stiff?"

When it felt right, I said, "Prunes . . ." The camera went in on Carson for the laughter and applause, and when it was dying down Jim cued the bandleader and began his first song from there, but that wasn't the part that got the fan mail. It was while Jim was singing. I leaned forward, still ogling, thinking the camera was off me until the end of the song, but then on went the little red light that meant my camera was hot. I ogled some more, and the cameras intercut us, Jim singing and moving down out of the band, and me apparently dumb with enjoyment listening. As Jim finished the number I fell off the couch.

It was naked camera-stealing, but the people who wrote the letters saw it as an example of brotherly love.

"How do you guys stand each other?" Carson said later.

THE BIRDS had smelled out their dinner. Over in the orchard, underneath the apricot tree. Grandpa lay dead on his side, his eyes wide open, his mouth loose and his tongue hanging out just a little bit. Jim saw him first, as we were about to go up to the house and get something to eat.

"Oh-oh," he said. "Grandpa's down!"

We ran over to the body and got on our knees in the dirt clods, but it was no use. He was clearly dead.

"Son of a bitch," I said. Jim took his feet and I took his arms and we carried him back up to the house. His head hung down and so I didn't look at him, except to be careful going up the porch steps not to bump him against the stairs. We laid him out on one of the big redwood loungers. He was awfully light.

"How old?" Jim asked.

"Mid-eighties," I said. "He was one of my favorite people."

"Well, he's dead now."

I sat down next to Grandpa's body and Jim went into the house. I looked up at the sky and saw the buzzards circling. I thought they only did that in cheap movies. Then suddenly there were thousands of black specks dancing in the light and my heart blew out of my chest and somebody right next to me was bellowing in anguish, it didn't take me very long to realize it was me because I could see my face in the windows, my eyes crazy and my teeth clenched, and then the glass disappeared with a helpless tinkle and I was swinging a huge chair against the French windows and crying out in pain, yet I was watching all this, unable to stop. Then Jim was there and I was sitting cross-legged on the porch crying into my hands.

After a while Jim handed me a box of Kleenex, which I used to wipe my eyes and blow my nose.

Then I could think again, calm inside. All the fuss and bother to come, the funeral, the arrangements, the lawyers, even for poor Grandpa the lawyers would come around, the selection of a plot, buying a coffin, all that crap. I thought maybe it would have been better not to have seen him lying there and let the birds have their feast. It would be easier, cleaner and cheaper, and Grandpa wouldn't mind, he wasn't there anymore, you only needed to look at the body to see that Grandpa wasn't in there anymore.

The anxious feeling began to go away. I was thinking: Well, it was a good way to die after a long life, out there scowling at the bugs on the trees and then wacko, no fuss, no muss, no long drawnout pain, no months or years in bed, Grandpa hated to have people wait on him, and now there would be none of that, he liked to get up at chickenfart, as he put it, and *get out there*, and *get to it*, and now he wouldn't have to lay in bed while everybody else got up and at it and he couldn't. It was a good way to die. No helplessness, no humiliation, no begging.

I reached out and shut his eyes and they stayed shut. I pushed the tip of his tongue back into his mouth and closed the lips, and he looked peaceful. I went into the kitchen. Jim had laid out six lines of coke on an ivory-backed hand mirror that belonged to Cousin Mallie, and gave me the mirror and a striped drinking straw.

"These are for you," he said.

I did the lines and felt better. We went out on the porch. The sun was high enough to put half the porch in shade, so we pulled up a couple of chairs by Grandpa and sat. It was still an utterly peaceful afternoon. The birds had gone away, maybe they knew they were out of luck here, I don't know, but the sky was blue and empty. We sat for a while, not talking. I cried a couple of times and had to go in the house and blow my nose, thinking how strange it was, I could think about Grandpa very calmly, how it was all right that he was gone, how it had to happen someday and this day was as good as any, and then these tears would rush up out of me and I would sort of yell and then sit there holding the sides of my chair and bellow, like, until the snot was running out of my nose, and then I'd get up and head for the bathroom. Jim paid no attention to me; he just sat there looking out over the view and rocking in his chair, like he had lived there all his life.

Finally I came back, my face all washed and my nose blown for about the fiftieth time, and I said, "That's all." I sat down again. Jim had a can of beer and offered it to me.

"No, thanks," I said. I giggled. "I'm trying to quit."

"Maybe we should bury Grandpa," Jim said.

"How do you mean?" I asked, but I knew what he meant.

"You know, just pick a pretty spot out by the trees, dig a hole, and bury him. There's some champagne in the refrigerator."

"I know," I said. "It's mine. They never touch it."

"We wouldn't have to tell anybody. Hell, it's nobody's business anyway, except Grandpa's . . ."

"And he can't complain," I said. "But what about the family? We'll be cheating them out of a funeral."

"Tough tiddy," Jim said. I took a sip of his beer. "We could tell them a story," Jim said.

"Grandpa ran off," I said.

"A big fat Avon lady, with a suitcase full of cosmetics," I said.

"She took one look at Grandpa, and he took one look at her . . ."

"And that's the last we saw of either of them."

"Just another missing person," I said.

"Meanwhile, he'll be safe in the ground," Jim said.

"Safe from Avon ladies and funeral homes," I said.

"Buzzards and relatives."

"Fuck it, let's *do* it."

"Grandpa would have had it *done*, by now. . . ."

"You know what?"

"What?"

"He died with his boots on."

There it was, I started bellowing again, went into the kitchen and started throwing things. Jim waited outside until I had made quite a mess, but I didn't feel so bad anymore.

I started to clean the kitchen but Jim said no, let him do it, and I did, opening a bottle of champagne and smoking a joint out on the porch by Grandpa. I could hear Jim cleaning up, sweeping the broken stuff off the floor, singing one of his damned songs about how great it was to be in love on such a wonderful day. Even after all these years and the events of the day, it was something to hear the way Jim could land on a note, not the greatest singer in the world, just a guy who could hit the notes and fill them out and make you glad to hear him do it.

I began to wonder where to put Grandpa, and after a while I let out a huge laugh, and Jim stuck his head out: "What's funny?"

"I was just thinking, the only place on the fucking mountainside where you can dig more'n a couple of inches is right about where Grandpa fell."

"You mean we carried him all the way up here for nothing?"

The burial itself came off pretty well. We got out long-handled shovels from under the porch, and I got Grandpa's old favorite patchwork quilt that I think his wife made before she died so long ago, and we wrapped Grandpa in the quilt and carried him back down to the orchard and then dug the hole for him. There was only about six inches of topsoil, most of it broken up into clods, and below that the ground was loose yellowish dirt, easy enough to dig. It was sometime after nightfall when we finally put Grandpa down into the hole and started shoveling dirt over him, and the moon had come up nearly full across the Valley of the Moon by the time we had packed him in and smoothed over the dirt. The champagne was almost gone. I held the last bottle up to the moonlight.

"There's enough for one last toast," I said. We each took a drink. My body was covered with sweat and dust, my nose hurt from all the cocaine, but in the moonlight everything looked eerie and beautiful.

"Grandpa," I said. "He was the spirit of the Old West."

"The last cowboy," Jim said.

"A real dirt farmer," I said.

"Do you know what?" Jim said. "Please don't take me wrong."

"I won't," I said. "What?"

"I think we should dance on his grave," Jim said. "Not as any kind of insult . . ."

"I understand," I said.

"You know, to kind of celebrate the number of graves Grandpa danced on in his time . . ."

But I was already holding out my hands, and Jim took them, and lightly, while he hummed "The Hora," we danced under the moon. There was nothing particularly appropriate about the music, it's just what Jim came up with. He hummed it faster and faster, and we danced faster and faster until I got dizzy and fell down. I watched Jim finish the dance himself, his eyes shut, his hands up in the air, circling slowly around the grave and the apricot tree. He wasn't singing "The Hora" anymore, it was just, *"Ah-yah! Ahhh-yah! Ahh-yah!"*

Later we carried the shovels back up to the house, and Jim went in to bed and actually got some sleep while I sat up in the living room at the old wicker table by the windows, writing a letter to my cousin Harold, telling him what we had done and where Grandpa was buried. If he wanted, I would come back for a regular funeral, but the odd thing was, after me and Jim got back to Hollywood, Harold called me up and told me the family had had their own funeral down at the gravesite, which Harold and a couple of the other men had done a better job of covering up, and that nothing else was planned. That strange Okie tact again, maybe.

JIM'S RENT-A-CAR was a little black bullet designed to go fast as hell for a couple of years and then fly apart. The next morning, somewhat after chick-enfart, we packed ourselves into the car and headed down the mountain. I had stuck my note where they would find it. Jim had read it over breakfast coffee and approved. With seven hours' sleep for three days, Jim had to do a little snorting to wake up properly, and I joined him. It was a bluesky day, warm and pleasant, running down the valley toward the Black Point cutoff. We didn't talk or play the radio, Jim just drove and I looked at the view, which I didn't normally get to do because usually I was behind the wheel. I did wonder if this wasn't going to be my last trip down to Hollywood, but I didn't bring the subject up. Jim knew my feelings and I knew his.

After Black Point we ran along the side of a slough, the road itself up on a levee, as we headed west toward the Coast Range, where we would pick up 101. There were lots of cattails and reeds in the slough, plenty of redwing blackbirds and some long-legged, long-beaked white birds that could have been cranes or egrets or something, beautiful as hell, wading slowly through the shallow water. I just got glimpses of them as we whizzed by, Jim having the car up to sixty or seventy most of the time. The traffic was light this time of day, although we whipped around a few farmers' trucks.

"This must be the last two-lane road in America," Jim said.

Just then a big white Chevy pickup truck whizzed past us barreling down the road, and I saw something funny:

"What the hell they doing?" I said.

Something sticking out the passenger side of the car, then I hear the *snap!* and see the white bird jerked away and over into the water, and we sped past the white bird in time to see a spreading stain of red on its feathers.

"They shot that bird!" I yelled at Jim. Another snapping sound, and looking ahead I could see that they had rifles out both sides. Jim speeded up.

"Pissants!" he yelled. The little black bullet car zoomed forward, almost breaking my neck.

We pulled up next to the white Chevy. I rolled down my window and looked up into the cab of the truck, seeing the tip of the rifle and the straw cowboy hat, the mean, unformed dumb young country face behind the wheel. There were three of them in there, and I could see the punk next to the driver lift up, grinning with all his gums and teeth.

Their faces just barely had time to register recognition when Jim swerved the rent-a-car sharply into the front fender of the Chevy pickup, hard, jamming, the metal screaming in shock, the pickup bucking like a scared horse as it passed over the gravel roadside and the lip of the slough, and then suddenly plunged down the bank and into the water.

I looked back just in time to see the truck go over on its side in the black muddy water, sending up a filthy spray and then quickly sinking in the mud. It was a miracle the driver was able to keep the truck from bashing into the bank and killing them all. I'm certain they were okay, maybe a broken arm or two, and I surely didn't give a shit.

"Let's turn on the radio," Jim said.

"Fuck, yes," I said.

THE TROUBLE with turning on the radio in a car with Jim is that he will either be gloomy because of what he hears (I guess) or he will sing along with the cut, especially if it's one of his, and you might think it would be a double blessing to be an audience of one for a popular singing star harmonizing with himself, but take my word for it, it isn't such a treat. You have to wear a fixed smile and wave your hand, or tap the dashboard to show that you are with it, or Jim will change the station in the middle of the tune—"You don't like it!"—and the whole thing starts again, or he will turn the radio off and drive along at forty miles an hour dead silent, and just as I am about to broach some topic or other, he will burst out *a capella* some new song or part of a song, and there you go again, forced to grin and tap your foot and nod your head, and when he yells at me, "Isn't that *great?*" I still have to worry about my response because one way he might brood for an hour and another he might just keep singing some awful song that will never be recorded.

These little snatches of songs are never the ones he records. They are always songs that are not his style, leading me to believe that Jim isn't all that comfortable with the "Isn't it wonderful to be in love on a day like this" songs, even though those are the ones that bring home the gold.

Jim drives fast or slow according to his mood, rather than traffic conditions, which adds an element of suspense to the whole business. Usually he is deep in thought and drives very slowly, slowly enough to make you crazy if you want to get somewhere, but just as you are about to speak up and ask him to drive faster or pay closer attention to the road he will burst out in song and the car will lurch forward and start weaving in and out among the trucks and police cars. Police don't bother Jim. They pull him over and he charms them out of giving him a ticket. Jim is never smartass with the cops, just humble and modest and agreeable, always admitting he was in the wrong and apologizing, with that little bit of a smile that makes you want to hug him, and the cops mostly would rather get his autograph than give him a ticket.

As we slid down 101 toward the Golden Gate Bridge Jim was singing along with himself, a happy love song, naturally, since it was on the radio, when he interrupted himself and yelled at me, "Hey there's a girl I use to know in Sausalito, okay?" and cut off the freeway in front of a truck at the Marin City exit. Jim talked enthusiastically about the girl, Linda or Susan her name was, and how they had had a fine time last time Jim had been through, as we drove past Gate Five, and while I was trying to remember how many years it had been since Jim had been in Sausalito, Jim tried to find her house. We drove up one street and down another, all the streets in Sausalito being on hills. We had KJAZ on the radio and the windows down and had just finished smoking a joint, so I felt pretty good, even though Jim did not seem to be able to find the place. Twice we stopped and he said, "This has got to be it," and we would get out, open the big wooden gate that both places had, walk through the expensive gardens, with the rhododendrons and azaleas, the hanging fuchsias, the cymbidiums and all, with the mockingbirds and finches singing their heads off in the sunlight and the big jaybirds squawking; up onto the big porches and knocking on the door, but neither place was the place, and after about an hour of hapless wanderings up and down the hills Jim said, "Well, maybe she moved," and we drove down to Caledonia and parked the car so we could get something to eat. Jim was a little pissed.

"I wonder where the hell she went?" he asked me as we walked into the big health food store. We were going to buy fruit and stuff to eat on the way to the airport instead of "wasting time" in a restaurant. Poor Jim.

Anyhow, it was a good thing we stopped in at the health food store, because while I was looking over the pippins, Jim picked up a couple of women. Their names were Lucie and Mimi, and they were probably housewives, dressed in their tennis clothes, buying stuff for their families.

Lucie was tall and blonde, with incredible tits, and Mimi was short and dark and hot-looking, with perfect legs. Obviously Mimi was for me, the way she kept staring at me with hot Spanish-looking eyes, her expression saying, "Relax, you're going to get just exactly what you want," as me and Jim kidded around and helped them pick their groceries. After we all got outside Jim offered to drive the girls home, but of course they had a car there, so Lucie said, "Why don't you come over to my place for a cup of coffee?" and we said yes and followed them. It was only a couple of blocks. Jim said nothing except, "Couple nice-looking tomatoes," and I agreed.

The apartment was all wooden beams and big expanses of blue linoleum, with a nice-looking terrace comfortable with redwood furniture like mine, looking out over the little bay and Tiburon beyond. The trees at the sides of the building gave the terrace a nice privacy, and we had our coffee out there, Mimi fixing mine and bringing it to me and sitting beside me giving me that soulful dark horny look from time to time. We answered their show biz questions with jokes and kept them laughing and having a good time through two or three cups of coffee apiece, and so when Jim and Lucie disappeared into the back of the apartment and were gone for about ten minutes, I knew it was time for love. I had to take an extraordinary piss. I excused myself and went inside, finding the bathroom door open and the bedroom door closed.

I could hear the murmur of voices coming from the bedroom, but I wasn't feeling all that hot about things. The fact is, I was pretty nervous. All Jim has to do is look at a woman and she melts. He can say the most outrageous things to any woman alive and she will only laugh or blush, and never be put off, as she would be if I said any such things. I have heard him say to wrinkled old hags in elevators, "goddamn, honey, I'd sure like to have you lick my cock!" and he'd grin and look her in the eye, and instead of hitting him or calling the police, she would throw her head back and laugh, and by the time we would get off the elevator they would be jabbering like old friends. I don't know what it is. One woman told me Jim had no meanness in him when he said these things and that women could sense that he really liked them, but there must be more to it than that.

Anyhow, I was feeling a bit nervous as I came out of the toilet and knew I had to make a pass at Mimi or sit and talk to her while we both knew what was going on in the bedroom, and how she would probably be disappointed if I did not make a pass at her—whether she took me up on it or not—and of course I was not always sure I could live up to billing, if you know what I mean.

But it was all right. When I got back to the terrace Mimi had taken off her top and was prone on one of the loungers. I sat next to her and talked to her, stroking her hair, until with a lovely smile and parted lips she turned toward me and I saw that she, too, had magnificent tits. God and nature took over.

Mimi and I had a rousing good time, and afterward she told me about her two little boys in Country Day School, and about her husband's good job and their boat and their two cars and the cabin at Alpine Meadows and the snowshoe trip all four of them were going to make through the High Sierras when the boys were old enough, and about singing whales and how awful the Japanese and the Russians were to kill such animals, and about the time she had played tennis with Herbert Gold and beaten him, and about Vitamin C and the common cold. I lay there with my eyes shut until she said, "I think I'll go see what they're doing," and I felt her get up off the lounge, leaving me more room to stretch. The sun was hitting my legs and felt good, so I lay there a while, about twenty minutes, and realized that Mimi had not come back, so the son of a bitch had them both in there.

I got dressed and let myself out and went for a walk. Down to Bridgeway and across to the yacht harbor, walking along the boardwalk looking at the hundreds of white sailboats in their slips. For a while I thought about my grandfather, who probably never set foot on a sailboat in his life, but then gradually I forgot about him. There were girls in summer shorts and tee shirts to think about, and by then I was out of the yacht harbor and walking down the street of shops among the tourists, my hands in my pockets, minding my own business. Jim can't do this because people always recognize him and always crowd around him, wanting to get part of him, I guess. This almost never happens to me. I don't want it to happen, and I think people understand this, except for the odd drunken asshole who is always so dumbfounded that you are shorter than your pictures, but Jim draws them like flies and cannot so much as go into a drugstore to buy a pair of sunglasses without attracting people. Maybe because of this I have a very short fuse about being interrupted, and a reputation for coldness, and Jim has developed into a master of diplomacy, getting out of more tight uncomfortable spots than you could imagine.

I walked all the way down to the Trident at the north end of town, went in for a piece of carrot cake and a big mug of apple juice and then back to Lucie's place. I was outside, about to ring the doorbell downstairs, when Jim leaned over the balcony and said, "Be right down," so I waited.

"Let's get rolling," he said.

We curled up out of Sausalito slowly, Jim quiet and tending to his driving, and onto the Golden Gate Bridge.

"This bridge is a fucking knockout," he said, when we were about halfway across. There was a bank of fog hanging off the coast, but on the bridge it was blue and sunny and brisk, the city all white and glistening like candy on one side and the ships down below passing under the bridge and out into the ocean and adventure—it was hard to believe that the people on those ships weren't heading into adventure, outward bound like that.

WE HAD a small argument about which was the best way to the airport. I said we should go down the 19th Avenue exit and take Park Presidio out through the Avenues and catch 280, which at this time of day was practically empty. Jim held out for Bloody Bayshore because he said the Avenues, as he remembered them, were a pain in the ass if you missed even one light, and a big hangup, etc&etc., but the argument wasn't serious. Jim was behind the wheel, so of course we went past the 19th Avenue exit and down to Lombard Street.

"Let's stop at Enrico's for lunch," he said.

We still had the bag of fruit, candy and pop in the back of the car, but I didn't bother to say anything. I didn't mind going to Enrico's; I hadn't been there in a long time, but I liked the place. And the Broadway exit led right to the Bayshore, so it was on the way.

Jack parked our car in the lot next door after giving us a big hello, still running the lot after all that time. Jim and I had gotten our start in North Beach and knew a lot of people there.

Enrico's is a sidewalk cafe on a major truckroute, and so you sit at the marble tables sipping your espresso while the big tractors and their loads rumble through the gears, and the walking wounded of the quarter lurch past on the sidewalk.

Most of the entertainers who come to San Francisco spend time at Enrico's; for one thing, nobody makes too much of a fuss over you, and for another, the place stays open until three or four in the morning, although not serving liquor after two. I started to walk through the sidewalk part, but sitting at one of the tables and looking like a little wooden dummy of himself sat Grimaldi, Pierre Grimaldi, Uncle Peter, with his beret, his tremble and his double Martini.

"Uncle Peter!" I yelled and went over to him.

"Uhn, godd*amn*, if it isn't, what's-his-name, Dick Ogilvie," Grimaldi muttered, and started to try to get to his feet. I pushed him back down in his chair and sat down. He was alone and looked terrible, old, shriveled, shaking, his chin in constant motion. But he sat as always erect, with his old hands folded neatly at the base of his Martini glass, and his eyes sparkled. "How are you, you old son of a bitch," he said to me. "Where's Doctor Jim?"

Jim came around the corner then and spotted us and broke out into a big dazzling smile and hugged Grimaldi, kissed him, peeked under his beret, took a sip of his Martini and generally made the old bastard feel like the King of England.

"Grimaldi, you old fart, I thought you were dead," Jim said.

"I *would* be dead if the women had their, uhn, way," Grimaldi said slowly.

Enrico came out of the back of the cafe and shook hands with us. "Hello, you old wop," he said to Grimaldi.

"I'm no wop, goddamn it," Grimaldi said. "I'm a fucking Swiss." But Enrico and his sidekick and a couple of dogs who had come out of the back of the place were gone by the time Grimaldi finished talking. He was always a slow talker, but now he was really slow. Back in the days when he had his club, Grimaldi always went around with at least one young pretty girl on his arm, even though he was already fifty or so and starting to totter from the combined effects of booze and tobacco. "I've drunk more kerosene than you've had liquor," he said once to some punk who had patronized him about the number of Martinis he put away. Grimaldi's club was where Jim and I first got our act together well enough to make a living at it, and in fact Jim had started in the house band there. But that was a long time ago.

Now Grimaldi didn't have any club. He had sold it at the height of the North Beach real estate boom, just before the topless craze turned Broadway into a war zone, and unlike a lot of the big sports who made money out of night clubs, he put a lot of it away and owned a couple or three apartment buildings on Russian Hill. "All full of Chinese," he told me with a trembling grin. "Pay in gold, weigh it out every Friday night, we share a glass of *Ng Ga Pai*, and everybody's happy."

"I think we should have a round of Martinis," Jim said. After we placed our order with the waiter, Jim said to Grimaldi, "What do you do for pussy?"

"Jesus, Jim, the same as always. I just walk around North Beach with the tip of a hundred dollar bill sticking up out of my pocket." But after a couple more raw jokes, Grimaldi told us he was living with a twenty-three-year-old girl. "She says she's Korean, but I don't believe her," he said.

"What do you reckon she is?" I asked.

"Just another, unh, Chinese," he said. He took out his cigarette lighter, an old gold Dunhill that had been fondled so much it glowed like an amulet. I must have watched Grimaldi go through this ritual a hundred times, but now it took him forever: taking out the lighter and putting it on the marble tabletop, then reaching into his inner pocket and coming out with his dark-stained old ivory cigarette holder, fooling with it, blowing through it and making sure it was clean, and then withdrawing a box of Benson & Hedges cigarettes out of his blazer side pocket and opening the box, removing the cigarette and slowly screwing it into the holder, both hands trembling enough to drive you crazy, and then finally putting the holder into his mouth and flicking the lighter.

Civilizations could rise and fall while Grimaldi lit his cigarette, a lonely old guy walking the streets of North Beach, having his regular stops, Gino & Carlo's for his first glass of beer in the morning, down the street to the Trieste for espresso and read the newspaper, and then across Columbus to the Chinatown part of Grant Street, slowly wandering from store to store, picking up the groceries and sundries of the day, and then up the stairs on Washington Street to the top floor flat where he kept his collection of Tiffany glass and local painters, the collection supposedly worth hundreds of thousands of dollars, I don't know, I've never seen it, and then out into the saloons for the rest of the afternoon and evenings, unless his story about living with a Chinese girl was true, and of course there was no way to know, but it doesn't matter, because Grimaldi was an important guy when he was giving starts to all kinds of things, his name was in the paper all the time, and he was interviewed on the television, and now that he didn't have his club anymore, those days long in the past.

We had a couple of Martinis apiece, the place was buzzing with the late lunch crowd, and then the waiter came out to our table and told me there was a phone call for me. Jim gave me a kind of funny look, and I went in to the bar and took the phone.

It was the studio. How they found us I don't know. I told them we were on our way, and they insisted that they were not worried, everything was fine, but of course they were worried sick, because we were late, not really late, but late on a schedule that allowed us to be late, just a little bit late. These couple of days late weren't costing them anything much on the production board, but if we were really late, say, a week late, then the blood would begin to flow, sixty people on salary doing nothing but being paid anyway is enough to drive any production supervisor right out of his mind. But we weren't that late, and I told them not to worry, we were going to have lunch here and then catch an afternoon commuter plane.

When I got back to the table, Grimaldi was alone. I finished my second Martini and was looking at the menu when it occurred to me that Jim might not have gone to the toilet.

"Where's Jim?" I asked Grimaldi.

"He went down the street," the old man said.

I ordered spinach crepes and another Martini. By the time I had finished lunch Grimaldi had gone on his way, moving down Broadway at about a foot a minute, and Jim had not showed up. I paid the check and left. The car was still in the parking lot so I took a stroll up to the all-night dirty bookstore and then across and down to City Lights Books and then to the Discovery bookstore where I used to work when it was a tiny place. I didn't recognize any of the kids working in among the stacks of used books and records, so I walked on down past the old Hungry i, the Purple Onion, Grimaldi's, and only the old Onion was still there, but I didn't go down the steps, it was too creepy for me, so I went back up to Vesuvio's and started drinking beer.

I had done comedy and theater in the service and got out of it because of the stage fright, but now everybody in North Beach seemed to be doing something great. San Francisco was full of young poets and folksingers, writers, vocalists and comedians; so me and Jim worked up a little act between us and he begged Grimaldi to let us try it out. Unfortunately, Jim got me stoned my first time, out in the alley before we went on, and by the time I was under the lights I was high and dry. I just stood there through the polite applause and then the silence and then some coughs and shifting in the seats, and then some of them thought it was funny and laughed, and then everybody laughed, and stopped and waited for me to say something. But all I could do was leer at them and try to remember where my mouth was, and they thought this was really funny and it brought down the house, applause and everything, and then they got quiet and Jim realized what had happened to me.

"What's the matter with you?" he said. "Some cat got your tongue?" and sang a couple of songs, talked to me, told jokes, charmed that audience practically one by one, and finally at the end, I said to Jim, "Thank you," and they ate it up.

So Grimaldi let us do it again the next night, somewhat different but the same basic plan, and we got the laughs. Ten days later Jim put his trumpet away.

I went back to Enrico's and drank more beer, and about seven in the evening Jim came back.

"You feel clean enough to make a dinner party?" he asked me.

"What's up?"

It seemed there was this actress.

🌴

THE DIMORRO mansion was well out Broadway in Pacific Heights, about as far west as you could go in San Francisco without crossing the fog line. While we were trying to find the bell, the door was opened by a Chinese butler, who gave us the fisheye until the hostess showed up and pulled the big door open wide and invited us in. Her name was Bianca diMorro, although it turned out she was just another longlegged San Jose girl. Her friends called her Binnie.

It was quite a nice house, and you could see that everything in it was authentic, from the paintings by Gainsborough and Picasso to the Rodin statue of Balzac shitting his pants, at least that's how it looked to me. I didn't even know it was Balzac until somebody told me. Most of the men in the house were dressed in dark blue suits and the women had on floor-length gowns and it was all very festive and pleasant, especially considering that Jim and I had filled in the early part of the evening with more beer-drinking at Enrico's, and had taken certain steps to insure that we would not fall asleep over dinner, if you gather my meaning.

The party was being given for a little Italian guy who was standing in the corner of the living room near Balzac wearing a light blue sweatshirt under a brown velvet jacket and a pair of gold-rimmed glasses hiked up above his eyebrows, which were bristling out over his nose like wings. I never really caught his name, but I found out he was in America directing a movie, and his two stars, including a certain actress, were along at the dinner. How Jim got us invited I don't know, but he seemed to be on good terms with nearly everybody in the place. I wasn't. I didn't know any of these people, and that made me somewhat uncomfortable. I sat in a corner and nursed a brandy and water, while everybody else laughed and chattered and moved from group to group.

The actress Jim was after was tall and blonde and dressed to kill in what looked to be a soft grey silk gown which matched her eyes, except for the soft part. Just for fun I watched her talking to this guy and that guy, nearly all of them millionaires, you would guess, and watched Jim work his way into the group she was with and start everybody laughing; but she didn't seem to be leaning on his every word, and in fact as far as I could tell, she wasn't impressed by Jim at all, which gave me a certain satisfaction. I wouldn't make a play for her myself, she wasn't my type, I learned right away when we were introduced. For one thing, she was a couple of inches taller than me, and for another, she reeled back visibly when she caught a whiff of my breath and seemed barely able to get control over herself enough to give my hand a tiny squeeze. And those eyes the color of killer-fog. Jim could have her, if he could get her. Which, as I say, did not seem to be happening.

After a couple of hours of hard drinking on everybody's part, Chinese servants came out of the woodwork and set up dining tables in a couple of rooms, me being seated at the regular dinner table, a big round number with a view of the Golden Gate Bridge from where I sat. I must have joined in the table talk but I can't remember any of it, except that when the Chinese servant poured me a glass of white wine at the beginning of dinner I was shocked at how good it was, far and away the best wine I had ever drunk, and I looked up in amazement, about to say something about the *great wine*, only to see that all the other people at the table were swilling it down without comment, probably because they drank wine that good every day of their lives. So I swilled away at it, too, like a good boy, and when the red came it was every bit as good and I swilled it, and when the champagne showed up, it was the best champagne I had ever drunk and I have drunk a hell of a lot of champagne, but swilled it on down without comment like everybody else. Jim and the actress weren't at the same table or even in the same room, but the little director was sitting to my right and talked to me in Italian for most of the dinner. But he could understand a little English: When some society woman across the table from us asked me why Jim and I didn't make better quality pictures and I answered by saying, "We'd like to, but the public won't let us," he laughed and pinched my cheeks. I liked him for that, and one day I will go see one of his movies, if I can only discover his name.

While people were swapping tables and carrying on various conversations at the tops of their lungs, Jim came and found me, and we went out into the big main hall looking for a toilet, finding one up by the front door. After we filled our noses I asked Jim how he was doing.

"Too early to tell," he said.

"Give her some snort and a couple of Quaaludes and she'll melt in your arms," I suggested.

"You trying to teach me how to suck eggs?" Jim said. He splashed cold water on his face, toweled off, and I did the same.

Later in the living room while everybody was sitting around in little groups, I tried to keep track of Jim but couldn't, because women, mostly around forty or sixty, would come over by me and sit, making conversation about one thing or another. After a while I realized Jim was missing, nowhere to be seen, out of sight for more than half an hour. The actress was still in the room, sitting on a little loveseat with half a dozen guys in dark suits at her feet or leaning over the couch, all redfaced and drunk.

But the hostess was missing. Bianca diMorro, long-legged, good tits, nice cascade of dark hair, so I thought maybe Jim was off someplace with her. The host, George diMorro, was right there hanging over the actress. I sat around for another half hour or so, and the hostess showed up again, there she was over by Balzac and the little director, all of them talking away a mile a minute in Italian.

I was heading for the toilet out by the front door when I happened to look up the big double staircase, with its old-looking Persian runner, and saw Jim at the top of the stairs, wearing a solemn expression and nothing else. I went on up the stairs.

"Is there a toilet on this floor?" I joked. He turned without saying anything and we walked down a hall with about fifteen doors, open and shut, on either side. A couple of them were toilets, I could see, but Jim didn't stop until we came to another little stairway. I followed him up and into an area that was obviously the diMorros' private suite. Then through another door into a big silken bedroom. Jim's clothes were all over the floor, and the bed, although made, was wrinkled and the pillows thrown about. Jim sat naked on the edge of the bed, looking mournful and lonesome. I went into the private bathroom and took my piss and came out and he was still sitting like that, so I went to a couch across from the bed and sat down.

I was about to say, "What's the matter?" when Jim spoke up, his voice so low I had to strain to hear him.

"It's all such shit," he said. "I get so tired sometimes." He went on in this vein for a while and I sat and listened to him, not having much to say myself, but nodding now and then to let Jim know I could hear him. Life was painful, life was boring, getting up in the morning was like crawling out from under a pile of rubble, etc&etc., until he suddenly jumped up and said, "I want to show you something," and he went over to a door that was partway open and opened it and went in. I followed him.

It was a closet, but not like any closet I had ever seen before, not just rows and rows of clothes on hangers, but rows and rows of rows and rows, and if that wasn't enough to hold all the dresses and gowns, above the rows of clothing were more, a whole second story of rows of clothes; and on the other side, all in this beautiful unfinished cedar, were these cubbyholes and shelves and cabinets, all full of stacks of sweaters, blouses, underwear of every description, and below that stacks of rows of shoes, so that all Bianca diMorro had to do in the morning was come into the closet and she could find *anything* she wanted. The one thing that got to me was the cashmere sweaters. I have always liked cashmere sweaters. She had so many of them stacked in their little cedar cubbyholes that they were color-graded, starting out with the whitest of white sweaters and going through the just plain white ones to the first hint of a shade of blue through dark blue, and then pink so soft it seemed almost white, getting pinker and pinker until finally, a couple of cubbyholes away you get at last to the red sweaters, and then the sweaters so dark red they seemed almost black, and so on until you get to a whole cubbyhole of nothing but black sweaters, all in all I would guess she had maybe two hundred and fifty cashmere sweaters.

Meanwhile, Jim was handling the underwear, which was as plentiful if not more so than the cashmeres, Jim running his hand over silk slips, brassieres, panties, the whole works, sometimes dropping an item of underwear on the floor of the closet, a nice thick beige rug, and then going on, looking around like a kid in a zoo. "Jesus, an underwear freak would have to die to get to a place like this," I said. Jim didn't say anything back, just kept looking around this closet, muttering to himself and making expressions of amazed disgust.

"You know what?" he said after a while. "You don't see any coats or jackets or furs, so she must have an entirely different closet for that crap."

It was true. I made a comment about what you could do with money if you really tried, and Jim snorted. "Shit. We could run this show for about a month, with our combined incomes."

"Don't be bitter," I said.

"I'm not bitter, I'm just dumbfounded and bored and sick of the whole shithouse mess."

We were out of the closet now, and Jim was putting on his clothes. A maid stuck her head in the door and then unstuck it. I waited for Jim to get dressed, and we went downstairs and made our goodbyes. While I was shaking hands with George diMorro, the Chinese butler stood about three feet from us waiting—I thought he was going to convoy us to the door, but he wanted to tell me that there was someone who wanted to talk to me. It turned out to be a tall skinny fellow in a chauffeur's uniform, with his hat in his hand. He was to be our driver. The studio had sent him.

We got all the stuff out of Jim's rental car and stuffed it into the back of the limousine and then got inside. The chauffeur said he would take care of getting the rental back to Hertz. He was to drive us to the airport if we could make the 12:30 Redeye Special, but if we couldn't he was to drive us to Los Angeles.

We had missed the Redeye by about an hour, so we slept in the back of the limousine, all the way to Hollywood.

"JESUS," SAID Jim, and turned on the lights.

My suite was filled with flowers and baskets of fruit, and somebody on the hotel staff had closed the windows, and somebody else on the staff had turned on the steam heat, so that it was about one-hundred degrees and the fruit had begun to stick to its cellophane.

I grabbed the nearest casement window and tussled with it until it sprung open with a rusty lurch and almost pulled me out eight stories over Los Angeles. I commented on this while Jim burned his fingers on the handle to the steam heat. The hotel telephone, not my private line but the one that goes through the switchboard, rang one long, very long, ring. I was naked and had all the windows open and Jim had managed to shut off all six steam outlets before I answered the phone, and it had rung that long ring the whole time. It was the desk, I was getting messages and they wanted to know if I was in or out. I told her I was out and to send up the messages, but I knew what they were before I saw them. Every year, the same thing, every subagent at the agency would send us a letter by messenger congratulating us on our movie, just a couple of typewritten lines in the middle of a sheet of the heavy crackly paper they use, a signature and the typist's initials below. One year I got sixty of them in two days, all from men I had never met and never would meet. This year it was only forty-six, but the agency business has gone all to hell, I hear.

I went around the room looking at the flowers and cartons and baskets of fruit. I happen not to like cut flowers, but none of the people who send this kind of crap ever seem to get the message. Jim and I put all the stuff out in the hall by the elevator, and after a while, after I had showered and brushed my teeth and combed my hair, the apartment began to be cool and fresh again. Jim had gone into the spare bedroom, and I left him alone.

The apartment has two terraces, one looking out over flat smoky L.A. and the other one at the back, overlooking the hillside covered with trees and people's houses. I stood looking down at a tiny man in a white jacket and dark pants watering a driveway back of the hotel. A mockingbird slowly and carefully went through his repertoire, and from somewhere in a copse of dark pines an owl gave a last contented sleepy hoot. It must have been about nine in the morning, and I felt pretty good. I dressed and walked down the street to Schwab's and sat at the counter for some coffee.

In Schwab's, the place to eat is the room with the booths, which opens at eight. The counter is reserved for people who don't have enough friends to fill a booth or for some reason want to be alone. Nearly everybody respects this; if you are at the counter you want to be alone. If you are sitting in a booth, particularly if you are sitting alone in a booth, looking nervously at the entryway every time somebody shows up, you want company. Lots of comedians and comic actors at Schwab's. People with series, coming in literally in sunglasses with literal entourages. To these people one must wave and smile, after all, they sat there a dozen years waiting for the chance to come in like this, who are you not to wave?

Guys who haven't worked in years. No more shades, no more laughing gang of hangers-on. There's always a big bunch of them at the table just to the right of the entrance of the booth section, and one by one they come over to me at the counter, this particular morning, say hello, the hand touching me lightly on the back, and I grin and shake hands, half-standing, and we exchange little jokes, and they go back to their booth, everybody's on a first-name basis at Schwab's. Dotty and Dorothy, Eddy, Bob, Jim, Jack, Jackie, Jackie and Jackie.

Two cups of coffee, a copy of the L.A. *Times*, a slow stroll back to the hotel past the former site of the Garden of Allah, small silent prayer for the ghost debauchers Bob, Scott, Dash, Des . . . up the slight hill to the hotel, out onto the shady morning terrace in the back to read my paper and get back into the civilized world. I had slept enough, but Jim was still in the spare room making up for the days he had lost, and the studio's happiness that Jim was at last here in place where he belonged would begin to fade under the realization that now we were here, we had to be worked, and that there would be a lot of executive unhappiness to be gotten through before everyone could heave a last sigh and start counting the profits.

BY TEN I had smoked a joint, taken my car up Sunset to the big carwash and run it through, gone to the Ralph's Market further up Sunset and done a big staples shop, come back to the hotel and put everything away and was in the middle of making breakfast—three eggs fried in butter, four strips of butcher's bacon, an English muffin split, buttered and broiled almost black, fresh orange juice and coffee—when I heard a tapping at the door to the suite. It wouldn't be the maid, she wouldn't knock, she'd ring and come on in, so I opened the door only a crack.

There was Karl Meador, our producer, standing out in the hall with his hands in his pockets:

"Hi, can I come in?"

It seemed he had spent the night in the hotel with a lady friend. I got back to the kitchen just in time to toss the eggs, with Karl behind me. I offered him coffee, juice, eggs, but he turned everything down.

"Trying to keep it off," he said, and sighed. Karl had gone through a fat period, and I didn't blame him not wanting to eat. Now of course he was slim and trim, wearing a silk shirt open to the third button, and you could see a couple of thin gold chains hanging in amongst his black chest hairs, Levi's that looked as though they had been tailored and washed out for him by the studio costumers and a pair of Puma running shoes. Karl was nothing if not fashionable. During his fat period he had also gone through his dopesmoking hippie period, and he had worn coveralls and plaid shirts to the office. Before that he had been in his Ivy League period, wearing all that three-piece-British boots drag.

Now he sat in my sunny dining room and watched me eat.

We talked about one thing and another, mostly girls. Karl was into fucking famous women and had fucked a whole string of them and was always getting into the papers this way, never failing to plug his latest picture. Karl makes a lot of movies, three or four a year sometimes, if things break right, but he is always the executive producer of our pictures since the first one ten years ago (Ivy League Period). He was very enthusiastic about the girl in suite 609, who had come to Hollywood from Texas via New York. The way Karl went on and on about her, she was probably going to get her big break in our movie.

While I was sopping up the last of the egg yolk with the last of the muffin, Karl said, "Listen, where's Jim? I called the lot and he's not there."

Jim keeps a bungalow on the lot.

"I haven't seen him today," I said.

Just then a toilet flushed in the back of the apartment, and Karl looked at me with that hatchetman look he can get sometimes, wiping it off his face as soon as he realized it was there, and said politely with a smile, "Who's in back?"

"That could be Jim," I admitted.

My private telephone rang and I went into the living room and answered it. It was my lawyer, who wanted to set up a series of meetings at my convenience, and as we talked I watched Karl getting nervous. It must have driven him crazy to have somebody else on the telephone in his presence and him with no telephone. After sitting straight and staring out the window and tapping his foot, he jumped up and went into the kitchen. I heard the bottled water belch as he drew himself a drink, and then saw him through the French windows walk over to the edge of the front terrace and peer out over the side, and then come back in and grab the house phone, and pretty soon he was having a low conversation of his own, probably with his service, because he kept saying, "No, keep that one" and "Give me that one again" and making little notes in a notebook with a tiny gold pencil.

All the time I had known Karl, ten years, he had been making notes in that same notebook with that same little gold pencil, or else he had a stash of them somewhere, thousands of them maybe, all alike, and got out a new one every morning, who knows? Karl is very secretive about some parts of his life.

Jim came into the living room naked and said, "I'm hungry as a bastard." He did a take when he saw Karl and glared at me.

"What the fuck is this?"

He strode out of the room and we heard him yell, "Get that asshole out of here, *pronto!*"

Karl hung up his telephone quickly and looked at me with big round eyes. "What's the matter?" he asked. I went on with my own call, and pretty soon Jim came out dressed and gave Karl another nasty glare:

"You still here?"

Karl stood up. Jim gave him a dazzling smile and hugged him. "Karl, you old bastard, how's your dad?"

Karl grinned, but I could tell he was really pissed off at Jim.

I hung up my telephone. Jim said, "I'm hungry enough to eat the ass out of a dead mule. Let's go somewhere and have a nice big lunch."

"I have a reservation at the Polo Lounge," Karl said.

"Fuck the Polo Lounge," Jim said.

"We could go to Schwab's . . ." I said. "Schwab's?" Karl asked. There was no enthusiasm in his voice.

"What's the matter with Schwab's?" I asked him.

"Nothing, it's just I've never been there," Karl said.

"Well, suck my nuts," Jim said. "We'll just have to take you to Schwab's!"

As far as I knew, Jim had never been there either.

"What about the girl?" I said to Karl.

"She already ate," he said.

"What girl?" Jim asked.

"What, the coffee and toast they bring you here?" I said. The hotel didn't have a regular kitchen, but you could get anything you wanted if you were willing to pay for it.

"I think she had juice, too," Karl said. "I was in the shower."

"What girl?" Jim said again. He went into the kitchen.

"Get me a beer, will you?" I called out to him, and picked up the house phone, dialing 609.

After a couple of rings she answered, a nice low voice with most of the Texas rubbed off.

"This is David Ogilvie," I said. "We're all going over to Schwab's for something to eat . . ."

"Here, let me talk to her," Karl said. He came over toward me holding out his hand for the telephone, but I backed away.

"You want a beer, Karl?" Jim called from the kitchen.

"No, thank you," Karl said.

". . . Me and Karl and Jim Larson," I said into the phone.

I heard the pops from the kitchen as Jim opened the beer, and felt a sudden wave of anxiety right down through my socks. "We'll pick you up," I said to the girl, and hung up.

Jim came out and handed me my beer. He smiled at Karl.

"Got a little piece of pussy stashed away here at the hotel, huh?"

"Little bit of the old Texas poontang," I said. "What the hell's her name?"

"Sonny Baer," Karl said. He spelled it out while Jim and I looked at him blankly. "It's her real name," he said. "You know those Texas people and their names. Rip Torn. Sissy Spacek. Candy Clark."

"And now Sonny Baer," Jim said. "She must be a real asshole."

"Karl probably wants to put her in our picture," I told Jim.

"Hell, I'm for it, if it gets Karl laid," Jim said.

"Maybe we ought to call Schwab's for a reservation," Karl said.

"Hey, it's a drugstore, man, you don't call for reservations," Jim said.

After we finished our beers I went into the bathroom and got a couple of joints out of my shaving kit and we drifted down to the sixth floor.

Sonny Baer was dressed in a plaid shirt and jeans. She had bushels of honeycolored hair, big deep blue eyes and a grin that cut the stunning effect of the rest of her and made it clear that Sonny Baer, whatever else, was no asshole. She grinned at me and shook my hand and said, "I see all of your movies at least twice."

"What?" I said.

Those eyes had never left mine, not even once, to look at Jim or Karl. "I love your movies. They're funny."

"What about *my* movies?" Jim asked.

Sonny said, "Oh, are you in the movies?" and won my heart forever. Jim laughed and shook her hand.

"Boy, you got great tits," he said, grinning and glinting.

"Give me a couple of minutes, okay?" she said, and went into the bathroom. Karl reached for the telephone and took it into Sonny's breakfast nook, and Jim turned on the television set. Jim and I watched a rerun while Karl talked in a low voice and made notes. Finally he came back in to where we were, looked from one of us to the other as if he wanted to say something, gave up and sat down and watched about thirty seconds of a commercial, then got up and went into the back of the apartment, then came out again, sat with us for another thirty seconds at least, and then went out onto Sonny's balcony, which overlooked the front of the hotel and Sunset, the same view as from my front terrace.

We were well into another rerun when Sonny came out, looking about the same, and we all jammed up at the door trying to open it for her.

"Wait a minute," she said. We all stopped and looked at her.

"Does anybody have a number? I'd really liked to get stoned."

I pulled out a joint and lit it, and Jim shut the door. It only took a minute for the three of us to smoke up the joint—Karl didn't smoke *anything* anymore, because, he said, it made him lose his feeling of control. Now he just waited patiently. Karl up in my apartment was one thing, he could never handle us somehow, but he didn't get where he was by being a jerk, and now, with an audience, it was more like the public Karl, smooth, darkly handsome, cool as ice. Karl was a real snooker player, and I should have known there was more to this whole Mickey Mouse morning than getting a part for his girlfriend.

"This is great dope," Sonny said. "What is it?" I could hear that Texas burr coming on a bit stronger now.

"Maui Zowie, the best marijuana in the world," I said, "and it hasn't even hit yet, give it another five minutes . . ."

"Hot damn," she said. "They got nothing like this in New York."

We all got into the elevator, and I pushed B for basement, but Sonny pushed L for lobby. "I want to check my mail," she said.

We waited and held the elevator door while she talked to the girl at the desk and finally came back to the elevator with a fat little letter, which she opened and glanced over quickly and then stuffed into her big leather purse.

"Letter from home?" I asked her.

"You're pretty smart," she said.

We walked down the little hill to the Liquor Locker, past the magazine and newspaper racks.

Jim said, "Anybody got any quarters?" and bought a dirty newspaper. Sonny looked at the cover and made a face.

"I want to go in here," I said, and went into the liquor store while everybody else stayed outside in the sun. I picked up a couple of pints of Old Crow and tossed one to Jim.

"Remind me I want to stop here on my way back," Sonny said to Karl.

"The prices are really terrible in there," Karl said. "You should shop over at the Chalet Gourmet."

"Anyway," she said.

🌴

BY THIS time of day Schwab's was packed, with a big double line of people waiting for booths in front of the cigar counter and every seat at the long counter filled. Lunch is different from breakfast. At breakfast the day is glittering with promise, the calls to be taken, the deals to be made, the mail yet to come; by lunch a lot of this has been taken care of, but never mind, lunch is *who are you with* and *who's in the room*; there's a need to maintain at least the appearance of being fully employed in this pleasant clatter and chatter of show business. Beginners come here to somehow be absorbed into the mainstream, longtime hangers-on come to be with their friends and equals, stars and hits come to keep themselves honest and to remember, *this is how it was and this is how it could be again.* And a lot of people come here to look at the others, and a lot of assholes and dimwits show up to confuse the issue.

I like Schwab's.

"We'll never get a seat," Sonny said, and moved off through the drugstore. Jim and Karl and I took our places at the end of the line, but of course when we had come by the window to the booth room and then in through the big double glass doors everybody did a take at us, as they do with everybody, and the energy of the room began its gradual shift.

I had to admire Karl. Here he was, a man with literally hundreds of jobs to dispense over the course of a year, brought half against his will into a room full-to-spilling with eager jobtakers—performers, showoffs, clowns, ladies and gentlemen who had been working all their lives at the fine art of attracting attention. A lesser man than Karl would have balked at the door when he sensed the energies inside, or would have refused to come at all. But not Karl. He knew personally at least a third of the crowd and most of the rest by sight, and he behaved like a champ, cool but not aloof, nodding and smiling with recognition, shaking hands and having something to say to everybody who came up to him.

Yet it was not like watching a master politician shedding his golden light on the chosen obscure, it was more like a tribal elder getting down with the troops; my God, this guy could put everybody in the room on easy street with a wiggle of his finger, he knew it and they knew it, and the energy coiled and surged.

Naturally, when everyone got over their surprise at seeing Karl they turned back to their own conversations, because nobody likes to get caught with his tongue hanging out. But it was as if everybody had sniffed cocaine in the interval between our arrival and the time we were seated in our booth, everyone a little happier, a little more jacked up, because *they* were *here* and *we* were *here* and big things must be happening. They would not have been nearly as turned on by just me and Jim, we're only jobtakers like them, but Karl was a Big Boss, and the best way to behave in front of a Big Boss is to appear friendly, fully employed, with a future full of projects.

Every conversation rose a couple of notches, and the fractured sounds bounced off the walls as the energy moved around the room gathering force.

And so of course it affected us, too, that wonderful sense of wellbeing, helped along only a little bit by the whiskey I poured into my coffee the minute Dorothy the waitress turned her back.

"Look who's drinkin' on New York time," somebody said, and the words ricocheted and everybody laughed, but not in chorus.

Jim read a couple of the raunchy sex ads from his little newspaper.

"Ugh," Sonny said. She had joined us as soon as the booth opened up. "Down in Texas we don't do stuff like that except to animals."

Jim read a couple more but nobody was listening, so he put the paper away and laced his own coffee.

A woman came by the table for autographs, she wanted all four signatures, she didn't give a damn who any of us were, but I had to feel sorry for Pops, back in the booth, red with shame.

While we waited for Dorothy to come back and get our orders, Sonny read her letter and Karl worked the room, making it around to everybody he had to stroke, giving it the personal touch and paying good dues. If somebody had seen him come into the place and then told his booth that he and Karl had this relationship, and Karl failed to acknowledge the relationship, the guy could be made to look foolish, and then some time in the future this could cause trouble. Making movies is trouble enough without trouble.

"When you consider he's got a heart the size of a beebee, he's doing all right," Jim admitted.

A couple of guys across the room reluctantly got up from their booth, but the pack was massing at the cigar counter and they had to leave. Instead of just going out, they took hold of one another and waltzed down past us and around the other row of booths and out that way, to a scattering of applause. Then a comic who was now working a police show as a straight actor came up to us, gave me a broad wink and bent over to whisper in Jim's ear.

Jim got serious at once. Karl slid back in the booth, strain showing around his eyes, and picked up a menu.

"Who was that?" he asked Jim.

"I don't know," Jim said. "He told me the poison was in the vessel with the pestle."

I happened to look out into the drugstore, and saw the fat face of a comic I had worked with years ago, out by the display of stuffed animals, in a place of concealment. He winked at me.

I excused myself from the booth and went out and over to him. Instead of shaking hands or anything, I pulled a long secret agent face and said, "The vessel with the pestle."

"Got it," he said, and moved off like a big fat Groucho toward the telephone in back.

Returning to the booth, one of the Jackies came up to me and said, out of the corner of his mouth, "Is it true?"

I nodded my head.

"The vessel with the . . . ?" He made stirring motions with his finger.

I nodded and slid back into the booth.

It was just silliness, but all over the place we were playing this dumbass game, and it spread from booth to booth, skipping only the newcomers and the tourists, the line from an old Danny Kaye movie getting all sorts of twists and obscene interpretations, and the big joke was, nobody would crack.

Karl was mystified. "What's going on?"

"Karl thinks everything has to do with him," I said to Sonny. "What a paranoid. Just because there are people skulking all over the drugstore . . ."

Then a comic wowowing like a redskin grabbed a big blue-and-white stuffed rabbit from the shelf back of the counter and ran through the drugstore with it. I looked at the woman behind the cash register. She was wearing the most noncommital expression I had ever seen.

"What'll you have, kids?" Dorothy asked.

Karl was still looking at the menu, probably trying to find the Cobb salad, which is what he liked to eat at the Polo Lounge, a Cobb salad being a regular salad that has been through a blender and looks, to me anyhow, as if it had already been eaten once. "What's good here?" he asked without looking up.

"The fish is good," Dorothy said.

Sonny ordered a bacon and avocado sandwich on toast, a big slice of melon and a pot of tea, Jim ordered a cheeseburger with fries and a vanilla milkshake and I had the same. Karl examined the menu front and back a couple of times while Dorothy shifted feet and tried to look patient, and finally ordered a small green salad and a glass of tomato juice. While we were ordering, a couple of girls came up and spoke to us, and I heard a guy in back yell, "Hey, gimme a *job*, man!" but he didn't get a laugh with it, and then there was a cracking sound and a yelp from the area of the cigar counter. The place went dead.

All I could see was a whitefaced guy lying on the floor, and then the mob surrounded him. But word spread rapidly. Some clown, all jacked up to the point of craziness, had somehow smashed the glass counter and cut himself badly. Gradually as the word got around, the babbling in the room started again, but now it was different, the energy had gone negative and there were waves of anger flying through the room, directed at us.

We had done this thing.

Everybody was showing off because we had brought this jobgiver into the room, and now some poor devil lay on the floor with his ass cut open.

Jim was up first and halfway over to the crowd before I got to my feet, hating it, not wanting to go over there but knowing I had to. When I got there Jim was kneeling beside the guy—I didn't recognize him, just another no-name guy—and the druggist was holding a gauze pad against the guy's cut-open pants. There was a good deal of blood on the floor, and I avoided it carefully as I knelt. I was afraid I would faint, but this once it didn't happen.

"The ambulance has been called," the druggist said to me. "They should be here."

The guy on the floor was grim. His eyes rolled around as he looked at the crowd of standees, Jim and me, the druggist, and another guy kneeling, probably the one he came in with. The guy on the floor had wanted to attract attention. Well, he had attracted quite a lot.

"How are you feeling?" Jim asked him.

"How should I feel?" the guy said bitterly. "I jump up on the counter like it's a horse and cut my ass open."

"What do you do for an encore?" I asked, hoping he would take it the right way. But he stayed bitter.

"Showing off," he said. "The story of my life. Show off and screw up."

"Amen," said Jim.

"I bet you're the first guy to get a Purple Heart in Schwab's drugstore," I said. Some of the crowd laughed, but the guy just looked at me.

Jim talked to him quietly for a while, learned his name, chatted with him about some people they knew in common, and then the two whitejacketed ambulance boys came trotting in and we helped get the wounded man onto the gurney.

"Goddamn lucky man," said one of the ambulance boys. "One more inch . . ."

We went back to our booth. The hostility was gone out of the room. By now everybody was seeing it as an event that might generate a little publicity, might make an item for Hank Grant or Army Archerd. Maybe even the wire services would pick it up, and I watched various people getting up and making their way back to the telephones. "I don't see why you like that place," Jim said to me after we left. He probably thought it was always like that.

OUT ON Sunset the sidewalks were empty and the street aswarm with cars. Karl and Sonny walked ahead of us, close together, talking. When we drew up to the Liquor Locker they both went in. Jim and I stood outside in the tiny parking lot. I took a nip from my pint and passed it to Jim.

"You said you had a lot of shit to do today," I said. "I'm still kind of shook up about that guy," he said.

"Me, too," I said.

"But I do have a plan," Jim said. "A way to get her shirt and pants off. I'd love to see those pretty little tits."

"What's the plan?"

"We'll go swimming," Jim said.

"I wonder if they have any film on her."

"What the fuck difference does it make?"

When they came out of the Liquor Locker both were carrying big paper bags full of stuff like deluxe mixed nuts, a quart of orange juice, bottle of Stolichnaya vodka, loaf of bread, milk, etc&etc. We moved slowly up toward the hotel.

"Well, I have meetings all afternoon," Karl said. "When's our first meeting, do you remember?"

"Isn't this it?" I said.

"I have a great idea," Jim said. "Let's all go for a swim."

"The pool here is too cold," Sonny said. "I tried it out a couple of times."

"Later in the year you'll appreciate it," I said.

"There's not a pond in Texas less than ninety degrees," she said. "Except when they're froze over."

"Why don't we head for the beach?" Jim said.

"Does anybody have any more grass?" Sonny asked. "I ran out a couple of days ago."

"Oh, hell yes," I said. "I still have a joint in my pocket." Which I took out and lit, passing it to Sonny.

"Hell," said Karl, "if you're going to go to the beach, you might as well come over to the house. I guarantee our pool is as warm as any Texas mudhole."

We walked lazily into the driveway past one of the staff watering the concrete and up to the elevators. Here, there was an uncomfortable pause while the three of us who smoked finished the joint. I swallowed the roach, washing it down with a bit of whiskey.

"My car's a two-seater," Karl said. "Unfortunately."

"Okay," I said, "then Sonny can ride with me, and we'll get acquainted, and you and Jim can talk business."

"Can't we all go in your car?" Jim asked me. Glint.

I laughed at him. "You want to sit in back with Karl, hugging your knees?"

So it was all decided. But this was no time to leave Karl alone with her. We all went up to 609 and had a nice musical comedy, putting her stuff away in the kitchen, drinking her beer and my whiskey, while she went in and changed and Karl got on the telephone. When she came out she seemed to be dressed exactly the same.

"Let's go," she said.

In the corridor I said to Karl, "You guys go ahead, Sonny and I will go up to the penthouse and get some more of my Maui," and I made it firm. Jim took Karl by the arm and off they went.

"Now, we are alone," I said.

"Let's go upstairs and get that weed," she said.

🌴

WHEN IT'S right, it's right and you can feel it in the air, when your bodies brush together the sparks fly and the ozone cooks; she cannot take her eyes off you, you cannot take your eyes off her, and nobody has to say a thing. As the elevator rose lurching slowly two flights, I wanted to put my hands on her shoulders and turn her toward me and watch her face tilt up and her lips part, I knew it would happen that way, that she would come in against me and I would press her against the elevator wall, and the kiss would be so hot and filled with excitement that we could slide to the floor unknowing and clutch each other melting into one soul.

Naturally, that's not what happened.

I didn't lay a glove on her in the elevator. We didn't even talk, I just looked at all that sweet honey-ginger hair and thought about the way it would feel against my skin. When the elevator door opened and I saw the maid's cart parked in front of my open door I wasn't even slightly phased, but touched Sonny with the tips of my fingers at the small of her back and she moved into the suite turning up to me and smiling. My knees almost buckled from the look in her eyes.

"Be done in a minute," the maid called from the kitchen.

"That's fine," I called to her. To Sonny I said, "Let's go out on the terrace," and when we were outside feeling the sweet warm winds, she said, "Oh, this is so beautiful," and I could have kissed her then, her face all lit up, but instead I said, "Let me get that weed," and went in the bedroom and got my bag of marijuana out of the cigar box I usually keep it in. I was rummaging around in one of my unpacked suitcases when she came to the door and said, "What are you looking for, papers? I have some down at my place."

"Aha," I said, and held up a package of papers and my little glass door-knob roach clip. She came over beside me and looked down at the long fronds of seedless weed. "That is so beautiful," she said softly.

I could hear the maid preparing to leave. Only a few minutes more.

"Let me go in here," she said, pointing to the bathroom. I was sitting on the bed, rolling a couple of joints on the glass top of the bedside table. By the time I finished rolling these and she got out of the bathroom the maid would be gone and we would be alone again. It made my fingers tremble so much I could hardly make them work, so the two joints were fat and messy. When I stood up my cock was bulging in my pants in an unmistakable fashion, and

I laughed, because it didn't matter at all, let it bulge, soon enough my pants would be gone and hers, too, and we would be on this big white-covered bed fucking like lightning bugs. My heart was about to blow a hole in my chest I felt so good. I didn't need or want any more marijuana, whiskey, anything; I just wanted that sweet lovely girl under me, on top of me, all over me.

Karoom, goes the toilet.

Click, snap, goes the front door.

Suddenly I knew she was going to come out of the bathroom naked, shimmering, ready for love. Here I was, still fully dressed, as if I hadn't got the message, as if I was impervious to the electricity of acceptance all over the room, and I sat down on the bed again and had one of my shoes off and was pulling at the other when she came out.

Dressed.

"What are you doing?" she asked me.

Now, here was a place where I could have used some advice. Maybe what I should have said was, "Changing my socks," or "Just want my feet to breathe a little." Something diplomatic.

But what I said was, "Putting on my birthday suit."

She laughed, grabbed one of the joints and went outside. I finished taking off my other shoe and both socks and went out there barefoot to see if there was any way, any way at all, I could get the magic back.

SHE SAID, "I wish I'd brought my dog. I didn't know they let you keep your dog here."

"That's what the hotel is famous for," I said.

She was looking down at the little curved street that moved up from Sunset to the entrance of the hotel and around behind. "I can see somebody down there now with their dog," she said.

"What kind of dog do you have?" I asked her. "I love dogs."

"Oh, just a little rabbit dog, a beagle," she said. "What's his name?"

"Pepper," she said.

"I was sitting out on the steps of the hotel one morning waiting for the limo to take me to the lot when this car came squealing out around the hotel and the guy behind the wheel threw a bagful of dog turds at me."

She gave me a strange look.

"Well, I guess he was really throwing the bag at the hotel," I said, "but I was the one sitting there."

"That's a weird story," she said, "but I can understand how he might do that, you know, people walking their dogs in front of your house and letting them crap on your lawn."

This conversation was careening off the track. "Pepper, huh?" I said. "Sounds like a cute little guy."

"He's the third or fourth Pepper we've had. My daddy takes them out rabbit hunting and gets drunk and excited and shoots the dog instead."

"Your daddy sounds like an interesting man," I said.

"Oh, Daddy loves to hunt rabbits. He says you can learn more hunting rabbits than you can going to college."

"Did you go to college?" I asked.

"No, and I didn't hunt no rabbits, either. They sent me to the New York City Ballet troupe when I was eleven, and after that drove me crazy I did underwear modeling until I had a nervous breakdown, then I went back to Texas and realized I hat'nt had a nervous breakdown at all, it was just New York. But no matter what, I like it better'n Texas."

She started talking about Texas and her daddy and her uncles, nothing big or important, just little conversational items about her family, leaning back with the sun hitting her face, relaxing; and I nodded and said uh-huh and picked at my toenails. Just a quiet day in L.A. My palms were dry again and I felt good. She seemed to have forgotten my stupid remark, in fact, she seemed to have forgotten we were supposed to be heading for the beach and Karl's house, just relaxed and beautiful.

"Oh, look," she said. "A butterfly way up here." She was pointing at a big yellow and black butterfly who was fooling around the jade plant the hotel had growing out of a big cement pot on the terrace.

"Aren't they *beautiful?*" I said.

She went on to talk about her life as a teenage model in New York and made me laugh a couple of times, not just to get her in the mood, but real laughs, this girl was pretty funny. The mood was coming back, everything was going to be all right.

Except for that goddamn butterfly, who had managed to get caught in the web of a spider under the overhang of the building right above the French doors, now open, that led to my bedroom. While she talked about life in Manhattan I sat still, praying she wouldn't turn around to see the spider rush out of his hole and grab the butterfly.

Maybe it went something like this:

BUTTERFLY: Oh, help, help!

SPIDER: I'm coming, I'm coming!

BUTTERFLY: Oh, help!

SPIDER: Here, let me give you some medication. There, does that feel better?

BUTTERFLY: Oh, thank you. I feel sleepy now.

SPIDER: Here, let me fold those wings of yours, you must be tired.

BUTTERFLY: Oh, so sleepy . . .

SPIDER: Let me just drag you here into the shade . . .

While all this was going on over my head, Sonny talked about herself and never noticed. I alternated between her face and the dinner show overhead. When the spider had finally folded the butterfly into a handy package and hauled it out of sight, I was sitting almost at her feet, listening rapt.

It was up to her to touch me, she knew what we were there for, and I was plenty close enough to touch, but she didn't touch me.

"Your hair," I heard myself say. I reached out and touched her hair. She turned toward me. There was no expression on her face, her mouth a little open, her eyes looking right into mine, eyes like blue opals, and I pulled her to me and kissed her.

First kiss.

Soft little mouth, I put my tongue into it and felt her shiver all over, and then my hand slipped and I fell on my knee beside her loungechair.

"*Ouch*, godd*amn* it!" I said. My knee really *hurt*. I stood up and she started to laugh and then saw the pain in my face.

"Oh, you *hurt* yourself," she said. "I'll run get something for it." She came out in a couple of minutes with a coldsoaked washrag. I was limping around the terrace cursing and crying.

"Here, sit down," she said.

I sat and pulled up my pantleg to where I had skinned my knee, and she pressed the cold washrag against it.

"Oh," I said, "that feels good."

"Do you have any iodine?" she asked me.

"I hope not," I said.

She was looking at me like I was a wounded Boy Scout and she was the nurse at school. I was not crazy about this, and hopped after her, through the bedroom and into the bathroom. The sun was streaming in the open window over the shower and bouncing off the white towels racked everywhere, making her glow. She had the cabinet over the sink open and was going through my shaving kit.

"I ain't got no iodine," I said.

"It's okay," she said, "I have some down at my place. It'll only take me a sec to run downstairs and get it. You don't want an infection."

She started past me and I grabbed her by the arm. "What's all this concern for my health?" I asked, and kissed her on the mouth, hard. This time I could feel her whole body tense up in resistance, and for some reason this pissed me off. The case was closed, we were going to fuck, skinned knee or no skinned knee, and I didn't care if it was in the bedroom or the bathroom, just as long as we got into it and over it.

She pulled away a few times but I just grabbed her some more and kept kissing her, and let my body sag so that we were both pulled down to the tile—it was the elevator dream all over again, only real this time, and cold, and angry, I don't know what got me so angry. While I was kissing I was also grabbing at her body, and she was trying to get me off her, grunting from the effort and talking whenever she could get her mouth free.

Finally she scraped her fingernail across my knee and made me howl, and then jumped back, into the bathtub.

"What the hell's the matter with you?" she asked me.

I got up and went after her. She tried to get around me, her eyes wild but not frightened, and I grabbed her and turned her around so that I was pressing up against her ass and that head of hair was crushed against my face. I could smell it, woman-smell, the first womansmell we all go crazy for as kids, clean hair and plenty of it, one arm around her waist and the other on her tits.

"goddamn you," she said, "You can't just up and fuck me . . ."

"Why not?" I asked her, and pulled her into the bedroom.

We didn't get as far as the bed, though. I started unzipping her jeans and had them down around her knees when we toppled over and hit the carpet, but even scraping my bleeding knee on the pile didn't stop me, I pulled her plaid shirt open, she didn't have anything on underneath, and her tits just sprung out at me. She was talking in grunts this whole time but I wasn't listening. I pulled down her underpants, ripping them a little, and then turned her over on her back and held her down with one arm around her while I pulled off my own pants.

"You can't . . . *do* this!"

"Like hell I can't," I said in an amazingly normal voice.

I stuck my cock deep into her, no hesitation bumps, just one long diving thrust to the bottom.

She was moist and tight and perfect heaven. She gave a long groan as I went into her, and then not a sound. I had her rammed up against the wall between the bed and the closet door, one leg up over my head and the other, with the jeans and torn underpants still on it, tucked under my arm.

"Oh, hell, you're right," I said, and I pulled out of her and got to my feet.

I was panting like I'd run up ten flights of stairs. She was still crammed up against the wall, her legs apart, her mouth open, her eyes on me.

She looked a little disappointed.

I went into the kitchen and popped open a beer.

"You want a beer?" I called to her. No answer. I drained off about half and went back into the bedroom. She was in almost the same position. I could hardly pretend not to be interested since my cock was dancing around in front of me, so I just stood there, sipping at my beer, while she got to her feet and pulled up her pants.

"That wasn't very nice," she said at last.

"I guess you're right," I said. I felt okay, and she didn't seem any the worse for wear. I sat on the edge of the bed and watched her finish dressing.

When she turned around from combing her hair in the mirror I stood up and started to tremble. "Texas bitch," I said, and we came together, touched and disappeared.

WE DIDN'T really disappear, it just felt that way. The next thing I knew everything was coming back into focus and I was lying next to the most beautiful creature I had ever seen. I won't describe the way we made love, there's only a limited number of choices after all, but what we did glowed and seemed brand-new, our experiment, our invention. Naturally, people have been inventing these sweet pastimes since the beginning and thinking they were unique. Is this love? Who knows?

But it sure felt good, and I wanted more, lots more. I didn't know how Sonny felt because I never know how other people feel, but she looked all rosy and clung to me and seemed to radiate hot love for me all the time we were in that room, and I wish we could have stayed there together forever, because nothing is ever the same.

THE MEADOR estate was on Fourth Street in Santa Monica, high on a cliff overlooking the beach, surrounded by cypress, pine and cedars of Lebanon, an old low rambling vanilla icecream plaster and red tile compound of buildings, tall skinny palm trees with little bursts of foliage at the top looking crazy next to the evergreens. Karl's little tan Mercedes two-seater was in the drive in front of the closed garage doors, and we pulled in next to it.

"Have you ever been here before?" I asked Sonny. I walked around the car to hold the door for her, but she was out and looking around by the time I got there.

"No," she said. Our arms and legs kept touching as we went around the side, through a little wooden gate and into the pool area.

"Probably out here swimming," I said. She touched my arm with her fingers. It was dark and cool beside the house, and I stopped to kiss her, just a couple of slow kisses, and we went on around the big greenhouse and out into the open. The Olympic pool was surrounded by lawn and garden. Here and there on the grass were groupings of furniture, but no Karl or Jim. At the far end of the pool the old man sat in his wheelchair talking to a big woman in white.

The old man, Max, Karl's father, with his dark-tanned skin, his sunglasses and the white towel draped around his neck, looked like Gandhi in a wheelchair. He had been knocked over by a heart attack thirty years ago and most people outside the business thought he was dead, the ones who didn't think he was crazy, but not Max Meador. Karl told me once that his old man made more money the first half-hour of the day than most people will ever see in a lifetime. He would sit out by the pool in the early morning, drinking coffee out of a tiny cup and glancing over the morning L.A. *Times, New York*

Times, Wall Street Journal, stock reports and whatnot, make a few calls to his broker or his banker, and huge chunks of wealth would be moved around here and there, drawing money like magnets, and then the old man would take a swim, helped in and out of the water by members of his staff.

"I like to keep busy," he told me once.

Sonny and I walked toward him across the lawn. "My God," Sonny whispered to me, "this grass is like moss, it's so soft."

I told her who she was about to meet and she stopped walking.

"It's like meeting the Pope," she whispered to me, and she was right. If Karl was a prince of Hollywood, then it was sure true that his old man was a king, and not deposed, either, just exiled to his own backyard, if you could call this a backyard, where he manipulated the corporations, conglomerates and supertrusts that in turn ran the movie companies.

"I have been kicked up," the old man once said to me. We used to sit and talk a lot, years before, when we were first getting to know each other. "A perfect field goal," he said, and laughed. Max had a soft guttural laugh with just a hint of the Lower East Side.

But I dragged her over and we stood a few feet away while the old man and the big woman continued their conversation.

"What language is that?" Sonny whispered to me.

"Swedish, I guess," I said. "Karl told me the old guy learned it just to please his nurse."

"Oh," she said, and I could feel her relax.

The nurse said hello to us and walked off toward the buildings.

The old man cocked his head. "I saw your partner a while ago," he said to me. "They're in the house."

I introduced Sonny, and the old man reached out a brown slim barely wrinkled hand and she shook it. No comment about her name, Max does not embarrass people unless there's something in it for him.

I kissed him on the forehead and said, "Another movie."

"Ah," he said. "You sound bitter."

Even with his dark glasses on I could see from the way he was looking at us that he knew about this afternoon. On impulse, I took Sonny's hand.

"So," Max said.

"Karl invited us to go swimming," I said.

"I didn't bring a suit," Sonny said. "I forgot."

I waved at the little pair of buildings just across the lawn. "Plenty of gear," I said, "but usually we swim naked. At least I do."

The old man said, "Don't mind me," and laughed.

"Why don't you come swimming with us," I said. "I'll throw you in the pool if you want."

"I guess I better find a suit," Sonny said.

I started pulling off my clothes, throwing them on the grass.

"Have the butler burn those," I said. The old man laughed again and I could see his teeth, a little stained, but all his.

"Do you think that stuff will still burn?" he said.

Sonny headed for the dressing cabanas and I jumped into the pool, nothing like that first shocking delicious crazy explosion into the water, and swam a couple of lengths ending up back by the old man, panting and hanging onto the edge. "Come on," I said to him.

"I swam," he said. "Let's see you do a hundred laps."

But I was distracted and only laughed politely. The truth was I already missed Sonny, and wanted her to come back out and be with me. He knew, too, the old bastard knew everything.

"She seems nice," he said.

SHE CAME out of the cabana wearing a shining blue bathing suit, hugging her arms in front of her and walking slowly barefoot across the grass. Maybe she was scared of Max. I pulled myself up out of the water. I knew Max was paying attention, even though he looked as if he had fallen asleep.

"Getting chilly?" I asked her.

She just looked at me shyly and I picked her up, so light, and dropped her in the water. After the splash and yelp, I could hear Max chuckling. I jumped in after her and we swam a couple of lengths together, and then I pulled myself up out of the water again and watched her lapping. She swam long slow strokes, textbook strokes, and I got the idea that if she decided to swim across the English Channel, she'd probably make it.

I said to Max, "Let me borrow that towel from around your neck."

"No," he said. "Get a fresh towel from the cabana. Are you afraid to leave her alone with me?"

There was a hoot from the direction of the house. I saw Jim and Karl coming across the grass, both in bathing suits. I yelled for them to bring over some towels, and Karl veered off for the cabanas and Jim came on toward us, grinning that lopsided shiteating grin that he got when he was really deeply drunk.

Jim grinned at me for a while, his hands on his hips.

"Have you been in, yet?" I asked him.

He fell lifelessly into the water and frogged his way to the other end, as I had done, and then swam a quick chopping lap back toward us, completely exhausting himself so that I had to help him up out of the pool. He didn't seem to have even noticed Sonny, although this whole swimming party had been his idea. Maybe that was what was making me nervous. Jim, magical Jim, Oh, how wonderful it is to be in love on a day like this Jim, idol of a million squirming females.

"*Oohfff, Jesus God!*" was all he could say, though, panting and rolling his eyes. He would never make it if he had to swim for her.

But of course like an asshole I had forgotten that she was Karl's girl, or at least Karl might think so. It was the handsome bastard coming this way with an armload of colorful towels that I had to look out for. Jim saw the way I was looking at Karl, and he turned to Sonny, still swimming, and then back to me, and said, "*Ah soooo . . .*"

That made everybody in on the big secret except Karl, and possibly Sonny. I guess it was all over my face and no amount of hamming around was going to do any good.

Jim said *sotto voce*, "Why not give him a kidney punch while his arms are full?"

I jumped in the water and swam a couple of furious laps, my eyes shut, not taking breaths, just plowing through the water, and when I finally came up, wiped the hair out of my eyes and looked around, Karl was kneeling by the pool next to Sonny, holding one of her hands and whispering to her. I sucked in a couple of lungfuls and sounded. I could see her legs against the tile sides of the pool, shimmering. I could frog over there and pull her under, or I could let the air out of my lungs and hang on to the filter hole grips at the bottom until I drowned, or I could come up and act like a man.

Frankly, none of the choices was particularly appealing.

He was helping her out of the pool when I climbed out by the ladder on the other side, but when I took a towel from the pile and sat down next to Max, Sonny came over and sat on my other side, her hand reaching out and touching mine. We looked at each other.

"Oh, relax," she said.

Karl came over, ever the gent in front of an audience, and asked her if she wanted anything. Coffee, fruit, a glass of champagne? She looked at me.

"Yeah," I said, "some champagne would be nice," and she turned back to Karl and said, "Yes, me, too," and Karl went over to the house phone by his father and gave the orders. Max and Karl had not exchanged a word, and I wondered if they were in the middle of one of their feuds. On Max's side of it, his son would have had a hard time getting a job in a gas station if it were not for the influence and guidance, however reluctant, of his father. From Karl's viewpoint, his father had never extended him any respect because no matter how good Karl got, no matter how much he learned, changed, advanced in the business, Max was always out there a hundred miles ahead of him and everybody else in the goddamn world. Any proper son of Max's would have had to outreach his father, possibly even destroy him, who knows, in order to get any respect.

But after all these years they still lived in the same house, even though Karl was a millionaire several times over on his own hook ("He doesn't have a hook to call his own!" I could hear Max saying with contempt), and if there was the suspicion that Karl was only the instrument to Max's wisdom, it was a suspicion held by people who had never seen Karl work, or who simply didn't understand the serpentine ways of moviemaking.

"Tell me what you think of the champagne," Max said to me, after a small man in a white jacket had poured for us and stuck the bottle back into its ice-bucket.

"No fair," I said, "I can't see the label."

"You drink a lot of champagne," he said. "Be a man and taste it."

I sat and watched the bubbles for a moment. "I had some in San Francisco a couple of days ago that was the best I ever tasted," I said. "So that's what this stuff is up against."

I asked Jim if he remembered the champagne, and he looked at me blankly. "From where?"

"The diMorros'," I said, faintly conscious of having dropped a name.

"I was out of my bird," was all Jim would say. He kept looking at Sonny, but I didn't mind. She was worth looking at. It was only when Karl looked at her . . . I sipped the champagne, rolled it around in my mouth and spit it into the grass.

"Tastes like shit," I said to Max. "You own the vineyard?"

Actually it was nice and cold, and champagne, which is enough for me.

"I'm sending you a case," Max said. "To your house up in the North Woods."

"Thank you," I said.

"The oil diMorros?" Karl asked me. "George?"

"God, I'd love to fuck you," Jim said.

I didn't have to turn around to guess who he was talking to.

IT WAS old Max Meador who rescued our careers back years ago by putting us in a movie. Everybody thinks it was Karl, but it was Max. Karl was executive in charge of television production at the studio at the time, and our management had brought us to him in a last desperate hope for a series. We had had series before, but they had blown out after the first season, and so after a couple of dry years where I lived in a motel room in Santa Monica and did bits and commercials and Jim went out on the road as a night club single, usually limping back with a lot of half-funny stories about small-town club owners, the agency called and asked if we would meet to discuss a low-budget film.

Jim and I hadn't been seeing much of each other. He was married and living in the Valley with the wife who had come to him at the peak of our success as entertainers, before we stupidly thought we could ease out of the hard life of clubs and into the insouciant luxury of video, and who now had to live with him during the economy years of only one car and no maid. It didn't bother Jim, he was raised on a tight budget, but Kitty made it pretty plain that she for one couldn't wait until we were all in the bigtime again. Meanwhile she gave parties for anybody she could get, and so Jim was pumped full of the gossip of the lower end of the business, where you are on a first-name basis with anybody you have ever seen, even at a considerable distance, and everybody has at least one major project in the works.

Just then a movie about some rats going crazy and running amok had scored big on a very small budget, so all the talk among dressers, grips, actors and secretaries was about crazy animal movies, cats going crazy, snakes going crazy, killer mongooses, elephants on rampages, whales coming ashore and running amok, etc&etc., and so when we met at the Beverly Hills Hotel, in the Polo Lounge, neither Jim nor I expected much. Kitty had come along, never one to miss a meal at the Polo Lounge, wearing tight pants that showed off her best feature, a perfect little blooming ass that invited you to grasp it and press it to your body, and Joe, the guy from the agency who is now out of the business, all of us trying not to peer around at the really important people in the room, sitting in our booth just opposite the entrance.

"There's Jimmy Stewart," Kitty said.

"That's not Jimmy Stewart," Jim said. "That's his stunt double, the biggest faggot in Hollywood, what's his name?"

"Michael Hunt," I said.

Kitty gave me a dirty look and said, "I haven't seen Jimmy since that benefit."

But we all knew we weren't in it, we were just sitting in it, like half the people there, trying to put together any small deal that would get us the big flashy smile from the greeter and the tablehops from the stars. You could see other tables like ours, with agents in dark blue suits and talent in sweaters and jeans, or even buckskins and beads, things were starting to loosen up in Hollywood, although not as much as later when even the agents started showing up for work in hippie costumes, and only one thing on God's green earth was certain, and that was that the agents would be picking up the checks.

"What is it?" Jim said to Joe. "Swarms of luminous green scorpions inundate Scottsdale, Arizona, causing the world market in fake turquoise to collapse?"

Joe laughed nervously and looked at his hands.

"A gigantic creature made entirely of petroleum products emerges from the La Brea tarpits and purchases the L.A. County Museum?" I asked.

"A couple of broken-down television comedians synthesize urine?" Jim asked.

Somebody in the next booth glared at us through the foliage.

"A couple of wacky guys dress up like women and fool half the police department, causing a scandal that reaches clear to Frederick's of Hollywood . . ."

"No," Joe said. "Close but no cigar."

Karl Meador came into the room, darksuited, goldrimmed glasses and the beginnings of the potbelly that would continue to grow for the next few years while marijuana sapped his will power. He did not say hello to anybody in the room or tablehop, but came straight toward us, frowning slightly as he was introduced to Kitty Larson. Joe was obviously worried that either Jim or I would blow the interview, but he didn't know us very well, he was just one of the dozens of guys at the agency who worked the not-so-hot clients before they were handed over to the mailboys, and I don't suppose he even expected to get us the job, but was polishing his handle on Karl Meador. However, the lunch went well, Kitty was fascinated by meeting the son of a mogul, and Karl seemed to know what he wanted, which was to get the hell out of television and into features and begin at long last that endless upward battle against his father, and Jim and I for once kept our mouths occupied with food—the food at the Beverly Hills is really delicious if you've been eating your own motel cooking for a couple of years. And so around the end of the meal, Karl said, "There's someone I want you two to meet," and then he looked at Joe and said, "You, too, of course," in a way that meant Joe was not invited to the next meeting, and we made the date, not wanting to ask with whom this second meeting would be. For all we knew it could have been the director, the writer, or anybody.

It was Max.

Jim picked me up in Santa Monica in the Rolls-Royce he had bought when we signed our first television contract and before our business manager got into the act and impoverished us with investments. Jim had paid cash for the car, but now the bank owned it and Jim drove. We got to the studio, which was on Olive off Sunset in those days before the move to Burbank, and the woman in Karl Meador's office made coffee for us and petted us and stroked us, gave us the trades to read, and then finally came out and said that Karl would not be coming in that day, and she knew it was a horrible inconvenience to us, but would we mind going out to the house? We would get there in time for lunch, she said, and we would be driven out in a studio limousine. As the limo passed my little motel I leaned forward and told the driver, "That's where I live," and he laughed and said, "Yes, sir."

I don't know why Karl didn't simply tell us we would meet at his home. We would not have guessed we were being brought to the old man, because everybody in the business thought the old man was crippled, crazy and retired.

Karl met us at the door and took us into a big greenhouse full of tropical plants, but the old man wasn't there. Karl got on a house telephone,
looking hot and irritated in his dark suit, while Jim and I looked around
at the various plants and tried not to do anything stupid. Eventually Karl
found out what he wanted to know, and saying to us, "Sorry, come on," left
the greenhouse with us trailing. We ended up at a paneled door, and Karl
stopped and knocked.

"Come in," said a rough guttural voice, and Karl opened the door and
stepped back so that we could enter first.

The old man was sitting in a wheelchair, all right, but he was at a small,
busy-looking desk and he was wearing a suit and tie. There were papers and
books and scripts all over the desk and behind the old man's chair a window
overlooking the cliffs and the ocean beyond.

"This is my father," Karl said from behind me. He pronounced our names
and Max nodded and said, "Sit down, gentlemen."

I had been nervous before, but now I was in shock. I glanced sideways
at Jim but he seemed perfectly calm, in fact, he seemed delighted at meeting
Max, where I had been trying to keep a straight face. Karl sat on a small
leather couch a bit back from the desk, where he could see all three faces,
pulled a pipe out of his pocket and started to fuss with it. Without looking at
him the old man said, "Don't light that thing in here," and Karl put the pipe
away, crossed his legs, recrossed them, clasped his knees and then folded his
arms, uncrossing his legs, and the old man said, "Stop moving around," and
Karl sat still. The old man smiled at me, his blue eyes twinkling; he looked
like a man who would have a high piping voice, but his was deep and strong.
He was darkly tanned even then and looked fit and sane.

"Mister Ogilvie, Mister Larson, would you like something to drink? Some
coffee? Beer? Tea? Didn't my son even offer you tea? Karl, go bring us all a
nice pot of tea."

Karl didn't move and I don't think the old man expected him to, but
pushed a button on his desk and yelled "Tea and coffee!" so surprisingly
loud that I must have jumped a little, because Max said to me, "Don't worry,
I wasn't yelling at you, I was yelling at a deaf old man in the kitchen."

Jim said, "He always thinks people are yelling at him."

I wished Jim hadn't said that. I looked over at Karl for the first time
since the humiliations had begun, and he threw me back such complete

understanding and sympathy that I have had a hard time hating him ever since, although he doesn't often give anybody reason to like him.

"Gentlemen," Max said, "do I address you singly or as a team? Who makes the decisions?" Without waiting for an answer, Max went on: "I've seen you on television and I'm surprised you were making a living at it, although God knows I don't understand why anybody makes a living at that business. I'm not trying to take you apart or hurt your feelings, but I want to make clear right away that I'm not interested in talking to the fellows I saw on television, but to a couple of young men who are willing to admit that up to now their careers have not set anybody on fire, much less the public. We start clean or don't start is the way I feel about this."

"What's the matter with our act?" I said.

"It depends on what you mean by that question. If you mean to defend, then I must tell you that what is basically wrong with your act is nobody wants to see it; if you are asking me, man-to-man, what's the matter with our act so we can get better, maybe I have something to tell you and maybe we can do business. Which is it?"

Jim and I looked at each other but had nothing to say.

Max said, "Well, you're listening, that's a good sign."

The coffee and tea came and we all fooled around getting what we wanted and settling back in our seats with the air full of hostility and cold fear. I had the feeling that we had been brought out here to entertain a bored old millionaire, and I was starting to get hot, but this was not the time to explode, so I paid a lot of attention to my coffee. The old man spent a lot of time squeezing his teabag and getting the right amount of lemon, etc., and then started talking:

"I see it a million times and it is always the same, young fellows with talent work hard out in the sticks and then get called to the attention of the people in this business, who drag them in out of the sticks and promise to make them rich and famous, only the young fellows must not continue doing their act, they must change, because the Hollywood people know what the people in the sticks want to see; so you think, they must be right, they are driving Cadillacs and sending their children to private schools, and you change your act around to suit every Tom, Dick and Harry who comes down the street. You are made to feel ignorant and stupid, they know what music to play, what jokes to tell, what clothes to wear, what guest stars to have on the show, and then comes the big night and you are out there on television alone, dripping crap all over the audience and wondering what happened to the geniuses who thought this all up, because it is not them the audience is throwing vegetables at. Am I right?"

"You are right," I said.

Max gave me a sharp look. "What you think right now isn't that important," he said. "Please accept my apology for pointing this out."

"I'm sorry," I said.

He laughed and sipped his tea. "It takes a man to make a mistake," he said. "Good for you."

"You're welcome," I said.

"You, Mister Larson," he said to Jim, "I have some of your records here and I listened to them. You have a nice voice, it bounces right along, and you are probably wondering why the teenage girls are not breaking doors to get at you and why the gold records go to the other fellows."

"The thought had crossed my mind," Jim said. His eyes were actually twinkling.

"Look," said Max, "you fool around, you sing this kind of song, that kind of song, but mostly you sing, 'Hello, I love you, let's get married,' and the records stack up in the warehouses, you know why? Because girls don't want to marry a fellow like you, that's the last thing in the world they want, a husband like a grasshopper: what they want from you is, 'Hello, let's fuck, and I'll see you later.' You start singing that song to them and they will kill to get at you."

Max turned his attention to me: "And you, my sarcastic friend. Has it ever occurred to you that being sarcastic works in kindergarten and almost no place else?"

"It works for Bob Hope," I said.

"If you want to spend the rest of your life doing Bob Hope's act, more power to you, but do not expect anybody to be listening because who needs you when they can get the original Mister Hope and his six-hundred gag writers any time they want?"

"I'm sorry," I said. "I didn't mean to crack wise."

"Cracking wise, yes, you better forget it, because frankly it makes people sick, people don't like to be told how wrong they are or how bad things are, even though God knows things couldn't be worse. No. You are the fellow the girls want to marry, that's the real you, kind of slow but not dumb, more like Mortimer Snerd than Charlie McCarthy but not stupid, just the kind of guy to bring home the paycheck and raise a little family of hayseeds. Am I making myself clear?"

But nobody wanted to speak. Karl looked from one of us to the other and we looked at Max, and he sipped his tea.

There was something about this meeting that was bothering me, not just Max's way of conducting a meeting, something else. . . . I tried to think of what it was and couldn't. Then, in the silence, it came to me: No telephone calls had been coming in. It is hard to tell you just what effect this had on me when I realized it, but I will try: normally anybody in Hollywood who is of any importance has hundreds of phone calls a day, and by the end of the day has a whole log of unanswered calls. In a normal meeting, that is to say, a meeting where nothing is going to happen, the Big Guy, the guy behind the desk, will take anywhere from one to ten calls while you are sitting there with your agent. Often, in fact, as soon as the Big Guy takes a call, your agent will pick up one of the instruments in the room and make a couple of calls himself, and then everyone apologizes for the interruptions and you get in about five minutes more of worthless meeting and the Big Guy's secretary apologetically interrupts again, because this is an *important call*: "Hello, Sidney!" And the Big Guy waves his cigar at you as if to say, "*Got* to talk to Sidney!" And the meeting goes on.

Of course the higher you are in the order of things, the less your meetings are interrupted, the theory being, I suppose, that the only calls that can interrupt your meeting are from people more important than either you or the Big Guy.

And of course if it is your office, you are the Big Guy.

So Max really wasn't taking any calls, and neither was Karl.

This made me realize the importance of the meeting.

"Well, *shit*, Max, may I call you *Max*?" I said.

"Of course you can call me anything you want," Max said coldly.

"You have a movie idea for us?"

"If you can control yourself I will tell you about it," he said. Karl was glaring at me.

"The world is full of trouble," Max said. "The war gets worse and worse and nobody feels any patriotism anymore. Kids are going crazy and parents hate to see them come home. Everything is getting impossible, so I think maybe a small movie that pays no attention to the facts of life but just goes down the road, a few songs, a few laughs, a small romance, nothing to disturb anybody, and if we keep the costs down maybe there's money to be made. A very old-fashioned kind of movie, a B picture. Are you interested?"

We were interested.

"It is the old story, older than Aesop, of City Mouse and Country Mouse," Max said. "Don't give the public new stories, give them new material. I don't trust new stories, the public don't know what to make of them, but a good old story that has fascinated people for a couple of thousand years, it can always be reworked to make people happy to hear it again. Mister Larson is the city slicker and Mister Ogilvie is the country bumpkin, it's as simple as that, except they love each other like brothers and they fall for the same girl. It looks like the city slicker has all the marbles, but at the end of the last reel country boy is married to the girl and everybody in the audience goes home happy. Is this too corny for you fellows?"

Not at all, not at all.

🌴

AFTER THAT first meeting with Max Meador, we rode back to the studio in the limousine and picked up Jim's car and then drove out to his place in the Valley. We didn't know if we had the jobs or not, although Max seemed confident, even told us we wouldn't make any money on the picture.

"This is my picture," Max said. "If I win, I win; if I lose, I lose. Either way, you boys will make your salaries. And forget about points, you get no points—points are for lawyers to divide up, nothing but a heartache."

Nobody said anything about Karl, sitting there, the producer of the picture, and even when he took us out to the limo he said nothing you could interpret as a fact.

Jim's house had a little aspen in the front yard, surrounded by burnt-out grass, double garage, faded green pseudo-shutters on the windows and a lot of cracks in the stucco, but the back was nice, several trees including a weeping willow, a nice swimming pool and some garden furniture in the shade. Kitty was out there wearing a bikini bottom and *zori*.

I waited in the house while Jim went out and told her they had a guest, although I did peek through the drapes at the pretty little tits she never grew tired of showing people unless they were obvious about looking and then she got mad, watched her slowly unravel the towel from around her hair while Jim stood talking, I couldn't hear him, but she nodded from time to time and pulled curlers and hairpins out of her hair for about twenty minutes.

I went into the kitchen and got a beer and came back and resumed my peeping, she still hadn't covered those tits, and I knew Jim would be upset if I just barged out there. The air conditioning was making me shiver. I finished my beer and went into the bathroom, marveling again and forever at the blue water in all the L.A. toilets, as if the inhabitants hated straight tapwater so bad they wouldn't even piss in it, and then went on outside, the hell with Jim, and she draped a towel over herself, but not quick enough.

C. C. "CHET" EUBANK was a chunky guy about my age, with brown hair that looked like he brushed it too much and pale blue eyes. He was from Connecticut somewhere and was supposed to be the President's favorite adviser on world affairs, as opposed to domestic affairs or foreign affairs, and also a former Kennedy person, whatever the hell that meant. Tonight at dinner with Karl Meador he seemed like a modest likeable guy, comfortable with the bizarre California types he found himself surrounded with, and I noticed on the sly that he didn't mind getting an occasional glimpse of the various ladies in the room earlier, when there had been a large gathering waiting to see Karl's latest movie in the screening room just off the big living room. The picture hadn't come from the studio in time, some kind of screwup with the director, who had opened up one of the reels to move something around, or maybe it was because the director hadn't been asked to the screening, or maybe the transportation man who was supposed to bring the print out got lost, it depended on who you talked to, and so Karl had to call off the screening and somehow get rid of the people he didn't want to feed, which was 90 percent of them, some drunker than others because they had been at it for a couple of hours while waiting for the print to arrive. But finally those of us who had been quietly invited to eat sat down at the table: me, Karl, Sonny, a guy named C. C. "Chet" Eubank, a couple of actresses I didn't know and Jim, who had spent the cocktail hour sacked out in a room upstairs and now looked sleepy and sullen across the table from me.

Also at the table was our Las Vegas boss, Gregory Galba, who didn't exactly own the Golconda and didn't exactly not own it, either, but when he barked everybody cringed, so it didn't matter, and Gregory barked a lot, a tall wrinkle-faced black-eyed man with a reddish rug that kept hiking up in the back like a mallard's ass, but of course he was Gregory Galba and so nobody would tell him, "Gregory, your toup's loose in back," so there it was, upflap in back, and it was hard not to laugh. There was a story going around that Gregory had a bad heart attack once and took the living heart out of another man in an operation south of the border somewhere. I never believed the story, but I had seen the deep red scar on his chest plenty of times. Gregory liked to play tennis without a shirt on, and he liked to play me because I never gave him a break.

Max, of course, was nowhere to be seen.

I had heard once that there was a little room behind the screen in the screening room, and that sometimes Max would sit there, not watching the movie so much as watching the faces of the audience, lit up from the picture; but the same guy who told me that story told me Max wasn't crippled, either, and only used the wheelchair to intimidate people, which, if true, made Max the greatest actor in Hollywood. But I wondered about that little room.

Eubank was telling a story about when he had been in the service, aboard a troopship heading for Japan during the Korean War, where a man had been murdered for wanting to keep the lights on so he could read in his bunk, and how the killer didn't do a nickel's worth of time after they let him out of the brig at Yokohama because the government couldn't locate any of the eighty or ninety witnesses.

The murder part of the story I recognized, because the same thing had happened on board the ship I was on, going the same way during the same war. I brought this up and it turned out that Eubank and I had been aboard the same ship, the U.S.S. *Mann*. He had been a member of the ship's newspaper staff, working two hours each morning putting out the little mimeograph sheet, the "Mann-U-Script," and spending the rest of the day topside, turning copies of the "Mann-U-Script" into gliders and sailing them off among the flying fish and porpoises.

Meanwhile, I was deep in the hold, breaking apart frozen chickens twelve hours a day.

Chet looked at me with a smile. "That was mighty good chicken, as I remember."

"The 'Mann-U-Script' wasn't bad, either," I said, and it turned out that Chet had a couple of copies at home in Connecticut and would send me Xeroxes.

Earlier, during the Long Wait, when we were introduced, Chet had made a point of telling me how much he enjoyed our pictures and Jim's singing, and couldn't wait to meet Jim, and how important it was to create little islands of relaxation, such as our movies, in this modern sea of trouble. Now that we were old pals from the service, he seemed even more interested in talking to me, and through the early part of the meal we jabbered away about Tokyo, where he had been in the 1st Radio Broadcasting & Leaflet Group, stationed right downtown, and about spending his days composing folk tales in Mandarin Chinese to bombard the People's Army with, so that their resolve would shatter under the impact of the voices on the radio and they would give up Communism and go home. He made it sound very funny, but he did spend two years doing just that, and it wasn't funny to them at the time.

"We thought we were more important than the real soldiers," he said. "We used to be proud of the fact that our unit had the highest educational level of any unit in the Far East."

"Our unit had the lowest," Jim said.

"Really?" said Chet, ready for a good joke.

But Jim just looked at him seriously and said, "Yeah, I was in the band," and went back to his food.

Since then Chet had actually been to China several times, first with Nixon, then with a group that stayed six months and worked in the fields and factories for a little while just to see what things were like, and then a couple of times for the State Department.

"I've been studying Chinese affairs for better than twenty years," he told me, "but it didn't prepare me in any way for the reality of the place."

"Are you ready to move there?" asked Gregory Galba from the other end of the table.

CHET SMILED over at Galba's big hard face. "Maybe that's not the question," he said. "Maybe the question is, Should we be doing here what they're doing there?"

"What's your answer, Chester?" the big man asked. It seemed clear that Galba didn't like C. C. Eubank, but Chet kept his party smile on. The other little conversations at the table stopped.

"Well, to answer *your* question, they'd have to catch me first," Chet said, and got a good laugh. "Which in a way is an admission that I regard my life as something less than devoted to the State—no matter which party is in power. The truth is, I like to eat high off the hog, and that is the one thing you can't do in China today."

Galba gave a snort and filled his mouth with about five pounds of food, which didn't stop him from commenting: "Then you're just like the rest of us, aren't you?"

"I hope so," Chet said. "I'm a little too old to start rehearsing Chinese rations."

"What about you, hotshot?" Gregory said to me. He grinned around at everyone, a big charming peasant grin. "This is my favorite political analyst, a man of the people," he said. "Give us your opinion of the world situation *vis à vis* the People's Republic of China," he said.

"When I go to China," I said, "I'm going to ask for a fork."

This got a nice laugh and the dinner broke again into little conversations, Jim being very serious with Sonny, Karl with Galba. The two of them had a vested interest in me and Jim, since when Karl was done with us we would go to Vegas and work for Gregory at the Golconda, which he didn't exactly own but had an interest in, a big enough interest to get him a floor of his own and make all the employees turn away from the glare of his majesty if he happened to be striding around the corridors, which he did sometimes, all six feet five of him, a Yugoslav by birth who spent the first years of his life in a Colorado mining town with other Yugoslavs and not speaking English until, as he told me once, "I figured out all the people with money were jabbering this foreign tongue, so I learned it myself." He learned it pretty good, too, enough to have an ocean of little iron men he could swing in and out of various businesses, causing the market to topple or rise according to his desires, or close to it.

Chet gave me a sly little look, as if to say, "Isn't he cute?" and started a conversation with the actress on the other side of him, leaving me with Jody McKeegan, the actress who came with Gregory, his more or less steady date these days, a woman of about thirty or thirty-five, who knows how old anybody is anymore? She was eating at a good pace, and held her hand up for me to wait until she swallowed her potatoes.

"You guys follow me at the Golconda," she said finally.

"That's so far away I hate to think about it," I said.

"I hope you'll come and see me," she said, and got back into her food.

"I hope so," I said without meaning it.

She flashed her eyes at me, and in an instant I could see why Galba ran around with her instead of the tasty younger women who must have been available to him. I watched her, having nothing better to do. She ate like an animal, not sloppy, just concentrated, shoveling the goods into her face with an expression of distant concentration, like, she would eat this food and then go find someplace to curl up and snooze for a couple of days, stretch, give herself a long lazy wash, and then back to the hunt.

"I know a great story about Max," Gregory said. "I hope you don't mind if I tell it . . ."

Karl laughed and dabbed at his lips with his white napkin. "Certainly not, I have a lot of stories about him myself."

"My favorite story about Max," Jim said, just about the first thing he had said to the table at large, so everybody is leaning forward listening to him, except Galba, who looked a little irritated, "is . . ." and Jim's head fell over, as if he had fallen asleep.

"Anyway," says Galba, "there was this Handsome Harry actor under contract to MGM, back a long time ago, in the seven-year-contract days, big fellow, could read and write English and sat good on a horse, getting important enough to be invited to some big parties. He brags one night in front of the wrong people that he would never on this earth work for a man like Max, an exploiter of the people, that his *integrity* was at stake, God knows what he thought of the people he was working for, but Max hears about this and lets it be known that he, Max, has a vehicle for this particular actor. The studio didn't want him, the director didn't want him, but Max says, 'Dis picture don't work widout Harry.' The brass at MGM figure they can get an arm and a leg out of Max in return for the guy's services, the poor actor gets his weekly wages and the studio keeps the rest.

"The actor hears the studio is negotiating with Max and blows his top. 'Never in a million years!' MGM suspends him immediately and he says he don't care, it's time to get out of this dirty business anyway, and he goes and lives with his sister in Santa Barbara, sailing her little boat out to the Channel Islands and shooting wild pigs with his .38 pistol to get himself in a relaxed state of mind. Meanwhile, MGM is going crazy, Max is offering them more and more money to produce this actor, 'alive and well,' on the first day of shooting.

"MGM sends an endless stream of executives up to Santa Barbara, each with a better offer for the actor, although not offering to share in the money Max is putting up, just perks and options to pick his next vehicle, veiled threats to poison his dog, you know, all bullshit of course, but the actor won't budge. 'I wouldn't work for that slavedriver for a thousand a day,' he would say, and then sail out into the channel with his pistol and a couple belts of ammunition around his neck to shoot the pigs. The studio people never followed him out there, probably afraid he might make a mistake in the fog and shoot one of them.

"Finally, Irving calls Max and asks him about the property, what is it that only Handsome Harry can do, and why is Max offering MGM so goddamn much money for an actor who frankly couldn't get arrested unless he was under contract?

"Max won't talk. He just tells Irving, 'Never mind, I think I can get along without him,' but still, through the agency involved, keeps trying to get the guy.

"This drives Irving crazy. He comes up to Max at a party and tries to jolly him, but Max just laughs and says, 'I never do business at parties,' which is the biggest crock of shit imaginable and only makes Irving hotter under the collar. Then the story is all over town that Max has gone up to Santa Barbara himself in a huge yacht he borrowed from a friend and cuts Harry off as Harry is sailing out for his daily pigshoot; I can just see them out there in the fog and the current, Max yelling at the actor, 'Come aboard or we'll sink you!' This is long before Max is crippled, of course.

"Max and Harry meet on the yacht for hours, sailing up and down the channel, with Max coming up on deck every once in a while to toss his cookies into the water, Max being very subject to seasickness, and then wipe his mouth, swear a little bit and head below again. But it was no use, Harry would not budge, even though Max is supposed to have told him, 'Listen, Harry, you are locked up in this situation. You think because two fellows like me and Irving are after you that you are somehow more valuable than you was before in terms of dollars and cents, but you ain't because you don't understand fellows like us. We get what we want because we don't stop at nothing. You're just an actor; what resources do you have? I can keep coming after you for years if need be, and how can you hold out? Family money? So what? Family money can't put you up on the silver screen, there ain't enough of it, and that's what you love most. I can and Irving can, and we can also keep you *off* the screen, as I am sure Irving has told you.'

"But the kid won't relent, at least so the story goes, and Max has to come back to Hollywood a beaten man. People know how serious it is when Max misses a few functions around town, staying home and brooding about the whole mess, and this is when Irving comes up with his generous offer: he will buy the script from Max and produce the picture himself."

Galba sat back and drained his glass of wine, keeping a straight face like any good storyteller. "Irving paid an arm and a leg for the script, sight unseen, so convinced was he that Max had his hands on a winner, and to make it seem even more likely, Max insisted on a percentage of the picture's profits for himself. The script, of course, was the worst dog Irving had ever seen, a complete piece of shit, which Max had paid too much for and couldn't figure out how to get out from under until he heard about this actor at MGM who had bragged that he would never work for Max in a million years."

"What happened to the movie?" I asked. "Did it get made?"

"Sure it got made. There sits Irving, knowing that Max can't lose—he's out from under the cost of the script and into profits, and if the movie by some miracle happens to succeed, he gets more from his percentage. Irving is stuck with making the picture to see if Max has screwed him royally, or if Max by some as yet unknown sense of what clicks with the public knew that this lousy script, plus this half-talent actor, will hit the public right in the eye. Sure it got made."

"Well," said Jody McKeegan, "drop the other shoe."

"This is the real point of the story," Karl said. "We don't know, or at least you don't. I happen to remember, because I was home from school that summer and I was aboard the yacht to Santa Barbara."

"You mean I just told a true story?" Gregory said, with a look of surprise.

"Sure it's a true story," Karl said. "Handsome Harry used to come over to the house every Saturday morning that summer to play billiards with my father, Hell, Max gave him his career. The picture was a big hit, a smash."

But Karl wouldn't tell us the guy's name. "What difference does it make?" Karl asked. "The man's dead now."

"I DON'T get it," Jody said. "Was Harry faking, under Max's direction? Acting? Or did he really refuse to work for Max?"

Gregory patted her hand. "Doesn't matter, does it? Suppose the kid really was the kind of idealist who would refuse to work for Max because of principles? If so, then Max said exactly the right things to him aboard the yacht: reminded him he wasn't going to starve, no matter what, and then all but accused him of excessive vanity, that he was just another egomaniac playing the game."

Chet laughed. "He wasn't buying an actor, he was selling a screenplay."

JIM LOOKED at me. "And so, by following a path of virtue, Harry became a star."

"And died," I said.

CHET EUBANK was talking to the table at large, but it seemed to me he was dwelling on Sonny.

"Suppose it went this way," he said. "Suppose you were a public figure, no, not just a public figure, but the subject of a myth, partly of your family's making and partly swelling up out of the people's need for mythic figures. And partly from the extraordinary nature of your martyred brothers. Suppose also that you were the clown of the family, the one who always got caught, a fixed position for you, glittering in the public eye, but always with your hand in the cookie jar. Now, with the martyred and worshipped brothers dead but far from gone, the family's power demonstrated to be stronger than that of many governments, sometimes including our own, you see yourself, will-I, nil-I, propelled into the center stage. People who never gave you a thought now cry when you touch their hand, and states you've never visited call you Favorite Son.

"But there's even more boiling under the surface: one brother has a sexual reputation that gives deep unconscious power to the myth, a young god trampling the boundaries, a genetic masterstag, Adonis to the women, Achilles to the men. In the public eye you are all devils with the women, no matter what the reality, and so one night you find yourself in a car with a young woman, she could be a secret concubine—the public would expect no less—or she could be a stranger—the myth would allow for that, too—on your way to a necking party, a tryst, whatever develops, and find other hands on the wheel, driving you into the cold dark fastrunning waters of death.

"The two of you escape from the car, and you can only wonder at the lubricity of your position, once again the comic, once again, with wet and baggy pants you pratfall on the world stage and everyone has a good laugh: 'Well, they're not *all* gods!' It takes a couple of hours for the two of you to make your way back to the party, and then more time is spent in confused and in some cases drunken congratulations and speculations, time, precious time, rolling past as you grow dryer and warmer and try to think of a way to keep this one botched attempt to be dashing out of the papers.

"And then they discover the missing girl. The girl who had been known to crawl into the back seats of cars at parties to sleep off the effect of a couple of glasses of beer. The girl who is missing.

"The others, as you rush to the water's edge, hope for the best, all except you. Your knowledge is based on a lifetime—you know she is in the car, you know she has passed from sleep into death, you know the trouble to come, that there will be no way to explain this, that all explanations are the same, that you did this and you will be blamed, and the blame is yours."

"So what this fellow is afraid of," said Gregory, "is not assassination but fucking up."

Chet looked as if Galba had hit him across the face with a whip—I saw the look because he turned toward me to keep Galba from seeing it. He composed himself quickly and smiled at us all and said, "Yes, I suppose so. At any rate, he's a damned good politician, probably a better legislator than either of his brothers . . ."

"But a fuckup," Galba said.

Chet sighed. "Yes," he said.

Sonny looked entranced. We had been exchanging under-the-table hand-clasps and toe-touches early in the meal, but not recently. I sent an exploratory toe out in her direction, but all I got was a wink from Jim.

"I want to sing a song," Jim said. His eyes were glittering. "I want to sing about tits and ass."

He stood up.

"Tits and ass," he sang, "tits and ass, raise a glass to tits and ass . . ."

We all raised our glasses, but I could see that Chet was a little offended by the language, and maybe the way Jim was stepping on his moment.

Galba noticed, too.

CHET AND Karl tried to keep things on an elevated level by talking more politics, but dinner had been running a long time and we were full of wine and food. Good old Gregory Galba put an end to the politeness for once and for all by tilting slightly in his chair and letting a series of explosive farts. It was worth it to have been there, just to see the various expressions, from Karl's sudden closing of his face to Chet's genuine shock. Galba showed his teeth to Chet:

And lo! he let flee a fart,
Both great and terrible,
And smote them full in the face. . . .

Jody McKeegan laughed immoderately, and Chet looked down at his plate.

Gregory said, "What's the matter, Chester, don't you recognize Geoffrey Chaucer? I thought you were Harvard, class of '52. . . . Don't they teach you the dirty parts?"

"The 'Miller's Tale,'" Chet said softly, "I'd forgotten that . . ."

"The trouble with you, Chester, is that you're a contradiction in terms, a political gentleman. You've probably never even killed anybody."

"At least not by that particular means," Chet said mildly, and the laughter was full of relief, but Galba would not be put off. He laughed too, drank some wine and refilled his glass. We were all tinkling over our wine and coffee, etc. Galba lifted his glass to the rest of us:

"Here's to tits and ass, without which none of us would even be here." Before he raised the glass to his mouth he said to Chet, "How about it? Are you willing to admit that a pair of nice glossy tits next to you in a warm bed is worth all the literature in the world?"

The comeback would have been easy enough, but now I saw what Galba had seen, that Chet wouldn't get dirty, wouldn't say certain words in front of women, that he was fighting with one hand tied behind his back, so to speak. And Galba was trying to hack off his head.

"'Sing, Muse, of the wrath of Achilles,'" Chet said in that mild voice, "I suppose you're right, because there, in the very first line of Western literature, you have a man so angry over having a woman taken away from him that he refuses to fight beside his allies . . ."

"Mighty interesting," Gregory said. He had drunk his wine by now and a shiny streak of it crossed his chin and made it look in the candlelight as if he was drooling, that mean heavy unrelenting face. "It was tits and ass then, and it is tits and ass now."

"Particularly tits," Jim said. "I love tits. I would do almost anything to kiss them, fondle them, even just look at them for a while. My God, here we are, sitting in the same room with three pair of tits, in some cases barely concealed but in all cases magnificent in their shape and, um, *attack*, shall we say, and yet we manage to talk of other things and look in other directions. Tits! Do you realize that when you were a baby, your mother's tits were the size of your *head?* Your first experience with food, with sex and with the sublime, all at the same time. goddamn!"

"Don't get carried away," I said. I was starting to feel a little embarrassed for the girls, although to tell the truth, they didn't seem to mind as much as Chet did; in fact, they didn't seem to mind at all.

"Big cocks are important, too," Jody McKeegan said.

"That's where you are wrong," Galba said. He appeared to be enjoying himself now, and not so much on the prod for Chet Eubank. "You are completely wrong, as you are on almost every possible issue, my dear, my sweet poppin, because if you were right, men would go around wearing clothes that showed off the size of their cocks the way women go around wearing clothes that show off their tits. No man ever got into a really high place because of his cock size."

"You have it all figured out," Jody said with a grin, "but you surprise me. I didn't know you noticed men's cocks all that much . . ."

"This conversation is descending a bit, don't you think?" said Karl. He was wearing an amused but willing to move on expression, and I could see the tip of his little finger lightly tapping the base of his champagne glass.

"Yeah," Jim said, wickedly charming. "Let's get back up to the tit line."

"You know," Chet said, "that's one of the astonishing things about China. Sex really doesn't seem to be as powerful, or maybe it's because the government has taken such complete control of the individual's sex life that the whole thing has gotten buried into the unconscious . . ."

"Yes," Galba said. "And then in a few years, everybody in China goes crazy and runs amok, raping and bayoneting everyone else . . ."

"Things are changing," Chet said.

"No, I admit you're right. By then the P.L.O. will be in charge of the world government, and they will do the raping and bayoneting."

"I wouldn't mind getting in on some of that," I said, but nobody laughed.

A SERVANT came in and whispered to Karl.

"Good news," said Karl. "The picture's here. They're racking it up now." He meant the movie we were supposed to have seen before dinner with the crowd of people who were now gone. "Why don't we take brandy and coffee in the screening room?"

"Beats popcorn," Jody said. Gregory Galba stood up, looming over all of us, and went around to hold Jody's chair out for her. She gave him one of those hot looks over her shoulder and they brushed against each other, and for some reason this made me like Galba in spite of everything, in spite of knowing him for years without hearing him say anything I agreed with, of working for him, of being patronized by him, snubbed, bored; that one little tickle of eroticism between him and Jody wiped it all out. He was just another guy with half a hardon.

But it turned out that something was wrong with the workprint we were about to see, the director himself was in the projection booth fiddling around with the first reel, blah blah, I didn't bother to listen but took a good big shot of brandy in a champagne glass and topped it with icecold champagne and wandered outside into a patio off the dining room. The moon was riding high in the west, no clouds, a warm Southern California night, the strong smell of some kind of nightblooming flowers almost but not quite too heavy. I found a bench in the darkness of an overhanging cluster of vines and sat down.

It was pleasant to be alone for a few minutes. It wouldn't do Sonny any harm to know that I was not always totally nuts about her, but had moments of sanity. Thinking about her, about the way she conducted herself, not trying to impress everybody, not trying to hold her own with the heavyweights and so holding her own quite well, like the other actress whose name I had either never learned or had forgotten, and you do not ask an actress her name. They had done pretty damned well and I felt warm for them both. But it was Jody who came out and sat next to me on the bench.

"God, fresh air," she said. "What are you drinking?"

I told her. "I learned to drink this in Japan. We used to call it *The Tokio Cannonball.* Booze was cheap, no U.S. taxes to pay, so what the hell, Armagnac for breakfast, champagne, Canadian Club . . ."

"Let me taste it." I gave her the glass.

"I think it's called a French '75 in polite society."

"Pretty good."

I offered to get her one but she said no, and we just sat there side by side looking out at the moonlit patio.

"This is a beautiful house," she said. "God, it's nice to have money."

"Amen."

The trouble is, I wanted very much to fuck her. It was wrong of me, it was bad, it was evil, it was even goddamn dangerous, but nevertheless I wanted to throw her to the bricks.

She looked at me and laughed. "Gimme another sip," she said. She laughed again and I felt her fingers on the back of my neck, gentle. She leaned in and kissed me.

"Maybe someday." She got up and walked away.

When I went back inside and down to the screening room, Sonny was sitting between Karl and Chet, with the other actress behind them, all laughing and chatting merrily. But Sonny looked like a kid after Jody McKeegan, her face unformed, her laughter almost too innocent. Jody and Galba weren't in the room, and Jim was sitting off by himself, down close to the screen. I flopped down beside him.

"Is he in there?" I asked.

"Who? Oh, Max? We should look." But neither of us got up.

"What's delaying things?" I asked.

"Maybe they're waiting for Max to zoom in," Jim said. "I don't know, but I'm getting mighty bored. Mighty bored."

I had nothing to say to that, so we just sat there and waited. Finally the lights went down, and the picture started. In the first five minutes I could tell that it was not the kind of movie I would bother to go see. Fortunately for me, a splice came undone and up came the lights again.

Chet walked down the aisle. "Let's go get a drink," he said. I didn't bother saying all we had to do for drinks was get on the phone, I just got up and followed him out.

🌴

"THE PRESIDENT really likes Larson and Ogilvie," Chet said. We were sitting in the little bar off the living room.

"You mentioned that before," I said. "Much thanks to the President." Chet was sipping his brandy, so into the silence I said, "You know, it's really nice to know somebody out there is watching."

"Well, I should tell you that when he learned I was going to be in Southern California for a few days, he telephoned me and asked specifically if I would be running into you fellows, and if so, to be sure to convey his best wishes."

"Well now that is flattering," I said.

"For me I think it's wonderful that he gets to sit down and relax with a film, even some television, if only for a couple of hours. Just a little relaxation, some laughs, can make all the difference."

Come on, I thought, drop the other shoe. What I said was, "That's what we're here for."

"Have you ever visited the White House? I know you haven't met the President because he mentioned the fact, almost wistfully, as if he hoped *he* could meet *you*."

"No," I said. "Never been there. We never even made Nixon's shitlist."

Chet laughed and looked at his watch openly. "I wonder when the picture's going to be ready."

"I'm not all that sure I care," I said. "Big day tomorrow."

"So have I. I'll be calling the White House early in the morning. Do you have any message in particular?"

"Um, hello, and keep up the good work?" I said, and he laughed again.

"As a matter of fact I'll make it even warmer than that, because I know that he's just like anybody else when it comes to being a fan, and in fact I think you might expect an invitation to the White House, the two of you, of course, sometime later this year, when things aren't quite so busy."

Thud.

I remarked about how flattering it all was and how I was sure Jim would be delighted, just as delighted as myself, and how I wanted Chet to be sure to convey to the President Jim's and my delight at the prospect of an invitation. Neither of us brought up the question of exactly when. He changed the subject to our old troopship, the U.S.S. *Mann*, and had me laughing at his description of the two-week poker game they conducted in the newspaper office, and then told me a couple of stories about life in Washington, looked at his watch again and said, "Well, back to the film, I suppose," pouring a little brandy into his pony.

"Don't cork that," said Gregory Galba. He came in through the curtain and sat down next to me, elbows on the bar, glass extended. The back of his rug was up, so he must have been scrooched down in his theater seat in the screening room. Chet and I exchanged looks. Heh heh.

"Pour a good honest shot, Chester, none of your conservative ways here," Galba said.

"Yes, sir," Chet said, and poured.

"That's a good boy. You must have been a waiter back at Harvard."

"Too busy studying the Orient," Chet said. He looked pleasant, except maybe a little grim around the mouth.

"You work with Ed?" Galba said.

"Worked with Ed," Chet said, his expression closed now. "Time to get back to the movie, I suppose," he said.

"You go ahead, I want to talk to Ogle," Galba said, taking charge of the room and everybody in it. He patted me heavily on the back. He assumed a droll obscene expression. "Saw you out kissing my lady friend, Ogle," he said. "What's going on here?"

"We plan to elope," I said. "You weren't supposed to know." But the hair on the back of my neck was standing up, and I could feel sweat popping out on my forehead. Not, I hoped, enough to show.

"I hope you can afford her," he said. "One of the goddamnedest women I ever met."

Chet was gone by now. Just me and good old Gregory.

"I'm worried about Jim," he said.

🌴

"WHY IS that?" I asked.

"Because of you, my young friend," Galba said. "How well acquainted are you with Jim's situation these days?"

"He seems okay to me," I said.

"Jim is what our Jewish friends would call a *macher*," Galba said, almost spitting on me with his Yiddish. "He likes things to happen, he likes to be there. He's always *on*, if you get my meaning."

I got that he was telling me about a man I had known nearly all my life, but I nodded and looked into my goblet and tried to keep from tapping my foot against the barstool. A servant came in and told us the picture was about to start again, and Galba waved him off.

"You're different," he said to me. Now he was going to tell me about somebody I *had* known all my life. No wonder he was a big success in business. "You're a relaxed kind of character, you've found your little niche, you do a picture, a couple of Tonite-type shows, a month at the club and you're happy. You seem to have a good sense of your own limits. In fact, I admire you. Under guidance you took a little bit of talent and made it pay off, like a man who don't lift nothing too heavy. I'm not insulting you, wipe that look off your face, I'm telling you a compliment, do you think I see myself as a genius? I'm a man who likes to gamble and hates to lose, that's the long and short of me, and you're in many ways a similar character. But Jim is different, you know that, Christ, you probably know Jim better than anybody else alive, except you maybe know him a little too well, and you forget he's different from you, touchier, more drive, a more mysterious personality, you know.

"Now, take this business of him not wanting to go out as a single," he said.

"Hum?" I said, or something like it.

"What is that all about, can you tell me? I need your advice in this matter and I'm not afraid to ask you. Why is Jim afraid to work without you?"

"I don't know that he is," I said. "Look, I really don't like to talk about my partner. . . ."

Galba smiled with charm. "I know, I understand, but *you* have to understand that Jim's *in* a lot more things than you, and some of the things are also personal involvements of mine, or say, for example, a situation where I might have recommended Jim to people, as an associate and employee of mine, with the understanding that certain things would happen that didn't happen. Like repayment. Don't look so shocked, Ogle, you know Jim can't handle money. What do you do with yours, by the way, I never see you at the tables and I never hear about you being in anything; what do you do, cash your check at the grocery store and bury the money in Mason jars?"

"I buy a lot of goat futures," I said, but Galba only looked impatient.

"Jim wants very much to expand activities," he said.

"That's fine," I said. "He seldom asks my advice about anything, so . . ."

"Any expansion, we've been led to believe, would have to involve you as his partner. I don't have to tell you what's out there, yen and pounds and marks . . ."

"Rubles and pice and francs . . ."

"Please shut up when I'm talking to you," he said warmly with a nice pat on the hand to remove the sting of the words. "Dollars are wonderful to have, but a world tour by you fellows . . ."

Thud. Thud.

". . . would bring in some really useful amounts of money. I don't have to tell you how well your pictures do in places like Japan and Afghanistan and around the world."

"Gregory," I said, and stood up. My hands were shaking. "My position on this is clear, and I think I made it clear: I don't want to talk about a world tour, or even a benefit or a weekend in Mexico."

The man could be a monster, but he could also charm you to death, and I feared the charm more. I backed away to the curtain.

He smiled and came toward me. "Don't be upset, David. But we must keep talking. I don't know if you have any idea how much trouble Jim is in . . ."

"Not enough to say anything to me about it," I said.

"But that's just it. You'd be the last person he could talk to. We know you boys, we know what you're like. If Jim came to you and said, 'Dave, old buddy, I need us to do some work overseas, just once, one world tour, for me to get healthy,' you would be forced not only to say yes, but to slap him on the back and pet him and kiss him and tell him the world is a wonderful place to tour. Isn't that right?"

"Not necessarily," I said weakly. I had left my goddamn goblet on the bar, and my mouth was dry.

"So he *can't* talk to you, because you can't refuse him."

"Gregory," I said. "You seem to have this all worked out, but to remind you of our contract . . ."

He didn't interrupt me with words, but he did look sad, like a Mafia Don who has to shoot his dog, and I shut up about the contract. It was no defense anyway; it just said that I would work here and there and nowhere else. This had all been tried before and would be tried again, I was not surprised by anything but the escalation—not just a couple of gigs in Reno or Atlantic City, not a command performance in Buckingham Palace, not a visit to a tennis tournament in Monaco, but a whole world tour, capped by a triumphant appearance at the White House, because I didn't doubt for a minute that the two things were connected, despite certain well-advertised animosities.

"Let's go see the movie," I said.

"I saw it," he said shortly. "Come back and sit down."

I came back and sat down.

"Is there some champagne under there?" I asked. There wasn't, and we had to send for some.

This was going to take a while. I rolled the bottle of champagne around in its bucket of ice and then poured myself a fresh goblet.

"Er, your toupee is up in back," I said.

THERE WERE a lot of gasoline explosions up on the screen when I got back to the screening room, and in their light I could see Karl and Sonny with their heads together, probably holding hands and twining toes, too. Next to them were Chet and the other actress, and right up by the door, Jody. Galba had gone to the toilet. I hissed at Jody and she came out with me.

"Where's Jim?" I said.

"He's left," she said. "While they were fixing the print he got up and sang us a song and then he said he was bored and left."

Galba bulged up into the corridor. "You two again," he said, and took Jody by the arm. To me he said as they went back inside, "You think about that," and I said, "I will."

Naturally, we had come to no conclusions over the brandy, Galba's harangues were just the first part of a continuing battle for me and Jim to expand our activities to the maximum dollar, as Galba might say. I wondered where Jim was, although I wasn't worried, I just wanted somebody to talk to. I wandered out in front and saw that my car was missing, and deduced that Jim and the Alfa were together. I didn't want to go back into the screening room, so I checked Karl's little two-seater Mercedes; there were the keys, so I got in and drove out through the big gates. Pretty soon I was on the Sunset Boulevard Speedway, with all the other Mercedes hotshots, heading for L.A.

I felt pretty bad, I guess. Instead of going on to the hotel, I turned off in Holmby Hills and stopped in front of another big set of gates, only these were closed, locked, and guarded by a big mirror that reflected your image to a television camera and showed you to the security people up at the House. I waited a minute and a scratchy voice asked me who I was, and I stuck my head out into the light better and grinned for the camera, and the gates swung open.

This was the entrance to the Playboy Mansion. When Hefner was in town there was nearly always a party going on, and Hefner was obviously in town or the gates never would have opened. When I got to the top of the drive, there were a couple of dozen cars parked in the circle, and I could see more in back, through the archway that leads to the rear exit. Also back there were the cyclone-fenced cages for the Dobermans, a small security measure taken by the staff since Manson. I was in perfect sympathy, and told Hefner so.

"Anybody who sneaks up to your house *ought* to be torn apart by dogs," I said.

Since my Alfa was among the cars outside, I knew Jim was somewhere around. Inside the House, a bunch of people were sitting on cushions on the floor of the living room, watching a movie, and I could see some of the faces of the pretty girls who strutted their tits and asses through *Playboy* magazine. I don't know why, but every time I saw one of those girls I got a twinge of anger; maybe, "There goes all that beautiful young pussy and I ain't getting any." Coming to the House you always saw them in bunches and bunches. There were guys who came over just to hang out by the pool, where the girls were encouraged, although they didn't need much encouraging, to swim, cavort and sunbathe naked, driving these guys out of their minds, because of course the girls were perfectly free to turn them down.

I didn't see Jim or Hefner among the movie watchers, although there were several wellknown faces and several people I knew personally. The parties at the House always had a lot of wellknown guys around, never the heart of the movie industry, but the cream of the egomaniacs. Jim and I fit right in.

I went out by the pool but nothing was happening, just a couple of couples, nobody I knew, so I went back in and ordered a Tokio Cannonball and sat and watched the movie. It was a picture that had been in release a few days, none of your workprints here, and it made me heavy-hearted to see where the laughs came, in this group. All the actors had to do was say, "Son-of-a-bitch!" or "Fuck!" and it brought the house down. These were real sophisticados, exclaiming with fright when the heroine was in danger, clapping and yelling like children when the hero comes over the wall, or up out of the hole, or through the window, guns blazing, fists akimbo. Sitting here on the floor hugging their knees or the nearest bunny were men who for a small profit would set fire to a village and light their cigars at the blaze; but now they were all honking like a bunch of goddamn geese at a scene so cynically sentimental I had to turn away to keep from sobbing myself.

In other words, just an average bunch of folks. Clearly, I was in a bad humor.

Jim made his entrance from somewhere in the upstairs part of the House just as the movie was coming to a close, the hero bloody but ready for a fuck and the heroine conveniently semiclad in his arms. Tears ran like glycerine down everybody's faces.

"All right, you motherfuckers!" Jim yelled. "This is a stickup!"

An hour later I was on the floor myself, clapping and singing along as Jim led the group in a community sing, waving my glass and alternately hugging the girl on my left and nuzzling the girl on my right.

Hefner still wasn't there. Somebody said he was upstairs asleep and somebody else said he was out. It made no difference to me, I was strangling my sorrows in champagne, brandy, perfume and the sweat of lovely young women.

THEN LATER we were sitting out on the lawn far enough away from the pool and the grotto to be out of the light. We were passing a bottle back and forth and talking. Jim was crosslegged and hunched over, and I was on one elbow. I don't know why, but I was trying to explain to Jim how hurt and upset I was about Sonny, how for once I had really fallen for a girl, a real instant crush, and couldn't shake it no matter what I tried, but

Jim wasn't paying much attention. Oh, he tried, sitting there rocking back and forth; knowing he was obliged to listen to me but bored by it, not wanting to hear it, wanting to tell me, "For Christ's sake, just grab one of the girls over there dancing naked in the moonlight, every last one of them is younger and prettier than Sonny, throw her into the weeds and slip her the meat and you will forget all about what's-her-name from Texas," but not saying it because it would be insulting to treat my emotions so lightly; bored, thinking about something else, shaking his foot, looking downward, jiggling his body not in rhythm to the music from poolside but against the rhythm, just itching to get away from me. But I would not let him go. I was drunk and wanted my pard to hear my sad message. He all but said, "Yeahyeahyeah."

"Shit, you don't care," I said finally, and took the bottle back from him and gurgled down an ounce or so.

"I do so care," he said. "What do you want me to do, pat you on the shoulder and tell you everything's gonna be all right?" I could see his teeth in the light from the pool. "It's not gonna be all right," he said. "Matters of the heart, my friend."

"Hell no," I said. "I want you to come with me. We'll go find the bitch. She's probably in Karl's fucking bed, right fucking now."

"I wonder what they're doing?"

"Waiting for us to come leaping in through the window," I said.

"Man," he said, "how long have you been on this planet? You don't know that's no way to treat a lady?"

"I don't want her back, the bitch, I just want to tell her goodbye . . ."

"Tell her she's out of the picture . . ." he said.

"No, that's bullshit, just goodbye . . ."

"See you on the set, bitch . . ."

"That's right. See you on the set, *cunt!*"

"Listen, Dave, I been around too long to jump into this one. If I agree with you, 'Yeah, fuck the bitch!' and say a lot of shit about her, and then you two make up, Christ, Man, she and Karl might be *friends*, did that ever occur to you, *friends*, who have little intimate secrets, and dinners together and phone each other up all the time, lean their heads together while watching a movie, shit, you don't know, you raving paranoid, but if it turns out that way and you're still hot for her tomorrow, you'll come looking for me with blood in your eye because of all the rotten things I said about *that goddess*. Take a hike, Man, I ain't gonna play."

"Some fucking friend."

"Yes, some fucking friend. Tomorrow you'll love me for keeping my mouth shut."

"I don't want you to talk, I want you to *accompany*. Me. Back to Karl's fucking house, and *get* the bitch, you can stay out in the fucking car if you want. All I want is company, is that too much to ask from you? Man, don't drift away now."

"I'm not drifting away, Davie, dear David, my pal. I'm just being super-fucking cautious."

I started crying about then, damn it.

"But I *want* her," I sobbed.

"Oh, I can't handle this," he said, and sprang up and fell over. I was sobbing and laughing at him, although I could not get up off the ground.

"I promise not to cry," I said. "Shit, I don't want to cry."

"Oh, Honeybear, you got a right to cry," he said, and made it to his feet. I knew what was coming:

"*YEW GOTTA RIGHT TEW CRAAAHHH!!!*" he sang, and fell back on the lawn.

Then we were in the back of Hefner's limousine, heading for Santa Monica. The moon was way over to the west, so it must have been pretty late. Jim and I sat with our feet up on the jumpseats. For some reason the people at the House would not let us get into our machines and drive.

"I can't wait to get there," Jim said. "My throat is dry."

"I'll just put it to her this way: Does she or does she not want a ride back to the hotel? That's, I think, the diplomatic thing to say, isn't it?"

Jim grinned. "Sure, we're standing over the bed, two fucking crazy men in the middle of the night, 'You wanna lift?' '*Aaaaggghhh! It's the Mansons!*'"

I had to grin at the sight myself. "Do you think they have dogs around? Maybe we'll be torn to bits . . ."

"Torn to bits," he sang, "torn to bits, into elbows and asses and tits . . ."

🌴

"DON'T WAIT for us," I said to the driver. I gave him a few dollars, and he said that two other drivers would be bringing our cars down here and he would take them back to Holmby Hills. I gave him some more money for the other guys and he got into the limo to wait. Jim and I went around the side of the house.

We tried a couple of doors but they were locked.

"Maybe we should go around front and ring the bell," Jim said.

"Naw, that would just scare people," I said. "Let's climb this tree, go over the roof to Karl's room and in through the window."

The tree was a huge branching oak with rough bark and dry stickery leaves, easy to climb, the kind of tree every California kid learns climbing on. I was up to the second floor in no time, and Jim was right behind me, then on up into the lighter branches and finally out a limb to the roof, which was red tile, not the flat kind, the half-round kind, easy to walk on. I let myself down onto the roof and walked up away from the tree to give Jim room, and he dropped out of the tree and fell over and rolled down almost to the edge.

"Nice fall," I whispered. I looked around. The hills and valleys of this huge house made an eerie landscape under the moon, but to the west you could see the entire Pacific Ocean, with a bright stripe of moonlight right down the middle. I could hear the surf at the bottom of the cliff, too, and for some reason it made me feel like Douglas Fairbanks or Errol Flynn.

"High adventure, 'ey, old sport?" I said to Jim.

"I think I skinned my knee," he said. He was rubbing the place tenderly.

"Which way to Karl's room, do you think?" I had been to Karl's part of the house many times, but from the roof and under moonlight the perspectives changed, and I was lost. There were chimneys and balconies and terraces and casements everywhere you looked.

"How the fuck should I know?" Jim asked. He was still rubbing his knee.

"You want a drink, don't you?" I said. "Let's get inside any old fucking way, have ourselves a brandy and then proceed to business. Indeed, Holmes, I daresay that is the only feasible course of action open to us."

"Bah," said Jim.

"Eloquent," I said. I moved off up the roof and down the other side of this particular section. I was looking for an open set of windows that I could lower myself into or a balcony I could drop onto without risking my life. Jim followed me at some distance, often going on all fours uphill and scrambling on his ass downhill. I came around some chimneys after a bit, stopped and turned to warn Jim by holding my fingers to my lips. But he was not looking and kept making noise, so I went back to him.

"Shush," I whispered, "and you will get to see a rare sight."

He misunderstood me and said, "Listen, maybe we better just go back."

"No, it's not like that at all. Come on."

We moved very quietly around the chimneys, and I stopped and pointed.

There was Karl, sitting on the roof hugging his knees. He was wearing a pair of pants and a white skullcap and staring out toward the ocean. His bare feet gleamed in the moonlight.

I looked back at Jim, and Jim looked at me. Then we both looked over at Karl.

"Hello, Karl," I said. "Out for a moonbath?"

KARL LOOKED over at us and smiled, as if he had been sitting there waiting. "Hello, boys," he said.

That stumped me. I couldn't think of anything funny to say, so I asked him, "What the hell are you doing on the roof?"

"I used to come up here all the time," he said. Jim and I sat down. "When I was a kid I once hid up here for three days. They looked all over the United States."

"What did you eat?" I asked him.

"I went inside when they were all asleep or out of the house. There was plenty to eat and it was warm."

He looked at me with great sadness in his eyes. "Don't ever send a small, beautiful boy to *military* school," he said.

"Oh, God," Jim said. "Did you have to go to military school?"

"Don't blame my father. What was he supposed to do? My mother died when I was born, so he had this kid on his hands."

"Yeah, but military school," Jim said.

"Well, I went to a couple of regular boarding schools, he didn't know, and I was always getting into trouble, so he got advice and the advice told him, military school, they'll take the boy and make a man out of him. Ha ha. They took the boy and made a girl of him. Jesus Christ, I hated it, too. I pretended to myself that I liked it, but I hated it. But, see, the only way I could look myself in the face was if I liked it. But it was terrible, you can't guess how many military school boys are nuts, really fruitcake, you have a phrase for it, Jim, what the hell is that phrase?"

"Out there," Jim said.

"That's the one."

"Have you been drinking?" I asked Karl.

"No, not drinking, nothing, no. It's just the weight; I can't stand the weight, it's too much for me."

"I am," I said, "drunk as a goat."

"Me, too," Jim said.

"We probably won't remember *anything* that happened tonight, *black-right-out*."

"I know I always do," Jim said.

"*Oh, fuck!*" Karl said, and with a deep moan he got to his feet and started running for the edge of the roof. He only got a few steps before I grabbed him, but Jim lost his balance and went careening down over the edge of the roof.

"Oh my God I've killed Jim Larson!" Karl said with horror.

"Siddown and shaddup," I said. I went to the edge of the roof. I hadn't heard any loud thump or any outcry from Jim, just the crackle of some greenery. I peered down into the treetops.

"Jim?" I said.

"Yeah?" came his voice.

"What's happening down there?"

"I'm in the tree," Jim said.

"You hurt?"

"Well, I don't really know."

I heard some more crackle, and then a light thump as Jim fell on down, or jumped, to the lawn below. I waited a couple of seconds.

"You okay?" I called.

"Yeah," he said. "I'm coming back up."

"How?"

"The old oak tree," he said.

I went up to Karl, who was just sitting there again. I shouldn't have left him alone like that. I sat down beside him.

"Everything's fine," I said. "Jim's okay, hell fire, the man's a trained acrobat."

"I'm sorry," Karl said. He began to weep into his hands. *"Oh God oh fuck oh God oh shit,"* he sobbed. It looked as if he was trying to dig his eyes out of his head so I took hold of his wrists, but he kept sobbing and beat his head against me. I didn't know what to do so I just held onto him.

"I want to *die!*" he cried. "I want to die, DIE!!"

"But I won't let you," I said. "So you can forget about that."

After a while I felt the tension go out of his wrists and I let go of him. He pulled a white handkerchief out of his pocket and wiped his eyes and blew his nose. I heard the clatter of tiles somewhere on the roof and assumed that trained acrobat Jim was on the way.

"I'm just crazy, aren't I?" Karl said. "This whole night is just craziness."

"Sure," I said. "Happens to me regularly, don't sweat it, pal, it's okay."

Jim showed up. He didn't look so bad. He grinned. "Fell three stories in two jumps, Christ, I ought to go out for the fucking paratroops."

"Stay here and talk to this asshole while I get us something to drink," I said. "Where's the nearest open window?" I asked Karl and he pointed.

Inside the house with just the night lighting, everything looked like old Spain, sedate, rich, powerful and impregnable, remote. The clown show on the roof was just not possible. I went through this corridor and that, looked into rooms that were spare bedrooms, drawing rooms, a room with a billiard table, and then into a place I had never been, but the door was wide open, so in I went, looking for Sonny, I guess, more than a brandy bottle, and on through the small comfortable room into a big bedroom with an empty but turned down bed in it, and past that, following the open doors, out onto a small balcony. There was Max in his wheelchair, one hand resting on a barrel-shaped telescope with an eyepiece halfway up the side. Max's eye wasn't on the eyepiece, though; he was just slumped over the goddamn thing dead.

In the last moonlight I could see the white of his eye.

"Oh, Max," I said.

WHY ME?

I am sitting in my dressing suite in the Golconda Hotel and Casino, Las Vegas, Nevada.

It is Opening Night. Fifteen minutes ago, Jim and I were supposed to appear on stage. The audience is out there, packed in solid, having a fine time watching the girls. The first couple of rows are cheek-to-cheek celebrities, comics, singers, friends of Management.

Jim, however, is not here.

I have not seen Jim in two weeks. Nobody has seen Jim in two weeks.

I remember once in Tokyo, we were drunk in a basement club called the Blue Shadows, listening to J. C. Heard and his jazz band. It was a great night and the band was really swinging, but we ran out of money. We ordered another round of beers and tried to figure a way out of our problem.

"Just wait here," Jim said to me after a while. "I'll be back in fifteen minutes at the latest."

"Where are you going?" I asked.

"Up into Tokyo," Jim said, "to get twenty-five hundred yen."

"From where?"

He winked. "A secret source. My ace-in-the-hole. Then we'll pay our bill here, get into a taxi and head for Rappongi, where I know a Mamasan who will let us stay the night with the girls of our choice, buy us beers, pay off the cab and even, by God, bring us a double order of *yaki-gyoza*."

"Sounds like a miracle," I said, and it must have been, because Jim never came back, and I didn't see him for a couple of months. I finally humiliated myself with promises to the management and even had to get J. C. to okay me, although we had just met that night, fan to musician, and he was obviously uncomfortable about it. Then through the snowswept nightstreets of Tokyo, fueled by rage, arriving at FEAF Headquarters just in time to miss the last bus to my base, and so had to spend the night huddled shivering with the other losers in the lobby of the HQ building.

Thanks, Jim.

BUT I shouldn't panic. Jim does not like the feel of the collar, he does not like to be prodded, he balks at enticement, but he doesn't betray his friends and he doesn't weasel out of agreements. So he should be coming in through the door any minute now, like a cat that's been missing and shows up scarred, exhausted and hungry, or maybe even plump and well groomed, and you aren't sure whether to pick him up and hug him or just toss him back out the window.

The door even opens, but it is not Jim, just a waitress in a cute black uniform, bringing me a jug of Perrier. I glower at her smile and watch the fear come into her eyes. Mustn't spill, mustn't disturb the star's concentration, mustn't look at all the crazy stuff around the room, just pour the Perrier and get the hell out. Especially since the star just sits there staring and doesn't say a word.

The ice cracks nervously in the tall glass as it cools the water. The air conditioner sighs with anxiety. My stomach groans in suffering. I should have said, "Thanks, Doris, how's your little girl," and given her a big tip, say, fifty dollars. But she's gone and wasn't Doris anyway. I drink from the tall glass and the ice cracks like knuckles.

"Relax," I say to the glass, "You'll be flat before you know it."

The bubbles hiss at me faintly. "So long, sucker," they seem to say.

I was in full makeup wearing what my grandfather would have called a monkey suit, with the jacket off. I sniffed my armpit. Two hours ago I had come out of the shower clean as a baby, and now I smelled, not just strong, but *rank*, oily and acid, screaming stink of fear. I had not eaten since yesterday and would not until tomorrow, so my guts had nothing stronger to grip down on than mineral water. I kept getting intestinal threats of diarrhea accompanied by a gaseous buildup I dared not tamper with for fear of disgracing myself in the eyes of my dresser, now long gone and probably out in the house with relatives, since I had told him over an hour ago to fuck off. I sat for a few minutes, enjoying the agony, daydreaming the scene where the dresser is called back, his relatives look up, ahh, he's an important fellow, no? Yes, he must go backstage and change his master's diaper for him—what a wonderful story to dine out on among friends. So not even a whisper must escape my body. I can fart after the show. I can do any goddamn thing I want after the show. Not *this* show, the last show. Not the last show of the evening, the last show of the run. Then I will fart, strip and run naked through the desert.

I confess to a little stage fright from time to time.

I stared at the telephone. If it rang I would jump out of my skin. If it did not ring I would go crazy. But I would be dipped in shit before I would make a worry call. Let the rest of them worry, Ogle is in Meditation until The Arrival.

Jim, you motherfucker, I'm going to knock your fucking teeth down your fucking throat if you do this to me one more time. Exclamation point.

The mantra for today is "motherfucker."

Everybody else backstage who has the slightest involvement in our act is probably going crazy, too, because among other stupidities, nobody gets to fret and wring their hands for fear of bringing on Nemesis. Everybody, from that master of methane Gregory Galba to Doris the waitress, has to go around smiling while their guts grind.

I insist on it.

Aw, hell, Dave, take a Valium, there's plenty of them in the medicine cabinet so thoughtfully stocked by Galba, certainly as a joke, but Gregory wouldn't mind if I went nuts. He had *filled* the medicine cabinet with drugs. It was a hit parade of stupefacients, the top ten of legal dope, the hall of fame for mindfuckers: Valiums, Percodans, Quaaludes, Benzedrine, Ritalin, amphetamines, biphetamine, the list goes on, and I won't touch a one of them. Not because I don't like the wonderful sensation of shredding apart, but ordinary precaution, like, if I take a Valium for this caper, what about tomorrow? Six Vals? Then on Tuesday I can have my convulsions. Screw that noise, screw Gregory, unctuous provider, and doublescrew Jim, who may have killed himself or God knows what while I am cursing him out.

No drugs. Not even marijuana, my dear old friend and teacher, the one who slowed me down; not cocaine, ol' nosedrip is back, not mushrooms, who wants to go out there and find a room full of flesh-plopping bipeds? No drugs. But God, how I would love to rush to the medicine cabinet or the secret compartment in my suitcase and stuff it all into my face and disappear into purple smoke.

I could even go out onstage while the drugs are getting ready to kick in and tell the audience that after a lifetime in show business I have chosen this moment to retire, and then, as the "AWWWWW!" rolls over me, spread my arms and sweetly fly out over their heads and . . .

I look up quickly. The door has spoken.

Click, it says.

I wait.

But, whoever it was decided to keep his head another day.

It certainly wouldn't have been Jim. Jim does not hesitate at doors.

Seventeen minutes late.

Laugh, laugh, laugh. Nobody gives a fuck about seventeen minutes; if the show started on time half the audience would faint from surprise. But you're supposed to *be* here.

But he's not really late until he's half an hour late.

Unless you think maybe he's two weeks late. Lying on the roadside trussed up in a dark green plastic bag, arms, legs, penis, head, severed; trunk, severed. Dead, oh, about *two weeks* . . .

For that matter, *I could sure use a drink*, for that matter. Three or four straight shots of 100-proof bonded whiskey would probably have some interesting effects on my stomach, and to keep the glow I could drink onstage, toasting the audience, slopping around, using the booze to get laughs. Then the second show. Um, how you feeling? Unghktlph . . .

The dressing room has four doors. One door leads to the bathroom, with tub and shower and a wicker basket full of corncobs, provided by Galba, beside the toilet, as well as a huge reading rack of the scummiest pornography he could find, water sports, enema clubs, child porn with outrageous titles like FAMILY PARTY, magazines full of women trussed up like hogs, strapped to crosses, bent into expository positions and wired down, magazines full of women in black leather costumes flicking plump, stupid-looking men with Sears, Roebuck riding crops, and on and on. And of course Gregory would not want me, at some fitful four a.m., to have to go to the drugstore for anything, so the bathroom was also equipped with a couple of huge enema bags and a set of extraordinary nozzles in a wall rack like dueling pistols; in a bowl on the counter with the two sinks was a wicker basket of assorted rubbers for "thrilling Milady with their deckle-edged plunger ripple action . . ." and a row of standing dildos of various sizes, textures and length and a bottle of amyl nitrite with a little hand-written card, IN CASE OF EMERGENCY, SNIFF TWICE AND INSERT OBJECT.

Gregory's crude mining-town scrawl, naturally.

Another door leads to the elevator that leads to backstage and also to Jim's dressing room suite, just down the hall. The door to the closet was open, and I could see, just by moving my head a little, some of the late-night finery he had provided, again, how much of this is what his press agent told him was "gargantuan humor" to go along with his reputation, and how much was paving stones for the road to hell? With Gregory you never knew. He might have thought that every entertainer was an emotional circus and liked to get up in women's underthings or rubber suits. There was also a very fine selection of resort clothes for me to wear around the pool or the gambling tables, although I never went to those places, and the row of identical monkey suits for me to work in.

The last door leads to the living room of the suite, with its own private entrance reached only by going through another special door with a cop to check your right to pass into the dazzle of backstage life. Right now I would guess the living room was full of friends and well-wishers, not the ones who were already at ringside out of politeness, but the close ones who were not exercising privilege but were giving me moral support, like, they were out there if I needed them. Ron and Jim, who write and direct our pictures and have for four years, a couple of real Hollywood guys, nice people who can deliver and who are able to say of something they have written, "Isn't that awful?" and not go home to the Valley and grind their guts about it. Jim spent his spare time writing mystery novels and indulging in domestic life with his family, and Ron was big in the Guild. They always came to our opening in Las Vegas and always brought their combined families and didn't demand six ringside tables, and I could always hear them laughing, Jim going *hughughug*, and Ron, *cackle cackle*, always on our side, always showing a cheerful front, getting a little thick through the middle, both of them, not doing what they had set out in life to do but making so much money they could hardly find it in their hearts to complain; they were out there, probably telling jokes to lighten things up. Of all people, they knew Jim and had faith in him.

But he has never done this before, Not two weeks. My own faith in Jim was not shaken, *trust your animal*, my grandpa used to say when the cat would run away, but *two weeks!* He left before we even wrapped picture, three days of pickups and some looping left to do, gone, snap, his apartment on the lot unlocked and empty, his home in Palm Springs still filled with his wife and her real estate salesman buddy.

Sure I fucked her. Out there in the backyard, while he went to get some champagne to celebrate.

The show biz hotels were checked out in order of rank and stature, first the Bel-Air, then the Beverly Hills, the Beverly Wilshire, L'Hermitage, the Chateau Marmont, the Sunset Marquis and finally the Montecito, but no Jim. The couple of times I exploded, thank God with nobody around, I wondered why if they could locate us at Enrico's in San Francisco without a clue, why were they having trouble now? The only possible reasons:

1. Jim does not want to be found.
2. Jim is kidnapped or dead.
3. They aren't telling me where he is.

Twenty-five minutes into Showtime.

I hit the Perrier button and picked up a copy of *Time* in order to appear to be doing something important. After a couple of hundredths of a second the waitress, this time it *was* Doris, hurried in with the tray and the fresh bottle and the bucket of fresh ice, even though I had my own icemaker over in the corner.

"Hi, Doris," I said. "How's your little girl?"

"She's just fine and dandy, Mister Ogle. Thank you for asking."

"Here's a little something, buy her a soda." I gave her the fifty-dollar bill I had gotten out.

"Oh, Mister Ogle, you don't have to do that," she said, but I forced the money on her with a good-natured chuckle and patted her hand like a pal and said, "God, I'm nervous, Doris, let's get somebody else to go out there."

She laughed shyly and blushed, a young pretty girl with a good job, and left the room without trying a comeback. She had taken the money so nicely and been so perfect, what with her daughter and all, I almost cried. People are so wonderful, I thought, I should just let my face fall into the big open jar of cold cream and die.

Jim, Jim, Jim, are you laid up with some Mexican whore in Tijuana? Are you doing three-way nipups with a couple of gigantic black transvestites in Long Beach? Are you on the Parker Center tower, hanging from the cornice and hoping for the courage to jump?

Are you in your dressing room? Dressing? Drunk? In secret communion with a priest?

Who else was out there? Ron and Jim, Marty, our line producer who had gone without drinking for six whole months and then on the day Jim vanishes, and Marty is to within about eight cents of budget, he goes across the street and has the big Bucket of Gin, just one, and comes back to begin to try to find a way to cut the picture without the pickups. Marty will be out there with his wife, Zelda.

My relatives had all come early and were now in their seats, not great seats, but good seats. If I knew them, they were making friends with the booths on either side, same kind of people up in those seats, big raw red American faces, now don't cry, Ogle, we know they're all swell folks, your fans.

The SALT of the FUCKING *EARTH!*

🌴

SONNY WAS out there. As a friend, of course. Sonny and I had come to Appomattox the day Max Meador died and we all had to help Karl get straight before the worlds of art and commerce heard the news and came at him. At first I thought Karl was just grief-stricken at the loss of his father. That, too, sure, grief and shock, loss, but not the same for a man that age as a younger person. I felt it for Max, the whole bottom falling out, a black hole in space where a man had been, not as strong as for my own grandfather but strong enough, and I'm sure Jim felt some of that, too, but Karl was going berserk. One minute he would be sitting calmly telling stories about Max and the next he would wail and fall to the floor or burst out, "I can't bear this!" and start to run out of the room. Once he looked as if he had had a heart attack right in front of us, gasping for air and grabbing at his throat, his face turning purple, etc. We finally figured it out, it was simple, of course, but we were drunk, shocked and confused at first.

Poor Karl had just had the control of an empire dumped on him, all the energies of a billion dollars landing flash and sizzle right in the middle of his soul. He told us the amount as we were driving him to my hotel that morning. We didn't want him to officially find the body of his father, and we sure as hell didn't want to be the finders. Let the staff find him in the due course of time, that was our philosophy, since we got the breaks and it could happen that way. So we got Karl in the back seat of my car and headed up Sunset. Most of the way he either cried or boasted about how much he was worth.

"It's not just money at that level, you know," he would say. "You don't inherit a huge wad of capital. It's all in things, goods, companies, services, people, agreements, letters, bits, God Almighty, it's all over the world and in every goddamn form you can *think* of!" Or he might laugh meanly and say, "People always wondered about me. Well, now they're gonna find out, all right, all right, certain people will find what can happen when a billion fuckin' dollars gets in the way!"

"There, there," I said at this point. Thinking, now that Max is gone, what is to become of *us?* What about Larceny & Ogle? Who's been running the show? I could see already the complications of getting into a shitstorm with Gregory, part owner of the studio and the Golconda and half of the rest of the world, a man perfectly capable of starting to work picking Karl clean before the funeral. And as if reading my mind, Karl would quail and quake and mutter, "Oh, my God, help!"

Up at my place we sat him on the couch and put some coffee into him.

"Now, Karl," Jim said. "You have to calm down."

"Don't worry, boys, don't worry, I'll be there when the shit hits the fan," he said. "And don't think I won't be grateful when the time comes, you boys are my best friends, do you know that? Nobody the fuck likes me. Oh God!" And he would be off again, rolling back and forth in agony, "Oh, my God, what an asshole I am, talking like this! My father! My father!"

He wept into his hands for a while, and then was calm again.

"This was no ordinary death," he said.

"What do you mean?"

"This man who died was no ordinary man, my father, Max Meador, this was one of the *kings* of the *world*, can I tell you something? You want to hear something? Max Meador produced over *three thousand movies!* Three thousand fucking movies. Nobody will ever do that again. Nobody. Ever."

He smiled, totally sane. "Certainly not me. We had a little game, from way back. He would pretend to be exasperated with me, act like I was a fool."

Jim and I must have looked embarrassed, especially me who can't control his face, because Karl looked at us fondly. "You boys," he said, "my friends. You never saw it, that Max and I would play it all between us."

Tears rolled down his face, but he was still sane, still smiling. "We put it over on everybody."

Including Karl, I thought, but said nothing, naturally.

He talked some more about his father, getting it out, getting over it, and then he went into another crazy fit, really frightened about the future. What was he going to do? He could not manage his estate, he couldn't even keep it from the people who were supposed to be protecting it, it was all twisted and unreal and political, oil wells here, land there, buried gold, numbered bank accounts, secrets, oh, it would be the death of him, and he would roll around in agony some more, with that billion dollars sitting on top of his head like a great electric elephant from outer space, buzzing and clicking, sucking him into its blazing guts . . . a billion dollars!

It even made *me* a little giddy.

So I dialed Sonny's number and after nine rings, she answered.

"You alone?" I joked. She mumbled something and I told her what was up. She arrived at the suite about ten minutes later.

"How is he?" she asked.

"He needs a mama," I said.

SO THAT was the end of me and Sonny Baer. I don't blame her, in fact, we like each other, but in the face of that billion dollars she was helpless. Trained all her life to respect money and bigness like every good American child she was just another beagle in life's drunken rabbit hunt. I told her so.

"Listen," I said. We were in the kitchen getting coffee. "Give me a chance. If I make a million a year, tax free, I'll be caught up to Karl in, let's see, just about one thousand years. Will you wait?"

"Sure I'll wait," she said.

Somehow, I did not believe her.

But the big changes were being rung on Karl himself, with that billion-dollar dildo headed his way, and Sonny did help to calm him down and get him ready for the assault by press, public and those ravening maniacs, his fellow super-rich, many of whom would become convinced that with Max dead his fortune was out in the open and unprotected. At first I didn't believe Karl's babbling about a billion dollars, that's a hell of a lot of money, three or four hundred million more than even Bob Hope, but after the funeral, which would have pleased Al Capone himself, the papers reported that Karl had inherited $60,000 in cash and securities and property worth "close to a million dollars." Ha.

I should have known, also, that Karl *was* actually his father's son, when after he was all calmed down and thanked us and begged for our support in his coming war against the universe, he asked us also to do something we had not done in years: to commit to three pictures instead of just one.

"I need you behind me," he said. "We don't have to sign anything, but if I come into the director's meeting with you guys tied up for three years, and maybe a couple of other deals already working for me, then I stand a better chance. Those people still think of me as Max's little boy, and it's time to step out there."

Jim smiled and said, "Or, you could take your money and retire to Mooréa, just off the coast of Tahiti."

"Huh?" Karl said.

He begged us some more, bringing up the fact that with his crazy confessions of the night before, we had him by the balls.

Jim and I looked at each other. What the hell, we could always weasel out later.

"Sure," I said to Karl.

He shook hands with us, and his palm was warm and dry.

"Thank you very much!" he said. My hackles rose. For the first time, I had heard a touch of the guttural in his voice.

Sonny and Karl went down to her place, hand-in-hand, to wait for the call from home. I probably looked woebegone, for Jim came up to me smiling and hit me on the back.

"Let's go get some breakfast!"

AFTER ALL the fussing about Max's death and the rumors that the studio would be sold, the actual making of our picture was an anticlimax. I won't bother you with the title or the plot, either you like our stuff or you don't, and the bald plots are not the meat of the thing. New songs and fresh jokes, that's our game.

The rumors were funny. Nobody seemed to trust Karl, nobody seemed to think he could run the place, and a lot of people were smug in the idea that Karl would go to pieces. Of course we knew better, but nobody asked us. This was *business*.

One rumor had Gregory Galba selling all his stock to a tribe of Beduin, another that he was only a Mafia front man whose major work was laundering money through the picture and entertainment businesses, and that if the stock continued to drop, he, too, would be dropped—into the bay in a barrel of concrete. Also a rumor that a bevy of superstars were putting their heads together and talking about taking over the studio as a forum for their artistic concepts, and basically would restore Hollywood to its golden age—the 1930s. Everyone got a good laugh out of that one.

For Karl, the rumors were good for business. He came down to Sound Stage Five, where we were doing all our interiors, at least once a day, scaring the hell out of everybody just by marching into the place with his gophers and acolytes trailing along. Karl was back into suits again, but with the silk shirt open in front so you could see all the little gold chains, and he would stand and talk to Marty or Ron while his followers would find other people to talk to, our agents, the pretty girls—there were always pretty girls on our sets, following another of Max's rules about making entertaining pictures: "All the women should have great tits, even the mammas and grandmammas, because it makes people emotional." This rule is followed on all the television comedies; you can check it out for yourself.

Anyway, Karl would come into my trailer and sit down and the charm would fall away like old skin, he would look exhausted and beg me for a cup of coffee, which I would pour him, and then he would say something like, "Oh, Christ, the shits are killing me!"

I would recommend Lomotil and he would give me a pained smile and start into a whining series of complaints. In a way it was flattering, because I suppose it was old Max he used to do this to, and now me. His complaints were as various as he could make them, considering where he stood on the world pamper index, and I would nod and sip coffee with him, glad for the chance to get my mind off my own gripes.

"Well, it happened again last night," he might start.

"What happened again last night?" I would ask sweetly. As long as Karl was in the trailer, nobody else would dare disturb me, so that was another positive.

"The damned *herpes*," he would say with the darkest frown you could imagine. "It's like a plague, an epidemic, a fucking invasion from outer space!"

"Oh, geez," I would say. "That's a shame . . ."

"Do you realize I can't screw?"

"Yeah, I realize that, Karl. Well, relax, they say the best way to get rid of the ol' herp is to relax . . ."

"How can I relax? I've got them again, twice in the same month! Do you know what it's like to get turned on by some lovely girl and then do your damnedest to get her into bed and then go for a piss and find you have these *ugly, red, pus-covered sores* all over your dick?"

"You can't buy happiness," I would remind him.

"*Shit!*"

Outside the trailer about twenty feet away, Sonny might be sitting in her chair, reading a paperback. For some reason it irritated me to have Karl in here pissing and moaning about his sore dick and all the beautiful girls he couldn't seduce, while she was out there. They "went together" for the whole shooting schedule, and then he dropped her during postproduction. During shooting she would arrive, when she had an early call, in Karl's big stretch Mercedes, and then it and the driver would go down to Santa Monica (or wherever Karl spent the night) and get him.

Karl grinned. "There's a guy in Europe," he said, "a doctor who has been curing a friend of mine from Palm Beach with a series of smallpox shots, a permanent cure." His smile was that of a man who has access to something the normal individual can't have. "Maybe after things around here get straightened out, I'll send for him."

"Rumors are flying," I said, to get off his herpes for a minute. "I heard the other day that Columbia and Warners are going to form a joint venture and buy you out when the stock gets low enough."

Karl laughed easily. "You just go on believing it," he said.

"I never said I believed it. And I don't believe the one that says somebody saw you ducking into a spiritualist's down in Santa Monica to have a chat with Max."

"That one was true," he said, with rare humor. "Every medium in town is working on her Max Meador impression." He looked at his watch. "How's the picture coming?"

"Ask Ron," I said. "He's the director."

He stood up and looked at his handsome, well-dressed self in my big mirror. "Well, you just keep those rumors flying," he said. "It helps the stock to drop, and that helps me to pick it up cheap."

"Maybe I'll buy a few million shares myself," I said. "I have the fullest confidence in your managerial abilities," and we would laugh and shake hands and he would open the door and step out, dropping the temperature on the sound stage fifty degrees, and I would close the door and sit down and let the sweat pop out all over me. Because Karl or no Karl, that billion bucks can make a fellow nervous, being cramped up in the same little room with it like that.

🌴

WE HAVE a happy set because we try to use the same people every year, everybody is making good money and there is plenty to talk about while the setting-up is going on because most of the crew are just getting back from location and have a lot of gossip, fresh juicy stuff about the big stars and lugubrious tales of life in America. When I say "happy set" I don't mean that people are going around whistling, it's just that the atmosphere of cold fear surrounding some productions is absent from ours except when guys like Karl show up and get everybody nervous. Even our picture could be canceled at any moment and no one told why, and there is nothing more ominous to the old hand than a bunch of front office types hanging around the set looking at their watches.

The making and selling of motion pictures isn't a very complicated process, and to run things does not require any particular genius, but like any other enterprise an air of quiet confidence is money in the bank. So, with Max's death and Karl's rise to power a certain uneasiness hounded us this particular year as it hadn't since our first picture, when nobody knew anything about the future, whether we would hit, miss or go into limbo.

Now the problem was, would we continue under the same management, which meant jobs for all, or would some crazy man like Gregory Galba or any of a dozen others come bowling into things with an army of campfollowers and screw everything up.

This made the crew a little tense; it made the production department terribly tense, for they are the ones who get blamed for high costs; it made the promotion department tense because they weren't sure on a daily basis what line to follow with an ever-curious world press; this made Marty the producer so nervous that he would sweat and this would make his tortoiseshell glasses slip down his nose so that he was always pushing them back up before speaking, which communicated his nervousness both upward and downward, and if anybody is charged with keeping the nervous element down, it is he; and this of course made Ron the director a little edgy, worried about the jokes, the blocking, the freshness of things, the time wasted getting it right; and this in turn would keep Jim the writer on the set making up one-liners or polishing our business, and it is tough to be funny under pressure.

Out of this whole bunch there was only one guy I really didn't like, but there was nothing I could do about it. This was Jim's camera standin, a guy he had known from the service, a former tenor saxophone player who called himself Baby Cakes, Jim's general size and shape, of course, but a broad crude sly untrustworthy face, a guy who only looked at you sideways, and always got a hurt, I-told-you-so look on his face when it appeared he was going to be cut out of things.

A movie set operates on a straight status basis, just like the Marine Corps, and usually privates don't hang out with generals, but this was different. Baby Cakes had known Jim from another life, and when he showed up in Hollywood a few years back to look up his wildly successful old dope-smoking buddy, Jim was glad to see him, polite to him, took him everywhere and fussed over him for a couple of days, until it became obvious that Baby Cakes was not going to leave without being thrown out, and if Jim said anything that might be thought of as a hint that the visit was over, he would pull a long face and start talking about how his life hadn't turned out as *lucky* as Jim's, etc&etc., until Jim's happy solution to hire him as his standin.

But Baby Cakes wasn't all that grateful and considered himself a cut above the rest of the crew, where in fact he was a buckass private in our little army. He was rude to the people he felt he could be rude to, and sucked up to the rest of us with a kind of growling whine that made you know he hated every minute of it and it was "just the breaks" that kept him from becoming a movie star or a big tycoon or something.

Naturally, since Baby Cakes felt he could walk into Jim's trailer at any time, tag along to recording sessions over at Paramount or even sit with us in the commissary without particularly being asked, people who wanted to get to Jim might first butter up Baby Cakes.

And did he like butter! If it was a woman trying to get to Jim, she would often first have to fight off Baby Cakes, and since he really thought of himself as a demon with the ladies, this might take a while, and if the girl was dumb, Baby Cakes might even score. Which meant we would all have to sit still for his tales of conquest.

By this year, Baby Cakes was on familiar terms with every low-grade hustler, con-artist and dimwit promoter in both the music and movie businesses.

One nice thing: he was barred from the Golconda, and effectively from Las Vegas. He had been caught doing a swipe-and-run among the blackjack tables. This is a hustle where you carry in your hand two cards adding up to blackjack and do a quick double shuffle on the dealer. Usually when some halfass tries this they merely beat him up and throw him out the back door, but Baby Cakes was brought to the boss, he insisted on it, made a big fuss, had Jim there and everything.

"You're eighty-six from the club," Galba said in a voice like tungsten steel. "I ever see you again I'll rip your head off."

Baby Cakes looked at Jim, shocked and hurt, but a little of the sly I-told-you-so in his eyes. Jim only shrugged.

But couldn't fire him. He just couldn't. And so Baby Cakes was on the set when Jim was around, a source of negative energy, a boil on our collective neck.

Now he popped up and opened my door, ducking his head at me like a goddamn servant from the Middle Ages, and said, not looking at me, "Hey, Ogle, I think Jim's on the way over here."

"I'm not home," I said. I had to be careful with the guy; he knew I didn't like him, and if I made it too obvious he would pout all day and make Jim feel bad.

"That's a good one," he said. "No wonder they give you all the jokes."

Jim came up behind Baby Cakes and pushed into the trailer around him. Outside on the set they were moving a couple of lights, nothing happening.

"What the fuck do you want?" I asked him.

He threw himself onto my couch, feet up, and pulled a joint out of his pocket. "You got a match?" he asked. There was a big bowl of matchbooks by his head, and he reached over and got some matches. Baby Cakes hovered in the doorway, waiting for somebody to ask him in. It wasn't going to be me, but I couldn't dismiss him, either. Jim took a deep hit at the weed and, holding his breath, offered the joint to me. I shook my head and he held the joint out toward Baby Cakes, who used it to segue himself into the chair by the couch.

"Great dope!" he said after exhaling.

Jim said to me, "How's that stash of yours?"

"What stash?" I said. Jim knew I always had coke and weed at the hotel, even when I was working, not to use, but for confidence, *just in case.*

"I could really use a couple of good snorts today," Jim hinted, and if it hadn't been for Baby Cakes I would have gotten one of the drivers to take us to the hotel and let Jim pack his nose. But as things were, Baby Cakes would have gone along, and the thought of my hard-gained Merck going up his nose was too much for me.

"Fresh out," I said.

The look Baby Cakes gave me meant, "You fuckin' liar!" which did not make me any happier. Jim, of course, took me at my word and didn't say anything more about it, and just for the hell of it we went over our next scene until Baby Cakes got bored and left.

"Thank Christ," Jim said.

If I hadn't been so pissed off, I would have taken Jim to the hotel then. I should have. We had a hell of a day ahead of us.

FOR A while things were slow and then they started to pick up. Marty came to the trailer a little after Baby Cakes left and said we were free until two o'clock because of an equipment problem, but there was nowhere I wanted to go and nothing I wanted to do. Well, I wanted to get drunk, but not with two o'clock staring me in the face. Marty stuck at the door, turning like he had just thought of something.

"You fellas up to seeing a few reporters? I could get a gang of them off my neck if you would."

"You mean a full-scale press conference? What for? We ain't done nothing yet," I said.

But Marty convinced us that if we would go to lunch now and come back at one o'clock, we could meet with the reporters and have the excuse of the shot at two o'clock, so the press people wouldn't hang on and nag us and try to get a good story.

"I don't give a rusty fuck," was Jim's attitude. After Marty left he said, "You wanna go get some lunch?"

We started talking about where to go for lunch. Time and distance meant nothing; a driver would take us anywhere in the Los Angeles basin and bring us back by one.

"How about Musso & Frank's?" I said. "Maybe get a big crab cocktail and some beer."

"I don't like the crabmeat in L.A.," Jim said. He sat up and started lightly to drum his fingers on the edge of the coffee table, not the way a normal person would, but like a musician, with paradiddles, rim-shots, fingernails against an empty glass, etc&etc. "I like the crabmeat in Florida," he said. "And Chesapeake Bay, goddamn, they got these little softshell bastards that just melt in your mouth, you can eat a hundred of them, with toast and butter, they make the west coast crabmeat taste like shit."

"Maybe you're talking about king crab, what do they call it? . . . Alaskan snow crab, which is tasteless as hell, I admit, but the crabmeat from around San Francisco is pretty good."

He blew me down by pointing out that the crabmeat in L.A. was frozen, anyway.

"You could have lasagna," I said.

"Naw, I'm all up for some of that Eastern seafood."

"Well, we sure can't fly to New York for lunch. How about the Studio Grill?"

Jim didn't want to go to the Studio Grill. No reason.

"Or across the street," I said. "I could eat some *ramaki*, glass of beer, sounds great to me . . ."

"You mean across the street from here?"

"No, across the street from the Studio Grill, the Formosa Cafe."

"We could just walk across the street from here," he said, "and get a big steak and potatoes."

"Make me sleepy," I said. "We could go to the health food place, what's it's name . . ."

"Or the Taco Bell . . ."

"Or El Coyote . . ."

"Polo Lounge . . ."

"Chez Jay's . . ."

"Schwab's . . ."

Obviously, neither of us was the least bit hungry, but if we didn't go eat we'd have to do it later. I was explaining this to Jim while he tapped a pencil against the side of an empty glass, beautifully but irritatingly, when the telephone buzzed. It is not supposed to buzz unless Los Angeles is falling into the ocean. It always made my stomach lurch, and I fell across my big overstuffed chair grabbing for the phone, saying, "goddamn, if we'd only got out of here . . ."

"Don't answer, we aren't here now," Jim said, but I had said hello by then.

🌴

WHAT I had for lunch was a soggy, fishy-smelling crab and avocado sandwich with shredded lettuce, Miracle Whip and tired-looking slices of tomato, all on this really bad French bread that cut the roof of my mouth and gave me the gut-rumbles for an hour. Also there was some pale champagne they must have recovered from the tomb of Tutankhamen.

"Luncheon" was in the office, across the lot, of Terrance Segebarth, truly one of the most repulsive and outrageous of Hollywood's collection of contemptibles, and the point of the meeting was to try to get Jim and me to participate in Segebarth's big annual telethon, which, of course, we refused to do. Segebarth was wearing a turtleneck sweater to cover up his real turtle neck, sunglasses to hide his little red eyes and clumps of transplanted hair all over his head that made him look more than ever like somebody assembled in Transylvania.

You probably get the idea I don't like this man. So true.

The walls of his office were covered with framed photographs—Roosevelt, Truman, Dewey, Eisenhower, Kennedy, Humphrey, Nixon, you get the idea—all these presidents and hopefuls shaking hands with Segebarth or grinning at him while he beams at the camera, senators, judges, international leaders, kings and heiresses, all beaming and grinning and smirking at the camera to testify that they were on the side of God, Charity and Terrance Segebarth.

There were no photographs of teenage girls. How strange.

Naturally, Segebarth was not without ammunition. We had refused to be on his telethon every year for quite a while, and so he knew that even to get us to a meeting he would have to have something. One year he came at us with a straight blackmail proposition, it seemed there was this *girl* and her *mother*, both well known to Segebarth, who had an interesting story to tell about Jim. It took the old crock about an hour to slime out the proposal and to get around to the *woman* and her *child*, and when he finally oozed it all out, Jim laughed and said, "Yeah, they're famous. They once fucked nineteen cops in one night, the two of them. You wanna put 'em on your show? I got the phone number here someplace . . ."

Didn't work.

This year Segebarth had managed to get to Jim's wife and put her, all fussed and twittering, onto the Committee to Save the Universe, or whatever the hell the old fart called his organization, and she was to be the crowbar that would get me and Jim to disgorge about fifty thousand dollars of free entertainment. She was at the meeting, Mrs. Larson, with her fox fur collar and her perfect ass, still perfect after all these years, a woman who just by walking past could make you grunt.

When Jim and I entered Segebarth's office we saw her sitting there with Karl on one side and Sonny Baer on the other, the three of them lined up on the couch. Karl jumped up, his eyes mighty nervous because he must have known how edgy the situation was, Jim never divorcing his wife, loyal to her or maybe just nasty stubborn, never visiting her and never complaining that she used his name in her activities as if they were practically inseparable; and of course Sonny was there for me, Sonny was going to get to be on the telethon *with* us, Karl said, his eyes glittering as he shook our hands. I love the way they do that. They begin the meeting as if it were all over and everything perfect; we have agreed, *of course*, to appear this year because it was really going to be a *family party*, just about everyone in the business would be present, everybody loved Larson & Ogilvie, and (never spoken, always under several layers of implication) we wouldn't want people to think we were *skinflints*, would we?

"Even Jack Benny did my telethon, heh heh," the old fart said.

I had to put things on an official basis right away by saying, "This isn't in our contract."

Karl grinned and said, "I was counting on you guys, this particular year." In other words, do it for poor dead Max, God rest his soul.

"I don't understand," I said. "What do you mean?"

Just then Segebarth's fat old secretary came in with the tray covered with sandwiches and the two bottles of pre-Ptolemaic champagne, and Segebarth "held sway" by cracking his own brand of one-liners, all filthy, all very funny, damn him, I hate him most when he's funny.

Jim, with a mouthful of stale king crab: "What the hell makes you think we'll play ball this year?" He is not looking at his wife.

But she replies, "I told them you were available. I hope that wasn't the wrong thing to do."

"What happens, do they kick you off the committee if I don't show up?"

Segebarth laughing: "Not that easy, but we do hope this year after all, it's the *kids* . . ."

"We don't have kids," I said. "Which makes it kind of impersonal."

Karl gave me a hurt look. "Let me ask you, Why is it you never want to do any things like this? You're not mean, you're not cheap, you have plenty of free time, and I think the American public has been pretty good to you . . ."

"Why don't *you* do the show, Karl?" I said.

"Yeah," said Jim. "You and my old lady could sing a duet."

Segebarth's face darkened. Storm clouds. If flattery and blackmail won't work, let's try a little good old paternalism:

"Boys, I'm getting a little tired of this problem. You aren't the only people in the business who won't cooperate, but you're among the biggest, and I think it's a goddamn shame you don't have any room in your heart for these kids."

"This sandwich is the worst I ever tasted," Jim said. He looked at me: "We should have gone to Musso's when we had the chance."

"Now, boys," Karl said.

"Lissen, Karl," I said, putting on a little heat, "us boys happen to be in the middle of shooting a movie for you, and we're goddamn sick and tired of being harassed by evil-smelling old farts!"

"I represent that remark," Segebarth said and cackled. You couldn't insult the man.

"You really aren't that strong," Karl said to me, cold.

"What is this, Gunfight at the OK Corral? In front of these women? Maybe we'll go someplace where they don't ask us to work free!"

"You shook hands," Karl said, trying to look shocked.

All through this Sonny is sitting there with her mouth shut and her hands in her lap. It must have been fun, watching these rich idiots, two of them in full makeup, waving their arms and yelling about what was, after all, a foregone conclusion. I thought it was charming myself and wanted nothing more than to be out of there, back in my trailer with my feet up, maybe a bottle of beer to calm my intestines. But no. If there was any one thing in this world I hated to be it was an imperious bastard.

SO THERE we were, the five of us, standing out in front of Producer XII, blinking in the sunlight. As far as I knew, Jim hadn't said anything directly to his wife, and nobody had said anything to Sonny. Karl's big metallic-blue stretch Mercedes was right there, the engine quietly mumbling, the driver, a nice guy named Jimmy, was leaning on the fender with his arms folded. We had been in Segebarth's office for a long time, and I for one was tired and irritated.

We were *not* doing the benefit. Another six months of being ignored and reviled by Terrance Segebarth.

At a glance from Karl, Jimmy straightened up and opened the back door.

Karl said, "Can I give you a lift back to Stage Five?"

I said, "No, I'm gonna walk across the lot."

"Me, too," said Jim.

"Aren't you going to see that I get home?" Jim's wife said to him.

Karl said, "Oh, Jimmy will take you home."

"Let him take her now," Jim said. He went over to Jimmy and shook his hand, whispering something in his ear. Jimmy laughed broadly and put his hand in his pocket, putting away the money Jim had given him.

"Get in the car," Jim said to his wife. To Karl he said, "Come on, walk across the lot with us."

Karl looked at his watch meaningfully, having to poke at it a couple of times to get the digits to appear and then hold it away from the sunlight so he could see the time.

"Oh, shit," I said. "Are you afraid to walk across your own lot?"

Jim closed the back door of the limo and patted it on the fender like a horse and the Mercedes moved off. Various people walking around or riding bicycles stared at the long famous car and tried to get a peek at its contents.

It was a nice pleasant walk on a sunny yet sweetly cool day, with, as I said, various types moving around on their own business. This was the new end of the lot, with acres of parking spaces and big military-looking two and three-story office buildings, some with lawns between them and little groups of secretaries and assistants, editors and whatnot sitting on the grass, making it almost look like a college campus. But not quite.

Here was a lot full of antique cars, everything from old Pierce-Arrows to 1922 Rolls-Royces, 1936 Ford three-windows, 1937 Chevy taxicabs, all kinds of old cars. I had spent many a blank afternoon looking over the old cars, enjoying their smell.

Then we were in the shady dim caverns between the enormous old brown sound stages, marching past the parked Mercedes and Jaguars of producers, directors and actors, each parking spot marked with a famous name, and sure enough, as we were striding by Stage Nine we saw a studio employee in grey pants and shirt pulling up the little sign with a guy's name on it, just uprooting the sign and tucking it under his arm, with one backward contemptuous glance at the little green 280SEL with its rusty crease on the front fender.

"*Sic transit Gloria Mundi,*" I said.

"Oh, was that her parking space?" Jim joked, but nobody laughed.

"Poor fucker'll come back from lunch all full of gin and plans, get into his office and find his secretary gone and a nice fat pink slip right in the middle of his desk," I said.

Karl was walking faster now, and we almost had to trot to keep up with him.

"Karl probably fired him before lunch," Jim said.

Our route took us past the little commissary just as a knot of people came out, and we saw a couple of apple-cheeked producers in cardigan sweaters look surprised to see Karl, and then wave and start toward us. Karl waved and grinned but was definitely not in the market for a conversation at this time. We sailed past the little group waving and grinning and not stopping, and watched the kissass grins turn to tight bitter lips.

Now we were in front of Stage Five, the huge door open and some of our crew out in front, lazying in the sun or playing with a Frisbee. They saw us round the corner like a color guard. They squinted at us but did not move.

Often when the crew is hanging around outside, it means that something is going on inside that they wish to disassociate themselves from, like a star tantrum or a royal ass-chewing, but we did not even suspect, or at least I didn't, and when Karl said, "You boys go on in, I want to speak to Sonny for a minute," we just went ahead. Since the crew was there, I kissed Sonny and said, "Don't let him put his hands on you."

She smiled at me sadly and I turned around and stumbled on some goddamn thing and went in. Jim was in his trailer by then, which was close to the door. I crossed the open area back of the set toward my own trailer and into the lights, which were blazing down on nobody, and heard out of the gloom over by the camera, "Yeah, well fuck you, and fuck your job!"

It was the voice of Baby Cakes, shrill with anger. Thank God we were about done with principal photography.

🌴

IT TOOK me a couple of minutes to get used to the darkness, and then I could see two groups of people. Over by the set were a handful of reporters and feature writers, looking mean as hell, God, don't ever offend one of these small-time Hollywood hacks because all they are sniffing for is some little hunk of nastiness they can magnify into a career-wrecking anecdote; just seeing them there and remembering that Marty had arranged the press conference pissed me off—a couple of hours of wrestling that toothless old shark across the lot had put me in a shitty mood anyway. And now the other group, which was two guys and Baby Cakes and Marty.

Nobody had seen me yet, so I stayed in the shadows for as long as I could. The two guys with Baby Cakes were obviously the cause of the trouble. They were black guys, not your average people but guys with LOSER stamped across their faces at birth, sunglasses, shapeless hats pulled down, dirty suits and shoes from out of the garbage can someplace, easy to tell from their swaying and murmuring, hands in bulging pockets, that they were drunk, I could almost smell the cheap boozy stink from where I was standing. One of them laughed at Marty's stiff face and showed a bunch of horrible teeth, and Marty stepped back, probably without even knowing it, and Baby Cakes said, "We'll wait in Jim's trailer, goddamn it."

Marty said stiffly, "The set's closed until after the press leaves, and I don't want you on the sound stage."

"Jim is expecting me, and he's gonna be royally pissed off you fired me," Baby Cakes said.

Naturally, the press is eating it up, though still uptight at being kept an hour. Marty, although it was obviously killing him, told Baby Cakes that he was not fired, he quit, and nobody believed him anyway, and to please clear the set with the rest of the crew. . . .

BABY CAKES: I'm not crew, you asshole . . .

ONE OF THE GUYS: Hey, man . . .

With wonderful timing, in came Karl Meador and Sonny, walking right into the middle of the mess. This stirred up the reporters and they broke formation and started toward Karl. Karl is good with reporters, although he hates them, and he went among them shaking hands, being introduced by the studio publicity guy, and I came out of the shadows and up to Marty and his group.

"What's happening?" I asked Marty. Baby Cakes backed away from the look on my face.

"We'll wait in Jim's trailer," Baby Cakes said.

Marty's eyes went to glass. "You'll *shit!*" he said, cold. "Get off the goddamn set before I have you thrown off!"

"Say that in front of Jim!" Baby Cakes said, and the two black guys weaved uncertainly and looked at each other. Now Marty could see all the reporters plus his boss Karl, and Sonny, a beautiful woman, watching. He turned to me:

"You throw them off the set!"

"Nobody's throwing me off any set," Baby Cakes said. "These are some people I want Jim to meet." He looked at me with terrible dislike and fear in his eyes. "And Jim wants to meet them, too!"

"Oh, fuck off," I said to him, and turned away. Marty and I walked over to where the reporters were milling around Karl and Sonny, and the PR guy said in a really fake cheery voice, "And here he is, ladies and gentlemen, David OGILVIE!"

I raised my hands like a champ and said, "Deelighted to be here, but just give me a little moment, perhaps you could pass the time most profitably by interviewing Miss Sonny Baer, and I hope you'll accept our apology for being late, but as you know, we're right at the tag end of making our picture and things are in a bit of a squeeze . . ."

I heard a girl reporter say in an amazed little voice, "Oh, he speaks so *fast!*" In character, I drawl.

Karl, bless him, took it up and began to introduce Sonny to them by quoting from the promotion handout, and I moved away and started toward Jim's trailer. Baby Cakes and the two guys were standing out in front. Baby Cakes looked upset and almost flinched when I grinned at him.

"Where's Jim?" I asked.

"Not in there," Baby Cakes said. "He wants to see us."

I walked around the trailer and beat on the toilet window, but no response. I went back and opened the unlocked door. No Jim inside.

I beckoned to Baby Cakes and the two guys to come in and sit down.

"Make yourselves comfortable," I said. I introduced myself and we all shook hands. "Would anybody like a drink?" I said. "Baby Cakes, how about being a good guy?"

In fifteen minutes we were all pals. The guys, it turned out, had something to sell to Jim, straight off the boat, uncut, topgrade stuff, only 125 dollars a gram, and after a nice warming drink of whiskey, I paid for two grams, folded into bindles in magazine paper, patted everybody on the back, winked at Baby Cakes and escorted the three of them to the door of the sound stage opposite to the one where the crew was hanging out. Then I went back to Jim's trailer and flushed the garbage down the drain.

I walked back to the press conference and answered stupid questions, trick questions and just plain ignorant questions for thirty minutes, and then Ron came out, smiling, from his little office, with Luigi the first assistant director and Leon the production manager. Luigi, as was his job, cleared out the reporters.

"Where were you when I needed you?" I said to Luigi.

"Huh?"

We waited two hours for Jim but he never did show up. That was when Marty crossed the street for his one big Bucket of Gin, and I began to fear that I might never see my partner again.

"I THINK I'm going crazy," he told me up at the ranch, in fact, he must have come to the ranch just to tell me that, but then other things happened and we never got back to it. Maybe we should have gotten back to it, I think as I sit in my dressing room waiting for the walls to explode. This year he disappears, what the fuck, one year he came down with some kind of insane virus and his face swelled up and turned red and he had a temperature of 104, an hour before we were due to make our opening night entrance at the Golconda. Galba had his pet doctor up there—I wasn't around for fear of catching it—but Jim told me later Galba really leaned on the doctor, like in a cheap movie, "Fix him up, Doc!" while the wounded bankrobber lays blub-bering about Mary Ann and the rain hits the windowpanes. Doc gave him a shot of something and we went on and that was the end of it.

Another time, it was me. Right in the middle of shooting our picture I went all cold inside and couldn't do anything. I've been depressed before but this was more like despair. It just didn't seem to matter. I mean, really, who gives a shit whether we make another movie or not? Who goes to see these things? What are we doing to their minds? I lay in bed in the motel and the despair was like a heavy airless weight on my chest; how long had I been alive, and what did it all mean? I had no wife, no children, my parents were long dead, I loved my relatives but I couldn't stand to be around them, what, really, had I contributed to existence? What had I done with my life except take my big paychecks and stow the money and ruthlessly screw everybody who came near me?

I didn't blame anybody but myself for the goddamn funk, so for a couple of days I would let them dress me up like a farmer (in this movie I was a farmer and Jim was my old army buddy from the big city) and lead me out onto the set, and everyone was very sweet to me, especially Jim, whose sweetness took the form of leaving me the hell alone, and they would fuss with the lighting and get everything right and Luigi would yell for everybody to be quiet, Ron would cue the camera, the sound man would quietly say, "Speed," the camera guy would clap the clapper, Ron would quietly say, "Action," and it was all up to me to speak my five words or look droll, or whatever, and I couldn't do it.

Fifty people standing around on salary waiting for me to chortle like an idiot, and I couldn't do it. I would be all cold in the middle and somehow not realize it was my turn to perform, and Ron would say quietly, "Keep rolling," and then to me, "You okay, Ogle?" and I would nod and say, "Sorry," and Jim and I would get back on our marks. "Action," and Jim would look expectantly at me and I would go all cold inside.

Later in my motel room I lay there and wondered if this wasn't the beginning of the end for me, not as a performer but as a human. From now on I would be nothing more than a humanoid. Why eat? Humanoids don't eat. Humanoids don't drink or take drugs or fuck or yell at people. They just move around until somebody unplugs them.

It lasted three days and everybody went nuts all the way back to Hollywood. Doctors were sent out, psychiatrists, holistic miracle workers, telephone calls from Karl *personally*, but I just lay in that room and sweated out my emptiness.

Then on the fourth morning I was fine. I didn't even notice until I was sitting in the motel coffee shop having a cup of coffee. Everybody around me was so pointedly not looking at me that I broke out laughing and made the waitress think I was nuts.

So maybe I should have listened to Jim.

The night he disappeared I dragged myself over to the hotel, preferring to walk the four or five miles because I was sick of sitting in the back of studio limos while the Teamster behind the wheel babbles his life story, which I don't give a rusty fuck about. Besides, walking took about an hour and a half, and gave Jim time to undisappear, show up in my apartment snorting my precious stash and laughing.

It didn't happen that way, of course. My apartment was empty and still. It was just getting dark outside. I kicked off my shoes and pulled the socks off and let my feet luxuriate in the twilight air. I sat on the terrace overlooking the city and wondering for the ten thousandth time why I allowed myself to get tense about this shit. Jim would show up or he wouldn't. I wiggled my toes in the cool air and they thanked me after the hot walk. Ten little toes. Hello, toes. A line of Lenny Bruce's: "It's so *good* to get out of the *box!*" I sat there a minute silently doing Lenny's act for an appreciative audience of ten.

I looked over the rooftops to the left: that was where Lenny got his start, cheap night club between strippers, making his jokes to the band because it was "a little Squaresville" out in front. I thought a minute about getting out his records and playing them, just to hear the guys in the band laughing at Lenny's nasty humor. Oh, balls, some other time. But he was a god to me, a sleazy dopy god. I looked to the right; just down the street is where Lenny died. I didn't want to die like that, half in and half out of the toilet, naked on the floor with a needle in my arm. God, I didn't want to die at all. I started crying.

"Lenny, you cocksucker," I cried to the dull red horizon, but I was really crying for myself.

I WENT into the kitchen and pulled open the refrigerator. Half an avocado, wrapped in plastic, three small hunks of different kinds of cheese, wrapped also in plastic—I have never been able to throw good food away, except, of course, drunkenly and deliberately throwing food—but any sliver or scrap of food in the house must be preserved until it is either dead and grey or eaten, perhaps at three in the morning, me standing in front of the refrigerator, the door open and its light spilling over my nakedness in the otherwise dark apartment, munching on a hunk of cheese and hoping I could get back to sleep from whatever woke me, drunken shouts from the drive below, sirens down Sunset, the sky opening up with a tremendous explosion and God reaching down, crushing L.A. under His paw. . . . It didn't take much to waken me in Hollywood, although on Sonoma Mountain I usually went to bed with the sunset and got up with the dawn, ten or twelve hours of sweet unbroken sleep.

There was also an unopened package of two T-bone steaks, a pound of ground round, a package of dinner franks, what my relatives called tube steaks, "Somebody's got to eat the ears and snouts!" my cousin Harold would say cheerfully, "no use throwing out good pig meat!"

These were all-beef.

There was half a jar of cucumber pickles, a couple of quarts of milk, three cans of Miller's High Life, and, in the freezer compartment, two trays of ice and half a pint of Dreyer's deadliest vanilla ice cream.

I could have called the desk and ordered dinner from Greenblatt's or Schwab's or for that matter Chasen's, all you have to do is pay for it, but instead I called down to Sonny's apartment. She answered right away. She'd had a tough day, too.

"Do you have any potatoes or salad stuff? I got some steaks," I said.

"I was just going to go to bed," she said. "I just got out of the tub."

"Did you have dinner?"

"I had a couple of cookies when I got home," she said. "I just thought I would read."

"What are you reading?"

"*Shogun*," she said.

"Can't you hear those steaks, sizzling in the pan?" I asked.

"You're talking me into it," she said.

I had time to take a nice hot shower before Sonny showed up with a big bowl full of salad and a baguette of bread. The television was on, Connie Chung with the news, and I was drinking a beer and watching.

"What's new?" Sonny said as she passed through to the kitchen. She was dressed in jeans and a faded pink sweatshirt, no shoes, her hair up under a scarf.

"Beats me," I said. My private phone rang, and for a second I thought it would be Jim and my low-down feeling of doom would go away. But it was Johnny Brokaw, a comedian friend. Johnny lived at the beach when he wasn't in residence in Vegas or touring, but right now he was in town with nothing to do. I asked him to dinner and told him to stop by the market and pick out his meat course. "We're having steaks," I said.

Johnny protested, saying he thought I'd probably want to be alone, but I laughed at him and said, "Come the fuck over." Johnny was a very funny man, naturally funny, handsome as hell although nobody really ever thinks of him that way when he's working; a damn good dresser, a doper and a good pal. Sonny had never heard of him.

"Jesus Christ," I said.

"Did you ask him to bring some wine?" she asked. I hadn't, of course, so I had to put on my *huaraches* and slip-slop down the hill to the Liquor Locker, where I picked up two bottles of grey Riesling, Wente Bros., a can of deluxe mixed nuts, and trudged back up the hill. Sonny had changed channels and was sitting watching the Dinah Shore Show. I sat next to her after getting a beer for myself. It was comfortable. Sonny and I had taken to spending quite a few of the dead dull weeknights together, watching television or even going to bed together. Karl was too busy to see her, although he claimed he loved her and she was the only girl for him. She knew what Karl was like, by now, and oddly, as friends, she and I had some remarkable times in bed.

There was a tapping at my door. I said, "That's Johnny," and went over to open the door, but it wasn't Johnny, it was an actor friend named Mike Leary, grinning, leaning against the wall.

"Hello," he said, "or is it goodbye?"

"It's hello and come on in," I said. We hadn't seen each other since last year, when he had gone to Hawaii. Mike was too good for our pictures, although he had appeared in a couple of them some years ago.

"Have you had supper?" I asked him.

"No, as a matter of fact, I haven't," he said. I introduced him to Sonny and they laughed and said they had met, at "the club," long ago, and had even been on a couple of casting calls together.

"What's 'the club'?" I asked.

"God, you mean to tell me you've never been to 'the *club*'?" Sonny said. She and Mike exchanged grins.

Mike said, "He's probably the only performer in America who's never been to 'the club,'" and I knew what he was talking about. Unemployment.

"I've done more time in the unemployment line than you've been in pictures," I said without originality.

"Tell us about it, Pops," Mike said, and grinned at Sonny, who patted the seat next to her. Mike sat down.

When I had gotten home I had wanted nothing but to be alone. Now I was in the mood for a party.

"Hey," I said to Mike as the three of us passed a joint, "let's call Phil and Oona and have 'em stop by the Hughes Allnight Supermarket. Oona can pick out whatever she likes, I'll pay for it when they get here. You could call Debbie and ask her to bring her cousin. We'll have a dinner!"

Sonny looked at me strangely.

"Fun!" I yelled. "Fun! Fun!"

"Oona's a great cook," Mike said. "Let me at that telephone."

Sonny sighed and went into the kitchen.

BY NINE or so there was a gang of people in the apartment, hanging out in the living room drinking the booze that various groups or individuals brought with them and watching the television or talking, moving in and out of the kitchen where Oona Naglio supervised the cooking, or out on the terrace where Mike had taken charge of the charcoal grill and a fifth of Wild Turkey. It was a good bunch of people, all working in show business one way or another. Nobody knew everybody, but that was all right, too. Johnny Brokaw showed up with a bag of groceries including a big jug of red wine and a couple more steaks, and on his arm was one of those beautiful long-legged Vegas line dancers that he liked so much even though they were all a few inches taller than Johnny, and right behind him came the Naglios, Phil and Oona, a writing team who lived over in Nichols Canyon; they had double armfuls of bulging sacks, having stopped at the Hughes Allnight Market, and Oona was carrying a big shallow bowl in case I didn't have one, for the main dish, which would be a rice and seafood conglomeration, and they had called Debbie (casting director) who had been in the middle of getting dinner for her cousin, her lovely cousin whose name I never learned, a secretary at Fox, and her cousin's date, Ford Hamilton, a rich boy turned comedian out from New York to make a picture at Fox and incidentally, a guy *Rolling Stone* had called "the hip David Ogilvie." During the first part of the evening Ford Hamilton and I sort of ducked around and didn't make any eye contact. I had been in the toilet when Debbie and What's-her-name and Hamilton arrived.

Then a few more people came, people who had called me for one reason or another: Marty, our producer, who had obviously come over to talk to me about business and finding himself in the middle of a loose friendly party, sat stiffly in a corner with a glass of Perrier talking to Sonny for at least ten minutes and then vanished. And others.

I was immoderately happy. These were all people I liked, even the ones I didn't know, and there was no pressure on me to be host. No civilians, no assholes, no cops. We had all eaten the salt of Hollywood and were alive to tell about it. For a while I hung out around the charcoal grill and listened to Mike and Phil talk about a hunting trip they were planning for the autumn in Eastern Washington where Phil came from, while on the grill were steaks, hamburgers and hotdogs, people coming out and grabbing what they wanted, Sonny's baguette of bread split, garlicked, toasted and gone, her salad wiped up in minutes and everybody still waiting for the seasmelling mystery wonderdish to emerge from the kitchen, where aside from Oona and Johnny's girl peeling shrimps and cracking crab, Debbie and Sonny sliced and quartered bananas, pineapple, strawberries, nuts and dates for the dessert, to accompany the two big ice cream nut rolls somebody had brought and put into the refrigerator. And more.

Naturally, there was a certain amount of marijuana being smoked, to keep everyone's appetite at a fever pitch, and plenty of beer and wine to keep throats from getting dry.

When it was finally time to sit down to the rice and seafood, everyone gathered in the living room and the big bowl was placed on the cleared-away coffee table, and Debbie dished. Mike put the television on to the Z Channel and we watched a firstrun movie, people making cracks like "Ooh, isn't she cute!" and "Boy, look at Larry's toup!" We were all insiders, naturally, and knew everybody. "Oh ho! He's the biggest dope dealer in Hollywood!" Or, "Look at those tits! Who are they kidding?" Not a set, not a line of dialog, not a makeup job, got past without somebody yelling something derisive. "Mike shadow! Mike shadow!" "I can see her scars, who lit this shit?" "Cut toooo . . ." "I was up for that job, but it was scale plus ten so fuck it." "Please pass the sliced tomatoes . . ."

And then we were done. The chatter died down and the movie, not bad, not good, ground on. Sonny and Debbie got coffee for everybody, putting the Chemex on the coffee table and getting out all my cups and some glasses. Somebody burped deeply and a couple of others chuckled with appreciation.

Well, here goes, I said to myself, and went into the bedroom, coming out with my remaining Merck, mirror, razorblade, silver fluted straw from Tiffany's, and walked over to where Ford Hamilton lay stupefied between Johnny's girl and Debbie's cousin. I gave him the mirror and the little bottle. The room sighed with hunger for the coke. Just one little hit after a big meal is the ultimate civilized touch, no?

"So you're the hip David Ogilvie, huh?" I said, looking him in the eye for the first time. "Why don't you cut us some lines?"

Ford looked up and ogled me like a master. I fell down laughing, not as a joke but because he was so funny to look at. The son of a bitch was really good. He grinned shyly, and Johnny Brokaw came in with his impeccable John Wayne impression: "You cowboys git tuh makin' love, there's gonna be blood on the saddle, fer sure!"

It was corny but everybody was in just the right mood for a little corn and we all laughed and slapped tables and knees, and nobody tried to top him.

By midnight everybody but Sonny was gone. While she was in the bathroom taking the pins out of her hair, I called Jim's apartment on the lot, just for the hell of it. Twenty rings and no answer. I hung up. The chill in my gut, the Vegas chill, began right about then, and I went into the bedroom, to Sonny, dreading it.

VEGAS. WELL, Vegas. Hmm, Vegas. "Lost Wages, Nevada." I've never been to Las Vegas, not really, and have no desire to go. I have never walked down Fremont Street, stopped just anywhere for a cheeseburger and dropped my change into the slot machine. I have never read a Las Vegas newspaper, nor have I gotten married or divorced in one of the neon houses of worship.

For me Las Vegas is a series of limousines and deep concrete garages, private elevators, endless carpeted canyons of shopping malls lit down so that people in evening clothes at ten a.m. don't look out of place, and air conditioned to a dry sweat chill. In all the years I have been coming here I have never left the Golconda grounds except in the back of a car, and never to go anywhere but the airport or somebody's posh suite through another pipeladen underground garage and up yet another private elevator.

Sunbathing? I had my own terrace, and I spent plenty of time there, giving myself a nice dry bake. If it happened to be nighttime I would use my private sauna, forty minutes of baking and I was ready for the night terrace and the crystal stars. Tennis? Galba's private court was mine to use, and the cyclone fence surrounding it was draped in green canvas, to keep the turkeys from gathering.

Turkeys. This is where the word originated, among the waitresses, busboys, bartenders, dealers and security cops who had to herd the turkeys hither and yon, seeing to it that they were housed, fed and stripped clean with a minimum of violence. The levels of contempt and tiredness from which the word developed are better left unthought about. Naturally, Galba and the other hotel and casino bosses wanted their highly-paid entertainers to mix with the turkeys, especially in the casinos, where a surprising number of performers left their paychecks, or, in a couple of cases, tried in vain every year to win back the money they had lost, wildly, entertainingly, and with great flair, in front of the turkeys last year, or even the last several years.

There are ladies and gentlemen of the entertainment persuasion who go out on the road every year to try to earn back what they have thrown away, and one of the things that bothered me, that Galba tried to make me believe, is that Jim is one of these, Jim a profligate and a wild gambler.

I never went into the casinos and never mixed. Jim and I argued about it once, and he called me "a real chickenshit," without any malice.

I never asked Jim about his financial affairs since years before we had been suckered into having a business manager who would call us into his office and enthusiastically pull the wool over our eyes. In those days Jim and I were both full of wisdom about various money schemes and talked about our "picture" all the time, but after the big crush, when we couldn't get work and had to withdraw from some of these profit-making ventures, and discovered that pulling out was *just not possible* without *wrecking everything*, we started keeping our own council, like the boys in *Treasure of the Sierra Madre* burying their gold in hidden places because they couldn't trust each other.

So I didn't know. Jim mixed when he felt like it, was always surrounded by people, and loved it. Jim truly enjoyed being in show business, even though it drove him crazy. I wished I did.

So we finished the picture without Jim, four days left on the shooting schedule, but a small rewrite and some close-ups of me, some voice-overs and we were covered. All this is an atmosphere of pretended calm, because, among other things, they didn't want me invading the cutting room to see what I could do about fixing the picture up. Fat chance. I wanted nothing more to do with the picture.

As for our act, we had rehearsed nearly every day of shooting and the only sore point with the hotel or Gerry, who managed the room, was that Jim wasn't there to work with the band, getting down the fine points. But hell, as I pointed out, Jim knew everybody in the band already, what more could you want?

They wanted him *there*, that's what they wanted.

Gerry, in his green-on-green polo shirt and lemon slacks, asked me one afternoon over tea, our opening three days away and Jim still not checked in, "Do you think perhaps, and I use the word perhaps because I can't think of a better word, that your *friend* might not be coming at all?"

Gerry was the only one who ever suggested this, and he did so only that once. I, of course, laughed lightly and said. "Well, if he doesn't, maybe I can break in as a single." Gerry's laugh was like rubbing two hunks of wood together.

As far as anybody was concerned, Jim simply hadn't checked in yet, had missed a week's rehearsals, which he hardly needed, and there was no connection between that and the fact that he hadn't shown up for the last shooting days of the picture.

Galba was wonderful. As we were walking through the underground passageway to the private entrance to his private tennis courts, he said, "My big party for you boys is tomorrow night, be sure to give Jim a call and remind him."

"I don't know where Jim is," I said.

"Of course you don't, but you can get the word to him, can't you?"

"I can't," I said.

He jerked open the big firedoor with a squeak and we both blinked in the brilliant heat.

"Maybe he's pissed off at you," Galba said, as we stepped into the light. "Maybe he's punishing you for being such a shit about things."

"Me, a shit?" I said. "For that you make no points."

Galba took off his shirt and stretched his arms upward. "Ye Gods this is beautiful!" he said loudly, and laughed. He grinned at me. "Do you know I'm eighteen inches taller than my father?"

Even so, I beat him in straight sets 6-2, 6-4, 6-2. His face was red and fierce and angry as we left the court, and all the way down the corridor to the elevator he walked ten feet in front of me, his head down, his racquet slapping his leg. Galba hates to lose.

I GOT a lot of phone calls the night of Galba's party. Galba never called, of course, because the conversation might have gone something like this:

"When are you coming up to the party? There's people here I want you to meet."

"I'm terribly sorry, Gregory, but I seem to be developing this *sore throat* . . ."

"Do you want me to send Dr. Glickman down?"

"No, I think bedrest . . ."

"This party is in your honor. . . ."

"Oh, please . . ." The party was really for his girlfriend Jody McKeegan, who closed that night.

"I want you to understand that I take this very seriously. . . ." And blah-blah-blah. He could hardly tell me I'd never work again, and even if he did, I would have to say, "That's great! Never work again? I love it!"

The truth is, I did go to bed early, after a quiet dinner in my suite and half a bottle of wine to help me get to sleep. Unfortunately, while the wine did work and I was snoozing comfortably with the television on, the telephone started to ring.

Jody called and begged me in her deep voice to come to the party. She even said that Jim was going to be there.

"You talk to him?" I asked her.

"Somebody did, he said he'd be right over," she said.

"In that case, I'll be right up," I said. "But otherwise no."

"You bastard," she said, "we have things to talk about . . ."

"Sometimes," I said to her, "the best parties are the ones we don't attend . . ."

"Shall I come down?"

"There's somebody here," I said in a low voice. The somebody was me, of course, but I didn't tell her that.

"See you in a year," she said. I asked her if she wasn't coming to our opening, feeling just a pang of fear that there wouldn't even be an opening, but she said she was working in England and would be packed and gone tomorrow. We made our goodbyes and hints of things to come, and I threw the covers back over my head.

But sleep was gone and I was left with that dry feeling of alertness and awareness, the rub of the sheets, the flutter of the air conditioning, the switched-off television set cracking as it cooled. The trouble with sleeping in total air conditioning is that you can't get away from it, sheets up or sheets down you feel about the same, and the hot side of the pillow never quite cools off.

Mike called from L.A., and I was glad to talk to somebody sane. He apologized for not coming up to Vegas for the opening, although he had never come before, and we talked about a job he was up for that would put him in Bora Bora for nine months. I told him to save up all the fungus that would grow on him during the long tropical nights, because it had medical value here in the States. "Or, you could dry it, roll it up and smoke it," I said. We made our peaceful goodbyes and I lay back again, grinning up into the darkness because I liked Mike, and was thinking wouldn't it be fun in the middle of winter just to show up in Bora Bora, take him and his pals on the picture out to dinner and drunkenness, and then fly out. I knew I'd never do it, but it was fun to think about for what seemed like a couple of hours but was really only twenty minutes.

Terrace. The air was buffeting hot outside. Back into bed, naked, on top of the covers. I could drink some more, but I knew from experience that late-night drinking to get to sleep could easily produce the opposite effect and leave me blistering drunk at eight a.m. Pills, there were plenty of pills, Galba had seen to that, through perhaps the ubiquitous Dr. Glickman, perhaps through a mob connection, or quite possibly Galba owned a couple of international pharmaceutical houses. Although Galba never really owned anything, he just took an *interest* . . .

I pulled the sheet without the blanket slowly up over me, and it felt good, just right, sleepy nice and comfortable. Down I began to sink, down and down, but just at the threshold of unconsciousness I felt a probing finger into my intestines, just that one little probing, but I knew what it could mean, and I arose into wakefulness quickly, dreading the next touch but knowing it would come, and then my mind drifting to other things as I almost slipped down and out again, but no, here came the twisting probing watery curl of my gut, the squeezeout, the leveler, the great common bond for all humanity: I had to get up and shit.

Here it came again, the death-dance of peristalsis, and I groaned in self-pity and belly anguish, got out of bed and started toward my toilet, my throne. The telephone rang again. It was Galba's gopher, a man named Phil Dickman, who wanted to know if I was "in touch with Baby Cakes."

"Christ no," I growled and hung up, just making it to the toilet in time.

I sat there in the darkness to keep from having to look at all the stupid crap Galba had decorated the bathroom with, and decided for the tenth time at least to have it all thrown out the next day. Then I thought about grizzly bears who expel their shit at the first sign of a fight and how a friend of mine up in Alaska had come around a corner on a trail someplace and run fullface into a grizzly, who wheeled, shit blueberries all over my friend, and fled. My friend was very lucky at that. Then Sonny called from the party and asked if I was coming over, and I told her no, hung up, felt guilty for a while, and then called down to have my phone shut off for the night. I sat quietly waiting for the next episode. The next squeeze, the next twisting agony. I thought about the former Shah of Iran sitting on his solid gold toilet feeling the same way I did, and all the soldiers in all the war novels I had eagerly consumed as a kid, feeling these agonies as well as their jungle sores, ulcers, terror from the dropping bombs. Quaking bowels.

Then, with a light cold sweat on my forehead and the back of my neck wet, I returned to bed to await developments. After only a few minutes I called downstairs and had them switch my telephone on again. I didn't want to say, "Only Jim Larson," out of some stupid kind of idiot pride because everybody in the hotel knew already what was going on, so who was I kidding anyway, and immediately the telephone rings, and I find myself talking to an old friend from years ago who happened to be in town . . . I was polite and glad to hear from him, glad about his marriage and his two kids and his uncle and sister-in-law, so glad that I told him there would be tickets to our show waiting for him, and then had to call downstairs to take care of *that*, and just while I was spelling everything out for Gracie the reservations girl, the second wave hit the beach and I doubled over with a sharp groan, got off the phone as quick as I could and stumbled helpless and humbled into the place where my only goddamn friend in the world was sitting squatly waiting for me.

I LOOK at the clock on the dressing-room table in front of me, big red glowing numerals. Silently, a minute dies and another is born. I depress the button on top of the clock and it shows the running of the seconds into minutes. I watch for a while, my fingertip white on the button. Once more I decide that if there is ever going to be an end to this madness I will quit the business, I will fake an accident, flaming wreck not enough left to identify and go live in the mountains with my grandpa. Then I remember he is dead. I take my finger off the button and the clock stares at me unblinking.

Jut for the fun of it, I slam the clock down into my big open jar of cold-cream, *wush!* The clock is facedown and I can't see it, but it grinds on, I can hear the tiny grinding noise inside. I pull the cord, kind of hard, I guess, because the clock flies across the room and hits the wall with a crack and a splat, and the cold cream jar goes rolling off the dressing table, hits my foot and rolls under the table. I screech, and then again, and the door opens.

Irony, again. It is not Jim the singer, Jim the straight man, Jim the head-liner, it is Jim the writer, his face carefully composed, his voice moderate. He looks at me sitting redfaced at my dresser, greywet at the armpits, little dabs and streaks of cold cream on my black knifecreased pants.

"Oh," he says, "I thought I heard a scream in here . . ."

I just stare at him.

After a while, he gives me a reassuring grin and closes the door again.

I should get up and go out there and apologize, make a little joke and come back in here to wait. Instead I change my pants and shirt. The shirt doesn't have any cold cream on it, but under the arms it is as fermy wet as if I'd been playing handball. "Whew, what a stink!" I say to myself. The new shirt is soft and confident against my skin, the new trousers even more razorsharp, and this makes me feel good as I look at myself in the full length mirror. I hold up my arms like a Spanish dancer and make a tiny stomp.

"*Hola!*" I whisper.

If Jim isn't here in five, no, *ten*, minutes, I'll send somebody out to make our apologies. Maybe Ford Hamilton, he's out in the house, roosting with the turkeys, and I grin like an evil bastard, because if there is one audience in the world that Ford Hamilton couldn't reach, it is out there now, waiting for its favorite cornballs.

For all I know, Jim is in his dressing room. Why hasn't he called me? He wouldn't. But somebody would tell him to call me, and he would say, "I don't want to talk to David, he's too crazy, he gets stage-fright, I don't want to be around him," and then somebody might say, "But he *has* to be told you're *here*, doesn't he?" and Jim grins and says, "Fuck'im, he trusts me or he doesn't," and the fantasy collapses because I know it wouldn't happen.

I dial Jim's suite. The line is busy. It is right down the hall, I can get up and go out through my circle of friends and down the hall and see who is on Jim's phone. But no, I can't. If he's there I'll hate him for the rest of our lives, and if he's not, I don't know what I'll do except scream and hit the walls.

I think to myself, if he wants me to stay in the business, this isn't the way to do it.

But if he hates me, my mind starts to say, if he hates me, has hated me for years, has swallowed his hatred because of his own terror of working alone, being alone, not succeeding, then the cruelty of this awfulness would be nothing more than what I deserved . . . The only way to reach David Ogilvie is through Jim Larson . . . for the wrongs he has committed, for his badness of character, but NO, GOD DAMN IT, JIM IS NOT THAT KIND OF MAN!!!

And it snaps. The weight is gone, my stomach sweetens. I look at my wristwatch. The time has come. I slip into my jacket, take one last vanity peek in the mirror. I open the door.

All eyes are upon me.

Then before I have a chance to say a word the outer door opens, and it is Jim. He grins at me, "Tried to call you, Man," he says, and I believe him. Behind him crowding into the room are Bianca and George diMorro, dazzling in their evening clothes, and more people crowding in behind them, and for a dizzy second I have a vision of Sonoma Mountain and the fine misty winter calm as I stand in the warm pool and look out over the valley. And then I find myself falling into the cold grey eyes of the actress who had snubbed us at the diMorro party, and look down to see her slim red-tipped fingers lightly on Jim's sleeve.

"Hello, everyone," I hear myself saying. "Now, don't be nervous," and it gets a great laugh, my old buddy C. C. Eubank squeezing in the door, charming with a lock of hair down over his eyes, Galba in his bug-green tuxedo, Karl Meador, relaxed and brilliant and handsome, where the hell has old Karl been these past few days, for that matter? He does not look over at Sonny, who got to her feet as the mob started pouring into the room. I go over to Sonny and give her a kiss, just brushing her lips and not looking into her eyes, and Jim grabs me by the arm and says, "Hey, no time for that, let's roll," and he pulls me through the people, through the door and down the corridor, his collar open and a small red stain on his ruffled shirt, like, while I've been here losing my sanity he's been eating spaghetti with the hotshots, come on, he hasn't been eating spaghetti for two weeks, has he, but he might have been romancing, by God . . . Or he might have been buried out in the desert with a stake through his heart, waiting for the right phase of the moon . . .

He's got me by the elbow now, and I'll never ask him where he's been; we half-walk, half-run down the corridor to our private elevator, and only the hottest of the hotshots are allowed on the elevator with us, the diMorros, of course, Karl, Galba, the grey-eyed actress who didn't like the way I smelled and who will not let go of Jim, and Chet. Jim turns to me in the packed elevator and says, "What's been happening?" and I say to him, "Not jack shit, my friend," and we laugh secretly and smell the anxious sweat that isn't ours for once and then the door opens and a hundred madeup faces flash past as we hurry, now just the two of us, through the held-open curtain and out into the blackness, and there they are. The last drop of fear inside me evaporates.

My light hits me, and I stand quite still. Jim's light follows him to the other side of the stage and the band starts to vamp.

I smile, a baby's first wide grin, and the house comes down.

This is love, my friends, and the hell with the rest.

THE TRUE LIFE STORY
OF JODY MCKEEGAN

For Marie and Julie

"The show must go on."—ANONYMOUS

PART ONE

ONE

WHEN SHE was fifteen, Jody McKeegan lived in a small house behind the Piggly Wiggly Market where her mother worked as a grocery checker. Her father did not exactly live with them, and Jody was glad of it. Every time Burt McKeegan showed up there would be trouble, even though he usually brought money and tried to make up for being gone. He would be drinking, as usual, and his dark red hair would be hanging down over his green eyes as he sat on the old overstuffed couch with his big hands holding the pint loosely between his legs. He would talk, telling stories about his life that Jody later decided were lies, because the only time Burt McKeegan ever had any money was when he won at the horse races, and of course whenever he did that he would show up. The stories were all about travels and adventures that cost money. Another dead giveaway, which Jody didn't even think about until she had traveled a little herself and told a few lies, was that Burt never told any stories in front of Eleanor. No, when Eleanor was home, and before the trouble would start, he would discuss plans for the future. Even though Burt was washed up and everybody knew it, he still had a lot of hope for the future. All her life Jody had this same unreasonable burning hope for the future, as if the mere passage of time would erase all the trouble and bring the joy she knew had to be out there somewhere waiting for her.

Burt, well, Burt had been cut down by time and circumstance, and she knew he was full of crap and would never amount to anything. He had been a body-and-fender man, a big young Irish galoot with freckles and a grin and a ball-peen hammer, happily whanging away at fenders and car doors when the Depression struck and took his job away, just after Jody's elder sister Lindy had been born. Out of work and with a new family to support—a family he had acquired by making love to Eleanor, then eighteen, behind some trees at a picnic at Blue Lake Park and then overjoyed when she told him she was pregnant because she was so pretty and he was ready to settle down anyway—laid off by the garage out on 82nd Avenue, fiery in his refusal to allow Eleanor to work by finally driven out of their house by the simple fact of poverty. It maddened him to have to sit home twiddling his thumbs, and so at first he would get up each morning, dress carefully as if he were going looking for work, take the lunch Eleanor had made for him and go to one of the taverns out Sandy Boulevard to sit around with other men. After a while he began going downtown and hanging around the pool halls. Burt was a pretty good pool player, but not good enough to make any money at it. He started drinking during the day and coming home later and later, and then not at all. Eleanor lived for a while on money given to her by her sister and her parents, and then finally she took a job and left Lindy at her sister's house. When Burt found out she was working in a stringbean cannery he got very drunk and came home and chased Eleanor around the house with a butcher knife, or so Lindy told Jody years later.

"Where did he get the money?" Jody wanted to know.

"Oh shit, drunks always have money," Lindy told her. Lindy was beautiful, and Jody, who was not, worshipped her. Lindy was short for Rosalind, and she had her father's dark red hair and milky skin, but her eyes were a deep rich dark brown, and by the time she was twelve men were following her down the street. But men did not trouble Lindy. Even during World War II, when they were living in a housing project and Eleanor was gone most of the time working at the Swan Island shipyard, Lindy had no trouble with the kind of men who hung around trying to get at her and the other young bobby soxers. She knew when to kick and where to kick, and she was smart enough to scream when that would work and smart enough to keep silent when only that would work, and just once was she overwhelmed, by three high school boys from St. Johns. They got her in the laundry room of one of the project buildings after school one day, and two of them raped her while she cursed and spit in their faces. The third one would have raped her too, but a neighborhood boy who was practicing his saxophone heard her cursing through the thin walls and came rushing in on the rich boys (boys who did not live in housing projects) and began flailing away with his instrument and screaming with rage. His name was Ron Higby and he was over six feet tall already, and so the rich boys made their retreat bleeding and threatening to call the police.

"Go ahead and call them, you dirty pimps!" Lindy yelled after them. "Are you hurt?" she asked Ron. He shook his head silently, his dented and bloody saxophone hanging brokenly from his hand. He was looking at her. She was wearing a pink cashmere sweater, now stained and dirty, pink bobby sox, saddle shoes and nothing else. Her skirt and torn underpants lay on the cement floor of the laundry room.

"Oh," she said. "Get out of here and let me dress, will you?" She threw him a smile. "I'll thank you later." She did—she thanked him. He admitted that he was in love with her and she smiled and said that she thought he was sweet, but that she only dated servicemen. But a couple of nights later she made a sailor pay her fifty dollars, and she gave the money to Ron. "Fix your horn," she told him. She was fifteen at the time.

Both Eleanor and Burt were working, but Eleanor was making more money as a spot welder than Burt was as a sweeper, and so they did not live together much of the time. Burt was only a sweeper because on the fourth of July, 1935, just before Jody was born, he blew the fingers off his right hand drunkenly fooling with firecrackers. He even got his picture in the paper, grinning and holding up his bandaged hand, but there went any chance of a career requiring ten fingers. He still had his right thumb and stubs of two fingers, and he could grasp a broom. If anyone started to commiserate with him about his missing fingers, Burt's green eyes would light up. "The goddam thing kept me out of the army, didn't it?" he would say, waggling the thumb and stubs.

Eleanor and her two girls were still living in the housing project when the war ended, and even though the economy seemed to be booming, Eleanor had a hard time finding work. To complicate matters, a man had fallen in love with her, and Burt was on one of his long absences from Portland. Eleanor said Burt was "out of town," but Lindy told her sister, "He's up at Rocky Butte, breakin rocks, I'll bet!"

Because she was hanging around downtown, Lindy knew a lot more about their father than their mother did. She knew where he drank and where he shot pool and the women he played around with, in Portland's smalltime coalition of bookies, pimps, gamblers and petty crooks. Lindy encouraged her mother to go out with Dick Westerhauser, and she even hinted that Eleanor ought to make it easier for Dick to give her money. He was always offering. He owned Westerhauser Buick in Beaverton, and since the end of the war he was rolling in money and did not know what to do with himself. He was a big man, bigger than Burt, for that matter, and old, perhaps as old as fifty, with a wife and a couple of grown children out in the suburbs. But he sought romance, and he would take Eleanor out to movies and dinners, and even to night clubs once in a while, bringing her home at four or five in the morning, where as likely as not little Jody would be alone, even though Lindy had promised to baby-sit. Once Eleanor came in from the motel where she had been making love to Dick Westerhaus and found Ron Higby asleep on the couch and Jody asleep in her bed with a saxophone cuddled in her arms. She was angry with Lindy for lying to her again, but not as angry as before, and Lindy told her, "Mom, for Christ's sake, who's going to come busting in our place?"

Dick Westerhaus offered to help Eleanor move to a bigger apartment—a real apartment instead of a housing project—probably so that he could comfortably spend the night once in a while instead of going to motels and having to get up at the crack of dawn to get her home, but Eleanor, after several days of putting off her decision, perhaps hoping that Burt would show up, called him at the Buick agency and told him not to come around anymore. Then, with only the twenty dollars a week unemployment, she moved her family out of the project and into a small but private apartment across the river in Vancouver, Washington, where she continued to look for work. This move almost broke up the family. Lindy could not stand Vancouver. As far as she was concerned it was the North Pole, and she would often disappear into Portland for days at a time. She began also wearing clothes which Jody had never seen before.

Lindy was supposed to be going to Vancouver High School, but she wasn't. On her second day she told her home room teacher to kiss her ass, and left school with a cigarette in the corner of her mouth. She found a boy hanging around outside the building and talked him into driving her across the river and down to Broadway and Yamhill, where she got out of the car and disappeared into the drugstore among her friends. She did not come home for nearly a week that time, and Eleanor almost called the police on her. But she didn't, because she understood what Lindy was after, or she thought she did. The world was a mess, and Lindy was too beautiful to waste her time in school. It broke Eleanor's heart to think of the punks and small-time gangsters Lindy ran around with, but she had a deep confidence in her daughter's native intelligence, and she was sure Lindy would get over it and move on to what they both hoped would be her career in motion pictures.

Lindy wanted very much to be a movie actress, and she knew that the best way to do it, if you were from Portland, was to be elected to the Rose Festival as a princess, and then be chosen as queen. That would get the national attention and the offers to come to Hollywood, and Lindy figured she could take it from there. But the only trouble was, Rose Festival princesses were selected from among high school seniors, and Lindy could never stay interested in school long enough to become a senior.

There were modeling agencies in Portland too, but Lindy walked up the long dark staircase to one of them and inside ten minutes, five waiting and five being interviewed by a woman she could tell was high on pills, Lindy realized the modeling agency was a racket, a mere front for a school where dumb-looking girls were taught to walk around with a book on their head for eighteen dollars an hour, or some such ridiculous amount. And prostitution. More than one pimp had promised to keep her in clothes and money, so that when the time came she could go to Hollywood in style, register at the Pasadena Playhouse and learn her craft, and then move on into pictures. In fact, most of the young pimps in Portland claimed to have Hollywood connections. Maybe they did; but Lindy never went for their stories. Not that she wouldn't take clothes or money from men, but she saw no reason to turn a percentage over to a pimp just so that he could sit around the Desert Room with the other pimps and whine about his girls. Lindy considered herself the equal of any pimp she ever met. And besides, she had no intention of becoming a hooker.

One day Lindy came home to the apartment in Vancouver in the middle of the afternoon. Jody was there alone. Eleanor was working part time at the public library, helping take inventory. Lindy looked very bad, with dark circles under her eyes, and as she sat at the kitchen table smoking cigarettes and drinking coffee Jody could see that her hands were trembling.

"What's the matter with you?" she asked.

"I'm okay. Just a little tired, honey."

"You're not even talking to me," Jody said. Usually she was anxious and unhappy until she knew where Lindy was, but this time Lindy was actually home, and she was still unhappy. Lindy smiled at her, and reached out to touch her on the forehead.

"Don't worry about me," she said. "I've been up for like five days, that's all. I just need some sleep."

But later, when Jody peeked into the bedroom, Lindy was lying on her back in the semidarkness with her eyes open. When Eleanor got home, she went into the bedroom, and Jody stayed in the kitchen, listening to the murmuring voices of her sister and her mother. She heard the word 'drugs' several times, but at the time she related the word to the kind of things you got from drug- stores, and so did not understand until some years later that they moved back to Portland not because the job opportunities were better but so that Eleanor could try to exert just a little more control over Lindy's life.

Eleanor was just past thirty-five when she got the job at the Piggly Wiggly, and although the money was not as good as the shipyard, she did not have to work so hard. The days went faster than she expected, because from the time she came to work until closing, the store was crammed with shoppers, and Eleanor was frantically busy unloading carts, slamming the keys on the cash register and sacking groceries. The fluorescent lighting was unearthly and the noise was constant, but Eleanor did not notice. Nor did she often notice the faces of the customers, unless they were trying to cash checks, and then all she really had to do those first months was wave for the assistant manager to okay the check. After a few weeks she even stopped being amazed at the kinds of things people put into their stomachs. For a while Eleanor sweated heavily while she worked, and she had to wear a bandanna around her head not only to keep her hair out of her eyes but to keep the sweat from rolling down her face and embarrassing her, but after she got more into the pace of her work she could make one uniform do for three days. This was important, because the faded yellow and green dresses had to be heavily starched, a job she hated.

But she was thirty-five years old, busy day and night raising her two chil- dren and working, and it had been a long time since she had been to bed with anybody. Actually, Burt had been around for a few days when she moved into the little house behind the store, helping connect the stove and painting the two tiny bedrooms, but although he slept in the same bed with her he did not try any lovemaking. Maybe it was just as well, she thought, because for the past few years sex with Burt hadn't amounted to much. Usually he was drunk and would fall into bed with a woozy grunt, grasp her and begin kissing her with a mouth that smelled foul with beer and potato chips. Burt never completely undressed in front of Eleanor, not even at his drunkest, and they always made love in the dark, so for Eleanor the sensual experience was limited to his bad breath, the way his stubbled cheek felt against hers, the heavy sound of his breathing and muttering, and the few pokes he would take at her with his usually half-erect penis. Burt was not the lover of her dreams. Nor was Dick Westerhaus, who never removed his undershirt and often ejaculated on her leg or her stomach, his lips pressed tightly together to keep him from making a sound. Eleanor was a very shy person and could not talk about sex. She wished sometimes that she could talk to Lindy about it, because Lindy seemed to have a much better time, and secretly Eleanor was pleased that her daughter was so attractive to so many men and took such unceasing advantage of it. In a different life Eleanor might have loved many men.

But in this life she was afraid her sex was going to dry up and blow away, and she would be an old woman. She knew a great deal more about menopause than she did about sex in general; a lot of the women she worked with in her life had been through it, or were going through it, and Eleanor dreaded the day. Sometimes she would lie in her bed, perhaps waiting for Lindy to come home or telephone, and she would suddenly grasp her breasts and clench her teeth in deep frustration. She wanted a man. She wanted somebody to wrap her legs around. Even Burt. She did not love Burt anymore, but she understood herself well enough to know that she would never divorce him. She just didn't have the guts, she told herself, to either end it with Burt or start it with somebody else. Dick Westerhaus had been an accident, a breezy but gentle automobile salesman who at least had a sense of romance and told her he loved her and sent her flowers. And of course she had been somewhat younger then.

Plenty of the men who came through her line at the store flirted with her, but she put them off with a laugh or a smart retort, and that was all most of them really wanted anyway, and with a smile she would imagine their surprise, these grocery-store romeos, if she had taken them up on any of their proposals. She was almost tempted to try it on some of the more offensive ones. Only once a man waited outside for the store to close and then followed her through the parking lot. When she got around the corner and saw him coming, she ran up the steps and into the house, locked the door and called the police, but he was gone when the patrol car got there twenty minutes later, and she never saw him again.

So she really did not expect anything to come of it when the nearly bald man with the beautiful eyes made jokes with her, even though these were the only little flirtations that made her blush. He looked about forty, and was a clean but sloppy dresser, always coming in the store wearing faded blue pants and a grey raincoat over his sport shirt. Often he would still have drops of water on his naked scalp, and she was tempted to make a joke about it but didn't because she felt he might be sensitive about his baldness. Aside from the lack of hair, he was a very good-looking man, with a sensitive mouth and a large firm nose, supported by a good wide chin. Except for the clothes, he looked like a doctor or a lawyer, at any rate from a class well above Eleanor's. He usually came in on Wednesday and Friday evenings just before closing, and he ate almost nothing but garbage—candy and bakery goods, prepared dinners and canned spaghetti or chili. Obviously not a married man.

Her name was stitched onto her uniforms, and he always called her Eleanor. "Well, Eleanor," he might say, "how do you like all that snow out there?"

"I'm glad I work indoors," she would say.

"You have a long drive to get home? Looks like it's going to snow for six months."

"Oh it won't be that bad."

"Oh you never can tell, Eleanor. You never can tell. Once in Cleveland it snowed for exactly three hundred and fifty-two days. Right through spring and summer, didn't stop snowing until Thanksgiving day."

"Must have piled up pretty high."

"Oh not at all. See, the temperature was always up in the eighties. Stuff melted as soon as it hit the ground."

She often wondered where he got his bizarre sense of humor, but when she found out that he was a professor up at Reed College, that seemed to explain it.

Then one night as she was crossing the parking lot against a slanting rain, with an armload of her own groceries, she heard him call out to her from a parked car.

"Eleanor!"

He was sitting behind the wheel of a little black Plymouth, his window open and the rain spattering his face as he looked up at her.

"Oh hello there," she said. She knew what was coming, and even though her feet hurt as usual and her back was sore, she felt a thrill of anticipation.

"Can I give you a lift? Or do you have a car of your own?"

"I just live a few doors away," she said.

"Then let me help you with your stuff." He opened his door, quickly rolled up the window and got out. "Here, gimme," he said. This was the moment, and instead of saying, "Oh that's all right," and ducking around him and going on home, Eleanor, for reasons she never questioned, handed him the sacks of groceries.

Jody did not like Quentin Corby. The eyes her mother thought beautiful were dark and shifty to Jody, and she did not like the fact that he was nearly bald or that his skin had a soft, almost silken look.

"That's a very nice-looking girl," Corby said after Jody had gone into her room to listen to the radio. Eleanor smiled and wished he would go away. She was exhausted, and the impulse that had allowed him into the house had faded now, under the very real possibility of getting her shoes off and having some dinner. Fortunately he was sensitive to this and after only twenty minutes or so, just enough time to drink his coffee and smoke a couple of cigarettes, he got up, politely took her hand, smiled and said, "Look, are you doing anything Saturday night? I'd like to take you to a movie."

Eleanor withdrew her hand and said, "Oh, I'm married."

Corby looked around the room. "I don't see anybody, is he really around?"

"Well, no, not really."

"Then come out with me. Please."

"Well, all right," she said, and tossed and turned all night dreaming about him.

Corby was a professor of humanities at the college and was forty years old. He lived on a houseboat in the small colony on the other side of the Sellwood bridge with his eight-year-old son. His wife, he told Eleanor, had collapsed under the pressure of what he called "Ph.D syndrome." She had worked as a file clerk in an insurance company office while he was attending graduate school at Boston University, and by the time he had gotten his master's and doctorate their worlds were so different they had nothing in common but their son. "This happens all the time," he told Eleanor over Italian food after the movie. "The man is constantly facing intellectual challenges and the woman's brain is being turned into a sack of sawdust. I blame myself for letting it happen to us, though. I shouldn't have let her take that damned job."

"Where is she?" Eleanor asked.

"I don't know," Corby said, and changed the subject. After they had dated several more times, though, he admitted to Eleanor that he really did not know where she was. One day he had come home from school and she was gone, taking all her things but leaving their son in his crib. "She only took six months off work to have the baby," Corby said. "I don't think she ever loved him."

On their third date they went to a tavern on Sellwood Boulevard and Eleanor drank too much and had to be helped into the car. She was not sick, but it was a work night and her exhaustion turned into silliness. She could not stop giggling, and then she got the hiccups, and while Quentin Corby was kissing her she hiccupped and broke away laughing and said, "Oh please!" and he drove her out to 82nd Avenue to a motel. On the way there her hiccups stopped of their own accord, and neither of them spoke as they drove carefully through the rain.

TWO

IN ALL her life up to now, Eleanor had never been made love to by a man who knew what he was doing. Quentin Corby shut off the lights, but for her sake rather than his own, and was very slow and very gentle, taking off all her clothes and all his and then lying beside her for a long time holding her and kissing her softly. The motel radio was turned to an all-night soft music station, and gradually Eleanor's nervous trembling stopped, and she began to respond less clumsily to him, touching his body with her fingertips and putting her tongue into his mouth when he kissed her. When he began sucking at her left breast she lay back in the darkened room with her eyes open and let the lovely forbidden feelings take control of her body, the feelings interrupted only briefly when she felt his hand cupping her, and then felt a finger slip inside her. She took hold of his head, to keep him at her breast for a while longer, and then, just as she felt she could no longer stand it, he came away from the breast, kissed her deeply on the mouth, and penetrated her. The shock of pleasure was so intense she almost cried out.

She expected him to push in and out a few times and then it would be all over and she would drift into that hazy, tense afterward feeling she had always felt before, but Quentin Corby was in no hurry, and instead of stroking rapidly in and out he moved so slowly that she could hardly sense the pressure until at the last moment he seemed to fill her entire body;

then the slow gradual withdrawal until that too became an excess of plea-sure. At the same time he was kissing her mouth, eyes, neck, breasts, even gently running his tongue into her armpit until she did not believe that she could stand anymore. She began to writhe and grind her hips around beneath him, and as she did so he increased his pacing. In a few moments they were bucking and heaving on the bed and she could no longer keep from panting heavily and making a sound in her throat. And then a very strange tension took over the center of her body, a kind of tightness that almost made her sick as it mounted and spread over her body, until at last it broke in wave after wave of pure pleasure. "OHHHH *CHRIST!*" she cried out. In a few moments she was weeping and holding him tightly. These had been the most exciting minutes of her life, and she wept with relief as well as joy.

But there was to be more. Quentin had not come yet; he merely stopped to allow her to have her orgasm in peace. After a few minutes, when she had stopped crying and had apologized without sounding the least bit sorry, he got into her again, heard her little moan of surprise and pleasure, and brought her to a second not quite as intense but still delightful orgasm. When he came, moments after she had, he was very emotional about it, crying out and grasping her shoulders in his hands. He did not seem able to speak for ten or fifteen minutes afterward, and when he did it was to say, in an awed voice, "God but you're beautiful!"

When he took her home at a little after two in the morning, they lingered on the front porch, kissing and holding each other.

"I want to see you again, very soon," Quentin told her, and when she got inside, she checked Jody, took a long hot shower in the cramped little shower stall and then put on her terrycloth bathrobe and sat in the living room another hour, thinking about what had happened to her, still feeling the release and the lazy sensuality in her body. She decided that she must be in love with Quentin, but she did not believe that he was in love with her. He did not have to be.

She was going to be his for the asking anytime he wanted. She was certainly not going to make any demands on him. After all, she was still married to Burt, and Quentin was probably still married to his wife, wherever she was. It gave Eleanor a little thrill to know that she was starting out on an affair.

But it was time to go to bed. She was due at work at noon the next day, and she had clothes to wash in the morning, and uniforms to starch and iron.

She got up from the couch with a grunt of aging bones and went to lock the front door. As she turned out the porch light she saw that it was snowing out, the sky black above the streetlamp and the snowflakes seeming to appear magically in the cone of light. Eleanor had all her life loved the first snows of winter, and now she leaned her cheek against the cold glass of her front door and wept at the beauty of her day. Then she went into the bathroom and blew her nose, grinned at herself in the mirror and went to bed.

THREE

LINDY HAD been living downtown in an apartment on SW Park for the past few weeks with a man named Eddie Dorkin, who traveled up and down the West Coast selling drugs to doctors—a "detail man." Although he supplied the doctors with a lot of routine medical supplies, the major part of his job was to talk the doctors into prescribing his brand of drugs to their patients. Lindy had met him at the Rialto Billiards, across the street and down the block. Eddie was a brilliant pool player and con artist, a bland, round-faced man in his late twenties who wore expensive inconspicuous clothes, and would often play an entire game of snooker or billiards with his hat and tweed topcoat still on.

Very few women came into the Rialto. For a while, a few of the girls who hung around Broadway and Yamhill with the local hard gang would come into the place to watch their boyfriends play pool with each other, and this is how Lindy happened to be in the room, sitting in a row of theater seats alongside the number one billiard table while Eddie Dorkin trimmed a couple of her tough young friends at a game of Thirty-one. She noticed Eddie looking at her a couple of times early in the game, and she stared back at him coldly. After that he did not look at her at all, but concentrated on his game, and she knew that he was playing to her, that everything he did, every funny remark, every gesture, even his billiard shots, were calculated to impress her. She was not impressed. He was not particularly good looking. But when it was all over and her friends happened to be out of earshot, he came over toward her, his hand in his topcoat pocket.

"You want something nice?" he asked her, and without waiting for the cutting answer Lindy was about to give him he removed his hand from the pocket and dropped a small bottle of pills into her lap. "Thank me later," he said, and left the poolroom. The bottle was full of little green heart-shaped benzedrine tablets.

The next time she saw him was in the Rialto also. It was close to midnight and she and a couple of girlfriends were drunk and had come up to have a hamburger at the long counter. The poolroom was full of smoke, loud talk and the clicking of the games, and the counter was crowded with people eating the excellent food. The three pretty girls had no trouble getting seats. Lindy was pouring catsup on her hamburger when Eddie came up behind her and said, "Did you like the pills?"

She turned on her stool and looked coldly at him. "Yes," she said. "Thanks a lot." Then she swung her stool back around and started eating.

"Little surprise in your pocket," he said into her ear. She shrugged irritatedly at his contact with her hair, and did not bother to reach into her pocket. The next day, at home in Sellwood, she happened to reach into the pocket and pulled out the piece of paper, which turned out to be a one-hundred-dollar bill with Eddie's name and address on it in red ink. Lindy laughed. She was delighted with the money, but she had no intention of going up to Eddie's apartment. He had probably gone home and undressed and waited for her, thinking he could get her for a hundred dollars. She laughed again, and split the money with her mother. Eleanor did not believe Lindy's story about where the money came from, but she needed it so she took it. And Lindy copied down Eddie's name and address. Just in case.

The next time they met was about two months later, in the palatial lobby of the Paramount Theater, on Broadway. It was late on a Tuesday afternoon and snowing heavily out on the street, the snow coming down in big wet clumps, Lindy wondering what to do with herself. She had come into the theater because there had been nothing to do that afternoon, and now she did not want to leave because there was still nothing to do. She was intensely bored with her present existence, but she did not know how to change it. Men were always asking her to go away with them, and others were always offering money to her for one thing or another, and yet, as beautiful as she was, as she knew she was, something was missing. None of her attempts to get into show business had panned out, because the men she always had to deal with wanted to fuck her, and she refused, not for any moral reasons but because she did not like being pushed against a wall by anybody. And besides, they were such greasy little men, the owners of the local night clubs, the managers, the bookers of talent. The pimps were a lot more handsome and a lot more fun to be with, but she was sick of pimps too. In fact she was sick of Broadway. Broadway! Broadway right in the middle of Portland, Oregon. And she was afraid to do what she knew she must if she wanted to get into show business, which was to get on a train and leave town. New York or Hollywood.

So she stood in the lobby of the Paramount, alone, watching the snow falling outside, while the ticket taker tried not to stare at her. When Eddie came up behind her and said, "Boo!," she did not jump but only turned around, bored to death, and let him take her to dinner.

FOUR

LINDY DID not want to be a bitch, but Eddie made it so easy for her she could not resist. He did not love her—he did not love anybody or anything— but he worshipped her beauty and paid no attention to the sarcastic cut of her voice or the limits of her interests. He gave her a gold wristwatch on a gold chain, charge accounts at Meier & Frank and Lipman Wolfe, all the drugs she wanted, his total attention when they were together, and all he asked in return was that she accompany him up and down the coast on his selling trips. She refused. Eddie could not stand to be alone for very long and he hated the emptiness of the road life, but he could not think of a better way to make lots of money legally, and so for most of his life he drove the highways between little towns, slept in motels and salesman's hotels, and learned the inside of every poolhall and bowling alley between Seattle and Crescent City. It would have been wonderful for him if, after a hard day jollying medical men, he could come home to the motel room and find this extravagantly beautiful eighteen-year-old girl. They could go to dinner, take in a movie perhaps, and then spend the night curled in each other's arms. On the long drives between towns they could talk to each other, sing, make up stories or just sit quietly together and watch the countryside roll by. But Lindy was goddamned if she was going to spend her precious life hanging around motel rooms all day while he was out selling. He was incredibly lucky that she would even live in his apartment alone for the three weeks out of four he was on the road, keeping things nice, feeding the goldfish and more or less waiting for him to get back.

The apartment was a godsend for Lindy, because it not only got her out of the tiny ramshackle house her mother and sister lived in, it gave her a place downtown where she could retreat from everybody if she wanted to. She never brought anybody there, although when she first started living with Eddie she expected to bring boyfriends to the apartment when Eddie was on the road. She did not remain anything like faithful to him, and he did not really expect her to. He never stopped asking her to come on trips with him, and she never stopped refusing. She loved her new-found privacy so much that for the first couple of days he would be gone, she might just stay home, listening to records, smoking his marijuana and lying around naked. All her life she had been surrounded by people, and this aloneness was the true luxury. She could not understand why Eddie was so intensely lonesome on the road.

But then she failed to understand much about Eddie. It was beyond her why he allowed her to treat him like dirt when he even admitted that he was not in love with her, and did not expect her to be in love with him. People were strange.

It was about this time that Jody cut school one day and took the big Sellwood trolley bus downtown to look for her sister. The weather had been unusually bad. Dirty snow was caked high along the streets and sidewalks, forming a thin grey sheet over the pavement, so that the bus made a cracking crunching sound along with the high whine of the overhead trolley. Jody was almost alone on the bus, with only a couple of bundled-up women on their way to town with umbrellas and shopping bags, sitting on the sideways seats up front, eyeing her with disapproval. Jody paid no attention to them. They were old. She was dressed in her cherry-red cap, checkered muffler and navy-blue coat. She had awakened early that morning and lay in bed thinking about the future. She wanted to become an actress. Lindy had told her to join the drama club and to study books about acting, but Lindy herself had never done any of these things, and for that matter had not even bothered to finish high school, although she was always telling Jody to get good grades so that she could win a scholarship to the Pasadena Playhouse, or go to college locally and get a degree in acting. But Jody was halfway through her first year in high school and already bored.

They were putting on two plays at Commercial High, Shakespeare's *Twelfth Night* and Oscar Wilde's *The Importance of Being Earnest*, and Jody had not been given a part in either one, although she had been the first to arrive at the auditions for the Shakespeare and nearly the first for the Wilde. They told her that freshman girls did not get parts right away and that she would have to paint flats, do makeup, scrounge props and all that sort of crap before she could win a role. But Jody noticed that Carole Spatz, who was also a freshman, had been offered both Olivia in the Shakespeare and Cecily Cardew in the Wilde and had to choose between them, and Carole Spatz couldn't act her way out of a charade, as far as Jody was concerned. But Spatz was very blonde and very beautiful, with cornflower-blue eyes and a thin clear voice and a way of walking with her pelvis thrust forward that seemed to drive the men on the teaching staff out of their minds. Jody did not actually mind that Spatz was getting good treatment because she was beautiful, she only minded that the faculty and the senior advisers were such a mealymouthed pack of hypocrites about it, and instead of telling Jody, "Listen, sister, you're too goddamn ugly to be on the stage," they went into that routine about apprenticeship and *could not look Jody in the eye.* That was the only good part.

Anyway, lying in bed at six in the morning, needing to pee but unwilling to be the first one out of bed and have to skip across the icy floor to the heater and get it going, lying there under her quilt with only her nose sticking out, Jody gave serious thought to quitting school. Facing facts, she was not the most popular girl in Commercial, and next year when she became eligible for a private girl's club she knew she would not be asked to join (along with eighty percent of the girls in school) and therefore any possible social career was blasted. Jody did not care about it except that if she had been popular she probably would not be thinking of quitting. Jody envied the popular girls because they seemed to lead trouble-free lives and always had plenty of cashmere sweaters and boyfriends. Not that Jody cared about boyfriends. Even though she was nearly fifteen she had not yet started bleeding, and she assumed that she would get interested in boys after the bleeding started. Her older sister certainly had.

But there were more reasons for quitting. Jody was not good in class. She had gotten a four in algebra, threes in PE, English and biology, and a five in art—probably the only five the art teacher had ever given out, so actually it was something to be proud of. Jody not only did not turn in any assignments, she created so much disturbance in her corner of the classroom that several other students' grades slipped, and Jody was sent to the vice-principal's office three times. She could not help it if she had a good sense of humor and made people laugh. Lots of things struck her funny, that was all, and the teacher, Mr. Sanders, tried to run the art class on an open free-form basis, letting the kids sit where they wanted and carry on conversations.

She was getting off to a bad start, there was no question about it. The vice-principal gave her plenty of excuses, telling her that it was difficult for a girl to move around as much as Jody had and have any friends in the class, and all that, but Jody did not need excuses for doing bad work, and she did not need a bunch of chums from grade school to support her morale. What she wanted was an even break in the drama club, and that seemed impossible. In fact, the only happy moment she had had in the drama club came after the meeting to announce the casting and crew assignments for *Earnest*, when she stupified the drama teacher, Mr. Quince, by the fact that she had read *My Life in Art*, by Stanislavsky.

Mr. Quince was a tall heavy apple-cheeked man whose sandy hair stood straight up.

"You've read Stanislavsky?" he said to her. She could tell he could not remember her name.

"Yes," she said. "Most of it."

"And, tell me, what did you think of it?"

Jody let that one pass. "I was fascinated," she said, and the center of attention drifted away. But at least now Quince knew the monkey-faced freshman girl he was not giving parts to was no ignoramus.

As far as Stanislavsky was concerned she could not see what all the fuss was about. It was perfectly natural to Jody that if you were going to be a good actress you would have to actually believe you were the person you were playing, and that seemed to be the message. She had read a lot of books about acting and the theater, and the one thing she really wanted to know— *how do you get them to pick you?*—was never discussed. So the books were pretty useless after all.

Of course Jody knew one way to get picked: be the picker. Choose a play and talk a bunch of kids into putting it on, with you as director. But if you were the director and you picked yourself for the juicy parts, you would be exactly the kind of phony Jody disliked the most, so that was out too.

The Sellwood bus was almost half full by the time it crossed the Willamette River, and with the people came the muggy smells of wet wool and suddenly perspiring bodies.

It was actually hot inside the bus, because nobody would open a window and let in a nice cool blast of frozen air. Jody snickered to herself, wondering what the people behind her on the bus would do if she worked open her window. But she didn't bother. Instead she leaned her cheek against the icy glass of the window, which magically cooled the rest of her.

Jody got off the bus at Fifth and Stark, all the way down in the midst of the big buildings. Down here too the streets were caked with ice, and cars went by, silent except for the thumming sounds of their motors, which echoed off the buildings eerily. Jody walked up to Broadway and caught a streetcar up the hill. There was a drugstore at the corner of Broadway and Yamhill that Lindy was supposed to hang around in, but standing outside with her hands in her coat pockets, Jody could see the row of stools along the counter empty except for a blond boy hunched over a cup of coffee. Jody was instantly depressed. For some reason she had allowed herself to think that Lindy would actually be in the drugstore. She had believed this from the moment she decided to cut school and come downtown. She entered the store, feeling the billowing warmth gratefully, and made her way through the crowded aisles to the counter, where she sat down four stools away from the blond boy. He looked up at her when she sat and then went back to his coffee, obviously uninterested. That was all right with Jody; he had thin lips and pimples around his mouth. But it was possible, he was about the right age, he might know Lindy.

A drab-looking woman of about twenty in a starched uniform that reminded Jody of her mother came over to her and said, "You have to go."

Jody was instantly embarrassed and could feel her face heating up, which always made her lose her temper. "Why?" she asked. She stood up, still looking at the waitress.

"They been rousting this place for kids during school hours," the waitress said. She smiled, and Jody saw a row of crooked teeth. She turned and left the drugstore, wondering where she would go and what she would do. She had eighty cents. She could go to a cheap movie later on, but for now it was only ten o'clock in the morning. She stood on the corner, the weight of empty time heavy on her. The only other place she could think of that her sister had mentioned was the Rialto poolhall, and Jody did not even know where it was. Anyway, she would have been afraid to go in. Maybe her father would be there; he hung around the poolhalls. But she definitely did not want to see her father. Lindy had told her about running into him a couple of times, once at the Rialto and once at Jolly Joan's, the all-night restaurant down Broadway. The time at the Rialto had been all right, Burt had been sober and playing snooker with a regular group of men, and he nodded and winked at his daughter and otherwise left her alone, but at Jolly Joan's it had been different, late at night and Burt drunk and with a woman (described by Lindy only as "an old hag"), which must have embarrassed Burt, because he came over to the booth where Lindy was sitting with a couple of friends and tried to get chummy, leaning over so that everybody could smell his rotten breath and telling Lindy how glad he was to see her and wanting to be introduced to her friends, while his own companion sat alone in her booth across the way, as embarrassed as Lindy and showing it. "I felt sorry for her," Lindy said, "and I finally had to tell Daddy to go away." Burt stopped what he was saying, straightened up, turned, and went to his own booth, and throughout his coffee and pie did not even look over toward Lindy, or speak to the woman he was with. That had been the last time any of them had seen him, a few months back.

As Jody drifted down Broadway, looking in store windows and theater display windows, she eventually came to Jolly Joan's. The place was packed with coffeebreakers, and Jody wondered if she would be thrown out if she went in, decided it was cold enough to risk it and went in anyway, and the first person she saw was her sister, seated at the curved counter by herself, drinking coffee and reading a newspaper. There was an empty stool next to Lindy and Jody took it.

"Do you think they'll throw me out?" she asked, and Lindy looked over at her with the irritated keep-off expression Jody knew so well, then did a double-take, or at least looked surprised, at seeing Jody's grinning monkey face.

FIVE

THE TWO sisters spent a happy day together. First they went up to Eddie Dorkin's apartment, which Jody was surprised to see was not as big as their house in Sellwood and even gloomier, with two windows looking out on the park blocks and the bedroom windows overlooking a light shaft. The furniture was massive and obviously came with the apartment, and the kitchen was only an alcove, now filled with dirty dishes and garbage bulging up out of a dark green metal wastebasket. Lindy said, "Oh Christ, I have to do those goddamn dishes one of these days," and Jody said, "I'll help. We could do them right now," and Lindy laughed and said, "I'll wait till Eddie gets back. Then he'll flip his lid and I'll look hurt and *he'll* do the dishes." But later she said Eddie wasn't due back for over a week, and so Jody wondered what her sister would eat from. Maybe that was why she was down at Jolly Joan's for breakfast. It would be fantastic, she thought, to eat all your meals in restaurants and never have to do another dish.

But the reason Lindy brought Jody back to the apartment was to show her all her clothes, and to see if there was anything that fitted Jody. They spent a good hour playing with the clothes, and Jody ended up one cardigan cashmere richer, a forest-green sweater that Lindy said didn't go with any of her other things. "I don't wear sweaters much anymore," she said, and then, still hanging things up, continued: "How's school? Do you like it?"

"It's a pain in the ass," Jody said. She sat down on the bed and explained to her sister in a not too roundabout way that she was thinking of quitting. By now the thought that she might be able to stay here in the apartment with Lindy had occurred to her, but Lindy was quick to insist that Jody finish school. "Listen," she said seriously, "you have to keep going, even if it makes you sick. It's all you have."

"You're doing okay without it."

"I am not. And besides, don't use me as your example. I don't want you living your life the way I live mine. God forbid, honey."

"What's the matter with your life? You spend half the day telling me how nice things are."

"That's me, not you. We're a lot more different than you think."

"You mean because you're beautiful?"

Lindy laughed. "That's right. You're going to drive men crazy, but nobody's ever going to call you beautiful."

Jody wanted to hear more about how she was going to drive men crazy, skinny and ugly as she was, but Lindy went on with the lecture about how Jody should stick to her studies and ignore the example set by herself. Jody was not bored or impatient only because it was Lindy giving the lecture.

Afterward they had lunch at the Pig 'n Whistle and then they went to a movie. In the break between the first and second features, Lindy said, "Don't you think you should call Momma and tell her where you are?" Jody squirmed around in her seat and looked up at the gigantic chandelier and the acres of gold leaf on the ceiling of the movie palace. "She's at work by now," she said.

"But she still calls home doesn't she? You could call her at work."

"She's got a new boyfriend," Jody said.

"Who, *Momma?*"

"Yeah. They go out and stay out until three or four in the morning. I hear Momma coming in sometimes."

"Who is he? What's he like?"

"He's nice. Bald as an egg, practically. I don't much like him, but he doesn't try to be buddies with me, which helps. He's about fifty I guess, a slob. You know."

"Has he got any gold?" Lindy wanted to know. "Maybe Momma can get out of the rut. She really blew it with the guy who owned the used car lot."

"I don't think so. He drives around in a little old black car. It's no Cadillac. And he dresses like a slob. I think he's a college teacher."

"Oh shit," Lindy said. "I wonder what he looks like."

Jody felt she had already answered that question, so she changed the subject, but when the news came on, Lindy got up and telephoned Eleanor at the supermarket. When she came back and sat down the cartoon was on. She leaned over and whispered to Jody, "I'm going to take you home. We'll have dinner with Momma."

Jody was glad. She had not been looking forward to the long bus ride alone.

Lindy was very fond of her little sister, although she did not hold out too much hope for her future. Jody just did not seem the type who would get anywhere. She was not really ugly, Lindy thought, but her face had just too much animality in it, reminding Lindy of a picture she had seen in Life magazine, little Italian children wearing hand-me-down rags and smoking cigarettes. They looked so old. It had been all right for Jody to imitate her big sister's ambitions and want to become an actress when she was little, but she was now entering into her teenage years, and it was time to get serious. Lindy felt that if Jody applied herself she could probably get office work of some type, which would put her in a good position to meet men of the right social level—not the kind of pukes and hustlers who hung around downtown nor the rich boys that go to college, but office workers, one of whom would marry Jody and provide her with a house to have babies in.

Lindy did not want a husband, even though at eighteen the dream of stardom was fading. She did not want to give her life over to anybody. What she really wanted was a lot of money so that she could travel, see things and meet people. Once in fact she and a friend named Nancy Lavery had planned to forge a lot of checks and run to San Francisco with the money, but when Nancy showed up at the drugstore flashing the book of checks she had stolen, Lindy cooled off on the whole idea. Nancy had gone ahead, with her boyfriend Frank Delaware and they had both been promptly caught, tried, sentenced and given probation, after which they disappeared. Crime was not the way. Lindy knew a lot of people mixed up in various kinds of crime, from the dark-eyed hook-nosed boy who would steal anything you wanted and used to walk into stores dressed in one suit and walk out wearing another, to people who worked for Faye Goman, the white-haired man with glasses who ran organized crime in the whole area and lived at the Benson Hotel. Lindy had only seen him once, talking to the mistress of the man who owned the Rialto, but she knew a few pimps who worked for him.

And of course that was no answer. Lindy knew at least five girls who had been turned out by the pimps, one of whom had married a vice squad cop, but they were all such stupid girls, either believing the line that they were the one and only true love of the pimp, or allowing themselves to pretend to believe it. Lindy just couldn't swallow the line; and even if she had, the first time a customer had asked for anything bizarre or behaved badly she would have spit in his eye and walked out.

Once, for twenty dollars, she had worked for one of the pimps, who had told her earnestly that the job required no actual sex at all. "Listen, all you got to do is walk into the dude's hotel room. He's in there layin in a coffin he's brought along with him. I don't know how the hell he gets it into the fucking room, probably used the freight elevator, but anyway, all you got to do is walk in there, he raises up, you scream like hell and run. That's it." It had sounded creepy to Lindy but she wanted the money, and so at the appointed time she tapped at the right door in the best hotel in Portland, heard the muffled, "Come in!," opened the door and entered.

There indeed was a coffin, on the floor of the living room of a beautiful suite, and there lying in the coffin was an old man with white hair and pink cheeks, dressed in a dark business suit, pretending to be dead.

"Hello?" Lindy said. She hadn't realized it but she was very nervous. She kept one hand on the doorknob, ready to scream and run, but when the man sat up, popping open his eyes at her, she started laughing hysterically and could not stop. She laughed, tears running down her face, while the man looked at her angrily and motioned at her with his hand. Finally she understood the frantic gesture to mean that he wanted her to shut the door. She shut it and put her hand over her mouth to stop the laughter.

"I'm sorry," she said. "I just thought of something. Can we go back and start over again or something?"

"I'm outraged," the man said. He looked it, like a stern parent with a wayward child, but it was so silly, this old man sitting there sternly in his coffin, that she started laughing again.

"It's just, I got to thinking," she said. "What if the bellhop came in by mistake?"

"I don't think it's funny," the man said gruffly. "You won't do. You won't do at all. You tell your associate that I'm not going to pay for this. I didn't pay for the last one, and I'm not going to pay for you."

Lindy said, "Are you the gentleman who ordered the ice?" And with a scream of laughter left the room and the sex business forever.

Now that she was living with Eddie Dorkin she did not have any more money worries, but she knew that the situation with Eddie could not last. She did not want it to last. She had been fascinated by Eddie because he knew so well how to get his way, but the fascination was ending for her, and apparently increasing for Eddie. The sex between them was very bad these days, with Eddie more the worshipper than the lover, looking at her with big sheep's eyes and muttering about how he loved her—even though at other times he told her he did not love anybody—and so it was getting time for Lindy to move on. But she was not going to make any moves without having a place to land.

Maybe she could get a job. She was seeing girls she had known in school, working as waitresses, salesgirls, ticket takers at movie houses, even usherettes, although that job was usually reserved for high school girls. Times were tough, Lindy knew, and getting a good job would not be easy, and she saw what working had done to her mother, turning her from a pretty girl to a washed-out woman. One of the reasons she was taking Jody home was to try to catch a glimpse of her mother's new boyfriend. Lindy wondered what kind of man would be available to a woman who worked in a supermarket. It gave Lindy an odd pang to think that the man, whoever he was, probably only took her mother out to screw her, and was probably filling her full of bullshit about loving her and leaving his own wife, etc. etc. Lindy was prepared to dislike the man, even though Jody had said he didn't seem so bad. What did Jody know about men? She was too young and too open.

SIX

THE GIRLS got out to Sellwood a little after seven. It was raining now, and most of the snow underfoot was turning to slush. They picked their way through the messy parking lot to the supermarket and bought hamburger and tomato sauce and spaghetti, said hello to their mother and went home to cook dinner for her. Eleanor got off work at eight-thirty, and when she came in, wet and tired, the house smelled delightfully of spaghetti and meatballs, and after Eleanor bawled Jody out for cutting school, they sat down to a happy dinner.

After dinner Jody took the telephone into her room and called her friend Patsy Wambaugh to tell her what she had been doing all day and to find out what she had missed at school, while Lindy and Eleanor did the dishes and cleaned up the kitchen. Then they went into the living room with coffee and cigarettes. Eleanor was glad Lindy had come home for dinner. She had long since given up trying to control her elder daughter's life, and now she was getting the feeling that it might be possible for the two of them to become friends. Eleanor was a quiet person who kept things to herself and did not have many friends. In fact there was no one with whom she was truly intimate.

"Jody says you have a boyfriend," Lindy said. Eleanor looked sharply at her daughter to see if there was any hint of mockery in her expression, but Lindy just looked interested. Eleanor patted her hair and said, "Well, it's true enough, I guess. There is a man I go to dinner with from time to time. I haven't seen your father in a long time," she added.

"You ought to divorce him," Lindy said. "He's not much good to you."

"You shouldn't talk about your father that way."

"Why not? My father's the joke of Portland. But anyway, tell me all about your new boyfriend!"

In spite of Lindy's eagerness and this godsent opportunity to get close to her daughter, Eleanor could not bring herself to talk about Quentin. She felt her face reddening as she thought wildly about trying to tell Lindy about their motel visits. There wasn't any way in the world she could tell her about her own sexual awakening and her own eagerness to get through dinner or the movie or whatever pretense they had used to avoid the admission that all either of them wanted was to make love.

"He's a very nice man, a professor of humanities at Reed College," she said, looking down at her coffee cup.

"Is he married?" Lindy wanted to know.

"He was. He's got a son living with him. I really don't know too much about him. We're just company for each other, you know."

"Oh Mama," Lindy said. She wanted to say, "Oh Mama, isn't he making love to you? Are you just letting yourself dry up?" but she could not, and a deep feeling of depression suddenly overcame her. She had a flash of herself in twenty years, worn out with some kind of drudgery, trying in her futile way to attract some middle-aged man. "Oh Mama," she said again, and lapsed into silence.

From Jody's room came a rill of girlish laughter, and Eleanor used it as a chance to change the subject.

"Isn't she getting pretty?" she said.

Lindy agreed, although she did not believe it, and the conversation drifted inevitably into a mother-daughter argument over what Lindy was doing with her life. Eleanor, without wanting to or even really meaning it, insisted once again that Lindy stop living with the drug salesman and get a job. She did not insist that Lindy come home to live, although she pointed out the economic advantages, and even suggested that with Lindy's income from her job, they could move to a slightly bigger house in a better neighborhood. This made Lindy feel guilty, which in turn made her angry.

"I don't want a job, Mama!"

"Well, be practical. What do you want?"

"Not some crappy job," was all Lindy would say. After an uncomfortable silence, they heard a car door slam outside, and Eleanor recognized the sound. Without thinking, she put a hand over her breast, and Lindy, looking at her, understood everything. Feet tramped up the wooden steps and a hand pressed the doorbell.

"I'll get it," Eleanor said. She did not say, "Who on earth?"—which was what she always said when the doorbell or the telephone rang. Lindy stood up as her mother opened the door to Quentin Corby.

"Hi," he said. "I was out at school for a meeting and I saw your lights on. Is it okay?" He stuck his rain-wet head in and grinned at Lindy. "You must be Rosalind," he said. "I'm Tin Corby."

The room suddenly did not seem big enough for all three of them, and with awkward embarrassment Quentin's raincoat was taken, he was offered coffee, and they sat down to a clumsy conversation that began with the curious coincidence that both Quentin and Lindy preferred the last halves of their first names. It served partially to break the ice until Eleanor said, "You never told me that, Quentin. I thought you went by your full name."

"Actually," he said, "I don't know why I introduced myself that way. I haven't been called Tin in years, since I came out to Portland."

"Where are you from?" Lindy asked him, and while he explained the devious routes of a scholar in search of grants, she watched her mother. Yes, her mother was either in love with the man or totally infatuated. She was nervous, her skin looked bad, and her eyes darted from Lindy to Quentin and then back again as if she was expecting one of them to pull a gun. Lindy was amused. He was a nice-looking guy, all right, probably very good in bed, now that she saw his eyes and his big soft-looking hands, but he must have been at least forty years old, and a corny dresser. Lindy felt better. It looked like her mother was getting laid after all. Abruptly she laughed, and when the others asked her why she just said, "Just something," and let it drop.

After a while Lindy said, "Well, I better get to the bus stop before they stop running."

Eleanor said, "Why don't you spend the night?," but Lindy didn't feel like sharing a bed with Jody. Her own bed had been dismantled and stored when she moved out of the house, and although Eleanor offered to make her a bed on the couch she said, "No, I have stuff to do in the morning," and Quentin said, "Come on, El, let's drive her home. Where do you live? Downtown?" But Eleanor was too tired to go out this late, and so Quentin drove her home by himself.

SEVEN

THE DRIVE through slashing rain took a little under an hour, and for the first thirty minutes or so Quentin kept Lindy laughing with stories about his crazy students at Reed College, but as they got closer to her place conversation lagged and the silences got longer, until at last, "Turn here," and "This is it," were the only things anyone had said in five minutes. Quentin pulled over into the white zone in front of the apartment building and Lindy said, "Thank you," and started to open the door, but Quentin said, "No, wait a sec," and reached across her and pulled the door shut again.

Lindy was not cynical—it could have been that he wanted to say something about her mother—and so she waited and looked at him in the darkness, his left hand holding onto the steering wheel and his head tilted to one side. "I really have to get in," she said finally, after another long pause.

"Listen," he said, "I'd like to see you again."

"Oh really? Shit." Lindy started to open the door again, but again he reached across her and pulled it shut, and at the same time brought his head right up next to hers. She had to pull away to keep his lips from touching her cheek. His hand kept the door shut.

"I'm sorry, Lindy, I really am. But goddamn it, I think I'm falling in love with you. The same thing I saw in Eleanor I see in you, only you're the real thing. Eleanor's—well, she's the forerunner. You're it. Listen, please, I hate talking to you like this. I know damned well what you're thinking and you're right. I'm betraying your mother, I'm playing a dirty trick on her and it would kill me if she found out about it. I'm a bastard, I admit it, but honest to God I've never felt about anybody the way I feel about you. I'm not sure it's love, maybe I'm just crazy about your youngness—"

"You must be a tiger with the little coeds," Lindy said cuttingly.

"I've never touched one of my students," Quentin said. He sounded tired and defeated, but he kept his hand on the door, and when she breathed her breasts rose up and touched his coatsleeve. She wondered if he could feel them. If he could it was probably driving him wild.

"Am I supposed to believe that?" she said.

"No. You don't have to believe anything I say. But for the love of Christ don't go until I finish what I have to say."

"You can't keep me here."

"I know it. Listen, you're so beautiful I can't stand to look at you. You're going to haunt me. I can tell. My peace is at an end. Jesus, I'm starting to sound like an old movie."

"A lousy old movie," she said. It was time to get out of the car. She took hold of his wrist so that her four fingers were on top and her thumb underneath and then squeezed so that her thumbnail cut into his flesh.

"Ouch! For Christ's sake!" he yelled, in genuine pain and anger. He pulled his arm away from her quickly and she opened the door and got out. Over the roar of the rain she said, "Keep away from me, you bastard!" and slammed the car door and ran into the apartment building.

The next morning she awakened early and could not fall back to sleep. Empty mornings were the worst for her, because there wasn't anybody around to talk to, there was no place to go, nothing to do. Everybody was either at work or asleep. She had not slept well, and thoughts of Quentin Corby kept coming into her mind. She did not believe anything the man had said. She believed that he wanted to fuck her, plain and simple. That he could meet her in her mother's house and then make a pass at her, when her mother had trusted him to take her home was more than disgusting, it was an outrage, and Lindy really did not know what to do about it. She did not want to ruin her mother's romance, but on the other hand, Eleanor had a right to know what kind of bastard she was running around with.

Lindy got dressed and wanted a cup of coffee, but everything was dirty. She did not want to go to Jolly Joan's for her breakfast, and so with a disgusted sigh and a gesture of defeat, she attacked the kitchen, and spent the whole morning cleaning up. By the time the kitchen was ready for breakfast she was ready for lunch, but there wasn't anything in the refrigerator but some old cheese and a few eggs. She looked out the window. It was grey overhead but no rain was falling, which meant that it was probably getting colder again. She put on a heavy coat and went out.

He was waiting for her across the street, sitting huddled on a park bench, his face grey with cold. When he saw her he got up and moved toward her as if his hinges were rusty. When she recognized him she stopped and turned toward him and waited. When he got up to her, his face was tense and anxious-looking.

"What do you want?" she asked. Maybe he actually wanted something.

"I have to apologize," he said. "Look, can we go inside somewhere? Coffee or something? I'm freezing."

"I have to do some things," she said. "You apologized. Okay. See you around." She started to walk away, but he hurried alongside her, his hands still in his topcoat pockets.

"No, please. Just a cup of coffee."

"What did you do, cut school or something?"

"Yes. I had to talk to you."

"'I had to talk to you. *Darling.*'"

"Please."

Oh shit, she thought. Why not? She had an idea of what he might want to say, anyway, and she wanted to hear him say it. They went into a little hotel coffeeshop on the corner and seated themselves in the window, where Lindy could look out at the people and the light traffic. Quentin took ten minutes to let himself warm up, sipping at his coffee and gingerly rubbing his cheeks with his fingertips before he spoke to her.

"I know you think I'm a bastard, and I guess I am," he began, in a voice that did not sound like its owner considered himself a bastard. "But years ago I stopped kidding myself and started trying to be honest with my feelings. I didn't sleep at all last night. I was torn between feeling terribly guilty about making a pass at you and feeling just absolutely goddamn delighted at making a pass at you. Because you're what I want. I really think I'm falling in love with you, and I'd rather be in love than not in love, frankly." He grinned quickly, and then went through the business of lighting a cigarette. Lindy just sat looking out the window. She was not going to speak unless she had good reason.

"Okay," he said. "Your mother."

Here it comes, Lindy thought. She turned to look at him.

"I've decided not to see her anymore. It isn't fair to her. I really like her, and we had—well. Anyway, I want to see you, and I promise that I won't see Eleanor again."

"That's sweet for Momma," Lindy said to him. "She thinks you're her boyfriend."

Quentin looked genuinely pained, and bit his lip. "I know. But how would it be if I went back to her and really all the time loved you? Wouldn't that be even more unfair?"

"Mister Corby," Lindy said slowly and deliberately, "I already have a boyfriend. I live with him. You know that. If I told him what you said to me he'd find you and break your fingers." She stood up. She wanted to add something absolutely killing, but couldn't think of anything good enough, so she just walked away from the table. He followed her, and when she turned at the door, she could see that their waitress was following him with a check. It was getting comical.

"Please!" he said again. "Please don't—tell your mother!"

"Don't worry," Lindy said. Then: *"I knew you'd say that!"* And she left.

EIGHT

THE NEXT night as usual Quentin bought groceries and went through Eleanor's checkstand. They had a date for that night, but Quentin's routine now was to buy his things and take them home, then pick Eleanor up later after she had showered and changed her clothes.

Eleanor asked him, "Did you get home late?"

"Not too," he said. "The rain was awful, though. I'm glad I drove Lindy home. She's a very nice girl. You told me she was beautiful but I thought, you know, just a proud mother talking."

"No, she's a real beauty," Eleanor said. "Oh, this onion's got a soft spot on it. Just a sec." And she trotted over to the produce section and picked him out a good big round yellow onion. When she got back to the checkstand she said, "Jody's not going to be home tonight. She's staying with her friend Patsy." Eleanor was too shy to look at him as she said this, because she knew he would understand her to mean that for the first time she was inviting him to make love to her at home.

"I didn't want to see the damned movie anyway," he said, and when she did look up at him he was grinning shyly. They had been going to go see *She Wore A Yellow Ribbon*, starring John Wayne.

As usual she was not hungry after work, but tonight there was a special sense of daring and excitement inside her. They were going to make love on her own bed, with her familiar sheets and her old patchwork quilt. She did not this night think about all the times she and Burt had made such hurried, embarrassed and furtive love in the same bed. She only thought about Quentin and the pleasures to come. Before she took her shower she changed the sheets and pillowcases, and then when she came out of the shower, her skin rosy with cold, she had an impulse to lie down on the fresh bed and wait for him that way, naked and sensual. But common sense told her not to be a fool, and she dressed as if they were going to the movie. After all, he might change his mind.

But he didn't. She heard the familiar car door slam and then his footsteps and she had the door open before he could knock. He kissed her right there, standing in the doorway and letting the cold air into the house, his tongue swelling into her mouth and one hand intimately grasping her as he pressed her against the doorjamb. My God, she thought with a thrill, we might not make it into the bedroom! But after that first passionate kiss Quentin laughed and said, "Let's shut the door before we freeze to death," and they went inside, and after only a few minutes of not looking at one another, moved on, holding hands, into the bedroom, where Quentin slowly undressed her and then himself as she lay on the bed with her arms delicately folded across her breasts.

He stood naked looking at her. "My God I love you," he said. He lay down next to her and took her into his arms and began kissing her breasts. She felt such an overwhelming love for him that she began to cry without making a sound and he only found out about it when he moved up and began kissing her mouth.

"What's the matter?" he whispered.

"Nothing. I love you," she said, and to prove it she moved down to kiss his belly, loving the way his hair felt against her lips and tongue, and then took his cock into her mouth. She knew he loved this best of all because he had saved it up to teach her last, saving it because he did not want to scare her off, and he had been right. If he had tried to get her to do this on their first evening she would have turned cold with disgust and fear. But now she loved the taste of his cock and the taste and smell of his sperm. Now she could feel him pressing his tongue up inside her, and she gave a deep satisfied internal grunt.

They made love for a couple of hours, holding one another and talking quietly between episodes. The subject of Lindy did not come up. Finally Eleanor was hungry, and she got up and made them both toasted cheese sandwiches, which they ate in the living room, listening to music on the radio. After he left she went back to bed and composed herself for sleep by daydreaming about what marriage to Quentin would be like. She knew she would not have any trouble getting a divorce from Burt. He would see reason. She could stay home and keep house, taking care of Quentin's son and Jody until they were out of school and away. Then she and Quentin could travel together. She had always wanted to travel, but as a matter of fact aside from a trip to Crater Lake before she had married Burt, Eleanor had never been outside the Willamette Valley. She had never even been to the ocean, although as a girl she had had many chances to go.

But of course none of this would actually happen. She would not ask him to marry her, and she did not think he would ask her. He had his life. He was a college professor and he moved in different circles. She would feel awful going to the kind of parties he told her about, with people sitting on the floor drinking wine and talking about communism. She even had a suspicion that Quentin was a communist, although to her he made fun of the campus radicals. No. Not marriage. But that was all right. Her life was full now.

NINE

EDDIE DORKIN came back from his road trip tired and irritable. He had been knocking back a little too much benzedrine, and for the past three days he had not been able to sleep without heavy doses of seconal, and after a brief staccato argument with Lindy he burst into tears and sat on the edge of the bed. "Oh God," he said to her, "I wish I was dead."

She had been about to tell him about Quentin to see if it would make him jealous, but when she saw his disconsolate face and pitiful little hands kneading each other in his lap she relented and sat beside him, putting her fingers on his neck and rubbing gently. "It's okay," she said, without even knowing what the problem was. He told her about all the pills, and about the terrors he had been experiencing in the middle of the night. "My life is a sham," he said, and started crying again. Lindy felt sorry for him. She helped him undress and climbed into bed with him but it was no use. "I'll probably have a limp cock for a week," he admitted. "Those goddamn drugs."

By the way Eddie looked and sounded, Lindy knew that she had it in her power to destroy him right then and there if she wanted to. All she would have to do would be to respond to this contemptuously, or even with false solicitude—anything that would let Eddie know she was repelled by his lack of manhood. She could gain complete control over Eddie if she played it right. But even while she was thinking about it she knew she could not. Instead she laughed and said, "I feel the same way sometimes. Lay back and cool it, and I'll fix you something to eat."

Later on he still was not able to sleep and did not want to take any more pills so he suggested that they smoke some marijuana. Lindy got out the Prince Albert can and the papers and rolled a couple of bombers. They smoked the first one and were halfway through the second, listening to some Stan Kenton records, when Eddie began to get the horrors.

"Oh Jesus God," he said in a wailing voice, "I can't stop thinking about it!" He put his hands over his eyes and rocked back and forth on the couch.

"You can't stop thinking about what?" she asked him.

"I can't talk about it," he said. "Oh God, the pot makes it worse!"

Lindy finished the joint by herself. She was feeling good and high and Eddie was quiet now, looking like a fat little gargoyle to Lindy. She did a few dance steps to the music and he stayed on the couch.

"Lindy!"

"Yes, baby?" She kept dancing.

"I'm dying."

She stopped. "What do you mean?"

"I started thinking about it in Medford. It just came to me. I'm gonna die and there's nothing I can do about it."

"Wait a minute. You mean you have a disease or something?"

He looked up at her and she could see the terror in his eyes. "No," he said. "Not a disease. It's just I never thought about it before, but we're all going to die."

Lindy could not help laughing. It was really outrageously funny. "Sure we're all gonna die! So what?"

"I know, I know, it's funny. I laughed myself when I couldn't get my mind off it, but it's true. I'm gonna die, you're gonna die, everybody's gonna die, and so what? *But I can't stop thinking about it!* Do you understand that? I lay in bed at night and think about what's gonna happen to me."

"Oh, crap, everybody does that once in a while. You'll get over it."

"Three days," Eddie said. "Three fucking days, and all I can think about is dying. Listen, I never told you this. I have a kid. A little boy. He lives in Bend with his mother, she works at the Greyhound depot there. He's five and a half. What I started thinking about was him. I saw him dead in my dream, his body all white as marble. He was laid out on this table, his eyes shut. There was no blood in him, he was just laying there dead. I couldn't get it out of my mind and there was nothing I could do about it. You don't know how helpless I felt. I spend my whole fucking life lying to those goddamn fucking doctors, smile smile, pretend to be educated, look sharp, dress cool, smile, smile, sell that shit! You don't know! Most of the time I see people as little parts in a puzzle, you know? I just take those little parts and fit 'em in where I want 'em, and if they don't quite fit I stick 'em in anyway. Just little pieces of wood, most of the time. I laugh and cry but I don't feel anything, and I think most people are faking it when they show their feelings. All the way through high school and college I work people around to do what I want; I get girls to do my term papers and I blackmail teachers into good grades if I can't get 'em any other way. Once, Oh God I never told this to anybody, once I made a teacher suck my cock and then I called up his wife on the telephone and told her about it, and he left school. I'm a motherfucker, that's all there is to that, and the sooner I die the better. My kid don't need me, nobody needs me. That's what I got to thinking about. Even if I did die, who would care?"

Tears were running down his face, and he looked absolutely terrified. "But I don't want to die!"

If Lindy hadn't been so stoned she might have slapped his face and said, "Stop feeling sorry for yourself, you little shit!" but instead she sat next to him and cradled him in her arms and said, "There, there, it's going to be okay, baby," while he cried.

Finally he shrugged her off and got up and went into the bathroom. She heard the water running for a long time, and eventually she could not push the thought out of her mind that Eddie was in there cutting his throat or his wrists and was bleeding to death into the sink. She giggled. What a silly idea! On the other hand, it had been a long long time, and that water was just running and running. She did not want to embarrass herself by knocking on the door and asking him what was the matter, but neither did she want to find his corpse on the floor and a sink full of blood. But it was impossible. He wouldn't kill himself. Why should he? He was just going through a little self-pity, that was all. Lindy often felt sorry for herself, and Eddie was no different. She could see why he got sick of his job, but he made heaps of money at it and what better job was waiting for him? He was just a salesman. She got to her feet and went to the bathroom door just as Eddie opened it and came out. His face was clean and blotched and his eyes bloodshot. He grinned sheepishly at her.

"God I'm an ugly bastard," he said in a hoarse voice. "What do you see in me?"

"Oh Eddie," she said, and hugged him.

It went on five more days. Eddie could not sleep that night, and she heard him get out of bed mumbling and cursing under his breath, go into the living room and rummage through his detail bag, and then heard the running water in the bathroom. She wondered how many reds he was taking. When he got back to bed she pretended to be asleep. Marijuana usually made her sleepy, but tonight she could not seem to drop off either. Eddie, after about twenty minutes of lying stiffly on his back, began to breathe deeply, and then heavily, a fluttering snore emerging from his slightly open mouth. Lindy debated whether to have more marijuana or to try the sleeping pills, but fell asleep before she could make up her mind.

The next morning and every morning while he was home, Eddie was down and logy until he had had four or five cups of black coffee and a few cigarettes, but he was making a conscious effort to stay away from the bennies. During the days he tried to spend more time with Lindy than he usually did, and they went to Mount Hood skiing once, to a couple of afternoon movies, and shopping. The skiing didn't work out too well because Eddie could not get warm enough to enjoy himself. They both rented good equipment and had plenty of warm ski clothes, but Eddie's feet simply would not warm up, and his face looked grey under the pink of his cheeks, and his eyes were sunken. He did not speak about death, but Lindy could tell it was on his mind more or less continuously.

The shopping was mostly for her. In the past it had been fun for them both. Lindy knew how to stretch it out, spending hour after hour trying on clothes she would never in a million years wear, such as full-length party gowns, cocktail dresses, furs and hats, and Eddie would watch her with the pride of a man who owns beauty; but this time he simply sat with his hands in his lap and stared dully at a point in the distance, and Lindy had to make all the fun herself. The truth was, she was getting a little tired of Eddie's death problems, and she coaxed him into buying her a lot of things she neither needed nor wanted. But Eddie would pay and kiss her absently on the cheek and they would move on.

Nights were the worst. They spent a lot of time in the Desert Room, The Shadows or The Cherokee Club, drinking and talking to the Portland night club people. Lindy was no longer proud of the way Eddie could handle himself. He was drinking far too much, and when men interested in her would needle Eddie, he would just nod and go back to his drinking. One night, just to see what he would do, she danced two hours with a shoe salesman named Ben Weintraub, who kept one hand on her ass and whispered into her ear that the two of them should meet when Eddie next went out of town. She ignored the hand and the whispers, and when they finally went back to the table, Eddie apparently had been ignoring them too, because he said nothing.

But the worst parts were when they got home to the apartment. Lindy was willing to let sex go for a few days, since Eddie was having all these problems, but he could not. Every night they had to go through the farce of attempting to make love. These days Eddie's breath was awful, and although she had mentioned it once and he had rushed into the bathroom and gargled, it got no better, and she had to stop mentioning it, deep inside afraid that he might, just might, commit suicide over the simple matter of bad breath. So she was not exactly in a sexy mood herself, and Eddie instead of confident was timid and tentative, which made her skin turn cold against his touch. She tried massaging him one night until her arms ached, but nothing worked. She wished it were her period, which would have solved everything because nobody was expected to make love then, but that wasn't for another couple of weeks.

After the attempts at lovemaking failed, Eddie would go through his nightly battle over the sleeping pills, which he always lost, but only after hours of pacing, talking, lying in bed stiffly and incidentally driving Lindy herself into insomnia. She kept expecting Eddie to wake up one morning his old cheery ironic self, but it just didn't happen, and finally she had to pack him off on the road again, rocky, shaky, dark rims under his eyes and terrified.

"I'll call you every night, baby," he said to her as he left the apartment with his bags, and after he had been gone ten minutes she understood why: he would call her to demonstrate that he had not yet killed himself. Jesus, she thought, he's really got *something*. Another ten minutes later the doorbell rang and, thinking it was Eddie returning, she pressed the buzzer without talking on the speaker. When she opened the front door to the apartment, she saw Quentin Corby standing there, a stupid grin on his face.

"I thought he'd never leave," he said. "Can I come in?"

Lindy thought about shutting the door in his face but for some reason she didn't. She really wanted to talk to somebody who was sane, somebody from the real world. "Oh hell, come on in," she said.

TEN

QUENTIN CORBY was the finest lover Lindy had ever been with, and she fell in love with him almost immediately. Not because of the lovemaking, she told herself, but because with him she felt for the first time truly alive and free. Her life had been closing down and now Quentin was opening it up again, showing her worlds she could enter and belong to. It was really so simple: all she had to do was register at Multnomah College's night high school, get her diploma, and then go on to college. No one had ever told her how intelligent she was, everyone up to now had concentrated on her beauty, but Quentin said, "Beauty's wonderful and you have enough of it to drive me crazy, but what's supposed to happen to you when you get to be thirty, forty, fifty? Life isn't over at twenty-five, you know. I'm forty years old myself, and the older I get the more I like my life and the more I want to live. You're a smart person, you're clever, and I'm just damned sure you're intelligent as hell."

"I don't know anything," she said. "Shit, I quit high school in the second year."

"School's got nothing to do with intelligence, only with learning. And you said 'shit' to make me think you're vulgar. Listen, I could show you some speeches in Shakespeare that would make even your ears burn."

He brought some tests over to the apartment, and Lindy found out to her delight and surprise that she really was pretty smart—a lot smarter than she had expected, anyway. "I'd like to get you a reading on the Stanford-Binet IQ test," he told her once, "but it's so damned expensive. I'm certain your IQ is up around a hundred-twenty, maybe a hundred-thirty."

"Is that good?" she asked.

"Mine is a hundred-forty-three," he said with a smile. "The average guy is around a hundred."

So for the first time in a while, Lindy was excited about her prospects for the future, and for the first time in her life she began to see the need for education.

"I don't blame you for being bored with all that crap they throw at you in high school," he told her one night as they lay in Eddie Dorkin's bed, "but when you get to night school you'll see that it's all cut down to the bone. They teach you what you have to know for that piece of paper, and that's that. You can handle it. When that bored feeling hits you in the gut, just say to yourself, 'I'm doing this for me!'"

Of course Lindy wanted to plan for a career right away. But Quentin said, "Don't think about things like that yet. You won't finish college for about five years, and things will be different then than they are now. And anyway, education's not just a way to get a job, it's an *education*. You learn to *know*."

This concept puzzled her, but Quentin seemed dead certain about it, and she was sure Quentin knew everything. He even knew what was the matter with Eddie.

According to Quentin, Eddie was suffering from world-pain. "He'll get over it. It's just that every once in a while a man sees through the facades of life, the shields we deliberately put up to keep from going crazy. It's happened to me a couple of times. Suddenly you realize that all around you people are starving, dying, being beaten, deprived of love, tortured, torn to pieces by insanity, all the horrors of the world. Then you see that it's all useless as well as horrible, because at the end of the road there's nothing at all. Just death. Get an image in your mind of a drunken father beating a child bloody because the child wet his bed or something. The kid doesn't know what's going on except he's fucked up again and Daddy's half killing him, and the poor father beats and crushes his child in a futile effort to ease the pain and terrors in his own heart, and of course it doesn't work, it just adds to the pile of guilt; and then remember that in a few years, a pitiful few years, both will be dead and gone, and all that pain and misery and sorrow was for nothing, got nobody anywhere, just perpetuated itself generation after generation without meaning or function."

"Jesus, you're a gloomy bastard," Lindy told him.

"I'm sorry," he said. "But that's probably what's eating your friend Eddie. Really, though, it's you."

"What do you mean?"

"Well, you're the only beauty in his life, aren't you? Really? And he knows you don't love him."

"How would he know that?" Lindy asked, feeling a twist of guilt in her stomach.

"Come on, don't lie to yourself. You know and he knows. People can't live together without knowing. Eddie feels useless, that's all. Locked up in solitary for the rest of his days, and so what? It's a hell of a feeling."

"Well, I hope I never feel that way."

"Baby, as much as I love you and want to protect you, you're going to feel that way some day. Everybody with half a brain does."

"Maybe not," she said.

But Eddie wasn't their big problem as lovers; in fact he was a convenience, gone most of the month and leaving them his apartment to conduct their affair in, even supporting Lindy while it lasted, just so long as he did not find out what was going on. Lindy was surprised at herself for not feeling guilty about this, but she reasoned that she actually loved Quentin, she could not help herself, he made her dizzy when she thought about him, and she did not love Eddie and she knew he didn't really love her, and so he got what he paid for, a pretty thing to fuck and show around. No, the big problem for them was Eleanor. But even that smoothed out as soon as Quentin explained things.

Quentin taught on Mondays, Wednesdays and Fridays, with student conferences scheduled all day Thursday, so he was free on Tuesdays and weekends, and he spent all or as much of that time as possible with Lindy, and yet continued to see Eleanor two nights a week. He told Lindy, "You have to understand that my feelings toward Eleanor are different from the way I feel about you. You make me sick with love sometimes, and sometimes I hate you; but Eleanor is like a wife and a sister all in one; I love her too, but in a tender sort of way. You know, your mother's never had much in her life. I couldn't hurt her. I wouldn't hurt her for anything." They were naked in bed and it was morning, the setting for many of their long conversations.

"It would kill me if she found out about us," Lindy said.

"Of course it would, and it should. But she'll never find out because we'll never tell her, and we'll never do anything indiscreet that would let her know."

"But God, I feel awful about taking you away from her. It's so unfair."

"Don't worry about that. You didn't take me away from her at all. I'm still with her, for one thing. For another, I'm really beginning to think that my love for both of you is actually one thing—that you're both part of the same idea, so to speak. Do you know what I mean? To me, you're one woman."

"But we're not," Lindy said. "I feel so bad about it."

Quentin put one of his big soft hands on her naked shoulder. "Do you want to stop seeing me?" he asked her gently.

"You know I don't," she said. "Oh God, I love you!"

With a chuckle he pulled her toward him and they began to make love again.

The first time Eddie Dorkin came home after Quentin and Lindy had become lovers he knew something was up, because she was simply a changed person, brighter, cooler somehow, less inclined to petulance and boredom. Eddie himself had been having a horrible time on the road, trying to break himself of barbiturates and consequently being unable to sleep at all. He had not slept in five days when he got home. He could not eat either, and so he had lost a lot of weight and he looked horrible. Horrible-looking salesmen do not do well in the medical field, and so his sales were off too. Lindy suggested that he take a couple of weeks' vacation and check into a hospital.

"They can fix you up," she told him. She did not mention his problem with death and neither did he, but she did not think he was over it, and she could imagine the horror of endless nights in motel rooms with the ghost of death sitting on the bedside.

But Eddie wanted no more sleepless nights, and went back on the pills. In a couple of days he was his old self again, and they even made love. Afterward she held him in her arms tightly until he fell asleep. His poor little body was so thin and his skin was so bad-looking she felt an almost overwhelming sorrow for him, as if Eddie actually were dying. But she was very glad when he went back out on the road and she could call Quentin at the college.

ELEVEN

THE FIRST thing Jody noticed was that her sister never came home anymore and had not even telephoned once since Jody had cut school and gone to visit her. Thanksgiving went past without any celebration, which was just exactly the way Jody liked it, but her mother seemed upset by the fact that they could not get hold of Lindy. "She's probably having dinner with that boyfriend of hers," Eleanor said, but her lips were thin and she looked almost angry. Her own boyfriend the professor from Reed College didn't show up either, and when Jody asked about it Eleanor said that he was involved in some kind of thing with his students. That was fine with Jody.

But when the Christmas vacation started and Jody still had not heard from her sister, she got worried and decided to go downtown once more and find out for herself. The apartment was messier than it had been the last time, with every ashtray filled and the kitchen smelling sour. Lindy's skin looked bad too, scratchy and grey. Jody stayed an hour and got Lindy's promise to at least come out Christmas Eve and relieve the boredom for Jody. The girls hugged each other at the door, something they almost never did, and Jody wondered why they had done it this time. It was almost like a farewell hug, she thought. And another thing worried her, although it really shouldn't have: Lindy smoked Herbert Taryton cigarettes, puffing nervously halfway through the cigarette and then crushing it out, so that her ashtrays were usually filled with half-cigarettes, lipstick-stained, bent and often broken. Jody's mother smoked Camels, taking a full puff and opening her mouth so that the smoke hung there for a moment before being sucked down her throat. When Eleanor put out her cigarettes they were usually about an inch long, and she put them out by tapping them gently until the coal was crushed. Eleanor's boyfriend, Professor Corby, sm

oked Lucky Strikes right down to the last fragment, and when he had been to visit the ashtrays around Jody's house would be full of the tiny stained butts. There were butts like that in Lindy's ashtrays too, and although Jody thought maybe that was the way men smoked and the butts belonged to Lindy's absent boyfriend, it still created a little tickle in the back of her mind that did not go away, and did not make her like Professor Corby very much more, either.

But she admitted to herself that she might be jealous of Quentin, or maybe jealous of her mother for having a boyfriend when Jody did not. Jody had gone to a couple of school dances in the gym, dragged along by her friend Patsy, who was very interested in boys, but by the time Jody would get to the dances she was so nervous and upset that all she could do was stand to one side and glower at everybody. When boys asked her to dance she would move out on the floor with them, put her arms up and go through the motions, sometimes not even speaking to the boy. The right ones never asked her to dance anyway, just the clods, boys who seemed all teeth and pimples. Most of them had erections when they danced with her, but Jody did not take it as a compliment, just as something else to be avoided, like hands that moved too low or cheeks that moved in too close. She assumed that most boys had erections most of the time.

The boys Jody wanted were unreachable. They were all juniors or seniors, all fraternity boys or athletes, the "wheels" of the school, who all dressed alike and all drove cars and went out with the beauties who were in sororities. These were the boys who were in control of everything, the celebrities, who would go on to college at the University of Oregon or Oregon State, get married, have children and live in the quiet dignified houses of the wealthy districts that Jody only saw from the window of the bus. There was one boy especially, far beyond Jody, but she daydreamed about him anyway, and then laughed at herself. He was the captain of the football team, of all things, a big dark surly boy with blue jaws and small dark eyes. He was All-State and expected to make a stir when he got to college. Jody had heard, as everyone around school had, that he had been offered sixty-seven scholarships, including Stanford and Cal.

His name was Jim Wintergreen and he was at all the dances with his steady girl. As far as Jody knew he had never looked at her and probably never would, but still she dreamed of a chance encounter, followed by a whirlwind romance, followed by Jody's possession of his fraternity pin and letterman sweater. Jody even admitted to herself that the best part of the fantasy was when she would come into class with the pin and sweater on, everybody—even the teacher—gaping at her. She wasn't really interested in Jim Wintergreen at all, just his loot, but he continued to serve as the focus for most of her daydreams about boys.

Jody had by now given up on the drama department and the drama club, and was just putting in her time until she finished formulating her plans to run away to New York City and become an actress. She had spent one day in the auditorium, painting flats with the other freshman and sophomore drama kids and it had driven her crazy with boredom. For one thing, all the other drama kids talked in British accents; kidding, but kidding on the square; as far as Jody could tell. And the worst part was she did it too when she was around them. You couldn't help yourself. And the smell of the waterpaints made her sick. Even though it was cold in the auditorium Jody sweated the whole time she was there, and was bitter about the fact that the students chosen for speaking roles were excused from working as stagehands, and were at that moment in a classroom rehearsing, having fun, while Jody sweated. She was sure that the Broadway theater did not put young actors and actresses through such paces. If you had the talent, you got the job. And Jody was sure she had the talent, even though she had never been on stage in her life, unless you counted those little kid pageants and things from grade school, and she didn't. She knew she had the talent. She *had* to have it, because she wanted it so much.

Jody did not go to movies very much, although she loved them, because she was usually so caught up in the story, the color, the glamour and the romance, that coming out of the theater she would be exhausted and spend hours wandering around depressed, fragments of the movie echoing in her mind. When she went to the school plays she would get so excited that she could hardly keep her seat, but not for the same reason. At the school plays it was frustration that agitated her, not romance or passion. She hated the kid actors for their terrible amateurishness. They had no right to get up there on stage before they knew what they were doing, and they especially had no business taking parts that Jody could have done beautifully and screwing them up so totally. But she could no more stay away from the plays than she could fly.

Patsy Wambaugh took a different view of things. She was a slender pretty blonde girl who lived only a few blocks from Jody and whose parents were divorced. Patsy lived with her mother, who worked downtown at Meier & Franks department store, so they had that much in common. Patsy too was a member of the drama club, and shared in the painting of flats. But she was also chosen as a super, who got to wear a beautiful costume in the Shakespeare. She was on stage in two scenes, and Jody hated her for it.

The Christmas holidays went by without incident for Jody, except that her sister did come home on Christmas Eve and sat very quietly in a corner drinking eggnog. The other guest was Quentin Corby, who entertained them with a long story about his experiences in London during the war, and left small, elegantly wrapped presents for all of them when he went home to spend the rest of the evening with his son. Jody's opinion that Quentin was a bizarre and dangerous person was reinforced when she opened her package to find a really thick sterling silver identification bracelet that must have weighed at least half a pound and was just exactly what Jody had wanted with such a passion that she had not even mentioned it to anyone. It was as if he had reached into her mind to discover her most secret desires. He had even had the good sense not to have the thing engraved. Jody jiggled it in the palm of her hand, loving its weight, and watched her sister open her package. It was a gold Dunhill cigarette lighter, really classy, but Lindy did not seem as delighted as she might have, and it was only the next morning that Jody wondered why he was giving such an expensive gift to a person he barely knew. The present for Eleanor was a pair of identification bracelets, both gold, one for the ankle and one for the wrist, and when Jody examined them she saw engraved on the wrist bracelet "Eleanor" on one side and "Quentin" on the other. The anklet was engraved "E" and "Q," and her mother seemed pleased with them. Possibly, Jody thought, he had reached into her mind too, for an old unsatisfied secret desire.

The holidays did not go quite so well for Lindy. Eddie chose to spend two whole weeks in Portland with her, and it was all she could do to keep him from coming over to her mother's house with her on Christmas Eve. "Holidays drive me crazy," he told her, and she was expected to nurse him through the season, insomnia, dreams of death and all.

Lindy was not sure she was up to it. She and Quentin had counted on his school holiday to give them at least three days together, but not only did Eddie decide to stay home but Quentin's son, who was supposed to visit a friend's family farm, decided not to go at the last minute, and so they actually saw less of each other instead of more, and Lindy was at the point now where she only felt alive when she was with Quentin.

Either she had never been in love before or this was something larger than love. But no matter what it was, it was destroying her. It was logical and rational for her to continue living with Eddie, because after all she couldn't exactly move back in with her mother, and she didn't have a job and couldn't have a place of her own, and she couldn't ask Quentin to support her. Things were best, he told her, at status quo, and she knew him well enough now to know that he probably did not love her half as much as she loved him. But she did believe he loved her, and she did believe that he loved her mother too, and so it was hopeless. She kept telling herself that sooner or later she would fall out of love with him and everything would be okay, but for right now she was being driven slightly mad by the crossfire of hypocrisy she found herself in most of the time. Eddie needed her love and support even though they never made love together anymore, and it was all she could do to keep from screaming at him sometimes.

And to top it off she got pregnant. There was no question about who was the father. She and Quentin had made love in a motel room out on 82nd Avenue one Tuesday afternoon during the holidays, and by that night she had known she was pregnant, although she pretended to herself for days that she was not. She had been wearing her diaphragm, but apparently it hadn't worked this one time. When she missed her period, she locked herself in the bathroom and cried (Eddie was on the bed, reading the papers) and then made an excuse and went across to the telephone booth and called Quentin. But as soon as she heard his slightly irritated voice she knew she could not tell him, at least not yet. Quentin said hello again, and she hung up without speaking and went back to Eddie.

It was so corny. Pregnant. When Eddie learned, would he throw her out into the snow? When Quentin learned, would he suddenly find business out of town, or quickly slip her a few hundred and a telephone number? Or would both of them, with tears of self-sacrifice in their eyes, offer to marry her and give the little bastard a name? Lindy had to laugh at that one; even the movies hesitated to show anything that far from reality. On the other hand, why did she have to tell either of them? Only for the money to see the abortionist, and maybe not even for that, if she could get the money some other way. She knew of an abortionist, the mother of one of the pimps who hung around the Desert Room. Her name was Elaine Benedict, and she was supposed to charge three hundred dollars. She did the local hookers all the time, and was supposed to be really good; fast, clean and efficient. That part would be easy. The tough part was getting the three hundred. She did not worry about what to tell Eddie or Quentin; she would just disappear for a couple of days, and when she came back she would damn them to find out where she had been. She was not so crippled by love that she had lost all her spirit. She could even tell them she had had an abortion and she didn't know who the father was, and let them sort it out in their own minds.

But she did none of those things, at least not right away. She didn't feel sick, and the pregnancy would not show for a long time, and she had at least two and probably three months until she had to get the operation done, so she let things slide, along with night school and the idea of going to college, which had once appealed to her so much, and now seemed such a silly dream. Even Quentin didn't talk about it anymore. They went through the winter and into the spring meeting two or three times a week, and that was about it. They made love, they talked, they argued, but there were no more plans for the future and no discussions about the hypocrisy of it all.

TWELVE

AT THE last minute, Lindy decided she wanted company for her trip to see Mrs. Benedict, and so she called her sister. Jody cut school the next day and they met at the bus stop at Fifth and Stark. It was a rare sunny spring day, and Jody got off the bus wearing Levi's cut and rolled almost to the knee, a print peasant blouse and her white windbreaker. Lindy was waiting for her. She had gotten the money not by asking anybody for it but by saving ten here, twenty there, from the money that Eddie Dorkin gave her to spend. The sisters walked up to Washington Street to catch the streetcar, and Jody very carefully did not ask where they were going or what the event was. Lindy had meant to tell her but the words came hard, and now, walking, it was impossible. Especially under this sunny sky. Lindy had not expected to be frightened but she was.

As the streetcar rolled up into the West Hills Lindy found the words. "I have to have a little operation," she said to Jody, as the houses of the rich people moved slowly by. "I guess you know what that means."

"I think so," Jody said. "How come your boyfriend doesn't go with you?"

"Eddie's out of town. He doesn't even know I'm pregnant," Lindy said.

"I'm glad you called me," Jody said. "You shouldn't go alone. Where did you get the money?"

Mrs. Benedict worked out of a small shingled frame house in the northwest section of Portland, on Johnson Street. Lindy had gotten the address from her son Bob, after sitting on a barstool at the Desert Room for three hours one afternoon waiting for him to come in. The house had a small covered porch, and on the porch were two old rotting wicker chairs. Jody said, "Maybe I should wait out here."

"Going chicken?" Lindy said with a grin. Together they went into the house. It was not much like a doctor's office and Elaine Benedict was not much like a doctor. She was a big woman, at least six feet. She had hard sharp intelligent blue eyes and a thin mouth covered with too much bright red lipstick, but the thing Lindy noticed most was her hands, which were large and beautifully shaped, the fingernails clear and trimmed. Elaine Benedict wore no jewelry, and was dressed in a brown tweed skirt and a pale yellow sweater set. "Do you have the money?" she asked Lindy in the small living room of the house. Lindy got the bills out of her purse and gave them to Mrs. Benedict.

"Who's this?" Mrs. Benedict said, without looking at Jody.

"My sister."

"Can she drive?"

"No. We came by streetcar."

"Oh shit. You should have somebody to drive you home. Oh well. I'll call somebody. Your sister can wait out here."

Suddenly, Mrs. Benedict looked into Jody's eyes, her expression almost fierce. "You can keep a secret, can't you?"

"Sure," Jody said. "That's why I'm here." She did not like this woman. She would have preferred a man doctor for Lindy, but Lindy had said that this woman was the best in the Pacific Northwest. The door closed behind her sister and Mrs. Benedict. Jody sat down, filled with the old doctor's-office dread everybody feels, and picked up a magazine. If she ever had to have an abortion, after she became an actress, she would have the operation done in Switzerland, by a top medical man. None of this sneaking around industrial districts.

Lindy was led to a bedroom that contained a pair of bunk beds, a dresser and some blue curtains on the window. The beds were covered with matching blue spreads with little sailboats, buoys and sailors, in white. There was a bathrobe laid across the bottom bunk, and Mrs. Benedict said, "Take off all your clothes and put on the bathrobe, and then wait for me." She handed Lindy a couple of little white pills. "The bathroom's in there. Take these right away."

"What are they?" Lindy asked.

"Pain killer," Mrs. Benedict said, and left the room. Lindy shrugged and went into the bathroom. She was used to pain killers.

After about twenty minutes of sitting on the bottom bunk, leaning forward to keep from bumping her head on the upper, Lindy began to feel high and woozy, and her worries slipped away. She smiled at her earlier fears. What she should have done was to hit Eddie's supply of codeine before she ever left the house; by now, and with the extra pills, she would have felt pretty great.

Ten minutes later Mrs. Benedict came back in, now wearing the white coat that Lindy had expected. Lindy stood up and said, "Ready when you are." Mrs. Benedict smiled and said, "You've got pretty good nerve. Come on."

Lindy followed her down the hall to another bedroom, this one done up as an examining room, except for the wallpaper, which depicted faded bunches of grapes. Lindy asked, "Do most of them act scared?"

"One way or another," Mrs. Benedict said. Lindy had expected to see more people, for some reason, but they were alone. There was a glass cabinet against one wall, and the black leather examining table, complete with knee stirrups, so that Lindy felt she was actually in a doctor's office. It made her feel even better. All the room lacked was a couple of framed diplomas.

"Take off the robe and lie down, hook your knees into the stirrups," Mrs. Benedict said. "You're lucky. It's nice and warm in here today."

"What's that smell?" Lindy said from the examining table.

"Ether," Mrs. Benedict said. She had a cotton pad in her hand. "Just breathe deeply."

"Getting all kinds of high today," Lindy said with a giggle. She breathed deeply into the cotton and felt her mind shredding. It was a delicious feeling, and the only bad part was a faint nausea in the pit of her stomach, but soon even that faded out, and she was alone inside a kind of cotton wool universe, all pink and glowing. Then there were a lot of people, mostly strangers, and then she was alone again, but in the country somewhere, among a lot of very tall trees. She could see way up in the tops of the trees the sun like a disk of burning gold, and she knew she shouldn't look at the sun because it would hurt her eyes, and so she went inside one of the trees where it was dark and warm. But out of the darkness somebody grabbed at her, no, some thing, and it had sharp claws, and one of the claws stuck in her and tore at her body. Then it was all right again and she was no place, just floating, and then she was awake again, on the examining table. The bathrobe was draped over her, and there was a very real throbbing pain deep inside her. She sat up, dizzy. She was wearing a Kotex and belt, and there was some blood. After a couple of minutes, while specks danced in front of her eyes, Mrs. Benedict came back into the room.

"How do you feel?" she asked.

"Rocky," Lindy said. "Is my sister still here?"

"She's waiting. I told her you'd have to lie down for a while. My son's coming to take you home." Mrs. Benedict smiled, and Lindy felt a warmth of affection for her.

"Can my sister come in and keep me company?" Lindy asked.

"You go in and get dressed and lie down."

After a while Jody, looking big-eyed, came into the bedroom where Lindy was stretched out on the bottom bunk. Jody stood in the doorway. "Are you okay?" she asked.

"My innards hurt," Lindy said. "But otherwise okay. Don't you ever let yourself get into this kind of spot."

Jody came over and sat down on the edge of the bed, and they waited for Bob Benedict. It was over an hour before he showed up, and Lindy had had to change her Kotex twice in that time. Once Mrs. Benedict came in, without her white coat, and asked if she was bleeding much. Lindy told her, and she nodded and went out again.

Bob Benedict's car was a sleek new black Mercury. Lindy sat next to him and Jody in back, where she concentrated on the boils on the back of Bob's neck. Bob had thick curly black hair combed into a duck's ass, a sharp face and a rasping voice. He did not look anything like his mother. They were driving down Burnside when Lindy said, "Oh, Christ, I'm bleeding right through my dress."

"Don't worry about the seat covers," Bob said.

"I guess you're used to it," Lindy said. "But kind of take it easy on the bumps, huh?"

Jody automatically helped her sister up the steps to the apartment house, and Lindy said, "People gonna think I'm drunk again." Jody laughed but she did not feel like laughing. Lindy's face was getting white.

Inside the apartment Jody helped her sister undress. Her panties were thoroughly bloody. Jody went into the bathroom and ran the hot water, soaking a washrag and wringing it out while Lindy, naked, crowded in behind her and searched through the medicine cabinet for codeine pills. Finally she found them. "Boy, I'm gonna take about two grains of this stuff," she said. Back in the bedroom Jody washed the blood from her sister's body. Lindy strapped on another clean Kotex and went to bed.

"Shit, I feel terrible," she said.

"Maybe we should call a doctor," Jody said.

"She said I'd probably bleed for a while," Lindy said. "I wish I had some morphine."

"Let's call a doctor," Jody said. "We could call Doctor Shoenbrun."

"He wouldn't come all the way downtown," Lindy said. "Anyway, I don't want any goddamn doctor in here prying around. It's a felony, you dig?"

"Maybe he knows a doctor down here," Jody said.

Lindy patted the bed for Jody to sit beside her. "Honey, don't be scared. This happens to girls all the time. Just stay with me, and let that codeine get to work. I'll be okay." But even the strain of talking seemed to be too much for her, and she settled back into the pillow, her lips blue and her eyes abnormally large.

"I'm going to call a doctor," Jody said. She went into the living room and looked for the telephone. It was on a table beside the couch. She could not find a telephone book, so she called information and asked for the telephone number of a doctor. The operator put on her supervisor, and the supervisor asked Jody where she was. Jody told her and the supervisor gave her the number of St. Vincent's Hospital. After several agonizing minutes, Jody was finally talking to an intern. "I think my sister's bleeding to death," she said, and as soon as the words came out of her mouth she realized they were true. The intern asked her questions and she answered them, wondering to herself why she was not crying. In this scene she should be crying. She should be hysterical and running around. The intern on the telephone should be talking briskly and telling her what to do, but all he actually said was that Jody should bring Lindy in for an examination.

Jody hung up and got information again and asked for the telephone number of a cab company, and then called for a taxi. The dispatcher told her it would be twenty minutes. Jody hung up and went back into the bedroom.

"I called a doctor," she said. "Do you have any money?" But even as she spoke she could see that Lindy was already dead. She went out and sat in the living room, waiting for the taxi to come. When the driver came she told him, "My sister's dead. I don't know what to do."

The driver was a young man with a sprig of daphne tucked into his hat. When he heard Jody's words he backed out and closed the door. Jody went back in and sat down. She really did not know what to do. She did not want to cry. She felt totally empty of emotion. One smart thing would be to walk out of that place and pretend she had never been there, but that would be deserting Lindy. Finally, she got on the telephone again and called the police.

They asked her a lot of questions, and finally they took her down to the police station and turned her over to a woman in the Juvenile Division. The woman took her into a small room furnished with only two chairs and a desk.

The woman said, "Are you going to be all right?"

Jody said, "Yes. I'm okay."

"The officers tell me the girl who passed away is your sister."

"That's right," Jody said.

"Do you have any idea what happened to her?"

"No, I don't."

"How did you happen to be there in her apartment? Isn't this a school day for you?"

"Yes. I cut school. I do it all the time."

"Then, as you told the officers, you simply came down to visit your sister and found her dead."

"No. I came and found her sick. She asked me to call for a doctor and I tried to but nobody would come. Then she died, so I called the police."

The woman was silent for a few moments, looking at Jody. Jody looked at the floor. Then the woman said, "Jody, listen to me. Your sister was killed. Somebody tried to perform an abortion on her and killed her. If you know anything about this, it's your duty and obligation to your sister to tell us, so that we can catch these people and keep them from killing other young girls. Do you understand me?"

"Yes," Jody said.

"Do you know anything about who did this to her?"

"No," Jody said.

The woman waited a few moments and then said, "Did you love your sister? Were you girls close?"

"Yes," Jody said.

"Then why won't you tell me what I want to know?"

"Because I don't know anything to tell you," Jody said.

After another pause, the woman said, "All right. I'm sorry about all this. But we want to find out who these people are and stop them. Do you understand?"

"Yes," Jody said.

"I didn't mean to be harsh or cruel."

Jody looked up at the woman. "I know it," she said.

The woman stood up. "Someone will take you to your mother," she said. "I'll leave you alone now."

Jody did not look forward to seeing her mother.

THIRTEEN

JODY DID not want to go to the funeral, but she could not think of any way out of it. She could not tell her mother that both she and Lindy believed funerals were a crock, that once you died you were dead and that was that. She did not know how to talk to her mother at all. Eleanor was playing the role that Jody could not: for three days she wept and thrashed and cried out, inconsolable and half insane with grief, watched over day and night by her cousin Annie who was a registered nurse and looked like a shorter version of Elaine Benedict; then on the fourth day Eleanor calmed down, and the day after that they had the funeral at a small funeral parlor on Tacoma Street, not two blocks from where they lived.

In the private curtained-off room to the right of the casket, Jody sat in her new navy-blue suit, sweating and uncomfortable. She was on a couch with her mother and her mother's cousin. In an overstuffed chair next to the couch sat poor old Burt McKeegan, looking sixty, his face and neck red and covered with hundreds of little criss-crossing blood vessels. Burt had obviously not had anything to drink that morning, and his whole body would shake from time to time. Jody wondered if part of it wasn't grief. Burt had always been nice enough to them when he had been around, and Jody felt sorry for him. It must have cost him a great deal to attend this funeral.

The chair and the couch were angled so that members of the immediate family could sit in scrimmed seclusion and yet still see both the casket surrounded by flowers and the more public seating—what Jody thought of to herself as the audience. There were quite a few people out in the audience, a lot more than Jody had expected. Most of them were a hard-looking crew of young people that Jody guessed were Lindy's Broadway friends, all of them sitting stiffly, looking forward, as if they were under obligation to attend but not to show any emotion, and Jody immediately felt a kinship with them. Jody looked in vain for Quentin Corby. He had been telephoned right away by a distraught Eleanor, but she was only on the phone with him for a few minutes. He was nowhere in sight now, and hadn't been for the entire five days.

Patsy Wambaugh and her mother were also in the audience, although Mrs. Wambaugh had never met Lindy. She was probably there because Patsy had been invited and she wanted to keep her company. Patsy looked very serious, but every once in a while she would covertly look around at the somewhat loudly dressed young people from downtown. Jody wondered if Patsy could see her, and once when Patsy seemed to be looking in her direction Jody made a discreet wave, but got no response.

After a while the music stopped and a man dressed in black whom Jody had never seen in her life came out and started talking about Rosalind. Jody did not like his skinny pinched face, and she did not like what he was saying about her sister. According to him, Lindy had been a sweet little girl, loved by all who knew her, full of spirits and the love of God. The speech was obviously a standard one used for girls of a certain age, padded out with the few fragments of Lindy's real life that were clean and decent enough for inclusion.

On he droned about her sister, and Jody, who thought she had her emotions under control, suddenly found that her head was bursting and that she could not stand to listen to another word of this.

"What a bunch of shit!" she said in a voice that could be heard all over the room, and stood up and walked out the back door. The preacher didn't miss a beat. Jody walked down a long corridor lined with ferns on white wicker stands and out into the lobby, where a member of the staff dressed in a black suit stood with his hands together over his crotch looking bored. He pretended not to notice Jody as she walked past him and out into the delicious air.

PART TWO

FOURTEEN

WHEN SHE was thirty-five Jody McKeegan lived with an out-of-work actor in a large one-room house behind a row of old wooden garages in Hollywood, a couple of blocks north of the Boulevard. The actor's name was Glenn Duveen, and he spent most of his time lying on their queen-sized bed smoking marijuana and listening to tapes from his collection of old radio shows. Duveen had been around Hollywood long enough to know that there is nothing an actor can do after a certain point except wait for the telephone to ring. It was through Glenn Duveen that Jody met the producer who was finally after all these years to put her into a movie.

One winter evening they went to a small party at the house of a record producer, well up into the hills above Laurel Canyon. The place was noisy with people, mostly in their twenties or thirties and dressed in expensive-looking eccentric clothes. Lots of cocaine was being passed around, and after Jody had gotten a noseful she drifted outside to the garden, which was separated from the house by a high privet hedge with an iron gate in its middle. Jody went through the gate to a narrow lawn surrounded on three sides by trees and shrubbery. At the far end there was a white wrought-iron love seat, placed so that when Jody sat down she could see the lights of Los Angeles below, between two cuts of canyon. She felt rich and powerful, as she nearly always did when she had some cocaine in her. This was a nice place to sit. She could only barely hear the music from the house, and there weren't any rock superstars or groupies or any of the other scum who hung around musicians. The house was full of them, and Jody was eternally tired of their company, so that when a man came out of the shadows and asked her for a match she thought he was one of them, and said coldly, "I don't smoke."

The man looked out at the view for a moment, seeming to ignore Jody, and she glanced up at him. He was older than most of them, and better dressed.

Perhaps forty, with lightish hair and thick dark eyebrows. He seemed to be a nice enough person, so she relented and gave him her cigarette lighter, taking out her package of Salems and letting him light her cigarette.

"Thank you," he said to her, and the two of them puffed on their cigarettes silently and looked out at the view. It was one of those clear cold nights, when the wind from the east had cleared the smog and mist away, and the lights of the city shone brightly, even more brightly for Jody, full of cocaine and marijuana. After a few minutes the man went away. Some time later Jody went back into the house and found a pillow to sit on in the living room, while people eddied around and talked. A couple of young men tried to hit on her, but she simply turned away from them. When somebody passed her a half-gallon of red wine she kept it, and over the next hour or two drank most of it before falling asleep on the couch. She did not see the man from the garden again, although he saw her, when Duveen woke her up and tried to get her to stand on her feet. Jody did not feel like standing up. Harry told her later, "I was walking through to get my coat when I heard you yell, 'Pigfucker! Get your goddamn hands off me!' I laughed to myself and went on out. I remember thinking how serene and deep in thought you had looked out in the yard, and then to see you with your eyes all bugged out and your mouth twisted up in rage, well . . ."

To Jody it did not matter whether she got drunk and made a fool of herself or not. These were not movie people, and so they did not matter. Jody only had to keep a tight control over herself if there was a chance for her to get into the movies. She did not know at the time that Harry Lexington was a producer, or she would definitely have given him a light the first time he asked, and she would have made room for him on the iron love seat, and she would have turned her eyes on him in a concentrated effort to get him to need her. She had learned years ago that many men are utterly helpless when reasonably beautiful women actively try to seduce them.

As it was, Glenn Duveen finally got her up off the couch and half-carried her out and down the path to where his car was parked with the other cars, hugging the clifflike roadway. Jody lay across the hood while he unlocked the car, and then slipped to the ground, giggling, while he cursed and tried to get her into the passenger door.

"I have to pee-pee," she said. "Can't I just get behind the car and take a little pee-pee?" While she was laughing at him he managed to stuff her into the car, and they drove home in silence.

The next time Harry Lexington and Jody saw each other was at the Hamburger Hamlet in Westwood. Jody and Duveen had been to the movies, and were sitting with their backs to the windows, having hot apple pie with ice cream on it. They were both very stoned and eating quietly when Harry Lexington came in with a fairly well-known actress named Susanne Hardardt and set the room to murmuring. Jody looked up and recognized Harry as they walked past and were seated in the middle of the room, where Jody could still see their heads and shoulders.

"Who's that?" she asked.

"Susanne Hardardt," Glenn Duveen said. "You've seen her before."

"I mean him."

"I don't know. Boyfriend? Agent? Pimp?"

"He was at that party we went to."

"Which party?"

"At the you-know, record business."

But it turned out that Glenn Duveen did not know the man at all, and so Jody gave up. She was interested in the man now. He had spoken to her, and now she was seeing him with a well-known actress. That meant to Jody that he was possibly in the movie business, possibly important, and possibly approachable. In a few minutes she said, "Give me the roach," and went into the women's room, being sure to walk past Harry's table. Jody knew how to walk. She did not wave her ass around like an amateur but walked with her head high, as if nobody in the room existed except herself. On her way back she was careful not to look in Harry's direction as she passed his table, but profiled him instead, making sure that if he *was* looking, he was seeing her at her best. Then, back at the table finishing her coffee, she waited for Harry to turn and make eye-contact. It took only a few minutes, and when their eyes met, she looked at him expressionlessly for a long moment and then turned and whispered something to Glenn Duveen. That was enough. She knew by now not to go further.

Then, one afternoon a few weeks later, Jody was sitting alone in one of the semicircular booths in the back room at the Cock 'n Bull, drinking a glass of white wine and waiting for Glenn Duveen. He was across the street in the highrise building that housed the International Famous Agency, where he was a sort of client, left over from the old Ashley-Famous days. Duveen had gotten up that morning in short temper and begun grousing about the way Jody kept house, although she was a good housekeeper and when she had moved in with him a few months before, he had been living in chaos and grime; then he had gone down to the Boulevard as usual for morning coffee, the L.A. *Times* and *Daily Variety*. When he came back he was furious. According to the papers, men of his approximate age, size and style were being cast in pictures and television shows, and he was not. He had been patient long enough, and it was time to raise hell with his agent, or maybe even change agencies. The rest of the morning went badly, and then when the mail came there was nothing, not a residual, not a bill, nothing.

"I don't even exist!" Duveen yelled, and spent the next hour bathing and dressing for his showdown with IFA. The only thing he said to Jody was, "Listen, do I need a haircut?"

"You look all right to me," she said.

Jody did not wait for him in the IFA waiting room because she was through with agents. None of the good ones would represent her because she was too old and had no picture experience, and the crummy ones only wanted to fuck her.

Jody liked the atmosphere of the back room of the Cock 'n Bull in contrast to the noisy darkness of the bar, and on this particular afternoon no one else was in the room except a waitress who was putting setups on the tables in preparation for the dinner crowd, until Harry Lexington came in with two men who looked like agents, and took the big round corner booth. When he saw Jody he smiled at her and she smiled back, and after the waitress had taken the drink orders for the three men, Harry came over to Jody and said, "I don't know your name, but we seem to keep running into each other. I'm Harry Lexington." He held out his hand for Jody to shake, and she introduced herself. "I'd ask you to join us," Harry said, "except I'm sure you're waiting for somebody, and we're talking business, at least for a few minutes." He stood waiting for her to say something, and when she only smiled up at him patiently, he grinned, gave a mock salute and went back to his table. After their drinks came, he got up again and came back to her. "Listen," he asked, "are you an actress, by any chance?"

"Yes," Jody said.

When Duveen dragged in another hour later, Harry and his party were gone and the room was full of loudly talking prosperous and successful movie people, but she had Harry's business card in her pocket, the card which identified him as a genuine producer. Business cards are a dime a dozen, but Harry's telephone number was the same as Meador Studios, 464-0056. He might still be a phony but at least he was a legitimate phony, and he had asked Jody to call him next week during business hours. She did not mention any of this to Duveen, who was sullen and quiet for hours, and then, at home, full of dope and self-pity, began crying and told her that he had barely managed to stay on IFA's client list.

FIFTEEN

HARRY LEXINGTON did not expect anything to come of Jody's visit to his office, although he was certain that she would show up, and she did. That year he was officed on the third floor of the old Writers Building, just inside the Olive Street gate to the lot, and at this stage of his current production he wanted to save as much money as possible, so he did not have a secretary, just a suite of three rooms, with the entrance through the middle room and his office on the left. Later on, if the project went, a director would probably occupy the other office, and by then of course they would have a secretary.

At this point, Harry's project consisted of a screen treatment, an okay from the production head of the studio to go ahead to screenplay, and tentative approval to start preliminary casting and budgeting, with the assistance of the production department. The treatment was twelve pages of vague and overdramatic prose, describing an almost routine cops-and-robbers thriller, just barely a cut above movie-for-television material, but what the treatment said and what Harry intended his production unit to shoot were not necessarily the same thing. Harry was forty-six years old and had been in and around the movies all his adult life. He knew that getting financing required one approach, and making successful films another.

The writer of the screenplay, Wilbur Garton, was sitting at home in Marina del Rey, assembling a screenplay that Harry believed would put them all into the big money, if only they were terribly lucky and worked terribly hard. Wilbur was an excellent film writer, but one who had a tendency to write hard in first drafts and then chicken out later, softening characters, eliminating scenes that might cause controversy and toning down the language. This was a highly successful formula used by many film writers, and Harry did not mind at all. He intended to film Wilbur's first draft, with certain inflexions of his own.

There actually was a part in the film for a woman of about Jody's age and description and Harry actually was having a difficult time casting the part in his mind. The character was that of a waitress in a small roadside restaurant. The three principals have already robbed a bank and, after various adventures, think they are safely away from harm. They are sitting in Jody's restaurant breathing easy and having lunch when two cops come in for coffee, become suspicious and get the drop on the gang. All would have been lost if Jody hadn't taken a shotgun from under the counter and held it on the cops. Then she joins the gang and is with them until the end. The woman has to be tough, hard, beautiful, but capable of playing the fact that she is stuck in this out-of-the-way gas station, and capable of playing the sudden change of character that leads her to reach under the counter for the shotgun, without blowing credulity. The studio thought this was a weak place in the story, and so did Wilbur, but Harry secretly felt that it was one of the bustout moments which made the picture worth shooting. He certainly wished he could find somebody good enough to play the part but cheap enough to cast. To bring in a name actress for this role would be to give away his game-plan.

As for Jody, she certainly had the look. She was beautiful all right, but you got the feeling that her beauty was assumed rather than real, almost an act of will; and underlying it was an animality, a fierceness, an independence, that Harry wished he could get onto the screen. But he was too experienced to hope. People who were marvels of charisma off screen often turned out to be dull and nervous once the cameras started to roll. So Harry's mind was divided: first, he wanted, hoped that this girl could carry off the role. On the other hand he knew she wouldn't be able to act (or she would have some credits, a woman her age) and so what he wanted was to fuck her. He assumed that she knew this, and if she showed it was both to read for the part and to allow him to make a pass at her.

But Harry had never done anything like this before. He had always been strictly professional in his relationships with actors, not out of any special rectitude but because the people he knew who did use their professional status to get laid irritated and annoyed him. It was contemptible, really, to take advantage of the fact that there are hundreds of pretty girls in Hollywood for every acting job and that many of these girls have no money and very little intelligence and next to no talent. It took a special kind of arrogance to seduce these young people with no intention of offering them work.

So Harry did not like himself very much when, at ten o'clock on Monday morning, there was Jody McKeegan in his office, all dressed and beautiful and shiny with expectation. Oddly, he felt even worse when she did not look around his office with surprise and say, "Just us? Where are the casting people? Where is the director?"—which is what she might have said if she had had any real experience. But instead she sat opposite his desk and smiled at him with a heartbreakingly wise and wonderful grin and said, "I hope I'm not too late." He would have felt much better if she had gushed over his last picture and touched his hand and pretended to be shy.

"I only have a few pages of what you might call first draft screenplay," he said to her. He shuffled through his papers looking for the right scene. "Ah, here it is," he said. He described the character of Helen the waitress to her and Jody laughed.

"I've been a waitress, God knows, but I never took a shotgun to anybody, at least not yet." She slowly read the two pages he finally handed to her, and then looked up at him and said, "Do you want me to just read her lines?"

"I'll help you," he said. He wished the whole interview was over. This was the most unprofessional thing he had ever done in his life. He felt like a shit. "All right," he said, "just take it easy and read the lines just for the sound, don't worry about the sense."

Jody put the pages on the desk where she could see them and then put her hands on her lap, seeming to steady herself, and then what happened next Harry was never able to figure out. As he remembered it, she seemed first to get a little larger, just sitting there in the chair, and when she spoke the hairs on the back of his neck stiffened, not that the quality or tone of the voice was so different, but that it seemed to be the voice of a different person coming out of her. Harry was used to actors' ability to mimic other people's voices but this wasn't the same, yet he did not know why it was not the same. He kept telling himself furiously as Jody read and reread the scene that if she could act as well as she seemed to be acting, he would have known about her before.

"That will be fine, thank you," he said at last. His face felt flushed and he was very nervous. He did not know what to tell her. She had changed from one person to another right in front of him and he did not know whether it was acting ability or his own overreacting imagination, guiltily imputing great talent to her because he did not have the guts to grab her and throw her onto the couch.

"Thank you very much for the reading," Jody said and stood up. She held her hand out for him to shake.

He stood up and took her hand and said, "Don't you have any film?"

"No," she said.

"I think you ought to have a screen test," he said. "You seem pretty good."

"Thank you very much," she said.

"Have dinner with me," he blurted, and blushed.

SIXTEEN

THE CHATEAU Bercy was only a few blocks from Glenn Duveen's house, but remote and isolated from the shabby neighborhood it dominated. When she had been living with Duveen, Jody often passed the hotel's glass-and-wrought-iron entrance on her way to the big all-night Hughes Market on Highland. The hotel was built in the twenties in the type of architecture known then as Mizener Spanish: red tile roofs, moorish arches and creamy stucco walls. Jody had several times peeked in through the wrought-iron windows to the big living room, filled with massive wooden furniture, Persian rugs and a big dark grand piano over in one corner, hoping to see movie people, because this hotel was famous for the New York and British talent who used it as their home while they worked on pictures. It was not exactly the place she would have chosen for herself—the Beverly Hills Hotel was more to her liking—but when Harry Lexington asked her to visit him in his permanent suite on the eighth floor, she decided that if things progressed to the point where he asked her to live with him she would accept.

It was not a question of no longer loving Glenn Duveen because she had never loved him. She had been very fond of him and grateful to him, but these days he was going slowly to pieces waiting for jobs, and so to keep body and soul together he was dealing a little marijuana, and kept harping on the idea of Jody getting a job somewhere. Jody did not want to get a job. She felt she had worked enough in her life, and so when Harry Lexington seemed to be interested in her, even though she had up to now refused to go to bed with him, she began feeling herself gradually moving from Glenn to Harry. Glenn was terribly unstable, and Jody was sure that he would find himself in deep trouble if he didn't get an acting job soon.

It was really too bad about Glenn Duveen. When he had mustered out of the Marine Corps in 1961 he had gone to acting school in New York, gotten a couple of small off-Broadway roles and then come West to do a Playhouse 90 segment. After a couple of empty months he got four featured roles in pretty good movies. His price went up and he was taken on by Ashley-Famous, who immediately got him all the jobs he could handle as a guest star on dramatic television shows. For a while he was seen on everything, and both NBC and CBS were thinking about him for his own series. And then, for no reason that Glenn could fathom, no one wanted to hire him anymore. For a long time he lived on residuals, and one summer he even went out on the road in a musical, but he really didn't like that kind of work and wasn't very good at it, so he came back to Hollywood and the game of waiting played by all actors. He got jobs from time to time, but the parts were never big or even interesting, and now they were coming less and less. His face could get him onto every lot in town, and so he sold cheap lids to secretaries and production people, never making much money and often lying awake nights afraid that the police were going to break into his house and arrest him.

When Jody had moved in with him he had been full of bright plans and promises. A friend of his was going to direct a movie to be shot in Israel as soon as financing could be arranged, and there were parts for both Jody and Glenn, another friend was working on a musical, even another was deep into the rebirth of dramatic radio; but as she got used to Hollywood Jody began to realize that everyone in and around the business was busy on some dreamy project, and so her hope of getting into the movies through Glenn faded, and with it her affection for him. He was just another dead-end boyfriend.

Harry Lexington, on the other hand, was actually working on an actual movie with a budget and everything. He had read her for a part and promised her a screen test, although that was a long way off, and Jody was half-sure all he really wanted was to make love to her in his fancy suite at the Chateau Bercy. That was all right, too. Harry was neither young nor handsome and he didn't make any special effort to be outgoing, but there was a kind of warmth radiating from him that made her feel very good, and she imagined he would be very passionate in bed, like many quiet men.

But there was no plan. When it happened, it just happened. A fierce argument with Glenn ended with her calling a taxi and standing at the open doorway with her suitcases and potted plants around her feet, her lip swollen from where Glenn had slapped her. Glenn spent most of the time on the bed, waiting for the taxi, staring at the ceiling. Finally he said, "Where do you think you're going? Who the hell do you know?"

"I'll land on my feet all right," she said. "Don't worry about me."

When the taxi came, Glenn got up and with a deep sob tried to grasp her hands but she turned away from him and would not even let him help with the suitcases and plants. She called Harry from a telephone booth in a gas station on Vine with the taxi idling nearby.

"He threw me into the street," she said.

"Come to my place," Harry said quickly.

SEVENTEEN

THE FIRST night Jody was upset and kept telling Harry that she would move out the next day, while he called downstairs to have a bed put back into the room he had been using as an office. A drink of whiskey to calm her nerves and Jody was in bed by eleven. "Thank you," she said to Harry. He was standing in the doorway looking down at her, her hair spread out on the pillow, a shy and yet knowing smile on her lips. He knew he was being taken for a ride, in fact he admired the way she had waited until she was actually out on the street before calling him. It showed a certain amount of style. They would have an affair, and when the pressures of preproduction got too intense, he would find some way to get rid of her. Nicely, of course. There was no question now of casting her as Helen. Harry did not cast girlfriends. Too bad, because the more he saw her the more she fitted the role.

The next day Jody spent out by the pool, and when Harry got back from the lot he said, "Let's go out to dinner and talk." While Jody dressed they had a couple of drinks in the suite and then went to the Aware Inn in the Valley, where Jody had two more drinks before dinner and a little better than half a bottle of wine. She ate almost nothing. Harry was confident that by the time they got back to the hotel and had a couple of brandies she would finally be in the mood to go to bed with him, but in the car she was sullen and in the basement garage of the hotel she did not seem able to get out of the car without assistance. The Mexican-American garage attendant politely tried to take her hand to help her, but she muttered, "Back off," and let her chin fall to her chest. The attendant looked helplessly over the car at Harry, who winked and said, "Thank you, Orfeo," and came around the car while the attendant faded back into the shadows. Harry reached in and tugged gently at Jody's arm. His heart was sinking as he remembered the night at the record producer's house.

"Get your fucking lunch hooks off me," Jody said quite clearly. She struggled her way out of the car and leaned against it, grinning at Harry, her eyes bright. "I can walk, you asshole," she said. She began to move toward the elevator in a slow sinuous walk, turning to glance at Harry over her shoulder. He shrugged and followed. In the elevator she did not speak to him until, "Eighth floor, men's notions!" She cackled and put her hand on Harry's shoulder. "Come on, pal, let's hit the old sack!"

But they did not hit the old sack. Harry undressed her (over curses and protests) and put her to bed by herself. In a few minutes she was snoring, and Harry drank his brandy alone, watching *The Pride of the Yankees* on television. Oddly he felt very warm toward Jody now, even though she had thwarted his plans. It was all right. He was looking forward to the next morning, to find out how she reacted with a hangover, or if perhaps she didn't even get hangovers.

When Harry awakened, his own head a little muzzy, he could smell bacon. He got up and pulled on his pants and went into the kitchen. Jody, in Levi's and a man's dark-blue tee shirt, was at the sink washing and stripping scallions. She turned toward him and gave him a lovely shy smile.

"I was awful, wasn't I?" she said. "I thought I'd try to make up for it by making you a good breakfast. Then I'll pack my clothes and get out of here."

"Shut up," Harry said, and kissed her on the mouth. She responded just exactly as if they had spent the night making love: warm and affectionate but not passionate. It was an intimate kiss and it surprised Harry. Her breath was awful, but then so was his. After the kiss she said, "These onions will probably help," and they both had a laugh.

After a lovely omelette of crumbled bacon, jack cheese and scallions, Harry spent a hard day at the lot, fighting a losing battle. When he got home Jody was curled up on the couch in a shining mallard-green robe watching television. Good smells came from the kitchen. Harry took a hot shower and when he came out Jody had a drink for him, but none for herself. "I don't really drink very much," she said with a smile. For the first time since he had been living in the hotel, the table was set in his dining room, and he and Jody ate what was an actual domestic meal. Up until then Harry had always either eaten out or picked up something at a take-out stand. The Chateau Bercy had neither a dining room nor a bar.

Jody was a good cook, and throughout the dinner they talked about food, shopping, cooking and other domestic matters. Not that Jody was crowding him. She still spoke of getting a job and her own place, where she would invite Harry over for the most fantastic dinners of his life. "I sometimes like to spend the whole day cooking," she told him, "and then I'll go for weeks eating out of a paper bag. In New York when I was modeling we used to make our dates take us to dinner and then we'd stuff half the food into our purses and take it home. *Steak*. Never any bullshit food, just good meat."

"How long were you a model?" Harry asked.

"Oh Christ," she said. "That was a long time ago. Before I was married."

"You were married?"

But it was time to clean off the table, and Jody did not answer him. She was still dressed in the green robe, and as she walked rapidly back and forth from the kitchen, the belt came loose and Harry could see her pubic hair in brief tantalizing flashes. He realized with a thrill that he was supposed to see her pubic hair, she was telling him that at last they would make love. He got up from the table very self-consciously and went into the living room to wait for her.

"Would you like coffee?" she called to him from the kitchen.

While he was sipping his coffee and thinking about the future, the telephone rang, and he spent over an hour in a conversation with his executive producer that left his hands shaking and the telephone where he had been gripping it covered with droplets of sweat. Harry noticed for the hundredth time the blistering on the telephone handpiece caused by the acid sweat of countless hands. Jody had been fluttering back and forth, pointedly leaving him alone in the living room with his telephone call, but now he could not see or hear her. He no longer wanted to make love. His mind was again filled with the problems of the day, and all he really wanted was a good stiff drink. But this was the big night, this was the night of love. Harry stood in the middle of his living room. He felt sexless. She was probably in his bed, naked, waiting for him. Or perhaps she was asleep. He really did not want to go in there and find out.

Jody had one small lamp on beside the big double bed in Harry's bedroom. She was under the covers, the white bedspread making the skin of her face dark and sensual. Harry stood in the doorway, hoping she could not see his face well enough to guess his feelings.

"Come to bed and we'll sleep," she said.

Harry undressed self-consciously, holding in his stomach and thinking how foolish men look in their socks and shorts. He could not turn away from her or she would know his feelings, and so, holding in his stomach, he hopped around trying to get his socks off without falling over (a problem he never had when he was alone) and then finally dropping the shorts and kicking them into the closet.

She drew back the covers and moved over. "I got this side warm for you," she said. He slipped into the warmth and she pulled the covers up over him and moved in so that her head rested gently on his shoulder. He could feel his skin moist against hers, and he was in a near panic that things would turn out badly, but she said, "Turn out the light, please?" and as they lay in the darkness he soon heard her regular breathing. Now he could relax.

The next morning when he woke up she was out of bed and making breakfast, quite cheerful, and when he said good morning she smiled and kissed him just as if they were lovers.

"I'm sorry we didn't make love last night," he said.

"You were tired and upset."

"I'm not tired now."

So they went into the bedroom and let the breakfast get cold.

EIGHTEEN

HARRY HAD been to bed with a lot of women, and he genuinely liked to make love, but nothing quite like this had ever happened to him. It was not that she knew any special tricks, in fact, their lovemaking was dull from a technical standpoint. But what happened to Harry was that he stopped thinking after a while and just humped like an animal while Jody groaned and clenched him and came time after time. When it was over and Harry lay flattened on top of her, the echo of his own near howl of climax still in his ears, he wondered what the hell he had gotten himself into. He was gasping for air. His whole body was still trembling and he could think only in fragments.

He was used to being very much in control of his lovemaking, and now he was almost ready to cry. The only thing in his life that even vaguely compared with it was the time he had been walking in the hills above Hollywood by himself and decided to try a primal scream. He screamed, but as he did so he knew he was holding something back, and so he screamed again, louder and longer, and then something took hold of his heart, and tears started from his eyes, and he really screamed. The scream trailed off into sobs and his knees were so weak he had to sit down on the ground. He wept for a while, his mind empty, and then blew his nose, got up and continued his walk. That was a lot like it. But not as strong. It was as if he had never really made love before, as if it had all been masturbation up to now. They made love twice again that morning and he was late for an appointment. All day he thought to himself, "I've really got to make up my mind about her," but when he got back to the hotel that night they did not even stop to have a drink but went straight to bed.

Jody really enjoyed the honeymoon. It lasted nearly a month, and Harry was like a kid. He bought her things, he took her to Chasen's and Matteo's, but mostly they made love. He had not said anything more to her about a screen test or a part in the picture, but this was not the time for her to bring it up. She could tell from his eyes when they made love that he was overwhelmed, and that satisfied her. He was a sweet and considerate man and really very good in bed, much better than Glenn Duveen, and she had to admit that she loved him a little bit, although neither of them mentioned the word for the first three weeks.

Harry was the first to say it. He was lying on top of her in the middle of a lazy Saturday afternoon, his face was half buried in a pillow. "Goddamn, you bitch, I think I'm falling in love," he muttered.

"Go fuck yourself," Jody said, and she laughed, digging her fingernails into his back. "So am I, so what's the matter with that?"

He pulled back and looked into her eyes. "It means that I can't cast you in the picture, for one thing," he said.

"I don't give a damn," she said, and she meant it because she did not believe him.

"Oh my God I love you," he said, and they were off again on another episode. But now it had been declared, and their relationship changed. When he came home from the lot there was no rushing off to bed. They had drinks, would go out to dinner or she would cook, and then on most evenings he would work and she would watch television. They would make love every night before going to sleep and every morning before getting up, and some-times he would come home for lunch, but it was not quite the same, and Jody counted the honeymoon over when for three nights in a row they did not make love at all. That was good. Now they were talking about *their* apartment, *their* things, but not yet about their future, and that was good too. But soon it would be time for Harry to start casting the picture, and Jody had no intention of letting this opportunity get past. Even though they had fallen in love.

NINETEEN

HARRY'S EXECUTIVE producer was an ex-agent named Fats Dunnigan. It was just another of the bitter and frustrating pills that Harry had to swallow to get his project going, and he had hoped that Fats would have been satisfied with the title and the honors, and would leave Harry to make the film. But no. Apparently Fats had found plenty of time in his busy schedule to interfere with nearly every detail of the pre-production madness that was beginning to engulf Harry.

The telephone call that had so unmanned Harry around the time Jody first moved in concerned the hiring of a director. Harry had wanted to hire a young television director named Calvin Fishler, who like most television directors wanted very badly to get into features, and Harry was confident that he could keep Fishler under control once they got out on location. Harry liked Fishler's work. Given the terrible problems of making television inter-esting to look at—the bright lighting, the scenes that were essentially two or three people standing somewhere talking, the hasty casting and even hastier blocking—Fishler managed to do a good and sometimes even exciting job.

Harry had had lunch with Fishler and his agent at the Polo Lounge, and had liked them both—Fishler about 30, with fine long dark hair and deep-blue eyes, a young man with the bright likable personality a director needs to make everybody work for him; and the agent short, bearded, smiling and silent. Fishler had liked the script and had had some good ideas about locations and seemed eager to have the job, and they all but shook hands on it right then and there. But fucking Fats Dunnigan. Fishler was not going to get the job, and it was a damned shame.

Fats had a new protégé, a young British director named Victor Ramdass Singh whose only credit was a semi-documentary on life in Soho. Weeks before, Fats had called Harry enthusiastically. "We have a great opportunity to give our little feature some class," he said, and Harry's heart had sunk. He spent part of the afternoon in a tiny screening room, watching the bad photography and even worse cutting of *Soho Blues*, and then there was supposed to have been a dinner with Singh but it got canceled, and after a while Harry figured Fats had given up. But no. A meeting with Victor Ramdass Singh was in the cards, as soon as he came back from New York. Fats reminded Harry that *Soho Blues* had cost seventy thousand dollars and so far had managed to gross over 4 million dollars. "He knows what people want," Fats said. "He'll be a definite positive asset to the picture—that is, if you want to hire him." The fiction was that Harry was the boss and Fats merely contributed the benefit of his thinking.

As far as Harry was concerned, Victor Ramdass Singh was just another Nervous Camera director, who worked tirelessly to make the audience realize at every moment that the picture was indeed being directed. What made the picture a hit, Harry figured, was all the creepy sex. Victor Ramdass Singh definitely had a feel for creepy sex, but he was being touted in the press as inventive, exciting and avant-garde. Harry wondered how much of it had to do with the fact that Singh wore a turban.

Even before their meeting, Harry decided that probably the only way he could get rid of Singh would be to make Singh not want to do the picture. But that would not be easy. Fats would probably alter the picture to suit Singh, he would probably raise the salary ceiling that was presently in the budget, and, Harry realized with a smile, he would probably fire Harry if necessary. Harry could not threaten to quit, because Fats would call him an artistic type and the picture would be made, God knows what it would look like, and Harry would be out on his ass.

The two other major problems facing Harry were the script and the production staff. Fortunately, Fats stayed out of both areas, preferring to read one-page synopses of the script (prepared by Harry) and let the studio production department worry about the little people. But the author of the script was already having second thoughts about the toughness of his story and, without really finishing the first draft, had gone back and started rewriting early scenes. Harry did not want him to do this. He wanted a whole clean first draft so that he and the production manager, whoever they got, could start to work on the production board, and in order to get it, Harry had to slightly terrorize the writer by telephone.

Wilbur Garton lived in an apartment facing the ocean a few blocks north of the Marina del Rey breakwater, and in the background, throughout the conversation, Harry could hear the squeals and laughter of people playing volleyball on the beach. Wilbur Garton's defense for not finishing the draft was that he had to alter early events to conform to what he wanted to put into the climax. Harry said, "But we all agreed that we like what goes on in the first act. We all agreed that the cops get shot because they're in the way."

"I don't want my people shooting cops," Wilbur Garton said. Over the telephone his tenor voice sounded even higher, and Harry could tell he was very nervous from the way he kept laughing and saying, "Okay okay!"

"But Wilbur, we agreed on this. The cops don't mean anything to these characters; they've seen the cops—"

"Okay okay! Listen, the whole point is, I really have been having nightmares about killing Wally off; so I thought maybe if Wally didn't actually have any part in the actual shooting of anybody, then it'd be okay if he gets away in the end."

"You want him to get away too? You want everybody to get away? What's the story about?"

"Well, ha ha, about some desperate people who are pushed into stealing. They aren't bad people, ha ha . . ."

"No, they're not bad. I never said they were bad. But they'll be fucking terrible if you turn them into a bunch of Disney bandits, for Christ's sake. Have you forgotten everything you knew about drama? The characters have to be interesting exciting people, or nobody will come to the theater to watch them. You put a bunch of namby-pambys in there, who cares? Now for Christ's sake get off your fat ass and finish the first draft. You have exactly two weeks to run on your contract."

After a silence, punctuated by the now eerie sounds of vollyball players, Wilbur said, "I thought we agreed I was to have autonomy over the script, and now you're talking about canning me."

"I wouldn't fire you, goddamn it, but if we don't turn in the script I've been pitching, and turn it in goddamn quick, I'm going get fired myself, and then out you go behind me. I mean it."

But the funny part was, all through the conversation Harry was really thinking more about Jody than the script, and thinking about her took the edge away, made things seem more trivial somehow, as if it didn't really matter, all that really mattered was Jody. That was the nice thing about falling in love. After he hung up from a whipped and beaten Wilbur, Harry called Jody at the hotel and told her he loved her, and then while she was still on the telephone, a man tapped lightly on his door and opened it, peeking in, a hesitant smile on his broad flat face.

"I have to run, honey," Harry said to Jody.

LEW GARGOLIAN looked like an Indian but he wasn't. He was an Armenian from Fresno and had been sent to Harry by the production department to audition for the job of production manager. Harry dreaded this particular interview, although he was courteous to Gargolian and stood up, shook hands and offered him a drink.

"No thanks," Gargolian said. He sat down on the edge of his chair, his large hairy hands folded primly on his lap. Gargolian was wearing a bright-red orlon sweater and checked slacks, darkly shined loafers and bright-red socks, a style of dress Harry thought of as Technician Mod. The reason he dreaded the interview was not because of anything he had heard about Gargolian but because he had wanted to hire an independent PM, one who would answer to him rather than to the studio, and in order to do this he was going to have to interview every PM the studio threw at him, find something wrong with each of them, and then come up with a man whom Peebles, head of the production department, could not simply dismiss by snorting, "That thief? You have to be out of your mind!"

But it turned out to be a nice day after all. Gargolian was a quiet sensitive man who had spent most of his professional life working out of London, which was why Harry did not know him, and after only a few feeling-out questions about past productions, Harry found himself warming to Gargolian and wondering why he was a studio man instead of staying independent. At the end of the interview he called Peebles and asked him.

"Lew's having trouble with his family," Peebles said. "Teenage kids."

"I like him. Is he a thief?"

"Would I send you a thief? He was an AD for Charlie Winkelmann for five years. He directed a couple things too. You know, location in Tibet or some goddamn place, the director gets antsy and they fire him and the PM takes over."

"What were the pictures, do you happen to remember?" Harry asked. He was pleased with this information. In the first place, Gargolian had said nothing about taking over the direction of two movies, which could either be from lack of pride, or modesty, and Harry did not think he lacked pride. And it never hurt to have a man on the set who could direct, just in case. Of course production managers were not known for artful direction and had a tendency to watch the budget more carefully than the actors, but Harry had no intention of actually using him as a director. Peebles did not know the name of the movies, but he said, "Listen, I think one of them wasn't released, some tax problem or other, and the other one was a two-hour movie for television. Does it matter? Are you looking at him for director?"

"I like him," Harry said, making up his mind. "Can we start on our budget tomorrow morning?"

TWENTY

JODY HAD been frightened by the sudden unexpected telephone call from Harry, because it had come while she was in the middle of a terrible debate with herself, whether she should go down to Hollywood Boulevard and have a couple of drinks. She had been getting dressed and made up while she was debating, and so she knew how it would come out, but then Harry called for no other reason than to tell her he loved her. She very much did not want to disappoint him. But she was tense and out of sorts, with really nothing much to do, and she could envision how much fun it would be to sit in some nice dark sleazy bar and have a few drinks while she listened to music and watched the freaks.

She had been talking to Harry about taking acting lessons over at the Actor's Studio, but Harry had not been very responsive about it, and she knew she couldn't get into the Studio without some professional people speaking up for her. So there was just nothing to do. Harry did not have any marijuana around the apartment, or at least if he did she had not been able to find it. In fact the only thing she had found in the apartment at all was a small cellophane-wrapped package of some pornographic pictures, still sealed, which Jody had discovered under some papers in Harry's bottom desk drawer. So there was nothing to smoke, and Jody did not like to drink alone. She thought about calling Glenn Duveen but she did not want to see him. If he came over he would probably think Jody had moved in with Harry Lexington because he was richer and had a better place to live, which was not exactly true.

Finally, if she was to resist Hollywood Boulevard she simply had to have some weed, and so she called Duveen. His telephone had been disconnected. Jody was so angry she did not think until she was seated at the end barstool of the Rainbow Room that an actor whose telephone has been shut off is in deep trouble.

The freaks were not very entertaining today. The bartender was only about twenty-five, with a thick bland face and a tight haircut, the kind of man Jody thought of as a rapist. He was wearing a white shirt and a small dark bowtie, and paid no attention to her except to bring her bourbon and water. The only other customer was an old man in a blue suit, bent over his drink as if in silent prayer. The man had an old-fashioned grey hat, a folded newspaper and an old cigar box on the bar next to his drink, and Jody wanted to ask him what was in the box, just for something to talk about, but decided not to disturb the man. She got up and crossed the dark room to the jukebox, idling over her selections like a teenager. She would play a dollar's worth of music, have a couple of drinks, and wend her way homeward, getting there in time to have a nice hot bath before Harry got home. Harry never got home before six-thirty, so she had plenty of time. She would even have time to go over to the Hughes Market and shop for dinner. They could have spareribs, cooked a special way she learned from a man she had lived with in Florida years ago, with pineapple chunks and green onions. She wished she had some grass; food always tasted so much better.

The music thumped heavily out of the jukebox, far louder than natural in this empty barroom, and Jody went back to her seat, ready to ask the bartender to turn it down, but three scruffy-looking homosexuals came in and started making a lot of noise at the bar, playing liar's dice and pretending to be macho, and so Jody just sat and listened to them make fools of themselves, and drank. Pretty soon some more people came into the place, and Jody found herself in conversation with a former stuntman who knew Glenn Duveen, and they had a couple of drinks and wondered what had ever happened to Glenn, and then it was time to go. But Bobby the former stuntman said that he knew a place where Jody could probably score some pretty good weed, and so with a bottle of wine they bought at a little corner market, they got into Bobby's old car and drove around the dark streets of Hollywood looking for a house Bobby had been to a couple of times, but each time either drunk or fucked up. It turned out that Bobby was actually looking for some heroin, and Jody was drunk but not so drunk that she wanted to get into that kind of a scene, so at the next stop-sign she just opened the car door on her side and got out. "Later," she said, and walked away from the car. Bobby did not try to follow, but simply drove off as if it had been arranged that way.

It took her an hour to walk back to the hotel, and she was less than drunk but more than sober when she came into Harry's apartment at ten-thirty. Harry was sitting in his favorite chair. The television was off. The radio was off. The apartment was silent and Harry was not working. He was just sitting there, looking up at her from across the room. She went in to take a shower after saying, "Hi!" over her shoulder, and Harry came into the bathroom while she was letting the hot water sluice down her body.

"Where have you been?" he shouted over the sound of the water.

"None of your goddamn business!" she shouted back.

TWENTY-ONE

LUNCH WITH Victor Ramdass Singh finally took place, but not in the Polo Lounge of the Beverly Hills Hotel. Instead, Fats Dunnigan told Harry to meet them at a place called the Peach Pit, on Sunset, and when Harry came up the steps from the parking lot behind the restaurant he could see Fats with a man and a woman, sitting around an outside table with a big orange umbrella shading it. Harry had to smile to himself: the group he was joining looked almost too Hollywood to be real. Fats Dunnigan, a gigantic man, bald on top but with long dark greasy-looking hair down over his collar, bright shirt, leather pants; Victor Ramdass Singh, wearing a dirty-looking pink turban, leather jacket and no shirt; and a woman whose name Harry never really got straight who was obviously with Singh, blonde, big-toothed, bland and pleasant, dressed in a black full-length gown with tight sleeves and a deeply plunging neckline. Singh looked about twenty years old except in the eyes, and the woman seemed to be somewhere over thirty. Harry shook hands and sat down and Victor Ramdass Singh said, "I think I'm going to like you after all. You might even find that you like me." He laughed.

Already he sounds more like an actor than a director, Harry thought, but he smiled and said something pleasant to Dunnigan. The menus came and they all ordered salads (the Peach Pit was a health food restaurant), and after the waitress went away Harry said to Singh, "Well, have you had a chance to read the story?"

"Not completely," Singh said. "I've gone through it, of course." He laughed again, his teeth bright against his dark skin. He looked into Harry's eyes and said, smiling politely, "Is this your conception of an important motion picture?"

"I don't know about important," Harry said. He thought he had detected a gleam of intelligent amusement in Singh's eyes, as if he and Harry were sharing a joke, that perhaps both of them were putting Dunnigan on. But Harry knew better than to act on it. "I think it's a pretty good story."

Dunnigan said, "Victor sees it as an opportunity to show the American predilection for violence in a new light. Would you explain for Mr. Lexington, Victor?"

"I thought the story was just garbage," the woman said softly.

"Yes, my love," Singh said, and went on quickly, "Yes, America's predilection for violence, yes. I think it would be an excellent idea to show the essential emotionlessness of these characters as they rob and kill. They feel nothing, of course, except for each other."

Harry said, "You mean, they're all psychopaths?"

"A word. Merely a word. Let us say their violence is existential instead of emotional. But those are only more words. I think the heart of this story— what are you calling it?"

"'Shooting Spree' is the working title," Harry said, "but we're planning on changing it as soon as somebody comes up with a better one."

"At any rate, I think the heart of this story lies in the fact that these people do not differentiate between their acts. To them, going to the toilet, eating, making love, killing a bank teller, all have the same distant quality. It should be a film that strikes one emotional note repeatedly, up until they themselves are wounded and hurt and killed. Then, on an emotional upsurge, they cry out in anguish and even rage."

"Why not call it *The Killers?*" the woman said. Singh put his hand on top of hers and patted it.

"Please mind your own business," he said to her.

"I like what Victor's saying," Dunnigan said. "What do you think? Isn't that just about what we had in mind for this story?"

"Wilbur Garton should be here," Harry said. "After all, it's his story. In fact, I think Wilbur ought to be invited to come along on location."

"I don't like to have writers around," Singh said. "They cause so much trouble. You ask them to rewrite and they get terribly upset, yet the sole reason for having them along is so that they can rewrite. Don't you think so?"

Harry did think so, but he didn't admit it. He was beginning to realize that perhaps Fats Dunnigan was not the person who wanted to see this young man assigned to the picture, that Fats might be looking for a way out too. Harry said, "Who do you see in the major roles?"

Singh had very definite ideas about casting. He wanted to use British actors for the two leading men, and when Harry said something about accents, Singh said, "American accents are easy to imitate." Fats kept smiling cheerfully and eating his salad, but Harry was now certain that he was furious. Singh must have had very powerful friends somewhere, because Dunnigan was not a man to hide his emotions unless there was a very good reason for it. Here he was, wasting his time on a bullshit meeting, holding in his emotions, eating what he probably considered to be rabbit food, and Harry began to suspect that maybe Dunnigan was under even more pressure than himself. Harry smiled and stuffed a large forkful of shredded cabbage into his mouth.

It turned out that Singh had his own British camera crew, and wanted to cut the film in London. "What would be the point of staying in Southern California for a year or so, when I can be where I am happiest?" he asked the table at large, and when lunch was over and they all stood up and shook hands with each other, Harry made sure he walked down to the parking lot with Dunnigan. Standing beside Dunnigan's big maroon Mercedes, Harry said in a matter-of-fact voice, "Fats, are you kidding?"

Dunnigan looked sour and said, "I think he's a very talented young man." He started to open the door to his car, but stopped and looked off into the distance. "I don't know," he said.

Harry knew better than to mention the pressure, but Dunnigan seemed to be waiting for him to say something. "He's going to be damned expensive," Harry said finally.

The next morning, while he and Jody were still making love, Harry got a telephone call from Dunnigan's secretary, telling him to meet Fats at Karl Meador's office at ten sharp. "All right," Harry said.

Karl Meador was the head of the studio and the son of the man who had founded it forty years before. Max, the father, had been a flamboyant tyrannical near-genius who had helped to create the Hollywood film industry. His son Karl was a graduate of Dartmouth, a bachelor and had the coldest eyes Harry had ever seen. Meador's office was always kept dark and cold and was not much larger than Harry's.

"I understand you gentlemen are having trouble finding a director for your project, is that true?" he said to Harry and Dunnigan, at a few minutes after ten.

Dunnigan was sitting beside Harry on the couch across the room from Meador's desk. He smiled with all the charm of a top agent and said, "We're not really experiencing any actual difficulties. In fact we had lunch yesterday with Victor Singh, and I might be wrong but I think the meeting was productive, don't you?" He was now looking at Harry, obviously throwing the ball to him.

Harry sat quietly and did not speak. Dunnigan was the executive producer; let him do the talking.

Karl Meador, behind his desk, was wearing a dark-blue suit with thin red stripes, pale-blue shirt with french cuffs and a black silk necktie. To Harry he looked like a stock broker. His cold eyes were half-hidden behind tinted rimless glasses, and his thin feminine mouth was slightly pursed as he waited for one or the other of them to speak. Finally Dunnigan broke down.

"I feel we had a most productive meeting," he said. "And I for one am ready to offer the man a contract."

Meador looked at Harry. "Does Singh meet with your approval?"

"No," Harry said. His palms were sweating and his crotch felt hot and damp. "I think it would be a mistake to hire Singh for this particular project, although I'd be interested in talking to him again about something more down his particular alley."

"What do you mean by that?" Meador asked.

"Bluntly," Harry said, "the man wants to turn our project into an anti-American picture. He wants to use it as a vehicle for some half-baked philosophical notions about American violence, which in my opinion he fails to understand. Also, he wants to use British actors, technicians, camera crew, and he wants to cut the picture in England."

"That's out of the question," Meador said. "Fats, how much were we going to offer him?"

"Fifty thousand with fringes," Dunnigan said, and added, "He got zip for that feature he did in England."

"For that kind of money he could work here and work with our people," Meador said. To Harry: "Did you have any particular candidate in mind?"

For one small moment Harry thought it was possible that he would get the director of his choice. "Calvin Fishler," he said.

"What's he done?"

"Well, a lot of television work . . ."

"Any features?"

"No, but . . ."

"I don't know his work," Meador said, and that was it for Calvin Fishler. Meador told them he would mull over the problem on the weekend and see if he couldn't come up with somebody everyone would be happy with, and they were dismissed. Harry walked Dunnigan down the long corridor to his office.

"Well, we got rid of the wog," Fats said. "Sorry you couldn't get that kid on the picture, but he's not the guy to handle the caliber of stars we are going to have to hire."

"I guess not," Harry said.

Lew Gargolian, with a worried look on his face, was waiting for them in Dunnigan's secretary's office. He was wondering if there was any way, at this point, to pin down the number and type of cars that were going to be wrecked in the course of the picture. "The way it looks he's wrecking about twelve cars," Gargolian said, meaning the script-writer. "In two places he specifies new Cadillacs."

"I'm sure you fellows can handle it without my assistance," Dunnigan said, and disappeared into his private office. Harry and Gargolian went over to the old Writers Building and spent the rest of the morning happily fighting over how many cars, and what type, were going to have to be destroyed in order to make this an authentic-looking and exciting major motion picture. Gargolian felt it could probably be done with six, and fake the rest. Harry wanted all twelve, if they could find some way to afford it. An honest difference of opinion.

TWENTY-TWO

IT WAS one of those horrible weekends. Jody had run into an old acquaintance from New York in Beverly Hills, a fashion photographer who was on the Coast trying to arrange financing for what he called "a tryptich of films" about the life of Buddha, which he wanted to shoot in India and Southeast Asia. He was full of enthusiasm and took Jody to the Beverly Wilshire for coffee, and from him Jody got the name and telephone number of a man who could sell her some marijuana. The fashion photographer was so full of himself that he did not ask Jody anything beyond, "What brings you to the Coast?" which she answered by asking him if he knew where she could get some dope.

When Harry got home that night, his undershirt soaked in the acid sweat of anxiety, she begged, cajoled and finally convinced him that he needed some good old drugs, and with a shrug he said, "I'm going to take a long hot bath. If you can buy something, go ahead."

"I need money," Jody said. He had given her money before, but this was the first time she had asked for any.

"Look in my wallet," he called out from the bathroom. The wallet was stuffed with money. Jody took three fifty dollar bills, planning to put back what she did not have to spend. After all, it was just possible that the dealer wouldn't deal anything under half a pound.

Jody really fell into it. The dealer knew a lot of the same people Jody knew from New York, and aside from having some of the best Asian marijuana, which was very hard to find in Southern California, he also had some really fine cocaine, and so Jody spent 130 dollars on drugs and the rest on cabfare. At the dealer's house in Laurel Canyon she snorted two lines of cocaine and smoked some of the weed, and so by the time she got back to the Chateau Bercy she was mellow, holding her chin in the air and smiling mysteriously.

Harry was out of the bathtub, wearing an old robe and halfway through his second fairly strong drink of Scotch. "I don't see how you can drink that stuff," she told him. "Do you have any papers?"

"No," he said. She could tell he was a little nervous about the marijuana because he became sarcastic: "I quit rolling my own when I came in off the range."

"Cute," she said. "Do you have a pipe? I could run down to the market and buy some papers, I guess."

"What about dinner?" Harry wanted to know. But dinner was very late that night, and came to the door in white paper cartons, delivered by a young Chinese. By the time it arrived Harry was in a fierce temper and Jody was stoned beyond her own recollections. Harry did not seem able to get high. First he smoked half a joint with Jody, and felt nothing beyond a tightening at his temples and an emptiness in the pit of his stomach, which could have been caused by his lack of dinner. He had another strong Scotch, and then Jody got out the cocaine. At first he was angry at her for spending so much of his money, but secretly he had always wanted to try cocaine, and so when she pulverized a small heap of the white powder on her hand-mirror and arranged it into lines with the tip of her knifeblade, he watched with interest and stopped making his bitching remarks.

Jody made four lines and then rolled up a dollar bill. She showed Harry how to stick the bill into his nose and sniff the powder, one line per nostril, and then did it herself. Harry tasted medicine in the back of his throat and felt his nose go cold and then numb. He felt nothing else.

"Are you sure this is cocaine?" he asked her. "They sell a lot of things *as* cocaine . . ."

"It's coke," she said. "Can't you get off?" She stood up. "Play some music, I want to boogie," she said.

When the Chinese food came and they smoked another joint between them, this one laced with coke, and Harry had a couple more drinks and felt pretty good. "That's all I needed," he said cheerfully. "I was hungry, that's all. Now I want to fuck you."

"You're going to have to do it right here," Jody said. "I can't move." They were on the living room couch, the television set flickering, the radio playing old-fashioned music. Harry felt mellow and distant, and he really did want to fuck her, only he didn't have the strength to get up. Thinking about fucking her was almost as good, he thought, and giggled. The stuff was affecting him after all. He had smoked marijuana before, but it had never really done anything for him. Perhaps it was the cocaine.

He awakened at near dawn, still on the couch in his bathrobe. The coffee table beside him was a litter of dirty plates and paper cartons, wadded napkins and glasses smelling horribly of whiskey. But he had no hangover, just a certain tiredness and a bad taste in his mouth. He got up and went to the bathroom, pissed and brushed his teeth and went to bed. Jody stirred when he got in beside her, and in minutes they were deep into making love. Afterward they lay back and Jody said, "You know, let's be evil. Let's just get into it. You want to?"

"Anything," he said. He had been about to start thinking about work. This would be a way not to. They smoked a couple of laced joints and went back to bed and made love again, and then Jody rolled up a few joints for them to take along, and they went off to breakfast at Schwab's. After breakfast they planned to go to some secluded beach and get even higher, but it was a bright clear sunny Saturday, and Harry said, "The beaches'll be murder. Let's go back to the hotel."

They had lunch delivered from Greenblatt's delicatessen, and just for the hell of it, a bottle of champagne, and spent the afternoon alternately dozing and watching old movies and cartoons on television. If the marijuana made Harry sleepy, the cocaine brought him fully awake and gave him a delicious sense of authority and power: there certainly weren't going to be any more problems on the picture because Harry knew now that all he really had to do was sniff a little coke and resume the reins of power. Indeed, as he watched the images on television he carried on in his mind several disjointed but seemingly clear fantasies about how to solve the major problems, which after a while faded out of his imagination and left him irritated and apprehensive. Jody was asleep on the couch, the late afternoon sunlight across her face, her mouth open as she snored lightly. He wanted to throw a glass of water onto her face and wake her up. It would be funny and she deserved it, for snoring. He actually got up and went into the kitchen for the water, but drank it instead, realizing that he was terribly thirsty. That was probably the champagne, he thought.

When Jody woke up it was dark again, and Harry was watching *The Sundowners* and crying silently, the tears running unchecked down his face. She watched him for a while and then said, "You're crying."

"Movies make me cry," he said. Jody got up and went in to take a shower.

Later they had a bitter argument about where to have dinner. Jody wanted to dress up and go to Chasen's and flash herself. Harry wanted to walk down to Musso & Franks, the image in his mind of the two of them strolling down the street arm-in-arm, stoned to the eyes, and then go into the quiet old wood-paneled room and have a lot of really rich and satisfying Italian food. The thing was, they wouldn't have to go to any trouble. But Jody was god-damned if she was going to put on clothes just to walk down to some joint on the Boulevard. Harry tried to explain to her that Musso & Franks was not some joint on the Boulevard, but a very high-class restaurant that had been a hang-out for Hollywood people since the Twenties. He even hinted that there might be some stars there, but Jody laughed at him. "Call the fucking Chinaman," she said. "And come here."

They went to bed and made love for a very long time, but neither of them seemed to have any desire to come, and so after it got actually boring, Harry pulled out and they lay together looking at the ceiling, until the doorbell buzzed with the Chinese food.

It was not possible to sleep that night. In fact the only thing Harry wanted to do was get deeper into the cocaine. He wasn't interested in the marijuana. It was all right for something to get high, but the cocaine was different. Now that he was into it, he could see how people could become addicted; not so much what it did to you, but everything was all right when you were coked. Harry could feel rivers of power flowing from his fingertips, and with utter clarity he realized at last, aided by the cocaine, why he was in the movie business, why he put up with the shit-eating, the back-biting, the sleepless emasculate nights, the awful, stomach-walloping changes in plan, the day-to-day crises: it was for this sense of power, this feeling of controlling destinies, not just his own but everybody's. This feeling he had now. Jody was there, he could exercise his power on her. He could talk to her, fuck her, cut her to pieces. He could order her out of his apartment. He could make her beg to stay. Ah, he thought, coming out of this odd reveries, some day I'm going to have to do just that, and the sense of power faded and Harry found that he was grinding his teeth. I need to brush my teeth, he thought.

He began to learn something of the other side of cocaine when he caught himself throwing his toothbrush into the shower stall in a fit of rage because the toothpaste had fallen off into the sink.

At around four in the morning Jody snapped off the television set and said, "I'm hungry again. Let's go to a Denny's or something."

"Oh God," Harry said. "I just got ripped again. I don't think I can drive."

"You can drive. Snort a little more lady."

So that was how it was done.

They slept until nearly two on Sunday afternoon. Jody talked about going out by the pool and spending the afternoon getting some sun, but by the time they had sent for breakfast, gotten stoned, made love and taken their baths, the idea was no longer charming, and the sun had almost gone down. For several hours Harry was under the impression that it was Saturday, and when "The FBI" came on the television Harry took hold of his head and rocked back and forth. "Jesus H. Christ," he said, "what the fuck kind of life is this?"

Jody did not take her eyes off the set. "I lived like this for a couple of years once," she said. "In New York. It's easy."

"You mean stoned every day and every night? What the hell's the point?"

Her eyes flicked over toward him, and then back to the screen. "My boyfriend was on skag," she said. "His mother used to send him money, and we'd go cash the check, score, and head back to the room. That went on for a couple of years."

Harry knew skag was heroin but he could not believe that Jody had been a heroin user. "What were you doing all that time?" he asked her. She just laughed drily and kept watching television. Harry said, "No, wait, I want to talk," and went over and shut off the set. Jody looked faintly irritated for a moment but then smiled and came over to Harry's side of the couch.

"What do you want to talk about?"

"Heroin," he said. "Did you actually use it?"

"Don't be a pest, I'm watching the show."

"No, goddamn it, I want to talk. You'll either talk to me or get your ass out of my apartment." He had not realized until he opened his mouth just how angry he was, but now, on his feet looking down at her, he could feel himself trembling with a rage that was almost joyous. "Did you hear me?" he said in his most cutting voice.

"Oh, you'll get over it," she said.

"Fucking bitch," he said, and went into the kitchen. He could not understand why he did not hit her. She had disobeyed him. This was his apartment and she should have either gotten out or cooperated with him. Instead she was sitting in there watching television. It occurred to him that he was helpless. Obviously he could not physically throw her out. He did not even want to throw her out. All he wanted was for her to do what he said. That was not too much to ask. But she would not do it.

"Hey," he said to her.

She looked up at him. "I'm sorry," she said. "The coke makes me into a bitch." She got up and turned off the television and came to him, putting her arms around his waist and her cheek against his chest. He could smell her hair and it made him dizzy with love. "I'm sorry, sweet baby," she said, and took him to bed. They made love for half an hour, their bodies slippery with cold sweat. Finally they just stopped moving, and as Harry lay on top of her he wondered if he could get to sleep without some more dope. But tomorrow was Monday and he would have to get back into it, so it would be better not to take any more. Not now. Not until next weekend in fact; but next weekend seemed years away. No more coke until next weekend. No more marijuana. And he should really quit drinking too.

But he felt a tickle of panic in his chest at the thought that he would not be able to sleep that night.

After what seemed hours, Jody asleep at his side, Harry got out of bed, went into the living room and, sitting in semi-darkness, smoked the last of the marijuana. Then he went to the window overlooking the city and saw that there was a nearly full moon in the western sky. He watched the moon for a while and then went to bed.

TWENTY-THREE

ON MONDAY morning things began to pop. Harry got to his office at a little before ten, still muzzy from the weekend, and found that a director had been picked, "subject to his approval, of course," and that Harry, the director, Lew Gargolian and the as-yet-unpicked cameraman were scheduled to leave for a location survey at the end of the week.

Harry had a secretary now, Alice Wanderove, whose long teeth and thin lips irritated him almost enough for him to complain to the studio, but Lew had recommended her highly as efficient beyond the requirements of the job, and so Harry swallowed his irritation (which, he realized, might be another side effect of his drug weekend anyway) and settled in to work on the budget with Lew.

The new director showed up for his appointment with Harry at a little after twelve, and they crossed the street to the Cinema Grille on Olive for a quick lunch. The director's name was Jack Meltzer. Harry had met him a couple of times through the years, once at the kiosk out in front of the commissary at Universal, where they were introduced by Martin Abramowitz, Jack Meltzer's agent, and the other time in the lobby of the Director's Guild, where the two men had arrived with separate parties to watch a screening of *Guess Who's Coming to Dinner*. Jack Meltzer had directed at least thirty pictures, Harry knew, and was regarded around the industry as a man who could shoot a fast clean movie, come in on budget, and most of all, as a man who had very little personal stake (ego involvement was how Fats put it) in the shape or consistency of his pictures. Jack was hired by producers who wanted to retain control over the shooting, and by stars whose pictures were less works of art and more personal vehicles.

Lunch was pleasant. Jack was not much older than Harry, and both men had been in the business most of their lives. They knew many people in common and more importantly, at least from Harry's viewpoint, they shared an attitude toward the industry, an attitude which Harry once summed up by saying, "Hollywood keeps changing but Hollywood remains the same." The remark had been made to a young woman who had been excited by the sudden outbreak of long hair and paisley fashions among studio executives some years ago. Over their hamburgers, Harry and Jack talked and laughed over the men who had come and gone the past few years—corporate geniuses sent from the East by conglomerates, boy-wonders who sprang from the agencies to take control, descendants of moguls, like Karl Meador, who had happened to suggest Jack Meltzer for this particular job.

Jack was a stocky man with a tanned lumpy face and small sharp blue eyes. He had a pronounced overbite which he knew how to use to make himself look stupid, but Harry was not fooled and neither was anybody else who had ever worked with Jack. Now he sat across from Harry in the tiny crowded restaurant holding his bottle of beer and smiling slightly so that his two front teeth showed their tips.

"I read the script last night," he told Harry. "It's not bad. Who do you have in mind, anybody?"

Harry very carefully kept the surprise off his face, and kept himself from asking Jack whether he meant the whole script or just the treatment. As far as Harry knew, the whole script had not yet been turned in. But it might have been, even over the weekend. It might have been turned in to Fats, which meant that something funny was going on. "I thought we'd wait for the director to cast," Harry said. "Nobody's tied to the project yet at all."

As they discussed the screenplay and possible actor choices Harry could tell that Jack had read the full version, and so he guessed that the first draft had indeed been turned in to Fats, probably over the weekend or perhaps even on Friday. It was even possible that Fats had gone down to Marina del Rey and gotten it from the writer. Harry wondered if Jack Meltzer knew that he had not himself yet read the full first draft, but there was no telling from anything Jack said. He was too careful for that.

And Karl Meador's selection of Jack. Was this all part of a plan to hand control of the picture over to Fats Dunnigan, was it a vote of approval for Harry or was it a simple downgrading of the project by Karl Meador after Meador himself read the script? Harry did not know. He knew only that Jack was not a first-class director and therefore had none of the problems attaching to a first-class director—staying up nights rewriting the script on location, hiring his own pet crew, etc.—and so either the picture was heading down or up. Harry smiled to himself.

"Did Karl talk any casting to you?" he asked Jack.

"I haven't talked to him. Fats brought out the script yesterday afternoon, all in a sweat over it. I guess he'd been out to Karl's place that morning. I don't really know." Jack looked at Harry steadily for a moment, drank a sip of beer and said, "Have you read it yet?"

"Nope," Harry said.

Harry shook hands with Jack and promised to get back to him, and walked onto the lot by himself, and just as he was passing the blue-uniformed gate guard, throwing him a mock salute, he thought of yet a fourth possibility—what if Karl Meador had decided to hire a big star for the picture?

That would explain Fats's behavior, Jack's presence, and maybe a couple of other things. Harry turned abruptly away from the old Writer's Building and headed for the Executive Building.

He waited in the office of the secretary to Karl Meador for only twenty minutes when Karl came in from lunch, his face ruddy with health and his hair wet after a shower. "Ah," he said to Harry, shaking his hand, "just the man I wanted to see."

Inside Karl's office they talked about tennis for a while, and then Karl said, "How do you like my idea?"

"What idea?" Harry said. He was sitting down, but he wished he was standing in front of Meador's desk, his hands behind his back, in the parade rest position. It would be more honest.

"Jack Meltzer," he said. "You people were having director troubles, so I assumed you might have use for a trouble director." He laughed. "A trouble-*free* director."

Harry laughed. "I like Jack," he said. "I've known him slightly for years. We just had lunch."

"Fine," Karl said. "Then I can leave the rest of it up to you and Fats?"

Harry hesitated, wanting to ask some questions; but this was not the time. "Of course," he said. Then, because he had to know, "How did you like the script?"

"I never read scripts," Karl said. He seemed no longer interested in the interview. Harry got out of there.

When he got back to his office he found a Xerox copy of the screenplay on top of his desk. Alice Wanderove told him Fats had brought it in and left it.

TWENTY-FOUR

JUST BEFORE he left on the location survey that would take him to several southeastern states, hoping to find a place that did not look like California, Harry had a long talk with Jody about casting. It had been a perfect evening so far, with dressing up and dinner at Matteo's, a late swim in the hotel's deserted pool and then a session of lovemaking that left both of them calm and clear-headed.

They were in bed, the only light coming dimly from the hallway leading to the living room. It was warm and slightly humid, so they were on top of the sheets, both still naked, when Harry began:

"Look this is not going to be an easy thing to talk about," he said.

"What isn't?"

"Well, let me get into it. Please just listen to me. Casting."

"I thought so," she said, and sat up so that her face was in shadow. "You listen," she said, in her sweetest calmest voice. "You don't have to cast me in your picture. You know that. I love you. Sure, I started going out with you because I was fascinated, you know. But now we love each other. It's all different. I know. Now you have to cast and you don't know how to tell me. Okay. I understand. I love you."

She kissed him deeply and then sat back, her face once again in shadow. She was sitting with her feet tucked under her legs, and he put a hand on her thigh.

"No," he said. "You got half of it. I knew we should have talked about this before. No, I'm going to do with you what I would do with anybody else. The reason I first got interested in you is that you look like this character Helen. I've been thinking of the character as looking like you. See, to me this character is the keystone to the whole plot—well, that's not something to talk about now—anyhow, you *are* the character. I don't mean that she acts like you—she *is* you, in a different life. Does that make any sense?"

"Sure," Jody said. "You want somebody *like* me."

"Almost. I want an *actress* like you. You don't know. You don't understand the pressures I'm under and I won't go into it now or I'll start crying, but the thing you have to understand is that even you, even the person I love most in the whole world, even you, I can't just stick in the picture. I can't walk up to Fats Dunnigan and say, 'Listen, Fats, I want to cast my girlfriend as Helen.' He'd laugh me out of his office. He'd think I just wanted somebody to screw on location, or that you had me pussywhipped into casting you. But I'd never get away with it."

Harry sighed, and Jody bent forward to kiss him on the end of his nose. "Don't worry," she said. "I told you. It's all different now."

"It is and it isn't," he said. "I still don't know if you can act or not. I don't think you know either. I've purposely kept from fucking around with this thing because I knew it was coming up and I wanted to do it right, so what we have to do, see, is put you in front of the director as a *candidate* for the part. Do you understand me? You'll be one of several girls selected for the part. You'll read for the director, along with the rest of the girls . . ."

"Cattle call?" Jody asked. "I won't go on any goddamn cattle call."

"No, for Christ's sake. You'll *read* for the part."

"It still sounds like a cattle call."

"Well, you can't expect to be hired without auditioning, can you?"

"Frankly, I don't expect to be hired at all. If you have to go through this rigamarole just to let me off the hook, go ahead. But you don't have to for my sake. You aren't going to hurt my feelings. Shit. You *can't* hurt my feelings. You don't know much about me, but I can tell you this right now, you can't hurt my feelings. That's all over with in my life."

"Oh baby," he said, and began kissing her. After a while, though, he could sense that she wanted to make love less and to talk more, so he pulled back, wanting to look into her eyes. But her face was in shadow again. "I know you've been hurt in your life, and I don't want to hurt you again. It's just that this is a terrible situation. Producers should never date actresses."

"I thought I wasn't an actress," she said.

So it was settled that when he came back from the location survey, she would have her audition in front of the director. Meanwhile, she was alone in his apartment on the eighth floor of the Chateau Bercy for two weeks.

TWENTY-FIVE

IT WAS not an easy time for her. All her life Jody had floated from job to job, man to man, not because she was a drifter but because she couldn't seem to keep things going without blowing the lid off. She knew that all she would have to do would be to sit still, maybe read, go to the movies, watch television and lay back, and he would return and she would have her audition. She would be competing with other women for the role, and if she was the best, she would get it. It wouldn't be up to Harry, she was now certain. The director, a man she had never heard of, would make the decision.

There would be no drugs, because Harry had said that he didn't want anymore for himself and hoped she wouldn't have any around the apartment. "Maybe after the movie," he had said to her. "But not now. They fuck up your brains and judgment." So she wanted to stay clean too, if only for Harry.

But she knew from experience with herself that sometimes the pressure just got too great and she would have to explode some way; maybe get drunk or do some running around. It was just that the boredom got so intense.

The first day was fine. She got up early, unable to sleep, and on impulse walked down to the Boulevard and had her morning coffee in a little hole-in-the-wall where the only other customer was the fry cook, sitting on the end stool in fresh whites, a thick sloppy-looking man with rolls of fat under his tight tee shirt and black greasy hair hanging out from under his white cap. He was bent over his morning newspaper and breakfast and gave her only a glance. Jody had her coffee and chatted with the tired-looking waitress, and then left a fifty-cent tip on a twenty-cent check. Jody had been a waitress for a while and she always left big tips when she could. She could certainly remember the depressed irritated feeling you got from giving customers good service and getting nothing for your trouble but a bent dime and a dirty wink. She remembered men who would pinch her on the ass in lieu of tip and others who thought that if they tipped ten percent they were entitled to get your address and telephone number. She had never worked in a place like this though. Jody's waitress jobs had always included costumes, panty hose and high heels.

After her coffee she walked along Hollywood to Vine, and then on impulse down Vine to the ABC Studios where she hoped they would be shooting a game show and she could get in and watch, but the building was quiet so she walked back up toward the Boulevard, already getting a little hot. She passed the Hollywood Public Library, stopped and decided maybe she should get some books on acting and refresh her memory. Then she laughed, thinking that the Hollywood branch library's copy of *My Life in Art* was probably pretty dog-eared by now.

After looking at some blouses in the Broadway Hale store on the corner and having the clerk, a little man with a mustache and long sideburns, offer to meet her that night, Jody lolled down the shady side of the Boulevard among the morning drunks, the sailors, the peroxided, the red-faced beefy Hell's Angel rejects and the rest of the Times Square-style riffraff, stopping for an orange juice, thinking about a morning movie and rejecting the idea because she did not want to come blinking out into the mid-afternoon heat, spending an hour in a record store dreaming of buying phonograph equipment and a dozen records, then thinking about Glenn Duveen, whose record collection she missed almost as much as she missed Glenn (and she had to admit that once in a while she missed him) and then on impulse crossing the street and heading up toward his house. His telephone had been disconnected last time she had tried to call him. Maybe he was sitting home on his bed, stoned, waiting for somebody to come and give him a job. But when she got there the man who owned the garages out in front of Glenn's house told her, leaning on his rake, that Glenn was in Hawaii, working on a television show.

Disappointed and now really wanting some marijuana to help the time pass, Jody trudged back to the hotel through the heat wondering whom she could telephone. She had impulsively thrown away the number of the only local dealer she knew. There were not that many other people she knew out here. In the apartment she took off all her clothes and drew the white drapes, letting the sunlight flood the couch, where she sat with the telephone wondering if she could call somebody in New York who would tell her the names of some people out here who could get her some dope, or at least might be interesting to talk to. But the maid buzzed the door and without waiting for an answer came in. Irritated, Jody ran to the bedroom and put on her bathing suit and went down by the pool.

The morning regulars were there, and they waved or nodded to Jody as she made herself comfortable on one of the rusty old garden chairs in the shade of the big avocado tree. The regulars were actors, mostly from New York, in town trying to get work. There was Phil, a man in his fifties, thin, brown and balding, whom Jody had seen in a hundred movies, although he never seemed to have more than one or two lines per movie. Phil was an old swish and a nice man, and he had been the first around the pool to speak to Jody when she moved into Harry's apartment. And there was Alonzo, whom Jody suspected of being on reds; at least he seemed pleasantly drunk most of the day, but she never saw him taking a drink. Alonzo had had one role thus far in his five-year career, and a lot of commercials. He was tall and handsome and full-lipped and cold-eyed, and he wore a tiny black bikini from which his thick nest of pubic hair bulged, leading to the masses of fine black curly hair on his chest. Alonzo was a very hairy man, very muscular in a lithe way, and must have really knocked them dead back home, wherever he came from. He was not knocking them dead in Hollywood.

Alonzo made his play for Jody only when one day they happened to be alone by the pool. He had come over to where she was sitting with her feet still in the water, sat beside her and dangled his own feet into the pool and said, "You're with Lexington up on eight, aren't you?"

"Yes," Jody said. She looked into his dead cold eyes and smiled.

"Yeah," he said. "I noticed you."

"Really?" Jody said with her smile in place.

"You got a good body, do you know that? Do you act?"

"A little," Jody said. He was close enough for her to smell his breath, but she couldn't, although he seemed almost woozy.

"How about coming up to my room later? We could have a couple of beers."

"No, thank you," Jody said, and Alonzo had looked relieved. Now, he sat across the pool from Jody, stretched out next to Phil, who was talking animatedly to a woman Jody had never seen before, young and quite beautiful in a white one-piece bathing suit, the kind people used to wear in the Forties. Phil had a copy of *Daily Variety* open across his stomach which he didn't seem to be into, so Jody walked over to him, said hello to everybody and asked Phil if he would mind if she read the paper.

"Oh, take it, take it," he said. "Nothing but gossip anyway." He looked from woman to woman and said, "Do you two know each other? Jody, love, I forgot your last name, this is Jan Kosky; both of you are aspiring actresses, I'm sure you have much in common." And while the two women were smiling at each other, Phil picked up his *Variety* and started reading again. Jan Kosky laughed and said, "I think I'll get into the water. It's so *hot!*" She was blonde, ten years younger than Jody, but there was something tough and nice about her. Jody went into the pool too, and they swam for a while and then got out on the opposite side from Phil and Alonzo. By now there were a couple of other regulars out by the pool, and the faded battered telephone in its little white wooden birdhouse by the gate was buzzing every five or ten minutes. Jan and Jody were stretched out on their towels on the hot concrete, but every time the telephone would buzz Jan would start and sit up, blinking under her sunglasses.

"I keep thinkin it's for me," she said with a grin. "Honest to Christ, you'd think I was Sally Kellerman or somebody."

"I would certainly like to smoke a jay right about now," Jody said. The hell with finesse.

"Oh, hey listen," Jan Kosky said, getting up on one elbow and looking down at Jody very seriously. "I've got about ten cents' worth of street weed up in my room if you want to split it with me." She smiled hopefully. "Or do you maybe have some yourself?"

"Fresh out," Jody said. "But I don't want to take your last . . ."

"Aw hell," Jan said. "I need somebody to smoke with anyway. I been in this hotel for three weeks and this is only the third time I've even been out by the pool. God, it's expensive, isn't it? Fourteen dollars a day and I have to pull my bed down out of the fucking wall. Come on, let's take another dip and go up to my room."

Jan lived on the second floor, in a room with a tiny kitchenette. "One rusty knife, fork and spoon," she said with a laugh. "Three plates, in case I have some company, a couple glasses. *Furnished*. What a laugh!"

The ten cents' worth of street dope turned out to be at least half an ounce of AAA Colombian Red, and while Jan rolled up a couple of tight little joints she explained to Jody that this man had given it to her, she didn't even know him that well, he worked as a casting director at one of the studios and she had met him in an elevator at 9200 Sunset, where she was trying to get herself an agent. He (the casting man) had been very nice to her, took her to dinner and then back to his apartment to smoke some of this really fantastic dope, and then he didn't even try to make a pass at her, but spent a couple of hours telling her how to get established in Hollywood. "Actually, he's a fantastic connection. I mean, he gets hired to do the actual casting of these movies. The director says something like, 'We need this blonde to play a hockey player,' or something, and then this guy Stan has all these lists and pictures of actresses, and he picks out a few and the director talks to them." She lit one of the joints, took a couple of deep puffs and handed it to Jody. After holding her breath for a while, Jan smiled impishly and said, "Gee, he was such a perfect guy about everything, I mean picking me up and dinner and all with no grabbing, I just leaned over and unzipped his pants and gave him some head." She giggled, and Jody would have laughed except that she was holding her breath. "I made him feel pretty good," Jan said. "It never hurts, you know."

"As long as he didn't grab at you," Jody said, and now she laughed. It was going to be great having Jan in the hotel.

"How come you're staying here?" Jody asked her. "Can you afford it?"

"My Dad sends me money from Detroit," she said. "The old guilt, you know? He's gonna give me a year to make it."

Jody was good and ripped. "Shall we go back down to the pool?" she asked. "Shall we flash our bodies?"

"Won't do much good," Jan said. "I think most of the guys in this place are queers anyway. At least the ones I've hit on. Either that or they're awful shy."

The women went back to the pool and swam lazily high until lunchtime. Jody found out that Jan's real name was Ingred Jankovski, "But they already have an Ingred, you know; Ingrid Bergman, only spelled with an 'i' instead of an 'e.'" She had been in Detroit little theater, had done some local commercials and modeling, and had come to Los Angeles only a month ago. "Oh well, I was married there for a couple years," she said with a shrug. "My old man, my husband I mean, he works for a glass company. When we split up he made an ass of himself wanting custody of the kid. Well, I let him have it. You should of seen the look on his face!"

"What are you girls laughing about?" Phil said from across the pool. He was sitting in the shade, with white ointment on his nose. "You sound positively evil!"

TWENTY-SIX

HARRY HAD left some money for Jody, and so that evening after a nap she telephoned down to Jan Kosky and invited her to dinner. "Come on up for a drink," she said, knowing how impressed Jan would be by the size and luxury of Harry's apartment. You had to live there a few days to see past the glamour to the cheap dishware, nappy carpets and somewhat lumpy hotel furniture. But it was worlds better than Jan's little room, and when she arrived Jan said, "Holy Christ, you live in a palace! Who did you say your old man is?"

"He's a producer," Jody said, and told Jan all about the movie Harry was working on while they had vodka over ice with a twist, one of Jody's favorite drinks.

"Are you going to get a part—oh, I shouldn't ask," Jan said.

"I'm up for one, but the director makes the final decision," Jody said, suddenly protective of Harry.

"I know," Jan said. "Stan Bird the casting man told me some really funny stories about casting. The old casting couch is really a reality, you know? Some of the chicks don't even wait to give their name, they just drop their knickers and wave their legs around in the air. I've never been up for a part, but I know better'n to do that."

Full of vodka and Jan's marijuana they drove in Jan's little red Fiat down to Tana's and had a gigantic Italian dinner. Two men across the narrow aisle started a conversation with them, obviously businessmen, and Jody saw with amusement that Jan became quite refined and delicate.

When one of the men told her she was very beautiful, Jan simply dropped her eyes and let a very small smile touch the corners of her mouth. Jody was quite demure too, although she did not know why she bothered. These men were not interesting, and even if they had been, Jody was not making any scenes with any men. Harry had been gone only one night.

After dinner they had dishes of spumoni, and the men across the way asked if they could donate a bottle of champagne and perhaps join them. Well that was a generous thing to do, and they weren't going to get anywhere anyway. The men came and sat by them, the one next to Jody the real talker of the two, florid and handsome, with dark curly hair and fine dark eyes. But he also had a roll of fat that bulged over his collar and soft moist pudgy hands, and he talked too loud. It hadn't been so bad when he had been over at the other table, but now he continued to shout into Jody's ear as they drank their champagne, and so when he suggested, at high volume, that they all go on to Dino's on the Strip, Jody said, "I can't."

"Aw, come on," the man said. "Be a sport. You don't want to be a party pooper, do you?"

"No," Jody said. "And we do appreciate the champagne. But my husband's union meeting will be over soon, and he's going to meet us."

"Your husband," the man said. "I didn't know you were married. Hell, you aren't married, you aren't wearing a wedding band. See?" He waved his own wedding band in front of Jody. "Besides, what the heck. You can meet him later. Union meeting? What does your husband do for a living, if I might ask? I thought you girls were in show business . . ."

"I am," Jody said. "But my husband's a Teamster organizer. We really have to go."

Jan said from across the table, "Yes, her husband beat her half to death last time she was late."

The two men found their way out of Tana's, and Jody and Jan finished the champagne.

"I hate to go home," Jan said. "This is the first good time I've had in California. Honest."

But it was late and virtuously they went home, smoked some more dope and said goodnight. The next day was not so good. Jody spent the morning by the pool, but got a little too much sun and developed a headache which aspirin could not cure. It was a hot muggy day and there was no breeze. Even the apartment was hot and stuffy. Only the bedroom had a window air conditioner, and it didn't work very well, making a clanging racket all the time it was on and breathing out only the mildest of cool breezes. Jody lay naked on the bed and sweated and hurt and wished she had something to knock her out. Jan was not around. She had said something the night before about some kind of appointment, but Jody could not remember what it was about. Jody did not want to do it, but all there was in the apartment was liquor. She hated to drink alone. She thought it would be better to eat first, but there was almost nothing in the refrigerator. She did not want to walk in this heat down to the Hughes Market, and so she telephoned for some Chinese food to be delivered and got right into the icy vodka. She was drunk when the food arrived and it reminded her of Harry, who had not telephoned, and so she sat watching television, drinking and eating Chinese food, sad and lonely.

Jan called and woke her up at seven in the evening. Jody asked her to hold the line. She sat up from the couch and rubbed her eyes. She was still naked. It occurred to her that she must have answered the door for the Chinese delivery man naked. She must have. She could not remember having put on any clothes. But on the other hand, the delivery man hadn't said anything to her.

"Hello," she said. "I was asleep, but thanks for waking me up. What time is it?"

"Dinner time. You want to go out, or am I making a pest of myself?"

"Come on up," Jody said. While she was on the way, Harry called. He was in Atlanta, hot, angry, tired and drunk. It had been a bitching two days. They had been out in the countryside and some of the natives had been openly hostile. "We could shoot the whole fucking picture ten minutes out of Atlanta," he said. "This is one swinging town." Nevertheless, the survey would continue southward, and Harry was not looking forward to the rednecks. "How about you, baby?" he finally asked. He sounded as if he wanted to go. Jody could hear music and people talking behind him.

"I'm fine," she said. "Don't worry about me. I found a friend." She described Jan, told Harry she loved him, and they hung up. Jan arrived a couple of minutes later and they went to dinner and a movie on the Boulevard, getting home around twelve. Jody said goodnight and went to bed without asking Jan for any of her dope, and of course she could not sleep.

She lay restlessly listening to the air conditioner, a sheet loosely pulled over most of her body, when the telephone rang. It was Alonzo.

"I've been calling for hours," he said in a calm intimate voice. "I thought you might like to come down for a drink or something."

"I was asleep in bed," Jody said.

"I could come up there," he said. "You could throw on a robe or something."

"No, really," she said. "I'll see you tomorrow or something."

There was a pause, then Alonzo said, "Aren't you a little lonely?"

"Listen," Jody said, "do you happen to have anything to help me get to sleep? Any reds or anything?"

"I have some fiorinal," he said. "It's supposed to be some kind of hangover cure, but it's got phenobarbital in it. Do you want me to bring some up for you?"

"I could come down," she said. "I'm just having a little trouble getting to sleep."

"No, I'll bring them up," he said.

She opened the door wearing her bathrobe. Alonzo stood grinning slyly out in the hallway, dressed in Levi's and a black tee shirt, no shoes. He had a little plastic vial of two-tone green capsules in his extended palm. "Can't I come in for a second?" he asked her.

She took the vial and said, "No baby, please. I really have to get to sleep . . ." She smiled tiredly.

"Okay," he said. "Rain check, right?"

She smiled again and shut the door. On the label it said to take two of the pills, so she took four, and after a while she drifted off.

The next morning it was just too damned hot to walk down to the Boulevard so Jody made breakfast for herself in the apartment, and then when she finished her shower and was about to get into her bathing suit she remembered about Alonzo's middle-of-the-night call and visit. He would be at the pool waiting for her. He would be attentive, and there would be that look in his eye, saying that they were soon going to go to bed together but that there was no hurry. She did not think she could put up with it. He had a fine body and she liked hairy men and she needed somebody to make love to, but not Alonzo. For some reason, just not Alonzo.

"Damn it all!" she said aloud. The maid was due, and she wanted to have someplace to go. She telephoned down to Jan and there was no answer. Looking out the window she could see a few people out by the pool, but the big avocado tree was partially in her way and she could not tell if Jan was there or not. She called the pool extension and saw Alonzo trot over to the phone.

"Central casting," Alonzo said.

"Is Jan Kosky out there?" Jody said. She would be goddamned if she would disguise her voice, but apparently he did not recognize her. She watched him turn away from the telephone, and then turn back. "Nope," he said.

It got hotter. When the maid came Jody threw on her bathing suit and went out by the pool. Maids embarrassed her.

Alonzo took her to a place just off Sunset where they had hamburgers and beer, and then down to Santa Monica to a bar crowded with unemployed actors and the kinds of people who liked to hang around with actors. They joined a group near the door, and when Alonzo went to the toilet two of the men propositioned her, one whispering in her ear and the other squeezing her hand and trying to get her to look into his eyes. She got drunk early and paid no attention to anybody, and when they got back to the Chateau Bercy Alonzo followed her into the apartment. She could not have cared less.

"I'm not going to fuck you, Alonzo," she said tiredly without looking at him. She went into the kitchen and got a bottle of whiskey, ice and two glasses. In the living room Alonzo was sitting in the middle of the couch. Jody sat next to him because it was convenient to put the things down on the coffee table. Alonzo took over at once, making the drinks.

"Do you have bottled water up here?" he asked her. "I used to order it but after a while it got too damned expensive. Besides, I think they just fill those special bottles from the tap. Don't you?"

"The water thing's in the dining room," she said. She decided to have her nightcap straight over ice. The bourbon tasted very good. Alonzo, seeing her already drinking, raised his glass in a salute.

"To us," he said.

"Jesus Christ," Jody muttered. She was drunk, but not that drunk. "I'm just not going to fuck you. Do you get the message? I thank you for the dinner and the drinks, but that's it."

"What makes you think I want to go to bed with you?" Alonzo asked in a light voice. He was smiling at her as if she had made some terrible social error and he, her only friend, was correcting her. Jody knew the look.

"Good, then you don't," she said.

"What makes you think I don't?"

She knew a good way to get rid of him: act aggressive. He was probably unmanned by aggressive women. She could lean over, give him a big wet tonguey kiss and then grope him. He'd probably jump a foot. Then she could murmur about needing a *real man*, the kind of man who could make love to her *endlessly*. She could tell him that her old man only gave it to her a couple, three times a night, and she was hot, endlessly hot, and needed the kind of loving Alonzo seemed to be promising. That would send him running. She laughed.

"What's funny?" he asked.

"Good night, Alonzo," she said. She drained her glass, got up and went down the long corridor to the bedroom. As she was undressing she heard her front door open and shut. Either he left, or he wanted her to think he had left. She giggled. He's probably behind the drapes, waiting for me to go to sleep. All right. Into bed and to sleep.

For the rest of the week she heard nothing from Alonzo. She and Jan went each morning to the beach just below Venice, near the Marina del Rey breakwater, spread their towels and things, including Jan's portable AM-FM radio. It was just too hot to stay in LA, and as long as they had the freedom, the beach was only an hour away. They were hit on regularly by men ranging in age from seventeen to sixty, singly and in pairs or threes, but after a while everyone who hung around this particular beach got to know them, and the hitting-on slowed down.

But Jan had a date Friday night with her casting friend Stan Bird. She promised to ask him where they could get some more marijuana. "See if he can score some coke too," Jody said.

"God, it's so expensive," Jan said on the telephone.

"Don't worry," Jody said. "Daddy will pay."

Jan loved it and promised to ask. Jody and Jan were getting along just fine and would sit ripped or drinking, watching television together and making nasty cracks about the actors and stories. But tonight Jody was alone. It was a Friday night, and she did not like to be home alone while everybody else was out boogie-ing.

By ten o'clock she was wound up tight, wired, ready to do anything but stay alone or sleep. Sleep was impossible. She was not hungry. The smell of booze would have been enough to make her sick and she had no dope. All the capsules Alonzo had given her were long gone. Jody paced up and down the apartment, trying to get her mind together enough to watch television. But the thought of it made her sick. She threw on some clothes and combed her hair and went down to the lobby. There wasn't anybody in the elevator, and nobody in the lobby except the clerk, a dried-up old person who could have been a man or a woman, Jody did not know or care. She leaned on the cigarette machine and folded her arms. No one came through the lobby while she was there. Eventually she got back into the elevator and went back up. She thought about getting off at four, where Alonzo lived, but pressed eight instead. When she got out of the elevators she heard the sirens outside, faintly, and when she got into the apartment, whose windows were open against the heavy warmth of the night, she could hear the fire equipment in the street right outside the hotel, on the opposite side from the swimming pool. She went to her window and looked down at a burning palm tree.

The palm was a tall one, with a cluster of dried and weary-looking fronds. Apparently somebody had thrown a cigarette out of a window and it had ignited the tree. As Jody watched, a fireman climbed a ladder and put out the blaze with a fire extinguisher. Jody could see a lot of people drifting out of the hotel and looking up at the fireman, so she went back downstairs and outside. At least it was something to do.

There must have been fifty people out on the sidewalk and leaning against parked cars, watching the firemen dismantle their equipment and prepare to leave. It was a very warm night, and the firemen looked hot in their helmets and protective coats, but the watchers from the hotel were dressed casually, some of them even in pajamas, and a couple of the men, including Alonzo, wearing only pants. Jody recognized most of their faces; they were the actors and actresses who filled the roles not taken by the stars. Jody even saw a couple of men who had had their own television series, way back in time. Now here they were, spending their exciting Hollywood Friday night watching the fire department put out a blaze in a palm tree. Some of them even looked as if they were hoping the television newsreel cameramen would come around. She was certain that Alonzo had taken his shirt off before coming outside. On the other hand, maybe she was being too cruel; maybe Alonzo was just loafing around his room naked, nothing to do. She thought about making her way over to him. If he had seen her he hadn't made any sign.

"Well, back to the rathole," said a voice from behind her. It belonged to a tall man with longish white hair, wearing a striped polo shirt and grey slacks. He seemed about fifty and sad, although he was smiling. He looked down at Jody and said, "I've been living here four years and this is the most exciting thing that's happened."

Jody liked him at once, and smiled at him. Without speaking further, the two of them began to drift back toward the lobby with a lot of other people. Jody looked back and saw Alonzo looking at her, and just at that moment the man with the white hair touched her elbow, as if to gently guide her. Giving Alonzo her profile she smiled again at the man and entered the lobby ahead of him.

"Eight?" the white-haired man said. It was not really a question. He got out with her.

"I'm not being forward," he said. "I happen to live on this floor myself." He walked her to her door, smiled faintly and said, "Harry would kill me," and put his hands on her shoulders and kissed her. It was a good kiss.

They looked at each other. He still had his hands on her shoulders. Jody knew that all she would have to do would be to say, "Come in," and he would follow her, she could have him. But they kept looking at each other, and neither said anything, and finally he dropped his hands and with that same almost sad smile said, "Good night, Jody," and went off down the hall. Jody went to sleep thinking about the way his hands had felt on her shoulders and his lips on her mouth.

TWENTY-SEVEN

JAN KOSKY was terribly excited. Over dinner her casting friend Stan Bird had told her that on Monday morning at eleven o'clock she had an appointment with F. Wayne Cole the famous director, who was casting a picture that would be shot in Durango, Mexico.

"The part I'm up for," she told Jody as they sped down the Los Angeles freeway toward the south coast, "is this chick who's captured by these Mexican bandits." She giggled. "I get tortured to death. Five days shooting for me. But the director and everybody else will be in Durango for at least two months, maybe three. Stan told me if Cole likes me, I mean if I get the part and he likes the stuff I do, I could maybe stick around for another week or two."

"It sounds great," Jody said. "How much money?"

"Oh, we didn't even get into that. Stan says that what I should do is after the audition if the director likes me he'll get me an agent. Stan will. He knows all the agents in town naturally, and they all want to do him favors. I never realized how much power these casting people have. God!"

It was a hot weekend and so they had decided not to go to any of the local beaches. Instead they were driving south, just to see the countryside. They got as far as San Juan Capistrano, where they had lunch and looked at the old mission with a group of other tourists. It was too late to go on and try to make Tijuana, so they turned around and headed back for Los Angeles.

"I didn't see any goddamn swallows," Jan said with a laugh. She drove with verve and style, weaving from lane to lane, keeping to a steady seventy miles per hour until they got back into the Los Angeles freeway complex. Then things slowed down. The air was thick and heavy and the traffic down to almost a standstill. Finally, by dusk, they were inching their way along the Harbor Freeway. Both Jan and Jody were hungry, tired and had to go to the toilet, but there was no way out of the mess. Neither of them knew the streets of the city well enough to venture off the freeway, and so they had to sit in the miasma, the car radio blasting out, until with darkness the traffic seemed to break up and once again they could make speed. They got to the hotel at nine-thirty.

Jody felt better after a long shower, and just as she came out of the bath-room, naked and loving the coolness of the air against her skin, the telephone rang. She thought immediately of the white-haired man from last night. But it was Harry, from Atlanta.

"I called to tell you I love you," he said. "I feel terrible."

"Are you all right?" she asked.

"Sure," he said. "Except that I feel terrible I'm fine. We've been beating around the backwoods. Gargolian almost got in a fight with some cracker in a bar. There was this sign behind the bar saying, 'track of the American chicken,' with a peace sign. It doesn't matter. We still have about twenty places to look."

"But you're back in Atlanta," she said.

Apparently the location survey was not going too well, except that the men were getting acquainted with each other's styles and that was good. Harry sounded hysterical and petulant, and Jody guessed that he was very tired.

"It's late there, isn't it?" she asked.

"Just past two, I think," Harry said. "What about you? Are you getting along okay? Do you have enough money?"

"I'm fine," she said. "Getting a lot of sun." She wanted to ask him about the white-haired man, but she did not, and after exchanging I-love-you's they hung up, leaving Jody feeling empty and somehow lost. Her skin was dry and hot now, except for trickles of sweat running from her armpits, and her palm, which had been cupping the telephone too tightly.

She could imagine Harry in his little hotel room, unable to sleep although he was terribly tired, calling her at two in the morning, in fact probably calling her all evening and not getting an answer (she was sure now the box in the lobby would be full of little message slips—she hadn't bothered to look), no one else to talk to except the men he had spent the day with. And Jody knew from her own brief visit to Atlanta a couple of years before with a man whose name she could not remember, that on Sunday Atlanta was dry as a bone, so Harry had nothing to look forward to but a day of lonely rest. Jody found herself wishing Harry would call a hooker and at least relieve himself. But then maybe he had, and that was why he was calling her to tell her he loved her. Jody had known men like that, probably most men were like that.

The doorbell rang and she opened it without thinking. Fortunately it was not the man with the white hair or Alonzo or anybody else but Jan.

"You look cool," was Jan's only comment. "Let's get on the phone to Stan and see about that dope!"

"Didn't you ask him the other day?"

"Yeah, but he told me to call him at home tonight."

Stan Bird arrived around midnight, with a friend and a pocketful of drugs. Bird was a small handsome man with grey eyes behind contact lenses and teeth so even Jody was certain that they were false, although they did not have the look of bad false teeth. They were probably caps, she thought. Looking down, she saw that he was also wearing shoes that built up his height about two inches. Around his middle was probably a combination girdle and moneybelt, she thought, and laughed aloud. Stan Bird was dressed Mod, and his friend, a large pale sweating man of about thirty in Hawaiian shirt and white drill pants. Jody guessed that the big man, introduced only as Tommy, was supposed to be for her. By this time Jody was wearing a faded blue man's shirt and her tightest palest Levi's, and she could see Tommy's eyes covertly looking at her body. Tommy did not look like a rich or powerful person. She wondered who he was and why Bird brought him.

"It's party time," Stan Bird announced, and pulled from one pocket a plastic bag filled with dark-red cleaned marijuana. "You got any papers here?"

Jody sat at the coffee table with the weed and papers and rolled a few joints while the others talked quietly. Jan wanted to talk about F. Wayne Cole and the picture, but Bird was evasive. Tommy did not join into any of the movie talk, and when Jody lit one of the joints and passed it to him, he waved a pudgy hand and said, "No, thanks. Emphysema." She did not believe it for a minute. While the others smoked, Tommy sat quietly sweating, looking from person to person, trying to appear interested but not joining into the conversation except to inject clichés like, "Well, what do you think of that!" or, "Sounds about par for the course."

After only a few tokes Jody knew this was very good weed. "Where can I buy some of this?" she asked Stan, and Stan grinned and pointed to Tommy. "This here's the man," he said.

"What do you want for it?" she asked Tommy. Now she recognized the type. He was a dealer but a square. He would run down to Mexico in his camper or motor home, square as a bear, probably with an uptight-looking woman with him, make his deal in Mazatlán or some other wide-open place, then cruise back, while the police were busting longhairs. If he was really smart he would buy his drugs directly from the police, paying well enough to guarantee, hopefully, that he would not be betrayed. And obviously he had not been. He looked no more like a dope dealer than the man in the moon.

"This is Panama Red," he said, as if describing an item in his sales catalog; "it's not tops, as you can tell, but the tops to this stuff went for fifty a lid."

"How much do you want for a good lid?" Jody persisted.

"Mostly it goes by the pound," he said, but she finally cornered him into admitting that he would part with an ounce of it for thirty dollars. Christ in Heaven, she thought, I'm glad it's not my money.

"Listen," Stan Bird said. He had his arm around Jan's shoulder and they had been whispering. "While you people conduct business, me and this one are going to use your bedroom, okay?"

Tommy had to go down to his car to pick up the lid, and as Jody was holding the door open for him she said, "Do you happen to have any coke?" She thought about Harry's desire never ever to see coke again. Well, if this man had any, she would conceal it from Harry, that was all.

"I have a little bit," Tommy said, and negotiations began as soon as Jody shut the door again. After he left to get the drugs, Jody sat down in the living room and tried not to listen to the faint sounds coming from the bedroom. It helped that all the windows in the apartment were open, and traffic noises from the nearby entrance to the Hollywood Freeway drifted up on the warm air; but it did not help enough. Jody was horny, that was all. She had been horny before, and she had gone without before.

But she was getting older. Thirty-five. Time was wasting and death was coming. She thought with a smile about seducing Tommy, the uptight businessman who happened to find himself in the dope business. Since he was overweight he was probably very uptight about women and sex, too. Maybe he carried all that extra weight on purpose, to thrust away the problems of sex. But then maybe not. Maybe he would be the one. Maybe it would be an act of kindness to seduce him, to be gentle to him and make love to him.

Jody caught herself gritting her teeth noisily. The doorbell buzzed and she opened it to Tommy, who smiled without looking at her and stood in the middle of the room, holding out the bag of marijuana and the gram of cocaine in its small plastic envelope. "Do you want to taste the coke?" he asked.

"Sure, but not from my gram," she said. They sat beside each other on the couch while he got out his own coke, contained in a small wooden carved box. He had a tiny silver coke spoon for her to use. She snorted a good pile into each nostril and felt the incredible, indescribable rush that first-class cocaine gave her. After a few moments she said, "Aren't you going to have any?"

"I just keep it for my friends," he said. He still would not look her in the eye, but it did not matter. From the bedroom came a cry and then another one. Tommy grinned at the floor and stood up. "Guess I better get out of here," he said.

"Don't be in a hurry," Jody said. "Don't you take *anything?*"

"I guess I'm just a sugar junkie," Tommy said. Now he looked at her. "There's a delicatessen down on Fairfax," he said, "with the best pastries you ever saw. Care to go have something to eat?"

"No, baby," she said. "I'm in the mood for love. You know what I mean?" His face reddened thickly and she said, "Oh hell, I was just kidding. Let's go eat."

Tommy brought her back to the hotel and up in the elevator, but he did not enter the apartment. Jody could not hear anything, so she walked quietly down to the bedroom and looked in. The bed was a mess but there was nobody in it. The air conditioner was on, clanging distantly, and the room was slightly cooler than the others. Jody sighed and went to bed.

TWENTY-EIGHT

IT WAS six o'clock Monday evening before Jan came up to tell Jody what had happened on her interview with F. Wayne Cole. Jody had just awakened from a nap and had not yet showered the sweat off her body, and she was about to ask Jan to come back a little later when she saw her face. Jan looked very bad. Jody opened the door wider and said, "What happened? Do you want a drink or anything?"

"I should have known," Jan said. She walked into the living room with her arms at her sides and sat down on the edge of the couch, as if she had to get up and go in a few minutes. She was dressed in jeans and a man's red tee shirt, so she had had time to change, and perhaps had been home for hours. Jody brought them drinks and sat beside her.

"Okay, spill it," Jody said. "You didn't get the part. Okay? You can't win them all."

"He wanted me to suck his cock," Jan said. "I came in his office and sat down and he said, 'Stan Bird tells me you give really good head.' I didn't know what to say. I just sat there. You hear about it, you know. But I never believed. He just kept looking at me. He's smaller than I thought and he has this full beard now and his eyes stick out a little. Then he says, 'Well, what do you have to say for yourself?' I asked him what else did Stan say about me and he says, "'That was about it, honey.'"

"Those sons of bitches," Jody said.

"Jody, I don't know what's the matter with me. I did it. I went over to him and kneeled down next to his desk and undid his pants and blew him. I wasn't even thinking, I just did it. It took a long time for him, but he squirted off in my mouth, and then when I'm spitting the stuff out into my hankie he says in this real distant voice, 'I wanted you to swallow it, honey.'"

She looked at Jody and smiled strangely. "That's when I finally caught on to what was happening. He was really auditioning me, but the person who gets the part has to be his girlfriend on the location. I guess when I didn't swallow his come I flunked." She laughed. "I used to *study* him in school! I'm such a goddamn idiot! What made me think I could make it out here, anyway?"

"Don't talk like that," Jody said. "He's just one bastard, that's all."

But Jan was crying now, and she grabbed Jody by the arms. "Oh, did you ever do anything like that, though? I feel so bad about myself! Why didn't I just say no thank you or something and walk out? I guess I really wanted that part bad, so bad I even shut off my mind. But I can't shut it off now, I think about those two calling each other up on the telephone and talking about me, like, 'She didn't work out, do you have any other girls?'"

"Did you talk to Stan Bird?" Jody asked. "I'd like to know what . . ."

"Oh, yes, that was the first thing I did. As soon as I got off the lot I went into this Chinese restaurant across the street and went in the can and cried, then I called Stan on the pay phone. He was very angry with me. He said it was all my own fault, for doing it to him the first time we went out. He said he thought I loved to do it and wouldn't mind. He told me that was how to get small parts and later on things would get better. He said I was stupid. I think he's right."

"I think he's a bastard," Jody said. "You're not stupid. You just happened to run into a couple of bad numbers, that's all. Don't be down on yourself."

"But I can't help it! There's thousands of women in this city trying to get parts! It's so hopeless! It's so stupid!"

She broke down again and for a while Jody held her by the shoulders while she cried. Automatically Jan reached for her shoulder-bag and got out a wadded-up handkerchief, and then started sobbing again, throwing the handkerchief across the room. It came to rest on the rug, and Jody looked at it while Jan went into the bathroom to finish crying and wash her face. She knew she should get rid of it, but she did not want to touch it. But she had to, before Jan returned. Jody held the handkerchief as if it was a dead rat, and dropped it into the wastebasket under the sink, and then came back into the living room and waited for Jan. She did not feel like drinking whiskey, and Jan had not touched hers.

When Jan came back she said, "I'm getting out of here."

"No," Jody said. "Stay. We'll go have dinner and a good time."

"No," Jan said. "I mean Hollywood. I'm getting out of here. Tonight. I mean, why wait? I mean, *fuck it!*"

With Jody to help her, Jan packed her things into two suitcases and one cardboard carton from the Hughes Market and stowed them in her car. She would be on the Hollywood Freeway before nine o'clock.

"Where are you going?" Jody asked her as they were standing beside the car in the parking lot.

"Anywhere but Detroit," she said. "I think maybe San Francisco or some-place like that."

"I'm going to miss you, baby," Jody said, but she did not ask her to stay. Jan was doing the right thing for a change.

"Oh Jody," Jan said, and hugged her tight. "I love you, Jody. I hope you get what you want. You're such a good person!"

Jody was startled. She had been called everything but that in her life. "I love you too, baby. Take care."

Jan got into her car, and after hesitating a moment, Jody said to her, "Wait. Listen. What you did. I've done a lot worse. And I'm okay." She laughed nervously. "It's just that I really hope I get in this picture of Harry's. I'm thirty-five years old, baby." She laughed again, the laugh almost out of control. "I sure need this part!"

In the elevator on the way back to her apartment, Jody could not understand why she had copped out on herself like that. She did not confide in people. Maybe I'm more shook up than I think I am. I know I'm shook up, but this is really bad.

In bed by eleven Jody smoked the last of a joint, wet out the roach and swallowed it, hoping it would help her sleep. But as good as the marijuana was, she could not feel it. There was no elation in her, just a deep sad feeling for Jan and for herself. She was really scared now. Harry was not going to give her a part. Intelligent men did not give parts to their girlfriends. And it was too late for Jody now. She had frittered her life away, trying this way and that way, but never just getting down to the hard work, always being the sexual object and never the smart determined intelligent person she knew she had to be to get anywhere in show business.

She had done worse, all right, lots worse. She had been a thief, a pimp, a blackmailer, a junkie, a liar and a cheat. She had pretended to love men she had despised. She had done it all, and none of it had worked. Every time she got into a place where she might have had a chance, something inside her fired up and she ruined her chances. Always. She thought about the time years before when she had been working as a dancer at the Copa in New York, and the headliner had come on to her, not the first star in her life, promising her a job in his traveling company when he took the show around the world, sending her expensive Dupont lighters and flowers and the whole bullshit business, but when he invited her to a party at his suite, and all she had to do was show up, look beautiful and then spend the night, what she actually did was drink champagne and screech at everybody until they threw her out. And that hadn't been the only time. Her whole life was a clutter of three-day jobs, punctured ambitions and drug-deadened hangovers.

"Oh Lindy," she cried out. "Help me! Help me!" She clenched her pillow and sobbed. It had been more than twenty years since she had shed any tears for anybody. Now these tears were for herself.

Harry got back on Friday, blossoming with optimism. They had found perfect locations, all in one site, and the whole area so remote and so filled with mosquitoes, rednecks and rotten heat that Fats Dunnigan, who had flown down there three days before, was not going to be a problem on the set. Suddenly Fats had business elsewhere.

"The picture's *mine!*" Harry said to Jody, his face ruddy with triumph and airline alcohol.

TWENTY-NINE

CASTING THE picture took six weeks, along with all the other thousand details of pre-production, and Harry would come home nights either heavy with whiskey from the couple of drinks he would share with Jack Meltzer and Lew Gargolian after work, or with the thick blue binder containing his master copy of the script. Either way he did not have much time for Jody, a fact he apologized for every time he thought of it. He was not worried about her though. She had been quiet and almost serene since his return from the Deep South.

The three leads were selected by conference and submission, Fats having decided that Karl Meador should at least be kept appraised of the narrowing-down process. They needed at least one actor who could draw, although nobody put it so bluntly, and their budget would not allow a superstar, and so Jack, Fats and Harry spent hours and days and evenings meeting with agents, having lunch with actors, trying to keep track of copies of the script, and having long two-against-one arguments every time somebody came up with a likely candidate.

Fats was the worst: he would call Harry and say, "What do you think about Bill Holden?" and Harry could not swear or hang up on him; he had to go through the travesty of pretending to consider Holden on his merits as an actor, ignoring the well-known fact that Holden was too expensive. When Harry finally would bring it up, Fats would be optimistic: "He's coming to town. I'll have dinner with him and we'll see. I know Bill wants to work." But of course nothing ever came of these ideas, and at last, with the terse approval of Karl Meador, they hired two men and a woman the studio felt were verging on outright stardom. The one box-office draw was Jonathan Bridger, who was willing to take a cut in pay because he liked the story and was fond of Jack Meltzer, and the female lead finally went to Elaine Rudman when Harry agreed to raise her salary to forty-five hundred a week with a six-week guarantee. The second male lead went to St. Francis Magnuson, who, it turned out, had not really worked much since receiving the Best Supporting Academy Award two years before.

Harry was better than satisfied; he was delighted. Bridger and Rudman were going to look well opposite each other, and neither had bad reputations; and Maggie Magnuson was one of the finest actors in the business. But the lesser roles were driving him mad. There were four parts they figured had to be cast here in Hollywood, with the bits and extras coming from Atlanta and the location.

The chief of these four parts, and almost big enough to cast a name, was Helen the waitress, the part Jody wanted and the one Harry saw as Jody. He had purposely underplayed the role in the first-draft screenplay to keep them from hiring a name, but damned Jack Meltzer had almost seen through him and said, "Listen, this part could be extended, you know. We could get some-body like Carol Korbel. She'd be dynamite, and I think she'd work cheap for a good spot."

"Too good for the part," Harry said carelessly and hoped Jack did not notice. But who would they get? The casting director, Peggy Spatenhaus, had set up a cattle call of "attractive but cheap-looking thirty-five-year-old women who can inspire compassion, humor, etc.," and Harry and Jack had sat through hour after hour of women reading for the part. But none of them satisfied Harry. Jack would have chosen two or three of them, but the furrow never left Harry's brow and the names on his mimeographed list were lined out one by one until there was just nobody left.

Then one evening Harry took Jack out for drinks, just the two of them, and said, "Jack, I'm living with a woman who'd be perfect for Helen if she can act."

Jack did not look up from his drink, but his shoulders dropped slightly, as if from sudden fatigue. This was an opening Jack had probably heard before. "Can she act?" he said.

"I don't know. But you know I'm in a funny position. I wouldn't even think of hiring her except that when I first met her I thought, 'Helen!' That's how I got interested."

"She on your back a little bit?"

"The thing is, I won't be happy with anybody we look at until we look at her, and look carefully," Harry said.

"If that's it, that's it," Jack said. "Do you want me to read her at your place? Have lunch with her or something, try to feel her out?"

"No, let's just have a regular reading, in the office," Harry said. "No special favors."

Jack, showing just the tips of his two front teeth, looked put-upon. "Oh come on," he said.

Harry was pretty embarrassed, but he tried to hide it under a laugh. "No, I mean it."

"If I think she's the shits, I can just tell you? Then what happens? You go home and no pussy for a month."

"Goddamn it, it's not like that!" Harry insisted, but Jack would only laugh at him.

Jody arrived at the lot twenty minutes early, paid off the cab at the drive-on gate and asked the officer where to find the production offices, but Harry came out from between two big sound stages and waved at her. She was dressed quietly and Harry was greatly relieved. He took her into a corner under a staircase and kissed her. She smelled of perfume but only faintly.

"Are you all right?" he asked.

"Yes," she said. "Nervous."

"This probably isn't going to work out, but we'll try."

"I'm sure you did your best for me," Jody said.

He kissed her again but she did not respond, and he let go of her and looked at her. She seemed calmer than he did. It was a fact, he was really tense and upset. He had never done anything like this in his professional career, and he sneered at the people who did.

"Okay, lady," he said. He led her up to the production offices, now busy with assistant directors, prop men, driver captains, gaffers and everybody else trying to get the bulk of their work done before the big move to the South. The reading was in the director's office, and when Harry introduced Jody to Jack he watched Jack carefully to see how he handled her. Jack was fine. He was polite to her, led her to the couch and sat next to her, quietly explaining the part and the scene. Peggy Spatenhaus was in Atlanta lining up lesser roles, so the only people in the room were Jody, Harry and Jack.

"Helen is a woman of middle age, a waitress in a little out-of-the-way roadside restaurant, you know? She hooks up with a gang of bank robbers and ends up getting killed in a big shoot-out with the police. Now, the scene we'll read from, Helen finds herself for the first time in a motel room with the man she's going to be with for the rest of the picture. This man will be played by Maggie Magnuson, so you can see that this is an important part, although she doesn't have all that many lines."

"I know the part," Jody said.

Harry sat behind Jack's desk with a copy of the script, and Jody was handed the few pages containing her scene.

"Harry will read Andy's lines, and we'll start at the top of the page," Jack said. "Any time, and don't worry, we'll read it a couple of times just for level."

INT.   MOTEL ROOM.   NIGHT.

Andy and Helen enter, both carrying luggage, gun-cases, etc.

ANDY
We'll bunk here for the night.

HELEN
You and me?

ANDY (grinning)
Well, you can see there's two beds.

HELEN
It's okay. I'll sleep with you.

After a beat and a take, Andy puts his things down and comes up to her. He tries to kiss her, but she still has her arms full of things. She laughs.

HELEN (con't)
Hey, give me a sec, huh?

ANDY
I'm a horny man . . .

He kisses her, and during the kiss she drops the things she is carrying and responds to the kiss. When they break:

ANDY
What's your name?

HELEN (SHY)
Helen.

ANDY (feelingly)
Come to bed, Helen . . .

CUT TO:

Harry sat across the room from Jody and read his lines clearly but without emotion. He did not want to look as if he was helping her more than he would help anybody else. Jody did not read from her part, she simply spoke the words to Harry. She must have memorized the entire part, because she had not known until just then what she would be reading. Harry hadn't told her because he hadn't known—the choice had been Jack's. But the most important thing was that she did not seem to be acting. When she finished and Harry said, "Come to bed, Helen," she looked at him and smiled.

"Was I okay?" she asked.

"That was a nice reading," Jack said. Harry could not tell how he felt. "Let's run through it again, and this time why don't you stand up? And by the way, I appreciate the fact that you know the lines."

Jody stood and they went through the scene again. Except for the slightest variations, it was the same.

"Very good," Jack said. He wrote something in his script and said, "All right, let's do it one more time, only Jody, will you give me just a little bit more?"

"Okay," she said. This time the character was harsher, cruder and even more vibrant. Harry realized that he was pulling his nose furiously. I must be terribly excited, he said to himself. Jack was making more notes and Jody stood in the middle of the room, her hands at her sides, seeming in perfect control of herself. I love her, Harry thought, maybe it's fucked up my judgment.

At last Jack said, "Well, thank you very much. That was a good reading. Have you done much acting?"

"Not really," Jody said. "A few things, you know, off-off Broadway. No movies, no hits." She laughed, and for the first time since entering the office, Harry could tell she was nervous. But Jack stood up and shook her hand and thanked her again, and Harry had the secretary call a cab. He took Jody out to the gate, kissed her and said he would see her later that night. She did not ask him anything.

When he got back to the office, taking the stairs two and three at a time, too impatient for the creaky elevator, Jack was sitting alone in his office frowning down at his desk top. Harry closed the door and sat down on the couch.

"Well?" he asked.

Jack's head was moving back and forth slowly in negation, and Harry's heart went cold. So she had been bad and he had not been able to see it.

But Jack said, "I just don't know. She's not an experienced actor, and that's what we really need. We don't have any film on her. I really wish we had some film. I wonder what she photographs like?"

"Did you think she was any good?" Harry said, and Jack's front teeth showed in a tiny smile.

"Oh fuck," he said. "You were sitting right here. She was fantastic and you know it. But God, do we really want to cast her?"

"It's up to you," Harry said, burning his bridges. Jack's lifted eyebrow was the only sign that he acknowledged this shift in power.

"I think she's earned a screen test," Jack said. "I can't make up my mind until I see her on film."

"That's a damn good idea," Harry said. "We can get some of our people together. I wonder if Maggie would come in and do a day's work?"

"I'll talk to wardrobe. When, next Friday?"

"Suits me."

They called in Lew Gargolian, who looked pained at the thought of renting all that equipment and paying all those people, but Harry explained that it was absolutely necessary, and besides, it would give Lew his first look at his crew in action, those of them who were already available, anyway. So it was set for Friday.

THIRTY

JODY SPENT Wednesday drunk, Thursday with a hangover, and Friday morning readying herself for the ordeal of the screen test. Harry was to come home and pick her up at two. She was dressed and ready by one, and the temptation to take a couple of drinks or snort some of her forbidden coke was almost overwhelming, but she did not. She sat on the couch and forced herself to watch television, remnants of a W.C. Fields comedy spliced between commercials for stone siding, toupees, upholstery and automobiles. She did not allow herself to think. Her stomach hurt and her palms were wet. Five times that morning she had run to the bathroom with excruciating spasms of diarrhea and she just hoped she could get through the afternoon without humiliating herself. It seemed so stupid. She had worked all her life for this damned cliché of a screen test and now she dreaded it, hated it and wished it were over. What a joke! Her entire life was a cliché.

She knew why they were testing her. She had known at the reading just how good she had been, and now all that mattered was if she could stand the pressure of acting in front of forty bored technicians, and if she photographed well enough to entertain millions of bored people, who did not want to see their friends and neighbors on the screen but wanted big dynamic exciting superpeople. Today's test was to discover if she was super. She did not feel super.

But when Harry came in twenty minutes early, his face drawn in anxiety, her own fears dropped away, and she stood up with a beautiful smile and said, "I'm all ready!"

"You look fine," Harry said, although he did not mean it. She was not wearing any makeup and her hair was pulled back and tied, giving her eyes an oriental look. But she kissed him anyway, and off they went.

Although it was extremely hot outside, the sound stage was clammy and musty. There were abandoned props and pieces of equipment all over the place, looming out of the shadows like gigantic worn-out toys. Jody felt fine. The makeup man was doing great things to her face, and the costume they had picked out for her, a faded green-and-white checked dress, fit loosely but made her figure all that much more attractive, as far as she was concerned. She did have a little run-in with the costumer, though. He was a small intense-looking man in skin-tight white pants, white deck shoes and a fresh white tee shirt. He stood back from Jody as she modeled the costume for him, his hand on his chin.

"I can see that panty line," he said. "Where the fabric brushes against you."

"Oh that's all right," Jody said. She could see Harry and the director standing next to the big camera talking to a couple of other men. St. Francis Magnuson, already in makeup, was poking around in the shadows somewhere, and the other people just seemed to be standing around waiting for her to get ready.

"No," the costumer said. His name was Bitts, she thought. "Those panties are going to have to come off."

"Okay," Jody said, and went into the trailer they had for her to change in. She slipped out of the panties and looked at herself in the oblong mirror on the back of the door. She could now see that if you looked carefully, if you were a pussy man, you would notice that she was not wearing any panties. Jody snorted and put them back on and went out. The costumer was gone, and so she went over to Jack.

"I'm ready," she said.

"That's fine," Jack said. He smiled warmly at her, and then introduced her to a bunch of technicians, and was about to get going when the costumer came back and took one look at her and bit his lip.

"I thought we were going to take those panties off," he said. He did not look at Jody. To Jack he said, "That panty line is unbelievably vulgar."

"So'm I!" Jody said and laughed.

"Leave them on," Jack said. "You're right. It's in character." The costumer gave her a dirty look and shrugged. Jack took her by the elbow and led her toward the set. "Have you met Maggie?" he asked her.

Maggie Magnuson was middle-sized and almost stocky. She had seen him in a few things and liked him. He grinned at her and shook her hand and said, "It's my first screen test, too, baby. We gotta help each other."

"No kidding?" Jack said. "You've never tested before?"

"I'm not testing now," Maggie said, "but you know what I mean." To Jody he said, "You know your lines?"

"Yes," she said.

"Then you know all there is to know about acting. Let's do it!"

"Do you mind if we sort of settle the lighting first?" Jack said with a puckish smile, and they spent the next hour under the lights, standing on their marks while the cameraman and electricians fiddled around. Harry was off in the gloom, sitting in an old easy chair, his hands formed into a steeple under his nose. While they stood around, Maggie Magnuson told Jody a string of filthy stories which he swore his twelve-year-old daughter had brought home from her private school in Switzerland. He was being kind to her, Jody knew, and keeping her entertained so that she would not be nervous. But she had not been nervous at all, not since Harry had come for her. But she liked Maggie for what he was trying to do. She knew he was a big-time actor and did not have to hang out while they fixed the lights. He was doing it so that she would get used to him and could play to him more naturally.

But something funny happened to Maggie while they were rehearsing the scene. It was such a short little scene, and so little happened in it that Jody wondered why they were making such an effort. It was the same scene she had read in the office. They come in, Maggie sort of propositions her, she goes for it, and they start to make love. Nothing to it, a compressed slice of life. But Maggie seemed to change, right after the first walk-through.

Jack came into the lighted area. "That was pretty nice," he said. "Maggie, would you sort of loosen up? You seemed to get a little tight there when you said, 'Come to bed, Helen,' like you really didn't want to take her to bed."

"Sorry," Maggie said. "I was thinking about something."

Then it was time for the take, and the man held the clapper and clapped it and Jack said very quietly, "All right, go ahead, action."

This time there seemed to be something the matter with Maggie all through the scene. His mouth seemed tight. If it had been real life, Jody would have suspected a little impotence problem; he hustles her into bed and then can't get it up. But if that was what Maggie was playing, he didn't say so when Jack asked him what was the matter. "I don't fucking know," was all he would say, and on the next take he was too enthusiastic, too macho, and he overwelmed her. Jody was beginning to sweat in the heat of the lights, and to lose her temper a little at Maggie, who was supposed to be such a great guy and who was fucking up her screen test.

On the fifth take, as they stood behind the door waiting for Jack to say action, Jody whispered to Maggie, "Watch out!" and when they came into the room, she threw her things onto one of the beds, and when he said, "We'll bunk here," she snorted at him and said, "You? And me?"— overplaying hard. Maggie caught it and threw it back to her, raising the level of his own performance, so that by the end of the scene they were practically shouting at each other.

"Cut, oh *fudge*, " Jack said. "Now we've all got it out of our systems, let's get a take and wrap." The next take was a good one, and they did one more for fun and it was good too, and Jody went into her trailer to be alone for a few minutes.

When she came out, Maggie was waiting for her. She could see Harry and Jack talking to the cameraman and the production manager.

"I want to apologize," Maggie said.

"You didn't do anything," she said. Jody was standing on the step of the trailer, looking down at Maggie. He had his hands in his back pockets, and now he grinned in the gloom.

"Who was that you were doing?" he asked.

"What do you mean?"

"That's somebody, isn't it? That character you did."

"Oh, that's my sister," Jody said.

"I'd like to meet her. I *think*," Maggie said. Jody just smiled down at him and he shifted his weight from one leg to the other and said, "Listen, you're really good. I want you to have good luck on this picture." When she still did not say anything, he added, "I'm quitting. I'm getting off the picture." He reached out and shook her hand and walked away.

THIRTY-ONE

MONDAY AFTERNOON after Harry got the official word from Maggie's agent he cursed for almost five minutes and then got into his car and drove out to Maggie's house in Brentwood.

"You have to tell me why you're quitting," he said. They were out in the back, near the pool. Maggie had a towel around his middle and sat on a white cast-iron chair under a striped umbrella. Harry stood.

"What'd my agent say?" Maggie asked cheerfully.

"He said a commitment from the past, something you really didn't think would come through, came through. Some spaghetti western or something."

"That's what we worked out," Maggie said. "Do you really want to go into it?"

"Yes."

"You're worried. I don't blame you, but don't worry. I mean, really, don't worry."

"But I am worried. You have to tell me."

Maggie tilted his head and began slapping it, to get the water out of his ear. Harry decided it was just an actor's trick to gain time, so he said, *"Schtik,"* and Maggie stopped and told him what had been the matter.

When Harry got home Jody wanted to know, and what he told her was that Maggie had been enthusiastic about doing the test for them because he had figured it would be a good way to get in solid with the producer—help him through his old lady's screen test. He had figured it would be like a lot of those scenes, the chick was making Harry's life miserable and so they had to go through the farce of giving her an expensive screen test, and then the director could play the villain and not cast her. Everybody would be off the hook and Maggie would look good—cooperative, humble, willing to work.

But when they got under the lights Jody had stunned him with her performance. Oh, no, it wasn't *that* good, but good enough to stun him. He had not expected acting. He had expected almost anything else, but not acting. After all, he told Harry, who was this chick anyway? Nobody had ever heard of her, how come she was so good? Anyhow, he had probably screwed up her screen test, and he knew he felt antagonistic and jealous toward her, and there really was this other job where he could spend three months in Spain making an Italian western, where he would be the *star*, where his name would appear *over* the title, and so what with one thing and another, Maggie felt it was right for him to drop out.

Harry explained to Jody that he had told Maggie that he was being foolish. After a few days together, he and Jody would work together fine, everything would be all right, and besides, they really wanted him in the picture and were willing to raise his salary to where it would be at least competitive with the Italian starring job, if you take into account all the cost of travel, etc., and Maggie laughed and agreed and apologized for being temperamental.

What Harry did not tell her was what Maggie had really said. Oh, he had said all the other things, but afterward Harry told him it was all bullshit and wanted to know the real reason.

"Are you sure?"

"Absolutely. What did you see?"

"You're right, I saw something. I sure did. Listen, man, I'm a trained mimic. I can do anything. You show me a little piece of business and I can do it. I can do a fifty-year-old man with a goiter on his neck drinking a lemon phosphate through two straws. I can do anything. Because I'm an observer. I walk down the street looking at the people. I really look at them, and sometimes it gets me into trouble, but when I look at them I see into them. Maybe it started out as self-protection when I was just a little kid, but I have it and I can do it. I watch a guy sitting at a bus stop and I can get into his mind, not know what he's thinking, but how he feels about himself, his life, all that shit. It's a lot in the way people hold themselves or dress themselves, and a lot of it's in the eyes."

"Okay," Harry said, "you're good."

"Listen, man, that chick is a loser. I don't care how well she can act. She's a stone loser. It's written all over her. It just spooked me, I just didn't want to be around for it, you know? I didn't want to work six, eight weeks on a picture waiting for that fucking timebomb to go off. She made me want to cry, man."

Harry knew what he meant. That afternoon in a tiny screening room in a remote corner of the lot he and Fats Dunnigan and Jack Meltzer had sat watching all the takes, less than ten minutes of film in all. It was Harry's job to watch everything—the direction, the camera work, the lighting—but he could not keep his eyes off Jody. Of course he was in love with her and it distorted his perceptions, but he had also been watching performances for better than twenty years, and Jody's performance was incredible for an untrained and unknown actress. In each of the takes she was a person, with twists and turns of character Harry had never dreamed of in her. She was vibrant, vital, alive, and yet she did not seem out of place as a waitress; in fact she would have seemed out of place as anything else.

Harry did not dare look over at Jack, who was sitting next to him in the back row of seats, with the fold-down table and telephone in front of him. Jack was scribbling in his notebook as usual, Harry could hear, but he kept himself from craning over to look at what Jack was writing. When they were at the end, Jack leaned forward and flipped the switch and said to the projectionist, "Thank you, would you run it again please?" and they sat through all the takes once more. By now Fats, alone in the row ahead of them, had gotten onto the telephone and was murmuring to somebody. Harry had to go to the toilet very badly, but he refused to leave the others alone until they had all discussed it. So far, Fats Dunnigan did not know Jody's relationship to Harry, and Harry dreaded having to tell him. Dreaded especially because now Harry was determined that Jody have the part. She was far and away the best actress they had looked at for the role.

"Thank you very much," Jack said into the intercom, "would you run the sixth take again for us?"

Harry thought the sixth take was the best one too, but wasn't Jack being more than thorough? Hadn't he seen enough to know whether he liked the performance or not? It took less than a minute to screen, and when it was over, Jack flipped on the houselights, thanked the projectionist, shut his notebook and put his pen into his shirt pocket.

"Well, boys," he said.

Fats hung up the telephone and turned to face them. He looked tired and harassed; he was executive for three projects in one stage or another, and it seemed to be telling on him.

"That the girl you want?" he asked.

"That's my Helen," Jack said flatly.

"Concur," Harry said.

"Jesus," Fats said. He got to his feet with a grunt. "Why'nt you pick somebody I heard of? I never heard of this person. What'er you paying her?"

"Scale," Harry said.

"Well," Fats said. "Looks like we got a movie."

THIRTY-TWO

JODY FLEW first class from Los Angeles to Atlanta sitting next to a man who said he was an electronics expert and who tried to teach her to play chess with a tiny magnetized board. He was in his fifties and dressed in a dark-blue suit and had a flat Texas accent. Three times he gave Jody his business card and once he turned the card over and wrote a telephone number she was to call if ever she was in Houston. He drank throughout the trip and slept for the last half-hour or so, a light snore coming from his babyish open mouth. Jody did not drink anything except a glass of red wine with her lunch.

She had a two-hour wait in the Atlanta airport, and after twenty minutes of hanging around the book and magazine counters she accepted a man's offer to help her pass the time by going upstairs to the lounge, but when the man tried to buy her one of the outrageously expensive drinks she smiled and said she just wanted a cup of coffee. The man was tall and thin and had carroty red hair and a scarred angry complexion. He seemed to be about forty and wore a white shirt, bow-tie and tweed suit. He was a professor of economics, he told her, a married man albeit an unhappy one, although he suspected that Jody heard that a lot from this man or that man. Jody smiled and said she supposed that most people who were married were unhappy in one way or another, and he agreed eagerly and told her that his wife was a fine woman but she had never been what you might call attractive and now with the children in high school she had just let herself run down and they had frankly not been engaging in any sexual activities at all for a considerable length of time. He had two drinks and continually ate handfuls of peanuts from the glass peanut dispenser on their table, and when he finally got up enough nerve to ask Jody to have dinner with him next time she was in Detroit and scribbled his name and a telephone number on the back of somebody else's business card he had in his pocket, he was so late for his plane that he had to make a rushed goodbye and lope out of the bar without waiting for her, leaving a twenty-dollar bill on the table to pay for everything.

Jody sat alone for ten minutes and then an Air Force lieutenant colonel sat down beside her and after only a minute smiled at her and asked if, like two ships passing in the night, they might have a drink together. He too was a married man, but out of sight, out of mind, he joked, and offered to buy Jody a drink, which she refused with a smile. He did not write down anything on a card for her, but he wondered if she wouldn't think him forward if he asked her to sleep with him that afternoon and catch a later plane to wherever she was going. He was not a man to mince words. He thought the two of them could have a hell of a good time in the sack. He considered himself to be an expert on lovemaking. He had made love to women of all ages in more than twenty countries. When Jody turned him down he told her she did not know what she was missing and for that matter he would pay her some money to go to bed with him, and by God if she didn't give the money back to him afterward and maybe add a few dollars of her own he was sadly mistaken. Jody laughed and said that she appreciated the offer, but no thank you, and he lost his temper and said between his teeth in a low voice, "You bitch, you have to. I need you. I have to do it at least twice a day, and my regular Atlanta girl didn't show up, damn her," and Jody signaled for the black cocktail waitress to come over, and said to her, "This man is drunk and offending me," got up, picked up the twenty dollars and left the colonel with the bill.

There was no first class in the little airplane that flew her from Atlanta to Montgomery, Alabama, and Jody sat between a fat black Army sergeant and a middle-aged woman who spent the entire time looking out the little window at the ground and working her lips.

At Montgomery Jody stepped out of the airplane directly into a wet oven blast of southern heat. It was almost dark and heavy clouds piled in the sky made it darker. There was a long covered walkway from the landing area to the terminal, with scattered handfuls of people greeting passengers or just lounging around, but Jody did not see anybody she knew. While she was waiting for her luggage at the other end of the terminal a plump young man rushed up to her out of breath and asked her if she was Jody McKeegan.

"Yes," she said. "Where's Harry?"

"Mister Lexington sent me. Ah'm Bobby, your driveh." They sped through the Alabama night north and west with Bobby behind the wheel and Jody alone in the back seat. Bobby asked her if she minded if he played the radio and she said no, and those were the last words they exchanged until they crossed a bridge some fifty miles from the airport and Bobby turned around and said, "This's the Alabama River, ma'm." On the other side of the river was the town of Selma and then they were out into the night again, speeding past acres of corn and cotton, the distant lights of an occasional farmhouse making Jody wonder who on earth could live here in the middle of nowhere. Then, at last, they crossed the Grissom County line and in another ten minutes arrived at the Sugartown Motel, on the eastern edge of Sugartown, Alabama. Bobby took the car through the motel drive entryway and up to a two-story row of units in back, stopped the car and turned to Jody.

"Now, ma'm, do you want to go to your room and maybe freshen up? They're shooting on the other side of town and Mr. Lexington asked me to ask you if you weren't too tired if maybe you might like to come out to the set. I'll wait for you here."

Jody sighed. She was exhausted from the trip, but she was too keyed up to go to bed and wait to see Harry when he came back from wherever he was.

"Let me just pop into the shower," she said to Bobby.

He had her key with him, and carried her luggage into the room. She looked around. A nice calm motel room, not classy but not crappy, and obviously all hers. She thought about asking Bobby where Harry's room was, but thought better of it. The poor kid probably didn't know they were living together. After he left she stripped off her clothes and stepped into the shower. One blessing: the shower threw a hard tight stream. She stood under it, letting the hot water hit the back of her neck for a long long time, getting the trip out of her nervous system, and then came out to lie on the bed for a few minutes.

When she awakened, Harry was looking down at her, one hand on his hip, one on his chin, his expression unreadable. "Hi," she said.

"Are you all right?" Harry asked her. His voice seemed high and strained and he did not sit down, take her in his arms, offer to kiss her or anything, just stood there.

"What did I do wrong?" Jody asked. She sat up.

"Nothing, only I've been waiting for you for a couple of hours is all," Harry said like a child.

"Oh baby," she said. "I just laid out for a minute and I must have fallen asleep." She smiled her best even though she was still sleepy and did not understand what was the matter with Harry, and held out her arms for him. Abruptly he turned and went to one of the two easy chairs beside the air conditioner and sat down stiffly. Jody sighed and went into the bathroom and threw some cold water on her face. "Christ, I have to unpack," she said to herself and came out into the room.

"I have to get back to the set," he said. "I shouldn't have left at all."

Jody turned on him, still naked. "Listen, goddamnit, I just spent the fucking day flying around and I got tired and fell asleep. If you don't like it, you can just fuck off."

Harry stood up and put his hands against his cheeks. "What's the matter with me?" he said in a strained voice. "I just got so goddamn mad on the set. I thought you either missed the plane or got drunk in Atlanta or something. It never occurred to me that you'd fall asleep and the kid wouldn't know enough to knock on your door. He's still out there waiting for you."

"Well, for your information I didn't have a single damned drink for the entire trip."

"Oh, baby, I'm sorry," he said and hugged her tightly. "Maybe you should just go on to bed and I'll see you tomorrow. We got another two hours tonight I think and we're behind schedule already."

"I can be dressed in five minutes," Jody said. "I want to come out to the set with you."

"You might as well," Harry said. "Everybody wants to get a look at you."

He still did not seem normal to her. Even under the worst pressures of pre-production he had not gotten this uptight. As they drove though the darkness he told her in rapid disconnected sentences about the problems they had been having—rainfall, a grip dropped a hammer on somebody's foot, a couple of locations had come unstuck, equipment on the Cinemobile had had to be sent back and they needed it—problems Jody did not think sounded nearly as urgent as Harry made them.

They were driving down a narrow dirt country road through forest until at last Jody could see in front of them a mass of light coming eerily through the mist and darkness, and then she could make out the bulk of trucks, buses and cars. Harry pulled up behind a big bus with the word CINEMOBILE on its side. Harry said, "Shit, I don't think they've lit the fucker yet," and got out of the car, leaving Jody to find her way over to the set by herself.

There were a lot of people Jody did not recognize standing around in the humid night while hundreds of insects flew in and out of the light from the big hissing arc lamp. There seemed to be around forty people there, and the only ones doing anything were apparently trying to get a little spotlight off in the woods to stand up by itself. Harry was with them and she could also see Lew Gargolian the production manager. She did not see any actors she recognized and she did not see Jack Meltzer, but after only a few minutes of standing there Jack came up to her from out of the gloom.

"Hey, I'm glad to see you!" he said. Unlike Harry, Jack seemed to be in excellent spirits. "Hey, come on, meet some of the people," he said, and took her back to a trailer where the three principals were sitting jammed into a tiny room overflowing with costumes, clothes, boots, hats, bottles and scripts. All three of them were covered with dried mud and makeup, their costumes in rags.

"Hello friend," Maggie Magnuson said to her with a happy grin. "You catch me in my trick suit."

Jonathan Bridger and Elaine Rudman were polite and shook hands with her, giving Jody a little thrill, as it always did, to be close to people whose faces she recognized; and then Jack said, "Hey, come on, I want to show you something," and took her hand.

"When are they going to be lit?" Jonathan Bridger asked.

"Any minute now," Jack said, and took Jody off with him to where there were five or six canvas chairs, all inhabited by people, lined up a few yards behind the big camera.

"Get your ass off that seat," Jack said not unkindly to a young man, and he jumped up and disappeared, leaving Jody looking down at her name, JODY McKEEGAN, on the chair.

"Sit down," Jack said proudly. "That's your chair."

Jody sat down and smiled up at him, and Harry came over grinning and said, "I see you found your chair," and the two men had a nice laugh together and then walked off into the woods talking quietly. Jody stayed in her chair and watched the electricians fiddling with the light. At last a man in a striped tee shirt yelled, "All right, settle down, people, this is going to be a take!" Nobody seemed to pay much attention to him. No one went near the camera. But then the three actors and Jack came out from behind Jody and went into the woods in front of the camera. "All right, SHUT UP, EVERYBODY!" the man in the striped tee shirt yelled. "THIS IS A REHEARSAL!"

Jack came back and threw himself into a chair, crossed his ankles and wiped his forehead. The three actors had disappeared into the woods. "All right," Jack said in a slightly-louder-than-normal voice, "Action . . ." While Jody watched, the three actors ran crashing through the underbrush, the girl falling down and being picked up by one of the men, and then they came to a forked tree where most of the lights seemed to be concentrated, and Bridger looked through the fork almost right into the camera.

"Cut," Jack said. "That was fine, let's do it." They shot two takes and then the little light they had been fussing with when Jody had arrived did something wrong and everything ground to a halt while the electrical crew tried to fix it.

"Don't we have it?" Maggie said to Jack. "I thought those were pretty good takes."

The man with the striped tee shirt walked past, saying in a loud voice, "If you people think we're going into golden time, you're sadly mistaken," and Jody heard one of the technicians say, "Aw, stick it."

"I want one more take," Jack said to Harry, who was standing next to Jody looking worried.

"What didn't you get?" Harry asked.

"Those face shadows are tricky," Jack said.

"Right," Harry said. Lew Gargolian came over from the light, his forehead creased in a frown. "I think we got it now," he said. He saw Jody and brightened. "Hi, friend. Glad you made it." He reached out a big hand and gave her a firm warm dry handshake. Then the smile vanished from his face and he said to Harry, "Can I see you a minute?"

Jack said to her, "Coffee or water's on the front end of the truck, there," and pointed. Then he too left her and she was alone. The three principals had disappeared as well, and so Jody wandered over to the truck and got herself a paper cup of bitter coffee and returned to her chair. She had just finished her coffee when the big insect hit the arc lamp and fell to the ground, fluttering like a wounded bird. Technicians gathered around like people at the scene of an accident.

"God, look at her flop!" said one man.

"The poor thing," said another.

Jody got up and went over to the light. The bug was on the ground, still flopping and clicking. Obviously the bug had hit the carbon arc and was dying. Jody took her paper coffee cup and trapped the insect inside. The thing was so big it almost filled the cup. Jody put the cup on the ground with the insect trapped under it and stamped down hard. The cup made a crunching sound.

Jody looked around at the circle of faces.

"Good God!" somebody said.

"Better off dead," Jody said and grinned. She went back to her chair and sat down. They shot the scene and Jack had what he wanted, and the man in the striped tee shirt said, "It's a wrap!"

Maggie Magnuson rode back to the motel with them. "Well, I guess everybody knows who you are now," he said to Jody. "Heh heh."

THIRTY-THREE

HARRY DID not get to see much of Jody the next day. Problems were mounting, and no matter how many times he had been through the process he always forgot how compelling each day's new set of troubles could become. He had been almost vicious to her when she had arrived, totally absorbed as he was in his own paranoia, and then when everything was all calmed down and they had gone to bed in her room, the motel operator had found him, in her sweet stupid way: "Ah was just *sure* ah'd fand you. Miss Rudman would like you to telephone her."

"Yes, thanks," Harry had said. He did not call Elaine Rudman though. He stayed in bed with Jody and hugged her until he fell asleep.

He was glad the next day that he had not answered Elaine Rudman's call, because it would have ruined his sleep. Accidentally on purpose he ran into her in the dining room at around nine and sat down opposite her. Elaine Rudman was a slender beautiful woman of thirty who had been in pictures for a dozen years.

"I hear you were looking for me late last night," Harry said. He picked up a piece of her toast and began eating it.

"I really wish you'd called me," she said. "Were you with your girlfriend or something?"

"What did you have in mind?"

"Well, I was talking to Burt last night. He's in Pittsburgh and he won't be able to come down here for at least another week."

Burt was her husband and business manager; as far as Harry knew he was also a highly successful investment broker. "Why does Burt have to be here?" he asked her, although in his heart he really knew. He had been dreading this moment, hoping this once it would not happen. But here it was. He could tell from her perfectly composed face that she was determined to win this argument.

"It's the riverbank scene," she said. "You know that I wanted Burt here to help me with my decision on this matter."

"What do you mean, your decision?" Harry asked, pretending that he did not understand her.

"About the clothes," she said.

And there it was. Elaine Rudman did not want to take off her clothes. It always happened.

"You mean the nudity?" Harry said, as if he could not believe that this is what was bothering her.

"I never appear nude," she said.

"But you signed a contract. You read the script. In fact if I remember correctly you even made some comment about how tasteful it was."

"I did. I think the script is beautiful. But I reserved, you can ask my agent, I reserved the right to discuss this matter with you and Jack with my husband here with me. And he can't be here for at least another week. So you're just going to have to postpone the riverbank scene."

Harry laughed and ran his piece of toast through her egg yolk and then ate it. After he finished he licked his fingers. "You're kidding," he said.

"This isn't a joke, Harry."

"You're too much of a pro to pull this shit on me," he said. "Think about it. The production board's a mess as it is. Remember those two days of rain? Well, you wouldn't believe what they did to our schedule. There is no way in the world we can take that scene and run it back a week. There is no room. Actors will be left hanging on the payroll. People who haven't even showed up would be needed. Don't kid me. You understand all this. What'er you pulling? What do you really want?"

"You know what I want."

"You can't have it. Period. We shoot this scene tomorrow, rain or shine."

"No, Harry," she said. "I'm warning you, I'll quit the picture first."

"Oh, Christ, now you threaten me with quitting. If you were a quitter I'd have known about it a long time ago. You're no quitter. But you are threatening me, and goddamnit, I don't like it. All right, all right, I know, you wouldn't have brought it up in the first place if it didn't mean a lot to you. So what is it, is it Jody McKeegan? Are you scared of working in the scene with her? Did Maggie tell you what happened with him?"

"That's not it at all," she said. "I simply do not think appearing nude is going to help my career . . ."

"Your career? You're a fucking star!"

"I do not think it is a good thing for me to do. I am perfectly willing to appear in the scene as if I were naked, you know, in the water all the time up to my shoulders, or perhaps a long shot of my back. You can't tell me there's an actual necessity for me to show my breasts. You tell me just what it is in that scene that requires the presence of nipples."

"It's Jody, isn't it. You know the scene belongs to her. It's not your scene and you're jealous."

"Now look who's doing the accusing. I've talked it over with Jack and he's on my side."

"What do you mean, he's on your side? You mean Jack doesn't want you to undress for the scene, or Jack is willing to put it off."

"Put it off," she said.

"Well, see, that's not Jack's department. Jack is the director. You may not know it, but Jack and Lew and myself spent quite a little bit of time on that production board, because we barely have enough money to make this movie as it is. We are spending approximately twenty thousand dollars a day whether we shoot or not. Every interference with that board costs us days, and days cost us money. Now, you're a star, and you're already on a lot of this film, but there's a break-even point, and when it costs more to have you than to lose you, well, you can see what happens. I'm really pissed off at you. I mean, to bring it up now."

"All I want is a week, so that Burt can come down," she said. She did not seem to be weakening at all. Harry had a feeling that she was going to stick to it, and he was going to have the heartbreaking task of redoing the board. Lew would probably freak out. He was already wondering why they had so many scenes in the picture, and why Harry was insisting on such full coverage of everything. In fact he had said to Harry only a few days into the production, "Man, you're shooting this like a four-million-dollar picture," and Harry had laughed and put him off. But it was almost true, and it was squeezing the board.

"Be practical," he said. "Are you willing to reimburse the production company for the money your week will cost?"

"No," she said. She had finished her breakfast, and she stood up. "I want my week."

And that was that. Harry was almost certain that Elaine had pulled it just to throw Jody off balance so that when the time came to film this admittedly delicate scene, Elaine would stand a better chance. But he could not brood about it; the day was short and he had a lot of things to do before they went back to the woods to finish up the night chase sequence, this time with the police and the dogs instead of the principals.

Harry did not knock on Jody's door as he went past on the way to the production office. Hopefully, she was asleep. Lew Gargolian and Bud Hanzer the assistant director were in the office going over the production board. Bud was holding five or six strips of cardboard on his hands, strips that represented scenes they had not managed to fit into the schedule yet.

"You ready?" Lew asked him.

"Let's go," he said. He did not have the heart to tell Lew and Bud that the whole board from the second week on would have to be ripped out and painstakingly put together again. Elaine's opening gun was going to cost them a lot of blood and sweat, but Harry could not really be angry with her. It was his own fault: this always happens when an actor has to appear naked for the first time. He should have allowed for it. The goddamn riverbank scene had not one but two women appearing naked for the first time, but fortunately Jody did not have the muscle or the know-how to cause a fuss. He hoped.

Harry and Lew drove through Sugartown and out the highway to Danny's Meadowbrook Cafe, pulling up into the graveled parking lot in front, the only car there at this time of day. Harry once again was amazed at how perfect a location the cafe was. This was the place where Jody and the others meet, in a scene they were going to probably have to shoot this week, but the owner had yesterday told the set dresser who had come around to look things over that he had reconsidered and would not let the company use his place. Lew and the local liaison man had gone to him immediately and Lew had offered more money while the local man had gently browbeaten the owner, but it had not worked, and so now it became Harry's problem.

They stepped into the air-conditioning of the cafe and sighed from their brief moments in the swelter of outside. The place was really too good: a row of cracked red leather stools, big glass counter full of pecan pies and stuffed plush toys for sale; a rack of Confederate flags and patriotic bumper stickers, two big revolving ceiling fans (no longer in use because of the air-conditioning, but Harry meant to have them on during the filming), and best of all, room to shoot in and room for their lighting equipment.

The owner came forward, wearing a white shirt and an apron over his dark pants. He was around fifty or sixty and appeared not to have any teeth. He did not want to meet Harry's eye.

"This is Mister Lexington," Lew said. "Maybe he can straighten things out." To Harry he said, "This is Mister Lorbun."

Harry said, without offering to shake hands, "What's the matter?"

"No trouble," Mr. Lorbun said. "We are just sorry but we can't let you use the place."

"Why not?"

Lorbun looked over at an old woman sitting at the counter, the only other person in the room. The woman sat looking at them without expression, and said nothing.

Lew said, "We had a deal."

"I can't help that," Mr. Lorbun said. He looked old and silly without his teeth, and kept looking over at the woman and getting no help from her.

"Do you feel we aren't compensating you properly?" Harry asked.

Lew said, "No, we discussed that yesterday, and Mr. Lorbun agreed that the compensation was more than adequate. More'n they'd make during the same time period."

"So it isn't money," Harry said. "Frankly, I'm at a loss to know why you are letting us down like this."

Harry stared at the old man until he finally, with one last eye-rolling glance at the woman, said, "Well, my wife she says it would be immoral."

Harry looked over at the woman. She was a mess, her skin blotchy, her hair greasy and stringy, her body soft and shapeless under her dress. She nodded to Harry, confirming her husband's admission. Harry walked over to her.

"Tell me," he said.

"It's immoral," she said, as if Harry had not heard correctly the first time.

"Do you mean," Harry said slowly, forcing himself to look into her hard little eyes, "that it is immoral for you to rent us the place for a couple of days, or it's immoral to make movies?"

She did not seem to want to answer such direct questions. She said, "You tell them," to her husband, and turned away from Harry. Lew looked at him as if to say, "You see?" and Harry said, "Well, it's a shame. I was not only hoping to use this place, I wanted you folks to be in the scene, sort of local atmosphere."

"We are not interested in such things," Mr. Lorbun said.

"You don't want us in your movie," the old woman said. "You're just trying to weasel us."

"All right," Harry said. "I don't have the time. I honestly do not think there is anything immoral going on, and you will certainly be present while we film. I'm going to offer you five hundred dollars per day to use your place, with a minimum guarantee of one thousand dollars. If you think there's anything even slightly immoral about it, why don't you talk to your minister? I'm sure he will tell you if anything funny is going on."

"Our church is over to Tuscaloosa," the old woman said.

"Call them at our expense," Harry said. It was going badly. He really did not want to give up this location. It would cost them too much time and sweat trying to dress, much less find, another place. This goddamn cafe was half their reason for picking Sugartown as their location in the first place; Harry could remember the marvelous breakfasts he and Lew and Jack and the cameraman had had on the location survey, when the old woman must have been out of town. But nothing was happening now, and he could see that the couple were frozen into a position they might really like to take back. On impulse, Harry put a five dollar bill on the counter beside the old woman.

"That's for the telephone call," he said.

"Well, I guess it would be all right," the old woman said.

Harry could never figure out what had worked. Maybe just the sight of real money. It did not matter: they had their location back, and Harry had work to do.

THIRTY-FOUR

WHEN HARRY got back to the production office the secretary told him Fats Dunnigan had called and wanted to speak to him. Harry's heart sank. Dunnigan had obviously been seeing the dailies as they sent them back, and now he was calling to scream. It was still relatively early in the morning on the Coast. But Donald Bitts the costumer was standing there looking tense and worried, and so Harry had to smile and pretend he liked the man and listen to another of his innumerable problems. Donald Bitts was not having a good time on location. In Hollywood he had been bitchy and self-important, with a reputation as an excellent man for the price, but since landing in Alabama he had been tense.

"Come out to the honeywagon," he said to Harry. "I want to show you something."

Harry held in the sharp retort and followed the smaller man out of the air conditioning and across the parking lot to the trailer used as a dressing room and toilet. Inside the dressing room it was terribly hot and stuffy. Donald Bitts waved his arm dramatically at the racks of clothing and said, "There!"

"All right," Harry said, and waited.

"Well, don't you see? There's nothing, absolutely nothing, for the Helen character! I mean somebody back in Hollywood absolutely fucked up, and I am not going to take the responsibility."

"You mean there's nothing for her at all?"

"Not a stitch. You remember, don't you? We waited so long to cast her there wasn't any time for me to take her for fittings. Remember, you said, I think it was you, that we could get things for the character down here, and now we're here and no one has spoken to me at all about taking her out and fitting her."

"Well, that would be a good thing to do today," Harry said.

"But my God she's in a scene tomorrow and the stores around here are the most godforsaken things I've ever seen. I've been to Selma and Montgomery and Tuscaloosa and they haven't got anything, and frankly I'm getting tired of mousing around those stores!"

"It's all right," Harry said.

"It is most definitely not all right!" Donald Bitts said. Sweat was running down his face and his lips were almost white with tension. "I'm the one who has to go out there all by myself and have those people staring at me. The pressure is unbelievable, and I've got all those things to get ready for the effects person, and I just do not have the time to run all over central Alabama with that woman looking for dresses!"

"Can't we get out of this heat?" Harry asked him.

"I just wanted you to see," Bitts said. "There's no air conditioning on those damned streets, either. I've been dying from the heat."

"Let's go back to the office," Harry suggested, but halfway there he patted Bitts on the shoulder and said, "You go ahead, I'll meet you there."

"I just don't have time," Bitts said, and walked off toward the office. Harry watched him. He wasn't even walking the same as he had in Hollywood: back there he had moved with a nice economy and a sense of personal style; here he was just dragging along, putting one foot in front of the other. Harry decided that Donald Bitts was going to be the first of them to flip. Of course by the time they wrapped the picture just about everybody would have flipped at least once. But Bias would be first, Harry would bet on it.

He knocked on Jody's door, and after a moment she opened it slightly. Her hair was wet and he could tell she was naked behind the door.

"I just jumped out of the shower," she said, and gave him a pretty smile. She opened the door and let Harry in. Actually, she was wearing a towel. He looked around her room. Since the night before she had unpacked everything and by putting her things around the room had managed to make it look less like a motel and more like a place to live. There were candles, a lovely old scarf thrown over the television set and some flowers in a water glass on her bedside table.

"I got those in the woods over there," Jody said, pointing across the parking lot.

"Listen," Harry said. "I have a problem and I could use some help. I fucked up and we don't have any clothes for your character. She needs the dress she wears as a waitress and runs off in, and some underwear that will be seen, shoes, purse, stuff like that. Just the things she would have at work."

"What happened?" she asked.

"It was just a simple fuckup. I thought we could buy the stuff down here and then I forgot to reserve the time. So, would you go with a driver and look around and buy three or four alternative costumes and stuff?"

"Sure," Jody said. "Give me a kiss." She held her arms out for him, and he kissed her. "I love you," she said.

Harry said, "I love you too, baby. I'll send the driver down in about thirty minutes, okay?"

"When do I have to go to work?" Jody asked. "I'm really getting up for it."

"I just don't know," Harry said. He kissed her lightly and left the room, snapping his fingers and wheeling to go back after only a few steps.

"Listen, what you have to do is get like three or four of the things you're going to wear. We're going to have to tear some, put squibs in, get them dirty; no, better get five of everything—shoes, dress, everything."

"Five of everything," Jody said. "Some little clerk's going to love me. But the clothes should be used, shouldn't they?"

"Bitts can age them," Harry said, and went back to the production office. Bitts was waiting for him.

"No sweat," Harry said. "Jody McKeegan will do the shopping, and you can get back to what you were doing."

"Her?" Bitts said. "She won't know what to buy!"

"Do you want to go with her?" Harry asked.

"I can't! I just don't have time this morning!"

"Then that's that." He broke eye contact with Bitts and said to Alice Wanderove, "Babe, get one of the drivers to run Jody around this morning, okay? And tell him to take her down to Selma to that new Sears first. Then get Fats for me, will you?"

Fats's voice sounded bland and noncommittal. After the *Hellos* and *How's it goings*, Fats said, "I like the dailies, Harry. You people are doing a hell of a job. How many setups a day are you getting?"

"About twenty-five," Harry said. "But it's getting better."

"The stuff is really pretty. Tell Jack for me. Really pour it on, okay? Let him know we support him all the way."

"Okay, Fats," Harry said, still waiting.

"You guys are really shooting up the film," Fats said. "How does the editor like it so far?"

"Why don't you ask him?" Harry said. "He's there on the lot with you, not down here."

"Right, but I wondered if you'd talked to him. He's probably as happy as can be, with all that film to work with. I certainly hope you people don't run out of stock before you get to the end of the picture."

"We can always get more," Harry said. "Film is cheap."

"Ha ha, it sure is, Harry. Well, keep up the good work. Listen, one piece of constructive criticism: the stuff is really great, the acting is great, but I wonder about the pace. It seems kind of soft to me, do you know what I mean?"

"It's all in the cutting," Harry said.

"Sure it's all in the cutting, these aren't my first dailies, Harry. I've seen uncut film before. This is not my first motion picture. What I mean to say is the pace is goddamned slow for a nice little action adventure movie of the type that we're making."

"I'll talk to Jack about it," Harry said. "But I think the pace is just fine."

"I just wanted to pass along that little piece of advice," Fats said. "We're not making *War and Peace* you know."

"I know," Harry said, and managed to get off the telephone. Two seconds later Fats was gone from his mind, as Lew Gargolian came into the office with the assistant director. For once, Lew's face was bright and cheerful.

"I think we found a place for one-thirty-five and one-thirty-six," he said. "Come over and look at the board."

"Lew, sit down," Harry said.

"Oh Jesus, what now?" Lew said, and threw himself into a chair.

"We're going to have to put back the riverbank scene at least a week," he said.

Lew closed his eyes for a long moment and then opened them, looking at nothing. His mouth was drawn down in fatigue and disappointment. "Somebody doesn't want to take off her shirt," he said in a low flat voice.

"That's right," Harry said. He did not explain who.

THIRTY-FIVE

JODY'S CALL for the riverbank scene was at ten, and she arrived in the production offices at nine, ready for her costume and makeup. She was wearing only her mallard-green robe, because the scene called for her to undress on camera and she would be wearing the things she had shopped for her first day in Alabama, just over a week ago. From then until now Jody had more or less imprisoned herself in her motel room. She hadn't lain by the pool because Harry had almost been angry at her for the tan she did have, and wanted her to lose as much as possible while she waited. She did not go out to the set every day because she did not want to appear to be just Harry's girlfriend, so she read, watched television, went crazy on a regular basis, worried about her part and wished there wasn't a bar just on the other side of the motel. When Harry was back at the motel he was usually in his own room working or down in the production office having one of his endless meetings. When he did come to her room it was either to sleep, holding her tightly, or a flying visit to check if she was drunk on the bed or glued to the ceiling on some kind of drug. As far as Jody knew, however, there were no drugs of any kind in the entire Deep South, and even if there had been she did not want any part of them.

The production office was jammed with people, and Jody made her way through to the back where Benny the makeup man was working on Elaine Rudman. Benny was a handsome tanned white-haired man of sixty who had been in the business since early silent movies. He turned to Jody and smiled and shook her hand. "I'm supposed to do Johnny Bridger next, and then you," he said. Jody moved into the background and watched him work on Elaine, who smiled at Jody once without really meeting her eyes and then went back to watching what Benny was doing to her in the big mirror.

They were all being made up to look as if they had spent the night crossing open fields and forest lands. The riverbank scene is where they clean off, wash their clothes and try to make themselves look as little like people on the run as possible. The makeup was subtle, and most of the effect was created by Nancy the hair stylist, who was working on Elaine in the next tall canvas chair while Benny worked on Jonathan Bridger. Bridger grinned and said hello to Jody and told her a Polish joke and read *Time* while he was being worked on.

When Jody's turn came most of the others were gone out to the set, leaving only the two women who worked in the production office, and after Jody's face and hair had been finished, Benny and Nancy went also, leaving her to wait for Donald Bitts and her costume. Jody sat in one of the high chairs and waited. Fifteen minutes and then half an hour went by, and still Bitts had not come back with her costume. Finally Alice Wanderove looked up from her work and said, "Hasn't that little bastard shown up yet?" and went looking for him. In another ten minutes she came back, followed by Donald Bitts carrying Jody's five different sets of costume, each set in a different condition, from clean and well-worn to filthy and ragged.

"I've been working my little tail off," he said to Jody in an accusatory tone. "These things you bought are really dreadful, but I think if I could just work on them a bit more, we at least wouldn't be embarrassing ourselves out on the set." He held up the cleanest of the dresses for Jody to look at. "See? I mean it's just nothing."

"It's what waitresses wear," Jody said.

"You should know, I suppose," Donald Bitts said and walked into the adjoining room for a moment. When he came back he said, "Well, get into it, dear. Do you expect me to help you dress?"

"Which one?" Jody asked.

"My God, the clean one, you've been out running through the woods all night, wear the clean one. Which one, for God's sake. Oh, you need me, all right." He picked one of the medium-soiled dresses and handed it to her and went out of the room again. Jody followed him.

"I need the underwear and shoes and stuff," she said.

"Oh God," said Donald Bitts.

Finally she was dressed and ready but Bitts made her turn around for him three or four times, sucking air in between his teeth and shaking his head.

"They are just all wrong," he said. "I should never have allowed you to pick out your own things."

"What have you got against me?" Jody asked him. She was getting nervous and she had missed her call. The driver named Tommy was sitting in the front of the office reading the paper and waiting for her.

Donald Bitts did not answer, but frowned as he looked at her clothes. "I think if I let out the waist you'd look a little less like a 1939 hooker and a little more what the part calls for. Take off the dress, please."

"I'm late for the scene," she said.

"I can't be responsible for that," he said. "The costume is hanging wrong and I'm going to fix it. Take it off, please."

"Does it really matter that much?" she asked him, but he went into the other room to wait for her to take it off. Forty-five minutes later he came back from his room, where he did his work, and said, "All right, now try it." She put the dress on and modeled for him. He was still looking at her and shaking his head when Harry came in. Harry's face was red from the heat, but otherwise he looked calm and even pleasant.

"You're fired," he said to Donald Bitts. He went up to Alice Wanderove in the front of the room and said, "Get him on the three o'clock plane to Atlanta. Lew will call for a replacement." He smiled at Jody.

"Sorry about the delay. Do you feel okay?"

Jody said, "I'm a little nervous."

"Let's go."

On the way out Harry told the driver Tommy that he was to wait around and take Bitts to meet his plane in Montgomery. Turning to Bitts, Harry said, "Do you need any cash or anything?"

"No," Bitts said. "Why are you doing this to me?"

Harry took Jody's arm and they left the office.

"What happened?" Jody asked him as they sat sweltering in his car waiting for the air conditioning to work.

"I called Alice to see what was holding you up," he said. "It's my fault. I should have waited. I knew he was getting ready to blow. He really wanted to get fired. He doesn't like this location one bit."

They drove out the highway that bisected Sugarville and then down a side road, passing through parklike open fields and woods, past small herds of black cattle and down red dirt roads through forests of pine trees almost buried in bright-green kudzu vines, making the forest look like a jungle. Finally they came to a clearing by the banks of the Alabama River where the big grip truck, the Cinemobile, the honeywagon and assorted cars and small trucks were parked.

Harry pulled his car into a small patch of shade and turned off the motor. "Well, here we are. How do you feel?"

Jody felt nervous and frightened. "Fine," she said.

Maggie, ragged and grimy, came over to the car and opened the door for Jody. "Missed you this morning," he said. "I got up early and came out with the camera crew. I hear the little twitch got fired."

"How did you know that?" Jody said.

"There's a gas station down the road about two miles," Maggie said. He seemed to be feeling good. "Can I take you to lunch?" he said.

"Good Christ," Harry said. "Is it lunch time?" In the shade of a gigantic mimosa the caterer's helpers were laying out the big tables, and two more were bringing the food out from the back of the catering truck. The meals were trucked in all the way from Selma, forty miles away, because there was no restaurant in Sugarville that either Harry or Lew would trust with the job. Even so everybody was already bitching about the food, Jody noticed. She herself did not eat but sat quietly waiting for things to start and listening to the conversations around her. Harry was gone doing something. Maggie sat beside her, eating a heaping plateful of food and talking to Doug the electrician about golf. When he was finally through he said to Jody, "Take a little walk with me, okay?"

There was a road cutting down the bank to the river's edge, and then a large gravel bar jutting out into the middle of the river, making a big green lagoon on this side. The opposite bank of the river was much higher and looked like green rock. She and Maggie walked down to the river and then out onto the gravel bar, where there seemed to be fewer insects to bother them, although out in the direct sunlight it was blistering hot. Jody did not mind though. She was feeling less nervous all the time. After all, she was among professionals and everybody else seemed okay.

Maggie said, his hands in his pockets, "Listen, I have to apologize to you. Remember that screen test, and I blow up and quit the picture? I want to apologize for that. The reason I blew was because I hadn't expected you to have any talent. But you do, you have a lot of talent, and I used my reaction to you as an excuse to jack a little more dough out of the studio. I don't know what Harry's told you about my little number, but I want you to be my friend. Okay?"

He held out his hand and Jody shook it, smiling at him to let him off the hook.

There was a new-looking raft of one-by-eights lashed to steel drums in the lagoon, and Maggie told her that they had spent most of the morning making it and deciding where and how to tether it for the camera. He told about the searches for snakes before some of the crew would come down to the river, and then they discovered that nobody in the company knew what a water moccasin looked like and so when they did scare loose a couple of snakes nobody knew if they were deadly or harmless. It did not matter; the snakes wriggled down into the dark green river and nobody had to try to kill them.

"Let's go sit in a car," Maggie said, and they were slowly walking up the bank when some of the crew started down. "I don't see any actors," Maggie said, "let's keep going."

"I want to be by myself for a while," Jody said, and so Maggie left her in Harry's car, with the door shut, and the engine and air conditioning running. She could see Harry in the shade, sitting at one of the now empty catering tables, leaning forward talking to Lew, and then he got up and came over to her. He got into the car beside her and sighed for a moment in the air conditioning.

"You ready for the big moment?" he asked her.

"Sure," she said. She was not nervous at all now, and not even impatient to begin. She had waited this long. She could wait.

"It all looks so goddamn beautiful when you're sitting in this air conditioning, but then when you step out into the bugs and heat, forget it."

"Are those turtles?" Jody asked. She pointed to a jagged stick jutting out from the willows below them along the inside bank of the lagoon. There they were, three shaggy and evil-looking turtles, sitting in the sun with their eyes shut and their necks stretched out.

"How the hell did they get there?" Harry said in an irritated voice. "We combed this area for a whole damn half-hour already." He got out of the car and a few minutes later Jody saw some of the technicians walking gingerly along the bank below, pushing the willows away from their faces and poking at the growth with long sticks. Jody's turtles slid off the bank with a single splash as soon as the men came near them, and nobody seemed to find anything else.

"Miss McKeegan?" said Bud Hanzer, the assistant director, wearing another of his striped tee shirts. "It's time to get ready." He led her to the honeywagon and knocked on the little door. "Miss Rudman?"

A handsome middle-aged man opened the door and smiled at Jody and let her in past him. She had met the man the night before at dinner in the motel, although she and Harry did not sit with them. He was Elaine Rudman's husband, Burt Keeling. Jody decided he had probably gone to Abercrombie and Fitch or some place like it and said, "Outfit me for Alabama." He was wearing a khaki suit, the jacket cut like a bush coat, the pants ending in high cuffs above new-looking lace-up boots.

"I'll leave you girls," he said in his cultivated Ivy-League voice, and started to close the door behind him.

"Send Harry," Elaine Rudman said. She looked more nervous than ever. To Jody she said, "Would you mind? I want to talk to Harry for a couple of minutes."

Jody went out just as Harry, with a little fixed smile, went in.

After twenty minutes or so, Lew Gargolian came huffing up the hill, his face shining and red, and asked Jody where everybody was. She pointed to the honeywagon and Lew knocked on the door. Harry stuck his head out, said something to Lew, and then closed the door again. Lew stamped his foot on the ground and then saw that Jody was watching him. He grinned crookedly and went off. A little while later he came back with Burt Keeling, who went into the honeywagon. By this time Jody was back in Harry's car with the motor running. She could see a few of the crew and the two actors ragged and dirty in their costumes out on the gravel bar playing with a frisbee. Another of the crew was skipping stones out into the river and the rest were hidden in the few shady places, although as the afternoon moved along, shadows grew longer across the bar.

The honeywagon door opened and Harry came out and over to Jody. He got into the car and sat for a minute, looking straight ahead.

"What's the matter?" Jody asked.

"She's frightened," Harry said. "She's never shown her tits on the screen before and she's worried that it will change her public image. She thinks it could cost her jobs."

"Will it?" Jody asked.

"I don't know. I don't think so. Anyway, it doesn't matter because she signed the contract and she knew what the job was. She's just afraid, that's all. Burt's talking to her. He's on our side."

And so eventually Burt and Elaine came out of the trailer, Elaine's head high and her eyes defiant, and they all went down the road to the gravel bar. Benny checked everybody's makeup and Nancy fussed with their hair, and out of nowhere came Jack, wearing a white golfing hat, no shirt and a pair of old Levi's. He took his four actors to one side.

"I'm sorry about all this," Elaine said.

"It's not your fault," Jack said. "Let's get to work."

He described to them the way he thought the scene ought to look, and walked them around to their marks on the bank and in the shrubbery. In the first setup of the scene the four of them appear over the bank and Jonathan says they have to clean themselves up, get their clothes as respectable as possible, before they attempt to go through town. They begin to undress.

But clouds were piling up in the west, cutting the light and heat, and before they had even finished a rehearsal, Bob Teague the cameraman, came over to Jack with his lips sucked into his mouth, shaking his head.

"We'll never make it this afternoon," he said.

"Oh fudge," Jack said, and then two of them went off.

"Well, fuck shit piss balls," Maggie said drily. "Who's got the frisbee?"

"Oh God, it's all my fault," Elaine said, looking at Jody. Jody smiled but said nothing.

Jack came back alone and took Jody and Elaine off to one side.

"Girls, we missed the light, and it wasn't your fault, and the person to blame was fired, so let's make the best of it. We can't shoot the beginning of the scene, but the light's going to be right pretty soon for the end of the scene. In fact, maybe everything worked out for the best, because those clouds might just give us a hell of a sunset to shoot into." The end of the scene shows three of them swimming in the twilight, relaxed and enjoying themselves, even though they are on the run. The only one not joining them is Jonathan, who sits alone on the bank, brooding about his responsibilities.

"Then we can wear our suits," Elaine said.

"You can," Jack said, "but not Jody. I want to shoot her standing in the water up to about her knees."

"Well, then, I won't either," Elaine said.

Benny took the makeup off them and they undressed, as soon as the camera had been moved onto the raft and the raft located in position. Jack was wet to the waist by now, and everybody who was not needed for the shot had gone up the hill and supposedly out of sight. There were only the actors, Jack, Bud Hanzer, the cameraman and his operator, and, over on the bank, Harry and Burt Keeling.

It was still so hot that the water felt icy and delightful against Jody's feet as she stepped into the river. On impulse she waded further out into the water until it came up almost to her waist and then abruptly she ducked under. She was in a patch of sunlight, and when she opened her eyes under water everything was eerie and green, the way she had hoped it would be. It reminded her of swimming parties in Portland, on the banks of the Willamette when she had been a child. But this was the Alabama River, and when she came up she would begin, at last, her career.

They shot the scene four times. Jody's part was to stand with the water up to her knees, her head tilted so that her wet hair hung down almost hiding her face. Maggie's part was to swim slowly past Jody and out of frame. Elaine's part was to sit in the water near the bank and be washing herself slowly, and of course Jonathan was up on the bank. They shot four times to catch four different arrangements of sun and clouds, and when they were finished, Jack was very happy.

"I think we got something," he said to Jody as he helped her out of the water and Bud Hanzer draped a large towel around her. "I think we really got some good footage."

Maggie came over to her and said, "See how easy it is?" and Elaine Rudman, when the two of them were in the honeywagon alone getting dressed, said, "Kind of an anticlimax, wasn't it? I mean, just standing there after all the hassle."

"I was a model for a while," Jody said. "I'm used to it."

Harry would never be able to get the picture out of his mind: Jody in the twilight, the sun behind her head, her skin shining like bronze.

THIRTY-SIX

THEN THINGS started getting better for a while. The next morning everyone arrived at the riverbank location in good spirits, partly because the weather had cooled a bit overnight (fall weather had been promised to them for weeks) and partly because the producer's girlfriend turned out not to be the problem everyone had expected. Harry had heard that members of the crew were calling Jody "The Dragon Lady" after she had so efficiently put the June-bug out of its misery her first night on location, but when she had waded out into the lagoon the night before and done her job and looked incredibly beautiful and serene when everybody knew that actresses have almost a right to blow up when they have to work naked, and of course everybody thought Jody was just the producer's girl, and now Maggie was going around telling the crew she was very talented.

Harry did not exactly feel as if a great weight had been lifted from his shoulders, but it was an enormous, incalculable relief not to have to worry about Jody. He knew he would never be entirely free of the worry that she would suddenly go to pieces under the strain, and frankly he would not have blamed her, but she seemed to be bearing up beautifully. Harry thought about all the years she had wasted in her life, when with a talent like hers she could have been a successful actress probably from the beginning. But then maybe that wasn't true. Maybe she had needed to throw her life away in exchange for the talent. Not every genius was a young genius. Of course Jody was no genius, just a damned talented actress, and once again Harry half-congratulated himself for seeing her and seeing talent in her.

By the time they wrapped that night up everybody was really in a good mood. After losing half of yesterday, the crew worked hard and the actors worked hard and they got their entire riverbank sequence, a matter of thirty-two setups, shot in a single day, and not even a full day at that since they couldn't use morning light.

The only one to complain was Jonathan Bridger, who took Harry aside after one of the rehearsals and said, "My reading of the script and yours must be different."

"How's that?" Harry asked, but he knew what Bridger meant. In the script, Jody's invitation to the others to come swimming and stop worrying seems like a minor point, a character point and a way to get out of the heaviness of the scene, but the way Jack had blocked the scene and the way the camera was being used, Jody's bit was becoming the actual point of the scene.

"It just seems a little out of proportion to me, that's all," Bridger said. "I thought the point of the scene was me on the bank unable to unbend."

"It's all in the cutting," Harry said lightly, and Bridger had to accept that as an explanation.

Most of the good feelings and energy seemed to come out of the actors, who after the first take really began to have fun with the scene, and there was a lot of rude splashing and horseplay between takes, and at one point Jack laughed so hard at a blown line that he almost fell off the raft, blindly grabbed at the camera, and was nearly responsible for dumping a thirty-thousand-dollar Mitchell into the Alabama River.

Jody was just great. She did not seem to know that she was naked, and being so unselfconscious herself she made Elaine and even Bridger and Maggie feel at ease with themselves. Nobody wore the flesh-colored suits, and when Jody suggested to Jack that if the women had to show their pubic hair then the men ought to also and Jack laughed and agreed, somebody went up the bank and found Harry and he agreed, and so after a great deal of fussing with reflectors and relocating the camera raft, the longest take in the swimming sequence was enlivened by a flashing glimpse of Maggie Magnuson's sex organ. And even so they came in on time, and when Bud Hanzer yelled, "It's a wrap!" everybody cheered and the actors dubbed themselves "The Four Prunes" and rode back together in Jonathan's car, drinking bottles of ice-cold beer from the tub the prop man kept ready for Bridger.

THIRTY-SEVEN

THIS WAS to be Jody's last scene in the picture: chased by the police, they crash into another car at a little country crossroads. Jody is pinned in the wreck, unconscious and fatally wounded. Jonathan Bridger forces Maggie Magnuson and Elaine Rudman to take the money and escape through the woods to the people who will take them out of the country to safety while he stands off the police in a final shoot-out. While he fires on the two police cars using the wrecks for a barricade, Jody comes to, makes her way dizzily out of the car and staggers into the line of fire. Bridger tries to save her and they are both killed.

The location Harry and Jack had picked was in the middle of a large plantation which occupied nearly a quarter of Grissom County and contained its own crossroads store and postoffice next to a huge rusting old cotton gin with a couple of empty cotton wagons out in front. The whole place looked as if it had been built and then abandoned in the Nineteen Thirties, but as a matter of fact the plantation was a bustling business, raising not only cotton but soy beans, millet and beef cattle. The attractiveness of this particular crossroads was that since it was on private property and both dirt roads were owned by the Sumner family, it would not be necessary to have Alabama State troopers present for the filming to direct traffic, and Harry did not want troopers around for any of the scenes involving the police. The police in the script were just dog heavies, not people at all, and Harry knew from experience that real policemen had a tendency to resent the theatrical kind.

But there were other advantages to the location. It was a beautiful setting, for one thing, and for another the usual collection of Sugarville people who had been watching most of the filming were not able to get out here, and Harry did not want any civilians around for these scenes. A lot of explosives were going to be used to make it look as if the cars and people were being riddled by gunfire, and Harry always hated the thought of anybody getting hurt, especially civilians.

The cars had been wrecked the day before, with cameras mounted inside the cars, strapped to trees, one on top of the Cinemobile and one inside the entrance to the little store, Harry was certain that they had gotten good coverage, although he would not really know until he got back to Hollywood, because they had received their last batch of location dailies three days before, and after they finished this scene, there were only a few pick-ups and run-bys to shoot. And they were only two days over schedule.

Now while the special effects man supervised the placing of the explosive charges for the first setup and the grips were building a long platform for the camera to roll along during the shot, Harry took a moment for himself to walk alone down the road toward a copse of oak trees. He did not know how he felt. Like everyone else he had gone crazy once or twice, and now he had an almost desperate longing for Hollywood, civilization, good food and peace, but there was a sense of regret in him too. This had not been the easiest picture he had ever worked on, but it certainly had the most potential, both commercially and artistically. His telephone calls to Bill Zimmerman the editor had been full of guarded enthusiasm, and of course Harry and everybody else had been seeing the uncut film in dailies shown down at the Sugartown Bijou two mornings a week. The photography was nothing short of brilliant as far as Harry was concerned, although Bob Teague the cameraman always squirmed and writhed in his seat during the screenings and seemed horribly relieved when people did not hate him. And the acting was right on the money, especially Magnuson and Jody.

In the shade of the oak trees Harry squatted down and rested for a moment, seeing the distant activity of the film company through the wavering heat of the morning. When he had been a little boy growing up in Nebraska he had often gone out into the countryside by himself, hunting arrowheads and imagining he was an Indian, and that was his true secret reason for coming over here now. A couple of days before a member of the crew had found some points—"arrowheads" he had called them—under these trees, and Harry really wanted to find some for himself, remains of the Alabama Indians who used to be all over this land. He had meant to go out hunting artifacts with the local expert, a druggist in the Selma shopping center, but it just hadn't worked out that way, and now this was going to be his last chance. He no longer worried about Jody at all. She had not had more than two drinks in a row for the entire six weeks, and although she was showing the strain of the production just like everyone else, she was certainly not the problem they had all expected. To the cast and crew she was just another actress in the company now, and the fact that she was the producer's girlfriend meant nothing. There were too many other things to gossip about: Bridger's and Elaine Rudman's brief but explosive affair after her husband had left; Maggie's sorties into the local communities; the crazy woman who kept going after Bridger's stunt double, and on and on, just like any other company on location.

He did not find any points, but he did gather a handful of potsherds which could have been anything from fifty to two thousand years old. They were light-brown clay, glazed or painted a dark brown on the outside. When Harry got back to the crossroads he went into the store where old Mr. Bill Sumner was behind the counter telling stories to Maggie and Jody. Harry lay the pieces of pot on the counter and the old man said, "Well, you seem to have found some of my cooking utensils," and with a slight twinkle in his old blue eyes he swore to Harry that the fragments were the remains of a terrible crockery battle between Sumner and his wife only last year. "I recall being hit on the head three or four times," he said to Harry, "and after the first few blows I began to lose track of what particular utensils were being employed."

Back out in the heat they were almost ready to go. Jack Meltzer, who like Harry had been averaging fifteen hours a day except Sundays when he would lock himself in his motel room and watch pro football all day sipping from a quart of Rebel Yell, was talking to the heavyset special effects man about the clouds of dust he wanted, to match the crash of yesterday. Harry listened for a few moments while the effects man explained that he personally would create the dust-cloud and Jody, inside the wrecked Chevrolet, would be asked to pull a wire that would cause steam to arise from the engine.

Harry moved on over to where Jonathan Bridger was sitting in his canvas chair in the shade of the honeywagon with the costumer, a stocky Italian who had flown in the day after Donald Bitts had gone home, made friends immediately and was now telling Bridger eggplant recipes that were guaranteed to "keep it up."

"How are you feeling, Johnny?" Harry asked him. Bridger nodded and grinned, and Harry moved along. He had long ago decided that Bridger was a cold fish, but thank God he wasn't temperamental, just a young Republican who was able to earn excellent sums of money by acting. There really wasn't anything for Harry to do. He was not a working part of the company, he was only the producer, and now that he had lied, stolen, cheated, wheedled and berated everybody and everything, there was nothing further for him to do but worry, and even the worrying was in far more capable hands with Lew Gargolian, who, even though they had only five or six days of work left, still wore the wrinkles of anxiety on his forehead. But that was his job. Harry's job here on location was really over until they wrapped the picture, when Harry and Lew would oversee the closing out of the location to see to it that Sugarville would not regret having had a film company in their town. Plenty of film companies left bad debts, pregnant girls and angered citizens in their wake.

BECAUSE THE explosive charges caused a matching problem they were going to have to shoot most of the scene in sequence from the moment of the crash: sending the dazed occupants of the other car to shelter; Maggie trying to pull Jody from the wreck; the arrival of the two police cars; the brief fierce fight between Maggie and Jonathan, ending with Jonathan pointing his gun at Maggie's belly and hissing, "Get going!"; the shoot-out, and then Jody staggering out of the car; she and Jonathan stitched by machine gun bullets and dying wordlessly in the dust. Later they would pick up the police action, Maggie and Elaine's escape and some close-ups. It promised to be a long hard day, and because of the explosives everybody sincerely hoped they could get everything in one take.

When they had Jody made up and in place in the wreck, Harry went over to her. She looked terrible, with blood on her face and in her hair. Harry touched her shoulder and said, "How do you feel?"

"Not so good," she said. She looked more nervous than she had since her first scene.

"Is there something the matter?"

"I don't know," she said. "I wish—well . . ." and she trailed off. "It's sure hot in this goddamn wreck," she finally said.

The other actors were getting into the car now, and the effects man wanted to make sure Jody knew how to tug the wire to make the steam work, and so Harry backed away and got into the shade. He was too keyed up to sit, so he stood with his hands in his pockets. Those damned explosives made everybody nervous.

By three in the afternoon everybody was limp and frazzled. The air was filled with the sharp odor of cordite and there was no wind, so the smell just hung over everything. They were now up to the toughest part of the scene, where Jody in a daze stumbles out of the car and Jonathan has to come out from behind and try to save her. Jody had been great all day, forced to sit for what seemed hours in the heat of the wreck with explosives going off all around her, playing unconscious. But now she and Jack were over on the porch of the store talking, and Harry could tell from the way Jody was standing that something was the matter. As he was walking over to see, Jack turned away from Jody and came to Harry.

"We've got a bit of a problem," Jack said. Jody stayed on the porch, her hands at her sides, looking at Harry without expression. He could tell she was determined about something.

"What's up?" he asked Jack.

"She doesn't like the way the scene goes," Jack said.

Harry laughed and waved him off, going up to the porch.

"What'd you do to poor old Jack?" he asked her. "He thinks you're trying to rewrite the script."

"I don't want to do that," Jody said. "But I don't like the way the scene ends."

Harry opened his mouth and then shut it again. He did not know what to say. This happened all the time, of course, one actor or another either trying to fatten his part or being genuinely concerned over the action. Sometimes the actors were right and changes had to be made, but this was the first time Jody had done anything but make little suggestions.

"Jack!" Harry called. "Come on over."

Jack said from the shade of the honeywagon, "Have you fixed things up?" Harry grinned and shrugged and Jack waved him off. "Straighten her out, she's your girlfriend," Jack said. So the gloves were off.

"What's the trouble?" Harry asked her.

"It's just so damned passive," Jody said. "I come out and stagger around and get shot down. I don't like it."

"But you see, it functions," Harry said. "It's very useful to the story." He laughed, poked Jody in the ribs and said in a low voice, "It gets that snotty son of a bitch killed, doesn't it? Doesn't that make it worth doing?"

But Jody would not be jollied out of it. "I just think it's too damned passive for Helen."

"Helen's not that important," Harry tried but that did not work either.

"She's important all right," Jody said. "I've watched you handling everybody for months now. You aren't going to handle me. I know you. Don't try it."

"All right, I'm sorry, you're right. Okay, tell me what you think ought to happen."

Jody bent over and picked up something out of the dust. "It looks like a piece of that Indian pottery," she said, handing it to Harry. "Keep it for me. I think I ought to pick up a gun or something and fire back. I mean, Helen for Christ's sake pulls a shotgun on a couple of cops just for the hell of it. She's not going to die like that, just staggering around looking for the lady's room or something. She'd go out shooting."

"But she's dazed," Harry said. Over Jody's shoulder he could see Lew's worried face as he pointed frantically at his wristwatch and then at the sun. "Come on," he said, "we don't want to lose the light. You don't want to have to work tomorrow, do you? Hell, this is your last scene. Tonight we celebrate."

"Goddamn it, Harry, cut that out. I really mean it. I think she should get a gun somewhere and shoot it out."

"You bitch, you're like every other goddamn actor in the fucking world," Harry said bitterly. He was not manipulating now, he was really mad. "You get a few thousand dollars worth of film on you, you know fucking well we can't kick you out of the picture, so all of a sudden you're an expert on story lines. Bullshit, lady! You're an actor. Get in there and do your acting and leave the script up to the writer!"

Jody laughed at him. "You mean the way you did?"

Harry was stunned. What she said was true. He was too angry to talk and too confused to turn away, so he stood in front of her taking short panting breaths until Jack came up to them.

"All solved?" he asked with a little smile.

"Give us a few more minutes," Harry said.

"Bob Teague's starting to bitch to Lew," Jack said, and walked back into the shade.

Harry looked at Jody's bloody dirty face and smiled, saying, "You know, it's kind of hard to argue with you when you're all made up like this. What I really want to do is put my arm around you and take you to the doctor."

"Please, Harry," she said. "It's hard enough for me to do this. But I really mean it. Way back in LA when I was sneaking looks at the script this scene bothered me, but I just didn't think you'd let it happen. I mean, it's all wrong. Please. Can't we shoot it my way and your way too? Then you could see what I mean."

Harry kicked at the dirt with his toe. Of course they had done that for Maggie a couple of times when he had had suggestions that Jack disagreed with; it was far easier and cheaper to indulge the actor sometimes. But not this time. It ground at Harry to have Jody pulling this on him in her last scene of the picture, but there was an even better reason:

"Baby, you're going to be wired up with explosive squibs and blood sacks. When they push the button you're going to have to do it right, or we blow the day. We just don't have time to do it both ways."

He took her by the arm and led her around to the front of the grip truck, where he drew them both tall paper cups of water. Others kept away from them, and out of the corner of his eye Harry could see a couple of the electricians starting to toss a frisbee.

"Look," he said. "I can understand your feelings. You're probably right for that matter, I just don't know. But you have to understand. We'd have to reblock the scene. We'd have to do close-ups on you getting the gun and stuff like that, carrying right over into tomorrow. We're right on schedule now. I mean you just have to realize that these things aren't just a simple matter of changing a little bit of business."

"Oh crap, Harry," she said. "There's supposed to be a fucking pistol in the glove box. All I have to do is come out of the car waving the gun, fire a couple of times and then get shot down. You don't even have to change his lines."

Harry threw his paper cup down and walked away from her. "Let's get going," he said to Jack. Jack got up and pulled Harry around the honeywagon out of hearing.

"Did you fix her?" he asked. "You look pretty pissed off."

"I am pissed off, and if she doesn't do the scene the way it's written the hell with her."

"Oh shit, you know better than that. Get a grip on yourself."

"Shoot the scene," Harry said, and walked away. He wanted to walk over to the oak trees and sit in the shade watching the whole thing from that distance, but the trees were in the shot. Instead he went into the store. Old Mr. Sumner was in back in his office and so Harry had the place to himself. He could hear the assistant directors yelling outside, so he knew they were setting up for the shot. Jody was probably being wired for her bullet holes now, and the effects man would be telling her how to react to them. He could not help worrying. He had seen enough actors damaged by those things. But you could not make a scene of violence anymore without showing the actual bullet wounds. People would laugh at you. He hoped she would not get hurt, especially after he had had to treat her roughly, but it was the amateurs who did get hurt, and for all her abilities and talent, she did still lack experience.

Standing in the dimness of the old country store with its half-empty shelves and its battered old Coca-Cola cooler, Harry allowed himself to think about the future. What was going to happen to Jody after this picture? Harry would definitely have to get her an agent. On the basis of the raw film they had shot on her so far, he was sure she could land one of the big agencies like IFA or CMA. She would not get a big star build-up or anything because she was too old, but she would be getting a lot more money and better billing. It even might be possible, Harry thought, to get some really good young writer to do a screenplay for her. Then he had to laugh at himself. Nobody did that sort of thing anymore.

In half an hour they were ready to shoot. Bridger was off pacing up and down getting himself up for the scene and Jody was inside the car, all wired up and made up and ready to go. Harry forced himself to walk over to her. She looked up at him coldly.

"I'm sorry, baby," he said. "How do you feel?"

Jody reached over to the glove compartment and pulled out the pistol, a worn old .38 with half the bluing worn off the barrel. She pointed the pistol at Harry's face, and automatically he pulled back.

"Where'd you get that?" he asked her. He saw her finger whiten on the trigger and heard the sharp *click*. "Why, goddamn you," he said and walked away. He found the prop man sitting on the back of the grip truck dangling his feet.

"Who told you to give Jody McKeegan that pistol?" he said.

The prop man was a flat-faced Australian with one drooping eyelid. He smiled at Harry, showing his teeth. "She said she wanted it for the scene."

"Do you realize that if that fucking thing had had any fucking blanks in it she might have blown my eye out?" Harry said angrily. "Get it away from her!"

The prop man pursed his lips and slid down off the gate. "Yas, Boss," he said sarcastically, and trudged off toward the wrecked cars. Harry followed him, aware that several members of the crew had heard him blow up. Fuck them, he thought. In a few days he would have the exquisite pleasure of saying goodbye forever to most of them.

He arrived just in time to hear Jack say, "Jody, if we don't get this scene in the next ten or fifteen minutes we aren't going to get it."

Jody, still in the car, said, "Then that's too bad." When she looked over and saw Harry she swung open the bent door of the car and stepped out. "I'm not going to do it, Harry," she said, and went over to the honeywagon and climbed in.

"Oh *fuck*," Jack said.

"Just a minute," Harry said, and went to the honey-wagon. Jody was sitting inside in the air conditioning, her face drawn. She looked at least her age, and maybe a couple of years older, Harry thought. The strain was tough on her. He had to admire her, though, even if she was wrong. He closed the door behind him and pushed some costumes off the other chair and sat down.

"Baby," he said. "I love you."

"Thanks," she said dully without looking at him.

"You must understand. This is not your scene. This scene belongs to Johnny Bridger, it's his big moment in the picture. You've already had your big moment, now it's his turn. He's the star of the movie. It was practically written for him, and this scene particularly. He's the cool one, the cold one, and now he dies trying to save your life. Your way it's different, the point gets lost. Do you understand what I mean? I know, from your point of view your way looks good, probably better than the script. But I have to keep an overview, I have to keep in mind what the whole picture's going to cut into; the balance, the tempo of the whole picture. You have to trust me: your way throws the whole thing out of kilter. Please. We only have a few more minutes."

"I don't know about any of that," Jody said. "But I know Helen and I know what she would do. She would not get out of that car and wander around while people are shooting at her. She would either lay there or shoot back. I mean it."

There was a knock at the door and Harry reached over and opened it, seeing the concerned face of Jonathan Bridger. He said to Harry, "Can I talk to her for a minute?"

"No," Harry said. "Oh, hell, come on in."

"I just wanted to tell her how much I've appreciated her work," Bridger said. He gave Jody his best slow grin and said, "You really helped us all, you know, by being a real pro. I guess that's all I had to say," and he left them alone again.

Into the silence Harry said, "Okay? Can we get our scene?"

"No," Jody said.

For the first time since the argument had started, Harry looked directly into her eyes. What he saw there convinced him that he had made a mistake. There would be no changing her mind and so it was Harry's fault that they were wasting the afternoon. He should have seen immediately that right or wrong Jody meant to have her way about this and he should have found a way to make it look all right.

"We've got enough time to shoot the scene once today," he said to her. "Do it my way, and I promise you that tomorrow we'll shoot it once your way before we pick up the close-ups. Deal?"

"If we shoot it my way tonight," Jody said, "you can see what I mean."

"All right," he said. "Let's go do it."

Outside he did not even bother to take Jack out of people's hearing. "Jack, we're going to shoot the scene her way tonight. Have we got time for one rehearsal?"

"Sure," Jack said. "Good. I like it."

The two of them found Jonathan Bridger and explained to him what was going to happen.

"I don't give a shit anymore," he said. "Let's just do it."

"That's the spirit," Harry said. He wanted very much to laugh. What difference did any of it make?

THIRTY-EIGHT

JODY GOT drunk that night in the motel's little bar. Everybody else must have been too tired to even come in, because she was the only member of the picture company in the place. She was glad she did not work here. Behind the bar was a thin bony woman of about Jody's age who said her husband was in the Air Force stationed in Alaska and she worked here for something to do as well as the money, and she had no intention of joining her husband in Alaska when he got enough time in grade to send for her, or whatever it took.

Jody and Harry were supposed to be celebrating tonight because today was supposed to have been her last day, except for a couple of shots where she didn't really do anything but sit there. But now she was going to have to do a repeat of the crossroads death scene, only their way, the script's way, a way the character Helen would never have died. So now Harry was angry at her and would not come out and drink with her. He was in his room fiddling with paperwork and pretending he was too busy, but she knew he was just punishing her for being a bitch today. But she was going to have her drinking party anyway, whether anybody joined her or not.

She had knocked at Maggie's door but he had not been there, so he had probably gone to town with some of the crew. There were a couple of raunchy clubs in Sugarville, and Jody was half-tempted to get a set of car keys from the production office and run into town herself. But no. Harry might get over his sulk and come over looking for her, and she wanted to be where he could find her without too much trouble. Later on that night she expected to want to make love. She usually did when she got drunk, unless she got too drunk, which did happen from time to time.

A couple of handfuls of peanuts from a dish on the bar was her dinner. She did not feel like eating. She felt like drinking and raising a little hell. She had been holding it in for a couple of months. That was practically a record for her. She had to congratulate herself. She had not really believed that she could actually get through this entire picture without fucking up. But she had done it, and she had even gotten them to make the crossroads scene the way she wanted, with Helen dying in a blaze of gunfire screaming curses at the police. She smiled to herself. She would have to wait for Hollywood to see the dailies on the scene, but it would be worth the wait. It was the best thing she had done on the picture and she was proud of it.

She had five of the little two-shot bottles of bourbon whiskey mixed with water and ice before Harry came in with that wary look on his face and told her that she had better get back to her room.

"I bet you think I'm drunk," she said and laughed, realizing as she said it that she was drunk, and it was a damned good thing Harry had come for her.

"Come on," he said. "Did you pay for your drinks?"

"Yes I paid for my drinks," Jody said, a little irritated at his question. "And I can walk without any help from you, either."

"Don't get mad," Harry said in his mild voice. Outside there was a nice chill in the air. They walked arm-in-arm around the pool and through the breezeway to her room.

"Aren't you coming in?" she asked Harry. He was standing at the door.

"You need some sleep," he said. "Big day tomorrow. Your last day on the picture."

"Yes, but I'm celebrating tonight," she said. "Come in, baby. I've missed you."

She went up to him and kissed him on the mouth and put her hands on his ass to pull his body up to hers. "Come in, lovey," she said to him. "I want to do something to you."

"Just for a minute," Harry said, and closed the door behind him. Jody kissed him again and felt him holding himself back. She put a little more into the kiss and then put her head against his chest and held on to him. She could feel him changing, and after a couple of moments he tilted her head up and kissed her, and then it was easy. She undressed him slowly the way she liked to do, kissing him and stroking him until his eyes went glassy, and then she took off her own clothes while he lay on the bed and watched her, and then they made love, for the first time in more than two weeks. This time it was good, very good for Jody. She came three times, each orgasm bigger than the last, until she was exhausted from it and he lay next to her panting happily.

"My Jesus Christ!" was all he could say.

They lay holding each other until Jody had to get up to get a glass of water. All the booze had made her thirsty, and of course she was still drunk as a fucking goat. But she could feel the edges of the hangover already creeping into her brain, and she wanted another drink to put it off.

"Do you have a bottle in your room?" she asked Harry.

"No," he said. "But you'd better get to sleep anyway." He got up and started to dress.

"Oh stay with me," she said.

"I have to get up three hours before you do," he said. "You're going to need the sleep." When he was dressed he came over to her on the bed and leaned down and kissed her. It was a very nice kiss, very tender and sweet.

"I love you," Harry said to her and left the room.

Jody's call was for ten and so she told the motel operator to wake her at eight-thirty, turned out the lights and faced the darkness, with nothing but the heavy breathing of the air conditioner for company. After a while she knew that she was not going to be able to get to sleep. The trouble was, it was still too damned early to go to sleep. She turned on the light again and dressed in a pair of tight blue jeans, her old paisley men's shirt and a pair of sandals and went outside.

The only light on in the row was Alice Wanderove's, and so Jody knocked, although she had not had much to do with Alice during the production. Alice opened the door wearing an old chenille bathrobe. Her television set was tuned to the Johnny Carson show.

"Hi, come on in," Alice said and stepped back to let Jody past. "I hear you were really good this afternoon."

"Who told you that?" Jody asked. "I thought everybody hated me."

Alice laughed and threw herself onto the bed. "Oh, no, the crew loves you."

"I love them too," Jody said. She sat down and for a couple of minutes watched the television. She did not see any bottles around the room. "I'm kind of on the loose tonight," she said. "I was over in the bar drinking but Harry came and got me and put me to bed."

"I guess they're closed now," Alice said. "They sure close early. Lew and I were over there drinking one night and they closed at ten thirty, just said, 'G'nat naow!' and threw us out."

"I can't sleep. I guess I'm still all keyed up from today," Jody said. "Do you have any sleeping pills or anything? What I'd really like is some good old country marijuana, though."

Alice laughed again and said, "I don't have any of that, but I guess about half the company's been buying the stuff from some of the drivers. I know when we first got here everybody was so scared about the Alabama police and stuff like the KKK and so nobody brought anything."

"I know," Jody said.

"I've got some seconal if you want one to get to sleep, though," Alice said. She got up and went into the bathroom, coming out with a plastic vial. "I practically live on these things sometimes," she said. "My husband he says they're no good for you, but out on location I really need something." The vial had seven or eight of the red capsules in it.

"I could use maybe three of them," Jody said, "if you can spare them."

"Oh heck," Alice said, "I'll be home in Van Nuys in a few days. Take all you want."

Jody took four and went into Alice's bathroom to wash them down. She swallowed two and put two in her shirt pocket.

"You didn't take all of those, did you?" Alice asked her. "You should only take one or two unless you're really used to them."

"I just took two," she said. "Two for tomorrow night, if that's okay."

"Sure," Alice said.

"Well, I better get back to my room before I fall out," Jody said. "Thanks a lot."

Just as she was putting the key in her door, one of the company cars drove up and parked with a squeal of brakes, and Maggie Magnuson got out. He had a big white bag from the McDonald's in his hand, and he looked drunk.

"Hello there!" he said to Jody. "You wanna cheeseburger?"

"Sure I do," Jody said.

"I'm going to invite you to my room, but you must not make a pass at me," Maggie said seriously. "The boss would kill me."

"I'll try to hold back," Jody said.

Even with the daily maid service Maggie's room was a mess, with clothes, guns, fishing rods, books, magazines and assorted junk lying all over. Maggie threw some things off one of the chairs and gestured grandly for Jody to sit down.

"You want a Big Mac or just a plain ordinary chickenshit cheeseburger?" he asked her.

"What I'd really like is some weed," she said. "I've been a good girl all the time, and now I really want to get ripped."

"Aw," Maggie said. "All I got left is one joint, local stuff. I bought a lid from the Goon about a week ago, after I got over my paranoia, but it's all gone but one joint. Everybody's been hitting on me." He opened a drawer in his desk and pulled out a fat marijuana cigarette, lit it and passed it to Jody.

"Goddamn, that tastes good," she said. Maggie turned on the television and sat watching, wolfing down cheeseburgers.

Jody did not want any of the food, but asked for and got a bathroom glass a quarter full of the Wild Turkey Maggie kept in his room. The 101-proof bourbon tasted delicious to Jody, and was so strong that it seemed to actually numb her mouth, but that might have been the effect of the reds. But the marijuana did not seem to be very good. She was not really high, just a little drunk and still wide awake. She really wanted to get high.

"Where'd you buy this dope?" she asked him.

"From the driver, you know, the guy they call the Goon, little nice-looking guy. The only genuine degenerate in the whole fucking town."

Jody knew him, a small bland quiet boy of about twenty whom everybody in the company liked. "He got fired, I heard," she said.

"Well, I don't blame them. He was always ripped. He was supposed to take some film to the Montgomery airport one afternoon you know, and he says to Lew, 'Ah jes' doan think ah kin *fand* th' goddam airpoat,' and so Lew fired his ass."

"Do you know where he lives?" Jody asked him. "I'd like to buy some weed, even though we're through tomorrow, at least I am."

"I'm too tired," Maggie said. "Have another belt of WT, you'll feel better."

Jody got to her feet. "No, goddamn it, I want to boogie," she said.

Maggie came up to her, putting his hands lightly on her hips. "I'll boogie with you," he said in a soft voice. "But after we all get back to California. You know?"

She kissed the tip of his nose and moved away from him. "I didn't mean that, Maggie. When I'm with somebody I'm with them all the way. And I'm with Harry Lexington for the present time anyway. So just don't make that mistake again, do you understand me?"

He grinned. "Sure. I was only kidding anyhow."

"Kidding my ass. You wanted to jump into bed with me, and I'll admit I like you. But no, baby. Now come on, let's run over to the Goon's place and see if he's got anything."

"You won't even pricktease me to get me to do it, will you," Maggie said. "Shit, you might as well. Anybody see you coming out of my room's going to think we've been balling anyway, won't they?"

"No I ain't going to pricktease you. I don't have to. You'll do it anyway."

Maggie took a belt from the open bottle of Wild Turkey and said, "I guess you're right. It's too far to walk, and you'd get lost anyway."

"Do you want me to drive?" Jody asked. "You look kind of drunk."

"I'm not as drunk as you are," Maggie said.

"That's true," Jody said. "Let's get that dope."

BUT THE Goon did not have any marijuana for sale. He lived in a small house-trailer in a lot filled with old car bodies out in back of a large frame boarding house. Maggie parked on the street and he and Jody walked down the dark path between cars and knocked at the door. After a moment the Goon opened up. He was sleepy-looking, wearing a white tee shirt and a pair of old shorts.

"Well hi," he said. "I was just laid back a little." They entered the tiny crowded trailer. Jody noticed the smell of old sweat hanging sourly over everything and shuddered, because it reminded her of the lower East Side.

"I hear you got fired," Maggie said to the Goon. They were all sitting down, Maggie and the Goon on the messy bed, Jody on a pile of clothes and records in the one chair.

"Well, they took my job away, but I don't mind," the Goon said. He smiled crookedly. "I have other sources of income."

"Well yeah," Maggie said. "We came over in fact hoping you might sell us some weed. Just a lid, or even less if you can."

"Man, I'll gladly share what I've got with you, but all it is is my personal stash. Things are drying up around here. I had to go clean to Mobile for that last pound I bought." He reached under the bed and brought out a shoebox lid covered with twigs, seeds and a little marijuana. "I think maybe we can get two joints out of this."

"We can't smoke your last weed," Maggie said. He got to his feet.

"The hell we can't," Jody said. "Don't be in such a hurry."

"Really, we shouldn't hang around," Maggie said, but Jody was watching the Goon's delicate fingers as he rolled the joints. As soon as the first one was finished he handed it to Jody, who lit it and passed it to Maggie, still standing by the door. It did not taste like the stuff they had had in Maggie's room. It seemed stronger and not as harsh.

"Good weed," she said as soon as she let out her breath. "God, I hope it's good anyway. I really need something."

"I hate to smoke and run," Maggie said. He looked nervous underneath the blandness, Jody thought. He was probably put off by the smell of sweat, and it probably made him nervous to be someplace where he was not protected by the movie company. Come to think of it, back home in California he lived in a big house with a swimming pool. The poverty probably offended him, too.

"You can go if you want," Jody said in a strained voice. She was trying to hold her breath and talk at the same time. "I'm going to hang out."

Maggie's lips went tight. She was sorry to see that; she had always liked this guy.

"I can't leave you here," Maggie said. He stuck his hands aggressively into his front pockets.

"Oh now, let's not talk like that," Jody said.

"You're both perfectly welcome to leave or stay," said the Goon. He finished rolling the second joint and stuck it between his teeth like a cigar and grinned at Jody. She lit a match and held it out to him and he bent forward cupping the joint in his hand and looking into her eyes as he sucked in the smoke. Trying a little of the old sexy look, she thought. He must be a terror with the local chicks, with his drugs and his reputation. He leaned back and blew a gigantic smoke ring, then leaned forward and sucked the smoke back into his mouth. Aha, Jody thought.

"Well, let's get the hell out of here, okay?" Maggie said.

"Oh, go fuck yourself," Jody said. She held a joint up to him but Maggie refused to take it. He looked pretty angry. "Can you drive her back to the motel?" he asked the Goon.

"Anything she wants, she gets," he said.

"All right then, goodbye," Maggie said and opened the door.

"Get if you're going," Jody said. She wanted him gone, he was nothing but a big bringdown now. She stood up and said, "Are you waiting for a kiss goodbye?"

Maggie got that look on his face that men get when they suddenly realize that three is a crowd, and went out the door backward, almost forgetting that there were two little metal steps to the ground, almost falling but hanging on to the door, and then slamming it shut with a tinny whack. She could hear his feet crunching angrily through the lot.

"God, I thought he'd never go," she said. "But don't you get any ideas. I really feel like talking. I've been up all night. You wouldn't believe the fucking day we had out there."

"I heard," the Goon said. He leaned back against his pillow, relaxed, and took another hit off the joint he was holding. Jody finished hers, wet it and swallowed the roach.

"Waste not, want not," she said. "Shit, I went all this time with no booze, no weed, not even a fucking glass of wine with my goddamn dinner, just to keep from fucking up this movie, did you know that?"

"I knew you wasn't running around much," he said. "I thought you'd be around, you know, you look like people, but then everybody else said you were really cold as hell, but I never believed it."

"You know me pretty well," she said. She did not want to stand and she did not want to sit, so she more or less paced up and down in the tiny floor-space between the bed and the door while the Goon lay stretched out. The weed was good, much better than she had expected, and Jody felt that rising sense of joyful expectation she almost always got from good marijuana, as if something wonderful was just about to happen. "Goddamn, I feel good," she said. "I haven't felt this good since I left California. I really did it to those bastards," she said. "I really knew I could do it. Nobody thought so but me, they always said, 'Baby, you're a good fuck, maybe even a great fuck, but you can't act for shit.' I never listened to them. Acting. What is it? You pretend to be somebody else for a while. I been somebody else all my life, haven't you? You ever show yourself to people? I never do. I did my sister in this movie. She was the one who wanted to be in the movies. I never did. I just wanted to do it because she wanted to do it, and then you know you wake up one day and that's all you can do, what you figured out for yourself when you were nothing but a goddamn kid. Fifteen years old, man, that's when I decided to really get into it. I done everything but act. You wouldn't believe. Maybe you would. Do you have any more dope? I really want to get it on. I'm not going to sleep tonight. I took a couple of reds and I'm still not sleepy, man. My head's racing. I did it. Do you know what I mean? I mean I really pulled it off. For the first time in my cheap fucking life I did what I said I was going to do. All my life I couldn't take the pressure, you know, but I took it. I ate the shit they asked me to eat and begged for more, because this time it was for me! Do you have any *drugs?*"

"I got some skag," he said. "Are you into it?"

Jody laughed. She could not stop pacing up and down the little room. "Skag? What the hell are you doing with skag in this fucking place?"

"We ain't that far out into the backwoods," he said. "A few of us take the stuff."

He went into his kitchen and rummaged around and came back with a hypodermic kit, and then went into the bathroom, closing the door with an arch look at Jody, as if to say, 'I trust you but you never know,' and then came out with a small yellow balloon.

"I haven't had a taste of that stuff since New York," Jody said. She stretched out on the bed while he fooled around getting the heroin cooked on his dirty little stove. "I used to live with a stone junkie, we'd just do smack, lay back and let life roll along, you know?"

"I'm not heavy into it," he said.

"I never thought I'd run into a shot of dope right out here in the middle of nowhere," she said. "But you have to take me back to the motel pretty quick, because I'm going to fade out. I have to work tomorrow, doing the goddamn scene their way, which is the most chickenshit way you ever heard of, with me dying like the queen of the wimps. But they'll see. I hated to do it, but I had to."

"Aren't you going to stay a little while with me?" the Goon asked without looking at her. He drew the clear liquid up into the outfit and threw the empty balloon over to her. "You want to tie off and go first?" he asked her.

"I'll just shoot it into my leg," she said, and sat up unbuttoning the top button on her jeans and then unzipping them and pulling them down around her ankles. She did not happen to be wearing any underpants, and she saw him sneaking a look at her pubic hair. "Don't get any big ideas," she said. "I love the man I'm with, and I don't sleep with nobody else. I'd fuck you if I felt like it, though. I just don't happen to feel like it. Gimme that needle," she said. "I got a favorite vein here on my leg." She found the vein and punched in, drawing back on the needle until blood showed in the glass tube.

"Ah," she said. Here it was, the easy death that had never been far from her hand.

"Are you gonna shoot?" the Goon asked.

"Bullshit," she said, and drew the needle from her leg. She handed it to him and immediately he began to tie off. Jody pulled up her Levi's. "I think I'll step aside and let this one go by," she said, but the Goon wasn't listening. She opened the door and went out, hoping that Maggie was waiting for her in the production car. But he wasn't, and so she had to walk all the way back to the motel. It took almost an hour, and by then she was ready for a good night's sleep.

TURNAROUND

This book is for Richard

"A man needs only to be turned around once with his eyes shut in this world to be lost."—HENRY DAVID THOREAU

PART ONE:
WEL OME TO HOL YWOOD

CHAPTER ONE

IT WAS just dawn as the black Porsche stopped with a sputter at the intersection of Mulholland and Laurel Canyon Boulevard. The engine was choking spitefully over something, as usual, but Jerry Rexford paid no attention. This was an important moment for him. Until now he had been driving down the length of California, and then the long predawn rolling emptiness of the San Fernando Valley, but from this intersection forward he would be in Hollywood, the mythical kingdom he had dreamed about all his life, the Movie Capital of the World.

At that moment, the engine died. If it was an omen, Jerry Rexford did not have time to reflect on it, because right then a police car with two young cross-belted cops pulled up to his left. Jerry waited for them to go ahead, but they didn't. They watched him. His face heating up under its all-night beard, he tried to get the engine started. The car was always skittish, and now seemed to be so carboned up that it would never go. *URurURurURurURur.* The cops were as silent as dummies in their car. Jerry looked around, realizing that from their viewpoint he was a man behaving in a suspicious manner, in an exclusive residential neighborhood in the Hollywood Hills at five a.m. A stranger in a black Porsche which he obviously did not know how to operate. He could feel the sweat running down his armpits as he twisted the key viciously and tramped once again on the accelerator. If it would only run just a little bit, he could get across the intersection and be on the downhill slope. Then he was sure he could coast all the way to Sunset Boulevard *(Sunset Boulevard!)* and then let the car have a little rest when he went for something to eat.

Jerry patted the dashboard. "Come on, honey," he said, and the engine coughed hesitantly and then, *thrum!* The tachometer smoothly ran up to 5000 and back down to 2500 RPMs. Jerry realized he had had his left foot pressing the clutch into the floor the whole time. He made sure he was in first gear and slid across the intersection in front of the immobile dummylike police officers and down into Hollywood. As he knew they would, the cops followed him all the way to Sunset. The Porsche, unused to the hairpin turns and long unbanked curves, rippled out a string of explosions into the teeth of the cop car.

Jerry Rexford called himself a writer, and thought of himself as a writer. When his various jobs made it possible he got up early in the morning and wrote. He wrote short stories, plays, poems, letters, essays, hopeful screenplays and novel fragments. But when the L.A. cops pulled him over and asked him what he did, while they ran him through R&I, and he said, "I'm a writer," the cop who was leaning against the Porsche tapped his teeth with a ballpoint pen and said, "Write anything lately I might have read?" and Jerry had to say no. "Laborer," the cop said as he wrote.

Obviously, R&I had nothing on him. The two cops stood there on the empty boulevard. Finally one of them bent down and said to Jerry, "Well, what the hell *are* you doing out at this hour?"

"I just drove down from up north."

"We got that. But why?"

"I'm just starting out," he said sheepishly. It couldn't get any worse, he might as well roll over on his back and wave his legs in the air, like a helpless goddamn dog. You got me! You got me! Scoop out my belly and be done with it!

Aloud, he said, "This is my first day in Hollywood. I'm sorry."

The cops grinned at each other knowingly. One said to Jerry, "Hey, don't have to be sorry. You just wanted to get an early start, huh?"

The other cop said, "In Hollywood, the early worm gets the bird."

Jerry found himself laughing, although *squeaking* might have been a better word for the sounds coming out of his mouth.

"That's a good one, Lew," the first cop said.

The other cop, obviously in a good humor now, said, "You proceed west here on Sunset for a few blocks, there's an all-night place."

The other cop said, "Yeah, Schwab's don't open for another couple hours," and snickered.

Jerry felt himself blushing again. It was true, the damn cop had pinned him, he *was* headed for Schwab's, and he hadn't known it was closed this early. That had all been part of the fantasy, driving down at night and that first hot Hollywood cup of coffee at the famous show business drugstore.

To add insult to injury, the sarcastic cop, Lew, pointed across the street, where Schwab's lay closed behind its big windows. "There's Schwab's," he said, and then pointing again, "There's the Chateau Marmont, there's Greenblatt's and over there, see that little park? That used to be the Garden of Allah."

"Thanks," Jerry said. At last rid of the cops he drove slowly down to the twenty-four-hour restaurant, the Porsche silent as a Rolls-Royce. He got out, stretched and went inside. His jockey underwear felt musty between his buttocks as he sat at the long curved counter, but it was too late to grab and pull.

Well, here I am, goddamn, he thought. The coffee was hot and strong, and cleared the oppressiveness from his head. There were others in the place, Hollywood people, people who got up at this hour routinely, maybe some of them were even in the Business, hell, they have to get to work real early . . . Jerry turned slightly, to look at the people in the red booths, and almost the first person he saw, sitting with a couple of other men, was Paul Newman. Jerry turned back and smiled down into his coffee. Seeing Paul Newman sitting there like anybody else, grim over coffee and breakfast, made Jerry's face turn beet red and made his heart pound, even though he knew damned well it couldn't actually be Paul Newman. After a sip of coffee, he turned for another peek, and they made eye contact. Those big blue eyes, it had to be Newman! Jerry broke the contact before Newman could break it, and took another sip of coffee, this time getting some of it on his chin and dripping down onto his pants. He sat there awhile frozen over the coffee, waiting for the powerful and unpleasant emotions to die down. What if it *was* Paul Newman? So what? The man goes to work just like everybody else, probably hates getting up at this hour, morning after morning, just like everybody else, this *is* Hollywood, the people who work in the movies are going to be around, walking, driving their cars, eating, drinking, buying toothpaste . . . He took another peek. Oh, hell, the man didn't look like Newman at all. He was too ordinary. He was an ordinary guy who looked a little like Paul Newman. People probably told him that all the time. But why did Jerry feel so overwhelmed, just by seeing supposedly Paul Newman eating breakfast?

Now that he knew it wasn't Newman after all, Jerry turned and boldly looked over at the booths. Other people were eating in booths on both sides of the putative Newman, and didn't even seem to notice the resemblance. Jerry felt completely recovered. Jezus, he thought, I better give some thought to being around these glamorous people . . . Daydreaming, he saw himself in the company of Newman, the real Newman, and being relaxed enough to go over the script with him while in the dim background everybody on the set waited expectantly . . .

"Hey, Paul!" a voice called out. Here were his two policemen, and Lew was grinning and waving to Paul Newman, who waved back, and Jerry felt himself going into a fugue again, just as Lew turned to him, pointed a finger and cocked his thumb and said, "Glad you could find the place, kid."

The two cops took a booth over by the window, and by the time Jerry got up his nerve to peep at Newman again, he and his party were at the cash register.

"Isn't he a beauty?" the waitress said to Jerry. "I could just eat him alive."

CHAPTER TWO

THAT SAME morning, but a little bit later and a couple of miles west Alexander Hellstrom lay quietly in his huge bed on the third floor of his Bel Air home and watched the ceiling turn pink with the dawn. Hellstrom grinned and stretched luxuriously. He loved to awaken at dawn, to know that he had not missed any of the day. He wiggled his toes and flexed his fingers. The woman next to him made a small sound and curled away, embracing her pillow. Carefully, so as not to disturb her, Hellstrom got out of bed, his feet touching the delicate silk pile of a Shiraz rug, which Hellstrom also liked. In fact, he liked nearly everything about his life, and especially enjoyed his enjoyment of it. "Nothing is too good for Alexander Hellstrom," he was fond of telling himself.

In the bathroom, with its hanging ferns and Mexican tiles, this morning's Los Angeles *Times, New York Times, Wall Street Journal, Barron's,* the *Daily Variety* and the *Hollywood Reporter* were all neatly in place, the newspapers hanging from racks and the trades and *Barron's* stacked on the table next to the dark green marbled toilet. After a brief examination of his big handsome face, to see if any poisons had risen to the surface overnight, Alexander dropped the bottoms to his striped silk pajamas and sat, picking up the *Wall Street Journal* first, to see if anything really important was going on.

Alexander enjoyed wearing silk pajamas. Women had asked him, more than once, why a man of his inclinations would also wear clothes to bed and he had never once told them the truth, that when he was a child, pajamas and flannel nightgowns in winter had always given him a deep secret pleasure of security, and that he still got a nostalgic coziness from them.

After twenty minutes or so of relaxed reading, Alexander stepped naked into the shower, five nozzles, malachite tiled walls, gold fixtures, and gave himself a bracing shower, just a bit too cold at first, and then after he had thoroughly soaped himself, a hot sluicing that made his skin ruddy under its heavy workman's tan.

He walked back into the bedroom. The girl was just a lump under the coverlet. A tiny snore came from her direction, like the distant humming of bees. It was a nice snore. Some women made horrible noises in their sleep, but not this one. Her name was Teresa di Veccio, a beautiful rich young lady from back East. Alexander had met her a couple of times in New York, and then again last night at a party in Holmby Hills. She had seemed like kind of a snob, with her nose up in the air most of the time and her lovely body concealed in a sensible dress, talking about painters Alexander had never heard of and did not want to hear of, but when he had suggested that she come home with him, promising, "I don't have a painting in the place worth more'n fifty bucks" (a damn lie), she had nodded modestly and placed her hand in his, trustingly, like a child, and he felt, for the first time that night, a tremendous eroticism. They can always get you with that perfect combination of beauty, innocence and trust, because you know that underneath is the hottest kind of fire.

Teresa di Veccio. She was probably used to sleeping until noon, and then lying in bed with her tray and her telephone until two or three, and then spending the rest of the day caring for her body or shopping. He wondered what she would think if he just got back into bed and started to fuck her. A lot of women, in Alexander Hellstrom's experience, did not like to make love in the morning. It made them grumpy to be pawed at and stuck into before their morning coffee. But she had indeed been *something else* the night before, and Alexander could feel himself swelling into readiness. He pulled the covers away from the girl.

She looked quite beautiful and innocent, her body childlike except for the knowing delicious swell of her breasts. Her eyes blinked open and her lips parted in a sleepy groan, but before she could ask what was happening, Alexander was on top of her, his big hands on her thighs, pulling them up and apart so that he could stuff himself into her. They both made loud groans at the same moment, and then after only a few collisions, Alexander gave an enormous cry and lay on top of her panting like a man who has just been rescued from drowning.

"Um, you're crushing me," she said after a few moments, but Alexander did not move. As a matter of fact, he was thinking about his morning's work at the studio. But these thoughts gradually disappeared in the pink mists of another surge of desire, the girl wriggling somewhat helplessly under him, and so they began again, only this time much slower, and together. And this time it was she who began the moaning.

Later he said, "Do you want to go for a swim?"

"It's too early in the morning," she said, and snuggled down into the covers again.

"Push that dingus on the bedside table for coffee," he said, and walked out the French doors naked and down the wrought-iron staircase to the white marble swimming pool, its water pale blue in the morning light.

ALEXANDER ENJOYED swimming alone in his big pool with its savage tangle of tropical vegetation at one end and the long rolling lawn that smoothly curved around the house and down to the front entrance. He enjoyed it particularly because his first work in Los Angeles years before had been swinging a pick on a swimming pool construction crew, trimming up the rough spots left by the big yellow scooper. It had been a hard job, in blistering sun or downpours of L.A. rain. Those rich people wanted their pools and they wanted them right now. But Alexander had never worked on a pool as beautiful as the one he owned and was floating in the middle of, with just his nose and toes sticking up out of the water.

Although he could not see them, Alexander knew there were two handsome seal-brown rabbits in the tangle of ferns and shrubbery behind him. The rabbits were not afraid to come out into the open when people were around; to the contrary, they seemed to enjoy company more than Alexander, and had often been photographed hopping around underfoot when the long linen-covered tables would be set up on the lawn for a garden party or a benefit luncheon. Alexander himself seldom spent more than a few minutes among his guests at these big flossy affairs, but the rabbits seemed to have fun, and seemed to enjoy being photographed almost as much as the hambones. The rabbits did not have set names, but Alexander could tell them apart by sex, although both were fixed. The male was slightly larger and seemed to get a lot more out of life, frequently jumping straight up in the air or bounding out of the vegetation unexpectedly and then sitting quite still, as if he had been there all the time. The female seemed brighter somehow and more forgiving about the conditions of her life. There was no way to explain to her that Belgian rabbits were bred specifically for meat and fur and that hers was a life of luxury by comparison, that the look in her eyes as she sat sideways panting, comfortable on the lawn, should have been gratitude rather than forgiveness. The male, when he was not having fun, would sometimes strike a pose, his nose up in the air wriggling—rabbits have a fantastic sense of smell—his legs poised for flight if only he would smell the right scent; that seemed almost tragic, as if he knew he was a rabbit, that he was fixed, and that his life would be forever in this luxuriant but somehow arid garden of paradise.

He wants to kick some ass, Alexander would think sometimes, he wants to get out there and make trouble, disembowel a couple of Dobermans, break into a greenhouse and eat all the orchids, get out onto the road and play the death game with the nightlights of fast-running automobiles . . .

Alexander pulled himself up out of the pool, not bothering to swim over to the broad steps, and threw himself into a garden chair, the thick white towel laid out for him by an invisible servant while he was doing his laps. He gave his head a vigorous rub and then lay back to let the morning sunlight dry him off. Shading his eyes, he tried to see into the darkness of the tropical shrubbery for a glimpse of his rabbits. He snicked his lips, although they had never come when he snicked before, and probably never would. He grinned. One of the things he liked best about his rabbits, as opposed to say dogs or cats, is that they were *prey*, and lived by the rules of prey, totally foreign to human thought. They would not come when you called, yet they were very loving when they did decide to come sit on your chest, or to sit beside you in the twilight enjoying the sunset, their legs kicked out in that relaxed way . . . and those legs were powerful; prey or not, a rabbit could kill with those legs or die of a snapped spine if they missed their target. Brave little bastards is what they were, independent, and funny.

"Here bunny bunny bunny, you sons of bitches," Alexander called softly.

The two rabbits, sleek and beautiful as seals, hopped out onto the lawn and began nibbling at the grass. Alexander laughed happily and went over and picked them up, carrying one on each big arm carefully around the lawn, talking to them and enjoying their company.

THE GARAGE was on the other side of the house, a white building with service quarters over it and all the big overhead doors open. In front of the garage was a brick courtyard, nearly surrounded by evergreens and one huge live oak, which had probably been there for a hundred years or more. Alexander came out of the back of the house through the service entrance, dressed in a dark blue three-piece suit and heavy black brogues. He was full of breakfast and had spent the usual seven minutes working on his teeth and gums. The question now before him was, which car to take to work? There were five of them, including his Mercedes 600 limousine, whose driver, Orfeo, was coming down the steps beside the garage building right now, wearing a uniform that made him resemble a South American general. Certain kinds of days required Orfeo and the 600; on others, Alexander preferred to drive himself.

Then there was the lady's car, pulled over at the corner of the courtyard, a cute little Alfa Spyder probably borrowed from somebody since she did not live in Southern California, but which meant Alexander would not have to either drive her home himself or detail Orfeo for this job.

Which would it be? thought the man whose first car had been a fifty-dollar pile of junk, into which he had sweatingly and patiently poured hours and hours of time after work and on Sundays, bruised knuckles, ingrained grease and precious cash until he had not only a workable 1947 Ford sedan, but a damned good one, too. He wished he had it still. The cars ranged in front of him like hookers at a Nevada whorehouse were all better than any '47 Ford, but there was a lot to be said for having done the work yourself. You knew what you were driving. Not that Orfeo wasn't a good mechanic, he was the best, but still things came up that would not have been surprises if Alexander was doing the work. For a moment, he envied Orfeo his basically happy-go-lucky life, and then of course laughed at himself.

Well, which car? The little Mercedes 380 SEL, which was more like a toy than a car? The Jaguar 4.5? The 1937 La Salle which was Orfeo's favorite? A beautiful old two-tone green convertible whose top groaned like an old man when you put it down, but was an object of art on a par with the Golden Gate Bridge . . . The Daimler-Benz, handmade and autographed, black, squat, his gangster car . . .?

Teresa di Veccio came out of the house, dressed as she had been the night before, in a dark cocktail dress and black heels.

"I thought you were gone," she said.

"Did you get any breakfast?" he asked her.

"I didn't want any, thank you. I hope I left the keys in the car," she said. "I can't find them on me."

Alexander remembered that he had driven the car home and Orfeo had gone for his. Naturally, he would have left the keys in the ignition. The two of them strolled over to the little Alfa, not as if they had been wildly making love an hour before, but just two people walking toward a car. A mockingbird started up in the oak tree, and Teresa di Veccio said, "Oh, what a beautiful sound!" and Alexander told her about mockingbirds. Orfeo's expression, as they walked past him, was deliberately noncommittal. Wouldn't it have been more natural for them to be arm in arm, touching, kissing, bumping together like lovers, instead of this sexless stroll? The truth was, Alexander barely knew the woman, certainly did not know her well enough to put his arm around her affectionately, or even lustfully, previous intimacies to the contrary notwithstanding. It seemed so stupid. The hell with it, he grabbed her and swept her up in a big kiss. She went stiff immediately and her lips flat and hard. Alexander dropped her.

"Yep, here's the keys," he said. "I'm late for a meeting, but I'll call you at the Beverly Hills . . ."

"All right," she said. She sounded a little disappointed. She got into her car, had a little trouble getting it started, then rumbled down the drive and out of sight.

Alexander scratched the top of his head. The woman meant nothing to him, an opportunity fuck, that was all, rich, young, beautiful and full of wiggles, but nothing special.

"I'll take the Daimler," he said to Orfeo without meeting his eye.

"Okay," Orfeo said without a trace of hidden meaning.

THE BLACK Daimler turned left onto Sunset Boulevard joining the early-morning swarm of expensive automobiles heading for Beverly Hills or on to Los Angeles. As always, it amused Alexander to see drivers of Mercedes, Rolls-Royces, Bentleys, Ferraris and Lamborghinis peer furtively into his car to see who it was in such a rarity. There were long snakelike curves on Sunset and it was a pleasure to take a fine automobile through them, but many of these drivers either lacked the experience or the proper nervous balance to execute this stretch of roadway with anything like style. Their cars were simply too much for them, and so they roared and squealed. Alexander, on the other hand, was an experienced driver of every kind of vehicle, from tanks to ten-speeds, even a few months driving a big rig on the Portland, Oregon–Chicago run. He had a natural affinity for mechanical transportation, and when he got behind the wheel of a fine car, it was as if his and the car's nervous system merged, becoming one creature, half metal and half flesh.

Every once in a while some jerk would try to race with Alexander Hellstrom, not knowing who he was, or perhaps filled with a wild ambition, knowing he was Alexander Hellstrom and hoping by this foolish plan to somehow come to his attention. Alexander, of course, paid no attention to them at all, beyond a disgusted snick of his lips and a resolve not to make eye contact as the two machines would pull up at some red light, the challenging race car or luxury sedan noisily making ready for the signal change, the Daimler silent and untrembling.

Then the traffic would surge again. Alexander seldom bothered with the speed indicator or the tachometer. He could feel how things were going, and without any sense of competition, although he was a very competitive man, had an awareness of the location of the other machines around him. But it was hard not to notice when somebody was so obviously keying on you and racing you even when you weren't racing, and it was difficult to hold down a grin when, light after light, you came out ahead, and yet never even had to put the brakes on hard. A glance in the mirror and there he would be, the challenger, helplessly stuck among the raffle of traffic backed up against the light.

Another advantage, hardly applicable, but nevertheless a point of interest: you could park a Daimler anywhere and no cop would dare give it a ticket. You never could tell who owned the damn things, but whoever they were, they had a lot of bucks, even for big rich Los Angeles a lot of bucks.

Alexander turned right just before coming to the big pink sprawl of the Beverly Hills Hotel, and once again thought about Teresa di Veccio. He wondered whose car she had borrowed. Some guy who hoped to get somewhere with her, and then hadn't even been invited to the party last night? More likely, judging from the type of automobile, somebody's wife, who had gone to school with Teresa and could struggle along with the station wagon for a few days. But Teresa herself, what about her? He envisioned her sitting alone in her hotel room, perhaps just out of the bath, nothing to do, too early to go out by the pool (she didn't have much of a tan), too self-conscious to turn on the television—she didn't seem like the kind of a girl who could order a big breakfast from room service and turn on the TV and the hell with what the waiter thought. Maybe she was reading a book or writing letters.

He would call her later:

"What did you do this morning?"

"Oh, wrote some letters, and read a little Fitzgerald. I'm rereading all my college favorites these days . . ."

Down the leafy street in the morning sunshine, past the homes of the not-quite-rich of Beverly Hills. Alexander decided to dismiss her from his mind until the afternoon call. He wondered if he would take her out. He would have to look at his calendar to see if there was anything appropriate within the few days she would be in town. (What was she *doing* here, anyway? She had never said.) He wondered if they would sleep together again. It had been very nice, now that he remembered. Not desperately show-off, like a hambone, or somebody on the everlasting make, but a soft kind of innocence, curious word to describe somebody as good at it as she, but it was the right word . . .

His chest began to glow and he felt a daring exuberance, as if he were a young boy, and about to jump off the roof with an umbrella for a parachute.

Well, here goes! he thought, and swung the car around on its remarkable wheelbase and headed back for the Beverly Hills. There was a telephone in the car, and he could have called his office and told them to back everything up for an hour, but he did not. He was excited now, thinking dizzily of her sleepy-eyed but suddenly tremendously desirable naked figure.

He pulled up the curved drive, left the engine running, opened the door himself as the boy in the garage greens rushed toward him. "Don't bury it," he said over his shoulder and entered the hotel. Black thoughts rushed into his head. She was *with* somebody, there was another man rooting around on that inexpressibly sweet girl, she was groaning with passion at this moment. He rushed down the corridor. He brushed past people who looked at him wide-eyed, as you would at a masked man carrying a gun. He felt hot all over, itchy-nervous. He rapped on her door, and, unable to stop himself, listened with his head tilted forward. Time passed. He knocked again. He should have telephoned from the lobby. She was not there, or they were in there holding themselves silently, giggling with their eyes and waiting for him to go away. More time passed, and he knocked again. Maybe she was out by the pool.

He was aswarm with doubts, but deep inside, where hid the secret cool individual who was never moved, he wondered what the hell was the matter. Was he being driven by some genetic combination that triggered this response whether he wanted it to or not? Was he helpless in the grip of a hundred thousand years of natural selection? He did not know, he only knew that he had knocked three times and she had not answered. Maybe out by the pool. He turned to go and a totally unexpected wave of depression passed through him like the ghost of some long-dead Beverly Hills Hotel lover spurned and dead by his own hand. And then the door opened and he was looking down into her fresh innocent face.

Teresa broke into a smile and the door opened wider. "Come in," she said. "I was just washing my face."

She did not seem surprised to see him, but that was how they trained them at college, he thought, as he grabbed her rudely and kissed her as hard as he could. This time she did not freeze and her lips did not harden. She melted into him, her belly warm beneath her robe, her leg moving between his, and the touch of her cool fingertips on the back of his neck.

Then they were on the bed, and Alexander felt as if his heart would burst with pleasure. They weren't even undressed, and he did not see how they would ever be undressed, because he was not going to let go of her, nor she of him. "I knew you would come," she said in a sweet smug tiny voice. He pulled her robe open and saw beauty incarnate, and that helped him get his own clothes off. He simply *had* to be touching her everywhere at once. He even took off his shoes and socks.

Everything in his love life up to now had been mere preparation, schooling for this unimaginable experience. Alexander was a man not unfamiliar with hyperbole, but this was beyond it all, into wordless pleasure. Even the man inside was impressed, so impressed that he too was silent. *This,* Alexander decided after he could catch his breath, and in that regretful but deeply satisfied moment when reality swims back into view, *must be love. That's it. Love. I thought I'd been in love before, but no. This was it.*

"Am I in love?" he said, half to himself.

She murmured something sweet and her puffed mouth brushed his nipple.

Pink joy radiated everywhere, and they were off again. He could laugh at himself later, as he sweetly reran moments of their lovemaking, he could laugh and feel lighthearted, but underneath it all he was stunned.

The day which had begun so well was now a disaster. Appointments were backed up, and naturally meetings would get shortened and some might even have to be cancelled. Alexander Hellstrom did not make a habit of cancelling, so God knew what people would think when told their meeting was off.

He pulled up to the entrance of the studio and paused for a moment's conversation with Charlie Devereaux, the guard captain, who had been a fellow pool-digger with Alexander back in the old days, had gone on the cops for a while and then moved into his present job. Devereaux had been working at the studio longer than Alexander, as a matter of fact, and this symbolic bit of seniority kept their relationship on a fairly even keel, where otherwise it might have collapsed. Alexander was always careful to defer to Charlie and never gave him orders, only requests; and Charlie, on his part, did not choose to attend most of the functions Alexander had him invited to—just a few key screenings and Alexander's New Year's Day party, which was just a bunch of hung-over guys getting drunk and watching football.

The two men liked each other, and their morning exchange of greetings was important to both. Today Charlie, in lieu of having a worried expression on his face, merely tapped the clock in front of him and said, "Big party last night?"

Alexander wanted to blurt, "Met a girl!" but didn't. There are certain things you don't burden people with, and a possible twenty-four-hour case of Hot Pants was one of them. At the thought he brightened. Hell, I might feel better by tonight, be laughing about the whole thing. He grinned up at Charlie. "How's the coffee this morning?"

"Tastes like shit," Charlie said, handing it to Alexander for a sip—his first of the day.

"Yeah, but what did they *do* to it?" Alexander joked, as usual, and tooled on into the lot. He drove slowly around the Administration Building, past the gigantic standing sets of the most expensive movie the studio had ever made, turrets and battlements, gun loops and weathervanes, an overweight extravaganza that was still limping around the world in scarred and noisy prints, trying in vain to keep up with the interest payments.

This had been under a previous administration, but Alexander ruled that the sets, which had turned out to be so criminally expensive, should stand, not only as a reminder of one of Alexander's favorite parables ("Sometimes it's cheaper to go to England") but also as something for the tourists to look at as they rode around the lot in their little elephant trains. This *was* one of Alexander's innovations, right after he became vice president in charge of production. "Universal does it, and it comes out profit, so what the hell."

A lot of people complained mightily that it was bush league and unprofessional and demeaning to have strings of tourists gawking at them as they worked, but the hambones didn't bitch, hell, it was their life, and for once Alexander agreed with them. And it was the hambones the tourists wanted to see, not some jerk who thought he was the new Shakespeare. He parked at the elevator door where the curb was painted red, and went up to the third floor to his office. He unlocked his private door and sat down behind his desk with a sigh. There was a cold cup of coffee sitting in the middle of his blotter, testament to his normal promptness. To be impulsive was to screw everything up, he thought a bit sadly, and then a rush of pleasure coursed through him as he remembered Teresa. He pressed the intercom: "This coffee's cold!" he said.

The first problem of the morning was, naturally, a picture that was running scared. The producer, the director, the writer and the production supervisor were ranged uncomfortably in Alexander's office, like boys who had been caught torturing frogs. They were slipping behind, and the production board was getting harder and harder to fit in with the star's commitments. According to the production supervisor, Ted Gage, an old salt thirty years in the business, if they lost any more days they would have to pay so much to the actor for his time that other aspects of the production would suffer, perhaps fatally.

Ted Gage put it strongly, while the producer stared at the rug. "We're gonna lose reality, we're gonna lose lighting time, and we may wind up having the actor unavailable for the loops we're gonna need if we have to rush through everything from this point on."

"In other words, you need more money," said Alexander, just to be saying something. The producer, Eric Seymour Katz, looked up hopefully.

Ted Gage said, "Time or money. *I would* prefer that we take another look at the script and see if we can't get a couple of extra days out of it."

That explained the presence of Dick Matthews, the writer.

"I just don't see it," the director said.

So there it was. Alexander looked at the sheaf of Daily Production Reports on his desk, glancing at the setup time, number of setups per day, shifts, changes and utilizations. It was obvious that the director had been taking a lot of time with each setup, but there was nothing criminal in his slowness. Alexander had seen dailies, and the stuff was coming out okay. It was simply that the budget was too tight. Gage had won too many victories in the preproduction battles, shortchanging department after department until the picture was anemic with economy. All in response to front-office pressure, of course. But Gage had been too good at his job.

Alexander had been a production supervisor; into the business as a grip, then location manager, production manager, Executive in Charge of Production for the whole lot, and now head of production. Not the king, but the prime minister. He knew what Gage wanted, a typical production-style solution. He wanted the script cut down again, therefore fewer days shooting. At sixty thousand dollars a day it mounted quickly.

Reaching out with one hand, Alexander adjusted the Venetian blinds so that he could see the towers and battlements across the way. It was a pleasant sight, and added to the unreality of it all. There was, he could see, a big yellow tabby cat sitting in an embrasure, giving himself a thorough wash. There were several furtive cats living on the lot, keeping the rats and mice down, and, Alexander had heard, a couple of humans who existed somehow without leaving the grounds. Living in Fairyland on crusts of bread.

Alexander could just smell the odor of Teresa di Veccio rising from his clothes, and he wondered if anybody else could. Matthews, the writer? Would he be entertaining the boys at the Cock 'N Bull with tales of his meeting with the Boss? "Dresses like a banker, smells like a fag . . ." Sure, we're all fags in Hollywood, sensitive folks, screw anything . . .

The scent caught at him again, and he could feel his penis swelling slightly at the memory invoked. He had already made up his mind to give them the money, God knows where he would find it, because the mistake was his. The buck stops here. Meanwhile, Alexander smelled the faint ripeness of rutting, and watched the cat at his bath . . .

CHAPTER THREE

NORTH OF Malibu, almost to the Trancas light, a lonely beach house jutted over the cliff, surrounded by sheltering windswept Monterey cypresses, the house itself old weathered lapstrake redwood, with a roof garage, a large wooden deck on three sides, potted shrubs and gaily striped beach furniture. From Highway 1 all you could see were two massive fieldstone pillars supporting a big double-doored automobile entrance, thick cypress, a dilapidated mailbox, and a fresh sign printed in bright red: KEEP OUT. TRESPASSERS WILL BE VIOLATED. This sign had several .22 bullet holes in it, but was still readable.

It was not a place you would enter unless you had a clear invitation.

Within, on this early Monday morning, were Richard Heidelberg and his lady love of the moment, Elektra Soong. Although it was just the kind of morning when one would love to walk down the sand-swept wooden steps to the beach and lie on a towel, getting a tan and listening to the radio, neither Rick nor Elektra was at all interested in the outside world, and every blind in the house that could be lowered was lowered, leaving the interior in semidarkness. Cold jazz trickled into every room from a network of loudspeakers, and in a couple of rooms there were color television sets making a morning soap opera visible but not audible. Rick and Elektra were in different rooms. Elektra was in the big master bedroom, reading a magazine, rapidly flipping the pages and rhythmically biting her reddened and puffed lips. She was also rubbing her toes together, making a sound like rats. This sound drove her crazy, but she would not or could not stop making it. The magazine was *Vogue* and she had read it thirty or forty times.

Rick was in the living room, still dressed in Arab costume made from sheets, bedspreads and scarves. He was trying his belt on around his forehead, looking critically at himself in the long mirror over the mantel. They were going to revolutionize the clothing industry, they had decided a couple of days before. It was simple, they would make Arab dress fashionable, and then corner the market. Rick wondered a hundred times why no one had thought of it before.

Satisfied that the belt did nothing for his costume, a decision he had made several times, Rick returned to the glass-topped table in front of the fireplace and kneeled beside it. On the table were the remains of a thousand dollars' worth of Peruvian pearl cocaine, and a variety of paraphernalia. He and Elektra had been having themselves a nonstop cocaine party, just the two of them, prepared for in advance: groceries, liquor, weed, the phones shut off, cover story (Tahoe) and all; and now they were down from the original half-ounce to a couple of grams. This was the fourth day. Neither had slept or wanted to, but they made sure they took their vitamins and drank a little milk or orange juice every hour. Rick wasn't feeling too bad. He was frightened, of course, by the fact that they were going to run out some time that afternoon, and that the curtains would have to be pulled back, the blinds lifted, and the *sunshine* let into the place. It made him shudder to think of the *sunshine*. The sun was God, after all, for any practical human purpose, and God is not mocked.

"Lines!" he called out, and started cutting four, then eight, lines of the cocaine, now chalky from the sea air.

Elektra drifted into the room, naked, perhaps the most beautiful girl Rick had ever seen, a mix of Portuguese, Chinese, Hawaiian, a real *hapahaole* from the streets of downtown Honolulu. "Oh, swell," she said, and got down beside him. He kissed her tiny shoulder affectionately and she gave his penis a squeeze. Then they snorted their lines.

Rick sat back against the couch. It would soon be over, this little trip into the white universe, but it had been a good one. No long nights of anxiety, no horrible thoughts crowding all pleasure from sight. Not much fucking, but long hours of quiet conversation about everything under the sun, both of them naked and hugging their knees. And of course the two great ideas. Rick often had great ideas when deep into cocaine, but sometimes you sobered up and the ideas turned out to be false. That was okay; this time, these two ideas would survive the *sunlight*.

The first was the Arab dress idea, and for two days they played costume and looked through books and magazines for anything having to do with dress or fashion. It all seemed so childishly simple: fashions were dictated by what the "people of the moment" were wearing, and right now Rick was a "person of the moment," and so, by extension, was Elektra. They were always being photographed and interviewed, and what they did became news. This would always work as long as they weren't pigs about it; the young public enjoyed success for its heroes, and Rick was certainly a hero. *The Endless Unicorn* had cost two hundred thousand dollars and had grossed worldwide something like forty million dollars, *because young people everywhere liked it*. Rick liked it, too, that's why he made the goddamn thing; he liked it and he forced it through, and it hit the bull's-eye. So even the establishment liked him, although it did not trust him.

Which brought his mind, now riding high on the new lines, to the second idea, which was not so simple as the first, but much more exciting to Rick. He would take over the studio, grab it away from Alexander Hellstrom, and with the whole creative power of the studio behind him, and with his friends, the young up-and-coming filmmakers of the world, he would begin a reign of moviemaking equal to the age of the pyramids.

At one point Rick laughed wildly and kissed Elektra and said, "We'll make *The Martian Chronicles,* with actual locations! On Mars!"

She loved it. "Can I be in the picture?"

It was time to blow the rocks out of his nose. Rick went into the bathroom off the bedroom, taking along a fresh wineglass, which he filled to the brim with warm water. He dipped his nose into the water, much as a bird might, and inhaled. Warm itchy water trickled down his throat, almost making him cough. He held the cough, and let the excess water drip from his nose. He looked at himself in the mirror. His eyes were feverish, big as prunes. He inhaled more water, repeating the process three times, and then with a shake of his head, blew. He could feel huge masses of wreckage up inside his head, and, closing off one nostril at a time, blew and blew. Once it started it rose to a torrent, and the sink was spattered with shiny crimson blobs and red rills of blood. God, but it felt good to blow that stuff out!

Rick cleaned the bowl thoroughly, reflecting on the fact that his snot was worth money. He was still high, and his nostrils felt like twin wind tunnels. In the bedroom Elektra was trying to get some sleep, lying on her side with the sheet up over her shoulder, breathing like a wounded buffalo. He did not disturb her, but walked on through to the living room and sat once again by the coffee table. Coffee table. There had been just about everything on that table but coffee. She was right. It was time to quit, even though there was a lot of coke left. His nose was clean and clear, even starting to hurt a bit; this was the time to take a double shot of 100-proof whiskey, lie back, and come gradually down.

Instead, he snorted three lines on each side and began riffling through a copy of *Playboy*. With Elektra snoozing there was twice as much coke for him, and somehow at the time it seemed like a good deal. She slept all day Monday while he sat in the living room, either going through magazines or thinking feverish thoughts, doubling his intake of the drug out of spite, going deeper and deeper into anxiety, fear of running out, fear of existence, fear of moving, fear that he was addicted to cocaine and would spend the rest of his life in this crippled trance, having an awful time. Later he started hitting the whiskey, and by midnight he was blistering drunk, helplessly throwing up into the toilet, somebody holding his shoulders and applying a hot washcloth to his temples; and then he was in bed, nauseated but able to keep the room from spinning, and then he was gone.

When he woke up, he felt as if somebody had been hitting him on the nose with a crowbar, but otherwise he was all right. He sat up. Elektra was not there. The magazines were all put away and the bedroom was neat and orderly for the first time in days. The smell of food was in the air. Food! Rick had not had an appetite for a long time. It was a delicious sensation. He got out of bed and walked, wobbling only a little, into the other part of the house.

Blinds were up, curtains open. All the mess was gone. He could hear the reassuring beat of the surf, and the sky stood richly blue against white clouds.

"You want some O.J.?" Elektra asked. She came out of the kitchen wearing a tee shirt and a bikini bottom. She smiled at Rick and kissed him lightly and gave him the big glass of orange juice, which he threw back all in one long gurgling gulp. "Can you eat yet?" she asked. "I had some bacon and eggs and muffins . ."

"Let's give it a try," Rick said. He followed her into the brightly lit kitchen and sat in the nook by the window that overlooked the cliff and the ocean beyond. Down the beach came a man riding horseback, galloping right along, a big older man with a mane of grey hair and a tan so dark he looked almost like a Kanaka. The man wore only faded jeans, and as he rode out of sight under the overhang of the cliff, Rick wondered if that was going to be the last few chapters of *his* life, rich enough to be able to horseback ride on this beach, bored enough to have to go ahead and do it.

Quietly he watched Elektra make his breakfast. Her timing and methodology were impeccable. While the bacon sizzled over a low flame in the black cast-iron frying pan on a back burner and the English muffins toasted in the toaster-oven on a shelf beside the stove, she put butter, salt and pepper into the long-handled French frying pan and shook the pan gently as the butter melted, bubbled and settled back down. Still holding the pan handle in her left hand she opened the refrigerator and took out two AA large brown eggs in her tiny hand, closing the refrigerator with a little swing of her hip, and broke the eggs one-handed into the pan, tossing the broken shells into the garbage sack at her feet. Quickly, but without splashing grease, she turned the bacon with her fork. The eggs began to bubble as she continued to shake the pan with her left hand, and now with the fork began stirring the eggs rapidly.

The heat was low and the eggs came together slowly, at first yellow and white, like mixed-up fried eggs. As she kept stirring, taking care to let no part of the eggs remain against the heat for long, they began to turn pale yellow and solidify. She turned off the heat, still stirring, and dumped the scrambled eggs on the plate. The toaster-oven popped open but she ignored it for the moment, scooping up the bacon and placing it aside on a folded paper napkin. Then she plucked the hot brown-crusted buttery muffins from the toaster-oven and onto the plate. Adding the bacon she slid the plate of food in front of Rick.

"Smell good?" she asked.

Rick nodded and murmured and started to eat. The eggs were the best he had ever had. The kitchen was neat and clean. Elektra had obviously been working away all the time he slept, quietly, so as not to disturb him, but working working working, where some other broad might have just headed for the beach and waited for the Mexican servants to show up. But not Elektra, and once again he congratulated himself on having her for a girl friend. God, this bacon was *just right!*

Was it love? He did not know. There was no reason to call it that. They said they loved each other all the time, but they also said they loved this and that, so the word was really just a way of expressing enthusiasm. Rick knew he wouldn't have had a chance with Elektra if he hadn't been Richard Heidelberg, and she wouldn't have stood a chance with him if she hadn't been so royally beautiful and so smart and so lucky. But of course what was the point of being Richard Heidelberg if not Elektra Soong?

"With a Soong in my heart," Rick sang mischievously.

"Oh, eat your meal," she said, and sat opposite him to watch. He ate with little yelps of joy at each new flavor, complimenting her on her cooking.

"Oh," she said, "eggs and bacon are easy. Someday I'll really cook for you, but you have to have about twelve people here or it's not worth it."

"That would be a swell party," he said, his mouth full of egg. "You in the kitchen slaving away."

"Oh, shit," she said. "I'm going down to the beach for a while. Are you gonna come down?"

Rick swallowed and suddenly remembered the Two Great Ideas. "Oh, Jesus," he said. He sipped his coffee, as Elektra watched him, her head cocked to one side.

"Remember the Arab clothes?" Rick looked embarrassed.

"Sure. That was fun."

"But not such a great idea, huh?"

She laughed. " 'My son, the Arab!'"

"Sweeping into Nate 'N Al's in our sheets and pillowcases!" Rick laughed. "Amidst the machine-gun fire . . ."

Another great idea down the drain.

But what about . . .

"Hey," he said to her.

"Yeah?"

"Let's go to bed . . ."

And off they went.

CHAPTER FOUR

THE TRADE journal had offices in the Hany Building, on Hollywood Boulevard near Cahuenga, a musty old building whose lobby was the only bright spot, with a florist on one side and a twenty-four-hour smut bookstore on the other. Jerry Rexford stood waiting for the elevator, looking at the orchids in the refrigeration case, just to keep from looking at the rows of specialty pornography and sex equipment displayed on the other side. Not that he wouldn't look at the sex stuff, but he didn't want the clerk to see him. They were always fairly degenerate types, and when they caught you ogling, they gave you this knowing look, somewhere between a leer and a sneer, as if to say, *"Ah, you're as filthy as the rest of us!"* Which was true, but why bring it up?

Jerry could hear the elevator arrive, but the doors didn't open for a few more seconds, as if it took all the machine's strength to force the door to the wall. Then there was a criss-cross steel door with a shiny worn brass handle to push, while the elevator creaked impatiently. Once inside and both doors closed, Jerry punched 5 and waited. A smell, something between stale ciga-rette smoke and tired feet, defied him to analyze it. He had plenty of time. No one got on or off as he slowly proceeded, laborious inch by inch, to the top story of the building.

Jerry's palms were wet. He hugged his briefcase, full of resumes and exem-plars of his writing, to his chest, feeling the strangling clutch of his necktie at his throat, tied too tight because since arriving in Los Angeles Jerry had gone up a size in necks and could not button his best shirt, the only one that worked with his blue suit, and had to use the tie, a nice maroon with white polkadots, to cover up.

The name of the trade journal was *Pet Care Hotline,* but Jerry did not laugh. Trade journals were a world to themselves, and a lot of them had laughable titles—if you went for that sort of humor. Indeed, to Jerry the hubris of calling yourself *Time* was funnier than *Pet Care Hotline.* Here they were, at the end of a long corridor of dirty white octagonal tiles and pebbled-glass doors. He could hear the sounds of routine office work faintly through the glass, and this reassured him. After the wonderments of getting settled in Hollywood, this was like home ground.

As Jerry politely sat waiting in one of a row of hard chairs the color of dead bananas, he looked over the office. A small bullpen, surrounded by "private" doorless offices glassed in to a height of about seven feet, and the real private offices at the other end. Five or six people milled around or sat at desks, looked up with disinterest. There were no handsome men and no good-looking women. The men were in shirtsleeves, with ties, the women a little less formal. One very large woman wore a slack suit, which in Jerry's opinion she shouldn't have been wearing. So here it was, a drab little office full of drab people doing a boring job. Also, the pay would be terrible.

But he knew how to do the work, and it took none of his attention, and having steady work was important. From a base like this, Jerry hoped to eventually make his way into the movie business. He would be, in Henry James's wonderful phrase, "one of those upon whom nothing is lost." He would keep his eyes and ears open, he would assimilate Hollywood through osmosis. Of this he was confident.

Mr. Harris, the president and publisher of *Pet Care Hotline,* was a small red-haired man in a stiffly starched white shirt. He shook Jerry's hand at the door to his office and ushered him in. "Please sit down, Mister Rexford," he said, and Jerry thanked him and sat and turned in time to see Harris rubbing his hands with a Kleenex and dropping the used tissue into a wastebasket beside his desk. The wastebasket was filled with white wads of Kleenex, and there was a box on the desk. Jerry's heart sank.

But he got the job.

"Tell me about yourself," Mr. Harris asked him with a shy boyish smile as he rocked back and forth in his truly impressive executive leather high-backed chair, the only impressive piece of furniture in the whole place.

"Well, I don't know a thing about pet care," Jerry said with a little smile. He knew he did not have to, to do his work. "But I can write and I can edit . . . I'm sure you've gone over my stuff," he said, pointing at the tearsheets in front of Mr. Harris.

"Yes, you do quite good work, that's certainly not at issue. Tell me, what brings you to the Sunny Southland?"

Jerry had been waiting for this one. He let a brief expression of pain cross his face, followed by what he hoped was manly determination. "New Horizons," he said. "Plus that sunshine you just mentioned."

"Married?"

Again the slight look of pain, quickly erased. "No," he said.

Harris tugged a Kleenex from its box and idly began to polish the glass top of his desk. "Tell me what you think you can accomplish at *Pet Care Hotline,* Mr. Rexford."

A tough order, but Jerry was ready for it. You have to treat the littlest publisher as if he were Henry Luce. Jerry gave Mr. Harris a verbal song-and-dance, hardly hearing the words himself. Beneath it all he was transmitting the information that he, Jerry Rexford, knew that selling advertising (not his job) was the important thing, and that the editorial columns did nothing much more than support those ads. To do this they had to be obsequious to advertisers and potential advertisers, hostile to government interference and sympathetic to the problems which beset those who provided pet care products to the public.

That was about the size of it for any small trade journal writer. His basic job was to rewrite press releases, publicity handouts and the illiterate, cliché-ridden and generally dreadful prose of those advertisers or potential advertisers whom Mr. Harris hoped to flatter by having their picture and byline over articles such as, "Are You Displaying Dog Toys at the Right Eye Level?"

He would also be expected to go to pet care conventions and to cover any hot fast-breaking stories relating to pet care, but these were few and far between, and if there was anything really hot, like a breakthrough in the tick situation, the boss would grab it for himself.

At the end of the meeting, Harris stood up and smiled at Jerry, holding out his hand.

"Welcome aboard," he said.

Jerry got out before catching Harris wiping off his hands, his desk and the chair Jerry had been sitting in. The wages were okay, nothing spectacular, and he started work tomorrow. Soon enough then to meet his fellow employees, and he made his way through the bullpen with downcast eyes, as if he had been turned down.

In the elevator he felt a lurch of nausea. This was not Hollywood, nor was it the world of Henry James. More like Dickens, and Jerry Rexford hated Dickens. Now more than ever.

THEN THE Los Angeles weather turned hot, and Jerry Rexford learned to hate the place. It was not the maddening heat of the East or the South, or the blistering desert heat he actually enjoyed; it was a stinging acrid flooding heat that made everything hot to the touch. You could not rub your eyes, he found out quickly, because that just rubbed it in. You could not go to the beach, because, as the Los Angeles *Times* and the *Examiner* were always telling you, "200,000 JAM BEACHES!"

It cooled down somewhat at night, but not enough to cover yourself with a sheet, until you woke at four a.m. chilled and sticky. The best you could do, he decided, was leave all the doors and windows in the little apartment open, and sit naked either reading or watching television—even though lights and television sets radiated volumes of heat themselves—one couldn't just sit there in the dark.

Jerry had finally found a place to live after depressing looks at a couple of really cheap but unbearable dumps. One on Del Mar in West Hollywood, Nathanael West country, a garage turned into a studio, with torn beaver-board walls and a toy kitchen but no insulation, so that when Jerry and the old man who lived in front and rented the place out looked at it, the heat billowed from the just-opened door as if they were entering a drying kiln. "Gets a little warm," the old man said. His breath had a smell of dead animals, and Jerry got away as quickly as possible. The other place was a converted attic down in the flat industrial section of Hollywood, near Technicolor (it had never occurred to Jerry that Technicolor might be a *factory—so* much for romance) and again there was no insulation but, as the stringy young woman pointed out, "You open the windows at both ends you get quite a little breeze in here." They were stooping under the sharp pitch of the roof, smiling at each other. The place was empty except for a big dark green cardboard wardrobe and a lot of wire coat hangers spilled across the linoleum.

So much for bargains. Jerry finally took a furnished apartment on a U-court on Fountain near La Cienega at a little more money than he had hoped, no air conditioning, but at least there was insulation, living room, bedroom, small but nice kitchen, and outside the part that secretly excited him, the life of the court around which the two-story building was built, a mysterious place with stepstones on lawn, trees, shrubbery, nooks and crannies, white wrought-iron garden furniture and a small kidney-shaped swimming pool. This was more like it.

Jerry had hoped, when he moved in, to be able to spend the warm evenings after work sitting around the pool, taking an occasional dip and meeting some of his fellow tenants, a couple of whom he had seen when the landlady, a nice woman with no gross physical deformities, had shown him the place. But he was too shy. He found out his first night, coming home from a fierce day at the office (no air conditioning—Harris was not throwing it away on overhead), taking a long cool shower that was marred only a couple of times by people flushing their toilets or running the tap, so that Jerry's shower dropped to a trickle or suddenly became unbearably hot, and then getting into his old faded green-and-yellow Hawaiian-style bathing trunks. Unfortunately, he happened to look in the mirror at himself. He did not like what he saw. He was a little overweight, just enough for a roll of soft white fat to hang over the top of his trunks, and his arms and legs were too thin. The man and woman he had seen sunning themselves had been darkly tanned, and the woman had a very attractive figure, what he could see of it. If he went out there they would see his slug-white body. And the trunks were just perfect, the kind of bathing suit some middle-class type would wear to a backyard barbecue. As a matter of fact he had bought the trunks to wear to a backyard barbecue, with matching Hawaiian-type shirt. But he had lost the shirt somewhere.

He took off the trunks reluctantly, feeling like an idiot. He was paying for the right to use the court and the pool, and now he was too embarrassed to do it. The heat wave continued, and Jerry kept to himself nights, often sitting in the semidarkness drinking from a tinkling glass of whiskey on the rocks. After the first few nights he did not bother turning on his own radio, because the person next door played his or her radio so loud he could hear it in every room of his apartment. Instead of going crazy and beating on the walls, Jerry decided he liked his neighbor's taste in music, and relaxed.

With the help of the whiskey and his exhaustion from the day's efforts, Jerry would often fall asleep early, sometimes on his couch, sometimes in bed, and then waken before dawn. For a while he would get up and make coffee and read the paper, but then he decided that he was too much alone, and started having his coffee after he had dressed and driven up to Hollywood Boulevard. There was a donut shop on the corner of Cahuenga and Hollywood that he liked at that hour of the morning. It was a tiny place with almost no decoration, a glassed-in donut counter in front, a row of stools along a short counter, and three tables, with fixed round stools. Everything was orange and white, including the uniform of Helen, the girl behind the counter. Jerry would come in and find a Los Angeles *Times* on the counter, serve himself a cup of fresh Farmer Bros. coffee, and half-eavesdrop as people came in for their donuts and coffee-to-go. There were others at the counter and tables, men and women in working clothes (some like Jerry in suit and tie), but they all seemed to know each other, and so Jerry kept quiet and listened to the banter and read the paper. It was enough, it kept him from being lonely, and after a bit he came to look forward to the early mornings as the best part of his day.

A couple of people from the office, including Lucille, the big fat woman, came into the donut shop just before time to go to work, and Jerry was friendly with them, in a distant sort of way. Frankly, they were not the sort of people he hoped to spend his off-work time with, although they were *all* friendly and the office was a happy ship whenever Harris was out selling advertising, which was most of the time. His fellow workers seemed to notice the slight distance he maintained, and tactfully did not try to breach it, although Richard, his fellow editor, had asked him home to dinner once.

Jerry had refused the invitation not because he didn't like Richard, but because that kind of life, home-cooked meals, kids yelling and running around, heavy joking about everything, was part of the past. At least so he hoped. And Richard didn't get mad, just grinned crookedly and said, "I guess you bachelor types got better things to do."

"Well, I write at night," Jerry said, although he didn't. That was to be the next thing to get going. Richard smiled, the light reflecting off his rimless glasses, and said, "Yeah, well, that's a good thing to do. I tried it for a while."

And after that they left him alone. They were shy, too, he thought over morning coffee, they didn't want their feelings hurt either.

If Jerry got there early enough, say, right around six a.m., there would be another familiar face at the counter, a scruffy young man with a long nose and dark hair down over his eyes. Usually he needed a shave, and he bent over his morning paper fiercely, drinking two or three cups of coffee rapidly and loping out of the place, yelling to Helen, "See ya!"

Jerry could not figure out where he knew this man from, but he *did* know him. The man never looked at him, or if they did make eye contact when Jerry came in, the man would break it immediately and go back to his sports section. And then one morning as Jerry was waiting for the elevator, keeping his eyes on the florist's shop as usual, he suddenly saw the man's reflection in the glass. Now, in reflection, the man was glaring at Jerry, and Jerry turned. There he was, the morning man at the all-night pornography store. Jerry went right past him every morning.

"Yeah, I thought you were a real stuck-up prick," Toby told him over coffee, now that they were acquainted.

"I'm sorry about that," Jerry admitted.

"Don't be sorry! Who the fuck wants to be caught lookin' in the window of a stroke shop? Jesus Christ, if I didn't have to work in the fuckin' place I wouldn't look in either!"

Once the ice was broken, Toby was a very friendly guy. He was a small man, perhaps only five feet three or four. In the shop he sat on a high stool back of the glassed-in counter containing the reels of motion picture and the more expensive sex toys. On the counter were copies of various racing periodicals, *Variety* and the trades. All around him, on racks and shelves and in the store window, were the books and magazines that made up the store's stock in trade. Toby did not allow any of this to embarrass him, nor did he defend his profession.

"You should meet some of the creeps who come into this place. Suits and ties, hats fer Chrissake, heavy operators, half the fuckin' movie stars in the world—you see 'em in here, then you see 'em on the screens of America, I'm tellin' you, it's enough to disillusion a Texan."

Jerry was fascinated by Toby for several reasons. First, it seemed he would say anything, anything at all, in front of anybody. Helen, the tall young girl behind the counter at the donut shop, was not the kind of person Jerry would say dirty words in front of, but Toby didn't mind. "Hey, Helen, where's za fuckin' donut holes?" he might say. She didn't appear to mind.

For another, Toby seemed to know everything about everybody in Hollywood, and once he understood Jerry's secret ambition—to crack the movies as a writer—his liking for Jerry doubled, and he agreed that Jerry should not talk about it around the office. "Fuck those assholes!" is the way he put it. Toby knew how to crack Hollywood. "You gotta have the right property," he said, ticking them off on his fingers, "the right connections, the right agent . . . and you got to be at the party."

"What's that mean?" Jerry asked.

"If you ain't at the party, why should they hire you? When they can hire one of their buddies? Don't make no mistake about it, man, things happen at parties, not at the goddamn studios. You could break your ass for ten years, writing dynamite property after dynamite property and never get within sniffin' distance of the big money. But if you get *fashionable*—" this word made Toby's lip curl—"it don't matter what you write, you're on the payroll . . ."

Jerry hoped this wasn't so.

"Hey, fuckface, you can't fight the system! I'm here to tell you!" Toby grinned. "But don't take it so hard. You'll make it . . ."

"Because you know *me!*"

Jerry did not see how knowing the morning man at a twenty-four-hour dirty bookstore was going to get him invited to "the party," but he didn't press the issue. Toby was too much fun to listen to.

CHAPTER FIVE

THE PARTY was a good one. There was none of this business of A list and B list, which Alexander hated, where the people on the A list would have a very formal sit-down dinner, smug in the knowledge that they were the *mucho importantes,* with the guests on the B list arriving at ten or eleven o'clock, often before the A list people had finished their meal, and often dressed more informally (after all, they hadn't been invited to a dinner, only a party) and generally made to look and feel inferior. Not that there weren't some satisfactions in seeing pompous millionaires and overfed hambones made to feel inferior, but God pity their wives and servants when they got home.

No, this party was okay, everybody had been invited for the same time and the same purpose, to celebrate the fortieth birthday of Kerry Dardenelle, as nice a man as you could hope to meet and one of the most interesting directors to come along in years, although Hollywood these days was overrun with brilliant young people. They came in waves, with their brilliant little personal pictures, usually financed out of town by doctor-and-dentist money. Sometimes they would strike gold, like Richard Heidelberg, and become immediately part of the industry; sometimes they would not make back their negative cost, but still impress the picture community. Then they would settle down to making commercial features and the hell with the personal stuff. A few of the very lucky ones would eventually rise to power for a while, and then submerge under the new wave. Or go on to become the grand old men of the industry at forty, like Kerry Dardenelle, plump and red-cheeked, balding and utterly charming to the ladies. The ladies saw him as a big overgrown baby who needed taking care of, although obviously he had been pampered by women all his life.

Kerry was a notorious pussy hound, and it gave Alexander a pang to see him standing in front of the big fireplace, obviously drunk, charming the pants off Teresa di Veccio. But Kerry was a friend, and Alexander didn't really think he was trying to steal his girl. Teresa's eyes were wide as she looked up into the cherubic face of Kerry Dardenelle, that way she had of listening with her complete attention . . . when she looked at Alexander like that he usually lost the trend of his thought in rising passion, and if they were where they could do it, fell into bed with a rush and a moan.

Alexander had never had such a physical affair in his life. Just the mere thought of it, here in this crowded living room, made him want to run over and grab her, take her somewhere and fuck her. And yet she was one of the brightest, most cultivated and urbane people he had ever met. Indeed, she was all superlatives. The best. The most. The highest. The fuckingest, if there was such a word, which there was, because Alexander had just used it. He smirked to himself. The room was full of important people, interesting people, the people he did business with, and instead of having a good time he was standing around mooning about Teresa.

Christ! The bitch! he thought wildly, and started over toward her. A man got in his way, wanting to introduce him to a woman, whose eyes shined and blinked with anticipation. He shook her hand softly, put his other hand on the man's shoulder and got through them.

Kerry and Teresa were talking about Edith Wharton, a subject which effectively cut Alexander out. He stood there beaming redly as they talked, and Teresa tucked her little hand into his. Now he just *had* to fuck her!

"Give us a minute, Kerry," he said, and they moved off toward the huge dining room, which had for the evening been turned into a dancehall, with a Cajun band flown down from San Francisco making a racket in the corner, and various people flipping themselves around in the muted red and blue light. At once, Teresa began to dance, and unable to stop himself, Alexander danced with her. Everybody was glistening with sweat, and everyone looked erotic. Teresa's eyes were on his, and she got the message, and they danced over toward the open French door and out into the garden, immediately coming together in a hot kiss in the shadows of the building. Naturally, the garden was full of people, too, and they made their way back down the garden path to the little recreation hut. There was a pool table in there, and some game machines. They could fuck on the pool table. But no, a couple of hambones were playing serious pool, money on the rail, their women sitting in silence watching the game. Of course when Alexander and Teresa came into the room, the other two women stood, but the hambones kept playing their game. Alexander saw that the bills on the edge of the table were hundreds. Dammit, he thought, waved cutely to the women, and backed out. They knew, too. He could see it in their eyes. So what!

"Where?" she whispered urgently.

"Upstairs!" he said, and they rushed back into the house, up the stairs and, at last, into an unoccupied bedroom. Alexander locked the door. "No sense letting 'em see me naked," he said, but his throat was contracting with emotion and the words came out fuzzy. He turned and she was almost undressed, her eyes hot on his as she slid down her panties. He went to her.

Afterward, and only afterward, did he feel he could enjoy the party. Downstairs later, dressed and sated for the moment, Alexander was able to join conversations, have a couple of drinks, eat a few of the delicious *ramaki* from the trays discreetly offered him by servants, and enjoy his life. Teresa was out of the room, but it no longer bothered him. He felt like scraping his feet on the rug like a rutting dog.

Then his face froze. Across the crowded room he saw the unmistakable bald shining dome of the little son of a bitch from the East, his boss, the Chairman of the Board. Mr. Donald E. Marrow. What the fuck was Don Marrow doing in California? Not that he didn't fly to the Coast often, but Alexander was always told of his movements, usually by a phone call from Marrow himself, his dry nasty voice blunt and succinct. "I'm coming out over that Hong Kong turnaround, be there ten hours." Or, "Meet me at the Fairmont in Frisco, two a.m. Tuesday. Can do?"

Although many found him charming, Alexander hated Marrow. And there he was, sarcastic grin stuck on his shiny face, dressed right out of the nearest Main Street department store, talking to Kerry and Paul Newman.

The sudden, unannounced presence of the Big Boss could throw some men into a panic, but Alexander was only irritated. Let the little son of a bitch play his paranoid power game; if he went too far, Alexander would let them have their studio back. Let *them* try to make it pay. It had been tried before, all over town, these hotshots from the East coming out with their graphs and charts and cheap suits, and either they got thoroughly fucked up over actresses or they went crazy trying to come up with a surefire formula for motion-picture success. In Hollywood, Alexander knew, squeezing a dollar often turned it into a dime. But these boys would look at you with eyes like marbles, making you think they thought you were stealing from the organization right and left. A few months would pass, and they would be carted off to the never-never land of independent production, or the loony bin, whichever seemed appropriate.

Smiling lightly, and with the memory of *her* to float on, Alexander made his way toward the little group by the fireplace, the group isolated and magnified by its power. It was a group only an Alexander Hellstrom could walk up to.

Newman was wearing a beautifully cut tuxedo, and shook hands warmly with Alexander. "How's tricks?" he said.

Kerry, red-faced, grinning and drunker than ever, said, "You should have seen him and his girl friend, running out of here with their pants on fire." They all laughed except Donald Marrow, who smirked.

"Who's the new one?" Marrow asked, like a prosecutor in a multiple murder trial.

Kerry said, "That rich bitch from your end of the country, what the hell's her name? Teresa di Veccio . . ."

Newman said, "I have to go to another party, Kerry . . ."

"Thus the monkey suit," Kerry said, "I knew you wouldn't dress up for little me . . ."

"You're so right, but I wanted to give you your birthday present," and he took something out of his pocket that, when he shook it out, turned into one of the worst-looking toupees Alexander had ever seen. Kerry laughed with delight and clapped it on his head. Newman adjusted it, and Kerry posed with his hands on his hips. "Aren't I cute as a button?" he asked.

"Just a last-minute thought," Newman said, with a straight face.

Alexander thought about the pile of expensive gifts in the library, including his own, a small painting by Larry Rivers that Teresa had picked out. Marrow interrupted his thought by saying, "Teresa di Veccio, huh? You're showing a little class there, Alex, a little class. Isn't she supposed to be of royal blood or something?"

"All those wops are related to some king or another," Kerry said, "if you go back far enough. Really, Paul, I can't thank you enough for your gift . . ."

"It's nothing," Newman said modestly.

Alexander was goddamned if he was going to ask Marrow why he was in town. Hell, maybe it didn't even have anything to do with business . . . no, everything Marrow did was connected to business, he did not have a private bone in his body.

"How is Jan?" he inquired.

"Fine, fine," Marrow said. Jan was his own rich but somewhat cowlike wife, whom Alexander liked. She was a modest, self-effacing woman who clearly adored her husband. Not for the first time, Alexander wondered what their lovemaking was like, the little dynamo wearing nothing but shoes, socks and digital watch, and Jan shy, tender, frightened of her plainness . . .

"Well, where is Miss di Veccio?" Marrow asked. "I'd like you to introduce me."

"Any time," Alexander said.

"Well, well, gentlemen," said a bright young voice, "what's this gathering all about? You guys planning a big movie?"

Alexander turned and saw Richard Heidelberg, grinning, dressed in tight jeans and a tee shirt that said BORN TO LOSE across the chest. Alexander could see the glitter in his eyes. He gave Heidelberg a limp handshake. After all, he wasn't really welcome and should have known it. These little one-shot geniuses could be a terrible pain in the ass. But Kerry put his arm around Heidelberg's shoulder and introduced him to Newman and Marrow. Alexander expected Marrow to be cold to him, but he wasn't, grinned and said, "Hey, I liked *The End of the Unicorn,* Heidelberg, nice picture . ."

"Rick the prick," said Kerry. "Where's that stunning little bitch of yours?"

"She's around somewhere," Rick said. "The name of the picture was *The Endless Unicorn,* Mister Marrow. And I hope you saw it in a theater and not in some little screening room. You have to see it with the public to really appreciate it."

Alexander had an image of Marrow going into a real theater with real people, and had to laugh.

"What's so funny?" Rick said, his eyes still glittering.

Newman made his goodbyes, and Alexander excused himself from the group. When he looked back, Heidelberg and Marrow were jabbering away a mile a minute.

Teresa was dancing with one of the Cajuns. Alexander stood in the doorway to the dining room and watched her comfortably. There were other couples dancing. It was nice to just stand there and watch. She saw him after a while, and smiled sweetly, but kept on dancing. A tray of *ramaki* appeared and he took a couple and popped them into his mouth. Delicious!

Then Kerry was dancing with a small beautiful oriental girl and the music was hot, much hotter than before. Everyone else stopped to watch the birthday boy get it on with this slim beauty. For a plump man, Kerry could really move around, but the girl was something else—tigerish, intense, never taking her eyes from Kerry's. The band caught on and the tempo increased. An odd idea occurred to Alexander. He looked down at Teresa next to him, her eyes bright. Alexander said into her ear, "It looks like that girl's trying to dance Kerry to death."

"What an interesting thought," she said back up to him, and took his hand.

But it wasn't a fancy, it seemed real. Kerry's face and the top of his head were a fierce shade of red and sweat flew off him as he contorted and stomped and jigged and jumped, always with his eyes on the girl. She went smoothly through her rhythms, pacing a little faster and a little faster, like a coyote encouraging a dog to chase it by running only a little faster than the dog, until at last the dog bursts his heart with effort and dies, while the coyote laughs from the underbrush.

Teresa was standing in front of him, against him, and he had his arms around her, cuddling, as they watched with complete attention.

But the oriental girl didn't kill Kerry, no matter what her intention, he seemed unkillable, and the music finally came to an end, and they both collapsed to the floor. Kerry's wife Janie came out and claimed her husband. "Now you have to dance with me, you worm!" she cried, and everyone laughed as Kerry collapsed to the floor again in mock exhaustion.

The little oriental girl was helped to her feet by Donald Marrow, whose face bore a horrible naked lust, but Heidelberg was there and took her off, so she was Heidelberg's girl. She was the best-looking woman at the party, next to Teresa, and for some reason this made Alexander like Heidelberg, feel a kind of comradeship.

Here came Marrow through the crowd, probably bent on meeting Teresa.

"Let's get the hell out of here," Alexander whispered to her and she squeezed his hand in assent. They beat it before Marrow got to them, and running down the driveway Alexander laughed like a schoolboy.

AND THEN she was gone. Alexander could not believe it. "What do you want to go to Paris for?" he asked weakly. They were sitting up in bed, his place. He never got her to give up her room at the Beverly Hills Hotel, because, she said, she needed an address of her own, and some place to store the things she had been buying, a bewildering mess of antique jewelry, pre-Columbian artifacts and paintings. "I only came out here for a raid," she told him tenderly, "I didn't expect to find you . . ."

"Well, *shit*," he said.

"Why don't you come with me? My sister would love you." One of her reasons for going to Paris was to visit her sister, Helene di Veccio.

"I have to work," Alexander said grumpily. "I can't just go flying around the goddamn planet."

"Well, I'm working, too," she said.

"You mean buying stuff?"

"And selling it."

So that was what she did with her time.

Once again he begged her to move in with him, for them to declare their companionship. He did not ask her to marry him. He had been married twice, and both episodes had been unfortunate. He was obviously attracted to active intelligent women, but once he married them his own pleasures in work tended to swamp his wives in social function and boredom. So both wives had bitten huge chunks out of his holdings and moved off, one to Chicago and the other to New York, to resume their own lives.

Teresa, touched but unmoved, said she had a lot of things to do and she would be back before he knew it.

"Or you could come to New York," she said, which thoroughly blackened his mood.

"You don't love me," he said bleakly. "You just proved it."

"But I do love you. And I know you love me, dear Alexander, come here and we'll prove it to each other."

Instead, he got out of bed and stood looking down at her. For once he did not want sex, sex was in the way. He wanted her not to go.

"I'm going to take a shower," he said in a grouchy voice, and wandered off toward the bathroom.

"Oh, darling," she said, just a tiny note of exasperation in her voice. He wandered back out of the bathroom, scratching the back of his neck.

"You could move in with me and still go to Paris," he said. "I wouldn't mind that. In fact, it's a great thing to do, and when I can find a hole in my schedule, I'll come along."

"But I live in New York, all my friends are there . . ."

"We can have a place in New York and a place here," he said, but he knew it wouldn't work even as he said it. "Damn!"

And so he went to the airport with her, the little Alfa returned to her girl friend, the two of them kissing hungrily in the back of Alexander's Mercedes 600, Orfeo at the wheel. In front of American Airlines, Alexander helped Orfeo with her luggage. Most of the stuff had been shipped already, so she only had half a dozen suitcases of various ages, all leathery and well traveled. After they got the eye of a greencap and were about to go inside, Orfeo did a strange thing: Alexander had expected him to say goodbye to Teresa and shake hands with her, for he had lent Orfeo to her several times for shopping expeditions, and they got along fine. Instead, however, Orfeo took both her hands in his, said something in soft Spanish, and when Teresa leaned forward, he kissed her lightly on the cheek. Then he went off with the skycap and the luggage.

"I'm no snob," Alexander said, "but wasn't that going a little far?"

"Oh, Alexander, you are too a snob," she said. In the terminal she bought a copy of *The New Yorker* and two packages of Reese's Peanut Butter Cups. "I'll just orgy on these all across the country," she said. "It's the only time I allow myself candy."

"I never do," Alexander said stiffly. She smiled at him and squeezed his hand, but his hand did not want to be squeezed. They walked toward the lounge. Some idiot recognized Alexander and started coming toward him, but Alexander glared at the man so fiercely that he was stopped in his tracks, frozen by the blast of icy dislike in Alexander's eyes.

"Are we going to the VIP lounge?" she asked him.

"The hell with that," he said. They would wait for the airplane with the rest of the suckers, at least that way there might be a few targets of opportunity for his growing rage. Yes, rage. Power. There was never enough. How trite.

So it was they sat on the little plastic molded seats among the hundreds who were flying to New York, he with his arms tight across his chest, she reading the columns of information in the front of *The New Yorker*.

It did seem to him, on the way home in the warm purring back of the limousine, that he had put more into the affair than she had. A good deal more. He glowered at the back of Orfeo's head. There was no way he could ask about that goodbye kiss. He could fire Orfeo, but why? Exercise of power? All he knew was that for three weeks she had screwed up his life every day, he had been missing appointments, screenings, lunches, even his exercise periods, all for the love of her, and now she was gone, leaving a hole the size of . . . well, he could not think of an appropriately gigantic metaphor, but a huge hole in his heart, as if he had been nailed right through the heart with a 50mm shell, like a bazooka blast through the heart. And left him lying there wounded on the battlefield of love.

He had to snicker. Wasn't there just a teeny touch of *gladness* down there at the bottom? Didn't he feel just the tiniest bit *relieved* that she was gone, and he could put his life in order again?

"Orfeo," he said. "What the hell was that big kiss about?"

"Oh, Boss," he said. "She and I got to be good friends, we talk Spanish while we drive around Beverly Hills. She has good Spanish. I hope you're not mad." There was nothing apologetic in his voice. Alex's heart brightened a bit. He had a pile of work on his desk. He would strip and shower, put on his comfortable old jeans and sweatshirt, some nice thick white cotton socks, and do a little working. That would be just fine! He would be feeling better in just a few minutes. He looked forward to the coziness of it all, and he probably wouldn't miss her much. Hell, it was just one of those things.

He was still running the tune through his head when Orfeo opened the back door of the car, and Alex felt the heat billowing in. How in the devil had he forgotten the heat?

CHAPTER SIX

SWEAT TRICKLED down Jerry Rexford's face as he sat hunched in front of his little electric SCM portable. Every window in his apartment was open, and through the screen door drifted the sounds of a radio somebody had on pretty loud out by the pool. Jerry was naked, sitting on a white towel spread over his kitchen chair to keep his ass from sticking to the plastic. Stacks of fresh paper, carbon paper and manuscript were arrayed on the little kitchen table, presenting the only order in the apartment. The sink was full of dirty dishes, the garbage sacks overflowing with aromatic grapefruit rinds and coffee grounds; the bathroom was all damp towels and dust rolls, and everywhere else were magazines, books, clothing—the dirty stuff rumpled in chairs and over the backs of everything, the fresh laundry sitting in ripped-open blue paper packages. Bachelor Hall.

But Jerry was truly oblivious. He was hacking away at his screenplay, and for once the ideas were coming thick and fast. No more did he worry about how the script "looked," whether his notation was correct, whether anyone would know how amateur he was by his clumsiness. The story was happening in his mind now, all by itself, the characters speaking and things moving. It was all he could do to get the stuff down on the page. Then, coming to the end of a scene, he sat up straight, sighed, and realized he was finished for the evening.

He picked up the stack of manuscript, collated out the carbons and put the pages in order. Good heavens, he had written seventeen pages tonight! That was a lot! He leaned over so he could see the little electric clock in the kitchen. He had been working three hours. And it only felt like a few minutes. He sniffed. He stunk. He sniffed again, and wrinkled his nose. His body smelled fermy and overripe, although he had taken a shower only a few hours ago, after getting home from the day's work.

Jerry unplugged the hot little typewriter, patting its side as if it were alive and saying, "Good baby, thanks a lot." He put the machine aside, leaving a cleared space for the editing process. This was going to be fun, seventeen pages to edit. Jerry loved to edit his own stuff. He sat happily sweating over his work for another hour. By then the radio out by the pool was silent and a bit of cool air was circulating in his apartment, making him shiver slightly.

That was all right. These pages, God save the mark, were "keepsies." The script was now seventeen pages longer. Not every night's work was half so good, and some of them ended bitterly, with Jerry tearing pages in half and dumping them in the overflowing wastebasket. Jerry looked around himself and saw the mess of his apartment, once again feeling the guilty pressure to clean things up a little, now that he was finished with his work session. But it was too depressing. A man who has had a seventeen-page day deserves better.

He thought about showering, dressing and going out. The bars were just getting started. But it would cost money. Sighing again, he looked in the refrigerator, removed a beer and popped it open. There were no clean glasses, so he had to gurgle his beer from the can, and got some of the icy sticky liquid down his front. Now it was definitely time to shower.

No! Now it was time to go swimming!

A quick sluice, another can of beer, and Jerry felt so good he just wandered out by the pool, a towel firm around his waist. If there was nobody around, he would have a little naked swim for himself.

But there was a couple on the lawn across the pool, wrapped up in each other, kissing, Jerry imagined. He quickly turned his back and returned to his apartment. His face was hot and he was very angry. Not with himself or even the necking couple. Just angry. He felt primed for action, something, anything but hanging around the clammy apartment staring at his mess (you couldn't close the door and windows when it got clammy like this, because the place would immediately turn unbearable again).

Jerry took stock. He was afraid. He was a very fearful person. He was afraid to go into a room full of strangers, like a bar, and he was still afraid of his own patio and pool, which he should not be. All he had to look forward to was six a.m. and the donut shop, a bit of friendly conversation and coffee, up to the office to open early, and settle down to the day's work. He had tried, for a while, to do his daily stint of writing in the early morning hours, when his mind was freshest, but that left his evenings a great yawning gap between dinner and sleep, a gap he simply could no longer fill with television or reading. So this way was working out better, but there was still a bit of a gap. Working left him tired but jacked up. For a while he had cured this by hitting the whiskey, but there was a horrible side-effect: he would awaken, instead of at five or six, at about three, and be wide awake until dawn. Then he might fall into a light snooze which would produce a string of vivid nightmares. He would waken late for work and off-key for the whole day.

So now instead of whiskey, he would have a few beers, which helped him over the hump without dashing him awake in the middle of the night.

Jerry flicked on the television and got a third beer. There were a bunch of Hollywood big shots on a panel show, and he watched them without much interest, except to think that these were the people he hoped to live and work among, these overdressed oafish people with their coiffed hair and braying voices. He hoped to become important among them, and he couldn't even take a swim in his own pool. But of course it would be different when he had a private pool, and it would be much different when people saw how well he wrote. Then he would have great confidence, and would be able to make his way among these people, go on television, plus his pictures, marry a movie star and become the First Earl of Rexford. "Lord Rexford?"

"Yes, Pimpleton?"

"The maid is here to brush your teeth . . ."

Jerry cackled to himself. He was beginning to feel pleasantly sleepy.

THE NEXT morning, when he got to the donut shop, it was empty. Jerry was a little disappointed, because he wanted to tell Toby about having a seventeen-page night. Toby could be tremendously encouraging because, sarcastic hipster that he was, he never belittled Jerry's efforts to become a Hollywood writer, and if Jerry confided to him some piece of news, such as a good night's work, he eyes would light up and he would say something encouraging, like, "Way to go, man!" or "Hot damn, they'll have yer star on the Boulevard by Christmas!"

But no Toby. Maybe he was stuck by a customer over at the dirty bookstore. Most of the customers, Jerry had been told, were furtive and wished to keep the transaction down to dollars and cents, but some of them, knowing they had a captive audience behind the counter, would hang around and burble about their lives while Toby sat dead in his chair, staring glassily into the middle distance, hoping the goddamn bore would finally get the message, pick out his porn and move along.

"Lonely assholes, most of 'em," Toby said gloomily.

Jerry filled his cup from the coffee self-service and smiled at Helen, the tall blonde waitress. She gave him a wonderful smile back and wished him good morning, and went back to her work, cleaning out the big metal container that held the glaze. Jerry stared at her ass for a while, fascinating in tight uniform slacks. At first, he had thought Helen was flirting with him, the way she would look deeply into his eyes when they spoke, and that had been part of why he had looked forward to coming to the donut shop in the mornings—she was the only person in Los Angeles giving him any kind of a tumble. He had feverish daydreams about her.

But over the days and weeks he came to believe that Helen was a very simple, very direct person, and looking deeply into his eyes only meant that she was paying attention to him, not flirting. Helen was not all that terrifically intelligent, he decided. When she spoke to customers over the donut counter in front, Jerry noticed after a while, she always said the same things in response to the same questions. This was natural. What made it interesting was that she did so freshly, not as if she were bored, or tired of saying the same things, or as if she had memorized every possible response to every simple donut-shop question. No, freshly, brightly, as if she had just heard the question for the first time, and was just thinking up the answer for the first time.

"Miss, how much are these donuts?"

She would recite the entire price list, always in the same order and the same manner:

"Anything with a hole in it is twenty-two cents, jelly donuts are twenty-eight cents, the twists are twenty-two cents and the cinnamon rolls are twenty-two. Holes are twelve cents apiece."

"How much are these right here?"

"Twenty-two cents."

"How about these?"

"Twenty-two cents. Everything with a hole in it is twenty-two cents."

"How about this one?"

"Twenty-two cents."

People buying donuts early in the morning were often very picky and inde-cisive. Some of them were clearly hostile, as if they expected Helen to give them an argument:

"I'd like a half-dozen donut holes . . ."

"Oh, with *your* waistline?"

But of course she never did, always had a smile for everyone, and sold them their poison cheerfully.

Now that Jerry was a regular, she took to telling him about her life, her boyfriend and his problems with motorcycles, her animals—Helen lived with her mother on a semi-chicken ranch out in the deep valley—her alarm clock, and her boss, a mystery figure who came in the darkest of night and made all the donuts, vanishing by six a.m., but calling once in a while on the tele-phone. Every time Helen mentioned her boss she would smile and roll her eyes. Exactly the same every time.

Jerry stopped fantasizing about Helen one morning at coffee break time, when he was down picking up everybody's coffee orders from the office. Helen was alone with a man of about forty, dressed like a dude, checked slacks and light tight leather jacket, his white hair curly and hip, his tan dark. Jerry did not like the man immediately, and kept staring at him out of the corner of his eyes while Helen filled his order.

"The usual?" she asked, and Jerry nodded. Helen could remember "the usual" for a bewildering array of people, so she wasn't all that dumb.

The man was talking to Helen about sex. This really bothered Jerry, but he kept his mouth shut.

"I bet you got a lot of boyfriends," the man said.

"Nope," said Helen, bent over the donut counter. Jerry saw the man ogling her ass and felt like going over there and punching him out. "Watch it, you old fart!" he wanted to snarl, but didn't.

"I bet you've got all the boys upset," the man persisted in a kidding tone.

"I guess so," Helen said. She was putting Jerry's order into a cardboard cup-carrier. The man got up and came over to her, reaching out to touch her on the side of the head, saying, "You've got the most beautiful head of hair."

Jerry was about to push him away, but Helen just stepped behind the counter and the man stumbled forward, and she laughed at him.

"Better watch your step," she said cheerfully, and the old gasbag had to sit down again, his face red as a maraschino cherry.

Helen exchanged a secret look and a wink with Jerry, and Jerry felt a thrill of comradeship.

SUNDAYS WERE the worst. On Saturday, Jerry could explore Los Angeles, those parts of it he wanted to know about, taking walks along Hollywood Boulevard among the throngs of inhabitants and misguided tourists, happily discovering that the Boulevard had a fine collection of new and used book-stores, from Larry Edmonds' old shop specializing in Hollywoodiana, to the Cherokee crowded with stacks of old comic books, big-little books and fantasy, occult and science fiction sections. Then there was a Pickwick, a gigantic store with all the new books and a fairly good backlist. Jerry had to be careful shopping, because he would have enjoyed taking home an armload of stuff every time he went out.

Then there were the hicks in front of Mann's Chinese Theater, gawking at the footprints, pawprints, titprints, etc., seeming less than immortal in the hot afternoon sunlight. Jerry was contemptuous of the tourists; after all, he was now an Angelino himself.

The Boulevard had a lot of movie theaters on it, and Jerry spent a lot of time in them until finally it became crippling to his work. He would go see a movie, and then all the way home he would compare it to his own screenplay, which would make him sweaty either because what he was doing was so much *better* or so much *worse* he felt he was losing his judgment. Pages would get ripped out, or other pages hastily written, Jerry grim and biting his nails as he sat naked on his towel, all to be sacrificed next time he saw another picture.

So there went going to the movies.

He liked to walk in downtown Beverly Hills, too, because it seemed like a regular city, with its expensive shops, tall buildings (but not too tall) and beautifully dressed people. It was here that Jerry made the delightful dis-covery that there was a street in Beverly Hills named Rexford Drive. Someday when he became famous people would say that it was named after him. What about Hayworth Street in Hollywood? Which came first? Rita or the street?

Naturally, Jerry wanted to meet girls. The ones on Hollywood Boulevard were a little too tough-looking. He had never been a man who could pick up a girl on the street, although he had not realized this fact until now. In Beverly Hills, where the women were extravagantly beautiful, perhaps the most beautiful women Jerry had ever seen, they would not even look at him. There was no eye contact with these lovely rich young women, who had nothing to do all day but shop and be picked up in their limos and go play tennis. There was no friendly banter in the stores, either. Jerry was used to having good relations with the girls who worked behind the counters of stores, but here in Beverly Hills they took one look at him and moved off. The trouble was, Jerry did not look rich. Finally he decided that downtown Beverly Hills was crass, and it was no longer fun to go there.

There were places to go in his Porsche, drives to be taken in the hills, or to places he had heard about all his life but never seen, like Capistrano or Palm Springs, but after a while he had seen all he could see from the car, and it was no fun hanging around without anybody to talk to. And the Porsche was acting up. It did not like Southern California at all, and hated the drive from Jerry's apartment to the Boulevard, always carboning up and threatening to stop dead in the middle of the street.

Jerry took it in to the repair place at Wilshire and Doheney, sitting with his hands between his legs in the big hangarlike garage watching the mechanics working on Ferraris and Lamborghinis. Finally somebody looked into his car, and Jerry started to get up and go over to find out what was the trouble, but in roared a long expensive automobile, and a rich man jumped out, and Jerry's mechanic left the Porsche with its back obscenely open and ran to make jokes with the rich man. Jerry sat and boiled. An hour later they told him his car was okay, nothing wrong with it.

"Take the sumbitch out and open 'er up once in a while," he was told. He had been driving too conservatively.

But Sundays were the absolute worst, because all he had to do on Sundays was sit in his apartment wishing he had the guts to go outside and make friends. Sundays were all for nothing, with the added pressure of Monday coming.

Gradually, his loneliness began to turn inward, in the form of self-dislike. He began to question his life-plan, his ambitions in the movie business.

He read the trades, he knew things were whirling on all around him, pictures were being made, men and women younger than Jerry finding themselves in the headlines for their accomplishments, while Jerry pecked and edited his life away at *Pet Care Hotline*. As for the screenplay he was writing so faithfully, what was it but a bunch of imitations, the same old whore of a plot with not even new clothes? It was a hunk of garbage, Jerry would think, lying miserably on his couch, dressed in his shorts and drinking beer. He should go over and throw it into the garbage sack.

Sometimes he would actually do it, and then feeling silly, take it back out and put it on the table. More than once this led him into a guilt storm of activity, and he would clean the apartment from one end to the other.

What a life!

"How did you make out with Adams, Ray & Rosenberg?" Toby asked him one Monday morning as they sat enjoying their coffee.

"Same as everybody else," Jerry said. "They'd be glad to see my screenplay when it's finished . . ."

"You talk to one of the boys?"

"No," Jerry admitted. "Just the girl at the door."

"Fuckers," Toby said, but not as if he were surprised. Toby seemed to think that a good agent should be able to tell from Jerry's sincerity that he would soon be a hot property, a surprisingly naive attitude considering its source.

"I'm not so sure I'm all that sincere," Jerry said. "Maybe I just want to score the big bucks like anybody else . . ."

Toby was amused. "Yeah, that's what I mean by sincere."

Jerry had come to realize that Toby was his only friend in Los Angeles, but even so, he was shy about asking him out for a drink, or even spending time with him at work, in the twenty-four-hour dirty bookstore. Toby did not mind, but Jerry imagined the customers were put off by having a man in a suit and tie standing there while they roamed among the pornography. So they saw one another only during the fifteen minutes or so in the morning when Toby would put the "BACK IN 10 MIN" sign on his door and duck out for coffee.

ON THIS particular morning, Toby was in rare good humor.

"Just the man I wanted to see," he said, and patted the stool next to him.

There was nobody else in the place except Helen, who was refilling the Orange Whip machine, but Toby looked around conspiratorially, and pulled a magazine from under his newspaper. Jerry moved to look at it, but Toby said, "Back off for a minute," and riffled the pages rapidly until getting the one he wanted. Then he pressed the magazine to the counter and said, "Okay, have a look . ."

Jerry looked, did a take, and looked again.

"Who does that look like to you?"

"It's Elektra Soong, isn't it?"

Toby's eyes wrinkled with cynical amusement. "Elektra Soong in a dirty magazine? With her ass up in the air?"

Jerry looked again. Elektra Soong had been on the cover of *Rolling Stone* a couple of issues back, with her boyfriend Richard Heidelberg. Jerry remembered that he and Toby had lusted over her photographs inside, and Toby had described her as "prime pussy." Jerry had to agree. Now, looking at the semipornographic photograph, he could not help but think he was looking at Elektra Soong—badly photographed and obscene. "Good God," he said.

"How much would you bet?" Toby teased.

"God, nothing. This picture could have been taken, you know, before she . . ." Jerry was not sure what he wanted to say.

"Before she made the big time, huh?"

"Yes. What a shame, to have it published now . . ."

"Shit, half the stars in Hollywood have pictures like this in the closet somewhere . . . but this ain't Elektra Soong."

Jerry said just the right thing: "Well, she looks enough like her to be her sister . . ."

Toby laughed wildly. "Yer close! Yer close!" Dramatically he opened the magazine and showed the rest of the photo layout, the headlines, the text. Jerry's skin went cold. The photo he had felt deliciously lustful over had been that of a man. A man who was the spit and image of Elektra Soong, but nevertheless a man. Jerry felt immediately furious at Toby for trapping him like this.

"Don't lose your cool," Toby said, "I fell for it, too. This is Elektra's brother, kid brother . . ."

"How do you know?" Jerry asked. "The name here is Karol Dupont."

"Would I waste your time with this crap? I met her, last night at a party."

"*Her?*"

"By courtesy," Toby said. "A bunch of drag queens at this party up in the hills, and she was there. I got to talkin' to her, nice bitch. Crazy about her sister."

"What's this got to do with me?" Jerry said a bit stiffly.

"Nothin', only this could be your connection, don't you get it?"

"My connection?"

"Yeah. Karol's in touch with her sister, her sister's livin' with Rick Heidelberg. I know Karol, you know me . . . get the picture?"

It made Jerry a little dizzy, but he got the picture. "You can't be serious," he said, but looking into Toby's feverish eyes, he knew that Toby *was* serious, and thought he was being a great help.

"You gimme your script, I pass it to Karol, Karol drops it on Elektra, and Elektra hands it to Rick."

Toby began to sing the Marine Hymn, but with new words:

> From the cesspools here in Hollywood,
> To the shores of Malibu . . .

He laughed wildly. "What a parlay!"

Jerry wondered how the hell he was going to keep this "parlay" from happening without losing Toby's friendship. Well, at first he would temporize. "I'm not finished yet," he said. "But when I do . ."

"Crap," said Toby.

Helen came over and turned her head to look at the magazine, *Queens on Parade,* but Toby slipped it under his newspaper again.

"Not for your tender eyes," he said to her.

"Oh golly, I've seen about everything," she said, but walked away blushing.

Toby turned back to Jerry. "Lemme ask you a question, what's this script of yours about?"

"Well, it's kind of complicated," Jerry said.

"Strip it down for me . . ."

Jerry did not want to.

Toby was impatient. "What is it, love story, fantasy, Western, gangsters, what?"

Blushing as redly as Helen, Jerry told him a bald, simplified version of the story he was working on. As he stripped it of its nuances Jerry realized once again how corny it was. After a couple of sentences he stopped.

Toby looked thoughtful, and then said, "Dynamite. It's a great idea. I think you got a property there, my boy."

"Don't say anything to anybody, okay?" Jerry asked. Toby had to get back. He slapped Jerry on the shoulder.

"Hurray for . . . Holly-wood!" he sang, and left.

Jerry looked helplessly at Helen, who blushed and stared into his eyes until he had to break contact.

CHAPTER SEVEN

RICK'S OFFICES were on the top floor of the Hendricks Building on La Brea just below Santa Monica, a four-floor building devoted to the motion-picture arts. Rick had the best suite, and his private office had belonged to a number of moguls before him, which accounted for the luxurious frosted blue glass backbar with the intaglio Venus emerging from the waves, and the huge (for an office) bathroom with its deep blue Mexican tile shower—big enough for two. There was even a tiny bedroom behind a sliding panel, with a view of the parking lot in back, and beyond that, the Goldwyn Studios, a block away.

With Rick's inhabitancy the office blossomed out in movie posters and modern art, furniture from the teens and twenties, all beautifully cared for and all in the best taste. It was normal for someone in pictures to put up movie posters, but only of movies one has worked on. Rick did more than that: he put up posters of movies he *wished* he had worked on. The biggest, right behind his desk and covering part of the panel which concealed the secret bedroom, was *The Treasure of the Sierra Madre*. Beneath the poster was a low credenza filled with books, and upon it was the golden Oscar Rick had won for the screenplay of *The Endless Unicorn*. Rick had also produced and directed the picture, but those awards went to others.

Rick was paying an arm and a leg for these offices, and although everyone who came to see him on business was terrifically impressed, still no deal had been made, and Rick was still a one-picture wonder boy, someone to be watched, but meanwhile, where was his next biggie? And the rent had to be paid.

In the other offices were Rick's employees, three secretaries, two script readers, and his friend Jose Gonzala, a graduate of the UCLA Film School (3.6 grade average) and a director looking for a project. They hoped of course to make a picture together, with Rick as executive producer, the marriage broker, as it were, but so far none of the properties they had looked at had rung any bells.

Input was tremendous, of course. First, when a new producer begins to make waves, the agents send him routinely all the loose scripts, in some cases stuff that has been lying around for years. In Rick's case, since he seemed to have a handle on the young, he got a lot of scripts and treatments for "youth-oriented projects"—most of it nakedly exploitive, some of it good but dated, but most of it just plain unreadable.

At first he swore he would read everything that came into the office, but in no time at all the huge stacks of red, blue, grey, black and green screenplays, the galley proofs from hopeful publishers, the old novels, the presentations and the treatments overwhelmed him, and he hired readers. Readers had been one of the things about "the old Hollywood" that irritated Rick. "You write a novel, see, break your ass on it;. and then some punk making fifty a day reduces it to a paragraph with a recommendation at the bottom, which the big boss reads while he's picking his teeth after lunch, and burp!—there goes your property!"

But he had to do it. Out of self-defense.

Jose Gonzala did not read any of this stuff. He spent his days searching for an original property among his friends. He was determined to find a project dealing with El Barrio in a reasonably commercial manner, and for this to happen, the writer, he felt, should live in El Barrio or at least have been raised there, as Jose had.

But a year had slipped away somehow, and Rick's telephone log got shorter. Not that he wasn't plagued with telephone calls, it's just that the calls were now coming in from people he had never heard of, or from agents who did not, frankly, represent the major talents in the business. Top agents and studio heads, first-run independent producers and heavy talent were not calling these days. One day Rick realized that he had called everybody back who had called him, and that he was even with the log. There had been a time when he left the office around six in the evening, with two hundred calls unanswered.

And the overhead rolled on. Jose alone was costing him a fortune, when you added up his deal, plus his secretary, who spent most of her days sitting out there making artificial bouquets of flowers out of tiny glass beads, plus the office rent, the rental on the hot-and-cold machine for coffee and water, and the refrigerator for the Dos Equis, telephone bill, etc. It had been a joyful moment when, a year ago, Rick had called Jose and coolly drawled out his offer, which Jose had leaped at. Rick had fancied that after a few weeks to settle down, Jose would begin his project, but alas, every script, every treatment, was somehow wrong. Fortunately, they were only paying the writers a little bit, flattering them with office space and daily conferences, but never signing a contract or paying Guild wages. Time enough for that when Jose and Rick approved the property. Then the sky would be the limit, the young novice writer would join the Guild, get an agent (if he didn't already have one) and start collecting the big dollar bills.

But somehow these underpaid young beginners did not seem to be able to come up with anything. Rick tilted back in his desk and looked up at a poster for *Gun Crazy*. John Dall with a gun. That was Hollywood at its best, the illusion beyond illusion.

Abruptly, Rick got to his feet. He did not knock on Jose's door, since it was open a crack. Jose was behind his desk in his totally Mexican office, his feet on his desk, a bottle of Dos Equis in one hand and an open book in the other.

"You're fired," Rick said.

"*No habla Englis,* " Jose said. He put down his beer and closed the book. His eyes betrayed no emotion. He folded his hands in front of him, his feet now carefully placed under the desk.

"It's not your fault, Jose," Rick said, his own hands in his hip pockets. "I been running this place on the wrong basis. The lawyers can work it out."

"Okay, fuck it," Jose said. He grinned and held out his hand. "I've been waiting for the axe to fall for months."

"You'll make your picture," Rick said.

"Yeah, but I'm not hungry enough, pal."

The two friends were delighted to discover that they were still friends, after the worst had happened. A little more conversation and Rick went back to his own office. He looked at his list of potential projects, the ones he had not yet given up hope on. To be an executive, you have to know how to make up your mind. Rick studied the list for a few minutes, and then picked one. He shuffled among the papers on his desk until he found the favored project—now in three-page treatment form. This he held in his hand. He pressed the intercom.

"Joyce, could you come in for a minute?"

His secretary came in, a wary look in her eyes. Word must have already leaked out. He smiled reassuringly.

"I want every project cleaned out of this office by the time I get back from lunch."

She stared at him.

"We're going into high fucking gear around here," he said.

When he got back from The Port, where he had feasted on chicken in wine sauce, all the projects were gone. He waited for Joyce to get back from lunch, reading and rereading his three-pager. Then he heard her come in.

"Joyce, see if you can get Alexander Hellstrom."

It would be an interesting test. Rick felt excited about his afternoon for the first time in a while. Would Hellstrom call him? He would have to sit there and wait. The odds were terrific that Hellstrom, if he called at all, would do so tomorrow or the next day. But he had to wait.

How important am I?

It is not often you can find out the answer to such a vital question.

"Joyce, see if you can reach Elektra . . ."

"Mr. Hellstrom on two," she said. "Do you still want me to try to reach Elektra?"

"Hell yes, and tell her to hold!"

Rick laughed wildly, and then had a sip of ice water to clear his throat. He pressed extension 2.

"Hello there," he said in his deep charming voice.

"Mr. Hellstrom will be with you in a moment," said a dry female voice. But before Rick could feel anything, the voice of Alexander Hellstrom boomed over the phone:

"What can I do for you, young man?"

"I thought we should make a picture together," Rick said charmingly.

"You don't need our help, from the way I hear it."

"I have to confess," Rick said, "this one is too big for me. I'd at least like a chance to talk to you about it, give you the property to read, and then maybe we could make a deal."

Sweat was pouring down Rick's body. Why? He did not know. There was a long silence at the other end. Finally:

"I looked at my schedule. How about lunch Friday?"

"Terrific." Rick started to say something else, but the telephone clicked. Busy man, no time for goodbyes.

Joyce: "Elektra Soong on three."

"I'll take it."

"Hi, baby," came Elektra's sleepy voice.

"Guess who just called me on the telephone!"

"JOYCE, SEE if you can reach David Novotny, please," said Rick into the intercom. David Novotny was his agent. He wondered how long it would take David to answer his call. Probably all afternoon, but that was all right. Things were starting to roll. He would have David exercise his option on the property, called so far *Witherspoon,* a love story about a daffy young man and the daffy ways he tries to attract the girl. Needed work, but it was something any young person would be attracted to, so long as they didn't soup it up too much, or treacle it down too much.

The screen treatment had been written by a college professor of English Literature at Florida University in Gainesville, a man who poured out a constant stream of low-grade short stories, movie treatments, screenplays, teleplays, series ideas, novels and articles. His success percentage was low but his output was high, so he must have been making pretty good money. He was also represented by David Novotny, and went under a number of aliases: H. J. Cromwell was the one attached to *Witherspoon.*

According to David, Cromwell (or whoever) had come to Hollywood once years ago, fresh-faced and eager, brought out by the producers of *Bonanza,* where he had sold several scripts. *Bonanza* wanted to try him out as a story editor, and set him down in a room at the Beverly-Wilshire Hotel with a failed script and instructions to "make it work" by Monday morning, when they had to start shooting. Cromwell came into the office at Paramount early Monday morning with a fine shooting script and a vicious hangover, and left Hollywood that night, forever.

Anyway, he was an old pro and would understand when they exercised their option, paid him his bucks and kissed him off the picture.

"Yes, Joyce?"

"David's office says he'll be in meetings all afternoon."

"That was nice of them."

"Uh, I told Elena about you and Alexander Hellstrom, was that all right?" Elena was David's secretary and a good friend of Joyce's.

"I think that was a very good thing to do," Rick said. "I'm out for the rest of the afternoon—no, I'm in a *meeting*," he laughed.

"In a meeting, yes, Rick."

The office was silent again. Rick went to the ornate and expensive equipment along one wall, turned on the FM radio. There was a black station that played good stuff. He fiddled around until he got it, and then went back to his desk and began rolling a joint from the crisp sensimilla he kept in a cherrywood box in his top desk drawer. Rick was good with his fingers and took pleasure in rolling cigarettes. He looked at his handiwork, a smooth medium-sized joint, admired it for a moment while Joe Williams sang the blues, and then lit up. A thin cloud of smoke drifted into the bars of sunlight that cut through the middle of the room.

"Ah," he said. The afternoon was his.

Joyce. Hm, Joyce. Thirty, blonde, good-looking, a little broad in the hips and slightly underbuilt in the breast department, but attractive. A damned good secretary, one of those cool efficient Hollywood secretaries who knew everybody in the business, could find anything, from a print of *Greed* to a reservation at Amelio's, in fifteen minutes, knew where all the bodies were buried, knew whom to put through and whom to put off. But of course she wanted to be a producer. Most of them, the good ones, wanted to be something else.

Joyce was married to a key grip who worked regularly over at CBS on a television series. Rick had met him once, a nice man, stocky, hairy and bland. He wondered if the guy thought Rick was fucking his wife.

Probably not, Rick thought.

There was a tapping at the door. Rick said, "Come in," and Joyce came in and closed the door behind her, leaning on it and looking at Rick through the smoke with a tentative smile.

"I just wanted to say congratulations," she said.

"What for?" Rick had smoked dope in front of her before, but up to now she had always refused him. He waved the joint at her in a vague gesture that could have meant anything. She smiled again and crossed the room, sitting on Rick's couch. Rick came over and sat beside her, offering her the joint. She took an expert pull at it, a double hit, and held it in. Slowly she exhaled, looking fondly at Rick.

"They want you," she said. "Every lot in town wants you. Did you see how fast he answered your call?"

They smoked marijuana quietly for a few minutes while Charlie Parker played for them.

Joyce said, "I'm just so happy for you."

Rick said, "Thank you. I'm so happy I could just fuck you." He hadn't meant to say that, it was just a joke. Why had he said that?

Joyce looked down and said, "Um, okay, I guess that would be all right."

Rick stood up, amazed, and watched as Joyce, ever the efficient secretary, opened the sliding panel without catching the corner of *The Treasure of the Sierra Madre,* checked to see that the little bed was made, gave Rick an encouraging smile and started to get out of her clothes. Rick had been wrong about her figure. In nothing but her underpants she had a wonderful body.

"Oh, just a sec," she said, and while Rick undressed she got on the telephone and had one of the other girls cover for her. "We're in a meeting," she said. She giggled and came into Rick's arms, soft and sweet and utterly relaxed.

"Boy, that's sure good marijuana," she purred as they fondled each other.

Rick had to suppress the desire to say, *"I'll send you a pound!"* He did not know where to find a pound of this stuff, and besides, this was not the time to play grandee.

"Wait a minute," Joyce said, sliding down his body, kissing his belly button lightly, "I've been wanting to do this for a *year!*" She began giving him a blow job.

That was fine with Rick. He lay back and watched her, amazed at what had been right there in the office all the time. She was good, my God, she was good, and she liked her work, letting her hair tickle him, looking up into his eyes from time to time, making little murmurs of delight. Rick responded to this kind of treatment enthusiastically, and when she seemed to have had her fill of straight cocksucking, he grabbed her and crammed himself into her with a savage grunt.

It was a terrific fuck, they both agreed afterward, and to seal the bargain they fucked again, and then later, drinking beer, very stoned and just a little zizzed, Joyce gave him the full-length slow-going thorough blow job he knew she had in her, making him come, even for the third time, with a fullness that made him cry out.

"God, I love to do that," she said. "I love men's cocks, they're so beautiful, even when they're little and soft."

"I can't get over how long we waited," Rick said.

"Oh, don't worry about me, I won't make trouble. We have a good thing going here, we have to protect ourselves. This is just my way of saying congratulations."

Later she dressed and kissed him and said she had to get back out there, ever the good secretary, sensing that he wanted to be alone.

Whew, thought Rick. What a day!

RICK SAT on the beach alone. He was naked and cross-legged on his towel, his hands resting gently on his knees. He faced the water, which was about twenty feet away, down a gentle slope of white sand. The sun was hot, but the slight breeze from the ocean kept it from being uncomfortable.

Therefore, why couldn't Rick meditate? He did not pursue the question, but put it out of his mind. He had told himself long ago that the ability to meditate was one of the few things he really wanted to accomplish in his life, one of the real challenges to his energy and intellect. It could free him the way money never could, and once he learned it, he would be beyond this world, the world of *samsara,* the wheel of sorrow, the suffering he knew was to come.

Did he see a whale? No. But he saw them often enough. Whales. No.

Sky. No.

Hey, Bob oh Rebop. No, no, Jesus.

Jesus loves me yes I, no.

See a big spot. Let the spot fill your mind. Here, Spot, come on, Spot, fill my mind, Spot, get bigger and bigger and . . .

It did not work, as usual. He knew what he wanted. He wanted to silence all the voices in his mind, all the inner dialogue, monologue, whatever it was. He was afraid of the silence in there, but he knew from his reading that this was the purpose of meditation, to get the silence, to lengthen it, to be able to relax in it. That's why Zen pupils sat, why dervishes whirled, why chanters chanted, why prayers prayed. It is why people paid good money to fakers from India who gave them a word to chew on—if the word they chewed on shut up the voices it didn't matter if the guy was a fake or not, the silence had been achieved.

Meanwhile, thinking about this, Rick knew he was no closer to meditation than the first time he had tried it, years before. It was his secret failure. Oh, he had told Elektra about it.

"I can't meditate," he said to her, deep in the night.

"I can," she said cheerfully.

He had been confessing a weakness, a failure, a battle lost, and she had taken it the same as if he had said, "I can't pitch a baseball."

She was down the beach somewhere, out of sight. Probably with a bunch of little kids. Elektra attracted children, especially the little ones, under five, and many of her days on the beach were spent amateur baby-sitting. There hadn't seemed to be that many little children around when Rick moved out here, but all Elektra had to do was show up and they would come up over the sand dunes, followed by their dogs, their mothers, their governesses and sometimes even their fathers, but after a while the parents and other adults would relax and leave Elektra in charge, and she and the little ones would walk up and down the beach, Elektra talking constantly. She knew them all by name and would address them: "Now, Susan, you're falling behind; Charles, take Susan by the hand; Billy, will you please pick up that big shell and give it to Gretchen? Thank you very much. Susan, you may look at the shell after Gretchen has looked at it . . ."

And on and on. Rick saw her often, looking down at the beach from his sun deck, her small figure trailed by four or five tiny figures. He wondered about her natural gift with children, and had asked her if she wanted any herself. She laughed and said no.

But this was not getting any meditating done. Maybe he was afraid of more than just the silence. Maybe he was scared of what would happen next. In his life. He *enjoyed* his life. He knew he was a rat and a slime, he knew he was a criminal and a degenerate, and he also knew he had rare gifts which made the world, the world of *samsara,* easy pickings.

A twinge of pain in his right knee. If he could meditate instead of think, the knot would dissolve.

What knot?

The one you can't untie with your mind, the one that keeps you here . . .

So much for the old knot metaphor.

Maybe the Zen people were right. Concentrate on some kind of nonsense until it becomes . . .

Now his mind was racing, and he bitterly felt the defeat. He stood up, his knees creaking. That was what bothered him. Defeat. Rick was the kind of man who could pick up a golf club, a Ping-Pong paddle, an oar, a chess piece, anything, and be good with it after only a few minutes of instruction. He could add columns of figures in his head, he could run the hundred in 9.5, he could make forty million dollars with a single movie.

But he couldn't meditate.

He couldn't even cheat and tell himself that he was meditating, because he would only be lying to himself, and when he did that, one of the voices in his head would laugh at him, *all* the voices in his head would laugh at him.

Maybe there was no such thing as meditating, and that was why he failed. But no, he could envision what it must be like, and he knew that the masters of philosophy and religion were not lying. This was no set of ideas, no philosophy, this was a real thing, like throwing a baseball, and it required training and practice, like throwing a baseball, and Rick only wished he had the time, and would not be embarrassed, by entering into a training program in some discipline. It didn't really matter to him which one. Zen would do. Or . . .

Rick had an image of Elektra dancing, the look she got in her eyes when she danced. Not gone, not hypnotized, but totally attentive, looking not through you but into you, and dancing . . .

The Disco Route to Samadhi.

He walked down and let the foamy water hiss around his feet. His feet sank a bit into the delicious cold sand. God, there were probably people all over the earth who could pass into and out of a state of Samadhi (empty brain but aware of surroundings) without even knowing it, just phase in and phase out. Elektra, he was sure, was one of them. That's what she liked about little kids. Clean little slates.

"Oh, fuck a duck," he said to himself.

He looked up, shading his eyes, at the sun. Feeling only a bit self-conscious, he made *namasti* to the sun, pressing his palms together, bowing his head and touching his fingertips to his nose. *Namasti* was his last thought, and then there was a tiny moment of emptiness just as his fingertips touched his nose. He opened his eyes and straightened up and returned to the world. He felt better. That always worked. He wondered if there was anything physiological about it, the pressing the palms together concentrating forces that were then directed into the center of the mind by the act of *namasti* . . . or whether it was just some Hindu nonsense . . .

Well. Wet feet, empty mind.

And here came Elektra, trailed by three tiny children in beach clothes, sunsuits, bonnets, etc.

"Say hello to Rick," Elektra said to the little ones.

Rick smiled at the children. They *were* nice, goddamn it. He said hello to each of them, as gravely as they said hello to him. Children did not find him as charming as adults.

Maybe they knew something.

PART TWO:
"ERROL FLYNN SLEPT HERE"

CHAPTER EIGHT

GRADUALLY THROUGHOUT the summer Jerry began to settle into the places he spent his life. He did so without recognition at first, maintaining his isolation like a fortress. Yet gradually the people around him became his friends. There was nothing he could do about it. At the office, on Hollywood Boulevard and in the U-court on Fountain, Jerry was accepted, and spent his days and nights among people who liked him.

He had been successfully able to avoid invitations to the homes of his fellow workers on the ground that he had to write, but this did not excuse him from the company Fourth of July picnic, which was held in a glade in Griffith Park. Everyone came with family or friends except Jerry, who could not think of anyone to ask. But this was highly satisfactory to Richard, his fellow editor, because Richard had brought his sister in the hope that she and Jerry would hit it off.

Her name was Barbara Tobin and she was twenty-eight, squarely built, with a high forehead, light blonde hair and dark blue eyes. She wore black-rimmed glasses and was dressed for picnic, in a nice plaid shirt and jeans. She did not seem to have a very good figure, with that squareness at the hips and shoulders and her blunt nose and chin, but she had a nice smile and a good low voice and Jerry wondered why she wasn't married and raising a lot of kids out in the Valley.

Richard, in his white shirt with the sleeves rolled up and dark green pants, looked like an off-duty bus driver, but he was obviously very fond of his sister, and started things off between Jerry and Barbara by embarrassing them both:

"You two singles sit here!" he said too loud, making people turn and stare at them. "What'll it be, beer, wine, Coke? There's Tab," he said to his sister too directly.

"I'll have beer," she said.

"Me too," said Jerry. He was a little mad because he felt he had to rescue the situation. Richard went off happily to fill their order and he said to Barbara without looking at her, "It's sure a great day for a picnic."

She didn't say anything, so he looked around at the others. There were children of all ages, some playing, some whining and clamoring for attention—everything he hated about domesticity—and there was his boss, Harris, informal in an all-brown ensemble Jerry suspected he must have bought just for the picnic, and Mrs. Harris, the tall slender hawk-nosed woman Jerry saw many times at the office, coming and going on errands Jerry knew nothing about and cared less.

"Gotta say hello to the boss," Jerry said, and grunted to his feet. He wondered how Harris was going to get through this day, with his clean-freak attitude. Would he wipe his hands off every time he touched somebody? Would he spend all afternoon brushing invisible specks of dirt from his clothing? This would probably be the most interesting thing to happen all day. Jerry waited politely while Harris talked to Sanchez the accountant and then shook hands.

"Glad to have you aboard," Harris said. He made no attempt to wipe his hand off. So he was going to rough it on the nation's birthday.

Sanchez was a nice man, thickset, grey-haired and short. He shook hands with Jerry and winked.

"The way to get you out of your hole is food, huh?"

"It sure smells great," Jerry said. He realized that the Fourth of July was one of his favorite holidays. He could smell hot dogs and firecrackers.

"The eating holidays are the ones I like," he said. The three men stood and watched as hot dogs, ribs and hamburgers sizzled on the Park Service grills. The old picnic table was covered with dishes of food, and there was more food in the shade of the table. Jerry's contribution, a case of Schlitz, was in a big tub of ice at the end of the table, with the jugs of white wine.

"Get your fingers out of that potato salad!" a woman screamed at a child, and Jerry grinned. In spite of himself, he was going to have a good time.

Up the slope aways, Barbara still sat, now holding two beers in her hands. Jerry went back up to her and sat down again.

"Is that for me?" he asked. She handed him the beer with a slight smile, but said nothing. Such a quiet person, he thought, and then his heart sank as he realized all the things Richard must have been saying to her, his unmarried sister, about the bachelor in the office who would be at the picnic and might be interested in her if she would only make herself interesting enough. He could imagine Richard, not the subtlest guy, saying, "Just don't sit there like a bump on a log, okay?" So what was there left for her to do but feel resentment toward this bachelor hunk of meat who was so obviously patronizing her?

"Your brother's quite a guy," he said lamely.

"Yes, he's the bright one in the family," she said.

God forbid, thought Jerry.

"Quite a guy," he said.

There was not a whole hell of a lot of eye contact going on between them. They sat and sipped their beers and watched the commonplace scene in front of them, the running children, the groups of men and women in relaxed conversation, the gentle breeze making the leaves dapple everything with shifting patterns. Smoke drifted on the wind, and the pleasant sound of firecrackers was everywhere. Not a bad moment. The alternative would have been to sit in his little apartment in his underwear and watch television until he drank himself to sleep. Not a bad moment at all, compared to that.

"What would you be doing today if you weren't here?" he asked Barbara. He peered into her eyes. She blinked.

"Oh, I'd be scrubbing the walls or something, I can't stand holidays," she said.

"What kind of work do you do?" he asked. Might as well get the interrogation over with, he thought heavily.

"I'm credit manager for Gelbhardt's Jewelry, downtown," she said.

"Oh, that sounds like interesting work."

"Oh, but it isn't, she said with a smile," she said with a smile, and Jerry had to laugh.

"Not that interesting, huh?"

"About as interesting as calling people up and trying to get them to pay for their wedding rings," she said, "long after they wished they hadn't gotten married at all, and certainly well after they thought they had to buy an expensive diamond for their sweetie."

"True, the way you put it, it does sort of sound like a drag," he said. "Is it as interesting as writing Tips for Retailers?"

"No, I don't imagine it's *quite* that interesting," she grinned, and they both drained their beers. Jerry's spirits continued to lift. This silly little banter would have gone right over Richard's head. He would have pinched his nose above his glasses and pointed out that writing Tips for Retailers had its interesting moments, and probably talking to people about their ring purchases must, also.

"I wish Richard was here," Barbara said.

"Really? Why?"

"So he could get us another couple of beers."

"Allow *me!*"

Sinking his hand up to the wrist in the icy water in the tub, Jerry stopped for a moment, an idea springing into his mind. He was going to *fuck* this girl. She was willing for him to fuck her, he could tell. She was shy, but so was he, and yet they had managed in only a few minutes to establish an intimacy, enough for him to delicately and gently lead her, step by step so as not to spook her, into his bed. Was his apartment neat enough for company? No. Then they would do it at her place.

He groped around and got out two cold cans of beer and carried them up to her. She smiled up into his eyes as he handed her the wet can of beer. With the idea of fucking her in his mind, she looked entirely different. Better. More womanly. Less Richard's sister.

"Skoal!" he said, raising his glass on high.

"Well, you two seem to be hitting it off," said Richard, hunkering down beside them. "How about having dinner at the house tonight? Just the four of us. We'll feed the kids and put 'em to bed and watch some television, huh?"

"Let's not and say we did," said Barbara, her eyes on Jerry's.

"Oh-oh, other plans, huh?" Richard said stupidly.

"I don't have a thing to do," Jerry said to her.

"Neither do I," she said to him.

"So why not come to the house?" Richard asked.

"Because we'll be helplessly drunk," Jerry said, taking a long pull at his beer. Barbara did the same.

"Helplessly drunk, and *abusive,*" Barbara said.

"Not fit to be around decent people," Jerry said.

"Bobby! *Bobby!* Get down from there!" Richard yelled, and left them alone. Jerry took her hand and squeezed it, and she squeezed back. Impulsively, he leaned forward and kissed her lightly on the lips. It made him dizzy, the way she smelled and felt, and the way her eyes half-closed for the kiss and then opened warm and lazy like the eyes of a female cat, even through her glasses. goddamn, Jerry thought. It had been a while.

"Do you want another beer?" he said shakily.

"We should have something to eat," she said in her low but quite beautiful voice.

"Yes, we should eat," he said distantly. "Or we really will get abusively drunk."

"And we don't want that. Not at the company picnic."

"The good old company picnic. Do you come here often?"

"Only to meet men," she said.

"Really? Why should a beautiful girl like you have to come to our little company picnic to meet men?"

"The ones I come into contact with at the office are, how shall I put it, not only married but deep in debt. Not attractive to me. Not at all attractive."

"I could eat about a dozen of them hot dogs," he said.

"May I fix yours for you? Don't get up, let me do it. A dozen? How do you want them? Gooey and dripping with mustard, pickles, tomato, onion and glop?"

"Make it two, and yes, dripping with glop."

He watched her walking down toward the food, her lovely fine square ass swinging to and fro. Pretty soon he was going to have his hands on that ass. He was entertaining fantasies about this when Harris came over and sat gingerly down.

"Having a good time?" he asked Jerry.

It took a minute to come back to reality. "Well, sure," he said. "Who wouldn't? It's a perfect day, we're all here, everybody's having a good time, the food smells great . . . Jesus, I'm having a ball!"

Harris's face changed, and Jerry remembered that he did not like the word *Jesus* to be used as a swear word. But Jerry felt too good to apologize. He drained his beer. To Harris he said, "What are you drinking?" and got to his feet.

"Oh, I'm still on the wagon," Harris said shyly.

"On the wagon?"

"Yes, I'm afraid I'm just a reformed drunk. But you go ahead."

For the first time, Harris seemed interesting. Jerry went down and stood beside Barbara while she prepared their hot dogs. He put his arm around her waist, and she moved closer to him, continuing her work.

Jerry looked around happily. These were swell people. They all knew that something had happened between himself and Barbara. Buzz buzz buzz and secret glances.

That was *all right!*

AND THEY did get royally drunk, and Jerry made a patriotic speech standing on the picnic table and almost put his foot into a big Tupperware bowl of cucumber salad, but Barbara, her eyes twinkling, steadied him, and he continued his speech until some boys came running through their area trailing strings of lit firecrackers, and Jerry climbed down to scattered applause and a fusillade of explosions. He kissed Barbara affectionately in full view of anybody who cared to watch and she wrapped her arms around him and hung on. Over they both went, in the dirt, and more applause.

"Did you bring a car?" he asked her.

"I came with Richard," she said.

"How about letting me drive you home?" He would have to be careful not to say anything stupid, just because he was full of beer. "Drive you home" was plenty.

"Of course," she said. "Is it time to go? Is the picnic over with?"

"Let's see," he said. "We ate, we drank, I made my speech about America, God bless 'er, yes, it's over. As far as I am personally concerned."

Without saying goodbye to anybody (why give Richard a chance to say something stupid?) they walked up the path under the trees toward the parking lot. It was too uphill to hold hands or touch comfortably, so they just trudged along. At one place they broke out into the open to see below them on an open meadow a boisterous game of touch football, which they stopped to watch while Jerry caught his breath. It was the usual Americana football game, except that it seemed to be played between a gang of motorcyclists and a band of homosexuals, and what had probably begun in a challenge of humor and mischief was now being played grimly, and for blood. Everyone was dirty and tight-lipped, and the couple of plays that Jerry and Barbara watched, between kisses, ended in sharp grunts of pain and pileups that had nothing to do with sex or fun. It was no longer motorcyclists and homo-sexuals, it was football.

Barbara's eyes glittered as she watched. Jerry wanted to suggest they leave, and was about to tug on her hand, when there was a long pass and then a heavy three-man tackle, and a loud snapping sound, really loud, as the three motorcyclists slowly got up from the ground and the homosexual didn't, but lay there broken and still. Others began running over toward the accident, and still others began drifting away.

"Let's get the hell out of here," Jerry said, and pulled her away. It took some pulling. *What was this?*

She admired his old black Porsche and loved the red leather interior and the comfort of the bucket seats, as they rode slowly in the dusty caravan of cars leaving the park. It was terribly hot in the car. Jerry had parked in the shade of a tree, but the shade had moved long ago and left it locked up tight in the burning sun for hours. Jerry was immediately sweat soaked and dizzy, and for a few minutes as they crawled along and Barbara talked about how nice his car was, he thought he was going to throw up. It became unbear-able, and he knew he must pull the car over to one side and *get out,* under the shade of a tree, into a pond, anything to get out of this oven. But there was no place to pull out of the string of equally baking automobiles. Jerry was stuck.

Then there came a wide spot on the road, but in it was a car, pulled over, with the driver hanging red-faced out the open door.

"Oh, the poor man," Barbara said.

"Couldn't take the heat," Jerry said grimly. Now he was goddamned if he was going to stop or pull over and collapse; it was not the manly thing to do.

Barbara was sweating, but she did not have the red face Jerry knew he had; she was not as affected by the heat. That was good. Horns started blaring up in front of them, and Jerry forced a grin. "That's a big help," he said.

"We should have brought along a couple of cold cans of beer," Barbara said, as the caravan stopped again. Kids raced by on bicycles, throwing fire-crackers into cars. Desperate redfaced men chased them. Jerry and Barbara were lucky: no firecrackers fell into the Porsche. While they waited, Jerry explained to an uninterested Barbara why he had not had air conditioning installed in his car, pointing out that the strain placed on the engine by adding the unit could make an already oversensitive machine even more cranky, and that Porsches did not come with factory air, as they called it.

"Factory air," he said. "Sounds a lot like L.A., huh?"

At last (at last!) they were out of Griffith Park, and moving fast enough to buffet a little cooling air into the car.

"Where do you live?" Jerry asked. "Or do you feel like going home yet? We could stop for a tall cold one somewhere . ."

"On the Fourth? Let's go to my place. I've got a fridge full of beer and wine, and I want to take a shower."

"Okay, where is this garden of paradise?"

She gave him instructions. She lived in a large apartment house in Studio City, a block off Ventura Boulevard. When Jerry pulled up in front, he managed to find a parking place in the shade of a big tree, just in case.

Her apartment was large and cool, Spanish-looking and a bit formal for Jerry's tastes, but he was grateful to be out of his car. Barbara breezed through to the kitchen and he could hear the percussive snap of a couple of cans of beer. She came out with his tall cold glass of beer on a little tray, with a folded napkin.

"If you'll excuse me," she said, "I'm going to plunge into the shower."

"I'll just take off my shoes, if you don't mind," Jerry said.

"If you'd like to shower off," she said, "I'll be out in just a minute."

"Sounds good to me," he said, and drained off half his beer. It was awfully good. He burped, tapped his chest, made a face, and drank some more. He could hear the shower going faintly from the direction of the bedroom. Her bedroom. He got up and went over and peeked in the door. Dark, cool, neat as a pin. The bathroom door was shut. Jerry decided not to undress and try to join her in the shower. Too pushy. And he did not feel the need to push.

When she came out she was in shorts and a tee shirt, her hair pulled back. She had very good legs, legs like a ballet dancer, long and muscled with full calves and unrippled thighs. Jerry had been afraid her thighs would be heavy, but no. He rose. "My turn," he said.

"There's fresh towels for you on the toilet," she called after him. The bathroom was damp and cozy, and the shower most refreshing, almost sobering Jerry up. He was really beginning to be interested in sex now, and she must be feeling the same way. This was wonderful, no fuss, no strain, two adults who desired each other and were civilized enough to be able to handle it without a lot of bullshit and social nonsense. He was amazed that Richard's sister should be so much more sophisticated than he was. The apartment alone showed that much. And her attitude. And the kissing and the intimacy.

Jerry looked at himself critically as he toweled off. Too bad his own body was not at its best. He resolved to get himself into shape before it was too late. He would have to begin exercising again, and restrain himself with food and drink. Especially drink. But not today. His mouth was dry again, and he wanted another beer. They would sip their beers, listen to music (he could hear music coming from the living room, classical music) and let the night gently fall.

But when he went to kiss her, as they sat on the couch side by side, he felt a restraint that had not been there before, and he pulled back, looking at her. Her eyes were downcast.

"What's the matter?" he asked.

"Nothing," she said.

He kissed her again. More restraint. He kissed harder, and the restraint became refusal, as she pulled away.

"I think I should tell you," she said.

His heart sank.

"I don't think we should make love," she said.

His heart sank further.

"On this, you know, first time we've met . ."

"I understand," he heard himself saying.

"I'm glad you do," she said, brightening and looking at him again. "So many men don't."

"I'm not that kind of a guy," he said.

"It's not *you*," she said, and took his clammy hand. "It's just the situation, you know?"

He patted her hand and looked at her miserably. They always did it to you, didn't they? No matter how or why, they always did it to you, and you were left holding the sack.

"Oh, hell," he said. "It's not the most important thing in my life. You're a human being, you have rights, you should be able to kiss a guy without taking him to bed. I guess."

"Do you think we shouldn't have kissed at all?" she asked.

"Yes," he said miserably. "I mean, no. I mean, we *should* have kissed."

He turned to face her and took both her hands in his. "You don't know me well enough to know this, but if we had, I mean, if we *did* make love, it wouldn't be something that would upset our relationship . . ."

She smiled. "You mean, you'd still respect me?"

That puckish sense of humor. Jerry smiled, getting the joke. He was a pretty funny guy, too.

"Well, I wouldn't *respect* you," he said, "But I wouldn't hate you, either . . ."

"Are you hungry? Can I fix us a snack?"

"That sounds swell," Jerry said, and she leaned toward him and kissed him inquisitively on the lips. Jerry didn't push it, he kissed her back but did not try for a big clinch. She got comfortable and kept on with the kiss, and Jerry touched her shoulder and then let his fingertips brush her breast under the tee shirt. With a thrill he felt her nipple rise immediately under his touch. He cupped her breast and felt her tongue slip inquisitively into his mouth.

CHAPTER NINE

NONE OF the doctors and dentists who formed the syndicate that paid for the making of *The Endless Unicorn* wanted to take their profits out, and so Richard Heidelberg was left in control of not only their original investments plus profits, but also the money being waved under his nose by the investors' friends. This gave Rick an immense pool of capital. He did not know how much. Most of the money had been filtered through a Dutch Antilles bank, and indeed, The Endless Unicorn Company was a Dutch Antilles corporation. The lawyers had their way of explaining what was going on, but to Rick it was just a case of pouring the money here and there to keep the IRS and everybody else from knowing just how much there was.

Plenty to make movies with, but Rick didn't want to just make movies. He had done that. He laughed with embarrassment (to himself) when he thought about his cocaine fantasy of toppling Alexander Hellstrom, but really, what was left to him? The idea of waking up in the morning with nothing to do genuinely frightened him. He was not a simple soul, he could not engage himself deeply in making breakfast eggs, like Elektra, or even in debauchery, like many of his friends. He had to be climbing.

So it was with high energy and a deeply concealed anxiety that he mounted his offensive against Hellstrom, hardly admitting to himself what he was doing.

Naturally every studio in town wanted Rick and the capital he controlled. They needed product, and Rick could provide it. The arrangement, after lunches and lawyers, was to be a negative pickup deal, with back-and-forth approvals. Rick would borrow money from banks, based on his company's assets, and produce his motion pictures, falling within a budget approved by the studio. The studio would provide facilities at a cost overhead of thirteen percent, make available to Rick their options and availabilities of properties, stars and directors and, when the negative was finished, pay Rick's costs to date plus a healthy fee. The studio would then distribute the film, adding to its share of the expense the cost of prints and advertising campaigns. The studio, through its overseas distributing company, also had the option of distributing the picture overseas itself or licensing another distributor, with a share of the profits to Rick's company.

It was a sweet deal, if everything worked. And if everything didn't work, Uncle Sam would take a screwing from all concerned. Rick's lawyers told him that by using money that would otherwise go into the government's purse they could make pictures for something like fifty cents on the dollar.

"So a ten-million-dollar picture, which used to cost about three million, would now only cost us five million," Rick said.

"Now you're catching on," said Lewis Corning, his main attorney. "But that's if the picture is a disaster. If it's a hit, everything is twice as expensive, strictly for the purposes of tax avoidance."

The property Rick had chosen, almost casually, was not particularly geared to these immense sums of money. In fact, when first submitted it had been an obvious candidate for a "little" picture, a personal effort by some director to show his stuff, a European picture. Daffy young man tries to attract sophisticated woman by daffy means. Ha ha, cute, but where are the mobs three thick around the block? Where were the repeat business and the newspapers full of free columns of chatter?

Rick intended to supply those himself. The world market for films, in his analysis, was most interested in two things: American Movie Stars and American Popular Culture. Rick would jam his project with plenty of both.

As he explained it to Alexander Hellstrom, "It's John Travolta, falling in love with the fifteen-year-old mistress of Paul Newman, with songs. It's the tortoise and the hare."

"What's the gimmick?" asked Hellstrom. They sat in his executive dining room at the studio; white tablecloths, white napkins, dull food from the commissary.

"The gimmick is," Rick said with a smile, "the tortoise wins."

"Newman gets the girl?"

"Maybe getting the girl isn't winning," Rick said. "Look at *Roman Holiday.*"

"Who's directing this picture?" Hellstrom wanted to know. "Haven't thought that much about it. There are half a dozen guys who could do it. I'm sure they're all on the list."

"What kind of budget do you see, above the line?"

Rick grinned shyly. "Well, this is one of the reasons we'd like to come to you. You're the best maker of budgets in the business. I don't see us flinging money around, but on the other hand, this has to be the kind of picture that goes full-race. Top stars, constant promotion, worldwide interest. It's going to cost some bucks."

At the end of the meal Rick had severe heartburn and a deal, although it would take the lawyers and agents several months to iron out the procedural matters. The two men who counted had shaken hands.

And the funny part was, Rick liked Alexander Hellstrom and felt relaxed around him. He felt almost as if Hellstrom would protect him, if things got rough. And at these prices, things could get very very rough. This deal would be scrutinized by large numbers of coldblooded men who knew nothing about movies, only about money, and these men would have to be convinced, layer after layer, all the way to answer print, that Rick Heidelberg could pull it off. Even though Rick and his company stood to lose the most, the studio's owners would look amiss at pouring several million dollars into a losing venture.

Rick drove the long winding drive back to the beach in his 1968 Mustang, listening to a cassette of Miles Davis. He could have a hit picture on his hands, another *Unicorn,* if everything went well. Yet many tried what he was trying, and most of them failed. The first picture makes it big because it somehow hits a public chord, people go because the picture is friendly and invites them in. Then, the guy who forced the picture through against all odds changes. No longer does he meet resistance everywhere—now it is obsequiousness, agreement, open doors. It becomes nearly impossible for him to get an honest opinion.

"Gosh, that's a *great* idea, Rick!" would be mild praise.

So the second picture is covered with insurance. The biggest stars, never mind, pay what it costs; a director who can work with stars, come in near budget and still grease his own ego. A script that works. The best songs, written by the hottest songwriters. A topflight advertising agency to carry the promotion. The works. Can't lose. The number is covered six ways from the middle.

The wheel rolls, and it turns out there are thirty-five more numbers out there waiting to catch the little ball.

But Rick trusted his instincts. He was not a middle-aged banker trying to psyche out the young, he was a young man who was setting out to make a movie he would want to see himself, would go see again and take his friends. That was the only kind of picture to make.

"*And then what?*" said a little voice.

He thought about Hellstrom, that calm likable man. If Rick was a general, leading his troops into battle, then Hellstrom was a general of generals, overseeing not the battle but the war itself, a man who must be able to commit to disaster *here* in order to reach victory *there,* a man to whom the death of a single picture is not the crucial matter, a man who knows that he can win a few and lose a few, just as long as profits continue to go up.

So in spite of all the cooperation, and the niceness of the man, Rick knew he could not count on Alexander Hellstrom in a last-ditch battle. He could only count on himself.

Getting home after the long drive, without even the rush-hour traffic to deal with, Rick once again asked himself why he lived at the beach. The answer was simple, of course. This had always been his vision of himself as a Hollywood big shot. The house at Malibu.

So he was living in a worn-out dream.

"Honey," he said to Elektra. "We have to move into town. This thing's going into high gear."

"Do I get a part?" she asked.

"No-you-don't-get-a-part," he said. "What's for snacks?"

"Eat this," she said, giving him the finger.

"No, thanks. Where's the coke?"

"All gone. I wouldn't tell you, anyway."

"You know anybody who's got any?"

"Nope."

Rick got out his address book, and felt a twinge of fear. To get busted in a dope deal now would be fatal. They would jail him. There was only one kind of millionaire they jailed, and Rick was it. But he wanted some coke.

After he had found somebody who would deal to him, he said to Elektra, "You better be nice to me when I get back, or I won't cut you in."

"I'll be nice," she said, and gave him a kiss to prove it.

RICK DROVE up the winding empty road through the Malibu hills, past the heavily gated entrance to the Enrique estate—now, in the post-Manson era, always double padlocked and chained—winding up and around a couple more of the brush-covered hillocks until he came to a cattle gate, held in place by a loop of plastic line. He got out of the car, opened the long gate, drove through, got out again and closed it, and then drove down the rutty dirt road until he could see the yellow lights coming from Tommy Cone's shack. He parked next to Tommy's beatup pickup truck and was about to get out of his car again when he heard a low warning growl. Rick could just see the dog's eyes in the light from the building.

"Nice boy," Rick said. He did not move. He felt a shiver, not at the dog, who was only doing his job, but at the remoteness of this place, this empty lonely spot, where anything could happen. Tommy Cone was the live-in care-taker and guardian of the Enrique estate. His cottage stood higher on the hill and looked down from its copse of trees over the garden and swimming pool area. Tommy had a dozen guns in his place, from .22 target pistols to a big ten-gauge double-barreled shotgun, and he had Enrique's permission to use them. Enrique himself owned a chain of small department stores throughout the West, lived with his family in their low rambling Spanish-style mansion, and was in deathly fear of being attacked and murdered in the night.

The dog was a Belgian shepherd, nine feet long and black as death, "The Hound of the Malibu Hills" Tommy cheerfully called him. No, he wasn't nine feet long, he could clear a nine-foot wall, or was it twelve feet? It didn't matter. Rick was glad enough when Tommy's door opened, spilling light onto the gravel. "It's okay, Tor," he said.

"Is it okay?" Rick asked.

"Sure, come on in."

Tor was seated beside Tommy in the doorway, getting his ears scratched by the time Rick got over to them.

"Nice warm night, huh?" Tommy said. Tommy Cone was a thin man who stooped his shoulders and had a pot belly, now much larger than the last time Rick had seen him. They moved into the house, leaving Tor to his duties, and Rick crossed to the big window overlooking the Enriques' back garden. The pool was lit and glowed like a gigantic aquamarine gem. The cottage was dark inside, except for the amber bulbs in the entryway and one red light over in a corner. Rock 'n' roll played softly in the background.

Tommy sat in his favorite chair, beside the big window. There were newspapers on the rug, stacks of magazines, candybar wrappers and a general sense of sloppy but hip bachelor living. Rick continued to look out over the lit pool. There were no lights in the house. Beyond, over a couple of hills, was the Pacific Ocean. Not for the first time, Rick wondered about the kind of man who would live up here and not build his house where it could look out over the ocean. Where there was all that fire danger. Where there were all those rattlers out in the brush. Where fear could come for him every night, even if nobody else did.

"They're all out of town some goddamn place," Tommy said. "We got the estate to ourselves. Want to go for a swim?"

"No, thanks," Rick said.

Tommy was slowly rolling a joint, and on the table beside his chair Rick could see a mirror and a little bottle of cocaine. He watched Tommy roll and twist the joint, hold it up to scrutiny and then stick it in his mouth.

"You want a hit?"

"I wouldn't mind trying the coke," Rick said. Tommy gave him a look. Coke dealers had such strange manners. Maybe you weren't supposed to bring it up right away, like that. Maybe you had to pretend to like the bastard before he'd get off the coke, as if you had driven up here just to see old Tommy, and not to make a deal.

"What's been happening, man?" Tommy wanted to know. "I ain't been down off this mountain except to get groceries in a week. How's Hollywood?"

"Hollywood is terrific," Rick said dryly. He could feel the cocaine urgency in his belly, now that it was lying there right in front of him.

"I gotta get back into show business," Tommy said. "This life's killing me." He lit up, puffed on the joint, and then handed it up to Rick, who took a polite puff and let it come out his nose immediately. Now Tommy was bending over the mirror, in the semidarkness, getting ready to cut some lines. He was incredibly slow about it. Tommy had been a lot of things in his young life, but he had always been a dealer and only a dealer as far as Rick was concerned. He had been a barber, with his own shop in Tallahassee, Florida, but his partner had run off with the money, or so he said. He had had a scuba rental business in Tarpon Springs, and he had been a "hick wrangler" for movie companies on location, rounding up and taking care of the extras, and then had come to Hollywood to get work as an assistant director. He worked on a couple of porn films, made a couple of trips to Colombia, owned part interest in a cabin cruiser, had tried to organize a rock 'n' roll band, and half a dozen other schemes, but always at bottom he dealt. That was where the eating money came from.

"Dealer to the stars," he called himself, with a little ironic Southern grin to take the edge off it. "Always the best stuff and always the best prices, and if you don't think so, try the competition."

Now he slowly and carefully chopped out six lines of rather chalky-looking stuff, and finally offered the mirror up to Rick.

"One and one?" Rick asked. Maybe there was a girl in the bathroom.

"Naw, that's all for you," Tommy said with a grin. "I just took a toot the moment you arrived. I'm high as a fuckin' lizard."

The stuff seared his nostrils and he felt that wonderful first medicinal rush that comes just from knowing the cocaine is on the way. Instant elation. Rick coughed and gasped, almost spilling the last two lines. But he got control of himself, and with more coughing and gagging, he did the last pair.

"Great stuff!" he wheezed. "Smooooth!"

Tommy laughed. It was an old coker's joke.

"It's the wash," he said. "The stuff s coming in like that, but it's good country dope."

Rick sat on the couch opposite Tommy and let the drug run through his system. Tommy sat quietly puffing on his joint (which Rick refused with a wave of his hand) and looked out the window, blackness everywhere except the glowing pool.

"I'd like a quarter of this stuff," Rick said, changing his mind. He had been thinking about only getting a gram. But here he was, and it *was* good stuff. He took out his wallet, shielding the contents from Tommy casually, and took out five one-hundred-dollar bills. Tommy got to his feet with a grunt and went into the back of the house. After a few minutes he came out and with a strange smile said, "Hey, you wanna see something?"

Rick followed him into the back of the house, expecting to be shown a large quantity of cocaine. But instead he found himself in a denlike room with glass terrariums racked up against the walls and on tables. There seemed to be twenty or thirty of them. On a cleared space on one of the tables Rick saw the open plastic ounce bag of cocaine, the scales and other paraphernalia of the coke dealer, lit by a powerful gooseneck lamp. Some of the terrariums were lit also.

"Not the coke," Tommy said. "Over here." He stood by one of the glass cages. "Look at that bastard, he's doin' a perfect coil."

Inside the cage a large rattlesnake sat bathed in its light, coiled. Its ugly broad flat head was erect, and the snake's tongue darted in and out.

"*Crotalus atrox,*" Tommy said proudly, "small for his kind, but who'd complain?"

"Where'd you get him?" Rick asked. The coke was just hitting, the real hit, and the snake frightened Rick very much.

"In the hills. That's where I got all of them. All these cages have rattlers in 'em, mostly the little Coast guys, but a couple of these big timber rattlers."

"You're collecting them?"

"It's muh new business, old boy. Rattlers for pets. Hell, people have tarantulas, pit bulls, fighting fish, why not make a fad of rattlesnakes? Shit, they're nature's lovely killers, wouldn't you like to have one of your own?"

It was Tommy's idea that if a few celebrities would buy snakes from him ("hell, I might even give a few away, to the right people") the resultant publicity could make Tommy's business a going concern.

"I could move out of this goddamn crypt and back to Beverly Hills," he said enthusiastically.

"How do you catch them?" Rick asked.

"Oh, they're easy to catch if you know what you're doing, but don't spread that around. Part of the price is the mystery, you know?"

Tommy went on about his proposed snake store in Beverly Hills, with flocks of movie stars and society types rolling up in their limos to buy snakes, as he weighed out Rick's quarter-ounce of cocaine.

"I figure all I need is twenty-five thousand, to start," he said.

"Twenty-five thousand snakes?" Rick asked, but he knew better. The big diamondback in the terrarium slowly began to uncoil as Rick watched with fascination. Eventually, the snake went under a pile of leaves in the corner of his cage. Rick counted the rattles as they slowly disappeared. Ten. That was some fucking snake. He wondered what Elektra would do if he came home with a ten-rattler.

Probably cook it for supper.

"Well?" Tommy said, after the deal was done and they were back in the living room.

"Well, what?" said Rick, but he knew what.

"Can you front me the twenty-five thousand?"

Rick laughed. "I can wish you luck," he said. He edged toward the door. "Listen, I got to go, Elektra's got dinner on."

Tommy said meanly, "You won't eat for days." He made no move toward the door, so, with some hesitation, Rick opened it himself.

"You going to take care of the dog?" Rick said after a while.

"Tor's all right," Tommy said. He was in his favorite chair again, staring out the window.

Well, shit. It was about twenty feet to the car. Rick said goodbye and left the front door open, crunching over the gravel, alert for the dog to rush him, fear high in his chest. *Here it came!* Rushing and growling low, across the patch of light toward Rick, who froze.

"Tor!" came Tommy's command from the darkness, and the dog stopped, a few feet from Rick. Slowly Rick got into his car.

"Thanks a lot, motherfucker," he said to Tommy, but only after he had driven up to the gate, opened and shut it, and was on the road back down out of the hills.

CHAPTER TEN

ALEXANDER TRIED TO keep busy in spite of his longing for Teresa di Veccio. At the same time he had to guard against lassitude, something he had never been troubled with before, and which frightened him by its insidious ways. He would wake up late and skip his laps in the pool, instead sitting up in bed with the papers, reading bad news and drinking coffee. Usually he waited until he got to the office to have coffee, but now he needed it just to get out of bed. Breakfast became a distasteful chore and so he skipped it in favor of more coffee and more bad news.

Of course he telephoned her almost every day, and if he didn't reach her, she would reach him. The only time they missed was when she went to Katmandu to attend a party (or was it several parties?), all for charity, all in a good cause, but still, halfway around the world to talk to the same people. It did not make sense to Alexander, especially since the time confusion left him without his daily contact. When she called the next day, the connection hadn't been all that good, and Alexander had been grumpy and sarcastic. By the end of the call, kiss-me's and I-love-you's to the contrary notwithstanding, he honestly did not know where they stood.

But soon she would be back on the West Coast, staying at the Lake Tahoe cabin of a friend, and Alexander would take time off from his work to run up and visit her. It would be fun, the two of them in a cozy mountain cabin. And then he hoped (but only hoped) to get her to come south for a while.

By eleven in the morning he was hungry and tired, coffeed out, impatient with the constant stream of ideas flowing past his office, just putting in the time until he could make his lunch appointment, wherever it was and whomever it was with, order impatiently, swill his drink, gobble his food, nod and agree, laugh and smile, and get back to the office in time to cancel a couple of appointments and take a short snooze. From this he would awaken in a furious temper, and until he began to realize things weren't quite right, those post-nap appointments were pretty hair-raising for all hands. It turned out better for everyone when he started scheduling screening-room time for right after his nap. He could sit there in the darkness, sipping Coca-Colas, and watch dailies or competition-product without biting anybody's head off.

It was getting harder and harder to see Alexander Hellstrom, which was probably a relief to all but those pitching projects.

Fortunately, by this time of day, New York had closed up and gone home. Conversations with Marrow or any of his people usually took place between nine and ten in the morning, although Marrow was capable of calling any time.

But even so, work was the best part of his life. In work he was the aggressor, the predator, no matter how it looked from the outside. Ideas for movies floated all around him, launched by a variety of agencies, coming from all directions in every possible form, from carefully worked out and expensive story boards, developed at producer's expense, which showed every key scene in cartoon form, to one-page outlines submitted by the studio's story department and culled from the hundreds of newly published books, and from the galley proofs of books the publishers thought were going to be hot.

There were all these ideas in the stream, and Alexander's job was to find among them the successful pictures of tomorrow. He was not alone in this. Every studio in town was looking at the same projects with the same idea in mind. And so it became, on a few projects, a matter of bidding. Once an agent knew he had a property that two or more studios wanted, the agent would spring into life, doing everything possible to stir up the competitive juices. Sometimes this resulted in extraordinary prices being paid for properties that weren't worth a nickel. Every studio had a backlog of expensive items they were slowly and carefully throwing more money into, hiring writers and directors to salvage the cold porridge of what had once been a hotly promising breakfast.

Alexander's pride was that most of what he bought got made, and most of what he made made money, and some of it, one or two pictures a year, made *lots and lots* of money.

It was all very well to use the computers and test-market situations and polls, but finally, the man who made the deals had to have a nose for it, and that was that.

Alexander was such a man, and he took great pride in it. His judgment launched the projects, employed thousands and brought in the steadily mounting tide of money that seemed the only way for the corporation to stay even.

He was not solely responsible for everything. He could go to picture on low- and medium-budget projects, but for the blockbusters he had to have the approval of New York, the approval of Donald Marrow.

On the Rick Heidelberg project Marrow was casual. Alexander outlined the project as a musical love story, a starring vehicle for some young singing star and a mature star (he did not use Rick's shorthand, but later suggested that Paul Newman and John Travolta would "give you an idea" of what they had in mind).

"I like it," Marrow said.

So that was approval, and Alexander didn't even have to go into the overhead angle or the lucrative possibilities of having Heidelberg's company on the lot.

"Everybody thinks you're doing a swell job," Marrow said over the telephone. As well he might. They had a picture out flogging the markets called *Hamadryad!* about an eighteen-foot king cobra, that was scaring millions out of the public, with a negative cost of five million dollars. It had been on the top of *Variety's* list of top-grossing films for six weeks now, and would stay there all summer. New York hadn't anything to do with the launching of this epic, it was all Alexander's baby, and so could do no wrong for at least a few weeks more. Which was a relief, because Alexander did not want to have to deal with a lot of meaningless pressure from the East for a while.

His social life was as fully planned as his days, a round of dinners, parties, screenings, charity board meetings, public affairs and openings. It went with the job. Alexander himself did not give a damn about charities and allowed his tax lawyers and public relations firm to decide what he would join, attend, give money to or represent as a board member. They came up with what his main tax lawyer called "an acceptable social services package," and Alexander signed the checks or attended the functions as he was told by his secretary.

But lately it had galled him. Until Teresa he had been able to carry out all these functions with ease, slipping his lady friends either into or between functions, carrying on like a pirate captain and still jumping out of bed at dawn full of piss and vinegar. Pirate captain. He liked that image for what he did, implying as it did that he bore down on the treasure ships and carried off his prizes with a high hand. But lately he had been thinking the metaphor was wrong. It was more like going to the butcher shop, poking the meat, counting your pennies and distrusting the butcher.

But that was not what was on his mind as he sat in the dark screening room behind his office watching a picture another studio was going to release in a week. It was a story with a good deal of flash—brief nudity—and every time a cute rear end or a pair of tits went by, Alexander would feel a flush of desire followed by something almost like revulsion.

At first he had not wanted any other woman. This was a rare feeling for him, and for several weeks he cherished it, remaining silently celibate with something like pride, but then at a party in Pacific Palisades a very young girl, a model who hoped to become an actress and who was very fashionable, made a play for him that he could hardly turn down. And so they went to his place, leaving behind the press agent who had brought her to the party. She was hip and funny and full of promise, but she was fresh from the New York modeling scene, and chattered about what was going on in New York until Alexander could think only of Teresa, and when they started fooling around in his den, he could not get an erection. Or did not want to get an erection. They had been watching late-night television and drinking brandy, and all he wanted to do was brush his teeth and go to bed.

"I'm exhausted," he admitted to the girl, and she said in a low purring voice, "I can take care of that," and started to give him a blow job, but he had to say, finally, "No."

"I understand," she said, and she did, for she kissed him lightly goodnight and called a taxi for herself. They parted friends, and if ever her name came up on the list, Alexander would hire her in a minute. Except the trouble with those goddamn beautiful New York fashion models was that they could not act and did not know it, and would never know it. Who would tell them?

But for Alexander it was his first nonerection in years. Since he had been last married, in fact.

Food for thought, there. What had Teresa done to him? Or was it a coincidence? Was he going to have to endure one of those nonerectile phases? What would happen when Teresa came west, to Tahoe? With all those tall trees for inspiration? He laughed to himself. At least I still have a sense of humor about it. Pardon me, darling, but what we need here is a good stunt-fucker to stand in for me. *Stand in* is good. Plague of Drooping Peter Strikes Film Capital. Maybe it was happening to everybody at once, and everybody was keeping it as secret as Alexander himself. Good picture. Although you could hardly.

Well, there were dick doctors. "Sir, you need more Vitamin E."

"It's simple, just say the word *manumission* under your breath for fifteen minutes every morning."

"Well, old fellow, a tongue-depressor and a couple of Band-Aids should do the trick."

Gasoline flames leaped skyward on the screen in front of him. The picture was coming to its climax. There went the hero's car through the flames and into the waters of the dismal swamp. So what? Would this picture make any money? Would it inspire imitations? Hardly, he thought, it was an imitation of an imitation already. But there was certainly no accounting for public taste. And the star was popular.

Alexander pressed the button putting him in touch with the projectionist:

"What do you think of this, Harry?" he asked. Back came the tinny-sounding voice:

"Piece a shit, Boss."

But Harry always said that.

ALEXANDER LOOKED at himself with horror. He had just stepped out of the shower and was toweling off when he happened to catch sight of his buttocks. And couldn't believe what he saw. He finished drying himself numbly, avoiding the full-length mirror as long as possible. But then there was no avoiding it. His tanned and once muscular buttocks were turning into two drooping bulbs of fat!

Old age was attacking him from the rear.

But it couldn't be old age, he wasn't old yet. He was a man in his fifties. His middle fifties. And he was turning into a fatass. Alexander drew himself up, filled his chest and flexed into tightness every muscle he could control. He still looked good, his muscles rippling under his tanned skin, his chest wide, his stomach narrow . . . he turned slowly, his buttocks flexed as tight as he could get them. But there it was, the sagging fatty ass, looking even sillier with the rest of his body in flexion. He relaxed and his buttocks quivered. Good God! There were stretch marks on his ass!

Stretch marks. He reached back and ran his fingertips over the soft flesh. Rippled, scarry. Ugly ass.

He looked anxiously at his face, and saw his anxious face peering back at him. The face was heating up and getting red. He looked away, embarrassed. He had never thought of himself as abnormally vain, and he had not spent much of his life in front of mirrors. But, he thought, that was because he *knew* what a handsome roughneck he was. Well, it was all crumbling, now. First his ass, then his belly, then rolls of fat would appear under his jawline and he would have *jowls*. Or he could go on a crash diet regimen, jogging around the lot in a grey sweatsuit and a white towel around his neck, desperately trying to keep ahead of the fat globules, knowing that he was really racing against time, and nobody won that one.

Might as well heave a sigh and get fat. He probably already waddled, and nobody would say anything to him, but they were laughing behind his back.

Had all this happened since he had last seen Teresa? What would she think of the new Alexander? Women don't care much about how men look, do they? *Bullshit.* Alexander was disgusted at himself for trying to make excuses. There was just no question about it. He would have to go back to lapping the pool every morning, eating his breakfast, cut down on the drinking and do more afternoon exercise. Daily tennis again. Cut out the nap. Push away sugar foods. Take vitamins. That was all there was to it. His own father had remained vigorous and lean into his eighties, and then fell over dead without a moment's illness. If he could do it, so could Alexander.

He dressed quickly in a three-piece Italian suit, a suit that made him look particularly dashing, and surveyed himself in the mirror. He turned sideways. Didn't the back panel of his jacket stick out a bit? As if the suit were just a tiny bit small? And, now that he thought of it, didn't that collar feel kind of tight? He buttoned the jacket. It did not want to button. Alexander had worn the same size suit for years. Would he have to go to his tailor and have everything remeasured? What good would that do if he was going to lose the weight anyway?

Vanity. Vanity.

He left the house and drove to work. At the gate, he said to his old friend Charlie Devereaux, "I'm turning into a fatass, Charlie."

Charlie, as usual, offered his paper coffee cup, but Alexander waved it away.

"How do you stay so slim, Charlie?" he asked.

Devereaux snorted. "You must be kidding, Alexander. I'm on my goddamn dogs all day in this fucking booth, is how I keep slim."

"Ha ha," said Alexander and drove on into the lot.

The first thing waiting for him on his desk was a memo from his production assistant, Dick Katzman, that there were "obligations but no availability" between Paul Newman and John Travolta. In other words, the studio had calls on the services of both actors, but there was no time within the next year when both were simultaneously available. So there went *Untitled Love Musical,* the Richard Heidelberg project. He wondered how much Heidelberg had into it, how much farther he would press the issue. Of course they could try to find a match for whichever of the actors they couldn't get, or they could go for two entirely new performers. But bankable actors were rare, and availability was even rarer. He had liked the idea of Newman and

Travolta. In his mind he had already nicknamed the picture *The Battle of the Peepers*. And NEWMAN SINGS! would make good copy. Hell, shit.

"Let me talk to Dick Katzman," he said over the intercom.

"Yes, sir. Richard Heidelberg on two, do you want me to put him on hold?"

"No, tell him I'll call him back."

When Katzman came on the phone, Alexander said, "Dick, is there any way we can buy Newman and Travolta?"

"There's no time interface," Dick said. Neither man could be broken out of his present commitments this year. "Next year is another ball game," he said.

"See what you can come up with for alternate casting," Alexander said. At least somebody would be working on it. He would get lists for days now, as Dick tried to make magical combinations of names for their picture premise.

"Do both of them have to be bankable?" Dick asked.

"Within reason," said Alexander, and hung up.

"Get me Richard Heidelberg," he said into the intercom. "Good morning, my young friend."

"Hello, Boss. How're we doing?"

"You must have second sight. We just pulled the plug on Newman and Travolta. Not available. Aren't you glad you don't have to pungle up three million dollars?"

"I'd be willing. Look, that casting was just a way of clarifying the project, I never really expected . . .

"Well, I did, and I'm sorely pissed off. And to quote my assistant, the viability parameter of this project is rapidly shrinking."

"The old shrinking parametric," came Heidelberg's amused voice. He did not seem bothered by this setback.

"Well," said Alexander, "let's have a meeting and see what we can come up with. Can you be at my office at about five-thirty? We'll drink company liquor and cast our crumbling project."

The next problem he had to face was also negative. Travis Morgan was balking on the set, to the tune of sixty thousand dollars a day. They were on location in Utah, making a Western that was already six million dollars over budget because the director, Sandor Kielmann, had been sitting up nights with a whiskey bottle, rewriting the script, and his buddy the cameraman was taking hours for every setup. It would be a disastrous situation except that Kielmann usually ended up with what the public wanted.

But this was different. Somebody on the location had gotten to Travis Morgan about the plight of the Indians, the threat to the ecology and assorted matters, and Morgan was making a lot of demands for script changes and attitude changes that were, to put it mildly, uninformed. Now, Morgan had flown home to Brentwood, the director had followed, and the first assistant director was shooting a lot of second unit stuff under the scornful eye of the cameraman. At least they hadn't had to shut down production. Yet.

Kielmann arrived first for their three-way meeting. He was a plump, sour-looking man with great rings under his eyes. He was dressed in dirty cords and a tee shirt advertising THE LIQUOR LOCKER. He had not shaved that morning. Alexander liked him.

"Well, my dear," he said to the director, who was slumped on the couch opposite Alexander's desk. "How are we going to trim this cowboy's sails?"

"He's probably at home, waiting for Brando to call," Kielmann said in a gravelly voice. He brightened. "Maybe I could pull it off. I do a pretty good Brando."

He did his Brando impression, and Alexander laughed. "We could try it."

"How's this: I pick up the phone and tell him, 'Hey, lissen, you punk, yer crabbin' my act . . .'"

The intercom buzzed. "Travis Morgan and David Novotny," she said.

Alexander got up and went to the door. Novotny, slender and handsome as ever, perhaps the best-articulated human body Alexander had ever seen, a tennis machine, a swimming champion, a delightful but always victorious poker and chess player and perhaps the best agent in Hollywood. The hilarious part was that David Novotny didn't have to work, his San Francisco-based family had been multimillionaires for generations, the family fortune coming from the mining camps of '49 and swollen by real estate dealings, oil property and Heaven knew what else. David worked because he loved the challenge of deal-making, he loved show people and he loved coming out on top.

Travis Morgan, Novotny's client, stood a bit behind his agent and grinned shyly, the same grin that had landed him in the top ten for six years running. He was dressed like a cowboy, boots, jeans and flannel shirt, while his agent looked as dapper as Alexander.

Novotny grinned and grasped Alexander's hand. "I thought I'd join you if you don't mind," he said smoothly. Alexander was delighted, but tried to keep it off his face. Novotny was at least a realist, and Alexander would not have to make his argument with this hambone's new conscience.

"Come into my office, gentlemen," Alexander said graciously. After they were all seated, orders for coffee delivered and morning pleasantries made, Alexander said, "Okay, now, why are you guys in Hollywood instead of freezing your asses off in the mountains?"

Novotny smiled politely and said, "I think this thing can be cleared up pretty fast. I advised my client to come home for a while."

"He's in breach," Alexander said politely.

"Come on, we're making a picture, not a deal." Novotny continued to control the meeting, and Alexander let him, knowing their interests were similar, if not identical. As he spoke, a picture emerged of what had been going on in the Utah mountains. Everybody was under terrific strain because of the cameraman's insistence on perfect light. Alexander had seen most of the dailies, and the stuff was utterly beautiful, but at enormous cost. There were Indians around, several of them had parts in the picture, and many of the cast and crew were bending over backward to let the Indians know they were appreciated, and that they had gotten a bad deal from the U.S. government. But this was normal and happened on nearly every set over something or other. What came out from under David Novotny's careful circumlocutions was that the cameraman, an old-line Commie, had openly ridiculed Travis Morgan, and had even called him "a dumb asshole" in front of half the crew.

Travis Morgan, then, overreacted by showing off his power, his power to alter the script, delay things and generally bully people around. Of course David didn't put it that way. He said, "They've all been working their asses off, they're all tired and on edge, and I thought Travis might feel better after a couple of days' rest. That's all. Blame me for the delay, although I hear you're getting some nice second unit stuff meanwhile, so no one's really hurt."

"Except your client's salary continues to run, and days are being put on the production board," Alexander said.

"I don't like being made a fool of," Travis said with great sincerity. He almost dug the toe of his boot into the rug.

"I don't see you as the villain of the piece," Alexander said. "I think that fucking Communist ought to go back to shooting commercials. Fire him."

"You can't fire him," Kielmann said stubbornly.

"We can buy out his contract. He'd love that. He loves money almost as much as he loves himself." That's it, Alexander said to himself, jump on the guy who isn't here.

"But it's personal," said Kielmann stubbornly.

"Then you should be the one to tell him," Alexander said gently, and the substantive part of the meeting was over. The dailies wouldn't be as good, but the picture would get done. That was what mattered.

Although Alexander strangely enough did not think any of it *really* mattered.

But you shouldn't call the star a dumb asshole.

LUNCH WAS in his private dining room, all business, putting together the final elements in a project that had stars, script, a start date, budget, location and crew, and needed only the final mesh of details to get rolling. There were ten men in the room, and they ate and worked in their shirtsleeves. This was the last chance for anybody to say his department wasn't ready, but nobody said it, and at the end of the two-hour meal, the producer of the picture gravely shook hands with Alexander.

"Looks like we have a picture." he said.

Alexander replied with equal gravity, slipped on his jacket and left the room first. I wonder if anybody noticed my ass, he found himself thinking.

"The Boss is packing quite a rumbleseat," nobody at all said behind his back.

Time for a wee snooze. If he did not shut the blinds and stretch out on the couch for an hour, he might fall asleep during dailies, and that would be bad. Alexander liked to keep track of not just everything on the lot, but location dailies and anything that could be stolen or borrowed from other film production units. It would have taken a fifty-hour day just in the screening room to accomplish this, so much of what went on had to be scrutinized in summary. Only the most important things passed through his screening room, and it would be bad news to fall asleep.

On this particular day there was nothing of any real interest to watch, just snips of film. He was slightly surprised to find at the end of the afternoon that he had drunk five Coca-Colas. He felt pretty good, though.

"Thank you," he said to Harry, and went back to his office. Rick Heidelberg was in the secretaries' office talking to Willi Gottlieb, his executive secretary, an attractive levelheaded woman whose father had been a driver captain over at Universal for years.

"Please don't bother the help," he said to Rick. He held his door open for Rick to enter. After Rick said hello and went past him, he said to Willi, "We'll be casting," which meant, don't interrupt us for anything, unless, of course . . .

Willi silently handed him his call log, and he glanced over his unanswered calls. There were three or four he knew he should really answer, and it would put Rick in his place if he had to sit there and listen, but no. Alexander did not feel like it. He wanted to relax and have a drink, right now. He handed the call log back to Willi and went into his office, closing the door.

"Let's open the blinds," he said. While he was doing this the intercom buzzed. Instead of answering it, he walked to the door and pulled it open. Willi was standing there next to David Novotny, who looked exhausted, but managed a smile.

"I talked her into it," he said. "I knew Rick was here, and I hoped I could get a free drink out of you."

"Of course," he said. "Come in and get off your feet."

Rick did not look surprised to see his agent, but got up from the couch and shook hands. Alexander went to the small bar and opened it. "Gentlemen?" he asked.

They sat quietly around the coffee table, Alexander on the couch next to Rick and David in a low armchair, listening to the ice crack in their drinks. The afternoon light made the battlements outside the window look romantic and remote. Alexander lifted his glass, and the others followed suit.

"Here's to the picture," he said. He took a healthy swig and so did Rick. But David merely sipped his.

David smiled tiredly. "I have to go out tonight," he said.

They talked business for a while. Naturally, since David was Rick's agent, he knew everything about the project and was not above putting in the names of other clients as director or stars. Some of his ideas were good, and some of the people he named were on Alexander's mental list, but Rick seemed restive and instead of just absorbing Novotny's ideas as Alexander did, he argued or looked negative.

"What's troubling you?" Alexander finally asked him.

"I want this picture to go," Rick said.

"We all do," David said dryly.

"But this isn't the way to cast it. Casting's the most important part of a movie like this. People will only want to go see it if they are promised a good time . . ."

"You're right," Alexander agreed, "it isn't exactly Hamlet we're doing here . . ."

"Thank God for small favors," David said.

"Okay," Rick said, with more animation. "A young guy falls in love with the young mistress of a rich and powerful middle-aged charmer, a guy who's got it made, had it made for years, and knows how to keep what he's got. The kid is funny, goofy and irresistible. The girl is attracted to him, the old guy stands to lose her. This is when we find out he really loves her. But he does nothing, and the girl falls deeper and deeper for the kid. They do crazy wonderful things together . . ."

"Yeah," said Alexander.

"There has to be magic in the casting," Rick said stubbornly.

Novotny winked at Alexander. "Terrance Segebarth opposite Richard Thomas," he said, naming a notoriously filthy old man and a notoriously clean young man.

Alexander laughed. "All right, we're getting too serious."

They all had another drink, although David only added fresh ice to his.

"Who's going to write this, anyway?" Novotny said.

"I think maybe I will," Rick said.

"There you are," said David. "An Academy Award screenwriter."

Rick shook his head. "That's not the point. The original story's set on a college campus, old prof, young students, and the old guy's played as a fool. I want to reverse that, make the young guy a fool, and I just think it would save time for me to write the script rather than to try to get my ideas across to some other writer. But before I proceed, I want some assurance that I'll have the casting I want. That's why Newman and Travolta were so appealing to me; I could *write* for them . . ."

"This won't be our last meeting on the subject," Alexander said, to take a little of the pressure off Rick. But Rick didn't want the pressure off.

"I want *that* casting, and I'm willing to pay for it."

"Learn the facts of life, sonny," Alexander said sharply. "Even you with all your doctors and dentists couldn't pay for *that* casting."

"Can't I just buy up the availabilities?"

"You would have to, in effect, *buy out* the pictures they're working on, and even then I'm not sure Fox and Columbia are all that willing to sell. They think they're making blockbusters, too, why the hell do you think they're casting those guys? It would cost you a hundred million dollars to just go in there and buy everybody out. *Forget it.*"

Rick looked as if somebody had let about half the air out of him, Alexander decided. He was feeling much better himself.

"Don't be dejected, kiddo," he said.

"I still think Raymond Carr and Dael Tennyson would make a nice combination," said David. "Ray's top ten, he's been top ten for a dozen years, and Dael is a very well-liked young man."

"But not a star," Alexander said.

"Yet," David said. "I'm going to send you some film tomorrow. You'll see a young man who can not only sing and dance, but charm the girls right out of their pants."

"You've had too much to drink," Alexander said, and laughed. David got up, leaving his glass half full. "Well, boys, my wife is waiting for me to come home and take a shower and dress up in my tuxedo."

"You'll be beautiful," Alexander said.

"Of course," David said modestly, and left.

"Let's have another drink, Richard, and stop being so serious."

Rick grinned. "I'm sorry. It all seems so trivial, you know?"

"And yet it must happen," Alexander said solemnly. "How do you like Carr and Tennyson? With maybe Brooke Shields?"

The casting talk went on, Rick finally loosening up under the impact of four drinks of bourbon. Both of us are kind of drunk, Alexander thought. "How about dinner?" he asked Rick.

Rick smiled. "My lady's going to meet me at the Roxy at ten, otherwise I don't have a thing to do."

"Swell. We'll go to Matteo's and fill up on fine Italian dishes. How is that lovely lady of yours?" he asked with a pang, thinking of his own fine lady.

"Oh, she's swell, only . . . well, shit, I have this slight problem with her. I want to move to town and she's supposed to be looking for a place for us, but she really likes it at the beach, you know?"

"Why not get some realtor to look for the house? Larry Goldman, for example."

"Yeah, but that's kind of going behind her back . . . you know? So I spend a lot of nights at my office . . ."

"If you want to do that, we have a couple of old apartments on this lot, you know . . ."

"No, I didn't know . . ."

"We don't advertise 'em," Alexander said. "Usually only top-line ham-bones with paranoid problems get to use 'em. But if you'll goddamn move your company over here like you're supposed to, and help me with my over-head problems, I'd let you have one of the places for during the week. Then you and your baby could weekend at the beach."

"Sounds interesting," said Rick.

"But not what you want to do, huh?"

"The thought of her stuck in some little apartment . . ."

"They ain't that little . . ."

"And she wants to be an actress . . ."

"Oh, Christ . . ."

"She gets offers. Not from me, but she gets them. You'd be surprised at the scumballs who want to hire her."

"If she wants to be an actress, how come she hasn't fallen for any of the scumballs?" Alexander liked that word *scumballs*.

Rick laughed. "Because she's my good baby, and she always asks my advice."

"Maybe it would do her good to be on the lot. We could run her a screen test and maybe put her to work . . ."

Rick said, "I just don't think she has it. She's an exotic, you know. What happens if you have an exotic cattle call around here?"

Alexander had to nod in agreement, even though it made his head swim a little. "Yeah, the same three Chinese girls show up."

"What kind of life is that for a girl who's been on the cover of *Rolling Stone?*"

"I see your point."

"But let's go look at those apartments, what the hell," said Rick. "One more drink and let's have a look."

They had two more drinks. Rick admitted he was screwing his secretary, which complicated the issue. He would come to the office and have to fuck Joyce and then go home and have to fuck Elektra. It was more than he could handle, sometimes, and so he would stay in the office alone. But Elektra wasn't born yesterday. If they all moved onto the lot, Rick felt things might reach a head at just the wrong time.

"But let's go look at the goddamn apartments anyhow," he said, and Alexander patted him affectionately on the back. This was a nice kid!

ALEXANDER HAD not been drunk to show it since he could remember. He had always been the man who drank along drink for drink and then helped the others into their cars. But this afternoon, with the sun hanging dimly in its grey-yellow atmosphere of smog, Alexander knew that he was definitely tipsy and would have to be on his guard. It wouldn't do for people to see him staggering around his own lot. Therefore he was very conscious of walking erectly and with dignity.

Then he remembered some advice he had once heard, an old actor telling a young actor, "The way to play a drunk is sober; the thing about drunks, see, is that they *want* to look sober." The very *attempt* to be dignified was suspicious.

"Do I look drunk to you?" he asked Rick Heidelberg.

"I'm pretty shit-faced myself," Rick replied.

They walked down a long narrow canyon between buildings, on one side Studio One, where pictures were scored. Outside the small fire door were a group of musicians, which, as they walked closer, became two groups of musicians, two knots of people on break, obviously not talking to each other. One group was black and one was white, but that did not seem to be the difference; there were a couple of women among the whites, and the men seemed older. The white group was talking in low tones and glancing at Alexander and Rick almost furtively as the two men bore down past them, but the black men, after a glance, did not pay any further attention.

"What's all that about?" Rick said.

"Strings and brass," Alexander said with a giggle.

"Of course," Rick said, and laughed.

"Best goddamn musicians in the world, right here in Hollywood," said Alexander with a flush of pride.

"Yeah, playing whole notes for those big dollar bills," said Rick.

"What are you so bitter about?"

"Don't you think it's a little ah, *shitty?* That the best musicians in the world are playing jingle dates and background music?"

"You like music, huh?"

"I like *everything!*" Rick almost shouted. "I like books, comic books, big-little books, records, live music, opera, rock, jazz, movies, plays, puppet shows, ice-capades, limited warfare and Christ knows what-all, I love it all."

"What about those little lingerie fashion shows women put on for themselves in department stores?"

"I love those best of all," Rick said with what Alexander saw as simple dignity. They turned a corner and the sun, a burnished aluminum disk behind its veil of smog, made them blink.

"How much farther?" Rick asked. There was the little red schoolhouse across the street, nestled in among its trees and shrubbery. Behind it was a typical small-town street, and beyond that the big New York street. They skirted the edges of the backlot where all the other facade standing sets had been for fifty years, and ducked into another alley between tall white-painted sound studios with outside iron staircases. Along one side of the street were parked a lot of trucks and actors' dressing-room trailers. People were standing around, and the red light over the door was on.

"Still shooting, this late at night?" said Alexander. He walked up to a white-haired man sitting with his legs dangling from the back of a truck.

"Mister Potter," Alexander said gravely.

"Why, hello, Boss," Potter said with surprise. He slid down off the truck. He was a prop man, had been on the lot for years.

"How's it going, Potter?"

"The mills of the gods, Boss. You can go in and see for yourself if you want."

Alexander looked over and saw that the red light had gone off.

"No," he said. He wondered if Potter could smell all the liquor on his breath. He and Rick kept moving, and were soon around another corner, where there was a white stucco staircase with red concrete steps.

"Up we go," Alexander said. He got out his key ring, for he carried the keys to this apartment all the time.

It was one of his secret hideaways.

He opened the heavy door and stood back for Rick to enter first. Alexander followed, grinning redly. This was in no way a test, understand, but he would be very interested in Rick's reaction to this apartment.

"It's a reaction medium," he said aloud.

"What?" asked Rick.

"Nothing."

They stood in the living room, and Alexander switched on the lights. The room sprung into life, a room preserved from the late thirties intact, decorated the way somebody with very good taste in those long-gone Art Deco days could decorate with an unlimited budget. Soft ivory silks, blue glass, silken lamps, wallpaper and woodwork, rich carpets and round windows. There was a faint odor of dried-to-dust roses.

Rick looked stunned. He had obviously expected some hot dust-ridden clunky apartment with a lot of discard furniture from the warehouse. Alexander went behind the bar where the small refrigerator hummed efficiently, got out some ice cubes and a bottle of bourbon from the backbar, while Rick wandered silently through the apartment. Alexander wondered how he liked the mirrored bedroom with its red and yellow silk wall panels, the big high old-fashioned bed, the Japanese prints of beautiful young maidens.

Alexander had their drinks ready when Rick wandered back into the living room. They solemnly clicked their glasses.

"Do you know who used to live in this apartment?" Alexander said softly.

"No," said Rick.

"Errol Flynn," said Alexander. Tears almost came to his eyes. "The man was one of my idols," he said.

It quite took Rick's breath away. He looked around again.

"It was a lot sloppier then, I think," said Alexander. "The kitchen full of garbage, broken glass in the carpets, blood and urine on the walls."

"How long did he live here?" Rick wanted to know.

"Not very, a few weeks, long enough for his purposes. But he lived here, Errol Flynn, one of my real heroes . . ."

"Mine, too," Rick said with awe, and then made a quick oriental praying gesture, touching his palms to his nose.

"Don't worry, there's no ghost here, just memories, and most of them false."

"It's still a religious moment for me," Rick said. *"Dawn Patrol. The Roots of Heaven."*

"Captain Blood, Robin Hood," said Alexander. He was liking this young man more and more. "Well, you want to move in for a while? Do you think Elektra would like it?"

"I think she'd love it, but I can't . . . move in here, I just couldn't . . ."

"Why not?"

"I couldn't live up to it. I'd be thinking all the time, Errol Flynn, Errol Flynn . . . nothing would get done. I'd be looking over my shoulder all the time. But thanks for the compliment, and I think it's an incredible compliment."

Rick fumbled in his pocket and came out with a little bottle. "I don't know about you," he said, "but I need a little of this Peruvian wakeup medicine."

Alexander had never tried cocaine. Now would be as good a time as any. Rick, using a tiny spoon, helped Alexander to snort the white powder.

"My first time," he admitted. "What should I look for?"

"First time, hey? Well, watch out for your throat closing up, you'll think you can't swallow, but you can, you just have to force it. And then in about fifteen minutes it will start seeping down into your gums . . ."

"My gums?" Alexander gave a lot of thought to his gums. Watch the gums and the teeth take care of themselves, he had been told, and it seemed to be working. "Will it hurt my gums?"

"It won't help them. But it'll just numb them at first."

"Some hell of a drug. Why do people take it?"

"I dunno. Stay awake, I guess," Rick said. "Do you keep the air conditioning on in the place all the time?"

"Uh, yeah, I guess so. I come here from time to time to get away from the office."

"Can I bring Elektra here, once?" Rick asked.

Alexander had never brought Teresa here. Why not? She might have loved it.

And then, to his great amazement, Alexander sat down on a small French love seat with a brocaded silk cover, and told Rick all about Teresa, and the doubts he was beginning to feel about himself. He felt wonderful doing it. The young man sat silent but sympathetic and listened to every word. And there were a lot of words, my, it just fairly poured out of him, and of course he realized later that this was one of the famous effects of the drug, to make you babble. Yet at the same time he felt a wonderful relief in spilling his misery to another human. It was not like him, it was downright dangerous to do, but it made him feel fine.

By now he had no appetite at all, and suggested they have another drink.

"What time is it?" Rick said. "I don't give a fuck, let's tie one on and hit the Roxy at ten. Some friends of mine are opening tonight."

"Rock and roll?" Alexander said.

"Rock and roll," Rick confirmed. "If you don't want to, the hell with it. I'll pick up Elektra and we'll go somewhere else."

"No," said Alexander. "Rock and roll is fine."

His head throbbed once, and the shock wave passed nauseatingly through his chest and intestines, ending with a vicious twist of his anus. For one shuddering moment it felt as if he were going to have an attack of diarrhea right there in the bed. If he did not throw up first. Alexander hadn't had a hangover in years, but he had one now. There was only one way to combat it. He had to get out of his bed, and in the chill of the early morning, go outside and jump into his swimming pool. Swim fifty hard chopping laps, and then eat a big breakfast. He steeled himself. Steeling himself didn't work. But in return his grateful body, which did not after all have to get up and go swimming, gave him a few moments of relief. He punched his pillow and buried his head in it.

As he rested, bits of picture and sound flitted through his mind, like Halloween ghosts. Would there be a headline in the L.A. *Times?*

FILM EXECUTIVE IN DISCO BRAWL

No. He had not brawled. And the Roxy was not a disco. He remembered sitting there beaming at everybody, all those young people, who were all beaming at him. He remembered buying a lot of drinks for people, and he remembered the cute waitresses, all of them, like sweet children. And he remembered loving the music, the three young, men in shining red costumes,

The Mercedes Effect they called themselves. Nobody had fawned on him, table-hopped him, or paid much attention to him. Why in his memory did there seem to be a brawl somewhere? Was he forgetting part of the evening? Had he blacked out?

He remembered sitting with Rick in Errol Flynn's old apartment on the lot, drinking whiskey and taking cocaine. They had talked about everything, movies past, present and future—Rick was as movie crazy as himself—and that was quite crazy; they talked about women and what a hellish problem they were. Alexander's stomach throbbed as he thought about some of the things he had admitted to Rick.

Then he remembered the girl at the Roxy, the one that had been sitting with them, blonde, blue-eyed, about twenty-two and stroking the back of his neck as they sat in the din. Carla. Something. She was going to come home with him and fuck him and bring him out of this goddamn business about not being able to get an erection. He remembered talking freely with her about this forbidden thing, Jesus, what had they had for dinner, well, they didn't eat at all, as it turned out, just some of Errol Flynn's left-over peanuts, and then headed late for Sunset Boulevard and the Roxy. Laughing and shaking hands with people as they made their way through the darkened room to their seats in the midst of the crowd. Then Carla with her stroking fingers and murmuring good cheer. And then he remembered, the fragments of memory like torn-up strips of newspaper, that Carla had come here with him, and so had Rick and Elektra, they had all sat in the den and Alexander racked up *Dawn Patrol* for them. Rick hadn't seen it in years. David Niven and Errol Flynn, so young, so bright, so sincere . . . He remembered crying in Carla's arms as she murmured nice things, and then he could remember no more of her. Had they made love? He knew in his bones that they hadn't.

Another failure. Add it to the pile. There comes a point in every man's life. Nausea. The real thing.

Cuddling his nausea, Alexander gradually drifted off to sleep.

The next time he wakened it wasn't so bad. He sat up and felt only a slight pain in his head. Rick had been wonderful. It had been in the doorway of the club, as they were leaving. Alexander had fallen down, and wildly grabbed at some people to keep from falling, and somebody had yelled and somebody else had cursed, and there was Rick at the center of it, protecting him, cooling off the man whose wife Alexander had pawed accidentally, helping Alexander to his feet, telling the manager, "This is a non-event, okay?"

Non-event. What a way to put it.

Alexander felt pretty good, now that he thought about it. The sunlight was brightening the drapes, so it must have been past eight o'clock. Did he have to be at the office today?

No. It was Saturday. Thank God.

Rick had been so enthusiastic, once he got rolling. He had other projects, other plans, the thing was all coming together, they would work together, Rick had the pulse of the young and Alexander had the power to make things happen the way they should happen. However, Alexander couldn't remember much about Rick's plans. He got out of bed and wobbled into the bathroom. He had to laugh. The kid probably thought he got Alexander doped and drunk and then pitched himself into a commanding position, but no. Alexander had gotten himself drunk and was not a high school boy who could be seduced by drugs.

And of course nothing was on paper. But he liked that kid.

Outside, he walked naked and a little dizzy toward his pool, fell into the water and had done a number of laps before he pulled over to the side, out of breath, and saw Elektra on the lawn, playing with his rabbits.

"Hello," he said. She was sitting in the sun, in only her underpants. The rabbits were having a bit of clover.

"Hello," she said.

Alexander remembered begging them to spend the night. And then suddenly he remembered getting Orfeo out of bed, taking Carla out to the cars, and having Orfeo drive the girl home. They had kissed in front of Orfeo.

"What do you call them?"

"The rabbits? Just rabbits. They don't have names."

Elektra stroked Mama Rabbit, who nibbled at the grass and clover contentedly. Papa Rabbit came over by Alexander who scratched him between the ears, those magnificent sensitive ears that could express so much, and then for no reason that Alexander could fathom, Papa Rabbit tore around the lawn in quick hops and sharp turns, ending with a jump straight into the air. And then went back to grazing as if none of it had happened. Alexander and Elektra laughed happily.

"I can see I'm gonna have to get some rabbits," Elektra said.

"Where's Rick?"

"Oh, he's snoozing. You boys really tied one on last night." Elektra did not seem concerned about it.

"I don't do that often," Alexander said.

"So you said, quite a few times," the beautiful girl said. She got to her feet and without any self-consciousness at all, slipped down her panties and came over to the pool. For an extraordinary moment, Alexander thought she was coming toward him, but it was only the swimming pool. She dived in, a smooth bubbling dive, and he could see her like a black-and-golden fish under water streaking to the other end and back. When she broke for air she pulled her long dark hair out of her eyes and grinned at Alexander like a child. "This is a great pool," she said. "Most pools aren't long enough to give you any workout." Then she started lapping in long slow strokes, and after only a moment, Alexander joined her.

Then they were out of the pool, sunning. Elektra was drying her hair with one of the white towels that had mysteriously appeared on the furniture.

"Am I nuts or were the towels here all the time?"

Alexander was pleased. "My staff likes to do things right," he said.

"Well," she said, "what do I call you? I don't want to call you Alec or Lex because I know you can't stand those names, but do I call you Mister Hellstrom or what? I can't call you Boss, because you aren't my boss."

"That's what most people call me," he said.

"I guess I'll just call you Alexander," she said. To Mama Rabbit she said, "And I'm going to call you Melissa, and your husband is Freddy."

Rick came out squinting into the sunlight, wearing pants and no shirt. "Hello, gang," he said.

"Look at the rabbits," Elektra said.

"Rabbits? Oh, yeah. I thought they were cats, the color, you know."

"Well, they are rabbits, and I want about six of them."

"Ha ha," said Rick. "Well, Boss, did we make a couple of assholes out of ourselves, or did we make a couple of assholes out of ourselves?"

"We did," said Alexander, "but I'm holding you to everything you said. If I could just remember what it was."

Rick actually looked embarrassed. "I'm sorry I pitched you. You must get tired of that."

"Do you men want me to get breakfast?" Elektra asked.

"Just pick up that telephone," Alexander said proudly. "Ask for the kitchen. We can eat out here."

"What a treat!" she said.

Rick went over and kissed her.

Alexander felt like an old man watching some natural wonder like a beautiful sunset for the ten thousandth time. The two broke their kiss and made a loving intimate eye contact, their foreheads touching.

"What do you want for breakfast?" he asked her eyes.

"Pig meat and poi," she said.

Alexander thought wildly of sending Orfeo down to Trader Vic's in Beverly Hills, make 'em open the kitchen early and bring them piping hot orders of pig meat and poi. But no. That was just the kind of Hollywood jive he scorned.

"Would you settle for bacon and Cream of Wheat?" he joked.

But the lovers did not even hear him.

CHAPTER ELEVEN

JERRY REXFORD was busy these days, and gradually the pattern he had allowed himself to fall into when he moved to Los Angeles changed; but he did not know if he was happier or just busier. She was at the bottom of it. Naturally. That was a joke, for she was a very natural woman, and tried, was trying and would continue to try, to make Jerry into a natural man. Gone was the morning hour at the donut shop; these days he only had time to jump in, grab a big plastic-topped paper cup of coffee to take up to the office, barely time to say hello to Helen, whose wine-dark eyes followed his every move while he was in the shop. Then bustle up to the office and knock out those editorials and articles, edit the crap, lay out the pages, paste up the art, lunch at his desk, prepared by Barbara, with cute little notes like, "Chew your food, you'll look good in the nude," pencilled on the bag. Nuts and vegetables, hard cheese, the kind of lunch to make you glad you were working anyway. But he loved her, and had to make allowances.

More and more he spent the nights at her place. She was a fine cook, in spite of her faddist ideas, and somehow he had convinced her that a man likes his red meat. He even quoted Kipling: "A man can't work on fruit!" So dinners would be spectacular feasts of steak or chicken, fillets of sole sautéed lightly in garlic and butter, with tiny new potatoes, and of course plenty of green and yellow vegetables, sliced tomatoes and sliced cucumbers in vinaigrette, desserts of extraordinary carrot cake or cheesecake, which passed the ban on sugar because, to quote Barbara, "Honey doesn't have any sugar in it."

Jerry had learned to keep his mouth shut about "quackery" and "faddism" and "pseudoscientific claptrap."

Also, they managed to get pretty drunk every night, for while she prepared the food, Jerry would sit in the kitchen with her, talking about the day's trivialities and sipping white wine. It was a lot of fun, and after dinner, as likely as not, they would climb into her big cool fresh-smelling bed and make love. Then, television, brandy and blotto.

There were only a couple of small flies in the soup. One was that she would drag him out of bed in the morning and make him go running with her, after guzzling a nauseating pint of "tiger's milk." There they would be, at six a.m., trotting down Ventura Boulevard. That was one fly; but not so bad, because Jerry's skin was tightening nicely, and the truth was, he felt lots better.

The other fly was that Barbara had a problem with sex. Magnificent as she was physically, there was something in her makeup that made it hard for her to have orgasms. Not impossible, just difficult, so that it generally became a race to see which of them would make it. Jerry's problem was that if he concentrated too much on lengthening the experience so that she would have an opportunity to climax, he would begin to suffer what he called privately "novocaine dick," a state of local numbness that made it possible for him to fuck on and on, but without pleasure. He began sweating when this happened. Sometimes they just had to give up.

She was a virtuoso of the penultimate cry, he thought bitterly one night, as they lay back to back after a particularly promising but eventually disappointing time. Queen of the unresolved chord. But it was not her fault, he reasoned, and to keep her from being too disappointed, he learned how to fake his own orgasms, which allowed him to give a great shout, lie there for a few moments, and then withdraw peacefully.

Then he learned to counterfeit simultaneous orgasm. This turned her on as nothing had before, and with her eyes gleaming in the semidarkness she told him it was because of his new diet. "Our bodies were out of synch," she said tenderly.

For a while he despaired of a return to natural open sex. Without any faking or lying. But then he learned another great secret. After faking an orgasm, he still had the power to make love again. Gradually, as her delight at his new "power" became more and more obvious, he became the most theatrical of lovers, episode after episode, bringing her to at least one and sometimes, miracle of miracles, two or three.

The more he faked it, the easier it was for her to come. But Jerry had acquired so great a control over himself that it became more and more difficult for him to come.

Of this Barbara was unaware. She only knew that she had taken a plump white-fleshed so-so lover and turned him into a suntanned, slim, damned good-looking *macho* man.

As for Jerry, he masturbated. But he was proud of the way he could make her feel. Sometimes it didn't even bother him that his love life was a sham.

There wasn't much time for writing. At first Jerry had weakly insisted that he should return to Fountain and his typewriter, at least a *few* nights a week, but she had gone through this with her brother Richard, and knew all the symptoms. "You'll get over it," she told him.

But they both agreed that he should keep his own place. A man has to have some place to get away, and Barbara didn't mind if Jerry had the hobby of trying to write screenplays. In Hollywood, nearly everybody does. Although she never said so, it was obvious that she didn't think he had a ghost of a chance. One night, drunkenly, he had left her house and driven over to Hollywood and gotten his first finished screenplay, a story about a couple of slum kids who rob a bank, make an enormous haul, far more than they had hoped for or expected, and then take the money to Vegas, where the professional hustlers take them for every cent and leave them for the cops. Jerry saw it as a tough hard uncompromising look at the world, but Barbara could hardly keep the boredom from her eyes as they sat in her living room sipping brandy and Jerry read to her in a flat nervous voice.

"You don't like it," he said at last. There were twenty pages to go.

"It's not that I don't like it," she said. And never finished the sentence. Jerry never read her anything again. For weeks he didn't write, and then one night, as he dropped by his apartment to get some laundry he wanted to run through the machines at Barbara's apartment, he sat down and sternly read the script again. It wasn't that bad. In fact, it was pretty good. Later in the week he stole a couple of big manila envelopes from the office and mailed his script, plus a politely worded note, to the office of Adams, Ray & Rosenberg, supposedly the best writers' agency in town.

Ten days later he had it back again, with an equally polite note explaining that the AR&R Agency was topheavy with clients. Not a word about the script itself. But by this time Jerry had begun to outline another script, and he was not so concerned. He just took the first one and put it into another envelope and sent it to the David Novotny Agency. *Five* days later, surely a record, he got it back with the same note—agent too busy, sorry. Off to Evarts Ziegler.

The second screenplay, written in dribs and drabs, was a hard-boiled story about a group of blacks in prison, revolving around an innocent youth who is finally set up and killed by the authorities because, in his innocence, he had become the focal point of a riot. It was a tough hard story and it came out fast. Jerry was amazed by its power. He cried with pity and rage every time he read it. Into the mail. Script #1 was back from Ziggie and off to Wm. Morris. Script #2 began to follow the same trail, and Jerry spent almost no time at home.

Then he got a phone call from the David Novotny Agency. Not from Novotny himself, of course, but from a subagent named Harriet Hardardt. Could Jerry please come and get his script, Harriet wanted to have a chat with him. Tomorrow would be fine.

Jerry was pretty excited, but he said nothing to anyone about the appointment. After all, she had said, "pick up your script." Maybe she just wanted to tell him to give up. Maybe she had taken pity on him and wanted to stop him before he wasted any more of anybody's time.

But no. When Jerry arrived at the luxurious offices on the twelfth floor of 9255 Sunset, dressed in his best dark blue suit even though it was eighty-five degrees out, he was quickly led by a beautiful secretary into a small office filled with books, where a handsome woman of fifty, red-haired and strong-chinned, reached across her desk and shook hands with him. Jerry's script was right there on top of her desk. It looked much thumbed.

"I'm Harriet Hardardt," she said, "and I'm *very* pleased to meet you. I'm always pleased to meet somebody who can *really* write."

Jerry sat, numbed by this greeting. "Thank you," he said, and numbly waited.

"Look," she said. "Let me get right down to business." But her phone buzzed, and with a wave to Jerry she answered it, talking in a low tone for at least ten minutes to somebody who seemed to be threatening to kill himself, or threatening to come to the office, Jerry couldn't tell which. She was soothing and firm, and finally got off the phone.

"You don't have what we consider a salable script here," she went on with Jerry, as if the telephone call had never happened. "But as I said, you write extremely well, and I just thought it would be a shame to let you go on submitting scripts that can't be filmed."

There was another interruption. This time, she sat there toying with a pencil and going, "Uh-huh." At last it was over.

"Tell me a little bit about yourself," she said. Jerry gave her a capsule biography. She nodded with approval when she heard he was gainfully employed, and as a writer and editor.

"That editorial experience," she said. "I knew it. Your work shows the fine Italian hand of a good editor."

"Thank you," Jerry said. "What's the matter with my stuff?"

"What's the matter is, to be blunt, you are writing expensive stories for small, discerning audiences. A movie has to earn an enormous return to make back the cost of filming, two and a half times as much as it cost to make. So one of the criteria for evaluating an original screenplay is, what will the picture cost, and who will go see it?"

Jerry's heart sank.

"Don't look sad," she said with a nice smile. "Just learn to incorporate that kind of thinking into your decision to write a particular script . . ."

"I'm afraid I don't know what makes an audience come into a theater," he said. "I just have to write what I think I can do best."

"Oh, phooey," she said. "Come off that. What do you really know about bank robbers and black prisoners?"

So she had read the first script, too. Jerry fought his depression. There were things to be learned here.

"Nothing," he said. "You're right, I'm acting like a jerk."

Her buzzer buzzed again, and Jerry waited without listening. At last she said, "I have an appointment now, but I want you to keep writing. Just try a little harder to evaluate what an audience, a very *large* audience, would pay to see."

He came out of the building, his script in his hands, his mind racing. This had been his first real brush with the real Hollywood, and he hadn't come off so badly, not so badly at all. He found a pink parking ticket tucked under the windshield of his Porsche, but it did not bother him. Cheap enough at the price.

HARRIET HARDARDT'S advice was good. There was no reason for Jerry to go on writing scripts that wouldn't get made, no matter how "good" or "interesting" they were. That word *interesting*. It used to be one of his favorite words. Now it made him think of people leaning forward slightly in their theater seats. These people were not wide-eyed or laughing or holding hands, they weren't even scared. They were watching an "interesting" movie.

"How did you like the picture?"

"Uh, it was very *interesting* . . ."

Jerry thrashed around for a project. While he thrashed, he stayed pretty much at Barbara's. There was no point in sitting at the typewriter when he didn't even have a project. And besides, their love life was improving. Maybe Jerry was just getting better used to her timing; whatever the reason, they were more in synch, and there was less reason for him to fake. This took much of the pressure off him, and he began enjoying himself more. It got so that during the day, at odd moments, he found himself staring off into space, thinking about Barbara sexually. He had never had erotic daydreams about somebody he had been going with. Always before they had been about hopelessly unobtainable women, whose images stared at him from the pages of magazines or shone down on him from theater screens. Now he was fancying, in his mind, catching her in an elevator, a full elevator, and crowding her over into a corner and actually fucking her, while she looks over his shoulder, her face reddening as she knows she is going to cry out . . .

And others. An open-field fantasy. One about love in a rainstorm, with mud and thunder . . .

"What's on your mind?" Richard might say to him. Pulling him back to reality.

"Oh, daydreaming different ways to fuck your sister," he definitely never did say.

"Dreams of lust and avarice," he would and did say.

Richard, with his fresh white shirt for every workday, all in bad taste, with backs that bulged out, instead of being tapered to Richard's waist. Jerry was getting pretty clothes conscious, since his figure had improved. Barbara loved to take him to a small men's store on Sunset, where the clerks, all gay as rats, fussed over him and acted as consultants. Jerry's wardrobe was definitely getting classier, a bit more color, European cuts, silk ties . . . Richard was getting on Jerry's nerves, with his assumption that Jerry was now "family," that Richard was the matchmaker and therefore entitled to eternal gratitude. One day when they were the last two in the office (they would dine at Richard's with the family and the television), Richard brought out a yellow-orange packet of Polaroid prints and started to show them to Jerry. Jerry could not believe his eyes. Badly photographed, with horrible highlights and shadows, red-eyed people, pornography that included not only Richard but his wife. And, Jerry recognized numbly, some of their neighbors.

"Just a little hobby of mine," Richard said proudly. "We belong to a swing group and I'm the official photographer."

Later Jerry asked Barbara if she knew about it, and she thought Jerry was making a bad joke. Finally he got mad at her.

"I'll steal some of the goddamn pictures and show them to you," he said.

"Oh, no, please don't!" she said. She didn't want to know.

So the pictures were an intimacy between Richard and himself. The first of a long line of confidences, he imagined. Well, what about it? Barbara was perfectly wonderful, and he could imagine that being married to her would be wonderful as well. Barbara would immediately want children. They could start a family, and with their combined incomes, live pretty well, nice house, good big enclosed yard, swimming pool, hot tub, grapefruit tree, the works.

But it would mean an end to his Hollywood ambitions. No, he thought furiously, it doesn't have to be that way! If he could succeed in Hollywood before getting married or making any foolish moves, then he would be in the driver's seat. That was the way to do it.

Then, at the donut shop one morning, he ran into Toby.

"A little late for you, isn't it?" Jerry said. He hadn't seen much of Toby lately.

"I'm trackin' you down," Toby said. Now that Jerry noticed, Toby was a really shabby dresser. Plaid yellow shirt, green pants with grease stains on them. Played-out tennis shoes. Jerry already was wondering why he had spent so much time with this man, only a little while before. Lonely, I guess.

Toby's eyes were glittering. "I got a connection for you," he said. "Remember Elektra Soong's brother? Karol Dupont? The little drag queen?"

Jerry remembered. He looked away from Toby with some embarrassment, and found himself staring into the eyes of Helen, the waitress. Helen smiled. Jerry looked back at Toby.

"She's makin' some goddamn movie down the street here, in the basement under one of those scum theaters."

"Yes?" said Jerry.

"Don't you get it, man? You could meet her!"

Toby was convinced that such a meeting would result in Jerry getting a "connection" with Richard Heidelberg. Jerry was not so sure, but Toby was all over him.

"You don't know Jack shit about how this town works!" He got a paper cup of coffee to take back to the bookstore.

"Meet me right here on Saturday morning, around ten," he said to Jerry. "We'll hit the set."

But Jerry did not show up. Although he was fascinated by the idea of watching a pornographic film shot, even with transvestites, he really could not spare the time. He didn't think Karol Dupont was a "connection" anyway.

His new idea was a good one, if he did say so himself. Instead of trying to write another original, he would adapt a novel. And not just any novel, one that had been made into a movie already, so that he would learn what worked and what didn't. It took him two weeks to find the right project, and then it was almost by accident. He was standing in the drugstore looking over the paperback rack for a copy of *The Big Sleep,* thinking to adapt it. Then he could compare it with the existing screenplay. There was much to be learned from such a process. But there were no copies of *The Big Sleep,* only some short stories and *The Lady in the Lake.* After some hesitation, he bought the novel and took it home to Barbara's house.

He stayed in the living room reading until after two. The book was fascinating, but what was more, there had not been a remake from the rather experimental movie of the mid-forties, in which the camera was Philip Marlowe. This picture did not make money.

Jerry thought he saw something in the story that had been ignored. His idea held all the way through the novel, and even held up when he got back to his own apartment and looked through his film books and confirmed what he had guessed.

The really successful detective movies, the ones that still played after thirty years, were the ones in which the detective had a strong love interest. Often bittersweet, often tragic. *The Big Sleep* was a terrific example of this, Bogart and Bacall, for Christ's sake! In the novel the love story was smaller, almost a by-product. In the movie it was everything, and nobody really cared who killed Rusty Regan. And even a better example, *The Maltese Falcon!* What was the greatest line in the picture, the one that got all the hankies wet?

"I'm sending you over, sweetheart!"

Tragic love in a detective story setting.

Marlowe has no love interest in *Lady in the Lake*.

Jerry would give him one. And not just a love interest. The villain of the novel is a woman, Muriel Chess, AKA Mildred Haviland, AKA Mildred Degarmo, a desperate woman who has killed and will kill again. Why couldn't Marlowe fall in love with her? He thinks she's somebody else, somebody dead, that he's falling in love with a murder victim, not the killer herself.

It ain't Chandler, he thought in the deep of the night, still so wrought up he knew he would not sleep without whiskey. It ain't Chandler, but it's sure Hollywood. My God, it takes elements from *Laura, The Big Sleep* and *The Maltese Falcon*. Not exactly petty larceny.

And then he remembered that it was only an experiment, just something to learn on. Nevertheless he tossed and turned. There was something about that scene, as yet unwritten, where Marlowe finds himself facing not just the woman he has come to love even though she was supposed to be dead, but the woman he must turn in for the murders. What a moment!

The next day at the office Richard held up the telephone with his hand cupped over the mouthpiece and said, "Richard Heidelberg, for you."

Jerry thought it was Toby, angry that Jerry had not shown up. He took the phone with a sinking heart. Everyone in the office was staring at him.

"Jerry Rexford," he said.

"Mister Rexford, will you hold for Richard Heidelberg?" said a warm confident female voice.

"Hello, my friend," came a warm male voice before Jerry could react.

"Hello, there," he said inanely. He grinned in a sickly way at Richard standing in front of him.

"I'm told you have a terrific idea for a movie," he heard the voice on the telephone say.

"Uh, yeah," he said.

"Tell me this. Suppose your idea got made into a movie. And that movie is sold to television. What's the one-sentence description of the movie that appears in the newspaper?"

"Huh?" Jerry thought of his two original screenplays, and shit-canned them forever.

"Give me your idea in one terrific sentence," Rick said.

"Well, it's based on a *novel,* it's just an experiment I'm trying . . . but it's Raymond Chandler's *The Lady in the Lake,* only as a love story, like *The Maltese Falcon.*"

Jerry listened miserably to the empty hum of the telephone. "What have you got on paper?" Rick said finally.

"Not a whole hell of a lot," Jerry said.

"Could you messenger it over to me? I'd like to read the material. It sounds like a major movie. Lots of stuff to check over, though. Availability of rights, stuff like that . . ."

It was Jerry's turn to speak. Swallowing what seemed like a mouthful of cotton, he said, "I'll—listen, give me a few days, okay? To smooth it out a little?"

To get it on paper, he meant.

Rick's voice said, "Okay, and I'll get back to you. Listen, Elektra says hello."

"Oh, hello to her, too," Jerry said, stunned. He hung up the phone. Nobody was looking at him, not even Richard.

So Toby had somehow burst the barrier. "Elektra says hello." What had Toby said? What was Jerry obligated to? Did Richard Heidelberg think Jerry was an associate of Karol Dupont? But even with all the confusion, Jerry felt a pleasurable tightening of his resolve.

That night he and Barbara got into a terrible fight on the telephone. He tried, without going into confusing or embarrassing detail, to explain that he *had* to work on his script tonight, that there was actual *interest* (although he cautiously held back the name Richard Heidelberg); and she was furious that he had not called her before. Good food was going to waste.

"I'm sorry," he said. But he wasn't.

RAIN CAME to Los Angeles, the swirling tips of subtropical storms brushing the great basin with torrents of pure water. It cleaned off the streets, the rooftops, the trees; it made mushrooms spring up on the glittering green highway dividers, it filled the concrete bed of the Los Angeles River and quickly flooded the vast underground run-off system, so that at the bottom of the hills, manholes would send up fountains of crystal water through the ring of one-inch holes in their covers. It rained and rained and rained, and erased one of the hottest, smoggiest summers in human memory. The first freshness created joy in people's hearts; perhaps it was negative ionization, perhaps it was just relief. But after a while there was a new smell in the air, and the smell carried with it a sullen dread, genetic dread of The Flood, dread of endless years of rain after endless years of ice and snow, with only some long-dead ancestor's tales to remind us of blue skies and sweet sunny days.

It was the smell of mildew.

Jerry's apartment was full of it. It came out of the plaster walls and settled in the dirty clothes at the bottom of the closet. It hung from the drapes. It moistened the garbage sacks, already overrun with streams of hungry ants, and encouraged cockroaches from their crevices. It made his typewriter keys stick together and it caused him to make a lot of typographical errors.

But Jerry did not care. He wrote, very rapidly, his first-draft screenplay of *The Lady in the Lake* just as the rain chose to begin. He wrote it on pure energy. He had never worked so hard in his life. Nor had he ever had so much fun. His gut rumbled and he wobbled on his legs as he made his way from toilet to typewriter to bed; he wrote all night and dozed with the dreams of scenes in his mind, and then got up without thinking and sat at the machine again and wrote again. Twenty, thirty pages a day, half of them thrown to the wind with enthusiasm as the new approach is tried and succeeds. He had never known it could be like this.

When he was done he mailed the script to Richard Heidelberg. He felt a twinge at doing this without consulting Harriet Hardardt, but after all, she had had nothing to do with his relationship to Heidelberg. Might as well ship a copy to Toby! Then he felt a twinge about Toby, whom he had not taken into his confidence. But what was there to say? Jerry had been around long enough now to hear the empty talk that was on everyone's lips, the deals about to be made, the parts one was "up" for, and Jerry definitely did not want to join the chorus.

Of course Barbara and his employer had to be kept in the dark as well. To finish his script, Jerry had said he had the flu, and over Barbara's protests that he bed down at her place and let her pamper him, Jerry weakly said, "I want to just lay here," and Barbara, obviously sensing rebuff, accepted his story.

So he was back working at *Pet Care Hotline,* but he was not back at Barbara's.

"I have a lot of writing to do," he told her.

"You could come here for dinner," she said, "and then go do your writing."

"I like to get right at it," Jerry said weakly. And, as weak and clumsy as it sounded, it was true. Without waiting for any response, Jerry was already into the second draft, working nights and weekends. Part of the weekends he spent with Barbara, dutiful, attentive, kind, loving, deliberately and with great effort putting the script out of his mind. Of course it wouldn't leave him alone. He might be spooning crabapple jelly on his hot muffin, Barbara enthusiastically describing their outing to the beach or desert, when it would steal into his brain. The jelly would drip off his knife and onto the tablecloth and he would apologize and Barbara would make jokes, but he knew she was bitter about it.

But then finally he would be free of her and able to go back to Fountain, strip, pull the cover from his machine and get back to work. He actually rubbed his hands together and chuckled. "Let's go, honey," he would say to the typewriter, and tickle her switch.

There was plenty to do. For one thing, he had thrown out too much Chandler, he hadn't seen how subtly Chandler had constructed his scenes, how easily he set up each scene, how important were the asides and apparent irrelevancies. So, back in went a lot of great stuff, and really only a few scenes had to be altered for the romantic overlay.

It was extraordinary fun to play with these ideas and have them come out right. Ideas flowed out of his mind onto the paper before he could think them, and for the first time, Jerry Rexford felt the awesome humility of a writer who realizes that he is not the train but the track.

In a way, it was a relief. He could read over something he had written and enjoy it fully, laugh or cry or feel anger, because he hadn't *really* written it, it had just come out of him.

It is like digging for buried treasure, he thought.

No, it is like milking a cow.

Now he understood why the writers of the Bible and other holy books thought they were inspired by God; they hadn't made it up, where else could it have come from?

He mailed off the second draft screenplay to Richard Heidelberg with a short note of apology for the first draft, and sat back and waited. The rain streamed down. He cleaned the apartment, got rid of the ants, caused the cockroaches to retreat to prepared positions, did his laundry and waited. The one attempt he made to get his relationship with Barbara back on some kind of friendly footing didn't work. She actively resented his long absence and was grumpy over dinner and impossible in bed.

He didn't blame her. She had just found out that no matter what, she came in second.

And then Harris began to complain about his work. He was getting sloppy. He was misspelling people's names, and in this business you can't do that. And his copy was too tame.

"I think you're perhaps giving a little too much to your, ah, other endeavors," said Harris politely. They were in his office. Jerry was barely paying attention. Harris did not ask him to stop writing at home. He was really very nice. He only asked that Jerry earn his paycheck. Everyone else had to. That was the way things were. Jerry nodded sullenly and went back to work. He hoped the old bastard would fall off the wagon and get off his back. It would be great to see Harris come in some afternoon, drunk as a goat, dirty, piss-wet pants and blood on his cheek.

But no, Jerry was ashamed for having such thoughts. Actually, he deserved firing; it was only Harris's niceness that kept him eating.

Once again, Jerry Rexford had screwed up his life.

But he waited to hear from Richard Heidelberg with the certain knowledge that everything would work out. He had fabulous daydreams of accepting his Academy Award, of appearing on the *Tonight* show and cracking everybody up; daydreams of an estate in Beverly Hills, Manhattan tower suite, his own jet airplane. The first thing he would do would be to move out of this dump. Oh, quit his job. Then move out of this dump. He would move into the Beverly Hills Hotel, at the studio's expense, of course. He would get rid of this little SCM, sweet machine that it was, and get himself a big IBM job, maybe the studio would furnish one free. He would be on the set every day, consulted by the actors and actresses wanting to know how to play the subtle aspects of their roles.

He cast the picture, oh, many times he cast the picture. You can't have just anyone play Philip Marlowe. No actor in the box-office top ten failed to pass before Jerry's scrutiny. Yet none of them measured up to the ultimate Marlowe, Bogart himself. So Jerry would always come back to envisioning Bogart in the role. In his mind's eye, as he wrote, and later as he feverishly went over every scene in his mind and waited for Richard Heidelberg to call him back, he saw Bogart's face.

And he drank, first to enhance the fantasies, and then to blot them out so he could sleep. You couldn't sleep with Bogart racing around in your mind, doing scenes you had written. So about five shots of 100-proof bourbon would knock him out.

All in all, he waited two months. In that time he learned how to hate. The person he hated was Richard Heidelberg. What a fool Jerry had been! He had not protected himself. When Heidelberg had said, "What's your idea?" Jerry should have covered himself. He should have pitched one of his original scripts, and then, when he had a relationship with the bastard, spring the Chandler idea. Jerry always got depressed thinking about that brief conversation, because he realized he could have done nothing to protect himself, he was out in the open with no help in sight. The idea did not belong to him. It belonged to Raymond Chandler, long dead, and M-G-M, not so dead, and logically after that, anyone who would pay M-G-M's fee to remake it. The more he thought about these things, the more foolish Jerry felt.

But he had *learned*. The idea he had started out with had been good. It was only the idiotic idea of trying to sell it that was bad. Now Jerry should go right out and write another original. With what he had learned on *The Lady in the Lake* he could probably write a selling script this time. But he could not think of anything to write about. Every idea was pale, drab, uncommercial. Compared to you-know-what.

Two full months. Rain all the time. Depression. Each day one more step to cold reality. He was sweating out a phone call from a man who had probably forgotten he existed.

Then one morning on the front page of *Daily Variety* there was an article about Richard Heidelberg and his just-announced relationship to Boss Hellstrom. Definitely not among the projects mentioned in the article (there were about ten of them) was "a remake of Raymond Chandler's *The Lady in the Lake.*"

The ants were trooping into Jerry's kitchen again, as the garbage mounted. Oh, hell, let them have it, he thought, heavily depressed. It's only garbage. He listened to the constant rain. He was a broken man.

That night Raymond Chandler appeared to him in a dream and told him to give up.

CHAPTER TWELVE

ONLY THE tension between himself and Elektra had caused Rick to telephone Jerry Rexford. Rick didn't know the man from Adam, and normally would have snorted and said, "Let your friend get an agent and do things right." But this was not the time for that. As a matter of fact, Rick had never actually been in this kind of a spot before. If a girl objected to the way he did things, or didn't want to do what he wanted her to do, he would smile and say goodbye. But he did not smile and say goodbye to Elektra. He *needed* her. Corny, huh?

He liked to stroke her ear and the curve of her neck while they lay in bed watching television. He liked to watch her cook. He liked to watch her repot plants. Elektra was good with plants, and the beach house was full of them. Orchids, begonias, bromeliads, hoyas, cactus, ferns, succulents. Sometimes, when one or another of the orchids was in bloom, the house would be filled with the ripe odor of perfume in the afternoon sunlight. "Add some rotten fruit, a little shit, some vomit, and it would smell just like Hotel Street," she said. She had been born in the rotting muck of downtown Honolulu, her mother a deranged prostitute and her father unknown, and Rick could not understand where she got her sense of humor. But she had it, and he needed it.

But mostly he needed her company. She was the best company he had ever had. They could do nothing for hours together. Or they could do *everything,* and it would be the same, their eyes would meet and affection, *love,* would shine back.

Okay, he *loved* her.

But he wanted to move to town and she resisted. She never actually came out and said she didn't want to move, she just inertly resisted. Rick's sensitivity to her made it impossible for him to just go ahead and hire a realtor and move. He knew he wouldn't lose her, but he would lose something, and whatever it was, he wanted to keep it.

So when she handed him a soiled piece of paper torn from a brown grocery bag with a name and phone number on it, and said, "Oh, would you call this guy? He's supposed to have a great idea for a picture . . ." he didn't just take it to throw away later.

"Who is the guy?" he asked her.

"Just some Hollywood dude," she said. "It's a favor."

There was not in Rick's mind the slightest thought that Elektra was messing around on the side, so it wasn't that. He shrugged and made the call, and now the project was a definite maybe. The first thing Rick had done was to call David Novotny. When the agent got back to him he said, "David, I'd like you to check out the availability of *The Lady in the Lake.*"

"M-G-M owns it," David said.

"Do you know if they have any plans to remake the picture?"

"No, at least, I haven't heard anything. But if you make them an offer, they'll sure look into it."

This happened all the time. A property would lie with its feet up in the studio vaults for years, and then a casual inquiry as to the rights would start the studio heads shaking and muttering, "What's this all about? What do they see in it? Maybe we should make this picture . . ." And a gigantic arglebargle would commence, gigantic sums offered and rejected, and then finally one day the press of business would make everybody lose interest, and the property would go back to the vault for another thirty years.

"Uh, what did you have in mind, if I may be so bold?" David said.

"A very successful formula," Rick said, carefully, for it was important to have David on his side. "We take a classic murder mystery, an absolute classic, and we present it as a tragic love story. But fun. Like *The Maltese Falcon.*"

"Who would do the script?" David asked, after a brief pause.

"I would," Rick said. He didn't mention Rexford's script. It was a damned good script and would be a lot better when Rick got done with it. But Rexford, whoever he was, was a total innocent. Let him stew, Rick thought with a smile. No point in telling him anything until there was something to tell. Once Rick owned the rights he would call the bastard and invite him to lunch.

It was only a couple of weeks later, right after Rick moved his operation onto the lot, that David was able to call and tell him that M-G-M was not interested in remaking *The Lady in the Lake* themselves (they weren't aware of the fun-tragic-love-story angle), but would sell the rights for a healthy fee. They didn't even care who was behind the inquiry.

"Buy it," Rick said.

"As your personal property, or for your company?" David wanted to know.

"Oh, the company, of course."

So began the complex, serpentine flow of energy that would ultimately result in the purchase, or not, of *The Lady in the Lake*. Rick relaxed and dropped the project from his mind. He would either get the rights or not, nothing for him to worry about. That was why David got ten percent.

Meanwhile something dramatic had happened, and for a couple of hours the studio was in an uproar. It was all because of Rick's company moving onto the lot. With him, of course, came his projects and his people, from Joyce his secretary to Jose Gonzala, who had finally found the script he was looking for.

The script had come to Jose through an old high school classmate, who thought Jose could help to get the classmate's uncle's novel published. The uncle was an old *camposino,* who worked the harvests from the Imperial Valley to Yakima and had written a book about it. The writing was dreadful and ignorant, but the scenes were innocently powerful. There was simple truth on every page, as well as a great number of grammatical and spelling errors. The old man had written the book over a period of years, in Scripto pads that were smudged and dirty from being carried through the valleys of the West Coast. Much was crossed out and much added in margins and over other words. There were over fifty of the Scripto pads, and the friend let Jose read them before having them typed up. It was part of the experience to begin reading in impatience and embarrassment for the old guy, and then find yourself in awe of him. He had painfully written it in English because all the best-sellers were in English.

The book was unpublishable, but the screenplay was going to be a master-piece. It would speak for farm laborers without ranting, it would describe a pastoral migratory existence that was more important than the larger issues of law and economics. It was about real people who loved their lives.

And it could be made cheap, without stars, and still clean up. It was a natural. It was *Romeo and Juliet*, *King Lear* and *Hamlet* all rolled into one. There were no Gringo villains, indeed, there were no Gringos at all. What it had was a *beat!* Rick could feel it as he pawed through the dirty old Scripto pads. A heartbeat. Young people would batter down walls to see it, if Rick did it right, the right music, the right casting, the right innocence.

So one morning as the rain poured down so hard you were wet to the skin the minute you stepped outdoors, a car arrived at the main gate of the studio, an old nondescript car jammed full of Mexicans. Young Mexicans, drinking beer and steaming up the windows of the car with their marijuana smoke. The man sitting next to the driver yelled to Charlie Devereaux that he was Jose Gonzala and the others were his staff and his guests. Charlie refused to let them on the lot. The rain poured down, and people in other cars waved past by Charlie peered through the rain at the carful of Mexicans.

Charlie finally called Rick, when he had a moment, and said he had a carful of Mexicans on his hands, what to do? True, there was a Drive-On Pass issued to Gonzala, but nothing was said about a *gang*.

"Oh, shit, Charlie," Rick said. "Let 'em on."

But Charlie was mad now. Thoroughly wet, with an undetermined number of Mexicanos glaring at him through the rain.

"I'll come out there," Rick said. He was soaking by the time he made it down to the main gate, and in not such a good temper himself.

"What the fuck is this?" he demanded of Charlie. "Do I have the right to let people on the lot, or not?"

"By name, sir, yes you do. By name."

Rick sighed and wiped some of the water off his face. He went around the car and tapped on the glass. The window rolled down and Jose's furious, embarrassed and humiliated face glowered up at him.

"We have to give the gate everybody's name," he started to explain.

"Fuck that noise" was Jose's reply.

Rick had to make a decision. He made it quickly, and said to Jose, "Okay." The window rolled back and Rick went around the car and up to the old man.

"Let them in, please. I'll be responsible."

But Charlie was pissed off, too. These punks had been glowering at him and yelling threats. He didn't know if they had weapons in there, either. He said to Rick, stiffly:

"Not without a list of their names. Sir."

"Get me Alexander Hellstrom, would you please? Or I can dial it myself."

"You may use the phone, yes, sir," Charlie said. Cars went by, and Charlie, stooping and peering, waved them by. Famous producers, directors, movie stars, all saw the car full of Mexicans stalled at the gate.

"Yes, Willi, tell him it's an emergency," Rick said into the telephone.

"I'm in a meeting," came Alexander's gruff voice.

Rick explained the situation as well as he could, with Charlie standing right there.

"The whole thing's gonna get spread all over the Spanish press," he said at last. "Jose's no pigeon."

"I'll come right down," Alexander said.

"He's coming right down," Rick said. He was sorry if this was going to cause the old man to lose his job.

Here came the Boss, through the mist and rain, head bent, fists clenched, sopping raincoat and overflowing shoes. He came straight up to the car and said loudly, "Gentlemen, I'd like to meet you and shake hands one at a time, but let's get the hell out of this rain, huh?" He dragged Charlie out of his hut and over to the car, grinning, his arm around the old man's shoulders.

"Charlie Devereaux here thought you guys were a bunch of *bandidos*. He was ready to shoot. He hasn't jacked that thing out for a long time, have you, Charlie? Come on, gentlemen, let's get dry and get some coffee and get acquainted."

It worked.

They all went to Alexander's offices and were served coffee and there was a general conversation about the project, and then a shuffling and shaking of hands, while Alexander begged each of them to feel free to visit the studio anytime and look things over. He made a point of telling Willi to give each a book of Studio Tour passes "for your families and friends," and it was over. Nothing in the Barrio press except a guardedly laudatory article about the project getting started, with a picture of Jose and the old man who had written the book shaking hands.

And it was a puzzlement, why the old guy at the gate hadn't gotten fired for pulling the Boss out of a meeting and into a rainstorm. Rick had to think about that one.

AND THEN, instead of winter, it became summer again. This was how Los Angeles fooled you. The new summer began bright and hot, with only a touch of the autumnal. The beaches south of Malibu were crowded again, and tens of thousands of happy Angelenos sat in open-air stadiums to cheer on their teams. But the smog still rose in gassy clouds over the freeways, and there would be sudden dense killer fogs, closing the airports and creating that too-cold, too-warm climate along the coast that drove a lot of people out of their minds and back to town.

At the beach you could hear the surf but not see the ocean. Rick couldn't stand it, and accepted Alexander's offer of the Errol Flynn apartment. Most nights during the week he wouldn't come home. Elektra was not all that lonely. For one thing, she was often in town running around or shopping, going to movies or visiting friends. And she was an important part of the beach life that included popular singing stars and musicians, movie people, dope dealers and a few of the idle rich. There were dinners and weekend parties for them to be involved in, and if Rick was not there, it was okay. These people understood the needs of art and profession, and someone was always coming back from London or New York, and someone else was always leaving for Australia. It was just what Elektra wanted whether Rick was there or not.

The project now called *Young Man, Old Man* had been through several evolutions. Rich had tackled the screenplay with vigor, the first writing he had done in a great while, and Joyce was under instructions to let no phone call, however important, interrupt the three sacred morning hours when he wrote. But the story didn't come along all that well. It seemed to run jaggedly between high comedy and something fit for a Daffy Duck cartoon. Casting was a problem. They were still trying to find two stars important enough and with the right qualifications to carry the project along.

Once Rick had even had to fly to London himself, for an audience with Mick Jagger, whose people had told Mick's American agency that he was looking for something along these lines to make a picture. Rick allowed himself to get excited on the flight. With Mick Jagger in the project, things would be different. Of course the young man–old man part would have to go, it would just be a naked power struggle between two beautiful men for a beautiful woman, with songs. But what about Rex Harrison? With that talky-singy voice he could break your heart in two seconds. The girl would have to be older (she would anyway, they never really considered a teenager, at least not a young one) but that was okay, maybe they could get a really good singer. On he dreamed as the Atlantic Ocean slipped under him.

But alas, personal matters kept Mick busy, and Rick fuming in the London Hilton, until a meeting was out of the question. Rick Heidelberg didn't wait around no hotel room for nobody, and Mick couldn't be found. Rick flew home and walked into the beach house with a heavy load of jet lag to find a dinner party in progress, Elektra in the kitchen and people all over the house, many of whom he knew.

"How's Mick?" somebody yelled at him from the crowd.

"Fucked," he said, and went into the bedroom.

Then the studio tried to force a casting on him, and he balked. Skye Davis and Dael Tennyson. As far as Rick was concerned, Skye couldn't get arrested. He had been top ten for a few years, a grizzled old drunk of a charmer. He lived in Nassau to work on his tan and be near his money, had a nice wife and numerous children, all in private boarding schools, and made a picture a year. Rick could not write with his big face in mind. It was like writing jokes for a grizzly bear.

Dael, he was a friend, almost, and would be fine as the young guy, but not with Skye Davis. But they had to have the interminable meetings of politely smiling agents and executives and sidekicks and lawyers before Rick could sense that things were easing off. And then one morning he read that Skye was going to make a picture at Universal.

"And we get stuck with a commitment we can't exercise," Alexander said grumpily.

"Are we in turnaround?" Rick asked him. They were in the apartment, having an after-work drink. Then they both had dinner. Rick liked Alexander a lot more than he had expected to, and found great comfort in the older man's calm sturdiness. So they got together quite a bit, considering the pressures on their time. But there were no more crazy drunken nights, and when Rick brought out his bottle of cocaine, Alexander waved it off.

"Makes my nose hurt," he said.

Gradually Rick had begun to sense that Alexander didn't like him doping on the lot, but was too nice to say anything about it. Rick decided to keep it out of sight.

"You'll be in turnaround if you don't get that script finished," Alexander said to him. "We'd have a lot better chance of snaring the top people if we had something better to show them. Like a great script."

But Rick wasn't worried so much about that. If he could just get the right images in his mind, everything would flow.

But he did not get the right images in his mind, and everything did not flow. Days turned into weeks. Rick finally had to tell Alexander, "Look, I'm going to hole up at the beach and get this thing rolling. Time's awasting."

He would get out his old Underwood, the one on which he had written *The Endless Unicorn,* and he would sit in the little room he used for an office at home, looking out over the Pacific, and beat this thing to the ground.

Elektra tended him with her silence and made conditions just about perfect. If ever a writer should be able to write his best, it was now. He became celibate, because it seemed like a good idea; he took long lonely walks on the beach, he abandoned drugs. The fogs came and went, the nice sunny days came and went, and Rick typed and typed. When he was done, he had a 151-page screenplay. That was all he could say about it. He titled it *Boy, Man and Girl* and sent it by messenger to David Novotny.

David called two days later and told him the script was magnificent and they were getting screwed on the price.

"If I had known you could write like this, I would have asked a quarter of a million," he said. He promised to have the script mimeographed and copies distributed.

Within only a few days, everyone from Alexander to Joyce had telephoned him and told him how great the script was. But he didn't fall for it. They didn't *really* know a good script from a bad one. If they did, things would be a lot easier in Hollywood. Rick knew the real test would be later, much later, because, goddamn it, you only knew what you had when the picture was finished. And even then, not a man on earth could tell you it would be a hit until the audience made it a hit.

That's why people like Rick had such tremendous power after one hit. Others had confidence in them, and if they acted with confidence themselves, they could stay at the top, getting on feature after feature, without ever having another success. *It happened once, it could happen again.*

Rick and Elektra had a romping reunion in their big bed, and Rick started coming in to the office again. Other projects were heating up, and even newer ones awaited his opinion, his injection of confidence.

Then Alexander called him into his office. He was beaming. "Well, young man, we're on the way. The corporation has just acquired the services of Peter Wellman for three motion pictures!" He laughed lightly and motioned for Rick to sit down. "Sit down, my friend, sit down."

Rick sat. Wellman would be perfect. Darkly handsome with those big soulful Jewish eyes, Mister Slick with the ladies yet immensely popular with men. And if not Top Ten, at least Top Eleven.

"Has he read the script?"

"My boy, we have to put two million dollars into his hands before he will read a script. There are meetings and meetings to go, but I can't think he'd balk at the role. He's not like some of these hambones, he doesn't claim to have literary genius. Only acting genius."

"What's the availability situation?" Rick asked.

"We can probably get him for fifteen days after he finishes the picture we just hired him for. Some time early in the spring."

"Is this an Alexander Hellstrom Production?"

"No. So far, it's a Donald Marrow Production. This deal was done in New York. That's why it happened so fast."

"You seem happy and confident," Rick said.

"Oh, that's different. My girl's coming out."

Rick grinned. Alexander grinned.

This was fun!

PART THREE: TURNAROUND

CHAPTER THIRTEEN

TAHOE HAD been magnificent, if he said so himself. Tahoe had been perfect. Tahoe could not have been better if Alexander had written, cast and directed it. Even though it started out badly and got worse. In the first place, Alexander took the wrong clothes, and because he felt himself to be right (although he was obviously wrong) and because he hated the kind of Hollywood gesture that would have allowed him to have proper wardrobe flown up to Reno and then driven over to the lake by messenger, he stood his ground in the clothing of his choice and won out magnificently.

If he said so himself.

What got him into trouble at first, he reasoned, was that during his lifetime he had never gotten around to taking the kind of vacation that would expose him to the circumstances of existence along the northwest shore of Lake Tahoe, and he just never happened to have visited the place. Summers, in his life, were for working, and skiing was not so much a winter sport as a way of getting the survivors of wrecked airplanes down out of the mountains. When Teresa di Veccio had invited him to join her in the cabin she was borrowing he had pictured a rustic retreat, perched up among the rocks, with forest, mountain and lake views. Perhaps a small dock with a rowboat tethered to it. His two suitcases contained lots of jeans, sweaters, plaid shirts, colorful tee shirts he wouldn't think of wearing in the city. Lots of wool socks. Boots and an old pair of loafers. A big pocket knife, in case they were attacked by bears.

They were, instead, attacked by suits and blazers. Alexander's pocket knife remained in his pocket. And the little cabin in the rocks had twenty rooms, three porches, sleeping accommodations for fifty people (a couple of the rooms were nothing more than fancy bunkhouses). There was a sauna for ten, more old stone fireplaces than Alexander bothered to count. But the lake, the forest and the mountains, were as imagined. The dock was a little larger than Alexander had envisioned, however, and had tethered to it a couple of speedboats, a sailboat and a large launch that looked a little like a floating streetcar.

And there were other guests, male and female. He was surprised by them because Teresa had said nothing. When she picked him up at the Reno airport she looked at his two suitcases and raised her eyes, but said nothing, and all the way over Mount Rose and around the Lake ("Let's take the scenic route!") they babbled like children. They hadn't seen each other for a while. Alexander thought they would be rolling through some countryside where on impulse they could pull the car over and make love among the Ponderosas, but it wasn't like that at all, the road was too wide, everything was too open, and there was far too much traffic.

There was so much traffic by the time they were beside the lake, that, once Alexander got over the beauty and size of it all, he was actually bored. They were in a big station wagon, Teresa behind the wheel, beautiful as ever and dressed in tight jeans and a plaid shirt, a wisp of hair down over her forehead. The traffic was terrible. They were stopped more than they were moving.

"Maybe we could get a bite to eat," he suggested.

"Oh, there's nowhere to eat along here," she said, even though they seemed to be passing restaurant after restaurant. True, all of them looked crowded and tacky. Now they were stopped beside a peewee golf course, a long stop, and Alexander was surprised to see a gigantic Buddha as one of the holes of the course, a plastic figure in the lotus position. You hit the ball into a hole in the base and it came out Buddha's mouth and landed in his lap, on a plate. Alexander watched several people do it.

"Isn't that awful?" Teresa said.

Finally they were past the crush, over a bridge by a dam, down a small private road that was nearly invisible from the main road, and in among the cabins of a very large compound, with massive cabins—no, you couldn't call them cabins—massive *structures,* with green roofs and natural wood sides and porches. Various cars were parked about, rugged-looking stuff, only a few Mercedes and sports cars.

"Home at last," Teresa said.

Carrying his suitcases, he followed her down a path to "Alta Verde"— their "cabin." As they came up onto the big wide front porch, in the shade of some really tall trees, Alexander saw a foursome playing bridge, and an older man with his feet out and his hat down over his eyes, apparently asleep. The foursome turned and waited expectantly, and so he put down his suitcases and went over to be introduced.

"Well, well, we've heard all about you," one of the men said politely, and he wondered if the guy meant "Boss Hellstrom" or "Teresa's Hollywood friend." Or both. They broke away with promises to see each other "at cocktails," and Teresa took him up to "his room."

"My room?" he said, looking around. There did not seem to be any of Teresa's things in the room. But she pressed up against him gently and murmured, "I'll be here, too, but I have a room of my own, it's so convenient," and they kissed fondly.

"I'm so damned glad to see you," he growled, his throat thickening. "goddamn it, I love you."

"I love you, my sweet man," she murmured into his chest.

"Close the door," he said thickly. "Never mind, I'll do it myself," and he closed the door and pushed her over onto the bed.

All too soon the passion was spent, and Alexander lay next to her listening to the sound of the wind in the trees. It was a good sound. He liked it. It was about the only thing he liked so far.

She told him what there was to do. Tennis, plenty of tennis. Swimming, sailing, hiking, bridge, drinking, dinners, backgammon, horseback riding . . .

"Sex," he said to her.

"Mmmm, sex with you . . ."

"That's all I want. I don't want to ride on any horse."

Then she helped him unpack and they had an argument. He had not brought his tennis clothes. He had not brought a dinner jacket. There were no suits in his luggage.

"I don't even have any jockey shorts," he said. "I thought we were going to rough it."

"You could send for your things." She indicated the telephone beside his bed. A telephone! He had told Willi he would be incommunicado!

He couldn't very well communicado Willi now and tell her to send up his tux and tennis gear.

"As far as I'm concerned," he said, "there's no telephone there, and there are no tennis courts outside."

"Well, I have a date to play in an hour, and so do you."

Alexander detected a petulant note. "You won't be mad at me if I just pig around in these things, will you?" he asked her.

"I have some calls to make," she said.

"Calls?"

"You know I have a lot of interests," she said. "If you need me, I'll be in my room. Dial nine and somebody will bring you sandwiches and beer, if you like."

Of course she had calls, she was as rich as hell and had to keep track of her interests. Sandwiches and beer. Probably brought up by a maid in full French costume, opera hose, high heels and all. Alexander made the call, ordered a steak sandwich and a glass of milk from a vaguely Chinese voice, discovered a small private bathroom behind a door and took a shower. The food was there when he came out.

Teresa looked in on him, immaculate in her whites, about an hour later. "Why don't you have a nice nap?" she asked. "I'll wake you when I get back from Squaw Valley."

Instead, he went downstairs after he was sure she was well away, and out onto the porch. The bridge players were still at it, although the sleeping man was gone.

"Is there a rowboat I can use?" he said.

There was a small debate, and the Chinese servant was sent for. Yes, there was a rowboat under the building, he would have someone get it and put it into the water.

"I'll do it," Alexander said, and spent the afternoon happily wresting the little rowboat out from the raffle of masts, furled sail, canoe paddles and junk under one of the side porches, dragging it down to the lake, sinking it, finding oars and oar-locks, seeing that the caulking was good and wet, floating the boat, and finally, just before Teresa got back, having a little row for himself. He was hot, sweaty, covered with small bruises and stuck with splinters, and happy as hell. This was more like it. He rowed out onto the icy clear water, enjoying the pull of the oars, the slap of water against the boat.

Then she was there, on the dock, waving at him. He rowed swiftly and well up to her.

"Come for a ride!" he yelled. Expertly and truly he reversed oars and made the little boat swirl around and offer its rear seat to Teresa.

"Oh, I'd love to," she said, "but we have to dress for dinner. Come on, I found somebody your size who'll lend you something."

Alexander had a moment to notice that the little boat was slowly leaking, filling up from the long-dry cracks in her bottom and sides. He would sink her overnight, and by tomorrow, she'd float like an angel. And then he lost his temper.

"I won't wear another man's clothes," he said ominously, in the voice he used to frighten gangsters and bankers.

"Oh, *shit!*" Teresa said and marched back to the "cabin."

"Oh, shit, yourself," Alexander said softly to the afternoon air.

BUT IT was only at cocktails and dinner that Alexander's wardrobe made him conspicuous. There was something almost every night requiring clothes, but he could have simply not gone. Teresa was prepared for him to behave this way, and so he didn't. Charm was the secret. Enough charm and you could show up naked, with cabalistic signs painted on your body, and people would forgive you.

Alexander made eyes at the women, treated the men as if he would like nothing better than to go into combat with them, told a lot of wonderful Hollywood stories, and generally acted like a sweetheart, if he did say so himself. Teresa had to forgive him.

It did not seem to be such a crime to wear a big woolly sweater to a lakeside cocktail party when everybody else was chilly and crowding around the open fire, and so he won them over almost completely. There were a few grouses, from old farts whose money had come from the dirty ragged miners of '49 or from the sundries and railroad pirates who followed, but in general, the "Tahoe crowd" turned out to be pretty nice people. Alexander wished them well.

He arose each morning and took his little rowboat out onto the lake, nothing violent, just a row before breakfast, and on the third morning wondered why he felt so extremely good. The nights with Teresa were of course magnificent, but there was something lying underneath the surface, some great pleasurable bubble which had yet to burst on his consciousness. It had something to do with Teresa. Of course he loved her, that was not it. Something that was about to be. But what?

Parts of the day were pretty good, too. Teresa had a full schedule, as if she were still in the city, but she had enough free time (or was it planned?) for the two of them to grab a car or Jeep and ride off into the mountains together, babbling about everything under the sun and fucking out on the rocks beneath the tall trees. Still, there was something to happen, some great event about to take place. But what?

When he finally did consent to play tennis, wearing his bathing suit, a narrow slip of blue fabric that barely covered his enlarging buttocks ("You can't drive a spike with a tack hammer!") he was a welcome addition to the courts. Alexander played a mean, hard game, and the local players were all pretty much used to each other. It took three days of hard tennis to find out where he fit in. They played on courts from Squaw Valley to the Tahoe Tavern, singles, mixed doubles and men's doubles, and Alexander became better known for his serve than his wardrobe. And best of all, there turned out to be three locals, at least three, all millionaires (although they did not think of themselves that way) who could clean his clock. At one time, tennis had been important to Alexander and he had played daily, thought about his game, dreamed about his game, but now he played only three or four times a week. sometimes even less. The three millionaire amateurs he enjoyed playing with most were in the same age group and situation as Alexander, all bemoaned their lost youth and dying game, and all played like animals.

These matches drew huge crowds, they were serious business, and he often forgot to wonder what it was his secretly joyful heart was concealing from him.

One evening, there was a dinner, as usual, this time at the home of a Sacramento publisher, and Alexander, as usual, showed up in jeans and a sweater. People had stopped even looking askance at him by now, but to his great delight, the three tennis players he was *sure* could beat him in the long run, showed up in their informal clothes, slacks and open shirts under tennis sweaters, and the four of them got royally drunk, tried to take out the sailboat tethered in front of the place, sank it and had to be rescued. That was maybe the best of the dinner parties, but the next time he saw his drinking companions they were back in their regular evening wear.

But all friends, fast friends, and many promises to get together "down below," as the real world was called.

And then it was Alexander's last day. He and Teresa were alone on a side porch, in the shade. They had just kissed, and a Steller's jay, a big blue bird with a black head and crest, hopped along the porch rail toward a nut dish. As Alexander watched the jaybird, he knew:

He was not going to ask Teresa to marry him.

He did not want to live among these people. Even half the time, even a quarter of the time, even a week at a time. And he knew he could never get Teresa away from them. It was a different world, a different life. Alexander was not even sure he had met all the people staying in the same building. He did not want to. They would be polite, they would be rich, from San Francisco or the East, they would exert enormous power, but it was not Alexander's kind of power. Alexander got down and wrestled in the mud compared to these people.

The joy this caused was because he recognized that he was not, after all, just another jerk searching for respectability. He had been afraid of that, and afraid that Teresa appealed to him so much because she *was* so respectable.

No, it was actually love.

Alexander beamed proudly at her. "Let's go to Los Angeles together," he said.

The jaybird hopped over closer to the nut dish and cocked his head.

"Oh, I can't," she said.

"But you must," he said affectionately. "I'm not through with you."

"Then stay a few days. Can't you call your office?"

"Time is money," he said.

"You'll be at the office and I'll be stuck alone. There's no one in Los Angeles this time of year."

They negotiated, amid kisses and complaints. Finally it was agreed that Teresa would come down after the following weekend, but only for a few days. Then back to New York.

The jaybird pounced. The nut dish fell off the railing onto the porch and broke. The jawbird squawked and flapped away, and Alexander gave a big, happy laugh.

For months now, he had been suppressing the desire to ask her to marry him. It would have been the worst possible marriage for them both, and Teresa was smart enough to know this, and enough in charge of herself to refuse him. And now he didn't even have to ask her.

"My dear Teresa," he said.

"My darling Alexander," she said.

They held a farewell party for him, and everyone dressed his way. It was sort of a costume party, each one dressing in his or her version of tacky. It was great fun, but Alexander somehow felt sorry for them. Many of them, he was sure, woke up in the morning with the dreadful fear that they were of no use to anyone, and all that kept them from having nothing to do was strict adherence to a schedule. Tennis, lunch, cocktails, extramarital affair, nap, cocktails, opera, dinner, drunk and to bed.

Alexander vastly preferred the scumballs of Hollywood, with their outrageous manners, disgusting perversions, unruly egos and uncontrollable behavior.

Poor Teresa. If she only knew what he was really like.

CHAPTER FOURTEEN

"TERESA, MAY I introduce Richard and Elektra?"

They were all pleased to meet each other. The meeting was taking place in the Polo Lounge of the Beverly Hills Hotel, where Teresa had taken a room. Rick at last saw the woman Boss had been talking about for weeks, and what he saw did not agree with what Hellstrom had described. Not at all. Did not agree with what he had heard about her, either. Italian countess, very highly placed in Eastern society, wealthy, intelligent and beautiful. Oh, beautiful, yes, nothing like Elektra, but a wonderful pouting lip and eyes as big and deceptive as a cat's. A real high-tone bitch with that uppity Eastern cant to her voice.

Also she gave Rick the eye. There was no question about it. Boss was red-faced and happy, sitting there telling stories about their time at Lake Tahoe, and this bitch was making it clear she'd like to fuck Rick at the first possible opportunity. Elektra didn't seem to notice anything. She sat laughing at Hellstrom's jokes and stories and shoveling food into her face. And here came Kerry Dardenelle and Peter Wellman from the bar, Kerry already a little smashed and Wellman's *darshan* glowing. More introductions, and they made room for the extra two, Rick conscious that every eye in the room watched their table.

Kerry took over the conversation at once, saying that they could only stay a moment, and then staying right through lunch, having drinks brought and babbling about all the horror of location in West Texas, where the two of them had been making a picture about life and love on a modern cotton farm, Texas-style. Kerry was terribly funny, as he always was, but Rick noticed a tremor in his hand and heavy deep circles under his eyes. Kerry worked as hard as he drank, and after a picture he was likely to disappear for a couple of months, some said into a hospital, others said into the tropics where he had his own island. Rick wanted both of them for his picture, but that was Boss Hellstrom's job.

Rick watched Teresa out of the corner of his eye. Would she give Peter Wellman the look? Peter was considered one of the handsomest men in the world, although a bit short at five six, almost an inch shorter than Rick. But he did not see anything happen, and when, from time to time, Teresa would look in his direction, there it would be, intact, that catlike invitation to get under the building and screw.

Frankly, it made him sweat with desire. He could almost smell her, he *could* smell her, he wondered what would happen if he brushed his hand against the inside of her thigh under the table. He looked over at Elektra. She was looking at Peter Wellman with undisguised interest. Wellman sat with half a drink, picking up bits of food here and there with a cocktail toothpick, laughing when the punch lines came and generally behaving like the star he was.

From the other tables it must look as if we're having just the most wonderful time, as befits our station in life, Rick thought. Kerry was now describing falling off one of the huge forklifts used to haul around these gigantic pallets of cotton, and they all laughed heartily, and everyone at the other tables cringed from being left out of the joke—see, they are rich and famous and funny and having the best time, is there no justice? Why don't they have ulcers and overweight and bad breath and sore egos and black rotting consciences?

Ha ha, well, too bad for you! They have more fun than anybody, and they don't mind shoving your nose in it.

"*Garçon!* A little more white wine and cracked crab!"

There was a television producer Rick had known a bit ago, staring at them from his own table of sycophants, ill-concealed venom in his eyes. Rick waved to him, winked, just to see the venom turn to a sweetly grin, eyes brighten with hope, the body half-rise in its seat, only to drop back down, disappointed by Rick's failure to wave "come on over and meet the gang!"

Somebody's gopher was going to have his ass ripped off that afternoon, Rick thought without charity.

Elektra caught his eye and nodded in the subtlest way toward Teresa di Veccio. Elektra's expression said much, with little apparent to an outsider. She had seen what Rick had seen. Not the flirtation, but the bitch quality. Elektra's sleepy eyes said, "Whew, what a bitch, huh?" and Rick signalled back, "Uh-*huh!*"

Was Teresa aiming at Wellman? Didn't seem so. Rick still had the inside track. There it was again, just a passing glance as her eyes went from Kerry across to Alexander for an intimate smile, pausing only long enough to plant one tiny erotic dart into Rick. *I promise,* it said, *I promise to make you feel as you've never felt before!*

Everybody at the table laughed, Rick included, although he hadn't paid attention to the story.

The luncheon party broke up in front of the hotel as they all waited for their cars to be brought around. Kerry and Wellman got away first, but not before Kerry had taken Rick aside, and with his pouched and unhealthy-looking eyes shifty under Rick's gaze, asked if Rick could get him some cocaine.

"We just need a l'il bit for a party," he said.

"Gee, I'll ask around," Rick lied.

"Are you going to be on the lot this afternoon? I'll be in my office." Kerry maintained offices at Fox, Universal, the Burbank Studios and Paramount, as well as at Hellstrom's studio.

"If I don't call you, that means nothing's happening," Rick said. He did not want to middle coke for Kerry or anybody else in the business. All it led to were midnight phone calls and a damaged reputation. Here came his Mustang, and Rick was amused to see how everyone wanted to hold the door open for Elektra.

"Oh, let me ride with you," Teresa said. "I'll sit in back. I want to ask Elektra some questions."

It was fine with everybody. Alexander said cheerfully, "I'll see you later in my office," and kissed her goodbye. Rick held the seat forward and Teresa ducked around him and brushed her body against him and smiled up hot enough to fry his brains.

They drove down the circular drive, and waited at the light. Elektra touched his hand on the gearshift briefly, as if to say, "I understand," and turned around in her seat to talk to Teresa. They babbled about clothes for the ten minutes it took to get to the lot. At the gate, Teresa leaned forward, her head just behind his, and said hello to Charlie, shook his hand, and you should have seen his face redden as he chuckled and waved and saluted them through. He hadn't even looked at Rick.

They drove around the Administration Building and Rick put his car under the tree reserved for him, not twenty feet from the back entrance to the building, a real prestige spot.

"What are you girls going to do this afternoon?" he asked politely. He thought they were going to watch some picture called *Headhunter!* about a man who sneaks through the night in this small town and beheads various people.

But no. Teresa, in her purring voice, took hold of Elektra's hand, and said to Rick, "Is there anyplace the three of us can go? I've had a passion for you both all through lunch."

She leaned forward and kissed Rick on the mouth, soft and moist, promising, a touch of tongue to his lips. Then she smiled up at him and turned and gave Elektra a kiss on the mouth, a deeper kiss, tongues engaged fully, her tiny hand on Elektra's neck.

Rick could see Elektra's one open eye, looking at him. "We could go to Errol Flynn's apartment," he said thickly.

"Ooh, that would be simply wonderful," said the Countess di Veccio.

Elektra responded by kissing Rick softly and saying shyly, "I'm kinda horny, too, I guess."

Rick's heart swelled in his chest. He started the engine of the car again and they drove slowly and carefully down the dark street between sound studios, twisting and turning until they came to the apartment. They were quiet in the car until Rick turned off the engine again, and then Teresa said, "I can't wait," and in they went.

Rick had been to bed with two girls before—once with three—but he had never gone through anything like this. Usually the girls competed for his attention, catered to him, spending all their efforts in pleasing him, and so there was a slight air of the track meet about the whole business. But Teresa, my God, she seemed to want to suck up all the sex in the world, to have it all again, to use them both as puppets in her dance of love.

By the time Rick had the lights adjusted and the music on, the girls were both naked on the bed, entwined, Teresa sucking noisily on Elektra's breasts.

He had seen Elektra with women before, at the orgies that used to be held up above Sunset at the home of Margo Liston, the orgies that lasted several years, with only two- or three-day breaks when Margo had a commercial or went out of town. In those days if Margo hadn't fucked your old lady you felt out of things. It's only sex, and it makes the guy hotter than blazes to see, a lot more erotic than seeing some big dude crawl on top of her. Rick had been to bed with a man and a woman, but it had been under the politest of circumstances—the other man always kept hands off, and they played it straight heterosexual, letting the girl blow each of them in turn.

But this was different. Elektra's eye bulged from desire and she waved frantically for Rick to join them, as Teresa's tongue licked her body and her fingers kneaded Elektra's breasts.

"Come to me, baby," she said.

"I will," he said, but he wanted to watch for a while. It was making him hornier than he had been in a long time, it was *evil*, the way this bitch went after what she wanted. But at last he crawled between them and found himself deep in a pleasure he had only guessed was possible.

They were still making their endless triangle on the bed, shiny with sweat and the stickiness of their juices, when Alexander walked in.

On Alexander's face was a prepared expression of rage that changed at once to amazement as he stared unbelieving at Elektra, and stammered out, "Wha—what the hell are *you* . . ."

They stopped. Rick at once understood he had betrayed Alexander, a thought which simply hadn't occurred to him up to now, as events flowed and Rick floated along. He looked at Teresa, whose lazy smile up at the baffled man included as much affection as contempt.

"Oh, Alexander," she said. "I'm so sorry you had to . . ."

"Shut up," he said without looking at her. He was still staring at Elektra. The radio took this moment to play "As Time Goes By."

"Aw," Elektra said. "Pull down your pants and join us."

"What?" said Alexander.

"Don't be such a stuck-up," she said.

"As long as you've caught us," Teresa said, and went back to caressing Elektra's shiny breast. The nipple was pink and hard from being bitten, and there were the beginnings of purple bruises.

"I'm sorry, Boss," Rick said.

"It's my fault," Alexander said. "I should have knocked." With a hopeless smile he said, without looking at Rick, "You're late for a meeting."

But that could not have been why Alexander had come down here. Rick's car was in front, he must have known Rick was inside. That look on his face. What had he expected to find?

Then he was gone.

Teresa said, "Oh, don't worry about him. He just doesn't understand about sex."

"What is there to understand?" Rick said.

"I have to be so careful with him," she said. "I love the man, but he's not . . . *sexual*. The way we are."

Lazily, and in that Up East voice, Teresa told them about having to duck and dodge around Alexander in order to fuck waiters, elevator boys, gardeners, chauffeurs, store clerks, bus drivers, masseurs, tennis partners, strangers and friends. Elektra listened to this disquisition on nymphomania as if Teresa were talking about her art collection, nodding politely and stroking Teresa's hair with one hand and Rick's thigh with the other.

As for Rick, he was disgusted with himself. He was not free enough to see things Elektra's way, and yet not enough of a hypocrite to pretend to be upset. He knew he had betrayed (that word again!) Alexander, but he didn't feel bad about it. He knew there was no end to the trouble to come, but at the same time he still couldn't believe that Alexander could be so naive about Teresa. *Whore* was written honestly across her face, along with *breeding, intelligence* and *arrogance*.

He got up and took a shower and when he came out the two girls were upside-down on each other and did not even sense that he was there. He dressed in the living room and got Joyce on the phone.

"I've been off the planet," he said. "What's new?"

"You missed a meeting," she said.

So did you, he thought, but said, "Has the Boss called?"

The Boss had called, once. Rick said he would be in the office in ten minutes.

"Oh, you're *down there?*" Joyce said in a hungry voice. Rick had brought her once to the apartment. Joyce had loved it, and was not a little upset that Elektra sometimes spent the night there with Rick. "I see it as our place," Joyce had said, which was not how Rick saw it at all.

He hung up. There were little murmurs coming from the bedroom. With a heavy sigh, he left the place. He had hardly expected to feel like *this,* so soon after *that.*

But he did.

RICK MADE a lot of phone calls that afternoon. He spoke to his agent, his business manager and the attorney who ran Endless Unicorn Company for him. The information he got was disturbing. It was going to be difficult, very difficult, to pull away from Alexander Hellstrom if it should become necessary. There had been "financial interbreeding," and the investors, under the guidance of their management team, were not as easily swayed by Rick's intuitions, now that they had a handful of a major studio.

"What if I cashed out?" Rick asked his business manager, Sherman Frieberg.

"You mean you personally cash out?"

"That's right."

"After the tax consequences?"

"Cash money."

Something under a million dollars. Probably more like half a million.

The trouble was, everybody liked the program, and this was no time to rock the boat.

As David Novotny put it, "What's the matter, Richard?"

Boy, Man and Girl was heating up and Peter Wellman's people were enthusiastic about the project and working with Rick's team. *The Lady in the Lake* was virtually bought, for a healthy whack of change, and everyone was pleased and proud to be associated with the Chicano project, now called *The Pickers,* even though no one expected it to be the financial blockbuster the other two projects were shaping into. But nonetheless it was a project you could take pride in.

So why the panic calls?

"Suppose, between you and me, that Boss Hellstrom took a sudden dislike to me?" Rick asked David.

"What the hell have you done?" David wanted to know.

"Nothing. But you know how it is."

"Richard, never bullshit your agent."

Rick sighed and told David a scrubbed-up version of the afternoon's events. It made him sweat, even though he left Elektra out of it, and only hinted that Teresa had been the aggressor.

"Can't you keep that thing in your pants?" David said with some irritation. "You could literally fuck yourself out of a pretty good deal."

"What's done is done," Rick said.

"Well, let me put it to you this way, young man. If the Boss decides to dump on you, you're going to have to fight. Everything's wired together. Your investors are not going to be happy that all the money we've spent up to now can be flushed down the toilet through your indiscretion. Their faith in you is all that keeps you in the driver's seat, as you well know, and their money is all that keeps you on this lot, at the front table, as it were."

"What can he do?"

"Stand in your way," David said coldly.

After hanging up, Rick sat quietly for a few minutes. He could walk out this afternoon, and land on his feet with over half a million tax-free American dollars. He saw himself on a lonely windswept road, the bag of money at his feet.

It ground his guts to think of quitting. What would he do with the half million? Open a chain of laundromats? Go back to square one and make another low-budget picture?

Half a million wouldn't even buy the house he was living in.

It made his skin crawl to think about being poor again.

So his skin crawled and his guts ground. He hiccupped sourly.

The buzzer buzzed and he almost jumped out of his chair. "Yes, Joyce?"

"Alexander Hellstrom on one."

Rick almost, almost but not quite, said, "I'm in a meeting."

"Hello, Boss," he said.

He heard Hellstrom's deep rich voice, almost in a chuckle: "If we put that little scene in a movie, they'd laugh us out of the business. Sorry about playing the heavy. I've got my wheels under me now."

But that was not why he had called. He had just been on the telephone to New York and everyone there liked the way *Boy, Man and Girl* was shaping up.

"I think we should strike while the iron's hot," he said, "and tie up Kerry and Peter and your friend Dael Tennyson. With them and your screenplay we can really go to the bank. The timing's just right. Kerry'll be through cutting his Texas pastoral, Peter will be available—by the way, what's the availability of Dael Tennyson?"

"We're safe on that," Rick lied. He would go see Dael as soon as possible and hogtie him.

The rest of the conversation had to do with the production department and Rick's presentation of a budget to the studio. Budgets often broke the backs of promising projects, but Hellstrom didn't seem worried. "Hell, that's my specialty," he told Rick. He truly did not seem bothered about the afternoon's doings. Rick decided to test him:

"Where's Teresa?" he asked, after they had gotten through the budget discussion.

"She's right here," Alexander purred.

"Then you're really not mad."

"These things happen," he said.

But the next phone call was not so pleasant. Jose had been trying to reach Rick all day, could they have a meeting?

"What for?" Rick asked.

It seemed that the Committee for the Screenplay of *The Pickers* had just ejected Jose unanimously. Except for Jose's vote, of course. The *Committee?*

JOSE'S TALE was a sad one. They sat in Rick's office in the late afternoon, drinking from beer bottles, Jose depressed and overwhelmed. His project was in danger of being cancelled, he knew, but he had to talk to somebody or burst.

"Somebody without a Spanish surname," he said with unaccustomed irony. Rick had always liked Jose, whose student thesis film at UCLA, *Tostada!* had won a lot of awards and attention for him. But that had been a few years ago. Jose's youth was deserting him as he broken-marched toward a project. Jose and Rick both believed there was a place for him in Hollywood, even though The System was corrupt and malicious.

But when The System came after him, it came from behind. Always an effective move when The System wants to break your balls.

Jose's own best friends were wrecking his movie.

Rick read over the five pages of treatment Jose had handed him, while Jose sat morosely sipping his Dos Equis. What had been a simple story about the classical themes to be found in the ordinary lives of produce workers—the passions, the family rivalries and hatreds, the madness of old age and the impetuosity of youth—was now, to be kind, a Marxist pamphlet. In a story entirely free of the presence of Gringos there were now Gringos aplenty, and each one of them eviler and stupider than the last. In this treatment nobody with a Spanish name did anything but get exploited. The end of the picture cried for bloody revolution.

"Good Christ," Rick said quietly. He dropped the pages onto his desk top and looked over at the miserable Jose.

"Yeah," said Jose. "There was just never a moment when I could tell them no. We were all in this together, see? Now I'm accused of greed, turning my back on my people and generally selling out to the lowest bidder."

"What about the old guy?" Rick asked. The man who had written the book.

"Oh, hell, he dumped us a long time ago. He's not the naive old guy I thought, damned intelligent, he's read everything in every library on the West Coast. He called the Committee a bunch of assholes and went to Fresno."

"Are they being paid?" Rick asked.

Jose hung his head. The Committee pooled his salary as director with the stipulated salary for writer on the project. But of course officially one of them was listed as the writer, and Jose cashed his own checks and divvied up.

"Okay," Rick said. "Here's what you got to do. Get rid of them. Clear up the financial mess. *You* bat out a treatment, a step outline anyway, from the original work. You get all this done in a couple of weeks and I'll try to save the picture. I won't talk to the Boss about it until then. Okay?"

"I don't know if I can fire them," Jose said.

"You have got to," Rick said. "If I do it, you go with them, and with you a lot of my money. Now, get off your dead ass."

As if on cue, Joyce buzzed Rick.

"Dael Tennyson on three," she said.

Jose got up, pained, like an old man, and hobbled out of the room, after a quick handshake and hug from Rick, who held the door open for him. Sigh. That would be the last of him.

"Hello, dear boy, how's everything at Hellstrom's Hellhole?" Dael's light voice was a relief.

"What are you doing for dinner? I want to get you loaded and signed. This deal is starting to cook."

Dael laughed lightly. How wonderful to be a young rising movie star, but so accustomed to the pace that it doesn't blow you out. Dael was a member of a show business family, many generations in the business. He was trained from birth to be a performer, his family delighted that he could sing and dance as well as act, but not surprised. They were all marvellously talented, father, mother, brothers, uncles, grandfather, all the way back into vaudeville and beyond, a pure strain of theatricality that probably descended from the chimpanzees or even before. A troupe of performing amoebas, Rick thought, oddly, as he and Dael tried to find a time to meet.

"The trouble is, Grandpa's here, the old fart . . . hey, why don't you come out to the ranch?"

"For dinner, or should I load up in advance?"

"Aw, grab Elektra and come out."

The ranch was north of Los Angeles, as easy to reach by the Coast Highway as the Ventura Freeway, and was quite close to the beach. It had been closer, but Dael's father, Eric Tennyson, had sold off several of the beach lots for a great deal of money, and the Tennysons contented themselves with one beach house for the whole family, five miles from the ranch proper. They raised horses and performers, they hunted and fished all over the world, they made friends everywhere they went and they didn't try to win the employment sweepstakes. Dael himself was content to make a picture a year. He had nominal representation by David Novotny, but what he had most was the Tennyson family (renamed from Smith by his great-grandfather, who felt they couldn't compete properly with the other Smiths in vaudeville) and the Tennyson family took care of its own.

Rick hoped he could get Dael's handshake that very night. The handshake would do it. The Tennysons kept their word.

People who raised racehorses were class to Rick. He loved the long acres of low white fence that surrounded their property, the neatness of the stables, the early-morning beauty of the animals themselves and the quiet expectation of the workouts . . . he knew he got all this from old movies, but he still felt it, and the Tennyson ranch *was* all those things, and the Tennysons didn't get it from old movies. Eric Tennyson's father, the grandpa who was visiting them from his own home, an apartment in New York City, whose name was a synonym for actor, old Clay Tennyson, had for years dutifully wasted all his money at the racetracks near New York and in the bookie joints around Times Square, but when he had first come to Southern California he had made so much money he desperately threw some of it into real estate and then forgot about it as he went back to Broadway.

Eric developed the property and bought the first horse. Now the old man reserved his wagers for family animals.

Rick followed the white picket fencing around the curve of the road and up toward the cluster of buildings and trees, the red roofs of the buildings just catching the late evening sunlight. Rick had not grabbed Elektra, in fact, he didn't know where she was. But it didn't matter, as long as she wasn't with Teresa. Rick liked Teresa, but he didn't want Elektra running around with her. He would drive down the Coast Highway to the beach house tonight, instead of trying to get back to town, and she would be there or not.

He had not been jealous of sharing her. It had all happened so quickly he hadn't had time to take stock of any feelings. And now he couldn't think about personal matters. He had to nail down Dael Tennyson, and it was not going to be easy.

RICK WAS admitted to the house by Dael's mother Kathryn and left to himself in the big low living room while a small boy was sent to find Dael. There were people all over the house, of all ages, busy with what they were doing, and there were at least six dogs, which had gathered around his legs in friendly fashion when he had gotten out of his car, and escorted him to the door, where Kathryn told them to stay outside, but they were not offended and came in anyway.

Although the Tennysons were obviously very rich, the house had a worn, used look, a banged-up look, Rick decided, that came from having a lot of boisterous children and animals knocking things over, spilling, shedding and breaking. There was a Picasso lithograph over the fireplace, under glass, and even up there the glass seemed to have a lick of dried saliva across its lower portion.

There went Eric Tennyson, movie star hero of the fifties, tall, lanky, grizzled, in dusty jeans and a dirty white tee shirt, an oily automobile part in his filthy greasy hand. "Where the hell is that roll of paper towels?" he asked the house in general, and soon Rick saw him heading out the front door with his roll of paper towels; a wink and a grin for Rick. Dogs and children came and went on various errands, and the smell of cooking came from the noisy kitchen. Not the homely smells of country cooking, but the rich dizzying odor of garlic frying in butter, and Rick felt a sudden leap of appetite.

Pretty soon Kathryn came out from the kitchen and said, "I think you'll find them out back."

Rick went along outside and around to the courtyard behind the house, where several men and boys surrounded a crippled automobile, its hood and trunk gaping open. Dael was among them, dirty and greasy from head to foot. He spotted Rick.

"Rick Heidelberg!" he shouted. Others looked up, friendly, and then back at the car. It was getting gloomy out here, even with the spotlights, and Rick wondered, not for the first time, what it was about automobiles that so fascinated a certain type of man so that they would stand around out here filthy dirty in the dark and talk about transmissions or carburetors and feel comfortable and satisfied that they were doing something. Rick himself cared nothing for the internal workings of his car, as long as the car performed. If it didn't he would pay to have it fixed. None of this standing around shifting from foot to foot talking about it.

"Rick's here to sell me the moon," Dael said to the group.

But it was not until after dinner and the family show that they could talk about business. Dinner was wonderful, plenty of everything, a big table for the grown-ups and two little tables for children. Dael's niece and nephew, called "the twins," were not at any of the tables, but were having their dinners in bed, watching television, because they had worked that day shooting a commercial in Santa Monica. Everybody in this family worked, even if the work was only indirectly show business. Eric's brother, called Stooge in the family but hopefully named Drew at birth and now seated at the end of the table scrubbed as clean as possible, had been Eric's lighting and stunt double for years, and when Eric stopped getting that much work, Stooge kept at it, doing stunts, until Dael became popular, and then became Dael's double. Kathryn had spent twenty years on the stage. Dael's brother Eric Jr. (not present) had been a television actor from the time he was ten years old, and was now working on a picture in England. *His* wife, the mother of the twins, had been a civilian and was now serving little red new potatoes ripe with garlic butter to Rick.

"Will you have another of these fine chops?" asked the grand old man, Clay Tennyson, in his deep voice. He presided at the head of the table and monopolized the conversation with stories about New York, which he was again threatening to leave. No one seemed to believe him, but the stories were funny and there was much laughter.

For dessert they had strawberry shortcake, giant helpings for everyone, and the old man waxed scornful.

"Strawberry shortcake at this time of year! My God!"

"I notice you're eating yours," Dael said.

"How do you stay so thin, Grandpa?" asked Stooge, who was making do with a cup of coffee. "I have to break my ass dieting to stay at one eighty-five."

"No one cares," Dael said with a puckish grin. "I'll just look a little fatter in the action shots."

Pandemonium from the nearby children's table as dogs overwhelmed a child and snatched her chop. Barking, crying, running around. Rick was the only one who seemed at all disturbed by this. He knew he would not have lasted a weekend in this kind of atmosphere, but still he envied them. They seemed to be a real family.

And after dinner on this particular night, they were having a family show, and Rick was honored to have been invited to watch. Not that it was private, but it was not a part of their lives that was for sale. There were plenty of things they would and could do for publicity—the horses for example—but the family shows were private.

With everyone gathered in the living room there must have been fifteen people there, all Tennysons except Rick and Brenda, the woman who helped Kathryn around the house. They sat in the semidarkened room and watched each other perform. A little girl danced to a record, her tutu white, her shoes black, gravity on her face along with the sweat of concentration. The family applauded her turn enthusiastically, and she ran to her great-grandfather to sit in his lap and hide her face from the applause. Then Dael's younger brother Philip, thirteen and redly pimpled, played his guitar and sang a song he had written. The song was awful, Rick thought, and the guitar playing not exactly up to family standards, but the applause was long and enthusiastic. Rick caught Dael's eye from across the room and saw, or thought he saw, an acknowledgment of the fact that Philip might not make it in show business. But Dael applauded as loudly as anyone, perhaps not quite as loudly as Kathryn, who was sitting next to Rick, but with great enthusiasm.

Then the quartet. Dael playing cello, Eric and Clay violins and Stooge on the French horn. Here was a surprise: to Rick's ear, all of them were excellent, symphony grade, especially Stooge. It sounded as if they were playing something by Mozart, and the long complex French horn parts were shatteringly beautiful. It was a formal piece of music, but the quartet worked the house, making eye contact with everybody and looking as if the music were being drawn up from their very souls. It was quite wonderful, *Mozart mit schmaltz,* and Rick had to get a Kleenex when they were done.

Then it was Grandpa's turn. Leaving the tiny ballerina in his big chair he went to the piano, spent a bit of time adjusting the gooseneck lamp so that it would illuminate his hands and not his face, and began to play, his long fingers light on the keys. He said, "I'm going to play a couple of Cole Porter tunes, just play them straight, the way they were written. We're so used to his stuff we forget sometimes the musical qualities."

Rick decided after a few minutes of listening to the simple notes of "Night and Day" that old Clay could have made it as a pianist, and then he lost himself in the music. The old man seemed to add nothing to the tune and seemed, by the lift of his shoulders and the tilt of his head, to be deeply moved. He finished and played a few quick little notes to prevent applause, a practiced old cocktail lounge piano man, and said, "Cole was a great one . . . most arrogant son of a bitch who ever lived, brave as a chow dog . . . this is called 'Miss Otis Regrets!' Old Clay played the tune, and in a voice pitched higher than his own, sang the homosexual lyric for gentle laughs. As he was singing it, there was a bustle in the back of the room, and Rick saw a woman in shadow move forward and sit down somewhere behind Rick, quiet, not interrupting the performance. It was a campy comic song, but the old man knew where to take it, and somehow the bitchy note of a refusal became a tragic admission and Clay was an old swish at an old piano making an age-old cry to the heavens.

His eyes twinkled in the wave of applause, and how he had done it, how he had turned the lamp to catch his eyes, Rick knew not.

"Thank you," he said, "thank you very much. Joanne, come up here, honey . . ." and the woman who had come in during the last song rose and went past Rick, kissed her grandfather and turned toward the audience. It was Dael's cousin, who worked under the name of Joanne Clay, an old hand on the Hollywood scene. She leaned against the piano, and after a whispered conversation with Clay and some adjustment of the gooseneck lamp, swung into "You Go to My Head," her voice torchy and deep, her tempo sexual. Rick hadn't ever heard her sing before, she had certainly never sung in a picture, and again, here it was, these terribly talented people could have made it big in lots of ways, this was no conglomeration of lucky-break artists, this was a gene pool of sheer talent.

Rick felt a wave of hopelessness pass through him like a ghost.

After the torch song and sustained applause and laughter, Dael brought up the lights from the switch by the kitchen door, and a generalized babble surrounded Joanne. When did she get in? How had the trip been? Had they rapped?

From the general tenor of it all, Rick concluded that Joanne had been away making a picture and had arrived unexpectedly. When, after a while, they were introduced, she met Rick's eye with frank curiosity.

"He's here to sell me the moon," Dael said.

It was decided to send the children all to bed, and the brandy bottle came out. The brandy had been passed around once or twice before, and so this round was greeted with mellow enthusiasm.

"Well, Joanne," the old man said, "sit down and enjoy yourself. Dael, give us a song, won't you?"

Dael arranged himself on a stool in front of the piano and Stooge dimmed the lights. Grandpa stayed on the piano bench, totally out of the light, and Rick marvelled. Even just among themselves they controlled that light. The gooseneck was tilted now, and showed Dael in high-key silhouette. Philip handed him the guitar, and Dael sang one of his own tunes, "Long Sweet Love." Rick watched Joanne out of the corner of his eye. She was extraordinary close up, wrinkled and tired, over-tanned and dry-haired, eyes that could sentence ten thousand people to death or glisten with mother love, a firm amused mouth and a chin both strong and feminine.

Rick wanted to make a pass at her.

True, she was older than he was, and probably stronger. And smarter and richer. And married. Where was her husband, Dillingham the Rich Boy? Everybody in the world knew they were happily married. Was everybody wrong, as usual? It gave Rick hope to think so.

Dael sang about passionate young love, and Rick plotted hotly against his cousin, the movie project utterly gone from his mind. Nothing could be done tonight, anyway, except let her know he wanted her. Then, if she decided to take him up on it, she would find a way. That was the good thing about a confident woman, she would find the way, and you did not have to make an asshole out of yourself.

Only once did their eyes meet during Dael's song, meet, lock for an intense moment and pass on. Rick had not put anything into his expression—it would already be there—and hers was unreadable, except for its duration. It seemed long, speculatively long, and Rick's heart leaped about in his chest.

Maybe!

As a guest in the house, Rick was politely asked if he would like to perform, and just as politely refused.

"I can't sing or anything," he said. "And even if I could I wouldn't, in front of such massive talent."

He made no attempt to catch Joanne's eye.

"Well, then," said Grandpa. "Shall we call it a night?"

"Grandpa," said Joanne, "I'd like to do a scene with you. Something meat-and-potatoes."

"How about Shakespeare?" the old man said with a sly grin.

"Yeah," said Eric, grinning himself. "I don't want to sit through Grandpa bellowing 'STELLA! STELLA!' again!"

The woman Rick decided he was falling in love with and the former king of the Broadway stage stood whispering together, and finally she turned to the house and said, "We'll do Macbeth and Lady Macbeth!"

Scattering of applause, and the audience sat back comfortably to watch these two performers take all the stops out of some of the most powerful scenes in the English language. Never did a brave man suffer such doubts, and never did a woman press her luck further. Rick was terrified by the thought of the bloody dead king offstage and the horrible powers this woman had over the confused warrior.

And then to break the mood, Macbeth sat at the piano and played "Over the Fence and Out."

The lights came up. More brandy was poured. Dael came over to Rick, who was still trying to pull himself up out of the terrifying experience.

"Time for our meeting," Dael said.

RICK FOUND himself facing six Tennysons, all sincere, all relaxed, all polite, sipping coffee or brandy and waiting for him to explain himself. Clay, Eric, Stooge, Kathryn, Joanne and Dael. Eric seemed to be in charge but everyone asked questions about the project, its financing, the intentions of the studio in regard to Dael's time during both shooting and a later promotional tour, Rick's role in the whole matter, and some particularly intense questions from Joanne about the plot of the picture and the other casting.

Up to now, Rick realized, he had been operating mostly on charm. But here in front of these people his charm was useless. These people were charm merchants. They knew all about charm. For a wild moment he thought of the great challenge: to charm these charmers on their own ground! To wrap them around his little finger and walk out of there with a commitment!

But no. He was not man enough. Or warlock enough. Or fool enough. He played it straight, and when he didn't know the answer to a question, he would say, "I don't know," and wait for the next. Finally, it came down to two things. The ending of the picture, which seemed, in Joanne's word, "flaccid," with the girl giving up her fling with Dael to go back to her "old man"—again, Joanne's words.

"Well," Rick said. "I'm willing certainly to listen to a better ending."

Old man Clay hadn't said much, but now he leaned forward with his big hands on his knees and intoned, "But the kids will want to see Dael get the girl, don't you think?"

Eric laughed. "And Peter Wellman's agent will want to see Peter get the girl."

Everyone had a good laugh, but nothing loosened up.

"That would seem to me to be a crucial point," Joanne said. "Naturally, Peter's people will tell him it doesn't do his image any good to lose the girl. Next you'll be asking him to play older parts."

"How close are you to signing Peter Wellman?" Kathryn wanted to know, and Rick had to look into those deep blue eyes and say he didn't know, pretty close, he guessed, the Boss was handling that end of things . . .

Kathryn looked at Eric and Eric looked kindly at Rick.

"Maybe we better have another meeting after Wellman's signed—hell, I'll give him a ring myself, he and Dael are good contrast . . ."

"And then you could work on that ending," Joanne said, and the meeting was over.

Tennyson, one. Heidelberg, zero.

Somewhere along the line tonight, Rick had failed some sort of test—or tests—and the Tennysons were not going to commit their leading money-earner to a project that might not serve his best interests, a project that might falter or collapse before getting on the screen, or worse, bomb in the theaters. For the first time Rick thought of his project in terms of failure and saw how it could be: investment of millions to put the thing together—both Wellman and Dael would have to be guaranteed their salaries no matter what else happened, and so would the director, whoever the hell he was going to be—and then it could all come tumbling down in squabbles over screenplay, budget, a million things.

The floor opened up and Rick stared down into the flames. "That first picture of his was great, but you know, the old story—he went commercial in a big way and flopped."

Flop. Like a dying chicken.

Cold sweat covered his body. Everyone could see it, even though they were talking about something else and not paying much attention to him. But that was only manners, they knew they had just killed his project.

And then Rick knew it. The project was dead.

What had the Boss said? "You nail down Dael Tennyson and we're on the way."

He had not nailed down Dael Tennyson. And they were not on the way.

He was frozen inside this thought when he noticed Dael looking at him, making a minute gesture that seemed to mean "Let's talk in the corner."

In the corner, Dael whispered, "You got any dope on you?"

"A jay for the road, why? You want to go outside?"

Dael winked, made a sign to Joanne, and the three found themselves out in the darkness by the cars, alone.

"Oh, good," said Joanne. "I wanted some dope pretty bad."

Rick pulled out his marijuana cigarette, lit it, and they passed it around silently. It was good stuff, of course, only the best for Rick Heidelberg.

"I guess the project is dead," he said. It didn't even hurt.

"Next time," Dael said.

"What did you want to make a cornball movie like that for in the first place?" Joanne asked.

"How come we're behind the barn smoking corn silk?" Rick wanted to say, but didn't. Joanne was standing right next to him, he could feel her warmth. Her eyes looked at his over the hot red coal as she inhaled.

"I know how it is," Joanne said with sympathy. "You get up to your ass in something, everybody around you tells you how good it is, nobody knows what the hell makes a hit, and so you find yourself with an armload of crap."

Crap. *Crap* ?

Yes, crap. Crapcrapcrap.

Rick laughed. "You're so right. Tell me, which test did I fail? Didn't I pet the dogs enough? Did I fail to get greasy out by the cars? Didn't eat enough helpings? Failed to applaud with sufficient vigor?"

Dael's teeth glittered in the darkness. "Naw, you smell terrible, that's all."

"Because I know fucking well you didn't have me out here just to kick my project to pieces. You would have gone for it if what?"

"You get Peter Wellman and watch our smoke," Joanne said without conviction.

"The hell with that. You and I all know this picture just died."

"Whoo," said Dael. "I'm going in and get some of them strawberries, if there's any left."

And he was gone. Rick handed the tiny roach to Joanne and she got a last puff of smoke out of it.

She was, what, five years older than Rick. He did not know, he only knew that this was his chance.

"Let's go for a walk, all right?"

"I'd like that," she said. "Down by the stables, I like the smell of horses."

They walked slowly under a row of pepper trees, not talking. Rick felt extraordinarily good. He felt *clean.* When they reached a gate at the end of the path under the trees, Joanne turned toward him and put her hands on his arms.

"I'm sorry, about my part in this," she said.

Rick didn't say anything, just leaned in and kissed her gently. She returned the pressure slightly and then moved back. This put her face in the light.

"Maybe we'd better not," she said.

"You're right," Rick said. Inside he was afire. Now if he could get her into his car. There was no place around there for them to go. Get her into the car. Talk awhile. Then drive down the road, anything, go to the all-night store for a quart of milk, just get off the premises.

"Walk me to my car?" he asked.

She took his arm and slowly they returned. Bodies touching. Rick felt like laughing wildly, but he kept his elation inside himself. Slowly, slowly, one step at a time, as if leading a lovely wild animal who can be spooked by sudden movement. He guided her to his car, and then said, "Let's talk, okay?"

He held the door open for her. Shyly she got in, and delicately he closed the door.

Rick walked around the car barely able to control himself. He wanted to jump and yell. The project was out of his mind now. All he could think about was Joanne.

He got in the driver's side, and with his door still open, kissed her. She responded shyly, wanting to be passionate but holding something back, some last trusting portion of her soul. He closed the door quietly and turned back to her. Her eyes glowed with a wondering and this kiss was deep and long, her lips wet and tender, her breathing growing deeper, her hands touching him, her smell in his nostrils.

"We better stop this," she said throatily.

"Let's drive down to the beach," Rick said, his own voice thickening.

"No," she said. They kissed again. Rick felt an urgency. She *must* know what she's doing!

"Please," he said.

"Maybe another time," she said, barely able to keep the passion out of her voice. She opened the car door. Rick almost grabbed it out of her hand and slammed it again, but didn't.

"Where are you going?" he begged her.

"Back to the house. You'd better come and say goodnight." He could not believe it.

Impossible.

But it happened. And zap! he was driving down the Coast Highway, alone, trying to accept that she had only been playing with him.

The Tennysons had nailed him, all right. The old one-two.

Wrecked his project and kicked him in the balls for good measure.

What kind of people *were* they?

His testicles ached throbbingly, as if in reply.

CHAPTER FIFTEEN

ALEXANDER SAT quietly listening to Dr. Fieldstone talk about how he had bruised his nipples painfully while body-surfing at Malibu and now wore a tank top to the beach. The good doctor, a man in his middle thirties and a general practitioner in the heart of Beverly Hills, made a fortune by calling on his practice in their homes or offices and by making himself available at any time of the day or night. He seemed very full of himself to Alexander, handsome, tanned, muscular, casually dropping famous names into his conversation without ever actually giving away any professional secrets. And he was good at his job, which he likened to that of a mechanic administering high-level pit stop repairs to his clientele so that they could get back out there on the track without a moment lost.

"I understand the Hollywood game," he said modestly, "because I'm the same myself. I work hard, play hard, sleep hard, and I give as good as I get."

Alexander sat quietly. If there was one thing he knew how to do, it was sit still and listen, his own emotions tucked away.

"To continue with the mechanical model," Dr. Fieldstone said abruptly, "think of what you put into yourself as fuel, and your innards as engine parts. Think of refined sugar products and alcohol as fast fuels." On he went, explaining the problems of aging and blood sugar in homely metaphors while Alexander half-listened and half-daydreamed about Teresa. It was because he was having trouble suppressing his rages, blind, sky-blackening rages, that he had summoned Dr. Fieldstone. The other night they had been making love out by the pool and in a moment of great passion he had grabbed her tiny neck in his hands and felt a delicious rush of pleasure at the thought of clamping down, crushing her throat, driving the life out of her squirming body just at the moment of orgasm.

She must have felt the power of his emotion.

"Do it!" she croaked, and her body writhed like a snake.

It was only a lifelong discipline over his emotions that kept him from sweet murder. And to murder Teresa di Veccio, even if he got away with it, would be to deprive himself of the only woman, apparently, who could inspire him to lovemaking. She was at once the sentence and the reprieve, and it was driving him crazy.

Now Dr. Fieldstone was telling him to quit drinking sugared soft drinks and to stop eating foods that contained refined sugar.

"Eat lots of protein, some fats, and get your carbohydrates from natural foods like orange juice. Go back to exercising every day, but don't try to break any records. And avoid caffeine."

"No medicine?" Alexander asked. What he had hoped for was some pill he could take, as Charlie Devereaux took his Inderal every day and seemed to be in great shape. "These emotional outbursts . ."

Dr. Fieldstone laughed lightly. "No medicine, unless you want to go around half-zizzed all day long. Just take care of your machine a little better. You're not hypoglycemic yet, my God, you should hear some of the things I hear . . ."

Alexander had not, of course, told him about the near-murder of Teresa.

"One director friend of mine, patient, really, lives on codeine while he's making a picture, gets 'em from Canada, calls 'em Royal Canadians, eats six or eight a day, has a couple of drinks, five or six cups of coffee and heads out for the set feeling pretty good. But then the picture's over and the pressure's off, and he starts to panic about possible addiction and comes to me for an easy way down the ladder. Well, there *ain't no easy way down the ladder,* as you must know, so he goes through a couple weeks of hell, drinking orange juice and dosing himself with gram after gram of Vitamin C. Then he's okay and can go into the cutting room, maintaining on beer. But one of these days, he's not going to make it off the codeine, and he's gonna come to me and ask my advice. Do you know what I'm gonna tell him?"

"No," said Alexander. He wanted very badly to tell Dr. Fieldstone to leave, please. But didn't. There must be a point to this story.

"I'm gonna tell him to move to Canada," Dr. Fieldstone said with a grin. He stood up and shook Alexander's hand. "I guess the moral of this tale is, this is no time to slacken up on your good habits. The more pressure you put on yourself the less you should rely on drugs or candy or booze, see what I mean?"

And then he was gone, and with a depressed sensation Alexander faced his afternoon's telephone calls. He had been neglecting business so badly he hadn't spent an afternoon in the screening room for a week, and he knew he was slipping behind, losing currency.

The trouble was, he couldn't just drop Teresa. He had gotten through the crisis of *that afternoon* strictly on automatic pilot, to use one of Dr. Fieldstone's metaphors, but for days he had been shaken, not by what he had seen, he was not that naive, and not even by the implications—that Teresa made a habit of this sort of thing—he could even handle that. He still loved her. Perhaps he loved her more, and she had been so sweet and so apologetic, blaming herself for it all and confessing to a hopeless nymphomania and swearing never to embarrass Alexander again—no, he could handle *that*.

It was something inside *himself* that really ate away at him, filled him with unpredictable rages and depressions and made him, for almost the first time in his life, wonder what kind of human being he was. The only words he could find for it were *moral outrage*. The three of them lying there wet and stinking. Not even embarrassed, just surprised. If he had had a sword he would have put them to death on the spot.

Who the hell did he think he was?

Slowly, filled with dread, he pulled himself up out of his personal life (such as it was) and back to business.

"Willi, bring me my calls and get Richard Heidelberg if you can."

He stared at the list of callers, which had grown by fifteen calls just since the arrival of Dr. Fieldstone, not counting, of course, the ones Willi hadn't bothered to log. These people wanted to butter him up, get him to solve their problems, help them with their power games. Only a couple, from men in the same position as himself, could be said to be friendly calls. Ted Ashley. Sidney Beckerman.

He called Sidney and had a good schmooze, laughing at Sidney's description of a cocktail party, and then Rick was on line 2.

"Gotta go, Sidney," he said abruptly and hung up without saying goodbye. "Hello, young man, I've been waiting to hear from you."

"Been busy," Rick's voice said.

"You don't sound happy," Alexander said.

"No Dael Tennyson," came Rick's reply.

Alexander had known that for a couple of days, but said nothing.

"Do you want to come over here and have a talk?" he said. Rick agreed to come by in a few minutes, and Alexander buzzed Willi. "Get me a nice Coca-Cola, huh?"

"Okay," she said with only a hint of reproval in her voice. "Donald Marrow on five."

"I'm in a meeting," Alexander said, and felt a guilty schoolboy pang. Willi came in and poured the cola into a glass of ice, and Alexander listened to the ice cracking and watched the bubbles subside with great impatience. Then, as an ironic gesture aimed at himself, raised the glass, "Here's to you, Doctor Fieldstone!" and drained his glass. Ah! Delicious!

It was too soon to talk to Marrow, anyway. He sat waiting for Rick, not knowing how he would respond to the young man's troubles. One part of him, of course, wanted to crush, humiliate and destroy him. Another part, perhaps the stronger, felt a fatherlike feeling for Rick; no, more brotherlike; no, he just plain *liked* him. And not for his phony charm, either. Rick really was, deep down inside, charming and nice, a good boy. With the morals of a cat. That's all.

My God, if you judged people by their behavior in this business, who would there be left to work with?

For some reason this made him think of the President of the United States, and he laughed, the first really good belly laugh he had had in a long time. On the tail end of it, in came Richard Heidelberg.

"Oh, excuse me," Alexander chuckled, and blew his nose. "I wasn't laughing at you."

"It's all right," Rick said, and sat.

"Willi, bring us a couple of Cokes, okay?"

"I'll have to send out for them," came her voice over the intercom. Had she been listening when Dr. Fieldstone had been talking to him? Maybe it was better not to know. "That's fine," he said, and turned once again to the young man trying to relax across the desk from him.

"So no Dael Tennyson," he said. "Travolta is still a possibility. And there are others."

Rick looked him right in the eye and said, "I've come to the conclusion that this project is fucked. The idea's weak and the script is boring. Let's not waste any more time on it."

Alexander's stomach sweetened and his mood rose sharply. This young man had guts!

ALEXANDER LISTENED quietly as Rick outlined his proposal to remake *The Lady in the Lake* and offer the part of Philip Marlowe to Peter Wellman. The thing was to be done period, World War II, and no expense would be spared developing the fun of period. Rick stressed the importance of the new tragic romance element and pointed out the popularity of *Witness for the Prosecution,* with its series of lurching volte-faces. That was to be the structure of *Lady,* too, with the additional shattering effect of having Marlowe confronted at once by the woman he has allowed himself to fall in love with because she is dead (with all that *that* implied) and the white knight ethic that makes him turn her in.

Alexander nodded gravely from time to time, but when Rick was finished with his pitch, he only said, "Let me sleep on it. Who owns the rights?"

"Endless Unicorn Company," Rick said. "We closed the deal with M-G-M yesterday."

"You can't shop this around town, you know," Alexander said. "You owe us a picture."

"I'm hip," Rick said.

"Well, I'll sleep on it."

Rick stood up. Alexander did not feel like standing up. He stared at the young man. The proposal was a candy store, of course, anybody who liked making movies would have a fine time with it. But whether it would make a profit Alexander could not foresee, and the little tickle of intuition he depended on in such matters tickled him not.

"I don't have to sleep on it," he said abruptly. *Let's see how tough this kid really is.* "I pass."

"You mean, no?"

Rick was actually goggling at him.

"I mean no," said Alexander. Now he was sure of himself. "And you can take it anywhere you want. I release you from your commitment."

Rick continued to goggle, and then he drew himself together. He looked tough now, like a street kid about to get into a knife fight. "You mean you're kicking me off the lot?"

Alexander laughed easily. "Oh, hell no, Rick. I'm just turning down your proposal, that's all. You aren't very much used to the word *no,* are you?"

Alexander stood up, just as Willi came in with the two Coca-Colas on a tray, with two glasses of ice.

"Make us a couple of drinks, will you, Willi?" he said. "What'll it be, Rick? Bourbon over ice?"

"I don't have to take this shit," Rick said, and started out the door, but Alexander's hand snaked out and grabbed him by the shoulder and turned him around. Alexander was smiling his deadliest smile, and his fingers gripped Rick's shoulder hard enough to really hurt. Rick did not flinch. The two men glared at each other, Alexander showing his teeth and Rick with his mouth a tight white line.

Willi made the drinks unobtrusively and got the hell out of there, closing the door behind her.

Alexander said, "Now I slap your face, and you say *'Thanks, I needed that.'*" He let go of the shoulder, picked up his drink and tossed about half of it down his throat. It burned sweetly. He walked over to the couch and plopped himself down. "Come on, kid, relax. It's not the end of the world. You just think it is."

Rick was making a visible effort to get control of himself.

Alexander finished his drink and watched him. Finally Rick sat and sipped his drink like a man.

"That's better," Alexander said. "We don't want to lose you, Rick, you're a good filmmaker and you're going to be a better one. Hell, someday you might have my job, you've got the makings of an executive, or whatever the hell it is I'm supposed to be. Did you know I was a tank commander in World War Two? Nineteen years old, breaking my ass for Georgie Patton?"

He regaled Rick with a couple of wild tank commander stories, hooked him completely, fascinated him as only Alexander, if he did say so himself, could fascinate. They each had another bourbon: "Bourbon's a man's drink!" Alexander drank both Coca-Colas, burped loudly and said, "Come on, we can't work anymore today, let's get the hell out of the office."

"I still don't understand why you turned me down," Rick said. "The project's really a good one."

"Quit pitching. I have to go watch some dailies, you want to come with me?"

But that was not to be the end of it. Alexander had assumed that Rick would take his project to another studio, with the whole town knowing that

Alexander had turned it down and that M-G-M had given the project up without a fight. Alexander didn't think he would have much luck against those odds, but you never knew, and he hoped it would all turn out well.

But no, that was not what happened.

Rick, instead, went to Donald Marrow. Right over Alexander's head, taking Elektra Soong and flying to New York the very next day.

By sheer coincidence, Teresa di Veccio was on the same plane.

CHAPTER SIXTEEN

JERRY COULD not live on hate. Gradually the seething disturbances in his belly went away and his life fell back into order. Richard Heidelberg should not be blamed. His silence was, if anything, informative. Making movies was a dirty business, and things like manners or politeness had no place. Thus, decent people like Jerry had no place. He moved back in with Barbara, got back into running and making love, and if Barbara did not understand his soul, perhaps that was the way it had to be. But every once in a while, he would feel a morsel of self-pity. Alas, the artist, even the unsuccessful artist, is ever misunderstood.

But then, without his willing the process to begin again, he found himself toying with a new idea, a tough idea, one that struck at the heart of our civilization. Jerry had long been fascinated and revulsed by the fate of chimpanzees, the funny cute little animals you see on television. Chimpanzees were very intelligent and very strong. Jerry had read somewhere that after the age of eight or nine, the animals were usually destroyed because they were likely (and with excellent reason) to turn on their captors. And then one day Jerry had found himself with a girl at a zoo, and out of curiosity, he looked up the chimpanzees. He was unprepared for what he saw. The animals were as big as he was, in strip cells, tiny cells containing nothing the animal could throw or destroy. For the animals wanted to throw and destroy, and having nothing else to throw, threw their own excrement at the humans. There was a sign out front warning the humans. Jerry made eye contact with one of the full-grown chimpanzees and saw with intuitive shock and horror that the animal knew where he was, and what was being done to him.

"What's the matter?" asked the girl he was with.

"I, uh . . ." was all he could say. He staggered to a bench and sat, horrified with himself, disgusted with humanity. "Jesus Christ, Jesus Christ," he said over and over.

The girl never did find out what was bothering him.

All right then. We have this full-grown chimpanzee (Jerry would never use the word "chimp" again) who is being used as part of a scientific experiment, something *clean*, like linguistics, to make the point all the sharper. The scientists in their white smocks see themselves as heroes, good guys, even though they have to lock down their animals and be extremely careful around them. So the chimpanzee, one dark night, escapes into the forest behind the university (Berkeley would be perfect). The movie would be about the chimpanzee's efforts to find his freedom, and the good-guy scientist who knows him so well he can think like him. Question: Which is the animal?

This was no *Planet of the Apes* movie. This was serious stuff. At first Jerry laughed at himself for having such an idea, but the idea wouldn't go away. Jerry kept seeing the eyes of that imprisoned animal, telling him in the universal telepathy of all animals, *Get me out of here!*

What the hell, it didn't matter if Jerry worked on the story or not, nobody was going to make the movie. Just another dreamland fantasy, just another gallop down the endless tatters of his mind.

He wrote eight pages and the script congealed. Nevertheless, to keep his freedom intact, he spent three nights a week at Fountain, mostly reading *Playboy*, drinking whiskey and wishing the script would write itself. It was either a piece of trash or a great idea. Enough whiskey and it was a great idea, but no son of a bitch like Richard Heidelberg was going to get his hands on it. First, complete the first-draft screenplay, then take it to Harriet Hardardt at the Novotny Agency. Insist on creative control, and because the script will be good enough, you'll get it. Direct the picture, and then won't they all eat their hearts out? Jerry had to laugh.

Now at Barbara's, Jerry sighed, took another drink of whiskey and lay back torpid on the couch. Walter Cronkite spoke to him of many wonders, and from the kitchen came the smells of corned beef and cabbage. Afterward, he knew, there would be a small scoop of delicious mint ice cream. Yet he was trimmer and firmer than ever, and he actually looked forward to his morning run before the hot shower and work.

Barbara was singing under her breath in the kitchen, Jerry did not recognize the tune. Obviously she was happy with the arrangement, and had said nothing about marriage for weeks. She was an ideal mate for him. Because he was such a child, and she mothered him. But when he needed to be treated like a man, she treated him like a man. And when he needed to be alone . . .

But she did not treat him like an artist.

Jerry sat up. There was one shot of whiskey left in the bottle. He drank it and went to the kitchen door.

"I'm gonna run down and get some booze," he said. "You need anything from the store?"

"Just hurry back, things are almost ready," she said without looking up. He gave her a warm gentle hug from behind as she chopped vegetables for the salad, kissed her on the nape of her neck, felt a momentary dizziness of desire, and left the place, forever.

Forever. And yet went to the big Ralph's market three blocks away and bought a bottle of Old Crow 100-proof and found himself driving back to Barbara's.

Bastard, but not bastard enough, was his thought as he pulled open the front door and was greeted by the exotic smells of freshly made corned beef and cabbage.

"I'm home!" he cried, not at all depressed.

It was as if he had been waiting for this test of his bastardliness, marking time until he could discover in himself some reason for thinking that what he did was important. Not just the after-hours pastime of a larger-than-average ego. Because Barbara didn't understand this part of him didn't mean he had to take failures out on her. He grinned to himself in the dark, and felt for her warmth. She made a little noise, and turned away from him. He could snuggle up to her spoon-fashion and ride that coziness into sleep.

The image of Richard Heidelberg, laughing, brought him up out of sleepiness, and a tickle of anger ran through his gut.

The next morning he asked for and got two hours off, driving through the ten o'clock Hollywood traffic to the west end of the Strip, Agent Country, driving down into the garage at 9255 as if he belonged there. He rode up in the elevator urging himself to have the guts to ask the girl to validate his parking ticket and then forgot all about it the moment he entered the cool silent dark-paneled but somehow terribly tacky offices of the David Novotny Agency.

Fifteen minutes of sitting sweating coldly into his clothes, and Harriet Hardardt came out of her office and wiggled her finger.

He jumped up and entered her office, with its homey atmosphere of books and scripts piled everywhere.

"I'm glad to see you," Harriet said. "Sit down and tell me in five seconds what's up, because I have to run downstairs to a screening about ten minutes ago."

But she sat down and smiled at him, and he was no longer nervous.

"I made a mistake, I think," he said. It no longer mattered to him that he would look foolish—the thing was to get that hatred off his back, and return to his writing. He explained what he had done.

"And you haven't heard a word from Mister Heidelberg?"

"Not a peep," he said. "I know how foolish I look."

"Don't worry about that. But you should have come to me . . . well, you were under pressure. I'll tell you what, I'll look into the matter and get back to you. Do I have a complete set of addresses and phone numbers for you?"

He gave her his numbers, including Barbara's place, and she stood up, grinning, and held out her hand.

"Welcome to the David Novotny Agency," she said.

My God, I have an agent! he thought with a thrill as the two of them waited for the elevator. Harriet shook his hand again when she got off at the second floor, and Jerry went on down to the garage numbly.

"I forgot to get validated," he said to the garage man. "I could go back up, I guess . . ."

"Naw, you look kinda distracted," the garageman said. Jerry tipped him two dollars and the man saluted with warm irony. "Careful out there," he said.

Sunset Boulevard never looked so fine.

"IT'S FOR you, Jerry," said Richard, handing him the phone but not tilting his chair back up, just sitting there waiting for the action. Jerry had no time for Richard, however.

"Jerry Rexford," he said.

"Will you hold for Harriet Hardardt?"

Within seconds: "Jerry, are you busy for lunch today?"

"Not at all," he said numbly.

"You work over on Hollywood Boulevard, why don't we meet at Musso's, in the bar, at twelve-thirty?"

"Sounds fine to me," Jerry said.

"David Novotny and Richard Heidelberg will be joining us," Harriet said.

"I'll be there," Jerry said. "Uh, where is it?"

"You've never been to Musso's? Well, this will be a double treat for you, then."

She told him how to find the place. It was two blocks down the boulevard. Jerry would never have guessed that an important Hollywood restaurant would be right here in the heart of Hollywood. But here it was, a frescoed high-ceilinged Italian restaurant, split down the middle, with the good room on the left and the *good* room on the right, red leatherette booths to one side, white tablecloths to the other. The place was beginning to fill up with industry people, many recognizable, and the busy warm chatter of busy people filled the place pleasantly.

Jerry walked up to the long bar and sat down. He was ten minutes early, and sweating. This would be a good place for a shot of bourbon—no, this would be a *terrible* spot for a shot.

"Perrier, please," he said to the barman. He turned on the bar stool and gave the room his frank appraisal. He had worn his best dark suit, and he was pleased to see that he did not look out of place.

At the tick of 12:30 Harriet Hardardt walked in from the back.

"I'm going to have to have a Martini," she said. "I have a full day. Well, how are you?"

"Just fine," Jerry said.

After Harriet had taken a sip of her drink she said, "Well, here's the basic situation. Richard Heidelberg didn't forget you. I suppose in his own way he was trying to be kind. So much of this business is bullshit, you know, he didn't want to bullshit you along and then have to backpedal if things went into turnaround. He's *just* gotten back from New York, with a deal to proceed with the development of *The Lady in the Lake* from Donald Marrow, and through me, he'll make you an offer."

Jerry wondered if he would ever know the truth of it. But what difference did that make? He was on the way to a deal. He asked Harriet a couple of questions and found out that Richard Heidelberg was also a client of the David Novotny Agency. He wondered how ethical all this was, but had the sense not to ask.

They were escorted to their pristine white-tableclothed corner table in less than ten minutes, and only moments later, in came Richard Heidelberg and David Novotny, stopping at only a few tables as they made their way across the room. Jerry did his best to appear calm, to appear as if he belonged in this room. He stood up to shake hands with the two new men, Richard in jeans and a soft blue velour and David, like himself, in dark blue three-piece. Only of course Novotny's suit made Jerry's look like something out of the free bin.

They all got themselves settled in a pleasant bustle of waiters and menus, and Jerry was conscious that a lot of people in the room were sneaking looks at *him*. Who was the lucky guy? Immediately he stopped sneaking looks at other tables. It was beneath his dignity, and besides, the conversation was starting to heat up.

"You probably want to kill me," Richard Heidelberg said with a friendly grin.

"Whatever for?" David Novotny said. He flashed Jerry a smile that Jerry could feel all the way down to his toes. "You only hung the man out to dry for a few months."

"Slowly twisting in the wind," Harriet said.

"Oh, I didn't mind," said Jerry.

"That second draft of yours is nothing short of brilliant," Richard said. "You have me crying all over the place, laughing, yelling. Damn good screenplay."

"Thank you," Jerry said.

"If we can make a deal, I'd like to collaborate with you on the next draft," Richard said. "I've got some dynamite ideas."

Jerry said, "If we make a deal?"

Harriet said, "We haven't decided on a price yet, and we have to take it to Marrow."

"It's not up to me," Richard said.

"But I'm sure Jerry isn't going to be more than usually greedy, nor Donald Marrow more than usually tight," David said. "So at least for the purposes of this lunch, we can assume, can't we, that Jerry has his deal?"

"But what's the matter with my script?" Jerry heard himself saying.

"It lacks experience," Richard said. "That's all. Some of the stuff you call for can't be done, or at least can't be done for the money. That's where I come in."

Jerry didn't know much, but he knew a little. He was amazed at himself, even so.

"Are you talking about splitting the screen credit with me?" David and Richard exchanged disappointed looks.

"Screen credits already," David said. He did not smile at Jerry.

"As a matter of cold hard fact," Richard said, looking right into Jerry's eyes, "you might not get a screen credit at all."

Jerry's heart sank. He looked at Harriet, who finished her Martini in silence.

The clatter of the room was abnormally loud, to Jerry. Their food came, and instead of enjoying his first meal at Musso & Frank's he could hardly remember it, except that it sat in his belly like a cannonball all afternoon.

But at last Harriet said, "I think you fellas are getting too serious." To Jerry she said, "Things will probably work out just the way you want them to, but you have to understand some things. What we're negotiating for is to sell, outright, your version of *The Lady in the Lake*. After that, anything can happen to it, but you'll have been paid for your work and your ideas."

"Nobody's trying to screw you, man," Richard said. "But you're like every newcomer, you're fuckin' paranoid. Relax. Make your deal, and we'll see what happens. Don't you know, I'm offering you a *good* deal by offering to collaborate. I'm not just buying up your ideas, I want *you* along."

"I'm sorry," Jerry said. "I'm acting like an idiot."

"Now you're talking!" David said, and once again he bestowed his smile on Jerry. It was like a pardon from the governor.

AT THE end of lunch, Jerry shook hands with the others and walked out the front door of Musso's, onto Hollywood Boulevard. The others presumably went out the back and got into their machines. For Jerry the shock was greater coming out than it had been going in. Here he was back among the skulkoids, the sleazos, the bad genetic material shuffling up and down the sidewalk, mobs of used cars roaming the streets, low-grade merchandise peering hopelessly from dirty store windows. And yet after a block Jerry was saying hello left and right to people he actually knew and who knew him, merchants, donut shop habitues, fellow tenants of this block of the Boulevard. By the time he turned into the entrance of the

Hany Building it was hard to remember the high-ceilinged room full of white tablecloths, red-jacketed waiters and the smooth bubbling relaxed hum of wealthy gab.

"Where you been, sport?" cried Toby from his throne.

"Musso's," he replied, pushing for the elevator. He did not want to talk to Toby right now.

"Hey man!" cried Toby. "You gettin' up there!"

There was no more curiosity about his affairs in the office, his fellow workers having concluded that it was real and therefore none of their business, and even Richard, his white shirt bulging out over his belt in back, stayed bent over the pasteup he was working on. Jerry slipped into his chair and reached into his IN box for a press release. It described a new kind of shovel-and-broom arrangement for getting dog shit off stubbornly resistant sidewalks. After reading it through rapidly once and seeing the notation blue-pencilled up in the corner—"1 par"—Jerry propped the release up beside his Royal Standard typewriter, reached over for the first sheet, carbon and second sheet, and began cutting the item down to one paragraph, as per editorial instruction. All around him was the clatter of typewriters and adding machines, the low bubble of voices. Within him was a numbness.

It is probably one of the basic fantasies. You find yourself among people who are not like you. You feel so different you are sure that you were plucked from your crib and spirited off. Someday you will be restored to your rightful place in the world. *No mere commoner he, but a prince of the royal blood . . .*

That's how Jerry felt. Right on the edge of being plucked from this unjust obscurity, just a few more days . . . a few weeks at the most.

He ripped the item from his typewriter angrily, quickly scanned the enormous number of typographical errors and threw the pages into his wastebasket, bending down and retrieving the carbon paper, stacking another deck and feeding it into the machine. This time he wrote a classically correct paragraph with not a single error, marked it up quickly with his grease pencil and dropped it into the OUT basket. Next item: But he did not want to read the next item. He had a full IN basket, lots of stuff, stuff he could plow his way through in about five hours at this pace, some of the items unconsciously funny, but most of them with a dull sincerity that made Jerry want to scream. And never must a note of irony creep into his prose, never a moment of fun or lighthearted phrase.

These people were goddamn serious about their products. Pushing pet care was a hard dollar in a tough world.

Jerry looked around the room. Everyone he saw would have looked out of place at Musso's. Did he look as out of place to them as they did to him? Did they know he was a prince in disguise?

"What are you laughing at?" Richard said in a friendly way.

Jerry wiped his eyes with a Kleenex and said, "Sometimes these weird thoughts come into my mind."

"I know what you mean," Richard said seriously. He tilted back in his swivel chair so that his mouth was closer to Jerry's ear. In a low voice he said, "I sometimes get these outrageous fantasies about my old lady . ."

He appeared to be willing to go on with this, so Jerry kidded him out of it:

"Have you seen this?" He handed Richard the copy about the dog shit invention. "You think we should replace the front page?"

Richard read the paragraph and the press release clipped to it. He looked up at Jerry seriously. "Nice item," he said.

By this time Jerry had picked up his new item, concerning a series of price hikes in grain ("2 para") and was well into typing it up.

But in his mind he was thinking about financial matters closer to home. How much was he going to get paid? There had been no time to discuss this with Harriet after lunch had broken up. How much did people get for scripts, anyway? Jerry read the trades and the press and knew that fabulous sums were often mentioned as having been paid for one property or another. Hundreds of thousands of dollars.

Jerry's skin went cold at the thought of all that money. He pulled his item out of the typewriter and checked it carefully with the press release to make sure he had all the names and numbers correct. A couple of hundred thousand dollars. A quarter of a million dollars.

A quarter of a million dollars?

A quarter of a million dollars?

When Richard, who could overhear him, left his desk, Jerry called Harriet Hardardt. The secretary said that Harriet was in a meeting and would get back to him. That killed the afternoon. Jerry worked mindlessly until six, a half-hour after everybody else had left, because he knew now that Hollywood worked until six, and then when the phone still didn't ring he dragged himself out of the place, wondering what in the holy hell he was going to tell Barbara.

Dinner was *arroz con pollo,* golden with saffron and picked out with bits of fresh pimento, utterly delicious, and followed by hot apple pie and coffee, brandy in the little pony glasses Jerry had bought for Barbara. During the meal she spoke of things at work, a romance between the head salesman and a new employee, a Korean girl who didn't seem to know how to avoid Blusterbuttocks, as Barbara called the salesman. Jerry ate his chicken and rice and half-listened to her. He had not made up his mind what to tell her, if anything. Indeed, the Heidelberg Approach might be the way to go. Say nothing until there is something to say.

Wouldn't her face go all funny if he said, apropos of nothing, "Hey, I made a quarter of a million dollars today. . . ."

Jerry helped himself to another piece of chicken, crispy where it had baked on top, soft and succulent where it had cuddled the rice. The steam rising from the freshly sundered meat was rich with herbs and butter. The white wine was chilled just enough to make him gulp happily after putting down his fork and *thoroughly chewing* his food.

Barbara watched him with approval. She had brought him a long way from the bachelor chomp-and-swallow of only a few months ago.

"My Jesus Christ this food is good!" he said with great enthusiasm. It was practically the only sincere thing he said to her the entire evening. He half-expected Harriet to call him there.

It threw a pall over their evening. He was obviously preoccupied about something he was unwilling to share. Even as they watched television in bed, she with a glass of white wine and he with a second and then a third brandy, his answer to her every remark, even those not aimed at him, was, "Huh?"

Finally she asked him. "Are you writing something again?"

"Yes," he said. It explained his preoccupation. Nevertheless, it worked as a wedge between them, and when it was time to decide whether to make love, both were looking for an excuse not to. Jerry lay awake after pretending to fall asleep, and he knew that Barbara, next to him in the darkness, was also pretending to sleep. He wondered how long they could go on like this, but soon slipped back into his mind's whirl of fragmentary ideas. Ideas of wealth, of change, worried thoughts of the future, dread at the thought that he was going to have to drag Barbara into Hollywood with him because he didn't have the guts to sever the thing right now.

Well, he didn't, and that was that. He was being oversensitive anyway.

None of this was really going to happen, at least not as he fantasied. He shifted uncomfortably in the bed. This has been one of the happiest days of my life, he told himself. Or it should have been. Why wasn't it? He shifted again. The pillow was awfully hot. Again his mind began to race, and he gave up the idea of sleeping. But he still had to lie there, as if asleep. For all he knew, Barbara might still be awake.

Things did not get better over the next few days, when Harriet Hardardt did not call, and Jerry, thin-lipped with anger, refused to call her. He spent three nights in a row over on Fountain, pretending to be working on his script, but he couldn't work. His mind was too full of fragments. Fountain was uncomfortable after Barbara's place, and compared to Barbara's cooking the stuff he fed himself was disgusting.

But the whiskey was just as good as ever, and he found himself drinking more and more, until he was up to a pint on his third night, drunk to the point of stumbling by nine o'clock, when Barbara called to say goodnight.

It was an embarrassing phone call because he was so drunk and had the foolish notion that he could hide it from her. The call ended with Barbara making an excuse and Jerry maudlin and loving and on the edge of tears.

And then days later Harriet Hardardt did call, and Jerry sat numbly as Harriet's voice explained to him that she had had to negotiate like a fiend to get him anything at all, with his lack of a track record and with the expense of buying the rights from M-G-M, and of course Rick's participation, so that the budget didn't allow much for script, but by dint of Harriet's all-out war, Jerry was to receive twenty-five thousand dollars for his work on *The Lady in the Lake,* including working with Rick and the production company getting the script into shooting shape.

"I think it's a good deal," Harriet said.

So this was reality!

But instead of telling Barbara that night, Jerry went back to Fountain and started in on a fresh bottle of whiskey.

The next morning he woke up early and listened to the mockingbird outside his window for nearly an hour before getting out of bed. His running shoes and sweatsuit were at Barbara's, thank God, so all he had to do was take a shower and get over to the donut shop for some life-giving coffee.

Everyone was still in place, as if he had never stopped coming in here. There was Helen behind the counter, sacking donuts, smiling at everyone, remembering people's favorites, making change, giving Jerry that same long loving look as he poured his own coffee and plunked himself down on a stool to wait for that first delicious just-too-hot sip.

Toby came in and sat down next to Jerry. Toby's breath was awful, reminding Jerry of the stench of a dead deer he had come across in the forest once. Jerry tried to shield himself, knowing his own breath might be just as bad.

"How's it goin' with you and Rick?" Toby asked, after wolfing down three donut holes.

"We have a deal," Jerry heard himself saying. Toby's eyes lit up.

"Hey, what'd I tell you! Man, that's great!"

Jerry told Toby all about it, warming up with the coffee in him, and pretty soon the two men were laughing and babbling about Jerry's first big break.

Then it got awful.

"Hey," Toby said, as if it had just occurred to him, "you got to take me with you!"

"What?"

"You got to take me with you. Assistant producer or some shit like that. You *got* to."

There was no doubt that Toby was sincere. His face was strained and anxious as he stared into Jerry's eyes.

"But I'm just the writer," Jerry said. It was true, yet he still felt like a betrayer.

"You got to take me with you, man! You can't leave me here! You think I wanna sell stroke books all my life? Hey, it was me that got you the gig!"

"I can't," Jerry said. He felt himself harden inside. He got up and paid for his coffee. His hands were shaking and he knew without looking that Toby was giving him a heavy guilt-inducing stare. At the door, Jerry turned and looked at Toby, but Toby was hunched over his coffee, staring at the back wall.

Helen was smiling at Jerry, though, and said "Goodbye!" brightly as he left.

AND SO, feeling a little like Dick Whittington's cat, Jerry Rexford went off to Hollywood to seek his fortune. He needn't have worried what to do about Barbara, because she dropped him like a hot potato as soon as she was reasonably sure he had a girl friend on the side. Nothing Jerry said could change her mind, and in a burst of cruelty she invited him over after work one evening—he thought for supper—and when he got there found all his things stacked up on her porch. Her brother Richard tried to be polite but it was clear that he, too, thought Jerry had gone astray. It was hard working beside the man, and then impossible.

Jerry went in to Mr. Harris and apologized for quitting. Mr. Harris, much to Jerry's surprise, only pretended to be sorry, and talked about how Jerry's work had been suffering these past few weeks, and perhaps it was all for the best. As Jerry left Mr. Harris's office he could hear the *fft!* of Kleenex being withdrawn from its box.

Twenty-five thousand dollars was plenty of money to get established, even though, as Harriet Hardardt had carefully explained, he would never actually see so much as half that sum, and no one part of it much more than the almost twenty-five hundred dollars he had already been paid. The gross amount had been five thousand. Jerry would get another check soon, and then, the first day of shooting, he would get another.

"What if the picture never gets made?" Jerry asked, in a rare moment of fiscal intelligence.

"Let's not be gloomy," Harriet said.

Jerry worked it out. If the picture went into turnaround (oh, he was picking up the language!) he stood to make a total of something under five thousand dollars, cash to him.

"But," as Harriet said with a small smile, "we'll get you a lot more for your next screenplay, a hell of a lot more."

"*If* the picture gets made, gets released and makes money," Jerry said cynically.

"Let's not rain on the ballpark," Harriet suggested.

Rick Heidelberg turned out to be one of the greatest people Jerry had ever met. He arranged a parking space right in front of the Administration Building, so that Jerry did not have to come in through the drive-on gate or walk halfway across the lot to his office. The production company had a shotgun row of four offices, but Jerry's was not one of these. His was across the hall and down the corridor. "Writers need their peace and quiet," Rick said, and Jerry agreed. Rick's was the corner one, a splendid office, with its bar, its posters of great old movies, its view of the battlements and turrets of the big medieval castle. The company's suite of offices was right under Boss Hellstrom's, and when the Boss came into the conversation, Rick would point upward with an ironic wink.

A funny thing happened the first day Jerry moved into his office. The place was tiny and bare, with its yellow oak desk and crippled-looking swivel chair, and the Royal Standard typewriter on the middle of the desk.

"It's not much," Rick said to him.

"Oh, gee, it's just fine," Jerry said, and as if to prove it, went over and sat on the swivel chair, which gave an angry squeak and almost dumped Jerry on the threadbare carpet. Jerry steadied himself, pulled over the typewriter and made as if to adjust it. He opened the top drawer looking for paper, but found only a couple of empty Dos Equis bottles.

"Former tenant?" he asked Rick, and Rick got this really funny look on his face. On another man's face it might have been called embarrassment, but Jerry couldn't imagine Rick embarrassed.

"The secretaries have all the supplies . . . just ask," Rick said, and left Jerry to contemplate his splendor.

The halcyon days lasted only a week, but what a week for Jerry Rexford! He would arrive fresh and bright at around eight o'clock, park in his slot, enter through the glassed-in police booth ("Good morning, Mister Rexford!"), past the seated double row of hopefuls, down the dim silent corridor that reminded him of nothing so much as a high school corridor except for the lack of lockers and the famous names on every door, up the staircase to the third floor, where Joyce, Rick's secretary and Roberta, *his* secretary, were just in and making the fresh aromatic coffee.

He would go down to his office, leaving the door open, and in a moment Roberta, his wide-mouthed, big-breasted secretary, would come with the trades and fresh coffee.

"Thank you, Roberta," he would say, and she would leave the office, gently shutting the door behind her.

Jerry would read about what the other folks in show business were doing (mentally discounting all figures by at least seventy-five percent) and then, his coffee percolating sweetly into his bloodstream, would turn to his typewriter and begin work on the day's pages.

Then lunch at the commissary or wherever Rick decided to take them that day. For that first week, anyway, Rick and Jerry had lunch together every day, and talked about the script. Rick knew how to compliment while criticizing, he knew how to get the most out of a negative situation, turn it positive; how to flatter without being destructive, and Jerry never learned so much about writing for the screen as he did during those five lunches. Technical matters. How to keep an eye out for the camera without pimping for it. To remember that lines are written to be spoken by actors. To refrain from attempting to direct the picture from his desk, and to forget employing camera terms he hardly understood, in favor of more diplomatic language. For Jerry it was a great relief not to have to fake camera language or directorial attitudes, and scene after scene was chopped and channelled into workmanlike shape, the script getting shorter and shorter all the time, until it had gone from 167 pages to 97.

"Isn't it too short now?"

"Naw," said Rick. They were at El Coyote, scooping in Mexican food. "It's still literary. Jesus, your first draft timed out at about four hours."

Jerry now knew that "literary" was not a snide insult, but a practical description of a kind of script with too much action per eighth of a page.

Often the two men spent the afternoon together in Rick's office, playing with the script, with Rick on the telephone most of the time and Jerry, happy on the couch, eavesdropping on the high-powered conversations.

And the screenings. At four each afternoon, they would walk down to Screening Room Twelve and watch hard-boiled private eye movies. It had become a tradition, in one week, that they take a six pack of Coors along, and each would drink three cans. Jerry could not help wondering if Rick had been just as cozy with the previous tenant of Jerry's office, a mysterious Mexican director whom nobody around the office wanted to talk about. But that was the way it was, old projects seemed deadly taboo.

So in one wonderful week they had gone clear through the script, and had something worth showing to the big bosses. Jerry could hardly wait for his next meeting with Rick.

Jerry hardly recognized his apartment, coming in Friday evening after that first week of intense work with Richard Heidelberg. Every night he had come home, slugged himself to sleep with whiskey, and awakened only in time to shower and dress for the next big important day. Now here he was with two days to fill, nowhere to go, no one to be with, nothing to do. All week, in fact, he had expected Rick to invite him to the beach, so that they could go on working. But it didn't happen, and here he was in the middle of this dirty, messy, smelly, dark little apartment with nothing but whiskey and television to keep him from going crazy.

Later that evening he learned a great truth—whiskey and television cannot do the trick. *Au contraire.* Sometimes television is a wonderful thing. You turn the switch and out comes great science, great art, wonderful comedy, exciting news. Etc., etc. Other times it is boring and stupid. Still other times, tonight for example, it is insistently, nauseatingly, rottenly, boorishly offensive. And whiskey, you know how sometimes the first sniff of the stuff makes you giddy and pleased, and how other times you can't get drunk on a carload? Well, there are other times, too, times like tonight, when no matter how much of the goddamn stuff you slop over your lip, it makes you sicker and wishing even more to get drunk and blot out reality. And yet you know that only the whiskey is keeping you awake.

But it cut the old-socks smell of his apartment, especially with the door open, and that was a sufficiency to keep the door in the open position. It was certainly unrealistic to expect him to stop drinking, now that he had aired the place out. But he cringed at the thought of having company in his place. He would have to move, just as soon as he got his hands on a good-sized check.

Now would be a swell time for a swim, before he got to thinking what he didn't want to think about, namely, his loneliness, the gigantic empty raw spot inside him where Barbara had been, the smaller but just as raw spot where Rick had bored his way into Jerry's heart. The dullness of his own life. He stripped but could not find his bathing suit. So what? Peeping out his windows he had often seen late-night nude bathers in the pool, so fuckum, he would do it too.

The dew-damp lawn felt great against his feet as he crossed toward the pool. He giggled, and somebody said,

"Who's that?"

"It's Jerry," he said, and stopped. Peering ahead, he saw a couple on the far side of the pool, on some towels. If they were not fucking, they should have been.

"Oh, excuse me all to hell," Jerry said. "I just wanted to go for a little swim."

"Well, go ahead, Jerry," the girl part of the tangle of humanity said.

With a giggle, Jerry half-jumped, half-fell into the warm sweet water of the pool. It felt wonderful to be naked in the water! He swam up and down, up and down, not getting tired, feeling his mind clear up, his depression, his emptiness vanish. He could barely pull himself up out of the water, and he sat on the concrete, running water and breathing deeply for quite a while before he even thought to open his eyes.

The couple was going at it, a mile a minute. Jerry dropped into the water and moved darkly to the other end, where he could sit on the underwater steps with only his head out. There were dim stars past the black branches of the trees in the patio. Another person came by, opened a screen door, *slap!* and flipped on an intimate amber light within.

And then the couple, still naked, jumped into the water and began to play with each other, giggles and splashes, while Jerry padded into his place and got a nice double shot of whiskey. This time it hit the spot and made him feel really quite goddamn delightful. Back out to the pool, naked as an opossum.

Jerry helped the girl out of the pool, watching the water run off her glinting breasts, and then, oddly, not wanting to intrude on her privacy, her right to be naked, averted his eyes from her sexual parts and looked at her attractive wet face. She lived next door to him.

"I'm Jerry," he said.

"I'm Brenda," she said, and introduced her naked companion as Jack.

"You're the one with the black Super 90, right?" asked Jack, a Porsche enthusiast. They talked eagerly about Porsches for a while, sitting around naked, and then the conversation drifted into the picture business (there were few civilians on Fountain) and Jerry was led to an opportunity to point out that he was working on a picture right *then*. To Brenda and Jack's excellent attention he told them all about it.

Jerry thought he saw a note of admiration creep into their eyes as he talked, and that made him shut up. Enough was enough. And so it was, the couple drifted into Brenda's apartment and Jerry into his, where in only a few minutes he could hear them through the wall, banging away on each other. Brenda murmured, *"Please . . . please . . . oh, please . . ."* and Jerry fell back into his desperately lonely funk.

The next day should have been terrible, what with Jerry's guilty hangover and the endless prospects of nothing to do. But it happened to be F. Scott Fitzgerald's birthday, or so at least they said, and it was a good excuse for a party. Everybody was invited.

IT BEGAN as a loose-knit group sitting in the sun by the pool, curing their hangovers from a couple of big pitchers of fresh orange juice and a gigantic bottle of vodka. It was a warm morning, with a gentle breeze and the sky robin's-egg blue above. Somebody went out and came back with several white sacks of bakery goods and somebody else passed around a joint of what was described as "Thai-stick shake," and there was a small argument as to whether it should be spelled "tie-stick," since the stuff was literally tied to a stick. Others held that since it was supposed to be from Thailand . . .

Jerry stepped out his door in jeans, tee shirt (unmarked) and *huaraches,* on his way to get a cup of coffee and the Sunday L.A. *Times.* Somebody from the pool group called to him and he waved and kept going toward the garage.

"Hey, Jerry," called Jack. He waved for Jerry to come over, and Jerry, head hanging, could not refuse.

"You all know Jerry," Jack said. He was tanned and grinning, with powdered sugar in his moustache. "The Phantom Writer." Everyone laughed easily, and Jerry realized he was an old character around here. He recognized most of the faces, from the garage, the walkway, the patio. People he nodded to. Now they all looked friendly and relaxed, and he laughed at the joke of being called The Phantom Writer. He kind of liked the title.

"How about one of these orange killer mamas?" Jack asked him.

"What's the occasion?" Jerry asked. He accepted his drink, and after the first tantalizing sip he tossed it off.

A dark man with a roll of fat peeping through his open Hawaiian shirt said, "The occasion, my friend, is that it's F. Scott Fitzgerald's birthday. We are all going to get bloody smashed."

Jerry accepted his second drink from Jack. A girl in an emerald one-piece bathing suit offered him a slice of apple strudel.

"No, thank you," Jerry said. His hangover was going away. He found a place to sit, and pretty soon he was no longer the center of attention. The conversation was full of names he did not know, but the activities being talked about were familiar enough. Who was getting together with whom, and how was it working out. Who was splitting up and who didn't care. It was a comfortable conversation. By his third drink Jerry was bloody smashed, and it was only just a little after noon. More people had been showing up all the time, and the patio was crowded and buzzing with conversation.

Jerry made a lot of friends when a newcomer, a short angry-looking man with a girl much too young for him, asked belligerently, "Who the hell's F. Scott Fitzgerald?" and Jerry just as belligerently said, "Why, man, he was the greatest silent film director the world has ever seen!" Jerry raised his glass, and so did nearly everybody else.

"Here's to . . . Effey!"

"Effey!"

It was not a wild party, it was just an empty Saturday onto which a party had been superimposed. No one really thought they were going to stay, and nearly everybody had afternoon plans. But the party took hold and it was fun to be there. People went out for more booze, and the girl with the fruit juicer kept grinding out the fresh orange juice. For Jerry what made it a party was the large number of good-looking girls, friendly girls, many of whom lived either here or nearby. He spent a lot of time talking to the girls, who were secretaries, actresses, waitresses, production workers, girl friends, unemployeds, and all fascinated by the fact that Jerry was working on a picture, and knew Richard Heidelberg personally.

"Rick and me are very tight," Jerry said at least a dozen times that day. When he thought back to the party he was embarrassed by the number of times he had said that, but another memory covered his embarrassment and made this particular Saturday one of the landmarks of his life. He played it over and over in his mind, unable ever to get it exactly right, or in sufficient detail, but playing it over anyway, because it make him feel so good.

The first one had followed him into his apartment when he had gone in to piss. He turned around and saw her standing in the middle of his messy apartment.

"I'm going to the toilet," he said.

"I'll wait here," she said, Short girl, lived down the street. Dressed in jeans and a shirt tied up under her breasts. Eyes drunk, mouth saucy. When Jerry came out of the toilet he said, "Your turn"—still not getting it— and she threw her arms around him and planted a big wet kiss on his mouth.

"Mmm, you're cute," she said.

Jerry took her into the bedroom, mess that it was, and within seconds the two of them were undressed and on the bed.

As they left Jerry's apartment he caught Brenda's eye, and she winked at him. He reddened, but did not care. Midge, the girl he had just fucked, disappeared into the crowd around the grill, where something was cooking, and Jerry loafed over to the grassy strip in front of the big banana tree and sat. Funny, making love had heightened his desires instead of satisfying them, and he looked around wolfishly at the female flesh everywhere to be seen.

Soon he was deep in conversation with a girl who worked at the studio as an assistant editor, and they gossiped happily about the stuff that was supposed to be going on at the studio, and then Jerry found himself asking her if she wouldn't like to go with him while he picked up some more booze. "Can't take a free ride all day," he said. "Come in while I change my duds," he said, and she followed him into his apartment. Jerry just didn't give a fuck, so he turned around and grabbed her and felt her slide into his arms with eagerness. And, so, little pink lights exploding in his mind, Jerry dragged her into the bedroom.

They came out of his apartment just as Brenda was passing by. Brenda's expression this time had a tinge of respect in it, and instead of winking, she merely raised her eyebrows.

When Jerry and the girl got back from their booze run, having traded phone numbers, kisses and promises of lunch at the commissary, Jerry got rid of her and found Brenda.

"Let's go," he whispered huskily.

"I thought you'd never ask," she murmured, and they slipped into Jerry's *boudoir*, where the smell of sex was thick.

"Where's Jack?" he asked, but did not care.

"I dunno, prob'ly fucking somebody in the bushes," Brenda said.

The party went on into the night, and Jerry made a couple of good friends among the residents. But there was no more sex. Jerry felt he had done his part. More than his part. When he finally went to bed he went alone, and the mingled odors wafted him into delicious sleep.

PART FOUR: WESTWOOD

CHAPTER SEVENTEEN

RICK'S GLOOMY mood was not improved by the front of the theater, even though already there were lines of young people stretching around the short Westwood block and out of sight, and a mob of "studio personnel" crowding their way in through a special velvet-roped open door. Above them the center of the marquee read not BRUIN! but RUIN! in blue neon script, and Rick was far from strong enough emotionally these days to see anything but an ominous omen.

RUIN! RUIN! RUIN! the blue neon blinked. Or maybe it was Rick blinking. He got out of the hired limousine after slipping a fifty to the driver *("Buy yourself a drink!")* and scooted into the lobby. Studio personnel crowded back to avoid his touch. Boss Hellstrom, standing by the candy counter in a beautiful grey suit, turned away from him. Elektra trailed six feet behind him, like a Japanese bride of twenty-five years ago.

Rick was *hot*.

He stooped over the drinking fountain and let the icy water chill his swollen lips. He barely felt like swallowing. But swallow he must, or strangle on his own anxiety. Somehow he had gotten it into his mind that tonight's reaction from this audience, mixed UCLA students, studio people and their guests, and the Brass, would determine the fate of *The Lady in the Lake*.

Rick looked around, half-expecting to see Donald Marrow.

At first, months ago, Marrow had been enthusiastic and full of ideas, actually moving west, taking up a bungalow at the Beverly Hills Hotel, occupying the big executive office across the hall from Rick's and generally bounding around like a jackrabbit. He was no longer dressing Main Street, so Teresa di Veccio must have gotten to him in more ways than one. She was his business partner and was putting up a lion's share of the bucks (Rick was not exactly certain how much) so that tonight's audience was being treated to

MARROW–DI VECCIO–RABALLO PRESENT

A RICHARD HEIDELBERG PRODUCTION

KERRY DARDENELLE'S

THE LADY IN THE LAKE

Raymond Chandler had somehow managed to elude this company of names, although way down in the billing he split a card with Jerry Rexford. Rick had decided at the last minute not to get in on the source card but stick to PRODUCED BY RICHARD HEIDELBERG. Perhaps it was the beginnings of a rudimentary modesty, although he doubted it. More likely preparation to lay the whole thing off onto Rexford if it was a disaster.

A disaster now would wreck Rick. He had long since worn out his welcome at the studio. The Boss must have hated him, although no one could have been more impeccable in his behavior than Hellstrom, who, once he found himself sandbagged, doubly sandbagged—not only overruled on the picture but finding the woman he had told Rick he loved in the delicate hands of a creep like Donald Marrow; nonetheless breaking his ass to make sure the picture had every advantage he could supply, from a miracle budget, utterly without padding, to a daily scrutiny to keep the little problems little, and waste at a minimum. And he got them the best below-the-line crew anybody had seen for years.

Rick had to admit that the production was first class because the Boss had made it so. Rick himself would have committed dozens of costly errors, and many times only the Boss's intervention had kept him from folly. And the Boss had been polite and never let anybody see the dislike he must have felt. Only Rick could feel the chill, and regretted the death of what might have been a lifelong friendship.

The Boss had even done his best to keep Marrow from forcing his idiotic notions down Rick's throat, once the production had started to roll. Jerry, whom Rick could see now across the lobby, grimmer around the eyes and firmer in the mouth than when he had come to Rick as a callow first-time writer some months ago, and now acknowledging Rick's wink with a flutter—no more—of his fingers and then pretending to be interested in a nearby tapestry, had feared Marrow more than any of them. Marrow would burst into Jerry's tiny cubicle with script changes and ideas that must have been baffling to Jerry—worse than baffling, surrealistic—because Jerry had not been to the screenings of new product from the other studios that Marrow had been to, and so did not know that he was being offered the Big Moments from these other pictures, the Moments where the screening room or theater or living room full of executives and their mates burst into laughter or applause.

Marrow was not one to stand back from a little judicious theft if it would improve the product, and he seemed to have no memory for yesterday's suggestions. Rick finally had to teach Jerry to nod and smile and make notes until Marrow ran down. Sometimes this worked and sometimes Jerry would get an awful tongue-lashing from Marrow and would have to sit and clench his knees while his face turned redder and redder and Marrow explained how he wanted things.

"This is a perfect chance for Jody McKeegan to *sing,* while she's working in Bakersfield in this country-western hole in the wall, see? I asked you to run that scene up before . . ."

Miserable Jerry would look at Rick and then at Marrow, squeeze his knees and say in a strained voice, "But I thought we agreed against any musical numbers . . ."

"Jody McKeegan can sing, the audience expects it of her," Marrow snapped.

McKeegan was playing Muriel Chess and had the biggest salary on the picture, although she was billed below Eric Tennyson.

Rick had actually fought casting McKeegan, on the grounds that she was too old, too expensive and too damn much trouble to work with, but the Boss had cut through all that by saying bluntly, "She's the best actor we can get for the money, and believe me, this part calls for an actor. The audience has to be fooled by Mrs. Fallbrook as much as Marlowe is."

The real stroke of genius had been Eric Tennyson for Philip Marlowe, if Rick said so himself, and he certainly did.

Rick looked around the crowded lobby. There wasn't a Tennyson in sight. He broke out into a light sweat.

"You better go to the toilet or something," Elektra said to him.

IT HADN'T exactly been Rick's idea to cast Eric Tennyson. Everybody wanted Peter Wellman, and Peter Wellman wanted to play Philip Marlowe very badly. The studio had a three-picture commitment from Wellman, and now that his Texas movie was finished, except for an afternoon's looping, Wellman was getting impatient for work. Rick had come down to his place in the Malibu Colony for lunch, with David Novotny and William Galaxy (Wellman's producing partner) and they had all had a fine time, ate a wonderful lunch, drank white wine and played some doubles. Rick was not a very good player, and let Novotny do it all, even unto throwing the match, because, as he said to Rick later, "You don't beat an actor on his own court, especially not with a terrible partner like yourself."

So Peter Wellman was hot to trot, and the item was leaked to Army Archard, on the instructions of Donald Marrow. Everyone, even Rick, groaned at this incompetence, and cringed while they waited.

They didn't have to wait long. Wellman's people marched in with their demands less than a week after *People* magazine copied Archard's item. Demand Number One: William Galaxy would not only produce the picture, under Rick's executive but not too active producership, but would enter into immediate conferences with Jerry Rexford ("Rexford's from a very fine old Los Angeles family, I don't know if you knew that . . .") and Heidelberg about the script and the changes that would have to be made to accommodate an actor of his stature, because among other things, Peter was *very* enthusiastic about playing the same role as Bogart and Mitchum and God knows who else, but it was felt that the old-fashioned notion of the private eye *loner* was passé, and most probably Marlowe ought to have a girl friend, maybe even a live-in girl friend.

So before Peter read the script and the studio was committed to paying him two million dollars, it would be very wise to have the script "Wellmanized," as Galaxy so ironically put it.

"Wellmanized my ass!" shouted Donald Marrow, the cause of all the trouble. "That man's off the picture! I never want to hear his name again! Get his people off the goddamned lot!" Marrow rushed into his bathroom to gobble Valium and Rick exchanged glances with Boss Hellstrom.

"Did he forget about the three-picture deal?"

"I'll remind him later," Hellstrom said. "Maybe while he's eating. Because he's sure going to have to either eat his words or eat the contract."

But that was the end of Wellman's involvement with *The Lady in the Lake,* and for a couple of days, Rick had that old feeling. The project, which had been so hot, was now cooling rapidly.

He sat in his air-conditioned office and sweated like a hog, his hands folded on the desk top. Joyce came in, and sensing his emotion, went back out again. Once more he reflected on what a fine secretary she was.

"Get me Elektra, will you, Joyce?"

"Elektra on one."

"Honey, I'm coming out to the beach. Is that all right?"

They had been having problems, nothing really out of line, but Rick's busyness and the pressure he was under conspired to leave him sexless and irritable. Lately he had been staying in Errol Flynn's apartment and Elektra had been living at the beach. But she sounded glad to hear from him, and cheerfully gave him a list of stuff to pick up at the Trancas Market.

It was lovely weather and the sun hung sweetly over the beach. Rick, in old jeans, barefoot, came down the steps to the dry piled sand, crossed it with sinking steps to the wet sand, wonderfully cool against his feet after the hot crossing—a thing he noticed every time, a part of his life that never changed, never deserted him. Maybe he should write a *haiku* about it. Only Rick did not know how to write *haiku*. He was not even sure if it was five seven five or seven five seven. One of those was a jet plane, another a poetry form. Never mind, *wet feet, wet feet, feels sweet, how neet, bleet bleet,* that's better than any goddamn *haiku.*

Rick laughed at himself, at his tense neck muscles.

When he got back to the house, exhausted from impulsively running halfway up the steps, Elektra told him he had had a phone call from Joanne Clay. He did not stop to think of the effect on Elektra but picked up the nearest telephone and dialed the number of the Tennyson ranch. Joanne was not there, and nobody there seemed to know her telephone number. But Elektra had it, and silently pushed the piece of paper with the message on it over to Rick and went into the kitchen.

"Joanne, this is Rick," he said in a strained voice.

"I'm glad you caught me, I was just heading for the market. Listen, I'm sorry about Peter and all that. I hear your picture's in trouble."

"Greatly exaggerated," Rick said.

"Why don't you come and have supper with me? I'd like to talk over a couple of ideas."

Rick got the address and the directions. Up Laurel Canyon, left on Kirkwood, up Weepah Way to the end.

"I'm sorry, honey bear, but I got to go out."

She looked up from her vegetable chopping. "You fucker," she said. The vegetable knife was huge in her tiny hand.

"It's pure business," he said lamely.

"You rotten fucker," she said.

THE HOUSE was almost invisible under a huge tree, and there was a small Datsun pickup truck and an old Buick convertible parked crookedly up against the trunk of the tree, so either she wasn't alone or these were her cars. Rick parked on a slant in the remaining dirt and gravel under the tree and got out cautiously. Dogs, you know. Most people up here protected themselves with dogs. But there was no barking, except in the distance, and Rick brushed his way through the drooping leafy branches to the front door, set in a white stucco arch, and, after finding the doorbell button rusted rigid, knocked on the door. Who would open the door? If it was Joanne, how would she be dressed? What was going on? Rick did not know. He had driven thirty miles after a day of exhausting anxiety and craziness, to have dinner with a woman who could easily twist him around anything she wanted to twist him around.

While he waited for his knock to be answered, Rick made up his mind that no matter what, he was going to be "impeccable" with Joanne Clay, and at once the great weight lifted from his chest. *Aha! That was the trick!* No skulking around trying to brush up against her. No bedroom eyes. No bargaining, with lust a butcher's thumb on the deal. He rapped again, this time with more authority, and the door opened so fast he almost lost his balance.

"Whoops!" he said.

"My God, you're not drunk, are you?" she asked with a smile.

"Just off balance," he said.

"Well, stumble on in here, and I'll *get* you drunk," she said, and held the door open wide.

The place was warm, amber lit, filled with the kind of possessions that are bought one at a time, carefully, with just so much money to spend, although Rick knew she had been well-off all her life. There were books and records and pictures, photographs and skeins of yarn and little statuettes, including unobtrusively in little niches her two Academy Awards; there was a tea cart covered with drinking equipment and bottles, a wine rack half-full of dark down-pointing bottles. Altogether it was a comfortable little house, much smaller than Rick had expected, much better lived-in, and overpoweringly Joanne's. She took him to the couch, just touching the tips of his fingers, and bade him sit. She sat next to him, drawing her knees up and facing him, dressed in a man's shirt and jeans, the most relaxed and comfortable and wonderfully used thing in the room.

Rick without thinking made *namasti* and thanked God he had left his seduction plans outside.

"We could smoke a joint," she said. "If you brought one with you."

"Don't you Tennysons ever buy your own dope?" he asked, withdrawing one of his beautiful almost tailor-made joints from his shirt pocket. Joanne took it from his fingers and licked it so that it wouldn't burn crookedly, and then lit it with a wooden match, struck on the side of the old-fashioned match holder that said Cinzano in red and blue.

"Mmmm," Joanne said, "you beach people got boss dope."

Rick laughed, and suddenly smelled dinner, a rich odor he finally separated out into meat loaf and scalloped potatoes.

"Let's get business out of the way," Joanne said, after they had finished the joint and she had brought them each a glass of white wine—amber it was, in the subdued amber light.

"You got it," Rick said.

"As I said on the phone, I heard your picture is just short of turnaround. I suppose it's true."

Rick had several choices. Give in to the marijuana and babble for fifteen minutes about all the troubles he was having. Lie. Divert. Answer with a question ("Who told you that?").

"Yes, " he said.

"My uncle wants that part," she said.

Rick's heart sank. The evening stretched out like the Sahara before him. There was, of course, no chance of hiring Eric Tennyson for the role, even though he qualified barely as an "older leading man." Eric Tennyson's vogue had been twenty years ago and he had been out of the business most of that time, except for the two years he did the Ford commercials and a couple of swings through the dinner-theater circuit.

"How would I get the studio to buy it?" he asked her quite honestly, and she nodded her head as if knowing that would be Rick's first question.

"That's the stumbler, all right. But Eric's willing to make a test for the part, and stand by the results. If that means anything to you."

"It means your uncle's got guts," Rick admitted. He could see Eric Tennyson on the screen in a Philip Marlowe hat and tie, with the dead staring faces of Boss Hellstrom and Donald Marrow in the flickering light, hard faces, unyielding faces, faces without romance or sentimentality or compassion. His own tough little face beside them. He remembered Eric as a natural actor who never seemed to be performing at all.

"I have a bonus to offer," Joanne said, and again Rick was glad he had left his heart on the porch.

"What?" he asked without looking at her.

"Grandpa will consent to play the old sheriff, what's his name?"

"Patton," Rick said. So she's done her homework pretty good! "Sheriff Patton's *fat*," he said stupidly.

Joanne laughed. "Grandpa'll make him *skinny* . . . and he's not volunteering to do this out of sentiment—Eric doesn't even know about it. Grandpa likes the role—that's a great scene he's got there at the end . . ."

A couple of Tennysons . . . in exchange for what?

Joanne seemed to understand. "Eric's tired of being out of the limelight."

The meat loaf got a little dry during their talk, but the scalloped potatoes took the opportunity to get even darker and crustier, and consequently more delicious. The steamed asparagus was perfect. They both ate like starving cats, and there was little conversation at the table. Rick did not even ask her where her husband was, or if he was still her husband. Rich people, he had noticed in the last couple of years, were likely to be worlds apart most of the time. After dinner Rick telephoned Elektra, in front of Joanne, and told her he would be home in an hour or so, whatever it took. She was cold on the phone, but he knew he could jolly her out of it. He felt wonderful. He had an instinct that this was all going to work out. Maybe it was that image in his mind, Eric in that Marlowe hat, that did it. It made Marlowe a little older, but that could add to the poignancy rather than take away from it. They would have to make the picture tasteful on every level, only the best character actors, loving detail on sets and costumes . . .

Donald Marrow's face intruded on his fantasy, and he had to say to Joanne, "Look, I'll do my best. If the studio buys him, I like him. And I'll try to get around that screen test idea, hell, Eric Tennyson shouldn't have to . . ."

"But they'll want him to," she said wisely.

They kissed goodnight, but it didn't mean a thing and she was right, they wanted that screen test, if only as a way of being polite to Eric Tennyson. And they were really hot for old Clay as Sheriff Patton, the quick-draw artist from the past.

Eric Tennyson was no fool. He knew he had only about a five percent chance of getting the part, but as he told Rick nervously, on the set for his screen test, "I'm tired of horse shit." He gave a fine restrained performance.

But Rick sincerely believed that if Donald Marrow had stuck around, things would have gone differently.

NO ONE really knew why Donald Marrow, after weeks of the closest interest, decided to disappear, or even why he had chosen to appear in the first place, except possibly his romance with Teresa di Veccio. Rick remembered with a rueful smile their little group at The Four Seasons, where Teresa was treated like royalty and the rest of them looked as if they would be more comfortable eating in the kitchen; how conscious he was of his own cheap-looking suit and Marrow's dull but somehow loud green suit; Marrow's lustful stares at both women, as if by the force of his eyeballs he could fuck them right there on the spot. It was hard to get Marrow to talk business. He kept saying things like "We'll have to go to Studio Fifty-four, I know everybody there, you'll love the place!" to Teresa's barely concealed boredom with the idea, to Elektra's simple placid acceptance of everything around her. Rick half-suspected that Elektra had been into his Quaaludes.

This is what gave him his wonderful idea, and while Marrow was making a telephone call and nobody else but Teresa seemed to be watching, Rick quickly spooned a tiny glittering pile of cocaine from his little bottle into Marrow's drink, winking at Teresa at the same time.

"I wish I had some," she said wistfully, and Rick passed her the bottle under the table.

"Coming, dear?" she asked Elektra, and off they went.

When Marrow came back, his swagger and smirk making it obvious that even in this place he was a famous fellow, Rick's last misgiving faded as Marrow sat down with a rude flourish and said, "Well, I'm free now; let's make a night of it!"

"I want to talk about this picture," Rick said. Marrow took a swig of his drink and soon was chatting like a jaybird. His enthusiasm rose to a crescendo under Rick's carefully tailored presentation, and within thirty minutes Marrow's hand was out shaking Rick's with wonderful vigor. The two women, who had been an enthusiastic claque for Rick and would have been even without the visit to the women's room, added their champagne glasses to the toast, as Marrow rose to his feet, almost continuing, Rick thought with amusement: the *himmelfahr* of Donald Marrow:

"To *The Lady in the Lake!*"

"People are looking at us," Teresa suggested.

"Let 'em look!" Marrow said. "We're the circus tonight!"

They went to Teresa's apartment high in the sky, an apartment so tasteful and European that it made Rick slightly queasy, and Rick got out the cocaine openly, only to get a Dutch-uncle lecture from Marrow on the uses of drugs and the terrible Draconian laws of the State of New York. He was thoroughly drunk by now, and pawing verbally at both women, winking at Rick as a co-conspirator and spilling champagne on the oriental rugs.

Rick was delighted to get out of there with Elektra in tow, and leave Teresa to get rid of him by herself.

But Teresa did not get rid of him. They were seen everywhere together for the next few days, and Rick's business talks with Marrow, conducted in his office in midtown, were uncluttered by high jinks or bad behavior. Marrow was a very intelligent man about some things, a tyrant, possibly even a tyrant-genius, and it was hard not to be impressed. Teresa herself told Rick that the man fascinated her. "He's a brilliant oaf," she said. "What used to be called a diamond in the rough."

"Is that anything like a chicken in the basket?" Rick wanted to know, and Teresa laughed. She probably thought he was a "rough diamond" too.

They had never been to bed together alone, and only once more as a threesome with Elektra. Rick was surprised—hell, astonished—to find himself thinking of Alexander Hellstrom's face when he broke in on them back in Hollywood. It was the face of a child who has learned suddenly and too early in his life that there is no Santa Claus. Of course Hellstrom had no right to the expression, he was fifty-odd years old and the head of a major studio. Where did he get off?

They were happier as business partners, anyway, and with a certain amount of "financial interbreeding" between Rick's company and the new company formed by Teresa and Marrow and an Italian syndicate under Teresa's control, Rick had about as tight a grip on the destiny of his picture as he could possibly hope for.

Even so, he knew he could be wiped out overnight, by any of a series of combinations of individuals, and it almost made him humble.

Maybe it was Teresa who brought Marrow west, and then maybe it was Marrow who brought Teresa. She was obviously crazy about him, and not afraid to walk right up to Boss Hellstrom and shake his hand and kiss his cheek and look at him like Vesuvius melting, and Hellstrom had to stand there and take it, grinning redly and being polite while Marrow all but slapped him on the back, called him "Alex," and barged into his office (as into Rick's) without so much as a warning.

But—wisdom from the sixties—what goes around, comes around, and the time came when Marrow began wearing that same strained, doubting face as all of Teresa's lovers; a time when he found himself subject to the whims of her coming and going, her disappearances, her bald lies and hypocritical evasions, and one day Rick ran into Hellstrom in the corridor of the third floor (on his way to a screening) and Hellstrom was actually whistling a merry little tune.

Revenge, even at second hand, can be awfully tasty.

Rick was returning from lunch with Donald Marrow and Teresa—a business lunch, of course—and in the back seat when they arrived at the drive-on gate, and Charlie Devereaux waved them past. It was a remarkable sight, and Rick was lucky enough to be alert and watching when it happened—it only took a couple of seconds—Charlie coming out of his guard house no longer an old man with a sinecure but a big, strong-shouldered, hard-bitten gentleman, carrying a gun he obviously knew how to use, like a mythical figure from the old West. And it was all for Teresa. Charlie, tall, proud, macho, saluted her gravely and waved the car on by.

It could only have meant one thing. Rick sat looking at the back of Marrow's neck trying to figure out if he had seen it, too. Obviously not. He kept babbling on about his big Doberman pinscher dog back home. And when Teresa turned and looked at Rick, there was nothing on her face but boredom.

RICK AND Elektra were in bed watching the eleven o'clock news, a coolness between them that kept Elektra from touching her toe to his leg under the covers as she usually did. It was the night after the screening of Eric Tennyson's test. Rick was worried. The Boss had been delighted with the test, but Donald Marrow's only comment as the three of them walked down the dim corridor was "Yeah but who *is* he?" And once again Rick could see his project put out to pasture, the impetus gone, the interest gone, like so many projects that are born in wild reckless enthusiasm and die quietly like abandoned babies.

At first it did not register on his mind, and he had to shake his head to drive away thoughts of the picture.

"What's the matter?" asked Elektra. She put down her magazine and looked at him. He stared at the screen and waved impatiently.

"Shut up and listen!" he said.

The story unfolding on the news was horrible—horrible. Rick sat hypnotized, his hands cold in his lap. Elektra kept muttering, "Oh my God, Oh my God."

The accident scene in the light of the television crews was in terrible high contrast and almost nothing could be seen except the wet pavement, the crushed and burned station wagon and the smashed but still arrogant silvery grill of the maroon Rolls-Royce that Rick recognized, that he had ridden in many times, the Rolls-Royce of Kerry Dardenelle.

Dardenelle was not injured. Rick saw him standing with several police and firemen in the lights, his face white as death, the shadowy crowd behind them. The accident had happened over an hour ago, and they had only just gotten the last body out of the burnt wreck of the station wagon.

It was worse than they could believe. Rick turned to another channel and heard the story once again, his face numb and cold:

Kerry Dardenelle, with Teresa di Veccio beside him, driving down Sunset Boulevard toward the beach, past the turnoff to his own home, and well past the Beverly Hills Hotel, had come rapidly around the long blind curve near Marymount and found himself rushing toward a station wagon stalled in the middle of the road. There were six nuns in the station wagon. Kerry did not have time to brake before he smashed broadside into the station wagon, which immediately exploded into flames.

What happened then Rick learned from Kerry himself and from the next day's newspapers. Neither Kerry nor Teresa was injured, although Kerry went into immediate shock. Teresa jumped from the car and ran forward, trying to pull open the doors to the station wagon. The women inside were screaming and the flames grew worse by the second. Somehow, no one knew actually how, Teresa managed to drag one of the women burning and shrieking from the car. Teresa smothered the flames with her own body, and then got up and rushed back to try to do it again. But by now the heat was too intense and there were no more screams.

Kerry Dardenelle had killed five nuns.

Teresa, blood-covered and scorched, went to the hospital in the same ambulance that took the surviving nun. Later she was asked many times how she had managed to do what she did, but she always said that she did not know. She had simply panicked.

"She panics," Kerry said to Rick later, "and rushes forward to drag a nun from a burning wreck. I panic and sit and watch her do it."

Neither of them, Kerry told Rick, had any memory of where they were going, or why. Kerry was not drunk, as a later test administered by the police proved. He had not been taking drugs and he was not a particularly careless driver. For the press, they said they were on the way to the beach for dinner and to discuss the picture, and maybe it was the truth. But they had no memory of it, remembering only the specter of that broadside station wagon and the faces within, lit by Kerry's headlights.

It was nightmare time. Teresa disappeared into the private sector of the UCLA Medical Center, and Kerry, after a brief try at secluding himself at home, where the press did everything but descend on him from helicopters, finally called Boss Hellstrom and begged him for a hideaway. The Boss let him have Errol Flynn's apartment on the lot, and for once a secret was kept, at least for as long as need be, and while the reporters skulked and sniffed and snooped, they did not find Kerry.

Some of the real inside Hollywood press corps knew where he was, of course, but kept it to themselves. They liked Kerry, everyone liked Kerry, and there was really nothing more to be gotten from hounding him.

Sister Mary Helene, the surviving nun, became the center of the story, her body and face badly burned, and the UCLA Medical Center public relations team made sure the press was well acquainted with the fact that UCLA had one of the world's most advanced burn centers, and that Sister Mary Helene was getting the world's best care. In ten days the press was assembled and told that she would definitely live and would probably not even be disfigured, although her right arm would probably never return to full articulation.

She was, at forty-six, the youngest of the nuns who had been in the station wagon.

Kerry was finally exonerated of any wrongdoing by the various police agencies involved, even though they wanted badly to hang it on him, according to insiders. They just couldn't. It wasn't his fault, and it wasn't really the fault of the nun driving the station wagon. It was a true accident.

That was when Donald Marrow vanished. No one really knew why. It might have been because Teresa was with Kerry, and they were obviously (once you knew Teresa it was obvious) heading for some rendezvous. It might have been that Marrow simply took advantage of the confusion and craziness to slip out of a situation that was bothering him; it might have been that he had plans on the other side of the world. He left without instructions, programs, advice or counsel.

Rick made an appointment with the Boss and went to his office.

"I want to hire Eric," Rick said.

"Go ahead," said the Boss. "You don't have to come to me."

"Well, with Marrow gone . . ." Rick said.

"You're on your own, until I hear otherwise from Marrow," Hellstrom said. He looked impatient. Rick got to his feet, almost unable to believe his ears. But he had one thing more to say.

"I'm keeping Kerry on the picture," he said. Hellstrom looked at him silently. "He's down there working on the script now. It's all that's keeping him from going nuts."

Hellstrom sighed and looked up at Rick with compassion in his eyes. "Well, your picture's blooded now."

"Yes," said Rick.

CHAPTER EIGHTEEN

AT LAST, here came the Tennysons! Alexander Hellstrom felt better, not that he had expected them to be late, and moved over toward the entrance of the Bruin Theater to greet them. What a mob! Three big black Cadillac limousines full of Tennysons pulled up to the cleared space in front of the theater, the doors open and Tennysons, famous ones and obscure ones, young and old, all grinning, all playing to the people waiting in line; Dael wearing his famous "stupid face" and causing the girls to swoon, Eric and Kathryn arm in arm, causing murmurs among the people who believed studio publicity; old Clay with his steel rod posture, Joanne Clay with her arm hooked under his, all of them extraordinarily attractive and seeming, even to hambone-hating Alexander Hellstrom, unbearably glamorous.

He came forward and took old Clay's hand, and kissed Joanne on the cheek. Just then a little girl of perhaps eleven dashed out of line and up to Dael, touched him on the arm with a squeal and started to dodge back into line. Dael swiftly grabbed her, picked her up and gave her a kiss on the cheek, whispered something to her and let her go. She ran red-faced and crying with happiness back to the line, and Dael intelligently disappeared into the theater to keep from causing a mob scene.

They threw open the doors to the theater proper on a signal from some-body and everybody trooped down into the roped-off section reserved for them, Alexander almost last. As Rick and Elektra went past him, Alexander smiled and patted Rick's shoulder. No harm in that. Now they opened the front doors to let the paying customers in, and Alexander slipped into his seat, between his administrative assistant and the empty seat reserved for Donald Marrow, should he choose to appear like magic. Alexander hoped he wouldn't.

After a bit, the lights went down. Alexander liked this moment, had liked it all his life. It was a moment of peace filled with anticipation. The big curtain hissed and the lights went even lower. Ah. Now came the studio logo. Alexander began to applaud the logo, and people around him picked it up, and soon, amid laughter, some of the students clapped, hissed or booed, as they felt. To Alexander, a preview was not a passive experience. He applauded the titles vigorously, as did many of the others, and was gratified to hear the volume of applause from the paying customers on the names Eric Tennyson (an old favorite with everyone from the late show) and Jody McKeegan, not present, and finally, with something like patriotism, the sustained applause for Kerry Dardenelle, seated between his wife and his eldest son, almost directly in front of Alexander, his balding head stiff and straight. He was not "making an appearance," he was working, listening for reactions, alert to the audience. Impulsively, Alexander leaned forward and patted him on the shoulder, as he had done with Rick. Kerry turned, eyeless behind glittering lenses, and smiled automatically for Alexander. The man had a lot of guts.

At first the wreck on Sunset had generated a lot of unfavorable publicity for the picture, and there were items in the trades and then in the Los Angeles *Times* when it was discovered that Kerry would be retained as director, and daily they all waited for the axe from New York to fall. But it never did, and they went on with preproduction.

Reporters, stringers and magazine writers kept snooping around, hoping to pry loose some interesting gossip, and Alexander decided to give them some. Jody McKeegan was in town, not working, just waiting for her part in the picture to come up on the production board, and so Alexander arranged for her to be photographed at lunch with himself and Eric Tennyson. When the photographs appeared, Alexander was not in them. It looked as if Eric and Jody were tête-a-tête and having a fine time of it. Both performers had been warned, and so there was no fuss. Eric's marriage was not up for grabs, and Jody had a boyfriend somewhere. Alexander did not inquire of her further, and she volunteered no information about her private life. Both performers were, in fact, glad the pictures were printed and the rumors circulated, because it would help the picture make an event of itself (not the easiest thing in the world) and because it took some of the heat off Kerry. Reporters would rather have a live romance—especially one that promised to do a little home-wrecking—than follow out a story that was basically already dead and gone.

When the timing was right, Alexander had the publicity department set up an interview with Eric in which he talked about his reviving career and denied the Jody McKeegan rumors. "Sure, we spend a lot of time together," he said, "but it's all work."

Soon a photo found its way into *People* magazine of Jody and Eric kissing and laughing at the same time. "All work?" was the caption.

It was not harmless stuff, but it was necessary, and ninety percent of the attempted publicity of this type is seen right through and ignored, so they were lucky it was being printed, and they kept it up. Alexander was very careful to be especially nice to Kathryn when she came on the set to watch her husband work, but she did not seem worried. This was, after all, not her first picture, nor were these the first deliberate lies printed about members of her family.

Alexander's next gimmick was to have a famous mystery writer, Dick

Landy, come down from San Francisco, all expenses paid, and hang around the set for a while. His article "The Return of the Hard-Boiled Hero" was printed in the Sunday *New York Times* and was a damned good piece of writing, as far as Alexander was concerned.

Week after week, the shooting went on, they carefully created an image for the picture as a major film, a work of art under the artistic direction of Kerry Dardenelle and yet a movie you would have to see just to take part in the romance between Eric and Jody, and the equally interesting romance of Eric's revived career.

Ballantine Books put out a paperback edition of *The Lady in the Lake* with Eric and Jody in costume on the cover, and so there they were, in every drugstore in America, sinking into the American consciousness well before the picture was released. Alexander felt they had a chance.

As for Kerry, he worked twenty hours a day, imparting that special importance to every scene that was his trademark, patiently shooting everything from several angles and keeping five takes, so that there were miles and miles of film to edit—a dangerous process in the hands of an egomaniac or a worrywart, but safe with a thorough and confident worker like Kerry. He also worked patiently with the performers and had a capacity for understanding and sympathy that was beyond most directors. Jody McKeegan, a notorious troublemaker, made no trouble for Kerry, and Eric was of course a master performer. Yet under Kerry's direction he found himself giving the best performance of his life. It was not the kind of flashy performance that has the crew applauding after every take, but in the screening rooms where the dailies were shown every night, the reactions were heartwarming.

Sometimes Alexander wondered why he put so much effort into a picture he had taken a pass on. There was, of course, his sense of craftsmanship. He just hated to see anything done half-assed. And, rationally, if the picture did turn out to be a disaster, it certainly would not be because Alexander Hellstrom had dragged his feet. And there was the question of loyalty. He was taking the company's money, great gobs of it, and his pride would not let him give less than one hundred percent.

And one last sneaking reason, which he didn't like to pull out and look at for fear it was true—was it possible that he had nixed *The Lady in the Lake* for personal reasons? If so, he was beneath his own contempt. No, he did not like to think about that, particularly since the emotions that might have interfered with his judgment had subsided considerably. He still loved her, yes, but it didn't burn anymore. In a way, he regretted it, regretted that he did not have the passions of a boy, to stand in the snow outside *her* window, and die of pneumonia. Indeed, sometimes he felt sadder about his lost emotions than his lost love.

And as for Rick, well, Alexander had his standards, and Rick met and exceeded them so energetically, took his buffets with such good cheer and bounced back so stubbornly to keep the work rolling that Alexander, in his secret heart, forgave him for going over his head, and even admired him a little for being able to get to Donald Marrow, to get Teresa to form the syndicate (something Alexander simply would not have thought of), although he surely would not let these feelings become apparent to Rick. Rick was cocky enough as it was, and clearly thirsted after Alexander's job.

Alexander chuckled at the thought. Let him have the job! That would be a good lesson for him! As for Alexander, he could walk off the lot tomorrow and have a good-paying manual labor job by Monday, if it became necessary. Which it wouldn't because Alexander had plenty of the hard stuff stored away, but it was part of his pride to be mentally prepared to go back to living alone in a room and working all day with his legs, back and hands.

Alexander squirmed pleasurably in his seat, remembering the terrible pain of overworked and cramping muscles, of lying in bed in furnished rooms with the light off, feeling the throbbing of his body. He could go back to that? You're damn right!

HIS PLEASURE deepened as the audience settled down and began to pay attention to the picture. The attentiveness was a good sign. Alexander waited for the first big joke:

KINGSLEY
I don't like your attitude, Marlowe . . .

MARLOWE
That's all right. I'm not selling it.
KINSLEY IS STUNNED.

The audience loved it. They always love to see pomposity punctured. And the timing was good—the laughter lasted about as long as Kerry held on

Kingsley's take, and then things flowed on. Alexander slumped down in the seat as he had when he was a kid and knew the movie was going to be good.

Well, what are you? his mind asked him. Never mind the picture in front of him—he had seen every frame half a dozen times, and the audience was completely in Kerry's hands. What about *you?* Fat-rumped, lazy, rolling over the hill, sex drive gone, bored with the perks and privileges . . . here was the perfect time of life to join ranks with the Hollywood Old Guard, those happy, smiling, cardboard millionaires who have nothing to do every day but go down to their offices and make life tough for their yes-men. "I'm writing a book, developing a property, eliminating hog pellagra, making the desert bloom; I'm having lunch, seeing my doctor, playing pinochle, getting to bed early, deflowering virgins and lying awake until five a.m., in the vast mistiness of my silk sheets, waiting for hell to define itself . . . I'm flashy at the benefit and the whole world knows my friends, I've got six cars. I'm hot stuff, with a Presidential Citation and a basement full of Krugerrands. When I walk in the front door of a restaurant the headwaiter commits suicide in my honor . . . I'm the guy who . . . *Who what?*

He thought about Teresa, not here tonight, busy in New York. He knew what she and Kerry were doing when they came around that blind curve, he knew his Teresa pretty well, grabbing Kerry by his dick and whispering hot nonsense in his ear, Kerry so hot his eyes about to come out of his head. And then coming around that curve, seeing those faces . . .

Teresa, brave bitch. He wished . . . well, he did not want to wish. He wanted his life back. But that wasn't going to happen. It was going to go on *this way,* and he would dry up and everybody would start telling him how *good* he looked. Which never seemed to come up in the conversation unless you looked half-dead . . .

MILLIONAIRE SUICIDE
Unbearable Ennui Cited

Well, no, he would not throw it away. They were going to have to pry it from his fingers.

The audience was roaring with laughter, and Alexander joined them. What the hell, we probably have a hit on our hands, let's enjoy it!

Little did he know how soon he would begin the enjoyment, little did he know. After the picture ended, everyone in the house half exhausted from the fun of it all, fools who did not know any better were crowding around him with their red-faced congratulations. Elektra made her way to him, and he bent down to hear what she had to say, putting his big paw on her tiny shoulder:

"Uh, can I stay at your place tonight?"

He looked his question and she said, "I was just hanging around long enough to see if he'd be all right. He'll be all right. You gotta hit here for sure."

Good old Elektra, hermit crab, darting from shell to shell. "Of course, my dear," he said fondly.

CHAPTER NINETEEN

JERRY REXFORD watched Boss Hellstrom hold the door open for the exquisitely beautiful Elektra Soong, and felt a pang of jealousy. He wondered where they were going. Probably to a party Jerry hadn't been invited to, even though he was currently working on a project for Hellstrom. He knew Hollywood better now, although it continued to mystify him and always would. He just wondered why he was so terribly depressed. There was no reason for it, except perhaps the butchered movie he had just seen.

But he should have felt wonderfully elated, because the audience had loved it and the commercial prospects were rosy. Jerry was working again, had money in the bank, a reasonably active sex life, why the long face? He looked around the lobby. Here were the Harrises, Richard and his wife, Barbara, even Toby, and Helen from the donut shop, all here to see Jerry triumph, to see him hobnobbing with the likes of Eric Tennyson and Joanne Clay. And it had all worked out the way Jerry dreamed it, with Eric sweeping him up after the picture was over and carrying him into the mob surrounding the Tennysons, and introducing him to Joanne Clay, who kissed him on the cheek and said, brightly, "You're a fine writer!"

Jerry could not help sneaking a look at Barbara, across the lobby. Yes, she had seen the kiss.

Barbara was with a man in a cheap business suit that looked about fifty-five inches around the waist. Probably her new boyfriend. Jerry had to grin to himself at the image of this tub of lard huffing down Ventura Boulevard in a gigantic grey sweatsuit, trying to catch up to the woman of his dreams.

The gang from the U-court where Jerry lived had left in a body the minute the picture was done. They were not hanging around like a bunch of civilians who had never seen a movie star. They were all over at the Hamburger Hamlet having hot apple pie and ice cream. Jerry was expected to join them but he doubted if he could swallow even one mouthful.

While Jerry was bent over the drinking fountain he heard Toby's voice behind him saying, "This is the guy I was tellin' you about." He turned, wiping the water from his chin, and saw Toby with a slim young oriental-looking kid with a hairline mustache and a bored expression in his flat black eyes. Jerry barely heard the name and forgot it immediately. The kid's handshake was limp and moist and unpleasant.

"How ya doin'?" Toby wanted to know.

"Well, you know," Jerry said.

"The picture was swell," Toby said without much conviction.

"Thanks," Jerry said.

"Look, there's Helen from the donut shop," Toby said. "You really spread them comps around."

Jerry saw Helen by the door to the men's room with a tall, mean-looking boy with greasy long hair and a black leather jacket. The boyfriend, she called him.

Rick Heidelberg came out of the men's room, looked around, saw Jerry and headed their way. Jerry was relieved that Toby and his friend moved off before Rick got there.

"Hello, my friend," Rick said to him. "How'd you like the picture?"

"Great, just great, Rick," he said, looking Rick right in the eye. Rick was not his friend, and had never been his friend. "Have you seen my old lady?"

"No," Jerry said, looking him right in the eye.

"Maybe she went out to the car," he said. The limos were all pulled up in a row outside, and a crowd of civilians, including Barbara and her boyfriend, were watching.

Rick grinned at Jerry and punched him lightly on the arm. "You feel like shit, right?"

Jerry nodded.

"You'll get over it. Just think, in a year or so, you can sue the studio for your points." Rick was being so charming Jerry could not help laughing. And then Rick was gone, and he turned to see Helen coming up to him, alone.

"You like the show?" he asked her cheerfully.

"Oh, I loved it!" she said, looking at him worshipfully, fondly, and—could it be?—erotically.

With a thrill, Jerry said, "Uh, you want to get together later?"

"Um, sure, just let me ditch the boyfriend," she said, and blushed beautifully.

They would meet in two hours, at his place. Jerry felt a squirm of pleasure as she carefully wrote down his address and apartment number and even his telephone number "just in case." She was really going to do it. She tossed him a last wonderful smile and went to find her boyfriend. Heigh ho, Jerry thought, another of life's little mysteries. Was it because he had sent her the invitation? Because his name was up there on the screen with the others? Because she had always liked him and he had been too dense to see it? Made no difference. At least he didn't feel sad anymore. Time for coffee with his friends at the Hamburger Hamlet.

Jerry walked out of the theater, past the still-loading limousines and the herd of onlookers, his head down, his hands in his pockets. He trudged along, avoiding his reflection in the Westwood store windows, avoiding contact with the swarms of young people out on this typically warm Los Angeles night. The young people avoided him, too, and once Jerry had to laugh as he heard the words "option the property" drifting through the night. So that was what they learned at the film schools! It was all such a screwing. Jerry hoped the young student whose property was being optioned had his feet firmly on the ground, because it could get hairy. Jerry knew, now. Jerry knew the extraordinary velocity that had to be achieved to leave Los Angeles and enter Hollywood. Escape velocity.

Well, Jerry had achieved escape velocity and was a member in good standing of the Hollywood community, Guild card and all, saddle sores and brand marks, floundered, blown out, run hard and put away wet, ah, never switch metaphors in the middle of a thought. Sloppy, sloppy, sloppy. But he felt a lot more like a broken horse than a rocket ship. The movie, which he had supposed would make him feel kingly, parental and proud, only made him sad and disappointed. Almost betrayed. And it was even worse that the audience seemed to love it, and did not miss Jerry's best efforts. Jerry had to grudgingly admire Dardenelle's way of developing a scene, of making a lot more of it than appeared to be there, but to counterbalance this, Jerry's heart sank when he heard the way the actors delivered the lines. Obviously the performers, even the most experienced, would do anything to keep the camera pointed at themselves, and would drag out their speeches or business until Jerry wanted to scream. But nobody else in the theater seemed to notice; in fact, they all loved the way Eric Tennyson would drawl out his lines, and it was obvious, even to Jerry, that Tennyson was going to be the most successful Marlowe since Bogart.

Well, that was all right. Jerry liked Eric Tennyson pretty much, more than the rest of the picture company put together. Tennyson and only Tennyson treated Jerry with any respect after the production got rolling.

"Oh, yer the writer, huh?" was his normal greeting when introduced to somebody on the set. If a technician, the person would become immediately impatient and nervous, and soon would get away from Jerry, as if they had been told he had a fatal disease. If a performer, they would either ask Jerry unforgivable questions about the script, or would beg him to write a part for them in his next movie.

Jerry was stunned at first by the fact that nobody wanted his comments on the script except the performers, and they were forbidden to ask him. This was the director's job, Jerry was told, and division of authority could be fatal. So instead of lording around the set, as he had imagined, he skulked, fearful that he would be barred. After a while, no one paid any attention to him.

The truth was, he had no business on the set, because there was nothing for him to do. The script was finished but the picture was just beginning. There were daily changes, of course, front-office changes, which never seemed to stop, and changes coming from Kerry Dardenelle, who, because of his recent tragedy, could not be argued with, and spent every night in his mystery apartment, making changes, changes, changes.

At first, Jerry had been invited to take part in the preproduction madness, and invited to production meetings, but instead of being a leading figure in these meetings, Jerry sat in the background, hugging his knees and listening to the incomprehensible conversations around him, having to do with the number of trucks, who was available, costs-per-diem, far more often than with the business of nailing down the script for once and for all.

And when Jerry was included, it was often not to his liking. In fact, it was like being whipped on the face with a wire coat hanger. Production people do not like writers. Writers make all the trouble. Mountains have to be moved. Expensive sets built. Large numbers of cars destroyed.

"Why does Degarmo have to run off the cliff?" Jerry was asked at a meeting, by the production supervisor, an irascible swarthy man named Dellorio. Everyone looked at Jerry impatiently. Rick Heidelberg seemed to have a gleam of humor, but nobody else. Looking at Rick for confirmation, Jerry said, "That's what happens in the book."

Dellorio sighed. "It's gonna cost us a lot of money, that scene."

Somebody suggested that the character should, instead of driving off a cliff, run into a tree.

"What's the advantage of that?" Jerry wanted to know.

Easier to control, he was told. And so over the first few weeks he learned that most of the people on the project were not devoted to getting the script on the screen, but were devoted to making a picture, any picture, so long as it was cheap.

It was a shock to Jerry, something he brooded about in his little office, where more and more he was being left to sit with nothing to do. Things were booming, actors swarming the offices for readings, but Jerry was not invited. So he brooded, and more often than not, when Rick Heidelberg or anybody else did ask his opinion, he would deliver it with curt sarcasm.

"What, you're asking the writer?"

Then the production got under way, and Eric Tennyson came into Jerry's life.

On the first day of shooting, everybody was excited, and Jerry got a sense of what it must be like to be in charge of the spending of millions of dollars. On the first day of principal photography, as they called it, the floodgates of money opened and the blood began to flow without the possibility of stanching it. There was a conscious sense of relaxation on the set that Jerry recognized with a thrill as the highest kind of tension, as people went about their work in a polite calm that was the descendant of many bloody battles, destroyed careers, mortally wounded productions; the war between the need to save time and the need for human beings to be treated decently at work.

As Jerry watched the lighting being set up, Eric came up to him out of the shadows.

"Jerry Rexford, you wrote one hell of a fine screenplay, and I thank you. You pulled my ass right out of the soup."

"Thank you very much," Jerry said, reddening.

"Just don't let the shits get to you," Eric said with a grin.

It was obvious that Eric, the old hand, was scared to death. How he could stand there and talk to Jerry was more than Jerry could understand. Under his makeup the man looked as if he needed to vomit. Jerry did not mention this.

Then the setup was complete, the camera in place, all the vast emptiness of the sound stage concentrated into this circle of hot light. Kerry Dardenelle came around a corner with a dozen people trailing him. He came right up to Eric, who was still standing next to Jerry.

The two men shook hands warmly, and then, as an afterthought, Kerry shook Jerry's hand. But his eyes were on Eric.

"Let's begin," he said in an oddly reverent voice, and the two men walked into the middle of the light.

Jerry looked around, moved by what was about to happen, the first film of a new motion picture. In a moment, Eric Tennyson was going to become Philip Marlowe. But first Eric had to help the young girl who was playing the switchboard operator. She was having some personal panic, and while thousands and thousands of dollars flowed helplessly through the hands of the producers, Eric chatted quietly with the girl.

The set glittered magnificently under its lights. It represented the lobby entrance to a perfume company and was filled with displays of perfume bottles and Art Deco furnishings. Jerry looked upon the set proudly, for he had fought like the devil for it. One day he had been told by Richard Heidelberg that the perfume lobby was "out of the picture" and, stunned, he asked why.

"Because it's a pain in the ass," Rick said. "We start with Marlowe in Kingsley's office, blam, L.A. out the window, and that saves us you don't know how much money."

It seemed Rick was more concerned these days about money than about the picture. All those little perfume bottles. A label would have to be designed—design fee—the shelves would have to be designed, the furniture picked out—all in all, Rick made it sound like an awesome task.

"But in the book," Jerry said weakly.

"Fuck the book," Rick said. "Why blow all that money for a set we use for about three seconds?"

They argued about it for weeks, on and off, and it had a lot to do with the cooling between Rick and Jerry, Jerry thought, although it was not Jerry but the director, Kerry Dardenelle, who put the scene back in the movie.

"What do you need it for?" Rick asked the director, in front of Jerry. They were all standing in Rick's secretary's office.

"Give me a break," Dardenelle said dryly. And the scene was back on the production board.

Jerry had been a little mystified at the time, but now he could see it. The director wanted something to play with, something flashing and glittering, to jack up the feeling here at the beginning of the film. It was not just slavish adherence to the book, as it had been for Jerry. Nor was it just for the camera, he thought, as he looked at Eric in costume on the set. Here's shabby but neat old Phil Marlowe in among these shining bottles, these walls of glass . . .

Eric had the girl calmed down now, and they were chatting easily. As if by secret signal, Dardenelle returned to the set, and everyone else took their positions. Jerry, along with many others, did not have a position, and so just stood out of the way.

The hush fell.

Sound rolled, camera rolled, the clacker clacked.

Jerry felt a welling of pleasure inside himself, intense pleasure, which he was absolutely certain everyone on the set shared.

"Action," said Kerry in the mildest of voices.

Tears came to Jerry's eyes, and he quickly backed away into the darkness, hoping no one had seen him.

But he needn't have worried. All eyes were on Eric Tennyson.

THEN THINGS got very bad very fast. Jerry had been living in a dream world. He had been thinking of himself as a member of the picture company. He came in to his little office every day, but most of the time he had nothing to do, and when he was brought into script-change conferences he was told rather than asked about the changes. Oh, from time to time he would be given little chores to do like rewriting runbys, a horribly boring business of setting up on paper a series of scenes in which nothing happens but a vehicle goes past:

EXTERIOR—MOUNTAIN ROAD   NIGHT.
The MOUNTAIN ROAD is empty.

MARLOWE'S CAR RUNS PAST.

DISSOLVE TO:

And so on and so on.

Jerry did not like writing runbys, but somebody had to do it. The runby had to be in the script. Because somebody had to budget for it, set aside time, provide equipment. The director and the cameraman had to go out and find the location, decide the angles. And then they all had to very literally show up and shoot it, because if they did not, and the director got to the editing room and found that he did not have it, and needed it, there would be hell to pay. So Jerry wrote runbys. But it did so remind him of *Pet Care Hotline*.

Afternoons, out of boredom, Jerry would either take long walks around the lot or visit the set. Actually, visiting the set was becoming something of a bore for him. Everybody knew him now, and most ignored him. Seldom was any shooting going on, hours and hours of setting up for minutes of rolling, and Jerry soon tired of the crew's jokes as they hauled cables or lights to and fro. He made a few tense visits to Eric Tennyson's trailer, and while Eric was nice to him, always offering him a beer or a soda, telling him to sit down and relax, Jerry could not quite fit himself into the busyness of Eric's life, for there was never a moment when Eric wasn't doing something, in his slow, lazy, masculine way—on the telephone, talking to the constant stream of businesspeople or front office people or publicity people who came through his trailer, studying his lines, or even just reading a book. Jerry finally stopped the visits.

Jerry was not on salary, his payment had been lumps, but long ago when he and Rick Heidelberg had been working so closely on the screenplay, they both agreed that it would be good for Jerry to hang around while the picture was being shot, even unto the postproduction to watch the cutting process, and all along it had been understood that when the company moved up to Big Bear Lake for the locations, Jerry would go.

It would be *fun*. You worked harder on location, the days were longer, but there was a cheerful expeditionlike feeling to the whole thing. Jerry should not miss it, Rick said more than once. And Jerry looked forward to it himself. But lately he had begun to worry.

Finally, one day, he called to make an appointment with Rick. First Joyce told him he could come over in an hour or so, but then she called him back and said, "Can you be here at eight tomorrow morning? Rick has a lot on his plate."

Jerry agreed to the morning meeting, and was in his office promptly at quarter to eight. At eight sharp he called Joyce.

"Listen, will you stay there and wait for Rick's call?" Joyce asked him. "He's got a crazy day."

"I want to talk to him about the location move," Jerry said helpfully.

"I'll get back to you," Joyce said.

Jerry sat back and waited for his telephone to ring. His own secretary, Roberta, had long since been reassigned to the production office when Jerry turned in the "final draft" of the screenplay, but Jerry didn't mind. It would have been horrible to have her sitting over there with nothing to type. So Jerry sat with his door ajar, wondering if he dared go down to the production office and beg a cup of coffee. But he did not want to be out of the office when Rick called. He might not be able to get hold of him again for days, and Jerry wanted this business settled. Was he going on location or was he not going on location?

Jerry waited impatiently for the telephone to ring. He thought about calling the production office and asking Roberta to bring him a cup of coffee. He knew she would do it. But even as he reached for the telephone a feeling of distaste came over him, and he let his hand drop into his lap. It would be playing *their* game, their goddamn status game, where three or four men would sit around talking about pussy while the only person in the office who actually has anything to do has to drop everything and fetch the men coffee. Jerry had always held aloof from this, not that he didn't let the secretaries make him coffee, but it was never that *drop everything* kind of situation. Come to think of it, neither was this. Jerry was kidding himself.

His telephone was not on the production company's set of lines. If Jerry was on the telephone, no one could call in. Jerry didn't want to call Roberta for fear that Rick might call and the line be busy and not call back.

What is this?

Jerry reached for the telephone, but his hand froze. Why not call Joyce and get a clarification about what Jerry was supposed to do? Wait here for Rick's call, she had said. Joyce was careful with words, so it meant just what it said.

He took his hand off the instrument and grinned to himself. Joyce is careful with words, huh?

"Joyce the writer, or Joyce the secretary?"

It was like dialogue from a Marx Brothers movie.

Jerry giggled. Well, what was he going to do while he waited? There was nothing to read but a stack of Los Angeles telephone directories in his bottom drawer. He hadn't picked up the trades that morning in his impatience to be on time, and he was not going to appear at Rick's office and ask Joyce if he could borrow Rick's copy. It would look as if he were hanging around, or pressing. He did not want to appear to press. Not that he gave a good goddamn anymore, it was obvious what was happening, Jerry was being stiffed, and stiffed good. Rick obviously had no intention of keeping his eight o'clock appointment, he probably wasn't even on the lot yet, that was why Joyce hadn't invited Jerry to wait in with her, sipping hot coffee and reading the trades.

Jerry could imagine the scene. Rick comes in late, and Joyce says, "You've got Jerry Rexford waiting," and Rick would say in an irritated voice, "Oh, shit, get him, will you? I totally forgot." And the phone would ring . . .

But the phone did not ring. Jerry could not quite believe that Rick was doing this on purpose, to put him in his place. It was too blunt and ugly a thing to do, too much the old Hollywood of myth and legend. Rick was just busy, and Jerry was hounding him. But this irritated Jerry. Rick was busy on other projects as well as their picture, and Jerry felt he should not be. Instead of running around setting up development deals, Rick should be paying more attention to the everyday problems of *The Lady in the Lake*. Including setting up Jerry's location trip.

Of course in his heart Jerry now knew that he was not going to get to go. And he had told everybody around the court that he was going. He had even hinted to Brenda that she might visit him, and she had been eagerly interested. Brenda, ah, Brenda, how nice it was to have a neighbor who would come over from time to time and give you a friendly little fuck, and then leave you to your life. Jerry and Jack never talked about this, but Jerry knew Jack knew, and it didn't seem to matter.

Maybe he should call Harriet Hardardt, no, don't want to tie up the line . . . but Harriet was the one to clarify this situation anyway, it was her goddamn job, just call Rick herself and say, "We want a hundred-twenty a day per diem for Jerry Rexford," and if Rick suggested that Jerry might not be going, just bull it through: "Of course he's going!"

Call Harriet. Don't worry about Rick calling. You have no business with Rick. Let Harriet do it.

He reached for the phone, but cold sweat between his shoulder blades reminded him that he was afraid. He was so afraid he wouldn't leave his office even for a cup of coffee, so afraid he wouldn't even go down the hall to piss, so afraid that until just this moment he hadn't even admitted to himself that he had to piss, and badly. But would not leave the room.

Jerry sat back and sighed. Now that it was out, he felt a certain relief. Yes, it was true, he was going to squat in his little corner until The Master called. Jerry had thought he was made of better stuff than this, but obviously he wasn't. He was a coward, hanging on by his fingernails. Anything to stay on the lot. Anything to stay with the picture. What else did he have waiting for him out there? He had no job and no prospects. His money was rapidly dribbling away. He had written nothing new, and his old screenplays were deadly bad stuff, he could not even bear to read them.

A heaviness settled on Jerry's chest as he sat glowering at the telephone. He had aimed his life at the movies, fired, and missed. No one would hire him. Especially after this picture came out. People would judge his writing by a script that had been butchered by so many hands Jerry could not remember them all. And now the actors and the director were down on the set, their hands blood-red from even further butchery.

For a moment, Jerry mourned his screenplay, and compared himself to the Old Man, with his great fish eaten by the brown sharks. Yes, that was a good image, brown sharks.

But Jerry couldn't quite make it into self-pity. Something inside him said, "You are to blame for everything that's happened to you. If there is somebody fucking up your life, it is only you." Jerry smiled sadly. Comparing himself to a Hemingway hero *was* a bit dicky. Next he would be comparing himself to Hemingway.

Jerry was in for a long wait, he knew that now, but he felt better. Even though his course of action was cowardly, he would follow it all the way to its cowardly conclusion.

Now that he knew what he was doing, he looked around for something to occupy his time. Not something short-term, but something he could get into. He opened the drawer of his desk to see if there was anything in there. There was. Paper. He could write. He pulled the typewriter over to him and carefully, lovingly, stuffed a piece of white paper, a piece of carbon paper, and a piece of yellow paper into the machine. This ole machine was the one he used to write runbys. He knew how to work this old bastard. He centered the paper and stuck his finger in his mouth.

What to write? Jerry had written a few unsuccessful short stories in his time, and of course like everyone who has the nerve to call himself a writer, he had begun several novels. Never finished one, though. He had always meant to get back to serious writing. In fact, long ago, that had been the dream, hadn't it? To come to Hollywood, make good money, and then have time to write fiction? Wasn't that what it was all about? He had a few bucks, not enough to write a novel, but sure as hell enough to work on a good short story, maybe several; short stories were the style perfecters that led to novels, anyway. He would be readying himself for his craft.

Jerry looked at the blank page in front of him and wondered what to write about. Minutes went by. Nothing came to his mind. Why was it he was always having ideas for books and stories when he was working on something, and the ideas were an interference, but now, when he searched eagerly for ideas, there wasn't one in sight?

He sat for a long time, trying to think, but his mind kept drifting away. He wasn't really trying to write. He was posing as a writer, to keep the humiliation of his position from overwhelming him. No wonder no ideas would come to his mind. It was a gross joke. Jerry, who had so much respect for fiction, now trying to use it as a shield. It was disgusting. Fiction did not rise from the wreckage of a hack writer.

Jerry had to face something now. It wasn't just fiction he was talking about. Anybody with a little training could write fiction. But great fiction was another matter. And Jerry had been hiding from himself all this time his passion to write greatly. Greatly. His burning young dream had been to stand beside Hemingway and Fitzgerald, Maupassant and Chekhov, Melville and Twain. Beside them as an equal.

Jerry now knew with terrible contempt for himself that he would never write any books. Something immense within him died. He looked at the blank piece of paper in his typewriter and saw his fate written there. The fate of nothing. To have been nothing, and to be nothing. And nothing to become.

At this moment, Jerry went a little crazy. He would always remember the moment not for his terrible self-knowledge but for the insanity that followed, even though he did nothing outwardly crazy. But he wanted to. There was a lamp: he wanted to grasp the hot bulb in his hand and crush it, crush the life out of it, cutting his hand. He wanted to piss in the desk drawer, on the Los Angeles county telephone books, and then leave the building forever. He wanted to break into Rick's office and in front of everybody gathered there stride madly across the room and grab Rick by his scrawny little neck and crunch the life out of him like a chicken, throw the lifeless body through the crashing glass and then turn and walk out and leave the lot. He wanted power to surge up out of his body, all the secret power he knew was there, all his atomic energy, for once at his disposal, to direct this energy in a wave of hatred at the studio itself, to see the whole place suddenly burst into flames, to explode with the violence of his intent, with himself in the middle, all the buildings smashed and quaking, all the people blown to bits, every tree knocked flat, devastation everywhere . . .

Jerry's eyes were glassy, and his face was pulled into a terrible mask of hatred. He could feel the muscles so tight they might snap. Consciously he relaxed his face muscles. He had seen people whose faces had fixed in awful expressions, and now he knew how it happened. He had to be careful. He didn't want to look like that.

And the insanity passed. Jerry had to laugh. Piss in the drawer! On the phone books! Blow up the studio with his secret energy! In a way it was all very frightening, and later when he looked back on it, it was even more frightening. He had been sitting there slathering in a mad rage for nearly half an hour.

And the telephone still hadn't rung.

For the first time in a while, Jerry thought about his chimpanzee, the one who escapes in his movie idea. Jerry felt tremendous sympathy for the chimpanzee, the animal in all of us, pursued relentlessly for our own good by civilization. That's something. The scientist should have a lot of really cultural stuff in his house, paintings, sculpture, tasteful little knickknacks to show that he is a civilized man, not just a man of science. And he must be shown to have great compassion for the chimpanzee as well, none of your Skinner Box mentality. He should be, indeed, a Renaissance Man, good with the ladies, tough as hell, magical personality; he should be a vastly superior human being, just as the chimpanzee should be a vastly superior ape.

But goddamn it, there's a hell of a problem here that can't be solved in screenplay, the matter of casting the ape and the way the actor will be made up. He should look like the actor, yes, but he should also look exactly like a real chimpanzee, or people would laugh at him and not feel the strong sympathy Jerry knew they would have to feel to accept the story. It was a bitch of a problem, and the only way Jerry could see out of it would be to produce the picture himself.

Scenes began forming in his mind, and quickly, with economy, he began putting them on paper. Unlike his last attempt he wrote narrative treatment instead of screenplay, just notes on each scene as he thought of it. Later he could write the dialogue, when he was sure of what he had. Jerry typed smoothly, pages mounting on the other side of the desk. It was easy. He was aware only of the emerging story and of the sweat trickling down from his armpits. All other sensations seemed to have vanished. The old typewriter clacked away, and Jerry wrote page after page. The day passed and the telephone did not ring, but Jerry was beyond caring. He knew without thinking about it that Rick would call him late in the day—six o'clock, as it turned out—and fire him off the picture with a few curt words, but it no longer mattered. This morning Jerry had been a man without a future, and now he had something to work on, something he believed in, and it did not matter if it was crap or gold, Jerry loved it.

So did Harriet Hardardt, who sold the twenty-nine-page treatment to Alexander Hellstrom, script and two sets of changes to follow, for eighty thousand dollars.